Works by Anthony Burgess

Fiction

THE LONG DAY WANES:
   A MALAYAN TRILOGY
THE RIGHT TO AN ANSWER
THE DOCTOR IS SICK
DEVIL OF A STATE
ONE HAND CLAPPING
A CLOCKWORK ORANGE
THE WANTING SEED
HONEY FOR THE BEARS
ENDERBY
NOTHING LIKE THE SUN:
   A STORY OF SHAKESPEARE'S LOVE-LIFE
THE EVE OF ST. VENUS
A VISION OF BATTLEMENTS
TREMOR OF INTENT
MF
NAPOLEON SYMPHONY
THE CLOCKWORK TESTAMENT
   OR ENDERBY'S END
MOSES
BEARD'S ROMAN WOMEN
ABBA ABBA
1985
MAN OF NAZARETH

For Children

A LONG TRIP TO TEATIME
THE LAND WHERE
   THE ICE CREAM GROWS

Nonfiction

ENGLISH LITERATURE:
   A SURVEY FOR STUDENTS
THEY WROTE IN ENGLISH
ENGLISH MADE PLAIN
RE JOYCE
THE NOVEL NOW
URGENT COPY: LITERARY STUDIES
SHAKESPEARE
JOYSPRICK: AN INTRODUCTION
   TO THE LANGUAGE OF JAMES JOYCE
NEW YORK
HEMINGWAY AND HIS WORLD

Translations

THE NEW ARISTOCRATS
(WITH LLEWELA BURGESS)
THE OLIVE TREES OF JUSTICE
(WITH LLEWELA BURGESS)
THE MAN WHO ROBBED POOR BOXES
CYRANO DE BERGERAC
OEDIPUS THE KING

Edited

THE GRAND TOUR
A SHORTER FINNEGANS WAKE

ANTHONY BURGESS

earthly powers

SIMON AND SCHUSTER · NEW YORK

Published by Simon and Schuster
A Division of Gulf & Western Corporation
Simon & Schuster Building
Rockefeller Center
1230 Avenue of the Americas
New York, New York 10020

SIMON AND SCHUSTER and colophon
are trademarks of Simon & Schuster

Designed by Clint Anglin

Title and chapter number calligraphy
derived from an alphabet in
Calligraphy by Arthur Baker,
published by Dover Publications, Inc.,
New York

Manufactured in the United States of America

Printed and bound by
Fairfield Graphics, Inc.

10 9 8 7 6 5 4 3 2 1

Library of Congress Cataloging in Publication Data

Burgess, Anthony, date.
  Earthly powers.

  I. Title.
PR6052.U638E2   1980   823'.914   80–20978

ISBN 0–671–41490–9

TO LIANA

one

It was the afternoon of my eighty-first birthday, and I was in bed with my catamite when Ali announced that the archbishop had come to see me.

"Very good, Ali," I quavered in Spanish through the closed door of the master bedroom. "Take him into the bar. Give him a drink."

"*Hay dos. Su capellán también.*"

"Very good, Ali. Give his chaplain a drink also."

I retired twelve years ago from the profession of novelist. Nevertheless you will be constrained to consider, if you know my work at all and take the trouble now to reread that first sentence, that I have lost none of my old cunning in the contrivance of what is known as *an arresting opening*. But there is really nothing of contrivance about it. Actuality sometimes plays into the hands of art. That I was eighty-one I could hardly doubt: congratulatory cables had been rubbing it in all through the forenoon. Geoffrey, who was already pulling on his overtight summer slacks, was, I supposed, my Ganymede or male lover as well as my secretary. The Spanish word *arzobispo* certainly means archbishop. The time was something after four o'clock on a Maltese June day—the twenty-third, to be exact and to spare the truly interested the trouble of consulting *Who's Who*.

Geoffrey sweated too much and was running to fat (why does one say *running*? Geoffrey never ran). The living, I supposed, was too easy for a boy of thirty-five. Well, the time for our separation could not, in the nature of things, be much longer delayed. Geoffrey would not be pleased when he attended the reading of my will. "The old bitch, my dear, and all I did for him." I would do for him too, though posthumously, posthumously.

I lay a little while, naked, mottled, sallow, emaciated, smoking a cigarette that should have been postcoital but was not. Geoffrey put on his sandals puffing, creasing his stomach into three bunches of fat, and then his flowery coatshirt. Finally he hid himself behind his sunglasses, which were of the insolent kind whose convexities flash metallic mirrors at the world. I observed my eighty-one-year-old face and neck quite clearly in them: the famous ancient grimness of one who had experienced life very keenly, the unfleshed tendons like cables, the anatomy of the jaws, the Fribourg and Treyer cigarette in its Dunhill holder relating me to an era when smoking had been an act to be performed with elegance. I looked without rancor on the double image while Geoffrey said:

"I wonder what his archbishship is after. Perhaps he's delivering a bull of excommunication. In a gaudy gift wrapper, of course."

"Sixty years too late," I said. I handed Geoffrey the half-smoked cigarette to stub out in one of the onyx ashtrays, and I noticed how he begrudged even that small service. I got out of bed, naked, mottled, sallow, emaciated. My summer slacks were, following nominal propriety, far from tight. The shirt of begonias and orchids was ridiculous on a man of my age, but I had long drawn the fang of Geoffrey's sneers by saying: "Dear boy, I must habituate myself to the prospect of reverential infloration." That phrase dated back to 1915. I had heard it in Lamb House, Rye, but it was less *echt* Henry James than Henry James mocking *echt* Meredith. He was remembering 1909 and some lady's sending Meredith too many flowers. "Reverential infloration, ho ho ho," James had mocked, rolling in mock mirth.

"The felicitations of the *faithful*, then."

I did not care at all for the aspirated stress Geoffrey laid on the word. It connoted sex and his own shameless infidelities; it was a word I had once used to him weeping; it carried for me a traditional moral seriousness that was no more than a camp joke to Geoffrey's generation.

"The *faithful*," I aspirated back, "are not supposed to read my books. Not here, on Saint Paul's holy island. Here I am immoral and anarchic and agnostic and rational. I think I can guess what the archbishop wants. And he wants it precisely because I am all of those things."

"Clever old devil, aren't you?" His mirrors caught golden stone from the Triq Il-Kbira, meaning Street the Big or Main Street, outside the open casement.

I said, "There is much neglected correspondence down below in what you call your office. Sickened by your sloth, I took it upon myself to open a letter or two, hot from the hands of the mailman. One of them bore a Vatican stamp."

"Ah, fuck you," Geoffrey smiled, or seemed to: I could not of course see his eyes. Then he mocked my slight lisp: "Thickened by your thloth." Then he said "Fuck you" again, this time sulkily.

"I think," I said, hearing the senile dry wavering and hating it, "I'd better sleep alone in future. It would be *seemly* at my age."

"Facing facts at last, dear?"

"Why"—I trembled at the big blue wall mirror, brushing back my scant strands—"do you make things sound mean and dirty? Warmth. Comfort. Love. Are those dirty words? Love, love. Is that dirty?"

"Matters of the *heart*," Geoffrey said, seeming to smile again. "We must watch that rather mature pump, must we not? Very well. Each of us sleeps in his sundered bed. And if you cry out in the night, who will hear you?"

Wer, wenn ich schrie . . . Who had said or written that? Of course, poor great dead Rilke. He had cried in my presence in a low beershop in Trieste, not far from the Aquarium. The tears had flowed mostly from his nose, and he had wiped his nose on his sleeve. "You have always managed to sleep soundly enough at my laboring side," I said. "Soundly enough not to be sensible even of the sharp prodding of my finger." And then, quavering shamefully: "Faithful, faithful." I was ready to weep again, the word was so loaded. I remembered poor Winston Churchill, who, at about my present age, would weep at words like *greatness*. It was called emotional lability, a disease of the senile.

Geoffrey did not mouth a smile now, nor set his jaw in weak truculence. The lower part of his face showed a sort of compassion, the upper the twin and broken me. *Poor old bugger*, he would be saying to himself and, later perhaps, to some friend or toady in the bar of the Corinthia Palace Hotel, *poor senile decrepit lonely old impotent sod*. To me, with kind briskness: "Come, dear. Your fly is properly fastened? Good."

"It would not show. Not inflorated as I am."

"Splendid. Let us then put on the mask of distinguished immoral author. His archbishship awaits." And he opened the heavy door which led straight into the airy upper salon. At my age I could, can, take any fierce amount of light and heat, and both these properties of the South roared in, like a Rossini finale in stereophony, from the open and unshuttered casements. To the right were the housetops and gaudy washing of Lija, a passing bus, quarreling children; to the left, beyond crystal and statuary and the upper terrace, the hiss and pump hum came up of the irrigation of my orange and lemon trees. In other words, I heard life going on, and it was a comfort. We trod cool marble, heavy white bear fur, marble, fur, marble. Over there was the William Foster harpsichord, which I had bought for my former friend and secretary, Ralph, faithless, some of its middle strings broken one night in a drunken tantrum by Geoffrey. On the walls were paintings by my great contemporaries—now fabulously valuable but all acquired cheap when, though still young, I had emerged from struggle. There were cases showing off jade, ivory, glass, metal *bibelots* or *objets d'art*. How the French terms, admitting their triviality, somehow cleansed them of it. The tangible fruits of success. The real fight, the struggle with form and expression, unwon.

Oh, my God—the *real* fight? I was thinking like an author, not like a human, though senile, being. As though conquering language mattered. As if, at the end of it all, there were anything more important than clichés. Faithful. You have failed to be faithful. You have lapsed, or fallen, into infidelity. I believe that a man should be faithful to his beliefs. O come all ye faithful. That could still evoke tearful nostalgia at Christmas. The reproduction in my father's surgery of that anecdotal horror—no, who was I to say it was a horror?: the wide-eyed soldier at his post while Pompeii fell. Faithful unto death. The felicitations of the *faithful*, then. The world of the homosexual has a complex language, brittle yet sometimes excruciatingly precise, fashioned out of the clichés of the other world. So, *cher maître*, these are the tangible fruits of your success.

Geoffrey shuffled into step with me, mockingly, as if to emphasize his, my dear, rôle of aide de *camp*. Side by side, tread by tread, in comic neatness, we descended the first marble flight. We arrived at a spacious landing with a Jacobean cupboard in which exquisite glassware hid—for use, dear, for actually imbibing out of—and an eighteenth-century chess table permanently set with men of Mexican obsidian (for show only, dear—his *playing* days are done), then turned right to engage the final marbled cataract. I looked at the gilt Maltese clock on the wall of the stairwell. It said nearly three.

"Nobody's come to repair it," I said, hearing my petulance. "It's been three days now. Not, of course, that it really matters."

We were three steps from the bottom. Geoffrey tapped the clock as if it were a barometer, then viciously mimed a punch at it.

"Bloody place," he said. "I loathe and detest the bloody place."

"Give it time, Geoffrey."

"We could have gone somewhere else. There are other islands if it's islands you bloody want."

"Later," I said. "We have visitors."

"We could bloody well have stayed in Tangier. We could have got the better of the bastards."

"We? It was you, Geoffrey, who were in trouble, not I."

"You could have damned well done something. *Faithful*. Don't use that bloody word *faithful* to me."

"I did do something. I took you away from Tangier."

"Why to this bloody place? Bloody priests and police working hand in bloody hand."

"There are two *bloody priests* waiting to see us. Moderate your tone."

"If you want to die here I bloody well don't."

"A man has to die somewhere, Geoffrey. Malta seems to me a reasonable kind of compromise."

"Why can't you die in bloody London?"

"Taxes, Geoffrey. Estate duty. Climate."

"God blast and bloody well damn this bloody stinking place."

I minced the three treads down to the hall, and he followed, damning and bloodying now merely under his breath. Three steps away, on a silver salver, blessed by a Chinese bowl full of flowers of the season, lay a fresh batch of felicitations brought by Cable and Wireless motorcyclists. The bar was across the hall, to the right, between the wreck of an office where Geoffrey neglected his secretarial work and my own fussily neat study. On the wall between the bar and the study was the Georges Rouault—a scrawled ugly ballerina, impatient thick black strokes and bitter washes. In Paris that time Maynard Keynes had hotly recommended that I buy it. He had known all about markets.

two

His Grace was quite at his ease in the bar. I had expected to find him sitting fidgeting at one of the tables with an untouched orange squash before him, but here he was perched at the counter on a fawn leather stool, neat little foot on the rail, neat little fat hand holding what looked like a neat scotch. He was talking loudly and affably with Ali—who, white-coated, stood behind as bar-tender—in, to my astonishment, Ali's own language. Was this a gift of the Pentecostal Paraclete? Then I remembered that Maltese and Moghrabi Arabic were sister dialects. His Grace began to climb down from his stool when he saw me, smiling and greeting in English:

"To meet you at last, Mr. Toomey. A privilege and a pleasure. I know I speak for the whole community when I wish you, as I do now, very many happy returns."

A swarthy young man in a plainer clerical habit than his superior's shouted from the far corner: "Happy birthday, sir, yes. It is an honor to wish it to you in person." The bar was small and there was no need to shout, but some of the Maltese use an abnormally high voice level even when whispering. He had been looking at my framed photographs on the walls, all of me with various of the great—Chaplin in Los Angeles, Thomas Mann in Princeton, Gertrude Lawrence at the close of one of my long London runs, H. G. Wells (with, of course, Odette Keun) at Lou Pidou, Ernest Hemingway on the *Pilar* off Key West. There were also framed posters of my stage successes—*He Paid His Way, The Gods in the Garden, Oedipus Higgins, Break Break Break*, others. Both clerics cheerfully raised their glasses at me. Then His Grace put his glass on the counter and ambled toward me somewhat slyly, his right hand raised horizontally at ring-kissing level. I shook it.

"My chaplain, Father Azzopardi."

"My secretary, Geoffrey Enright."

The archbishop was a few years younger than myself, evidently vigorous though very plump; being plump, not much lined or wrinkled. We eyed each other with friendly wariness, opposed in trade but united in our generation. I noted, in my frivolous way, that we all made up a reasonable poker hand—two pairs, Ali discarded. I said to Ali in Spanish: "Gin and tonic. Then you can go."

His Grace sat now at one of the three tables, draining his glass first then rocking it humorously in his hand. He was very much at home. This was, after all, his archdiocese.

I said, "It's perhaps, after all, too early for drinks. Would you like tea?"

"Oh yes," the chaplain cried, turning with eagerness from myself and Mae West outside Grauman's Chinese Theater, "tea would be very nice."

"Drinks," pronounced the archbishop. And he told Ali, in Maltese-Moghrabi, to give him the same again. Then, he seemed to say, Ali could go. "This lovely house," he said. "These lovely gardens and orchard. I have visited here often. In the time of Sir Edward Hubert Canning. In the time of the late Mrs. Tagliaferro. Father Azzopardi, I know, would be very delighted to be shown all around or about it, everything, by Mr. . . . by your young friend here with the mirrors on his eyes. The young, is it not, Mr. Toomey? These young people. The house was, this you may not know or perhaps may know, it was built in 1798 when Buonaparte invaded. He sent the Knights away. He tried to restrict or constrict the powers of the clergy." His Grace chuckled grimly. "He did not succeed. The Maltese people would not have it. There were incidents. There were deaths."

I took my gin and tonic from Ali and brought it to the table. I sat down opposite the archbishop, who had already been served with a large neat Claymore. "Well," I said to Geoffrey, "you have your instructions. Show his ah reverence around the house and gardens. Give him tea."

Father Azzopardi drained his glass of whatever it was with nervous haste and began to cough. Geoffrey banged him on the back with excessive energy, saying at each stroke of his fist, "Through my fault, through my fault, through my most *grievous* fault."

"Geoffrey," I said sharply, "that is not funny."

Geoffrey put out his tongue and led coughing Father Azzopardi off. His Grace made one final Semitic joke at Ali, who too, laughing, went off. "A good boy," His Grace said, "one can see that. These young people," he added, nodding toward Geoffrey's voice that could be heard, full of aspirated stresses, moving toward green and sunlight. And then: "You play bridge here, I should think. A room pleasantly appointed for the playing of bridge," his eyes on the shelves full of bottles. "A harmless and civilized pastime." He raised his fat hand in what seemed to be both a blessing on the game and a gesture of regret that he could not accept, ever, an invitation to come and play. "I played. I play no longer. I have far too much work. His late Holiness too played. And then he too had far too much work. This you will know." His modest smile was meant, I assumed, to diminish the comparison.

So, as I had been foretold in that Vatican letter, the visit was to be about His late Holiness. I said, "When Carlo was raised so high, his bridge-playing days were already over. Far too much work, as you say, as he said. But he had been a superb player—very clever and fierce. Like Mrs. Battle, you know."

His Grace had not heard of the lady. "Ah yes, I can believe that. Clever and fierce. But also human, or is it humane? Perhaps both. But also a saint." He looked at me with small unwilling awe. *Carlo*, I had said.

I was ready to joke about there being no bridge saints, but that would have been cheap and unworthy. Instead, I said, "I know of the proposal, naturally. I gather there is still much to be done."

His Grace waved the hand that was not holding his drink. "I speak, of course, of course—"

"Proleptically?"

"You are a master of the language, Mr. Toomey. It will, I fear, be always a foreign language to me. The language of the Protestant, if you will forgive me. That you are a master is well known. I have little time, of course, for reading. I have been often told that you are a master of the English language."

"Something," I said, "that most Maltese must be content to be told. Those interested, I mean. They are forbidden to find out for themselves."

"Oh, one or two of your books are permitted. This I know. But our people must be protected, Mr. Toomey. But I think that soon our censorship may be a little bit relaxed. There is a new spirit abroad, at home as well, aha. Already you may now buy the works freely of the atheist Monsieur Voltaire. In French, too."

"Deist, not atheist." I knew what he was here for, but I decided to use pretended ignorance to get a point in. "Archbishop," I said, "I take it you are not here in any shall I say pastoral capacity? You will know, I think, that I was born in the faith. But I propose to die out of it. I have lived long enough out of it. I ought to make my position absolutely clear." And yet I gulped on that *faith*.

"You propose," he said cheerfully. "Man proposes." And then: "No no no, oh no. One thing I have learned, we are all learning, His late Holiness was, aha, very clever and fierce in teaching us all, one thing is that there are many ways to salvation. But let me put it this way to you, Mr. Toomey. You *know* the Church. Whatever you are now, you are not a Protestant. Certain doctrines, words, terms—these have meaning for you. I am right, I think."

"Permit me to give you more whisky," I said, taking his glass and getting up, stiff, an old man. "Allow me to offer you a cigar. Or a cigarette."

"A lethal action, smoking," he said without irony. "Smoking makes the life shorter. Just a little drop, then." I took a cigarette for myself from the Florentine leatherbound box on the counter. There was also a huge wooden bowl from Central Africa full of matchbooks, trophies of the world's airlines and hotels. I had toyed once with the notion of a travel book arranged on the aleatory taking out of matchbooks from this bowl, rather like filthy Norman Douglas's autobiography based on the random selection of visiting cards. It had come to nothing. There is sense, however, in keeping a bowl full of such trophies: there are addresses and telephone numbers there, as well as a palpable record of travel helpful to an old man's memory. I lighted my cigarette with a match from La Grande Scène, a restaurant at the top of the Kennedy Center in Washington,

833–8870. I could not for the life of me remember having been there. I puffed and shortened my life. Then I gave His Grace his whisky. He took it without thanks, a kind of intimacy. He said, as I sat down again:

"The word *miracle*, for example." He looked at me sharply and brightly.

"Ah, that. Yes, well, I received a letter, a note rather, from my old bridge-playing acquaintance Monsignor O'Shaughnessy."

"Ah, the bridge I did not know about. Interesting."

"He mentioned the virtues of the personal approach. I see his point. Some things do not go well on paper. For all that, they seem to be building up a vast dossier of saintly evidence. A piece of evidence from a known apostate and self-proclaimed rationalist and agnostic would be of far greater value than the testimony of some superstitious old peasant woman in black. This is what Monsignor O'Shaughnessy's note seemed to imply."

His Grace swayed rather gracefully on his bottom, flashing his rings. "To me," he said, "he spoke when I was in Rome. It is strange, Mr. Toomey, you must admit it, it is even bizarre, if that is the word—yourself, I mean. I mean a man who has rejected God—that is what they would say in the old days, now we are more careful—and yet had such close contacts with— I mean, you could write a book, is not that true?"

"About Carlo? Ah, Your Grace, how do you know I haven't? In any case, it would never get into Malta, would it—a book by Kenneth Marchal Toomey about the late Pope. It would be bound to be—well, not hagiography."

"Monsignor O'Shaughnessy mentioned to me that you have already written some little thing. You wrote it while he was still alive. Before he became what he at last became."

"I wrote a certain short story," I said. "About a priest who— Look, my Lord Archbishop, you can read the story for yourself. It's in my three volumes of collected stories. My secretary could hunt you out a copy."

He looked at me. Was there bitterness there, was there shame? One should never say that one had no time for reading. It meant, with him, no time for my kind of irreligious trash. But there were times when even a great cleric should be prepared to do his homework. "Monsignor O'Shaughnessy," he mumbled in a very un-Maltese manner, "telephoned to me yesterday, saying that he had read somewhere that it was your birthday today. That it was a good day for me to come. There was some article on you, he said, in an English newspaper."

"Last Sunday's *Observer*. The article has not, officially speaking, been read by anyone in Malta. The reverse page carried a large article, copiously illustrated, on ladies' swimwear. The censors at Luqa Airport cut it out. They thus also cut out the little birthday article on myself. I received an uncensored copy through the British High Commission. In the bag, as they put it."

"Yes yes, I see. But our people must be protected. But some of these men with their scissors at the airport are not of the most educated. However, there it is."

"While we're on the subject, I may as well tell you that the General Post Office in Valletta have, after some trouble, kindly allowed me to have a copy of the poems of Thomas Campion that was sent to me, a limited edition of some value. They said that they had at last discovered that Thomas Campion was a great English martyr, so it must be all right."

"Good, that is good, then."

"No, not good. The great English martyr was Edmund, not Thomas. Thomas Campion wrote some rather dirty little songs. Clean songs too, of course, but some quite erotic."

He nodded and nodded, not displeased. Something or other, my agnostic depravity probably, was confirmed from my own mouth. He seemed unabashed at his ignorance of English martyrology.

"Well, now, that is very interesting. But it is the other thing we are concerned about." He was right, the conversational economy of the confessional against the author's tendency to divagate. "And, of course, to wish you a happy birthday yet again." He toasted me, smiling plumply. Absentmindedly, I toasted myself.

"Monsignor O'Shaughnessy says that you are said to have said in some interview or somewhere about there not being any doubt of the miracle. That you witnessed it. And so I am to offer you every facility to set down, to write, to make some little—"

"Deposition?"

He played an invisible concertina for two seconds. "Your mastery of the language. Canonization. Miracles. It is the usual thing. Your Thomas More, man of all seasons. Joan of Arc."

"In what way are you to offer me *every facility*? I have paper, a pen, a sort of memory. Ah, I think I know what is meant. I am not to put off doing it. I am to be prodded. The saint-making is somewhat urgent."

"No no no no, you are to take your time."

I smiled at him, seeing my jawed grimness in the fine old mirror over the bar, a genuine antique that advertised Sullivan's Whiskey. "So I, who don't believe in saints, am involved in the making of a saint. Very piquant. Bizarre, to use your own term."

"It is surely only a matter of the fact. It is not even a matter of you using the word *miracle*. It is a matter of you saying that you saw something that could not by normal means be explained." He seemed to be growing bored already with his assignment, but suddenly a spark of professional concern animated his brown droll eyes. "And yet surely *miracle* is the only word for what is seen clearly to be happening but cannot be explained except except—"

"—As the intervention of some force unknown to common sense or to science."

"Yes yes, you will admit that?"

"Not altogether. The world was once all miracle. Then everything started to be explained. Everything will be explained in time. It's just a matter of waiting."

"But this. It was in a hospital somewhere, was it not? And the doctors had despaired of the life of whoever it was? Yes?"

"It happened a long time ago," I said. "And I don't know whether you, Your Grace, would understand this, but writers of fiction often have difficulty in deciding between what really happened and what they imagine as having happened. That is why, in my sad trade, we can never be really devout or pious. We lie for a living. This, as you can imagine, makes us good believers—credulous, anyway. But it has nothing to do with *faith*." I shut up; I could feel my voice beginning to crack on that word.

"Aaaaah," he sighed. "But there will be witnesses other than yourself. People who do not lie for a living." What was meant to be a mere echo of my own words took on in his voice the tone of frivolous sin. "If you can get witnesses, it will be the better. There are hard men, you see, who must pretend that they do not want the canonization. They are called the advocates of the devil." That too sounded terrible.

"Witnesses?" I said. "Oh, heavens, it was so long ago. I honestly think you'd better go to some old peasant woman in black."

"No hurry," he said. His glass emptied, he got up. I got up with him. "You cannot be *forced*. You are to consider it, at least consider. That is all." He pointed his archiepiscopal ring toward the picture gallery of myself and the great. "I see," he said, "that he is not there." He had had a look at them then, a minor bit of homework, the cheating kind done in a rush in school just before the teacher comes in, seeking a picture of Voltaire and Christ together, smiling, godless artists and actresses all about.

"That," I said with finicking care, "is a *secular* portrait gallery. Although there, you see, is Aldous Huxley." And I gestured at myself grim and the stone-eyed mescaline saint laughing.

"Yes yes." He did not seem to have heard of him. He beamed through the tall window at the garden scene: Father Azzopardi and Geoffrey taking tea together at a small green table under a white umbrella, Geoffrey talking and gesturing with animation, Father Azzopardi nodding, taking it all in. "These young people," said His Grace. And then, prodding my ribs very familiarly: "No hurry, I say. But still please regard the matter as urgent." One of those contradictions that come easily to the religious mind, God being quite as large as Walt Whitman.

three

The gardeners kissed his ring, the maids kissed his ring, Joey Grima the cook kissed his ring. Ali did not but was shaken hands with very cordially and treated to a final Semitic quip. And when Geoffrey and I escorted His Grace to his Daimler, which was parked by Percius's Garage, the Triq Il-Kbira being narrow and my house possessing no forecourt, many villagers came running to kiss his ring—the two Borg sisters from the corner grocery, the entire staff of the police station opposite, an ancient squat known atheist in a flat cap who, all dusty, looked like some effigy from Malta's Paleolithic past newly exhumed, embarrassed children pushed to it by their mothers, even the drivers and conductors of three converging buses whose passages the emerged Daimler blocked. I would now be thought better of in Lija and even neighboring Attard and Balzan. The retired brigadier down the road, who, so Geoffrey had told me, despised me as a man grown rich on the writing of filthy yarns, was not so graced by archiepiscopal visitations. Geoffrey was saying, too loudly, to Father Azzopardi:

"We could arrange a private showing for you. We have all the gear here. You'll never see it in the public cinemas. But for Christ's sake don't tell the archbish." Father Azzopardi laughed terribly heartily. To me His Grace said:

"I'll be happy to see your deposition then. Mastery of the English language. Many happy birthdays once more. And please tell your young friend to be careful." No fool, then: he did not miss much. Father Azzopardi got in front with the driver, His Grace waved and blessed from the dead middle of the rear cushions, and the holy car sped soundlessly toward, say, Birkirkara.

"Poor young swine," Geoffrey said as we went indoors. "I told him all about copulating priests and nuns in hot pants in the States. He doesn't know his arse from his elbow. What was it all about then?"

"As I foresaw, I am to assist in the canonization of the late Pope."

"Oh God, oh my God, oh my dear God, you? Oh, Christ help us."

"Don't be silly, Geoffrey. You forget certain facts of my biography, if you ever, which I am inclined to doubt, knew them."

"Ah, getting all stuffy now, are we?"

"His Grace also asked me to tell you to watch your step."

"Did, did he? I see. Highly honored. Has his bulldogs sniffing round Strait Street, does he? Oh Jesus Lucifer Beelzebub Almighty, how I loathe and detest this bloody place."

"You mean, I think, that there is no decent tradition of Islamic pederasty here. The whole place is dedicated to good Catholic family making. It is also, you would say, excessively hippy and bosomy. No dirty little boys with bodies like straight sharp knives."

"You fucking hypocrite." He said this with little malice and followed it with a snigger. "None of that, eh? You must accompany me to the Gut sometime, dear."

"The Gut?"

"What the sailors call Strait Street."

"I see, I see." We walked out into the garden with its fine high thick walls, walls built by men used to sieges. "I think the archbishop was right to ask me to ask you to watch your step," I said.

"Fucking shithouse of a bloody place."

I said, as we strolled down a shaded path, seeing the three cats play ambushes: "You know, Geoffrey, if you're *really* unhappy—"

"Yes yes, dear. Percy in the Bahamas would be only too ready to have me, and there's Frank palpitating for friendship in Lausanne. The vicariously literary life of Geoff Enright, or from pillow to post office among the expatriate *masters*." He kicked a pruned twig out of his path. "I suppose, though, I *have* been just a bit wayward. The mail's piling up, as I am well aware. There are probably one or two royalty checks lying under the scum. But tomorrow morning—*early*—on the stroke of ten—I will really get down to the grind again." Knowing, of course, perfectly well, of course, that the old bitch hadn't much longer to go and one might as well, my dear, see the whole bloody business through. "Because you see, Kenneth"—he aspirated and nasalized my name and made it campily preposterous—"I am, in spite of my frequently quite unvolitional and usually deeply regretted misdemeanors, the thing you have averred rather too often that I am not. I mean *faithful*." I felt tears again ready to prick at that word. "Spiritually, I mean, I think I mean. I mean, what do you call it when it isn't just physical? That other thing doesn't really matter, does it? You've positively *sermonized* on that yourself, isn't that so? And, correct me if I'm wrong, but didn't you announce this very afternoon that that sort of thing was all over? For you, that is. All all, ah, over."

We had arrived at a massive siege wall crawling with greenery, so we turned about, seeing the ambushing cats from another angle. The two gardeners, Mr. Borg and Mr. Grima—these seemed to be very nearly the only two surnames in Lija—were still placidly irrigating.

I said, "Why don't we at least look at the more important letters after dinner? I've always, as you know, tried to be—"

"Gentlemanly and punctilious, yes dear. But we're dining out. And there is to be a birthday cake, though not, I surmise, with eighty-one candles."

"I didn't know. I'm not going. I'm not up to it."

"But you have to be up to it, dear. It's the British Council man, Ralph Ovington, and the *Poet Laureate*, no less, is on a visit."

"Oh, my God. And who defers to whom?"

"A nice point, isn't it? You're the senior, of course. But he has the O.M."

Yes, Dawson Wignall had the O.M. I saw myself in Geoffrey's twin mirrors —quite cold, not at all bitter. Willie Maugham, poor old bastard, had always maintained that the Order of Merit was really the Order of Morals. Three years previously I had been made, like him, a Companion of Honour and then heard the door of official laureation bang shut on me. The C.H. is about what the old bitch is worth, I'd say. As for the Nobel, I did not write inelegantly or tendentiously enough. I was not, like Boris Dyengizhdat, in political chains— which, I felt sure, he would break soon enough when the dollar royalties had mounted sufficiently. I did not, like Chaim Manon or J. Raha Jaatinen, belong to a gallant little nation that, possessing no strategical resources, had to be compensated with a great writer. I was, they had always said, cynical, not given to deep feelings or high thoughts. But I still sold well enough. Geoffrey's office bulged with as yet unanswered fan mail; my birthday had been very adequately remembered. I fulfilled a need, and that was for some reason wrong.

I said, sulkily, "I didn't know about this. Nobody told me."

"You held Ralph Ovington's note in your very own hand, dear. You said nice of him nice of him or some such rubbish. You forget, you know, you forget things."

"I'm entitled not to be well enough."

"Listen, dear," Geoffrey said. "Have we not here the most delicious *classical* bit of psychowhatsit of everyday life? It's *Ralph*, isn't it, the name *Ralph*?" I looked at him. Strangely enough, it was true. Strangely, because I thought I'd got over Freud. I'd even dreamt of Freudian interpretations of the dreams I had just been dreaming. And there I had been kicking Ovington's name and note and invitation out of my head because of an onomastic coincidence. "Black bastard," Geoffrey said with no tone of malice. "Black bitch. Dear, you really must show yourself as often as possible at your advanced age, you know. Oh, you and I know you're alive and well and, well, wonderful really, but it's a good thing to show it to the Poet Laureate, who's an awful little gossip. If you didn't turn up he'd take it back home, you know, that the old bugger's on his way off to the neverneverland, and you'd have the newspapers sharpening their obituaries. Terrible thing, that."

I sighed deeply. "Very well. I'll rest a little before dressing. In the study. Get Ali to bring me in some strong tea and a few pastries."

"Is that wise, dear?" There was the old harridan in a terminal coma, oozing with goo.

"Of course it's not wise. Nothing I do will be wise any more."

four

On the walls of my study I had a Willem de Kooning female in mostly red crayon and one of the first sketches Picasso had done for *Les Demoiselles d'Avignon*, also an Egon Schiele wash drawing of ugly lovers and an abstract composition by Hans Hartung. I had two oxblood leather club chairs and a matching couch, old-fashioned and chunky. Also books in glass cases, mostly of the well-thumbed-favorite variety: the main library was next to the upper salon. Near the original Quiller-Couch edition stood, not well-thumbed, not favorite, the revised *Oxford Book of English Verse*, bloody Val Wrigley as editor. I took this down and lay on the couch with it, looking for the inevitable selection from Dawson Wignall. I did not much care for what I found—insular, ingrown, formally traditional, products of a stunted mind. Wignall's themes derived from Anglican church services, the Christmas parties of his childhood, his public school pubescence, suburban shopping streets; they occasionally exhibited perverse velleities of a fetischistic order, though his droolings over girls' bicycles and gym tunics and black woolen stockings were chilled by whimsical ingenuities of diction. For this sort of thing, then, he had been honored by the monarch:

> *Thus kneeling at the altar rail*
> *We ate the Word's white papery wafer.*
> *Here, so I thought, desire must fail,*
> *My chastity be never safer.*
> *But then I saw your tongue protrude*
> *To catch the wisp of angel's food.*
> *Dear God! I reeled beneath the shock:*
> *My Eton suit, your party frock,*
> *Christmas, the dark, and postman's knock!*

I returned the book to the shelf and took down *Who's Who*, nearly staggering under its weight. I humped it over to what I called my Directory escritory and laid it on the blotting pad. There he was: Wignall, Percival Dawson—not yet O.M. but tinkling with other awards. His list of literary achievements was exiguous enough, spare output being the mark of a gentleman writer, but the autobiographical epic called *Lying in Grass* was probably the dehydrated equivalent of ten of my watery novels. I turned to my own entry and gloomed proudly over a whole column of overproduction. Wignall was also Harrow and

Trinity College; I was the Thomas More Memorial School and nothing. Ali knocked and I called *adelante*. While he placed the tea tray on the coffee table I heaved *Who's Who* back, shouldered rather. The aroma was of Twining's Breakfast Tea, which I took at all times except breakfast; at breakfast I drank Blue Mountain. Ali stood waiting as I poured.

"*Si?*"

He was troubled about something but found difficulty in expressing it. Something metaphysical then, not wages or women or living conditions. At length he said, "Allah."

"Allah, Ali?"

"*Éste país,*" he said, "*es católico, pero se dice Allah.*"

"Yes, Ali." The cakes were Kunzel, imported in dainty packets of six. It was a comfort to be on a sort of British soil again. "Their word for God is evidently the same as yours, but it means the Christian version of the Almighty, not the Muslim one."

This clearly troubled him. He said excitedly that there was no God but Allah, but Allah was not worshiped in churches, only in mosques, and that Allah was certainly not, so to speak, administered by *arzobispos*. In Tangier, he said, the whole situation had been perfectly understandable. The Christians had spoken of *Dios*. He understood that in their churches they had spoken of *Deus*—the same name almost. Here, however, in their churches—the *arzobispo* had told him in the bar there, while he drank deep in the manner of Christians —they referred to God as Allah. He did not understand. Not, of course, as I well knew, that he was what one might term a religious man. But the situation here struck him as strange. He had been taught as a boy that there was no God but Allah, and the Tangerine Christians had said there was no God but *Dios* or *Deus*. But these Maltese Christians said, just like Muslims, that there was no God but Allah. In churches. It was a strange situation. More, it was what might be termed a *bad* situation. That I should properly understand this, Ali gave me all available ways of putting it: *mala—malvada—maligna—aciaga.*

I had now eaten my third Kunzel cake, enough. I said: "Once, Ali, in Catholic churches all over the world, they used the Latin name *Deus*. But now they have what is called the vernacular, since very few ordinary people know Latin. In mosques all over the world they say *Allah*, but in Catholic churches all over the world they use the vernacular. In Serbo-Croat *Bog*, in Finnish *Jumala*, I think, and in Swahili, I know, *Mungu*. Now here in Malta their language is a kind of Arabic, though it uses the alphabet of the Romans. And in Arabic and Maltese the word for God is the same—*Allah*. Is that moderately clear?"

It was clear, he said, but it seemed somehow bad. Still, presumably the big men—*arzobispos* and so on—knew what they were doing, but nevertheless it did not seem right for Catholics in their churches to be calling on Allah. Then he changed the subject by taking from his white jacket pocket a small parcel and shyly handing it to me. It was a little *regalo*, he said, today being my *cumpleaños*. I checked the emotional lability by wondering why he had not made the presentation earlier. Perhaps because he knew that Geoffrey would say something sneering about it and this was the first time today he had found me alone. "Thank you, Ali, very very much," unwrapping it. It was pretty horrible, of course, by the standards of the sneerers of the world: a cigarette lighter of cheap metal encrusted with a Maltese cross. "Beautiful," I said. Ali waited. I struck it and it worked. Ali waited. I got myself a cigarette and lighted it. "Wonderful," I said, having drawn deeply. "It imparts a special taste to the tobacco." This was the kind of manifestly insincere response that Ali's culture required. Satisfied, he nodded and went out, saying something with *Allah* in it, perhaps appropriate to a birthday. So. It looked as if it were not going to be easy to get away from His late Holinesss Pope Gregory XVII today, meaning fat little Don Carlo Campanati. His reforms were upsetting even Ali.

I lay on the couch shortening my life and clutching Ali's gift like some token of faith—not inappositely, considering the Maltese cross. I thought of my brother Tom, who had smoked three cigarettes in his entire career and yet had died of lung cancer at forty-four. Tommy Toomey. With a name like that he had been destined to set up as a professional comedian, and he had done well enough, especially on the British radio in the 1930s. But the cough had become increasingly a hindrance to his sharp bright somewhat high-pitched delivery. Comedians of the old demotic school, like George Formby, Sr., had been able to make comic capital out of audibly dying ("Coughing better today, lads" and so on), but Tom's way had been one of rapid wit. His specialty had been the surrealist reshaping of English history, and this had presupposed an audience of some education. Such an audience was ceasing to exist when Tom's on-stage or in-studio coughing began to be uncontrollable. He had had the best of his time when he came to die, and he knew it. He died in the faith in a hospital near Hendon, having tried to joke some few hours before about a special niche in Purgatory for British Catholic comedians. He died clutching something—rosary beads, probably. I put Ali's gift in my trouser pocket. I supposed that Tom might find it easier to get out of Purgatory—if the now much impaired eschatology of fat Carlo's Church still admitted its existence—if he had a saint more or less in the family, or should I say more precisely had a saint as brother to his sister's husband. Then, having doused my life-shortener, I savored an old man's doze.

five

The residence of the British Council representative was in a quieter and perhaps more patrician part of Lija than my own. Geoffrey, sitting tied and jacketed next to Ali, who was driving, pointed this out, adding however that the whole bloody island was bloody terrible and he bloody hated it. Having arrived, we told Ali to come back in two hours, and then Geoffrey rang the doorbell, composing his sullen face, now unadorned by twin mirrors, to a twinkling vacuity. The British Council representative appeared, together with his wife. Mrs. Ovington was a big fair woman in a long candy-striped dress, her face bronzed and wrinkled. The bronze and, to some extent, the wrinkles were a badge of long service in the sunnier and duller stations of the world. They had had Warsaw for a couple of years, and there had once been talk of their being sent to Paris, but it had usually been places like Beirut and Baghdad. The wrinkles could also be accounted for by the long professional habit of insincere smiling. Ovington, who had a sun-and-tobacco-bleached stallion forelock falling onto his forehead, was also a smiler, but only with his teeth, which were of various shapes and colors and usually, as now, had a hearty Dunhill pipe stuck between them. They greeted me with laughs and shouts of "Got here, then?" and "Jolly good" but no happy returns. They were no strangers to me. They had presided over the Writers' Week that I had been asked to inaugurate, all of twelve years back, in Sydney. Sydney was regarded as a great British Council plum, but Ovington had not got on with the Aussies. They had also come to see me when I had been settling in here in Malta, with "Jolly good" and a jar of homemade cognac-flavored orange and lemon marmalade. It was good marmalade and I had not yet quite finished it. They were good people.

Ann Ovington dramatically stopped wrinkling and dragged me out into the forecourt. "Rather unfortunate," she said rapidly. "But you'll understand, and he won't. Sciberras, the Maltese poet, I mean. We had to have him along to meet Dawson, and he took the wrong turning out of the loo and barged into the kitchen, and there he saw the damned cake. Then he said how thoughtful and kind and the rest of it. Apparently it's his birthday today as well as yours, and he doesn't know it's yours, happy birthday by the way, and—well, you see the awkwardness of it. I've already primed everybody else—well, not your Geoffrey yet of course, but I will, no good leaving it to Ralph, he'd take all night explaining anyway. I know you'll see it as, well, you know, humorous. Short story stuff."

"Indeed," I said. With sadness I saw it as (indeed) short story stuff. If these had still been my writing days I would have itched to go off with that little seed of fiction, abandoning the party, knowing that what I was to invent would be far more entertaining and, in a sense, truer than the impending reality. "Does this Mr. er—"

"Sciberras."

"Does he know me? My work, I mean."

"I don't think so. You know what these people are like."

"A job for the British Council."

"How right you are. No lady guests, by the way. Except John's girl friend. I hope that's in order."

"Why what how—"

"Your Geoffrey said something about giants of literature meeting and no damned nonsense about sexual symmetry."

"But this is absurd. Also insolent. I would never make such a stipulation. This you know."

"I'm inclined to agree with your Geoffrey. All you bachelors. I discovered there was a Mrs. Sciberras, but it's the poet's mother. She speaks only Maltese and prefers to watch television anyway. So that's all right."

"I'll have a word with that damned Geoffrey."

"Oh, don't spoil your evening." She wrinkled and took my arm and urged me in. In the mold-smelling downstairs salon the two other writers were on their feet, drinking. Dawson Wignall O.M. decided we had met before, which we hadn't, and came for me with a hand out at shoulder level, the other hand tremoloing an iced whisky like a little bell (I tintinnabulate for you/A birthday wish that's warm and true).

"What?" he laughed. "Eh?" Question tags, not questions: British upper-class greetings often sound like confirmations of something. I gave him hearty congratulations without specifying on what, and he said, with mock-embarrassed mock seriousness, "Well—you know." Then he was all laughter again, a round duck-down-headed hamster-toothed children's book illustration of a benign humanoid who held the office John Dryden had once held. Sciberras, the Maltese poet, was introduced to me, or it may have been the other way round. I was given a sturdy gin and tonic in a rummer almost too heavy for me to hold. I got in first at Sciberras with many happy returns and he must forgive my not knowing his work, I hadn't had time yet to start trying to learn Maltese.

"Ah, but I write in Italian too," he shouted conversationally. "You must start to learn Italian."

"Then," the Poet Laureate said, with a tartness that made me want to like him, "he could read Dante as well as you."

"I know some Italian," I said. "Indeed, we once had Italians in the family."

"I know," Dawson Wignall said somewhat irritably. "Of course I know." Meaning that we great public men had no secrets from each other.

"I was saying that to him," I said. "Mr. Scribble er ass here."

"And I was saying what I said to him too," Dawson Wignall said.

"Yes yes," I said. "I understand—a *mot*." Sciberras looked from one to the other of us, sipping a cold drink as if it were a hot one. "A *mot*," I repeated, straight at him. "The French word for a word. But perhaps you write also in French."

"In Maltese and in Italian," Sciberras said more loudly, as if I had not clearly understood him the first time. "Only good night in Malta do we say in French. The French were not here long. The Maltese people made the French to go."

"Yes," I said. "So your archbishop told me. The Maltese people got rid of the French. One of my mother's ancestors just missed being one of the French that the Maltese got rid of, by the way. He was got rid of very nastily by the Mamelukes. In Egypt. The same expedition." I saw Geoffrey down a whisky mac in one draft and then give me an exaggerated wink. I stared coldly back. God knew how much tanking up he had done before leaving home. No ladies, indeed.

"But you are British," Sciberras said.

"My mother was French."

"The Maltese people got rid of the French," Sciberras shouted.

"When you got rid of them," Wignall said, "did you perhaps arrange that they were got rid of at night? So you could say *bon soir* to them?" I was beginning to find Wignall tolerable.

"It is *bonne nuit* we say. And in the daytime it is *buon giorno*. That is Italian."

"Go to bed French," Wignall said, "and wake up Italian. The best of both worlds. And in the middle you're Maltese. Jolly good."

Ann Ovington stood by us, benign, wrinkling away. Literary giants meeting. Then she said, "Well, must see how things are getting on."

"I look forward to my cake," Sciberras shouted roguishly, as though he already knew that he would not much care for the preceding courses.

"Jolly good," she said, wrinkling at him, leaving.

"He's looking forward to his cake," said Wignall very seriously. "Talking of your family, by the way. Mrs. Campanati sends her love."

"It is not pronounced like that," declared Sciberras. "It is not *neighty* but *nahty*. I know the name. It is an Italian name."

"And so you should know the name," Wignall said. "But in America it rhymes with *weighty*."

"Hortense?" I said. "You met Hortense?" I pronounced the name in the French way our mother had always insisted on.

"They call her Hortense over there," rhyming with *pence*. "There used to be a song about my sweet Hortense, as I remember. Got no money and got no sense. Not true of yours, of course. She looked very well, I thought you might like to know. I'd say she looked very modern, very smart and slim and so on. She sends fond regards and so on."

"What were you doing in Bronxville?"

"Reading poems, some of them mine. At Sarah Lawrence. She was at the little party afterwards. Not so little, really. Long, anyway. She seemed to me to be very well." But he nodded somewhat sadly.

"Not," I said in old man's candor, "knocking it back? Not getting stoned or blind or anything?"

"Very fit, I thought. A few, yes. Not too many. She seemed to me to be very well. I told her I'd be going to Malta. She said to say happy birthday and so on. When the time comes, that is." Wignall raised his glass at me and drank. Wignall, I decided, was a very tolerable person. Poet, that was a different matter, but who was I after all really to say?

Geoffrey was talking with Ovington, just by the drinks table, already on his third whisky mac. "She's probably written," I said. "We haven't had time to go over the mail lately, have we, Geoffrey?" He made a vulgar gesture of staggering against the ropes. I introduced him. Wignall said jolly good and Sciberras shouted something cordial and unidiomatic. Wignall said, slowly and clearly, to Sciberras:

"Mr. Toomey, besides being perhaps the most distinguished living writer in the British Commonwealth, was also related by marriage to His late Holiness Pope Gregory the Seventeenth."

It was little fat Carlo's day all right. "That I did not know," Sciberras said. Most people were awed on the revelation, but Sciberras kept whatever feelings he had well in check. "I wrote a *sonetto* about him. It is a strange story, also wonderful. He came to me in a dream and said to write it. So I wrote it." He started to shout it out:

> "*Sempre ch' io veda nel bel cielo azzurro*
> *levarsi bianca vetta scintillante*
> *quel radioso di Sua bontà gigante*
> *al cuore mi rammenta in pio sussurro . . .*"

Both Wignall and I listened in embarrassment, our eyes surveying the icescapes of our drinks. Wignall was not going to let him get away with the whole thing: he was, after all, Poet Laureate. He said, "Very profound. It needs to be looked at, I can tell, and really pored over. Pity to waste it just by blurting it out. Jolly good sonnet, I can tell, though."

"There is also," cried Sciberras, "the wonder of the visit in the dream."

"Yes, I see that. Remarkable, when you come to think of it."

The Ovington boy and his girl friend had not greeted us. She wore a dirty

Mother Hubbard and had neglected damp straw hair about her shoulders. John Ovington's hair was not neglected: it was contained in a headband glistening with bits of colored glass. He wore what I can only think of as a Natty Bumppo outfit, though his long soiled feet disdained moccasins. Home for the holidays, both, I presumed. The two young people sat tailorwise in the far corner on the floor, sharing a hand-rolled cigarette that stank of autumn twitchfires. Geoffrey kept leering at the boy, but the boy was not interested. Geoffrey was saying to Ralph Ovington:

"Don't know how you stand the bloody place. Bloody place gives me the bloody creeps." He could be more himself without lady guests.

"There are worse." Ovington smiled, his pipe pluming away as if dinner were over. "You can put up with any place if you have to be in it. If you have to be there you look for the good side. It's being too free that's the trouble perhaps." He swiveled his smiling head toward the boy and girl, who whispered together, shackled in the conformism of the young. "If you're free you're never satisfied. I've never been free."

"Oh, bloody Christ. The call of duty and all that balls."

The word *duty* made my eyes prick, just like *faith* and its derivatives. There was a line of Walt Whitman that—"There's a line of Walt Whitman," I said to Wignall, "that always brings tears to my eyes. Something about 'all intrepid captains and mates, and those who went down doing their duty.'" And there, to prove it, were the tears in my eyes.

"Stock response," said Wignall. "The Cambridge School invented the phrase, but only to sneer at. It's a useful phrase. And you can't make literature without the stock response."

Geoffrey was sniggering at me. "Those who *went down*," he sniggered. "Dear old Walt knew all about going down."

"Shut up, Geoffrey," I found myself saying with prep schoolmaster's sharpness. "Do you hear me? Shut up."

"Sorry, dear. But you must admit it's a bit comic, going down, doing his duty. Nurse Walt. A whale of a time in the war."

"It is not to be laughed at," cried Sciberras. "We did our duty. We did not go down. Except to the air-raid shelter."

"Yes yes yes," said the Poet Laureate, somewhat unhappy, but not half as unhappy as I. "We're all very proud of you, yes yes. The George Cross and all that. Jolly brave people, you Maltese."

"Who is he, then?" Geoffrey said. "This George Cross character, I mean."

"It is not a person but a thing," Sciberras shouted. "For valor in the Second World War, the whole island. I wrote a *sonetto*—"

"In Italian too?" said Wignall. "Jolly forgiving of you."

"No relation to Double Cross," Geoffrey said, helping himself to his fifth or sixth whisky mac, "the bugger who always came twice? And while we're on notable personalities, did you ever meet Joe Plush, the man with the velvet—"

"I said *stop it*, Geoffrey," I ground out. "Stop this nonsense *at once*."

"Or Chunky, the man with the pineapple ballocks?"

"Not heard that one before," Wignall lied. "Jolly good."

"The names," Sciberras called, "are not familiar to me."

"Oh Jesus bloody Belial Beelzebub, Lord of the Open Flies. Where's your bloody sense of bloody humor?"

Ovington kept smiling, pipe gripped hard. His wife came in, wrinkling jollily, to say: "Grub's up, chaps."

"Bring that in," Ovington said to Geoffrey, pipe gripped hard.

"Not worth it, old boy old boy," and he drained it. "Now lead me to the costly vintages."

"Maltese wines tonight," Ovington said. "You did say you wanted to try some, Dawson. Improved a lot lately."

Geoffrey quietened down when the imported cod fillets were brought on, and this had much to do with the Maltese wine. He insulted everybody during the avocado course, and the insults were taken with good humor by all except me and Sciberras. First he ribbed young John Ovington about his presumed philosophy of life: "I mean, we can't all be bloody parasites, can we? Got to be a host, hasn't there, to be parasitic on, right? So it won't work for everybody, so that means there's got to be a parasitic élite, which doesn't change the bloody world much, does it? Too right, it doesn't, sport." To the Mother Hubbard girl, whose name seemed to be Janie: "It becomes you, it does really, that chunk of filthy butter muslin, but then you're the sort of girl who could get away with anything, even having one tit bigger than the other." He did a comic oenophile act with the bottle of Marsovin: "Oh, I'd definitely say those raisins came from Grima's backyard not Fenech's, the north side where that diabetic tomcat goes for a piss, wouldn't you?" He told Sciberras that the Maltese language sounded like somebody sicking it all up, and no bleeding wonder, mate. It was ill-advised of him to make the similitude. He was telling the Poet Laureate that he ought to give the Maltese and the expats, if any of the sods turned up, and he wouldn't blame the buggers if they didn't, a recital of Great Filthy Poems, instead of the muck about sniffing little girls' knickers that he was probably going to drone out, when his color changed radically. Everybody noticed it but only Sciberras remarked on it.

"You are now very bloody green, mate," he shouted. He was no fool, despite the *sonetti* and the not going down. Subdued Geoffrey got up, saying nothing, and left the table with speed but dignity.

"You know where it is," called Ovington. To me, who had said nothing, he said, "Not at all, think nothing of it. He's a good chap, I know. Overworking, a little overexcited perhaps. It happens to the best of us."

"He hates us," Sciberras declared, with a bit of cod on his tongue. "This I can see. He hates both Malta and the Maltese. He thinks we are a small island and an inferior people."

"You are, you know," Wignall said. "A small island, I mean. No getting away from that."

"It is no reason to despise or for hate. 'This precious jewel set in the sea.'"

"Jolly good, very apt bit of quotation." Wignall finished his fish. To me he suddenly said, "When are you coming home?"

Home. Another of those damned emotive words. I must give up seeing people, I told myself, sniffing the tears back. All the old bitch can do these days is lay on the weepy-weepies. Self-pity, you know. "I doubt if I'll see England again," I said. "I'll perhaps have my cremation there. Or in France. I don't know. I suppose I'd better start making up my mind."

"You look jolly fit to me," Ann Ovington said. "Ah, talking of ah incinceration—" She meant the pork chops that were now being brought in by a mustached Maltese matron, each chop topped with a pineapple slice. She saw that that was probably tactless.

Wignall said, nodding, grinning at me, "Chunky, eh? I hadn't heard that one."

"A sort of anthropophagous aura hovering." I smiled, consciously thinly. Wignall was delighted.

He said, "Yes yes yes. Significant perhaps that the Real Presence is on its way to becoming the Real Absence. Except for a few like me. It must be because secular cannibalism is on its way in." Sciberras looked bewildered, chomping away at his chop. "I refer," Wignall told him, "to the population explosion and so on. Cans of *Mensch* in the supermarkets." Sciberras was still bewildered. "Kosher for those who want it. Nothing in Leviticus or Deuteronomy against it, is there? Or *Munch*, perhaps. Or *Manch*, even. But that sounds like canned Mancunian." He was disclosing a talent submerged in a nobler vocation. "Or a whole line of dressed meats presided over by Ann Thropp. Like Sara Lee, you know," he said to Sciberras, who did not know. I noticed that the two young people of the party took only vegetables. This would not, of course, be Wignall putting them off; this would be an aspect of their lifestyle, as it was called. The girl Janie, who was on my left, said:

"You're the Great Writer, aren't you? What do you write?"

"I'm retired now. Very old, as you can see."

"What sort of things did you write when you did write?" She had quite clean fingernails and a slight venerean strabismus, rather like— No. Wait.

"Novels, plays, short stories. Some of the stories were filmed. Did you ever see *Fitful Fever* or *Down Came a Blackbird*? Or *Duet* or *Terzetto*?" No to all those, and I couldn't really blame her. "Do you like reading?"

"I like Hermann Hesse."

"Good God," I said, surprised. "There's hope for us all. I knew Hesse."

"*You knew him?*" Her jaw dropped, showing half-chewed greens. She goggled and then cried across the table, "Johnny. He *knew* Hermann Hesse."

"Who did?" He had his own family-size bottle of Coca-Cola to help the greens down.

"Him here. Mr. er—"

I was not quite all things to all men, but I had plenty to offer: for the Catholics a potential saint as good as in the family; for the young a much overrated German novelist of my acquaintance. And there was always my own work for those who cared for that sort of thing.

"Hesse is great," John Ovington pronounced.

"You've read him in German?" asked cunning Wignall.

"He's above language," John Ovington pronounced.

"There I must respectfully beg to differ," said Wignall. "No writer is above language. Writers *are* language. Each is his own language." I was impressed to hear a slight tremor of what I took to be vocational conviction.

"It's the ideas," the boy told us. "They count, not the words."

"And how about Shakespeare's ideas? Damn it, Shakespeare had no ideas worth talking about." Trembling more, rightly.

"Perhaps that's why we don't read him." The boy swigged straight from his family-size bottle.

"*Dig* is what you used to say, dear," wrinkled his mother.

"Following," said his father, smilingly chewing, "the behest of the bard himself. 'Good friend for Jesus' sake forbear to dig the dust enclosed here.'" He looked round for approval and got a sort of grin from me. Sciberras looked blankly from face to talking face, eating heartily though.

"A dead scene," the boy said. He made the gesture of being willing to pass his bottle across to Janie, but she shook her locks at him.

"A dead shakescene," smiled his father. Wignall's jowls shook as he prepared unguestly reproof, outrage, disgust, something, so I got in quickly with, addressing Sciberras out of politeness:

"He was a nice rather unhappy old man when I saw him last. It must be all of fifteen years ago. In Lausanne or Geneva or somewhere. He was as old then as I am now. He didn't seem to care much for his work any more. He wondered if he'd done the right thing in getting out of Germany and concentrating on fake orientalism and higher games."

"What higher games?" Janie asked and, simultaneously, John pronounced, "I'm quite sure he didn't say *fake*."

"*Das Glasperlenspiel*," I said, "for which he got the Nobel. And no, he didn't say *fake*, he said *ersatz*."

"This cannot be so," Sciberras said, and I could see he thought I was referring to Shakespeare.

"The East, the East," in a manner wailed Wignall, and I feared he was starting to recite a poem. But then, "You think you've wrung the West dry, you kids."

"Wrung us dry," John said, pleased, smirking.

"What do you know about the East?" I said, angry at the smirk, also at last feeling the sugary acid of the wine bite, sickened by Geoffrey's behavior and by a birthday that was going to end miserably, remembering too late that the Ovington boy had been born in Kuala Lumpur and now undoubtedly to be told that the girl Janie, smirking—

"I was born in New Delhi."

"Oh, it was the sahib's East for both of them," Ovington admitted. "I should have mentioned that Janie's father is the Assistant High Commissioner. This new orientalism has nothing to do with being children of the Foreign Service. I think they're partly right, I think they've been let down."

"Oh my God," Wignall said, "who hasn't been let down? But don't think that it's a system or a culture or a state or a person that does the letting down. It's our expectations that let us down. It begins in the warmth of the womb and the discovery that it's cold outside. But it's not the cold's fault that it's cold." I felt sure that he must have written a poem on some such theme. Nay, perhaps his entire oeuvre was erected on it. Anger I could not well explain started to bubble in me. I was about to say, angrily, that we'd all let down our past, our culture, our faith when Sciberras saved me from public tears by speaking quite quietly over his emptied plate.

He said, "I will tell you this. It is as follows. It is that we must look for what we want where we are and not in some other place." I gaped at that good sense as if this comic Maltese had turned into an oracle. Then I saw him as a symbol that, had I still been writing, would have been of immense potency: the whole incarnated Mediterranean—Phoenician, Arabic-speaking, inheritor of Greek philosophy, Roman stoicism, a provincial faith promulgated in Aramaic that had built its own empire. "It is also that we do not sneer at duty and at the faith we are taught at home."

Ah, that terrible emotive trinity. The force of the words was softened by the comic Mediterranean accent, otherwise the tears that started would have flooded onto the congealed sauce on my plate. And then we were all saved, except the children, who were past saving, by the appearance of the birthday cake, brought in by Ann Ovington herself, its shape that of an open book, three candles only on top out of, I presumed, deference to my shortness of breath. Sciberras, beaming now, had plenty of breath. The children la-lahed "Happy Birthday to You" with a knife-on-bottle punctuation from John Ovington while Sciberras, a smiling moon of delight, blew out and commenced cutting.

He said, "Where is our friend? Perhaps now he will be less bloody green."

"I think," I said, starting to rise, "I'd better go and—"

"Leave it to me," Ovington said, quicker. Wignall nodded and nodded, putting crumbs of the cake to his mouth, smiling down some long vista of the years at perhaps some fateful childhood party in Hampstead or an as yet uncorrupted Golders Green. I settled myself again and brought out, thinking to give pleasure to their author, the lines I had read that afternoon:

> *"But then I saw your tongue protrude*
> *To catch the wisp of angel's food.*
> *Ah God! I quailed beneath the shock:*
> *Your something something party frock—"*

"Shut it," he cried. *Shock* was right. "Shut it, shut it. It's nothing to you except a chunk of—" His eyes now were the ones to fill. "All over, it's all over. Sorry," he sniffed to his hostess, who wrinkled painfully though not in bewilderment: she had entertained plenty of authors in her time. And then to me: "Sorry. It's just that— Growing old isn't easy," he said loudly to the children, who had been crumbling cake in what I took to be embarrassment. He was all of sixteen years my junior. "Everything's spat upon now. Everything." Then Geoffrey came in, ahead of Ovington, pale and with a big damp patch on his jacket where, I assumed, vomit had been hastily wiped off with a face flannel. Ovington was trying to steer him into the salon, saying something about coffee, but Geoffrey said:

"Just in time for that thing, I see. Won't have any, though. Just a beaker of that shitty local raisin juice." And he went back to the place he had vacated at the time of the fish course.

"Is that wise?" his hostess asked.

"It will either settle the guts or effect a definitive ah purgation," said Geoffrey in what I took to be a parody of my voice. He helped himself. "How's my booful lil boy?" he leered at John Ovington. Then he swigged.

"Stop that, Geoffrey," I said, very weary. But then something hit out at the weariness, something a man of my age ought not to have had, namely a twinge of toothache. It was the cake, of which I had tasted the smallest possible fragment. It seemed unfair somehow, injury to insult.

Geoffrey said, "Yes dear of course dear. Behaved badly, haven't I? It's this bloody place, you know. Shitty nasty little bloody island. Still, it *is* your birthday, after all." Oh my God. "Should have behaved better on Grand Old Man's bloody birthday."

Sciberras cut into the general shock with: "You make a mistake. It is *my* birthday. But I do not think you are able to get anything right. You have a mind very badly arranged."

"Deranged you mean," Geoffrey said. "You're not the only bugger in the world or even on this shitheap of an island to have a birthday today. If you knew anything about anything you'd know whose birthday it primarily bloody well is." He raised a recharged glass. "Many happy returns, *cher maître*, and all that shit," he leered at me. Sciberras had to be made to take all this as a very tasteless joke.

"A tasteless joke," Wignall soothed a fellow poet, "but still a joke. It's *your* birthday," patting Sciberras blindly. "That's right, isn't it, Toomey? His and his only, isn't it?"

I had given up many things in my time but had never yet had to deny the most basic fact of my life. "Certainly not mine," I said. I heard, thank God, what could only be our car coming back for us.

seven

I was stupid not to go straight to bed, initiating the new regime of sleeping alone, instead of having it lengthily and dangerously out with Geoffrey. In the upper salon he sat at the untuned harpsichord, picking at ensoured harmonies while I tried to address him with calm, to treat him as some errant character of my own fiction. But my inner agitation was too strong to permit me to sit. I tottered up and down on the fur and marble, a weak nightcap whisky and water atremble in my claw.

"It was deliberate, wasn't it? An attempt, highly successful, to make me look a fool. What I want to know is *why*. But I think I know why. This is my punishment for making you leave Tangier. A punishment for consulting your own interest and, indeed, safety. And, as far as that matter is concerned, you are very far from being out of the wood. But still I had to be punished."

"Oh, bloody balls." And, as if this were opera buffa recitative, he struck a sort of chord. He had his mirror glasses back on, though the salon lights were dim enough. His stomach seemed to have settled, and his speech was unblurred.

"Stop that. Stop that stupid noise."

He twanged a foul fortissimo cadence and got up. Shambling over to the leather couch he said, before falling onto it, "Things just got a bit out of control, that's all." He lay glooming up at the dead chandelier. "Didn't care much for the atmosphere. Hostile. That stupid bloody poet too. Making you hand over your birthday like that. It was on your behalf really. Got irritated, got pissed."

"Well, it obviously can't go on, can it? I obviously can't afford to let it go on."

"You mean peace in your declining years, tranquil twilit fulfillment and the rest of the bloody crap. Honor and fucking dignity. You mean I've got to go."

"You're not happy here." I was being very reasonable. "And I've no intention of making another move. This one was shattering enough."

"You're bloody well telling *me* it was bloody shattering. So I have to go."

"Oh, I don't really want you to go, you must know that. But it's a matter of . . . it's a matter of self-preservation."

"Very cold words, sir, after all those former hot avowals. Right right right. Go. Pack my pitiful possessions and go. London first, I think, sort myself out from there. And then Percy in the Bahamas or that epileptic snuffling sod in Lausanne. Good good good. I shall need some money."

"Three months' salary. That seems to me just and reasonable."

"Yes," he said quietly. He took off his mirrors to eye me coldly. "A just and reasonable bastard, that's what you are. And when you've snuffed it I'll be just and reasonable too. Ten thousand quid's what I want, dear."

"You're joking."

"No, not really. As a matter of fact, you foresaw all this. You set it all down in that stupid bloody sentimental shitbag of a novel called *The Affairs of Men*, fucking silly pretentious bloody title. You know, this just and reasonable writer bastard who's getting old but has the O.M. and the Nobel and his best friend goes in for the term as I remember is posthumous blackmail. And there's all this guff about when the writer's dead he's finished with and it doesn't matter a monkey's ballock what anybody writes about him so up your arse Jack and publish and be damned. Then he bethinks himself that he's a Great Writer and doesn't want to go down in history as a Right Bastard so he pays up in return for a Solemn Promise in Writing to produce nothing of a haha Biographical

Nature after the great writer sod has snuffed it. And the great big subtle marvelous point is that he knows there's nothing to stop this shit of a best friend spewing all the muck up when he's kicked but at least he'll go to his tomb in Westminster Abbey knowing that if the shit is shoveled out at least it is Unjust."

The nightcap was spilling. I sat on the edge of the armchair and tried to drink it but could not. I could see Geoffrey grinning with a film gangster's laziness at the tremolo of teeth and glass. I put the glass down on the fretted Indian table with care and difficulty. "Bastard," I choked. "Bastard bastard."

"A bastard who's read your books," he said. "And a prissy old-fashioned load of fucking codswallop they are. Things have changed, my old darling. Now we're allowed to set it all down stark and bare, not in ah ah *elegant periphrases,* your term I think. About a dirty old man trying to get it up and in and crying because he can't come. And snuffling about darling boy oh this is such ecstasy. You just and reasonable bastard, you."

"Go on," I said, rising. "Out. Get out now. Before I put you out."

"You and whose fucking army?"

"I'm ordering you to go, Geoffrey. You can spend the night at a hotel and have the bill sent here. You can pack your bags tomorrow. I shall not be around. A check will be waiting for you on the hall table. Three months' salary and enough for your air fare to London. Now get out." I had to sit down again.

"Ten thousand nicker here and now and I'll be on my merry way. Didn't you write some fearful shitty nonsense called *On Our Merry Way* or was it that bloody twerp Beverley? Never mind." He grimaced and painfully belched. "Christ, that bloody muck. Alum and cat piss. Cheeseparing sods."

"Out of my house, go on."

"I've got a fair amount done already, dear. You always said that my letters showed I could have *flair* if I got down to it. That business at Rabat makes quite a nice paragraph—you know, when pocky little Mahmud literally shat on you."

"Go on, go." Then I collapsed into sniveling. "To think of all I've done for you—the faith—the trust—"

"Ah, here we go: faith and duty and the rest of the boxroom junk. Boo hoo hoo. Tears idle tears. You do really, you know, cry most bee-ootah-flah. England, home and duty. Jesus Christ on the fucking cross. Owwwwwwww."

"Out of my house—" I was on my feet again, hands blindly seeking something to hold on to. He lay there comfortably, admiring the shaking ineffectual pathetic shrunken trembling mannikin. "There's a police station across the street. I can have you thrown out."

"I'll scream bloody blue murder, dear. I'll tell them you were trying to bugger me. It's the death penalty here, I believe."

There was no time for me to see clearly what Geoffrey's real intention could be. The rage was too fierce a tenant. I felt collapse impending but held it off. "You want me to die," I gasped. "That's it. Easier that way."

"Very neat, to do that on your birthday. Like Shakespeare, if he really did. And then that Maltese sod can write a *sonetto* about it. A homo generoso. He gave me his birthday, cake and all."

"Don't. Can't."

"Do control yourself, dear. You've gone all blue around the lips." And then, in a deliberately bad parody of my dictating: "Geoffrey lay unperturbed on the ah settee while his aged friend exhibited all the symptoms of an approaching ah cardiac ah spasm. In impeccable cockney he remarked: 'Yer've gawn owe bleeoo abaht ve—' " And then, getting up in concern: "Oh God, no."

"Get me the . . . can't . . . it's the . . ." An obscene shaft of indigestion followed by mild toothache followed by agony that shot from clavicle to wrist, all on the left side, the right serenely aloof. I went down to the rugs as neatly as in a stage fall but without syncope.

"All right, dear, the white ones, I know—" He was into the bedroom to the bathroom, I heard the click of the medicine cupboard door. Then I passed out, as it were, volitionally. I came to, it seemed, no more than a second later, but I was in pajamas and bed and Dr. Borg or Grima, it had to be one or the other, was taking my pulse. When I opened my eyes I saw Geoffrey standing there. He gave me a sweet and loving smile. Dr. Borg or Grima was also wearing pajamas but an egg-stained dressing gown as well. He was severely unshaven and had a cigarette in his mouth. I had once seen an Andalusian priest conducting a burial service unshaven with a cigarette in his mouth. It took the seriousness out of things.

He dropped my wrist and his own, which had a wristwatch on it. He said, "No excitement. Eighty-one is a good age, but my father is ninety-five. I tell him no excitement but the television programs sometimes excite him. The Italian ones, not the Maltese. It is the girls who make the announcements even that excite him. I give him," he said, "simple sedatives," taking out and dousing his cigarette, a presumable sign that the examination was over.

"He did get excited," Geoffrey said. "It was what you might call literary excitement. But I'll make quite sure there's no more of that."

"Yes, and next time please telephone me. You woke up the family with the knocking."

"I can't telephone," Geoffrey said with his dangerous sweetness, "because we have no telephone. They tell us there is a long waiting list for the telephone. They say we have to wait at least eighteen months for a telephone. Or even longer, for a telephone. During the day, if I wish to telephone, I go to the shop at the corner, which has a telephone and allows me to use the telephone. But when that shop is shut I cannot telephone. That is why I did not telephone."

"There is always the police station."

"Yes," Geoffrey said, "and a right lot of snotty bastards they are."

I found that I could not speak.

"Well," the doctor said, "this is Malta."

"You're bloody well telling me that it's bloody well bloody Malta."

I found that I could speak.

"Please, Geoffrey, no."

"No excitement," the doctor ordered.

"I'll watch him," Geoffrey said.

This intention went unfulfilled that night, although, despite my avowed purpose of the afternoon, I did not sleep alone. I did not, for that matter, sleep very much. After an hour or so I woke ridiculously refreshed and, as it were, cathartized, and none of the properties of the Maltese night conduced to sleep's resumption. The electric mosquito-repellers whirred and clicked and puffed, and public clocks all over the island announced in imperfect unison the full hour or the part hour and, as an exordium to the part hour, the full hour which had already been completed. I watched Geoffrey, instead of he me. He was snoring irregularly, his fat back turned to me, and occasionally forgetting how to breathe, remembering only in a bed-shaking spasm. At one point he started to breathe easily and then he said something in Latin. It sounded like *"Solitam . . . Minotauro . . . pro caris corpus . . ."* I listened with care and surprise, having believed that he had attended a minor public school that despised the classical tongues and taught in their stead a kind of elementary anthropological linguistics.

I took a cigarette from the silver box, a gift from the Sultan of Kelantan, that stood on the night table, seeing it clearly in the very rich moonlight, and, to my vague astonishment, was able to light it with Ali's flaring gift that lay beside it. I had, I thought, left that below in my study. The big flame seemed to impinge on Geoffrey's sleeping mind, for he flailed as if fighting it and then turned toward me. After a pause he snored out a ghastly odor that was neither vinous nor vomitory, more ferrous in its basic tone, with indefinable harmonics of gross decay. It puzzled more than appalled me: it was remotely familiar.

Moonlight showed a heavy sweat on Geoffrey's nakedness, which was now too close for my comfort. I had not, on my first waking, been sure whether to encourage a certain vague hunger for tea and a sandwich to attain a solidity that demanded satisfaction; now I was quite sure. I got out of bed on firm legs and found my slippers and dressing gown. The bed was all Geoffrey's now. I felt for him none of the bitter resentful loathing I might properly, in spite of his eventual yielding to duty or fear, be expected to feel and, indeed, expected to feel. I felt only the generalized pity one always feels for the defenseless prisoner of sleep, seeing in him the defenseless prisoner of life. Man does not ask for nightmares, he does not ask to be bad. He does not will his own willfulness. If that is contradiction, it is because human language disposes to contradiction. I told myself, untruthfully perhaps, that I knew the world and had learned tolerance. That it was too late for me to take human passions seriously, including my own. But I remembered saying something of that kind publicly at the age of forty-five. Give us peace in our time, whatever the time. Which logically meant throwing Geoffrey out. And then feeling no peace because of a lack of charity, of awareness that I was, all said and done, a dithering nuisance, a hypocrite, a prissy product of a bad period, ludicrous in my senile sensuality, everything that, in blunter language, Geoffrey had termed me. Let him sleep, let it all sleep.

I went down and entered the great white kitchen, its surgicality qualified by the ghosts of spices, softly, very softly. Ali's room was just beyond it and he was, the desert life only three generations behind him, a featherweight sleeper. Very softly I boiled water, made a sandwich from the remains of the luncheon roast chicken, scalded the Twining creature. Then I softly carried my bever to the study on a tray, helped by moonlight to toe-on the footswitch of the standard lamp. It was not urgency but curiosity, as well as a disquiet that would clarify itself later, that made me want to look again at the story of the priestly miracle. I munched while I searched for the three volumes of my collected shorter fiction, beautifully leatherbound and tooled, my American publisher's ten-year-old Christmas gift. That it was in the second volume I knew, since the first was given over to tales with a European setting, the third to the harvest of my Eastern travels, and the second to the Americas. The event on which the story had been based had taken place in Chicago in the twenties, this I knew, but the title I had totally forgotten. It turned out to be *Laying on of Hands* and the style more slipshod even than I remembered. A thousand-dollar effort done hastily for a long-dead illustrated monthly. I read with shame, sipping and chewing, trying to reach the tones of a reality under the shabby professionalism.

The faceless and nameless narrator (I apologize to those who know the story already) is a British journalist visiting Chicago to write about the Reverend Elmer Williams, publisher of *Lightnin'*, a periodical devoted to the exposure of gangsterism and corrupt politics. In the foyer of the Palmer House Hotel he renews acquaintance with a priest, Father Salvaggiani, whom he knew ten years previously on the Italian front, the priest a chaplain, the journalist an ambulance driver. The priest, a fat undistinguished little man who smells of garlic and speaks comic English, is distressed. He has come all the way from Italy to see his brother, who is dying in a private ward in a hospital from multiple cranial fractures and ice-pick wounds in the stomach. The narrator realizes that the brother, Ed Salvaggiani, is a noted gangster and, scenting material for a little color story, goes along to the hospital with the priest. Father Salvaggiani gives his brother the final comforts of the Church and, knowing that he cannot last much longer, weeps. Passing through a public ward he hears terrible screams from a child dying of tuberculous meningitis. The doctors shake their heads: nothing can be done. But Father Salvaggiani lays his hands on the child and prays. The screaming lessens and eventually ceases and the sufferer falls into a deep sleep. To the surprise of the doctors there is a progressive improvement, recorded each day as the priest comes to weep over his dying brother. The brother dies but the child recovers. The faithful among the hospital staff do not doubt that this was a miracle. But Father Salvaggiani talks, in his comic English, of the terrible unintelligibility of God's will. Why could he do nothing for his brother, whom he loved, and yet be the agent of divine mercy for a total stranger? Perhaps the Lord intends this child to grow into a vessel of his own redemptive purpose and has used this meanest of his priestly servants to defeat nature and initiate the accomplishment of that end. He thinks these thoughts aloud at his brother's funeral, a great affair of flowers and unshaven mourners. The narrator thinks such speculations are idle. Life is a mystery and God probably does not exist.

I fitted a cigarette into my holder and flared Ali's lighter, which, for some reason, I had brought down with me in my dressing-gown pocket. There was hardly a table in the whole house that did not have its own cigarette box and matching heavy Ronson, Queen Anne silver or chunky onyx. Ali ought to be pleased. I thought about the story and could not for the life of me reassemble all the historical facts upon which the fiction was founded. There had certainly been a magazine called *Lightnin'*, and its publisher had been the Reverend Elmer Williams. Father Salvaggiani had really been Monsignor Campanati, at that time a kind of wandering chairman of the Association for the—was it the Propagation of the Faith? His elder brother, Raffaele, had indeed died of gangster violence in Chicago, but as a loud and annoying voice of decency and incorrupt politics. I had been in Chicago, staying at the Palmer House, but not to write about brave crusaders against cruel racketeers. I had come to see the Manet and Monet and Renoir collection of the Chicago grande dame Mrs. Potter Palmer, so much I remembered. To write about it? To buy from it? Sell to it? This had disappeared from my mind. I saw clearly still the agonized face of Raffaele, whom I had, though with certain qualifications, admired but who had never much cared for me. This had everything to do with my homosexuality, which, in the manner of decent Latins, he believed was a matter of free election in brutal sinfulness. Carlo was never so censorious. He never *saw* my homosexuality in, as it were, action; he was not inclined to be interested in stories retailed about me. The sins of libido he knew of were strictly limited to the heterosexual sphere and were two in number. If men desired little boys or each other, that was because they were deprived of the company of women. Or perhaps, though rarely, they might have been set upon by exorcizable demons of buggery. As for those with a holy vocation who had chosen the celibate way, God's grace sustained them like quinine, and that was that. Of such is the kingdom. I Campanati were a highly moral family, except for the youngest boy, Domenico, whom my sister married. The only daughter, Luigia, became a very martinetish mother superior.

Which hospital had it been? Had the miracle, if it was a miracle, been after all so spectacular? Was the disease in my story the same as the disease in fact? Might it not have been some disease not quite so lethal, its course reversible under the influence of a powerful benign will united to the wavering will of the sufferer? I had, of course, no real need to puzzle all this business out; I was under no obligation at all to help turn Carlo Campanati, a good but greedy man, into a saint. But there was this niggling matter of the truth. The term *truth* did not flood my eyes as did *faith* and *duty* and sometimes *home*, but a man who serves language, however imperfectly, should always serve truth, and, though my days in the service of language were over, I could not deny the other, timeless, allegiance. But I was less concerned now with that deeper truth, the traditional attribute of God, which literature can best serve by telling lies, than with the shallower truth we call factuality. What had happened in Chicago? I was not sure.

There were records. There had been witnesses. They could be found, consulted, though with trouble. But the real question for me was: how far could I claim a true knowledge of the factuality of my own past, as opposed to pointing to an artistic enhancing of it, meaning a crafty falsification? In two ways my memory was not to be trusted: I was an old man, I was a writer. Writers in time transfer the mendacity of their craft to the other areas of their lives. In that trivial area of barroom biographical anecdotage, it is so much easier and so much more gratifying to shape, reorder, impose climax and dénouement, augment here, diminish there, play for applause and laughter than to recount the bald treadmill facts as they happened. Ernest Hemingway, as I remembered well (but what do I mean by remembering well?), reached a stage where, even though he had virtually ceased to produce fiction, he was totally in thrall to its contrivances. He told me, and he was only in his fifties at the time, some years my junior, that he had slept with the beautiful spy Mata Hari and that she had been "good though a little heavy in the thigh." I knew, and records could confirm, that Hemingway had not yet even paid his first visit to Europe at the time when Mata Hari was executed.

I had, it is true, been in the habit of keeping certain records, especially in my first twenty years as a professional writer of fiction. The little notebook in the waistcoat pocket, Samuel Butler said, betokens the true writer. And so I had jotted down *mots*, ideas for stories, descriptions of leaves, the flue on women's arms, dogmerds, the play of light on gin bottles, slang, technical terms, naked factualities of time and place (the better to fix some extraordinary, to use Jim Joyce's term, epiphany), and these notebooks survived, though not in my possession. The notebooks of Kenneth Marchal Toomey were lodged in the archives of some American university, to be published—probably with all the trimmings of scholarship—after my death. I did not object to the opening up of the junkshop of my brain when that brain had ceased to be mine and had become merely part of the economy of the soil; for the present, considerations of reserve and privacy prevailed. Now which was the university? There were letters to and from that university on file, also details of the few thousand dollars paid for the dubious treasure, but my files, thanks to the hurried move from Tangier but also, and mainly, to Geoffrey's inefficiency, were in total disorder. I did not want to bring on another heart attack by insisting on at least a minimal sorting-out, though Geoffrey could be reminded of his grudging promise of the afternoon. What afternoon? What day? Did I? Geoffrey lived entirely in the present; he had shed, perhaps wisely in his case, the burden of being burdened by memory. No, not strictly true: he remembered, far more clearly than I, what it suited him to remember. I trembled again as I remembered what things he had decided to remember about me.

Best let Carlo achieve sainthood through other miracles, better attested. But then *faith* and *duty* trumpeted a muted two-part invention in a chamber of my brain. Saint Gregory, enthroned to some extent by grace of the attestations of K. M. Toomey, Companion of Honour, pray for us. Pray for me, hypocrite, lecher, waster of seed in sterile embraces. Not just faith (lacking now, long volitionally discarded, but, because of a new and final sterility, contemplating return). Not just duty (servant of faith and hence disregarded, but reread that last sentence). Fear then, a kind of fear.

I knew what I would find in Geoffrey's office. A ghastly mess of toppling files, a snow of unopened letters, corded bundles of the same, books, periodicals, press cuttings, earnest theses with titles like *K. M. Toomey and the Thanatic Snydrome*, filing cabinets lying on their sides like dead square dogs (*K. M. Tooney and Figurative Ineptitude*), empty bottles, heel-ground cigarette-ends, a desk covered with "gay" periodicals showing naked simpering boys and frank scenes of pedication, a chair sticky as with semen. Nevertheless, I took several deep breaths, and then some Peveril of the Peak watered from the tap in my adjoining washroom. Then I softfooted into the hallway, passed the bar, and entered Geoffrey's office. I switched on the light, whose rawness flooded the foul leer of chaos. I expected to be appalled but not so appalled as I was.

nine

The crackling of the letter in my left dressing-gown pocket was a crackling as of fire. But I was maintaining calm pretty well. The letter had, to cool the metaphor, ignited my cerebral engine, which was throbbing away nicely. I had everything worked out, I thought. When Ali rose at dawn, he found me seated at the kitchen table sipping Blue Mountain. He respected, as ever, my preference for total morning silence and merely nodded a *buenos dias*. Nor was he surprised to see me there so early: he knew my scant need of sleep. He nodded and nodded as I poured coffee into another cup, added ample sugar, filled a glass with orange juice from the refrigerator, and put the two eye-openers on a tray. Geoffrey's were the eyes that had to be opened. I left the kitchen, balancing the tray with an admirable (I admired) control of nerves, and mounted to the master bedroom.

Geoffrey lay across the bed, his head over the edge like a man lapping from a pool. I put down the tray and shook him. He made foul noises and at last awoke, blinking down at the floor as if wondering what it was. Then he forced himself onto his back in a crucifixion posture, groaned, coughed, blinked rapidly, then almost sightlessly grasped the orange juice I proffered. He drained it blind, smacked, shuddered, belched, shivered, sighed deeply and handed back the emptied glass. I gave him his coffee. He was half awake now.

He sipped, then muttered "Cat piss." He did not mean the coffee. "Mouth like a fucking all-in wrestler's jockstrap. Awfully kind, dear." I sustained my morning silence. "Any more there?" He blinked for the tray and, he hoped, coffeepot. I gave him a cigarette and lighted it with Ali's lighter. He coughed long and obscenely and then said, "Better. Much." Then he lay down again and smoked, rolling the dirty whites of his eyes at me. "To what do I owe the inestimable so to speak fucking honor?" I cleared my throat and spoke my first words of the day, saying:

"Last night you asked me for ten thousand pounds."

"Did I? Did I really? A nocturnal inspiration, as they say." And then, "Oh yes, my God, last night. Behaved badly, I seem to recall. It was that bloody Maltese raisin jam and vinegar." He recalled more. "Ah yes, indeed." He appraised me, who was sitting on the edge of the bed. "You seem fit, dear. Does you good, that sort of fuse-blow, so it would appear, yes. Must do it more often. What's that about ten thousand pounds?"

"Geoffrey," I said. "Listen with very great care and do not say anything until I have finished. First, you shall have your ten thousand pounds."

"Jesus Beelzebub, are you serious?"

"I said no interruptions, didn't I? Attention now, please, close attention."

"Hanging on to your lips, sir."

"In the early hours I was in your office, which, I may say, was and still is in an unbelievable state of squalor and disorder. It was by sheer chance that I found this letter on the floor, a cigarette-end crushed into it by, I presume, your heel." I took out the dirty envelope and, from that, the letter. "This is from Everard Huntley in Rabat."

"That shit."

"Geoffrey, please. You have no conception of the effort I am expending on keeping calm. I will not read out the letter, which is to me but altogether concerns you. I will merely tell you what it says. It says that a certain Abdul-bakar called on the British consulate in great and indeed tearful distress. He spoke of the death of his son, Mahmud."

Geoffrey went terribly pale and whispered, "Oh bloody Jesus."

"Yes, Geoffrey, the injuries you inflicted in what you termed *play* proved lethal. This letter, I must inform you, is already a month old, and I have no knowledge of what has happened since. However, Abdulbakar quickly modu-lated his distress to cries and angry shouts and demands that justice be done. He expected justice to be done by the consular representative of Her Britannic Majesty. First, though, he had gone searching for you in Tangier, finding at length our house, only just vacated by us and already in the possession of the expatriate painter Withers."

"Oh Christ, get on with it."

"That was while Mahmud, poor boy, was still alive and in hospital with an even chance of recovery after his operation."

"What operation for God's sake? Oh Christ, yes—"

"Abdulbakar had only a garbled version of your name. My name fits easily into Arabic, as you know. The teller of tales Tumi, so said Withers, had departed. Abdulbakar will have no difficulty in finding out where he is now, though Huntley kindly kept quiet about it. Huntley says that you, Geoffrey, are in grave danger."

"Bugger it, I wasn't the only one. You had a go at pocky little Mahmud yourself, prissy bastard that you are."

"Abdulbakar's instinct is not to leave justice to the law, which he, reasonably considering his background, does not trust."

"Bloody pimp. Pimping for his own kid, bastard."

"He is much more likely, thinks Huntley, to effect, or try to effect, or have effected, a wild justice of his own. Of course, in desperation at not being able to afford a fare to Malta, where he will have no trouble, incidentally, in finding the house of Tumi, he may bring in the police. You cannot be charged with murder, perhaps not even with manslaughter, but there is a very nasty penalty attached in most countries to Grievous Bodily Harm Resulting in Death. Extraditable, surely. Have I made myself clear so far?"

"Right, right, I've got to skip."

"If I were you I should get washed, shaved, dressed and packed now. This is goodbye, Geoffrey. You're leaving the place you detest so much. A plane departs for London at midday. With luck you should get a seat on that plane. You must first go to Sliema to the travel agency on the High Street. I am making out a check for you, in Maltese pounds. I shall give you another check, on the National Westminster Bank, Stanhope Gate, to cover expenses in London prior to your leaving London and traveling to the United States. That check will also take care of a return ticket, tourist class of course, to Chicago via New York. I trust you are taking all this in."

"Chicago? Chic— What the fucking hell am I to go to Chicago for? Return, you said. I'm to return here? To get fucking done in by Abdulfucking-bakar?"

"There's a job of work you have to do for me in the United States. I'll give you yet another check on the Chemical Bank, New York, for five thousand dollars. You may have to travel around, it all depends on what you discover in Chicago. As for return, I mean return to London. In London you will render your report, to me in person—Wignall asked me when I was *coming home*, I did not think I would be *coming home* so soon—and, if I find you have worked diligently, you will be given a final check. This will be for the ten thousand pounds you ah desiderated last night."

Geoffrey was on his second cigarette and in control of the situation, lolling easy, even faintly grinning. "Such fucking decency and ah charity, such a colossal change of heart." As he would not be sleeping here again, he stubbed the cigarette out on the polished cedarwood of the bedside table.

"I have plenty of money, Geoffrey. You know exactly how much is in the British account. I found the most recent bank statement mixed up with your pornographic magazines. Cognate, I suppose you would say, equally exciting or obscene reading. I have other accounts too, of which even you know nothing. I think, for all my wealth, that ten thousand pounds is sufficiently generous. But you have to do a little work for it. Not hard, but, to me, important."

"What work, dear?"

"I'll tell you over breakfast. It has something to do with the archbishop's visit of yesterday."

"Oh fucking Christ. Very well, sir. I shall get up." And he got out of bed, naked, not hairy, running to fat (why *running*? Geoffrey never *ran*). The living had been too easy for him.

ten

It was the tooth that had begun to twinge at the Ovingtons' dinner party. It was now aching intolerably, and the gum above it was swollen and tender. The tooth itself was loose. An abscess, probably. Cognac quietened it, also some essence of cloves that Ali bought me from Grima or Borg the pharmacist, conveniently next door to my house. Toothache was, I supposed, a kind of luxury to a man of my age. My father had been a dental surgeon; he had lectured his children on the importance of healthy dentition as other men lectured theirs on the importance of getting on in the world and being discreet where they could not be moral. For all that, I had never taken special care of my teeth, yet here I was in my eighty-second year with twenty-six of them, discolored but sharp and sound, except for this rebellious premolar. I thought that even this might be saved, but I could not risk going to a strange dentist, the waiting room full of aromatic Maltese, in Birkirkara or Valletta. I needed my regular dentist, Dr. Pes, on the Piazza Bologna in Rome. Pes is a Sardinian name, less fitting for a dental surgeon perhaps than a podiatrist. A monied gentleman of my generation naturally kept *faith* with such tenders of his health, comfort and utilitarian needs as had proved their own faith in the metaphysics of skill and quality. Distance no object. Teeth in Rome, silk shirts in Kuala Lumpur, leather goods in Florence, tea in Mincing Lane. I had to go to Rome, unaccompanied.

Both the pain and the prospect of traveling for the cure of its cause had come at the right time. I was lonely without Geoffrey, and not even his behavior at the airport, a final and spectacular performance as it were, could altogether quell my bitter affection. Ali and I took him there in plenty of time for his plane, and this perhaps was a mistake. First he quarreled with the police who wanted to stamp his passport with an exit chop, shouting that he refused to have anything further of his defiled by the fucking Maltese, and what would they do if he wouldn't have it, shove him in bloody jail? He got away with an undefiled passport but, in the bar, he treated me and all around us to a loud recapitulation, based loosely on the visas and entry permits in his passport, of the more scandalous elements of our life together. "New York, dear, and that pissy-arsed publisher of yours who tried to stop me going to the fistfuck party, dangerous he said, lethal, stupid sod. Toronto, that was where we had little whatsit at the same time, remember, lovely kind of henna color, half-Indian half-French, not an ounce of bloody Anglo-Saxon blood, remember." He got drunk very rapidly on undiluted Pernod. "The man on the *Washington Post* who once had it off with a ghost. At the point of orgasm the pale ectoplasm shrieked 'Coming I'm coming—almost.' " We soon had the bar to ourselves.

"That's your plane there, Geoffrey."

"Got to unload the bugger first, haven't they? Too right they have. Time for another ah ah imbibition."

"Have you got everything?"

"Too right, sport." He slapped and slapped the old Gucci case I had given him as a parting present. "All in here positively aching to be encashed. And all the Pope Buggerlugs twaddle."

Geoffrey was the last to board the plane. He attempted to give the airport staff a voluble account, highly rhetorical and very loud, of my virtues, summing the vices up in: "Sentimentality and bloody prissiness as well as fucking ingrained hypocrisy, product of a bad bloody period. Apologies, ladies, for that *bloody period*. No, I don't fucking apologize. Malta is bloody lucky to have great international writer on its sanctimonious soil. And to Malta *this*." The lip fart he let off was monstrous; at the same time he pronged two devil's horn fingers at the roof. "Up all of yours and the very best of British arseholing luck. Look after Toomey, you bastards." At last he could be seen weaving across the tarmac, while the engine turned over and the ground menials waited to wheel away the steps. He tried to do a kind of staircase dance but was at length persuaded to get aboard. I did not envy either the stewardess or his fellow passengers.

And then the toothache. As I was here I might as well book my passage to Rome. I would have to wait till the day after tomorrow, I was told. Two parties of Maltese going off for a papal blesssing. I collected my ticket and paid by check. When I got back to the car Ali and I looked at each other. I had no doubt of Ali's cordial detestation of Geoffrey, but Ali had never indicated, in word, gesture, sigh or eyelift, his dislike or resentment. But now Ali nodded at me, his eyes fully on mine, took in a quart of air and then released it swiftly. "Home," I said, or rather "*A casa.*" There was nothing in that to bring tears to my eyes. Halfway home the bad tooth sang a forte measure of rage. It was a prompt surrogate for Geoffrey. One o'clock, June 24, 1971. My eighty-second year lay all before me.

eleven

"The point is, Father," I said, "that I shall never have any hope of making a good act of contrition. Not until the urge fails, or libido, as some call it. And why, for that matter, should I have to be contrite about the way God made me?"

Father Frobisher, S.J., gave me another glass of Amontillado. That was kind of him, because sherry was short, everything was short and growing shorter. We sat in an ugly dark parlor on Farm Street. My chair was a penitentially hard Windsor, but his was big and deep as a bed, old and with creaking springs, covered in dirty chintz. It was just before that green and muggy Christmas of 1916, when full graveyards were promised. Just one month before, the battle of the Somme had ended, with British losses estimated at nearly half a million. A green Christmas represented a kind of civilian expiation.

Father Frobisher said, "Who was it who sent you to me?"

"A man called Hueffer, Ford rather—he changed his name because of the war. An editor, poet, novelist." Father Frobisher frowned, couldn't seem to recall the man.

He said, "I've had one or two shall I say literary personages sent to me with precisely your problem. It's always such people who have the problem. Actors, too, though not musicians. You're a writer?"

"A novelist, reviewer, that sort of thing."

"Well, the situation is the same for writers as for dustmen, if dustmen ever have this problem, which I doubt. Heavy exercise and beer, Mr. Toomey, are remarkable solvents of of of." He was a heavy man and could have carried dustbins himself with ease. His scalp was nearly nude but his eyebrows thrust out stiff filaments in all directions. His clerical black was filthy. "Holy Writ," he said, "is perfectly clear about *the way God made us*. Male and female created He them. The sexual urge was designed for the peopling of heaven with human souls. Aberrations are the work of men, not God. God gives us free will. We use it or we abuse it. You, from what you tell me, have been abusing it."

"You're wrong, Father. With respect. I did not will myself into being the way I am. From puberty on I was driven away from what the world and the Church would call the sexual norm."

"Have you prayed?"

"Of course I've prayed. Prayed to be attracted to what I find distasteful. Prayed even sometimes to be led into the carnal sins of the norm."

"You must never pray to be led into temptation, Mr. Toomey." He pulled out a cheap snuffbox and offered it to me. I did not know whether it represented an alternative to sex or a type of sensual temptation. I shook my head. He fed a great pinch of what looked like white dust, though it smelt of pepperment, into each of his hairy nostrils. Then he carked and spluttered and pleasurably shivered. He drew a handkerchief of surprising snowiness from his sleeve and trumpeted into it. Then he said, with the smugness of one who has overcome the flesh, "I think you make too much of sexuality. It is a fault of your generation. Of the artists and poets of your generation. You have read the poems of Rupert Brooke? Distressingly—physical."

"Heterosexually so. He's paid for all that, Father." He had too, at Skyros the previous year. "Perhaps," I said, "we make too much of sexuality, as you put it, because there's so much death going on. Oh, I know what you'll say—that my sort of sexuality is sterile. But there's only the one fundamental urge. *Alma Venus*, and so on."

"Why," he said, as impertinently as any strange woman on a bus, "are you not in the army?"

"You mean that an army chaplain would know more of my problem? Or that an untimely death might solve it? The fact is," I said, "that the medical officers don't care much for my heart. The rhythm is irregular. Doubtless, if we have any more Somme disasters, it will be heard to beat healthful enough music. But may I return to the problem? What does the Church say?"

"First," Father Frobisher said very briskly, his hands folded in his lap and his thumbs rolling round each other, "all fornication is sinful outside the married state. You are therefore in ah the same position as any any any."

"Yes, but a *normally* sexed person can at least marry rather than burn. I cannot marry. Marriage would be a mockery and a sin. Yes, a sin."

"I will indulge your ah ah metaphor. But there is no knowing what the love and yes help of a good woman might achieve. You must pray for God's grace. You have no right to assume that your present present present represents a permanent and unchangeable state. God's mercy works strangely. You know nothing of what the future holds. You are still very young."

"Twenty-six, father."

"You are still very young. But old enough, may I say, to be beyond the expectation, I say the expectation—"

I finished it for him impatiently. "The expectation of loopholes, the hope of clauses of exemption and distinguished precedents, and all the rest of it." Just behind Father Frobisher and seeming, in his post-snuff tranquillity, to be riding on the apex of his scalp, was a dim reproduction of Michelangelo's *Last Judgment*—a Christ with wrestler's shoulders condemning everybody, impervious to his blessed mother's pleas, the painter himself standing in the foreground of the blessed, though as Saint Bartholomew grasping his own flayed-off hide. "Where," I asked, "is Michelangelo? In hell? He had dealings with men and wrote passionate sonnets about homosexual love. God made him what he was, a homosexual and an artist. He's one of the glories of the Church. Am I not right in supposing that the Church used to take the sins of the flesh less seriously, in a humane spirit of humorous resignation? There was a bishop, I've forgotten his name, who spoke of a man and a girl in a garden of a May morning, and if God would not forgive it he would. Meaning, I think, that God would forgive it. If God cares at all, which I doubt."

Father Frobisher spoke loud words now. "God *does* care. Man bears in himself the miracle of the seed planted there by the Creator. The power of generating new human souls for God's kingdom. The wanton spilling of the seed in the sin of Onan, or in the pseudo-Hellenic embraces of your your your." Then: "I never heard of this bishop. But he referred to a man and a girl. You must give up this deadly sin. You must vow never to commit it again. Do you hear me?"

"I have," with equal loudness, "regularly vowed to give it up. I have gone dutifully to confession once a month, sometimes more, and repented of impure thoughts or impure acts. And then I have regularly fallen again. This cannot go on forever."

"It certainly cannot. It certainly."

"So I have to make a choice. It is not easy. Are you, Father, a Catholic from your cradle?"

"That is not to the purpose. But no, I am a convert. As Newman was a convert. But it is not to the."

"My father too is a convert. He became a Catholic when he married my mother, who is French. But on my mother's side I look back to a thousand years or more of unswerving devotion to the faith. Oh, there was the odd deviation—Catharism, Jansenism, if that's truly a deviation. But now I face the breaking of my mother's heart, since I cannot both be true to my nature as God made it and a faithful son of the Church. For even if I committed myself, as you have done, to a life of celibacy, where would be my spiritual reward? I lack your vocation. I have another vocation, at least I consider it to be that, but it can't be fulfilled in priestly seclusion from the life of the flesh. To which God do I listen—the God who made me what I am or the God whose voice is filtered through the edicts of the Church?"

"There is no difference, you must not say that, this is wholly wholly wholly."

I looked at him disbelieving for a second, hearing the wrong word.

"Heretical, blasphemous," picking up the Amontillado bottle. "It is finished," he said, in the very tones he would have used on Good Friday. Then: "We are living in terrible times. Thousands, millions, dead on the battlefields of Europe, the German blockades attempting to starve us into submission. There are men coming back from the front maimed, limbless, their lungs rotted with gas, blind, paralyzed, physically condemned to celibacy. Who are you to talk of a spiritual reward?"

I sighed and, without seeking permission, lighted a Gold Flake with a Swan vesta. He had himself taken in tobacco, and in a dirtier form. I blew out smoke with the pleasure he had shown in carking on the irritant. One substance, two forms. "I have to put it all off," I said. "Faith, grace, salvation. Perhaps when I'm sixty, if I reach that age, and the fires are burnt out, perhaps then I can come back. What did Saint Augustine pray—to be made pure, but not yet?"

"This is no occasion for frivolity or cynicism. You're in deadly peril."

"I no longer believe that, Father," I said, but the hand holding the Gold Flake shook. "Thank you for your time and help. For you *have* helped."

"I think you had better come back and see me again. Next week. Having prayed and meditated. Pray to our Holy Mother for the grace of purity. She will listen."

"Embarrassing, Father. I'd prefer to address a saint who knew about these things. Are there any? Or perhaps Our Lord himself. He, if what Renan hints at is true—"

"I know what you're going to say. Don't say it. I see already the way you're going. God help you. You've withdrawn, by a perverse act of the will, from the opportunity of grace. So quickly can these things happen. Come, we'll kneel, we'll pray together now." And he got up from his creaking chair and indicated the fireside rug.

"No, Father. Too late. Or too soon. It won't be easy, I can assure you. I'll always have a kind of—" It was my mother's language that came out, though the English word was available. "—*nostalgie*. But I can't come home. Not yet. Not for a long time yet." And I got out of the place as quickly as I could.

twelve

The above must not, of course, be taken as a verbatim account of what happened. I cannot remember the name of the priest or whether the cigarettes I smoked in those days were Gold Flake or whether he or I took tobacco in that Farm Street room, one substance, two forms. But the gist is true. I walked through Mayfair shakily, with the sense that my feet belonged to somebody else, and my haed spun as though it were with a doctor's negative prognosis. On Berkeley Street the *Star* poster of a newspaper vendor said NIVELLE RE-PLACES JOFFRE. Yes, of course, there was a Great War going on, and here I had been trying to reconcile my sexual urges with my religious faith. LLOYD GEORGE WAR CABINET SITS. I turned onto Piccadilly. Outside Green Park station holly and chrysanthemums were being sold. A barrel organ in a side street played "Keep the Home Fires Burning." A middle-aged woman of the governing classes, whaleboned rigid, her hat a froth of feathers, gave me a hard look. She saw a fit, even jauntily fit, young man in a good gray suit with an open gray dustcoat, the wide-brimmed hat of the "arty" set back on his head like a halo. I bought an evening paper in the station and went down the stairs to get my train to Baron's Court. A trio of Tommies on leave, tipsy, their uniform collars undone, came up abreast and forced me to press myself against the stair-rail. One of them began to sing, and the others raggedly joined in:

> *"You was with the wenches*
> *When we was in the trenches*
> *Afacing our German foe—"*

It might or might not have been meant for me.

In the train I opened my paper and read:

On getting into the flat the prisoner lit a gas fire, sat on a chair, and then committed the offense complained of. Witness did not say anything but tried several times to get away, but prisoner pulled him back. Prisoner kissed him and gave him a shilling, also a screwdriver, telling him the latter was a keepsake from him.

That was Norman Douglas of the *English Review*, to which I sometimes contributed. Douglas, who was getting on for fifty, spent much of his spare time picking up little boys. He had been unlucky on this occasion. I was no casual pederast and would never, I believed, put myself in danger; still, I shivered. I had said goodbye to my warm loving mother and elected for cold, uncertainty, sin, the horror of the normal and respectable, their claws, latent but acute.

How ironic it was that the small reputation I had so far made for myself had begun with the publication of a novel considered heterosexually assertive, also daring, even scandalous. This was, as some of you may know, *Once Departed*, published by Martin Secker (three printings of 1,500 each, with 4,000 sets of sheets sold to the United States). The epigraph was from Fitz-Gerald's *Omar Khayyám* ("You know how little time we have to stay . . .") and the story dealt (*deals*, I should say, but I cannot help thinking of the book as a dead letter) with a young man due to die from an incurable though not super-ficially obnoxious disease who is determined to drain the cup before he goes. His sexual exploits, with girls great-limbed and firm-breasted under their 1911 carapaces, their hair tumbling in an odorous cataract on the removal of the innumerable pins, I described with a suggestiveness regarded as shocking by many, and the invocation of the powers of the Public Prosecutor was seriously urged in, I think, *John Bull*. It was a tyro work, published just after my twenty-second birthday, and it was composed as a cold and deliberate exercise in the presentation of heterosexual passion. It was assumed by many, especially by the young women I met at parties, that it mirrored my own tastes and appetites. I told no one that I could bring myself to compose the more intimate scenes only by imagining them as homosexual, though this was sometimes difficult with torrents of scented hair and swinging breasts getting in the way. What, of course, I was trying to prove was the limitlessness of the creative artist's province, his capacity for imagining feelings and situations totally beyond his personal encompassment.

This young man who was, cynically some might think, prepared to force his name on the reading public with a work of scandalous eroticism (or what passed for it in the year of *Pygmalion*, the loss of the *Titanic*, and Scott's last expedition) was still a deeply religious being, confessing and communicating weekly, hearing mass on occasions when the Church did not oblige him to, scrupulous in examining his conscience nightly, always on guard against sin. He had, naturally, no control over his dreams, which tended to the homosexually extravagant, nor over the spontaneous floodings of semen which they occasioned. The books he wrote and intended to write could, he considered, be justified as cathartics, or warnings (the hero of *Once Departed* died, or dies, not of his fatal disease but of knife wounds in a Madagascar brothel). My second novel, *Before the Hemlock*, dealt with Socrates and Alcibiades and had naked males embracing offstage, but Socrates was found guilty of the corruption of youth and condemned to death. My novels could, in a word, at a pinch, be defended as instruments of morality. And yet I suppose they had something to do with my spiritual corruption, my eventual ability to throw off faith by an act of the will. But my sexual orientation was the true instigator of apostasy. God forced me to reject God.

Yet in the time of my faith I was, and I must make this clear, faithful to a degree hardly known in the countries of the Mediterranean (which Norman Douglas maintained to be, to their credit, wholly pagan), though Catholics of the North have not infrequently exercised belief to the excruciating limit. Having accepted the major premise about the divine foundation of the Church, they must of need accept everything it teaches, from Limbo to Ember Days. I had no doubt at all that, if I persevered in the sexual courses which had been planted on my inescapable path, I would end in hell. I knew what hell was: it was having an infinitude of teeth drawn without cocaine. It was a live coal falling on my six-year-old fingers when I was pickin a celluloid blow-football ball out of the grate. But, since God had made me homosexual, I had to believe that there was another God forbidding me to be so. I may say also that I had to believe there were two Christs—one the implacable judge of the Sistine fresco, the other the mild-eyed friend of the disciple John. You will not be surprised to know that this second Christ played occasional parts in my erotic dreams.

However and anyway, as I climbed the steps of the station at Baron's Court, it was with the guilty lightness of one who knows he has gone the way he had to go. I had done my best, the God of the Church could hardly deny it. He and the God of my glands were, perhaps at that moment, conferring about my case. They would have to conclude that I must be left alone to practice a vocation (in the service of a divine attribute) which was inconsistent with celibacy and that a deathbed repentance was more than in the cards. So there it was, *Deo gratias*.

Now, entering the apartment house on Baron's Court Road, climbing the stairs to my top-floor flat, I was free to think about another kind of faith or faithfulness. Val Wrigley was to spend the night with me, as he did at least once a month. We were friends, we were lovers, but he was not free to enter the homosexual equivalent of the married state. He was nineteen years old and lived at home with possessive parents. He was a poet by vocation and worked in Willett's bookshop on Regent Street. He was fair, delicate, and very beautiful. He was fine-skinned and weak-lunged. He had read an article I had contributed to the *English Review* on the poetry of Edward Thomas and had written me a letter saying that he had thought himself to be the only admirer of Thomas's work and he took the liberty of enclosing three little poems much, he believed, in Thomas's style. One of the poems, as I seem to remember, contained the lines:

I had not thought to hear
A thrush in the heart of Ealing
Like a heart throbbing, unsealing
My waxed London ear.

We met for tea and buns in a shop of the Aerated Bread Company and then went to the Queen's Hall where, I think, the first British performance of *Le Sacre du Printemps* was given. I may be wrong, but I seem to associate the final movement with his cool hand touching mine in excitement. We became lovers almost at once.

He was able to spend the occasional night with me because his parents (his home, of course, was in Ealing) believed he did voluntary duty at the tea urn in the Salvation Army all-night troops' canteen at Euston station. He shared the shift, so he told his parents on my recommendation, with a nice harmless bookish man called Toomey. This was not too risky a tale: his parents, who had no right of access to a troops' canteen, could never check on it, and he could discuss me and recount my dicta without fear. In other words, he would not have to lie too much. "And this Mr. Toomey, dear—is he married?" "I don't know, Mother, I never asked." "You must ask him to tea sometime." But I never went to tea in Ealing. Val left my flat early to go home to breakfast looking dog-tired. The deception worked well.

I unlocked my flat door, went in, and lighted the gaslight and the gasfire. Mrs. Pereira, my Portuguese landlady, had been in already to leave post—a couple of books for review and a letter from my mother in Battle, Sussex. It was Mrs. Pereira's snooping privilege to enter whenever she liked, but she preferred the pretext of performing a little service. She regarded me as a good tenant—I paid regularly and never brought women into my room.

At seven Val knocked—three shorts and a long, out of the scherzo of Beethoven's Fifth—and I rushed to open. "I'm starved. What are you giving us, old thing?"

It was gas-ring cookery. "A kind of ragout. A tin of bully beef with onions and carrots. And the remains of the Médoc."

"I'm starved." Like myself, Val spoke with a slight lisp. Telling Geoffrey of my past, I had mentioned this. Geoffrey had been delighted and did a fine cruel parody. "Thuch ecthtathy." "Yeth, it wath, wathn't it, my thweet thweet boy." Val threw his long limbs into the shabby armchair and read the paper. He was not much interested in the war news, except when it got into the literary columns with the deaths of poets. He was a little distrait this evening, peevish. He went through the pages irritably, going *ts-ts* occasionally. It was as if he expected to be mentioned in the paper and, through editorial enmity, was not.

"What's the matter, dear? A bad day in the shop?"

"Oh, the usual, old thing. The only books people want to buy are *Beat the Hun in the Vegetable Plot* and the *Pip Squeak and Wilfred Annual*. Which reminds me. What are you giving me for Christmas?"

"I hadn't thought. There's not much to buy, is there?"

"You hadn't thought, no. There are one or two things about. If you don't want the trouble of going round the shops, you could always give me the money, you know."

"What's the matter with you tonight, Val?" I set the ragout on the small round table by the window. A District Line train hammered by.

"Ah, I see this friend of yours is in trouble." He found the item about Norman Douglas. He came to the table reading it.

"He's no friend. A colleague, you could call him." I served; the ragout had a faint odor of metal.

"Wasn't careful, was he? I say, this stew thing smells of army mess tins or something."

"The bully's army issue. But the civilian stuff's just the same."

"Why can't we eat out occasionally? Soho or somewhere. It's not nice having to sleep in the odor of bully. And onions." He forked in the stew listlessly. He was supposed to be starved.

"What's into you, Val?"

"Not quite your usual loving boy, am I? Oh, I'm a little depressed. Hole in the corner stuff. Not much in life, is there?"

"Love, Val, love. Try this cider."

"Windy stuff. All right, a little. Ah, I wrote something today." And he took a scrap of paper from his inner pocket. "Listen.

> *Do ye the savage old law deny.*
> *Let me repay, in age or youth—*
> *An infinitude of eyes for an eye,*
> *An infinitude of teeth for a tooth.*

It needs tidying up a little, of course." He smiled, not at me, but in pleasure at his performance.

"Strafing Jesus again," I said. "I'm not impressed. Besides, that means nothing any more. I gave it all up today. I went to Farm Street and had it all out, or up. I made my choice. You can't shock me any more with your adolescent atheism."

"Fergus in the shop told me that in the army they split up the different religions by saying Catholics this side, C. of E. that, and fancy buggers in the middle. So you and I are now both fancy buggers." He giggled. "And you gave up Jesus for me."

"I gave up the Church because of the inescapability of living in sin. If you like, you can say I did it for you."

"Charmed, old thing. Awfully flattered." He forked his stew with a boy's spoiled pout making him look silly and ugly, also desirable. "I say, this is awful muck. Why don't we go and eat out? Celebrate being fancy buggers together."

"A matter of money, Val. I have exactly two shillings and ninepence farthing."

"Wouldn't take us very far, would it?"

"You said you were starved. This seems edible enough." I ate some. "Many a starving German would give his back teeth for it."

"Wouldn't need any teeth at all, would he? It's just mush." He spooned some of the thin gray sauce out of the ragout dish and deliberately let it slowly ooze onto the tablecloth.

"Don't do that, laundry costs money. That's a silly thing to do."

"Anyway, I don't believe the Germans are starving. I think it's just government lies. Oh, this horrible war. When's it going to be all over?"

"Nineteen nineteen. Nineteen twenty-one. Does it matter? You're not going to be in it."

"Nor are you. Well, I'm hungry, but not hungry enough for that muck. I think I'll go home. I can always say I'd a pain in my chest and they let me off tonight. Mother got a nice leg of lamb. Father managed to find some Christmas whisky for the butcher, ten years in the vat or something. Novelists don't have anything to barter, do they?"

"Nor poets."

"Except their lives, except their lives, except their lives. Die on the Somme or at Gallipoli and your poetic name is made forever. Still, I'm in the Keats tradition. A poet with phthisis."

"You're talking silly nonsense. You could have bread and margarine and jam if you like. And a nice cup of tea." I put my hand persuasively on his. He snatched his hand away. "What *is* the matter with you, Val?"

"I don't know. Don't maul me. I don't like being mauled."

"Val, Val." I got out of my chair and on my knees beside him. I took his hands, which were limp enough, and kissed each in turn, over and over.

"Slobberer. Making me all wet."

"There's something on your mind. Something's happened. Tell me."

"I'm going home." He started to get up, but I pushed him back into his chair, saying:

"No. Don't say that. Don't break my heart."

"There speaks the popular novelist. 'And then he tried to take him in his arms, slobbering over him.' No, that's not popular novel stuff, is it? Not yet." (Did he say *not yet*? The danger of memory is that it can turn anyone into a prophet. I nearly wrote, some lines back, "1918. November the something. Does it matter?")

"Be honest with me, Val, darling. Tell me what the matter is."

"Go and sit down. You must get used to not kneeling any more."

"Some things have to be done kneeling." It was a coarse thing to say; it was the spray off a mounting wave of desire. He ignored that but looked at me with a lifted upper lip. I went to the gas ring and put the kettle on for tea. I had no coffee.

Val said, "It's all take with you and no give."

"I give my love, my devotion. But I take it that you've begun to want more."

"Not *me*. Not *want*. I'm tired of having only an audience of one for my poems."

"Ah. I see. So you're letting that come between us. I've tried to place them, you know that. I've shown you the letters of rejection. But they all say you must keep on writing."

"Jack Ketteridge, that pal of Ezra Pound's. He's been given an old hand-press. By someone both loving and generous."

"I'd give you an old handpress if I had one. I'd give you anything."

"I don't mean that, silly. I don't want a handpress. I want to be printed, not to print. Ketteridge is calling his little enterprise the Svastica Press. Apparently the svastica is a Hindu sun symbol. It means good luck too. He'll do my volume for twenty pounds. Two hundred copies. That's cheap, I think."

"So that's what all the sulks were about. I never give you anything. And you know I can't give you twenty pounds. Why don't you ask your father?"

"I prefer to go," Val said, "to those who say they *love* me. And I don't mean what my father calls love, which is just possession and bossiness."

"I'll get the money. Somehow. An advance on royalties, perhaps. Though I'm not really ready to start the next novel—the one I've told you about, the modern Abelard and Eloise—"

"I know, the man who has his pillocks blown off at Suvla Bay. I know too that you don't like taking money in advance. You've told me often enough about it making you resent **doing** the work when you've spent the money and thus doing it badly. I know, I know, Ken. You needn't bother. I just want you to know my motives, that's all."

My heart sank, the water bubbled cheerfully. Faith. Faithfulness. I had stemmed the thought at the very moment of unwinding the can of corned beef: what right had I to expect fidelity if I was myself withdrawing it? Superstition was already replacing faith. And here it was coming now, my punishment. Men are right to be superstitious. I said nothing for the moment, keeping my back to Val, making tea, weak tea because I was near the end of the packet of Lipton's Victory Blend. At length I said, in what in my fiction in those days ("And in your later days too, dear"—Geoffrey) I would have termed a strangled voice: "Who is it?"

"I want you to understand me properly, Ken. Do turn round and look me in the eye. I want money, not for myself, but for what I think's important. Oh, I may be stupid thinking it's important, but it's all I have."

"You have me." I looked into the pot to see how the tea was drawing. "Had me."

"This is different, Ken, you old stupid, you know it's different. Anything for art. Bernard Shaw said something about it's right to starve your wife and children for the sake of art, art comes first."

"No, no, it doesn't." I poured two cups of tea and put canned milk and gray wartime sugar on the table. "Love first, faith, I mean fidelity. Who is it? I want to know who it is."

"You won't know him. He comes into the shop, he has an account. A great seeker of first editions of Huysmans. He knew Wilde, or so he says. Older than you, of course."

"And richer. Prostitute," I then said. "Whoring. You don't know what love is."

"Oh yes I do. It's eating corned beef stew, or not eating it, and then getting cramps in a single bed and smelling the ghost of onions at dawn. Sounds a bit like *Blast*, doesn't it? That Rhapsody on a Windy Night man. Well," and he cocked his head at me whorishly, "do you fancy a bit of a farewell tumble, dearie?"

"Why do you do this? Why?"

"Perhaps," he said solemnly, "it's to make you turn against me. That tea looks awful. Warm cat piss. One thing anyway. No more Saturday afternoon tumbles and the odd night with the onions. My dear father and mother have known nothing, guessed nothing. Caution, Ken, is it right to be so cautious? Well, no more caution. After the leg of lamb tonight—and I'd better go now or I'll have to eat it cold—I tell them I'm leaving. Yes, leaving. We always have dinner late and then father gets somnolent. This will wake him up."

I, during the above, moved with the slowness of a tired old man to the bed with its harlequin cover and sat on the edge. The tea steamed untasted. "You propose telling them you're going to live with another man?"

"Ah yes, but they're so innocent. They'll think: Well, at least he's not going off to live in sin with a woman. What I'll say is that I'm sick of living at home. I want to come home as late as I please. And if they say young, you're too young, I say: Yes, young, but not so young as some killed at Ypres and on the bloody Somme. This, I'll say, is the new age, the modern world. Two men sharing a flat in Bloomsbury. Though, between you and me, Ken dear, it isn't a flat. It's quite a nice little house full of books and bibelots."

"Who is it? I want to know who it is."

"You've asked that already, in exactly those words. 'A certain monotony of locution.' Who was the beastly reviewer who said that? Ah, the *Times Lit Supp*, wasn't it, no names no packdrill. Look, a last loving kiss and then I must fly. I'm starving."

And so he left me starving. I lay on the bed and wet the pillow. Then I smoked a cigarette (I had almost written: lighted a cigarette with Ali's Maltese-cross present). I had given him no last loving kiss, the little whore. I brooded less on Val's perfidy than on the injustice of the what I would have called had the term been available then Sexual Establishment. Nothing to hold together two male lovers, or female either, no offspring, no sense of the perpetuation of a name and a family face over the centuries. But of course I had nothing to offer a wife or wife surrogate—no house, no income. The great clanking chains of Justice sounded from without, a Piccadilly Line train supplying the basic fantasizable datum. My washed eyes took in my mother's letter, the French scrivener's hand in violet ink on the envelope, the Battle postmark on the decollated head of George V. Home, warmth, the bleeding patients passing from the surgery through the hall, my mild father with blood on his hands, my mother's precise English with the Lille tonalities. I had gone out into the world and the world was making me bleed.

thirteen

My mother said in her letter that they were managing, but her heart was torn with the tearing of France. They had enough to eat, an advantage of living in a farming district, and Father, rather in the manner of Irish country doctors, was prepared to take his fees occasionally in eggs and butter. Tom, my brother, in the Royal Army Medical Corps at Boyce Barracks, had completed a gas corporal's course, whatever that was. My sister Hortense, named for my mother as I had been named for my father, had had as good a sixteenth birthday party as could be expected in these sugarless times. Father Callaghan of St. Anthony's in St. Leonards had heard from Dublin that his cousin Patrick's appeal had been rejected and that he was to hang for his part in the abortive rising of last Easter. My mother hoped I was happy in London and was herself so happy that I would be coming home for Christmas. If only Tom too could get leave, but that apparently was too much to ask for. All this was written in neat violet-inked French, making the news about Father Callaghan's cousin somewhat remote and literary, and even the butter and eggs seemed to belong to *Un Coeur Simple*.

I finished the letter, buried my head in the pillow for another passionate cry, this as much to do with lost innocence and the mess of the world as with Val's defection. Then I dried my tears, smoked another Gold Flake, and got up to look at my eyes in the cracked blue mirror of Mrs. Pereira. Then I washed them in warm water from the kettle, soaking a tea towel corner for the purpose, and afterwards took several deep breaths. I had books for review; I could review them more comfortably in Battle than here, in the smell of onions and among the remembered smells and sounds of Val. I had money enough for a single fare to Battle; there was, I knew, a train from Charing Cross just after nine.

And so I packed my little bag, put on my arty hat and my warm coat, and went out into the dark that was crowned by a zeppelin moon to Baron's Court station. I traveled to Earl's Court, changed, arrived at Charing Cross. The station milled with soldiers and sailors, many of them drunk. There were whores in trim boots and boas, also grim respectable ladies ready with grim looks for fit young civilians. Such patriots had once been ready with white feathers, but there had been too much handing of that badge of cowardice to men blinded at Ypres not well able to understand the meaning of the proffer. I was looked at, but no more. I decided, as I sometimes did, to limp to the train. It was as much a certificate of immunity as a uniform.

There were not many on the Hastings train, and I had a compartment to myself. I was traveling back to my youth via Tonbridge, Tunbridge Wells,

Frant, Stonegate, Etchingham, Robertsbridge, via defecting Val and two boys I had myself betrayed, the young man met on a station platform who had given me a look to which I had responded and about which I had been mistaken and who had shouted aloud and made me scurry off scarlet and trembling. I was traveling back to the origin of it all, my back turned for the moment (for I preferred perversely to sit facing the engine) to a future I did not care to think about.

I had been seduced at the age of fourteen in, of all places, the city where Father Callaghan's cousin was to be hanged. Not at the Thomas More Memorial School, where there were ravening priests enough and an Irish headmaster who did his share of cautious fumbling, but in a fair city which regularly exported its sexual perverts to London and Paris. We were all there in Ireland that June of my fourteenth birthday, Mother, Father, little Hortense and growing Tom, myself in a school blazer and flannel trousers and a blue cap with a TMMS badge in yellow stitching. For the evening I had a stiff grown-up-style suit that was becoming short in the leg. We stayed in the Dolphin Hotel. My father was taking his annual holiday early because he could find no locum tenens for July or August; also Tom had had severe bronchitis and had been recommended a quiet couple of weeks by the sea. My father had once enjoyed a stay in Kingstown, now called Dun Laoghaire, and my mother was curious to see an English-speaking Catholic capital. She had also read *Les Voyages de Gulliver* and been moved by the brief account of Swift's life prefixed to the edition she had. We stayed some days, as I remember, in Wicklow and then in Dublin before moving north to Balbriggan.

I was tired of poor still-coughing Tom and my noisy drawer-wetting little sister. My parents proposed a trip to the Phoenix Park; I elected to stay in the hotel, though the weather was gorgeous, and read an old bound *Boy's Own Paper* I had picked up for twopence on a bookstall. So I sat in the lounge of the Dolphin, sucked lemon toffee, read. I was alone there. From the bar came hearty noise, Dublin being a bibulous town. And then there was a man sitting quietly beside me. He was in early middle age (thirty-seven, as I was to discover later), bearded, wearing curious clothes that, again later, I found out were homespun. He had a rather pleasant smell of peat and peppermint overlaid with Irish whiskey (I knew even then the difference between Irish and scotch) and he seemed desirous of talking.

He said, "Reading, I see. But would you not consider it to be very trashy stuff?" For he could see it was the *Boy's Own Paper*.

"I like it. The stories are exciting."

"Yes, inculcating the imperial virtues, games and discipline and cold baths in a cold dawn. And all but the British very comic, comic niggers and froggies and even micks and paddies. Amn't I right?"

"Well, yes." I couldn't help smiling. What he said was a plausible, if biased, summary of the ethos of the *B.O.P.*

"But you're young, of course, and out for excitement and not much concerned with the world as it truly is. How old would you be?"

"Nearly fourteen. Fourteen a week from today."

"A fine age to be, my boy, and the world before you. And there will be changes in your life, you will see." He had a pleasant soft voice with blurred consonants. "It will be a different world from what the trash you are reading bids you believe is the fixed and unchanging one. But never mind, never mind. In youth is pleasure." He searched in his pockets for something, perhaps a pipe or snuffbox, and came up with a drawing of a pig lined like a map with frontiers and named regions—hock, ham, saddle and so on. *"The Pig's Paper* they call the journal I edit, not at all like the one you're reading. Our friend *Sus scrofa*, Ireland's friend, the gintleman that pays the rent. I'm in damnable need of a wash and brush-up," he then said. "Are you staying in the hotel? A room of your own? Who's with you?" I told him of the Phoenix Park outing. "A bathroom up there, is there? I don't know the upper regions. I should be grateful if you'd show me the way."

So I took him upstairs and, to cut a long story short, he came into my room to borrow my comb for his beard, and said, all glowing from his wash, "Now there's just time to show you a bit of Irish wrestling from the County Meath, for I'm due soon at the offices of the *Homestead*. Now this we do stripped, as we may well do on a warm day like today. So strip then and I'll show you some of the holds." One of the holds involved what I was to learn later was called fellation, a term not found in the *B.O.P.* nor, for that matter, in any dictionary of the time. There seemed to be no Irish name for it, though this pigman used the word *blathach* for what was stimulated to burst and flow. He gave me a shilling for myself before leaving and said, "Now you may resume reading your imperialistic trash, though I'll wager it will seem less exciting after today." And, smiling kindly, he went.

Jim Joyce devoted a whole big novel to the Dublin day on which I was seduced. I have never been able to take this book seriously, as I told him myself in Paris. All the inner broodings and exterior acts of the work seem so innocent. I remember none of the public events described or reported—the viceregal cavalcade (though I seem to recall a distant military band shrilling and thudding), the charity bazaar fireworks, news about the sinking of the *General Slocum* in the East River and Throwaway winning the Ascot Gold Cup at very long odds, nor the evening rain nor the heaventree of stars appearing later hung with humid nightblue fruit. My mother that evening stayed in with the younger children; my father took me to see an excessively dull melodrama called *Leah*.

I said to Joyce in a bar in Paris in 1924: "Well, you gave George Russell an eternal and unbreakable alibi for that afternoon. But I know and he knows that he was not in the National Library."

"I wouldn't want to call you a liar," Joyce said, his eyes as cloudy as the ghastly cocktail he had before him (absinthe with kümmel in lieu of water), "but I'd always thought Russell more likely to commit sodomy with a pig than a boy. Ach, the world is full of surprises."

I liked Jim Joyce but not his demented experiments with language. He threw away the chance of becoming a great novelist in the great tradition of Stendhal. He was always trying to make literature a substitute for religion. But we met in an area of *nostalgie*. His common-law wife Nora was a strong-minded and strong-jawed woman who would not put up for long with his nonsense. I took him back drunk one day, and Nora was waiting for him like thunder. As soon as the door shut I could hear the hitting begin.

fourteen

I walked from Battle station to my father's combined surgery and residence on the High Street, a stone's throw from the abbey. A railway porter going off duty walked two hundred yards behind me, singing, to the tune of "Pretty Redwing":

> "*Oh the moon shines bright on*
>   *Charlie Chaplin,*
> *His boots are cracking*
> *For want of blacking,*
> *And his little baggy trousers they'll*
>   *want mending*
> *Before they send him*
> *To the Dardanelles.*"

I arrived. There was a holly wreath encircling the door-knocker. I knocked and was benignly pricked. Then I heard my sister Hortense running, calling, "It's him, I know it's him." And then I was encircled by arms and the odors of home.

The smells of that time, the smell of that time. I have always cherished the smells of places and eras. Singapore—hot dishrags and cat piss. Moscow—

builder's size and the unflushed stools of the smokers of cheap cigars. Dublin—
roasting coffee which turns out to be roasting barley. The whole of 1916 had a
mingled smell of unaired rooms, unwashed socks, bloody khaki, musty mufti,
the rotting armpits of women's dresses, margarine, cheap gaspers made of floor-
sweepings, floors swept with the aid of damp tea leaves. It was a very un-Ameri-
can smell, one might say. The smell of my father's house, however, mingled the
neutral surgical and the Anglo-French domestic. As I entered I met the ghost of
a gigot for dinner, well-garlicked, and caramel, and hovering over the distracted
faint fumes of cocaine and nitrous oxide. The two worlds met in the aroma of
oil of cloves. And then there was my mother, the familiar odor of a red wine on
her breath (like the priest bending with the host at the altar rail) and the
delicate envelope of eau de cologne.

"What a surprise, what a lovely surprise," said Hortense, who adored me.
"You said you wouldn't be coming till the twenty-first."

"I got Mother's letter this afternoon. And then I thought: Why not now?
There was nothing to keep me in London." My eyes pricked.

"Lonely, a lonely place," said my mother with her deep voice. And my
father, in his alpaca house jacket, watch chain flashing on his growing paunch,
smiled from a kind of shy distance. We were now in the parlor, where a fire of
pearwood explained another delicious odor I had not been able to place. Hortense, home from school, had festooned the room with paper chains. Holly and
mistletoe and ivy. A Christmas tree in the corner with little dangerous candles
not yet to be lighted.

"Belated happy birthday," I said to Hortense. I took the parcel out of my
bag.

"A book, I can tell," she said, but without rancor. "Always a book."

"I'm only rich in books," I said. "Review copies at that. But it's the thought
that counts, so they tell me." Hortense's present was a new edition of *The Diary of
a Nobody*. We needed laughter in those days, but we had to go to the Victorians
for it. Oh, there was W. W. Jacobs, there was P. G. Wodehouse, but their
humor was thin with a touch of the defensive about it, an apology for purveying
the stuff of escape.

"You must be starved," my father said. I shook my head, I could not trust
myself to speak. "Perhaps you could give him a cut off the cold gigot," he said
to my mother. I shook my head vigorously. My mother appraised me with
solemn brown eyes. Being a woman, she saw more than my father saw. I wish I
could see her clearly now, but all I can see is an elongated fashion plate of the
time—the long brown dress low-waisted, unfrivolous in deference to a period
that badly needed true frivolity, not the gruesome insouciance of the politicians
and the General Staff, the pearls that had belonged to her Aunt Charlotte, the
soft brown graying hair up-piled.

She said, "I think you are not very happy there. You seem to me thin and tired. You do not have to be in London in order to write. You were happier working on the Hastings newspaper. At least you were home each night and also well fed."

"It's a question of being close to the literary life," I said. It was, of course, untrue. It was a question of, a matter of, it was.

"We're very proud and so on," my father said, shaking his head, "but it's not a profession. We've been talking about it, your mother and I."

"Oh come, Dad," I said, "you can't take a university degree or a licentiate and set up as a writer with a brass plate, but it's as honorable a profession as drawing teeth."

"How *are* your teeth, by the way?"

"Splendid," I said, showing them. "Mother," I said, turning to her graceful solemnity, "you'd not denigrate Flaubert and Balzac and Hugo? I want to be like them."

"I do not read novels," she said. "I read yours, naturally, but that is different. That first one of yours. Mrs. Hanson took it from the circulating library and was rude to me about it. Of course, because I am French she thinks I have brought you up to be immoral."

"Sister Agnes," said Hortense, in her clear young candid voice, "said it was very artificial and was obviously by a very young man. She said it was not believable."

"Sister Agnes is," I said, "a very shrewd critic."

"Oh she is, she's always criticizing."

"You look *extenué*, Kenneth," my mother said. "I will make cocoa for all of us, and then we shall go to bed. Your room is always ready for you but I will put in a hot water bottle. There is all tomorrow for talking."

"And the next day and the next," said Hortense. "Oh, it's lovely to have you home." Hortense, her hair in what was to be called by Yeats honey-colored ramparts at her ear, promised great beauty. She had a slight venerean strabismus and a strong straight French nose. Then she said, "*Heimat*. A lovely word." There was a brief breath of embarrassment from my parents.

My mother said, "If you would not speak German in the house, Hortense, I should be much happier."

"Now you're getting like the other parents," said Hortense. "Sister Gertrude says that to blame the German language for the war is like blaming German sausage. Anyway, there are still three of us doing German. And we're reading a book by Hermann Hesse, and he's a pacifist in Switzerland or somewhere. Is that wrong?"

"Henry James stopped taking walks with his dachshund," I said. "And even the royal family had to change its name. It's all very stupid."

"If you were French—" began my mother.

"I'm half French."

"That reminds me," said my father. "Talking of Mr. James, I mean. There's something that was sent over from Rye for you." He put on his nipnose glasses and went out.

My mother said, "Cocoa. And a hot bottle." And went out too. Hortense smiled at me with a girl's radiance. The madness of it all was that if there was any girl to whom I could feel attracted it was Hortense. My capacity for love was hedged in by all the thundering edicts of Moses.

"You promise fair," I said ridiculously. "I mean, don't let them make you all burly and beefy and land-army. Hockey and so on." She blushed. "Sorry," I said.

She said, blushing deeper—it was as if the bush already there for one cause might as well be used for another—"Do you have *affairs* in London?"

"I get on with my work," I said. "Such as it is. I can't afford *affairs*. I mean, affairs begin with dinner and wine and candlelight and continue in commodious apartments. I live in one room and sleep in the smell of gas-ring cookery."

She put her fingers to her lips; I blinked the water back; Father had come back in again with a letter. "They were tidying his things up," he said. "Apparently there were a lot of letters he'd written but hadn't sent off yet. Here."

It was the usual involved periphrastic infinitely qualified Henry James, O.M. He had made his major pronouncement about the contemporary British novel (of which, with his naturalization of 1915, he became the great though retrospective luminary) in a couple of articles in the *Times Literary Supplement*. I had written a mild protest in a stand-in literary column in *The Illustrated London News*, the regular man being ill and incapable: I had found as much fault with his imagery as with his judgment. He had spoken of the fine play of oar of Compton Mackenzie and Hugh Walpole and had D. H. Lawrence bringing up "the dusty rear." He had hit on a "persistent simile" of an orange and said it was "remarkably sweet" in the hands of Walpole. The great stylist could not be allowed to get away with that. He had replied to me but had delayed sending the letter off, or perhaps, obsessed with his Napoleonic fantasies, he had just forgotten he had written it. Well, here it was—my dear young friend and the rest of it. I bow my head with shame at your naked rebuke (the bowing, alas, comes all too naturally, though from the physiological causes altogether appropriate in one whose advanced age and concomitant bodily decay bid him increasingly look earthwards) but would say in feeble extenuation that the exigencies imposed by frantic copy editors, et cetera, et cetera.

My mother brought in the cocoa.

fifteen

It was a mistake to go home for Christmas. For much of the rest of the world the feast was sentimentally pagan, and tears at the birth of the prince of peace were altogether compatible with rage at the Hun. For me, for the family, the redeemer was born, and I had the intolerable task of keeping to myself my recent decision not to believe that the redeemer was born. The carolers came round singing "O Come All Ye Faithful," words which to them were a means of earning odd coppers for a winter-woolies-for-our-brave-boys fund or of being invited in for hot eggnog and mince pies. To me they were a reminder of my voluntary but ineluctable exclusion from the world of the faithful.

When Christmas Eve came, my mother said, "This evening we take the train for St. Leonards and go to confession. Your father will finish his surgery early. And then tomorrow morning we all go to communion together."

"Can't we stay in St. Leonards and go to the kinema and then go to midnight mass?" asked Hortense. Kinema. Pedantic nuns, I supposed.

"There will be no trains," said my mother. "No. Very early mass tomorrow. And then we come back to our special Christmas breakfast and then put in the oven the turkey."

My heart was sinking all through this. And I can see how you, my readers, will sigh with another kind of sinking of the heart. We are into Graham Greene territory, are we not? Or, since the betrayal of a mother is involved, James Joyce territory (*A Portrait of the Artist as a Young Man* had been published that year, to be mainly misunderstood but fulsomely praised as "Swiftian" by H. G. Wells). Some things, may I remind you, are anterior to literature. Literature does not manufacture them. Literature about them is there because they are there. Graham Greene invented a kind of Roman Catholicism, but not a kind easily intelligible to Catholics of 1916.

I said, "I shan't be going to confession."

"No sins on your soul?" teased my sister. "Unspotted by sinful London?"

"When did you last go to confession?" my mother asked.

"I could say, Mother, that that is a matter between me and my soul," I said gently, smiling. "But in fact I was in Farm Street only a few days ago."

"Well then, if you think you are still in a state of grace—"

"I'll stay home and write my review." It was a long one on the oeuvre to date of Eden Phillpotts, a writer then thought important, especially by Arnold Bennett, who called him "a master of the long sentence."

"But it is fine weather and very mild, and we can walk a little by the sea."

"I must pay my rent, Mother, and I was promised payment on receipt of the article."

"Very well, then." And I sat by the fire writing the rough draft in pencil on a pad on my knee, chewing dates, sipping sherry. My father's house was short of very little.

I lay awake that night, juggling agonizedly with alternative courses of action. If I no longer *believed*, then the host on my tongue would be no more than a bit of bread, and the family would be happy, all having taken Christmas communion together. But I knew that the host was more than a bit of a bread, and I could not take it cynically. A sacrilegious communion—terrible phrase. In the morning I prayed briefly to the God of my glands: Help thou my unbelief. Unbelief takes time, I know, but please make the time short. I heard the family stirring. It was still dark, and the electric light was on on the landing. My father came in, lather on his face. "The train goes in half an hour, son." The God of my glands was already responding. "You don't look well," said my father. I had switched on my bedside lamp. It showed, I did not doubt, pallor and hollow eyes.

"I don't," I said, "feel all that well. I don't think, somehow, I can . . . a slight stomach upset. I'm not used to good food."

My mother came in, ready dressed and cologned. "You are sick? Perhaps you should not have eaten so much of the"—she pronounced the name of the dish in, as it were, quotation marks: an item in a barbarous cuisine, cooked because my father liked it, admissible just about, Christmas Eve being, despite the wartime dispensation, a day of abstinence for us—"fish pie."

"I'll go tomorrow. Tomorrow's Saint Stephen's Day."

"If you are better you can go to the last mass today. And good, yes, Saint-Étienne Protomartyr. And the feast of your poor uncle Étienne. We will go together." Hortense came in, full of a young girl's morning energy and Christmas radiance.

"Merry Christmas. I *knew* somehow you wouldn't come. It's all London's fault. *Gottlose Stadt*, Sister Gertrude calls it."

"And probably Kaiser Bill too," warned my father, studding his stiff white collar.

"Please, child. No German. Especially this day."

"*Entschuldige. Je demande bien ton pardon.* Leave him to rot in his sin, then. Come on, we'll miss the train."

They went, and I lay rotting a while longer while the house, creaking rebuke, let in the mild dawn and the milder daylight of my *Gottlose* Christmas. I was ravenous. I dressed (stiff collar and tie, always formal, even when declaring the love that durst not speak its name) and went down to the kitchen, where the stove was banked and hot. I made strong tea and toast, opening the window to discharge the crumbs and the smell of burning, then made the fire in the dining and living rooms. Then I put my presents by the Christmas tree—*Mr. Britling Sees It Through* for my father; a new edition of *Three Men in a Boat* for my sister; for my mother a homage-to-a-brave-ally anthology called *La Belle France*, with a parody of Mallarmé by Beerbohm, a tactless polemic on the sins of France by Bernard Shaw, a pastiche of Debussy by Cyril Scott. It was perhaps not a good choice; it would make my mother tearful. I peeled a lot of potatoes. The surgery bell buzzed loudly. There was a middle-aged man at the door, a kind of ostler to judge from his oaty smell. He had a raging toothache; he needed my father.

"He's gone to St. Leonards. To church."

"What for? Want me Christmas dinner like everybody else. It ain't fair."

I took him into the surgery. The soldier on the wall looked in fearful exophthalmia at burning Pompeii. "You should look after your teeth," I said. "You should get your teeth ready for Christmas." I looked for oil of cloves but could see none. There were forceps there, though, neatly laid in lines, shining in the Christmas morning light. "Sit in that chair," I ordered. "Let's have a look at it."

"Here, it's the dentist I want. You're not the dentist."

"Like Christian baptism," I said. "Anybody can do it in case of emergency. Open." He opened and let out a hogo of medicinal rum and beer. The bad tooth was a premolar. It wobbled when I fingered it.

"Hurts, that does, ow."

"You don't want an anesthetic, do you? It may upset your stomach."

"I want something what will kill the pain."

"Through fire," I said, "to peace and cool and light." I took the largest forceps in my right hand, pushed back the chair, inserted the pincers and caught the tooth, squeezing hard to hold it. He kept his mouth well open in protest and pain, ow for both. I worked the tooth to and fro, felt it loosen and then break from its moorings, and then pulled it out. "Spit," I said. He spat, howling from a pursed mouth. "Rinse," I said. I gave him cold water. "Better," I said. "Better now, eh?" I showed him the decayed horror at the end of the tongs.

When he could speak he said, "There ought to be a law."

"Don't grumble. I'm not charging you anything. Call this a Christmas gift."

He went off bleeding, grousing about bloody butchers. I threw the tooth into the kitchen stove and rinsed the forceps under the kitchen tap. There was blood on my fingers but I did not at first wash it off. A corporal work of mercy and the badge thereof. If I were to be good in this my post-Christian life, it must be totally without hope of reward.

I said nothing of what I had done when the family came home. Yes, better, a little better, but I could not stomach eggs, bacon and sausages. I missed last Christmas mass. I ate heartily of Christmas dinner, though. Better, much better.

In the evening there was a little party—Dr. Brown and his wife and three slackmouthed children, Mackenzie the bachelor bank manager, a Belgian evacuee widow whom my mother had befriended. I wore the tie my mother had given me, smoked the Muratti Turkish from my sister, crackled in my trouser pocket the five one-pound notes, God bless him, from my father. Cold turkey and stuffing, ham, trifle, Christmas cake, mince pies, a punch of burgundy and fizzy lemonade for the children, Beaune and Pouilly-Fuissé for the rest of us, a toast to the end of war, absent friends, absent Tom. My mother held back her tears. I went to bed a little fuddled.

My mother came, not at all fuddled, into my bedroom and switched on the main light. Electric light in those days was surely softer, pinker, more intimate, even when it shone from the ceiling. My mother wore her new dressing gown, a gift from my father, cornflower blue and frilled at wrists and lapels. She sat on the edge of the bed and looked at me with sober eyes. Throughout our colloquy she spoke not one word of English.

"No confession, no communion. Indeed, no mass. This is the first time it is so at home at Christmas. I do not believe you were not well, my son."

"I was not well in my body perhaps because I was not well in my soul." I was grateful for French; it distanced a little, though not enough. Acting the vowels and the intonation, I was also acting the predicament. But French was literally my mother tongue. It had the power to knock down solid-seeming English, language of my education and street games and craft, disclosing the solidities as mere stage-flats. It had this power because it had fluted and hurled through my fetal bones and flavored my milk and soothed me to sleep. But it was still a language of the brain; its words for *faith* and *duty* and *home* would never make me cry.

"You lied too. You said you were at confession in London. I want to know what is wrong."

"I was scrupulous in not lying. I said I was at Farm Street, where the Jesuits are. I talked with a priest."

"What did you talk about?"

"I talked about the necessity of giving up my faith."

"Necessity? Necessity?" The word hissed like gaslight.

I set up a pasteboard shield. "It is a necessity that many Christians are talking of. We pray to the same God as the Germans. Must God answer only the prayers of the French and the English? Is the sacrifice of the mass offered only that *we* may be granted grace?"

"This is a just war."

"It began as a just war. I and many others believe that it is being prolonged for reasons other than justice."

"You have not talked of this before, to me or to your father. If you are convinced of what you say it should have come bursting out of you, as so many things you were convinced of came bursting out of you on other of your visits home. There is something else. Are you perhaps living in sin?"

"We are all living in sin, Mother."

"Very clever, but you know very precisely what I mean. Are you keeping house with some woman?"

"No woman, Mother. No woman, no woman." And then it came, as it had to, bursting out. She listened at first with disbelief and then puzzlement. I did not speak French much these days; perhaps I was not expressing myself correctly. But I was expressing myself all too correctly. Then her machine would not play my record. She smashed the shellac on the floor.

"What you're saying makes no sense. You have been drinking too much wine. You took also three glasses of cognac after supper. You are making a very silly stupid joke. In the morning perhaps you will speak reasonably."

"You want to know the truth, Mother. I'm telling you the truth. Some men are made this way. Some women too, as I have seen for myself in London."

"London, yes. I can believe many things of London. But this I will not believe. Not of you."

"Mother, Mother, I cannot help it. It is some strange freak of the chemistry of the glands. I am far from alone in this, other men have been so, great men, writers, artists, Michelange, Shakespeare, Oscar Wilde. Wilde suffered for it, in prison. It is not a thing a man would want to choose. Not in a world like this, which looks with horror on it."

She did not hear the latter half of that. She picked on the *grands hommes* and repeated the phrase in distaste. "So, because the great men were like that, you must be like that too." Then belatedly she took in *Oscar Wilde*, remembering the scandal well enough. "If he was a great man, then it would be best for you to have ambitions to be a very little man. I cannot," she said, "believe, I cannot take this into my head."

"I'm sorry, Mother. I do not know how long I could have kept this secret from you or from Father, but I wished it to be a secret. Now you have probed and asked and been given the truth you sought."

Her tears were a sign that she was beginning to accept the unacceptable. "Your father," she said, "he must not know." And she muffled her sobs in a cologne-smelling square of cambric she took from her sleeve.

"Father will know sometime," I said, "but let him rest in his ignorance for now. There is sometimes neither goodness nor beauty in truth."

She could not resist crying aloud at that. "You try to be clever, you try to be the *great man* like Oscar Wilde. And you will end like him because you will think it clever to be what you say you are. Oh my God. What have I done, why should this happen to me?"

"I have no doubt, Mother," I said with some coldness, "that Tom will make a good marriage and provide you with grandchildren. Hortense, too."

"That innocent child. If you breathe, if you hint—" She looked very old now. "But all must know sooner or later. There will be scandal. The police. The newspapers." And then: "Poor Tom, serving his country, both his countries. And you being the great man with your scandalous books in London."

"I am sorry, Mother, that the authorities have found me unfit to go and be slaughtered. I cannot help that either. I cannot help my heart being the way it is any more than I can help the other thing. It would solve so many problems, your unworthy wrongly made elder son dying for his country or countries. It may happen yet. The medical officers may be kinder or less kind to my poor heart next time. Next month, indeed. I report again next month. I hope everything will work out to your satisfaction."

"Now you add viciousness and cruelty to the other wrong."

"That's right, Mother. All my fault. There's a line from a poem I shall copy out neatly for you and frame." I gave it her as it was, in English: " 'Gently dip, but not too deep.' " And then back to French with: "You asked for all this. I volunteered nothing. Tomorrow is the feast of the first martyr, but I shall be going to neither mass nor communion. I shall get the first train back to town. Whether you wish to see me again is entirely up to you."

She heard noises I did not hear, holding herself straight the better to listen. "Guns," she said. "Across the Channel. Nothing but ruin, ruin. And Christmas ruined." She got up and looked at her face in my dressing-table mirror. "My face in ruins." It sounded less melodramatic in French. "I hope to God your father is already asleep. I am a bad actress."

"A good mother, though," I said, "a good mother."

She went out without bidding or kissing me good night, leaving it to me to get out of bed and turn the light off.

sixteen

Nineteen seventeen was, among other things, the year in which I began to make money. The medical board convened in Hounslow, to which I was summoned on January 16, found my heart still unacceptable and condemned me to the continued shameful life of a civilian. One of the medical officers, a patriot with a sewn-in whisky smell, insolently recommended that I take up "real war work," meaning the manufacture of guns and bullets, instead of merely trying to keep British culture alive. I told him that I proposed helping the country's morale by writing something humorous for the stage. They all shook their heads sadly.

In my one room on Baron's Court Road, with a view of the tube trains clashing along aboveground, I wrestled with my piece. I was sustained, as before, by bully beef, army issue, sold to me by the office boy at the *English Review*. His uncle was a quartermaster sergeant in the Service Corps. I wrote, in very cold blood, never once even smiling at the cunning hilarity of my lines, a kind of French farce, not much of a tribute to the culture of my mother's native land. A married woman pretends to leave Paris for a few days in order to see her sick mother in Lille, but she actually spends the time with her lover in a little hotel in the Old Marais. Her husband, a singer with an artificial leg who she believes is performing in a concert in Dijon to raise money for soldier comforts, turns up with his mistress at the same hotel. The manager of the hotel has lost his voice as a consequence of the shock of hearing Big Bertha boom, his wife is huge and domineering but becomes gentle and amorous if you can find a particular trigger-point on her ample bottom and press it firmly. The sinning husband faints if he sees eggs, having been pecked by a hen as a child. The lover cannot bear to hear talk of rats. Say "All arks eventually reach their Ararats" and he starts to scream. At the end of the play the husband sings a song about rats and boiled eggs are served for breakfast. The landlord recovers his voice when Big Bertha booms again. There are epigrammatic cadenzas which have little to do with the action. I called this work, constructed in three brief acts, *Jig a Jig Tray Bon*. Reg Hardy at the Comedy Theatre loved the play but hated the title, which he thought vulgar. It was rechristened *Parleyvoo*.

I finished it on February 1, the day when unrestricted submarine warfare began. The full dress rehearsal was held on March 11, when British troops occupied Baghdad. The play opened, along with the Russian Revolution, on March 12. When, on April 6, the United States declared war on Germany, much applause was accorded the specially inserted pro-American gags. On April 13, the search for the *patron*'s wife's trigger-point was presented in terms of the Battle of Arras and the taking of Vimy Ridge. When the Third Battle of Ypres began at the beginning of that hot July, the play seemed likely to run as long as *The Bing Boys* if not *Chu Chin Chow*. I was making money and writing a new play in a more commodious apartment where, like Mr. Ivor Novello, I served cocktails in a silk dressing gown. This was at Albany Mansions. I also had a new lover, Rodney Selkirk, who played the part of the singing husband and for whom the role had, in a sense, been created. He was himself in real life a husband and also a father. He had joined the Artists' Rifles in August 1914, run a concert party at Mauberge, had a pelvic bone splintered at Mons, lost his left leg on the Marne. He bravely made comedy out of his new stiff walk in Grigson's farce *Teeny Weeny Winny*, that ran for six weeks at the Lyric in the autumn of 1916 and in which I saw the returned hero act for the first time. He pretended to his wife that a wound in the prostate rendered him totally incapable of a husband's office. He was three years older than myself, talented, witty, charming, ugly. We spent many Sunday nights together, he having usually feigned to his wife a troops concert in the North or Midlands. Real life, like drama, has few devices for the encompassing of clandestine sin. Sin? Such nonsense.

The British theater is full of homosexuals and also of Catholics, and sometimes the two areas of conviction seem to conjoin with none of the gloomy Cartesian misgivings that had led to my apostasy. Albert Wiscomb, who played the lover in my farce, arrived cheerfully late at one of the evening rehearsals with "Sorry, darlings. I went to have my pan scraped and it tsook rather a tsime"—the latter phrase done simperingly and uproariously suggesting a load of sin which that small and elegant body seemed singularly unfitted to bear. Wiscomb was a happy and lucky pederast who loved lacy altar boys. I spoke to him one early evening in his dressing room while he was making carefully up.

"You confess it?"

"Sins of impurity, dear? Oh yes. I don't specify, of course, and I'm always properly penitent. I mean, we have to *try*, don't we? But no more than try. Can't go against our nature, can we?"

"That's not how it was put to me."

"Yes, but you're a great fusspot and everything has to be just right for you, doesn't it? Me, I'm not fussy, and I don't think the Almighty is, either." And he carefully gave himself black eyebrows. Me, I could not take it so easy.

My father came up to see the play, catching the last train back to Battle immediately afterwards. He thought it vulgar but he laughed. My mother did not come, but she wrote to me in English just before Easter:

I have tried hard to keep to myself the shock. Your father I am certain suspects nothing and thinks we saw little of you at Christmas and hear little from you because you are busy working to become famous in the great but bad city. I must warn you again to say no word of what you say you are to Hortense, though I fear you must have said something since she mentioned a book about a man who loves a boy in Venice and she had known of such things before. It is a German book. I think she must leave that school because the nuns are more on the side of the Germans than should be allowed. You are still my son and I love you with all a mother's heart but I think you must stay away from home until I can live with the shock. I pray that it is only a temporary thing as is sometimes so with boys in English schools and that it will end soon. Tom has been on a short leave and it was a comfort to have him. He says he is to be a permanent gas instructor at Boyce Barracks in Aldershot. It is now Easter and I pray for the miracle that you will say I will change and be pleasing to God and make my duty. We are all well though I have little fainting fits which I am sure come from the shock. I send you my love. I pray for you.

The new play I wrote had as its setting a dentist's waiting room. I had already travestied my mother's country as a place of silly fornication and intrigue; now I was to make people laugh at my father's profession. The comedy was a loose adaptation of Molière's *Le Médecin Malgré Lui*, and its germ was my own corporal work of mercy on the Battle ostler. It opened, with Charles M. Brewster in the lead, at the Criterion on October 24, the day on which the Austrians defeated the Italians with great severity at Caporetto. It was successful. Soon (on November 7, in fact, the day of the Bolshevik Revolution) the *Daily Mail* honored me by mentioning the new comedy in its editorial: "We can assure the Kaiser that the principle of a tooth for a tooth will be fulfilled to the limit, and there will be no Mr. Toomey to sweeten the extractions with laughter." My play was in fact called *A Tooth for a Tooth*—a title I considered grim, if not blasphemous, but Brewster, as actor-manager, insisted on it.

I was already working on a new comedy as Christmas approached. Willie Maugham had had, in 1908, four plays running in London at the same time, prompting a Bernard Partridge cartoon in *Punch* that showed Will Shakespeare not too happy about his namesake's success. I was not so ambitious. I still regarded myself as a novelist making plays somewhat cynically for money, and three plays would be, for the time being anyway, quite enough. I was working in my silk dressing gown on the day when the Russo-German armistice was signed, smoking cigarettes continually and refreshing myself with an endless stream of green tea. It was eleven in the morning. Who should come to the door but my sister Hortense.

She was just seventeen and very pretty. We embraced fondly. She was dressed as a smart young lady and not as a schoolgirl. She had brought luggage with her. "You're staying?" I said.

"May I? For a few days, anyway. Then we can go home together for Christmas."

"I am not," I said, "going home for Christmas. I have a play to write. I have two plays to touch up with topical references."

She sat on the settee, yellow with black stripes, and bumped herself up and down to relish its springiness. "Golly, you *are* doing well," she said, taking it all in. "The rewards of literature." She pronounced this with a German accent, so I took it to be a phrase used by one of her nuns.

"No, dearest Hortense," I said. "The wages of prostitution, if you know the term."

"I know the term all right." She looked at me sparkling. It evoked in her sweet innocent young mind images of wholesome sexual freedom and female elegance. She had probably read *Mrs. Warren's Profession* without under-standing it.

"That," I said sternly, "is a lubricious look. I mean that I'm sacrificing my talents in the service of a very doubtful art but a highly commercial craft."

"Will you take me to see your plays?"

"Of course, and also to smart places for lunch and dinner. And to the Café Royal too if you're a good girl."

She said, as I'd expected, "I didn't think good girls went to the Café Royal."

"Sweetest little sister, won't Mother be annoyed at your not going straight home? And, moreover, staying with your bad brother? For I *am* bad, you know. I'm celebrating my first year out of the Church."

"I *knew*," she said. "I *knew* when you said you were ill last Christmas. Sister Agathe said there was a lot of terrible atheism these days among young men, and it was all because of the war. But they'll get over it, she said, when the war's over."

"And when does the knowledgeable Sister Agathe think the war will be over?"

"Oh, she says next summer the German army will try one more great offen-sive and it will be the last, and the English and French and Americans and Canadians and Australians will either push back or they won't, and everything will depend on this great offensive, she says."

"Would you like tea or coffee and biscuits or a glass of sherry or something?" I asked.

"I'd like you to show me my room and then I'll unpack and bath and change, and then it will be time for lunch." She was very sure of herself, little minx, and I said so. "*Minsk*, Sister Gertrude says it really is. She says it's German for hussy. Hallo, this is all very tremendous luxury." She meant the master bed-room, the door of which was open and which we had to pass on the way to the little spare one. Then she saw something it would have been better for her not to have seen, namely Rodney's spare, original really, artificial leg, lying on the right side of the bed as if to establish, like the living leg of the old manorial lords, a droit du seigneur. It was more comfortable, Rodney said, than his later one, or Mark Two, better cushioned where it met the fleshy stump, but, with the gradual subsidence of the tissues of that part, it had become a little too short. He did not normally keep it here but at home. Why was it here now and in that particular place? Was it really there or is memory speaking false? I think it really was there, the Mark One, an ingenious structure of straps, springs and metal, with a rich red leather cushion, a little darkened by sweat, for the thigh-stump. It caught Hortense's eye at once.

I said, "That belongs to the leading actor in the French-style farce I shall take you to see tonight. He is a fine actor, also a war hero mutilated in a bloody battle."

"Does he live here with you?"

"No, he lives with his wife and children, but his house is in Swiss Cottage and he finds it convenient sometimes to come here, this flat being so central, to freshen up before or after a performance. Does that answer your question, madam?"

"Very stuffy. Sometimes I don't know whether you're joking or not. Poor man. Easier for a man, though. Sister Agathe says that skirts will be very short after the war because of the shortage of material. It seems to be made very well, that leg, a very nicely made artificial leg. I've never seen one before." And she looked at me acutely as though she more than half divined what was going on. I very nearly said: *There's nothing going on, you know.*

She divined further that evening at the Comedy Theatre. She had had a reasonably good dinner at Frith's, where they often had a very fair game pie, into whose contents it was imprudent to enquire too particularly. She'd had also a tinselly dessert which was really no more than a cleverly disguised bread pudding, and had shared with me a bottle of something eely and alumy and North African with a Pommard label. And then she had loved the first act of *Parleyvoo*, even the heavy jokes about the Balfour Declaration and the fall of Jerusalem. In the first interval she came with me into the vestibule, flushed and bright-eyed and proud of her brother. I was proud of her too, in her dressy waistless gown with sequins, something she wore for the once-a-term all-girl dances at her school, probably with Sister Agathe or Gertrude being grimly efficient on the piano with the Turkey Trot. She also had an eye-matching bandeau round her honey-colored hair and a very little rouge on her lips. I was given an awed nod by some I did not know who had been told by some who did know that this was he, the author. And there, one of those who did know me and very well too, was Val Wrigley, my former boy-lover. I felt no bitterness. He seemed to be alone. He seemed also not very well, thinner, his sunken chest sunk further, the points of his cheekbones crimson.

"Well, Kenneth dear." Hortense was all attention. "Not what you and I used to mean when we talked of the glory of literature, is it?"

I did the introductions. "Where," I asked, "is your *friend?*"

"Oh, he's gone off. Left as soon as you fired that little joke about an asylum for the Jews. Not funny, he thought. Nor me."

"Ah," I said, "but you stayed."

"Saw you coming in, old thing. With this delightful girl on your arm. *Hortense*, eh? Always proud of the French blood, weren't you, dear?" Hortense giggled. "Thought it might be nice," Val leered, "to renew an old friendship."

"Did you get your little book printed?"

"Some small difficulties, old thing. But I doubt not that they'll be overcome in God's good time." The stress he laid on the holy name indicated an all too mortal tyranny. "But soft," he then said, "whom have we here?" I felt dirty. I felt my linen was already grimy from the sweat of guilty embarrassment that had at first trickled but now gushed. Linda Selkirk was there, very beautiful, her eyes of a preternatural blue, her fine abundant black hair in a chignon. Her companion was Phil Kemble, whose father had been plain Watson but who had dug out the Kemble from his mother's side, invoking the name of a great theatrical family to prime the engine of his own theatrical career. I had heard, though, that his mother's Kembles had nothing to do with Fanny and Charles but were really Campbells, small distillers with a Kelvinside accent. Phil was a good actor, though difficult to suit with his aptitude for tragedy and his long comic body. Seeing him and Linda together, I felt the thought flash: *They are lovers.* Was this artist's intuition or the wishful thinking of my own guilt?

Val had recognized Kemble but did not know him. I introduced everybody to everybody. Phil pulled me into a space between the box office and the *house full* notice. "You never replied," he reproached.

"I'm still thinking about it, Phil. I'm not sure whether it's the sort of thing I can do. I can see that that kind of part would be right, of course—" It would, too; Phil could make a very moving, complex and unusual William Pitt. He had something of the look of Pitt in the Gillray cartoon, where he and Boney are carving the pudding of the world. "There's the question too of not offending the French," I said.

"The war will be over next spring," Phil said. "We'll be able to offend the French all we want to, mean-souled bastards that they are. A spring opening, think, the first big play of the peace—patriotic, comic, tragic. 'England has saved herself by her exertions.' " He made a kind of Pitt arise out of that line; people began looking at him. I was aware, and was uneasy about it, that Val was doing a lot of talking and Hortense was doing a lot of talking, while Linda listened, smiling. She turned, caught my eye, then did not smile. I didn't like this. Phil went on about good plain straight John Drinkwater dialogue without *prithee* and *egad* and who could play Fox and who George III till the bell went.

I said, "This your first visit to this?"

"Yes. Awful tripe, as you'll be the first to admit, old lad, but who can blame you? We all have to eat, if you can call it eating these days. Linda's first too, did you know? Had to drag her here practically. Things not going so well in that household, but you know better than I, I should imagine. Well, we'll give it another couple of weary gags or so and then I'll take her to supper." He nodded pleasantly and went to collect Linda. Val left, waving sadly at me. I took Hortense in.

After the performance, back at the apartment, I gave Hortense a large cup of hot strong milky cocoa. She was overexcited, she would not sleep without some such nursery nightcap. I had picked up the last mail delivery of the evening from the table downstairs. "Here's news," I said, while she sipped shoeless on the striped couch, feet tucked under her. "My agent says that Bourreau wants to do it in Paris. As a typical piece of English farce."

"That means a lot more money," she said.

"Dearest Hortense," I said, putting the letter down, "I realize I've been very selfish and neglectful. All I gave you for your birthday last year was a book. For Christmas too. And the books didn't even cost me anything. Tomorrow we must go out and buy really magnificent presents for you. And for Father and Mother as well. And Tom. But what would *you* like?"

"Not the way you give presents, that," she said. "Presents are meant to be surprises. *Nice* surprises." And then: "Why did Mrs. Whatsit seem *nastily* surprised tonight?"

"Selkirk? Linda Selkirk? How? What about?"

"Well, you know one babbles things out when one's nervous, I mean Mrs. Whatsit is a bit overwhelming, blue eyes and raven hair, very unusual that, and I was being complimentary about her husband's acting and the stiff walk was funny but tragic really. She said it was an artificial leg and I said I knew and I'd seen his spare one and . . . There was nothing wrong in saying that, I thought, but she went all white. Why? And that poet boy, I'm sure he's consumptive, trying to be like Keats I suppose, laughed in a very strange way. He said better to wake up to that than to onions. What did he mean? Was he trying to be modern like Sister Anastasia's favorite poet? You know, the one who has smells of steaks in passageways—"

I too had, I knew, gone white. I tried to breathe easily. Hortense's eyes, too bright for this time of night, grew wider.

She said, "Oh golly, oh saints in heaven, it's not possible, is it?"

"What, Hortense? What is not possible?"

"The Café Royal, Oscar and Bosie, oh my dear Lord, are you one of those?"

"One of what, Hortense?"

"You know, you know. So this boy deserted you because you had no money, and now you're making money, and he said it was all his fault you turning from great literature and writing muck for the stage. Oh my dear dear Lord in heaven, it all fits in."

"You," I said carefully, "are having a modern education. Mother and Father —it would never be possible for them to—too late, I mean. If you told them that in prisoner of war camps man and man were driven by sheer necessity . . . but apart from that, there are, and I suppose they're comparatively rare, cases, I mean . . . what I mean is, your mother knows and is inexpressibly shocked. Father doesn't and, says your mother, mustn't. As for corrupting poor innocent Hortense, she said—"

"Well." She tucked her feet under more comfortably. "It is a bit of a surprise, my own brother, that is. Oh, I'll shut up about it at home, pretend not to know. It happens in schools, I know. Jill Lipton's brother. And with girls. Two of our girls were caught, fourth-formers, immature, inexperienced, it's silly to get caught."

"I've got caught, haven't I?"

She looked at me with adult seriousness. "Not like Oscar. Bosie got away with it, didn't he, being a lord. Oh my dear Lord, you must be careful." And then, with a pose of scientific curiosity which her shining eyes and flushed cheeks belied, "What exactly is it that men *do* together?"

seventeen

I lived a celibate life from Christmas till Shrovetide. This was not a matter of caution: what went on behind locked doors was nobody's business but the consenting participants'. But Rodney had already given warning that he would leave the play in the new year, handing over his part to Fred Martins. He had been invited to appear in a sort of trial production of Shaw's *Heartbreak House* in Manchester, taking what most considered to be the totally unsuitable role of Captain Shotover—a role that nevertheless fascinated him and which he was determined to attempt. Val tried to make a pathetic return into my life, finding his present friend tyrannical and parsimonious, but I was stern in my rejection of his advances. I was far from lonely; I had my work, I had my friends in the theater.

The new comedy broke, for me, unexpected ground. When I showed the draft first act to J. J. Mannering, he breathed on me his chronic odor of cigars and said, "Lad, it's a musical comedy."

"Never."

"Oh yes. Look—parallel love stories, those people there could be blown up into a chorus, this boozer character is pure rich low comedy. God, even some of these speeches suggest lyrics. Have you ever written lyrics?"

"Well, I wrote poetry at school."

"That's all musical comedy lyrics are, lad—poetry you write at school. Drury Lane, get that into your noddle, big stage, open out, let the thing breathe, dancing, singing, get down to it. Duets, patter songs, choruses. You start with a chorus and end with a chorus. Two acts. Second act in Monte Carlo, Biarritz, somewhere naughty and foreign. Do the lyrics, you know, you know the word, along with the book, let them spring out of the book, you know the word—"

"Pari passu?"

"Knew you'd know the word. Joe Porson's itching for a job. Wasn't his fault *Tilly Tulip* closed after a month. At least three good numbers in it, he has the gift, Joe, Jerome Kern touch, Irving Berlin, jazzy, we're past that *Chu Chin Chow* muck. Get down to it, lad."

I was being driven further and further away from literature all the time. You could hardly call this sort of thing literature:

> *Waking and sleeping*
> *It's always the same,*
> *Sleeping and waking*
> *I call on your name.*
> *Sleeping I cry,*
> *Waking I sigh,*
> *Knowing there's no reply.*

What would Henry James have said? I remembered, or perhaps it is now I remember, walking with him in the autumn garden of Lamb House after the publication of my Socrates novel, him saying, "Keep away from the stony bosom of the theater, my dear young friend, is the considered advice of one who has suffered the agonies of the damned from the— There is a nakedness, there is a laying on of whips, there is a—" Emotion would not let him get the words out. He shuddered, his mouth opened and shut. He picked up his dachshund Max and clasped him to his unstony bosom as if to protect him too from the theater. He was, I could tell, remembering the hoots and howls that greeted *Guy Domville*, himself responding in innocence to the cruel call of "Author," standing there to be ridiculed, his mouth opening and shutting. Oh for the concealing warmth of the novel, the tortuous caverns of style wherein to hide. Nakedness was right.

The musical comedy was called *Say It, Cecil* and was based on a very silly idea. A young man named Cecil loves a young girl called Cecilia but cannot bring himself to utter the ultimate endearment. In August 1914 he said *I love you* to a girl and immediately war broke out. In France he said *Je t'aime* to a girl and the surrounding village was blasted to smithereens. Somebody taught him to try *Ya vas lublu* and his brought about the Russian Revolution. Cecilia thinks she loves him but refuses to be sure until she hears him utter the unequivocal formula. He says *Ich liebe dich*, despite the snarls of the patriotic, and this brings about the collapse of Germany. Great jubilation, but he still dare not say *I love you*. He has a song with chorus—"What I want to say"—and the chorus sings it for him, but this still will not do. The problem is solved (I blush, I still blush) through a trick involving the names of islands. Isle of Man, Isle of Wight, Isle of Capri, Isle of You. No further disasters. Final reprise of chorus

"Oh, say it, Cecil" as "You've said it, Cecil." Is it possible for the reader to imagine anything stupider? I was haunted throughout the writing by an image of the great stone head of Henry James, unmoved, unmoving, eye and brow all eternal reproach.

I finished the final chorus on Sunday, February 24:

We're versing and voicing
Our heartfelt rejoicing,
Your troubles belong to the past.
So nuzzle and nestle,
For you've said it, Cecil,
At last.

Curtain. The shame, the salivation at the prospect of more money.

There was a knock at the door.

"Rodney, dearest. Such a lovely lovely surprise."

Kiss. "Angel, it's seemed like a long time." He put down his bag.

"But why the diffident knock?"

"No keys. The whole damned bunch of them disappeared just before I went northwards. No matter. Must have a drink, angel. Parched." And he mixed himself Haig and water. Strange to consider that we had no refrigerators in those days. He drank and poured himself more. Then he sat on the striped couch, his artificial leg grotesquely stiff before him. "One of my bad days, angel. The bloody chafing."

"Take it off, Rodney. We shan't be going out, shall we? I managed to get hold of a nice piece of mutton. *And* capers. And a virtually immaculate cauliflower. We'll have a pleasant dinner." I looked on him with love, neat and compact in his stiff gray suit, humorously ugly, tanned as though he'd been to summer Blackpool, not Manchester. "How was it?"

"Messed up as from Thursday. Dear Mabel, Mrs. Hushabye you know, got a telegram, War Office. Poor bitch, I'd met Frank, nice lad. She did the brave little woman, the show must go on, but she forgot her lines and broke down, nerve-racking. What Manchester thinks today London will think tomorrow. Manchester says pshaw to Shaw. And it wasn't really my part, not my part at all. You writing something for me?" He saw the manuscript on the desk.

"This is singing and dancing. Do take that leg off."

"You? Singing and dancing? Well, I suppose it had to happen. I can sing, as you know, angel. A peglegged dance might bring the house down. But no, I have to get down to Claudius for Bentinck. God, I'm so thirsty." I mixed him a fresh drink. "Had the shivers on the train. Cold early train in the dark of foredawn. A bit feverish. Feel my head."

"Hot. Get nearer the fire. Sweat it out."

He had a bad cold, sure enough. He could eat little dinner. I got him to bed with a hot water bottle and a tumbler of grog. I lay beside him. He threshed, he mumbled his Captain Shotover lines in the night.

"Nothing but the smash of the drunken skipper's ship on the rocks, the splintering of her rotten timbers, the tearing of her rusty plates, the drowning of the crew like rats in a trap."

"Rodney, Rodney dear—"

"The captain is in his bunk, drinking bottled ditch-water, and the crew is gambling in the forecastle. She will strike and sink and split. Do you think the laws of God will be suspended in favor of England because you were born in it?"

He sweated in gushes, soaking the sheets, then woke raging with thirst. I gave him tepid barley water. "Thanks, angel. A bit better, I think. Sweated a lot of it out. God, we'd better do something about this bed." I got him out of his soaked pajamas and made him sit, shivering now, wrapped in the counterpane while I turned the mattress over and fetched fresh sheets. Then, both naked, we got back in and clasped each other, and I soothed his poor aching stump with stroking fingers. So embraced, we finally slept, lullabyed by the first milk floats.

In full winter morning rainlight I dreamed that the bedroom door was open and that there were people standing there. Was I sickening too? No, it was no dream. There were people in the room, three, two men and a woman.

"I see. Filth," said Linda Selkirk in sable coat and sable toque. The two men might have been younger and elder brother, both with glum Old Bill whiskers, in drab herringbone overcoats, one, the elder, with his bowler hat on.

"Get out," I said to them all, pulling my numbed arm from under sleeping Rodney. "You've no right in here. You broke in, I'll have you for trespass." One never says the right things. Linda Selkirk bitterly jingled a keyring from the end of her gloved right index finger. Rodney began to snore to compete with the voices.

She said, "Trespass. A wife has a right to be with her husband. Have you gentlemen," she asked her companions, "seen enough?"

The elder, he with the hat on, said in a Thameside whine: "There's certain differences, madam. If that gentleman there was a lady . . ." pointing at me. "You see the difference, madam. Soldiers sharing a bivouac, that's not adultery."

"What are you two?" I tried to shout. "Police officers? Where's your warrant?"

"Ah, expected police officers, did you?" said the other one. "And why would that be, sir?"

"As for entering without permission," the still-hatted one said, "the lady was frightened of violence. Any citizen has the right to protect. And she has a right to be in here."

"You two look," said Linda, "and remember. Men in bed, their arms round each other, disgusting. He comes straight here, ignoring his wife and children, wallowing in filth."

I nearly said, *We changed the sheets*. Infection from my trade. I said, "Here you see a sick man." Unfortunately Rodney was now awake, audible licking a parched mouth, looking with wide-eyed hate on his wife. He did not seem surprised at her presence here; he did not seem to see the two whiskered men. "He came here sick. I've spent the entire night looking after him. Your job," I said stupidly to Linda Selkirk.

"He can act sick," she said. "He's acted sick before, just as he's acted love. And don't you tell me what my job is, you filthy sodomite."

"Careful, madam," said the unbowlered.

Rodney was trying to sit up, well-backed by pillows. There we were, two men in bed, clearly naked from the waist up. I grabbed my dressing gown from the bedside chair and, like any spinster, covered my breasts.

"Prothero Agency, eleven Wardour Street," the hatted man said, making the gesture of getting ready to produce a card from an inner pocket. "Witnessing an act of infidelity being the purpose of our business."

"Take that bloody hat off in my house," I cried.

"Yes, sir." And he took it off. He seemed to have dyed his hair some time past; the dye was working out; there were patches of dirty gray and dead black and a residual henna glow. "Madam," he said, "you can lay an evidence. Perhaps you've been told that already."

Rodney now seemed to be acting a well though demented man. "Bitch," he said, "you can go to bloody Kemble as he calls himself. He has two legs and he can shove them both between yours. Leave us alone, we're all right as we are."

"I'll leave you alone," she said, "and I'll make sure you leave the children alone. Have you," she said to the two witnesses, "seen enough?"

"The act's always hard to prove," said the younger. "That's well-known in law. It's all circumstantial."

"You heard that," she said, "from his own filthy mouth. About leaving them together."

"Yes," Rodney said, getting out of bed. "Get out, go on. You can have Kemble, making a bloody fool of me all over London."

"Discretion of the court," muttered the younger witness. He looked at Rodney getting out of bed naked, lacking a leg. "Ah," he said. The other shook his head sadly, as in pity, as at the hopelessness of our situation, the leglessness being an added perversity. Rodney, hissing "Bitch bitch," hopped two paces, holding on to the bed, ready to spring and hold on to her for support while strangling her. Then he fell and could not get up.

"Do you admit," said Linda to me, "that you're sodomizing my husband, you swine?"

"Not at the moment," I said. The farce had really entered my blood. Then, putting on my dressing gown, I went over to poor Rodney. The dressing gown lacked its belt. I might as well have been naked. I heard one of the men going tut-tut while I got hold of Rodney's artificial leg. The idea perhaps was to strap it on to him and enable him to get over there, naked and legged, to strangle Linda.

Linda said, "I want to be sick. I want to vomit. The filth. Trying to be Oscar Wilde. I'll break you, I'll ruin you both. Jail for both of you, filth. I'll have it all over the newspapers, everything."

"Law of obscenity," muttered the younger.

I grasped the artificial leg like a club and raised it to hit, my dressing gown open, showing all I had. Rodney on the floor groaned and tried to get up. His poor arms were too feeble to take the strain of lifting. He collapsed again. The two witnesses sturdily placed themselves in front of their agency's client as I came forward diffidently. I lowered the leg and seemed to be presenting it as a seller of legs, lovely leg here madam admire the action, as one who offered the leg as a legal defense, blame it all on the war. Linda showed her teeth in disgust.

She said, "You'll hear. You'll be punished. You can keep him." And then: "Can't, can you? You'll be in different cells, they'll send you to different prisons." Then she neatly spat, turned her back, and went out. She herself, of course, had been a small actress, not successful, abandoning art for marriage. The two men put their hats on, nodded, made tentative hand gestures of goodbye, all in very fair comic synchronization. Then they too went. I followed, seeing them off the premises. They did not look back. I returned to Rodney and got him into bed. He was both burning and shivering and could say nothing but *bitch* and *bloody bitch*. I went to the kitchen and made tea. The sad Monday rainlight would not ray down rain; it was a harsh and costive February sky. I made toast and spread real butter, gift of an Irish admirer. I still refused to think. I took in a tray to Rodney. He could eat nothing but drank thirstily of the milk-cooled tea. Then it was my turn to tremble, though with fear.

I said, "What's she going to do?"

"Bitch, the bloody bitch. I have to get up, I have to go and see Bentinck." He tried to get out of bed but I pushed him back. "We're reading at two. I want my bag, I want my *Hamlet*."

"You're staying here," I said. "I'll ring Bentinck. I'm also ringing the doctor."

"I don't want a bloody doctor."

"What's she going to do?" I said again.

"She can do what she bloody well likes. I'm finished with her. Give me more tea, angel."

He drained three more breakfast cups and then slept uneasily. His forehead flamed. I dressed and went below to the hall telephone. I could not get Bentinck but left a message with his wife. Dr. Chambers said it sounded like a bad attack of flu and he would be around when he could; flu was on the rampage, I'd better watch myself. I went back to Rodney. He slept and oozed, and there was a bubbling noise in his chest. It seemed natural for me now to set my affairs in order. A phase of my life was coming to an end, perhaps in brutal public scandal, the leers of my enemies, tears of my family, the whips of the vindictive state. They had devoured Wilde like a great meat meal; me they would swallow as a Continental breakfast. I packed *Say It, Cecil* in a heavy legal envelope and addressed it to J. J. Mannering, stamped it and took it below to the hall table for the porter to post. The morning mail had already been laid out on that table, but there was nothing for me. It was as though a silence premonitory of violence was already setting in. It still would not rain.

I sat by Rodney and thought. As always with me, thought expressed itself in dramatic images. Two grave men in ulsters and bowlers arrived with a warrant. "If you would come quietly sir and make no fuss it would be better no point in protesting to us sir we are merely indifferent arms of the law." One of the men had a twitch in his left cheek. Or if it were merely a matter of divorce then there would be a long wait before the civil action bred the criminal one. The scandal. How would the newspapers put it? Patients in my father's waiting room reading the papers there, going into the surgery, noting my father's slight tremor, eyes lowered to his instruments in shame. "Needn't say Mr. Toomey how much we sympathize my wife asked me to tell you terrible thing who would have thought it yes that's the one hurts when I eat anything sweet." No, the mere act of filing divorce action would entail the laying of an information, if that was the term. I sweated as I saw myself with heavy baggage at Dover or Folkestone, furtively climbing the gangplank in merciful seafog. When the doorbell below rang at noon I sat frozen. My door was knocked impatiently. I sat frozen. No good, they had the right to force an entry. I went to the door on legs of oatmeal. It was, of course, Dr. Chambers, dressed in doctor's old style with top hat in bad need of reblocking.

"He lives here?" he asked sternly, looking down on bleary rambling Rodney.

"No," I said blushing. "He came on a visit. He arrived yesterday. From Manchester."

"The flu's bad up there. A new strain, very tough. Don't at all like the sound of that chest. His face looks familiar."

"He's Rodney Selkirk. The actor. He was in one of my plays."

"Not seen any play of yours." The guilt mounted. "Must have been something else I saw him in."

"Very likely. What can be done for him?"

"I'll have to get him a bed."

"This is a bed." Oh God, a laugh in every line, Mr. Toomey excels himself, 365th hilarious performance.

"I mean in the London Clinic. Ambulance too. He obviously can't walk."

"He has only one leg. On the Marne. A war hero, you know."

"Ah, war hero, eh?" Nothing sounded too good. "Danger of pneumonia. A killer, that. Needs careful nursing. Even so, even so." He shook his head. My heart fell; I felt the beginnings of the exhilaration of treacherous liberty; dead Rodney, no divorce action, no criminal action. Oh Christ: dead Rodney, Rodney dead. "Can I use your phone?"

"Downstairs. You don't mean that, do you?"

"Mean what?"

"A killer, you said."

"Mark my words," he said loudly, poking his finger at me. "It's going to be a very sour peace when it comes if it comes. Epidemic proportions, you mark my words. You don't look any too good yourself." And sternly he went down to the telephone.

When they took Rodney away he was too delirious to know where he was or who I was.

"Do you think the laws of God will be will be." And then he was King Claudius. "Who, impotent and bedrid, impotent and bedrid, what the hell comes next, prompt, damn it."

"Rodney, Rodney."

The rear stretcher-bearer shook his grizzled head. The ambulance driver carried Rodney's bag downstairs, but I forgot to give him the artificial limb. I told Brett, the porter, that I was going away for a time and gave him five pounds to pack my books and household effects into boxes and stow these in the cellars. I scribbled a note to the landlord terminating my lease. Secret war service, I said, an urgent posting. God knows what happened to poor Rodney's leg.

eighteen

I registered at the Marmion Hotel in Bloomsbury under the name of Henry M. James. The M., chosen randomly, I later discovered stood for the dachshund Max. I had a few words with Humbert Wolfe, poet and civil servant, who eased my way to obtaining a visa from the consular department of the French Embassy. We were, after all, at war, and only the doomed had free access to the fields of France. I could claim a sort of business in Paris: the British farce *Goddam*, freely adapted from my French farce *Parleyvoo*, was going into rehearsal at the Odéon, with André Claudel in the lead, and it seemed reasonable that I should at least look in and protect such features of the original as I valued. I got my visa without trouble and then wondered whether I dared risk visiting poor Rodney to tell him of my impending flight. But the police might already be seated by his bed, awaiting me. I telephoned and learned that he was "very poorly."

It was on the packet from Folkestone that I read of his death. The boat was really War Department transport taking odds and sods to the other shore—officers with strange specializations, journalists, two men of the French War Ministry, nursing sisters, a platoon of intellectual-looking weeds called an Extraordinary Offence Unit, a bearded but uniformed war artist who left his *Evening Standard* on one of the deck benches. It was in this newspaper that I read the few lines dedicated to the untimely demise of a notable actor. I wept in the windy marine dark; I had loved him and he, I believed, me. It must be hard for my younger readers to take in the fact that a man could die of influenza. We of that age had electricity, gas, automobiles, rotary printing presses, the novels of P. G. Wodehouse, canned goods, Gold Flake cigarettes, mass destruction, airplanes, but we did not have antibiotics. Millions were to die of influenza before that year was out. This was, in art, the modern age, the age of Eliot, Pound, Joyce, surrealism, atonality, but of science we knew very little. Even our war was waged on the medieval assumption that the enemy was encastled on a hill that was called Central Europe, and that the hill had to be climbed painfully, trench by trench. As for homosexual love, this was a sin against society. I did not know whether, with poor Rodney dead, I was still in danger from Mrs. Selkirk and the law, but there was no turning back now. I had committed myself to exile. Save for odd business visits, I would never see England again.

The train journey from Boulogne to Paris was wretched, full of stops and jerks and railwaymen's shouts in the night. The war artist sat next to me, charcoal-sketching in the dim light a kind of general outline of a scene of slaughter. A fat Belgian opposite had an inexplicable supply of powdery Turkish delight, which he would offer from a sticky palm. An old lady smoked what looked and smelled like Russian *papirosi*. When we arrived I had difficulty in finding a taxi. The only motor vehicles around seemed to be Red Cross ambulances. The blackout was intenser than London's. Of the few blue-clad porters at least half wore black bands of mourning. I must get my own black band, I told myself.

The crippled cabdriver found with difficulty the little Hôtel Récamier, which hid in a corner near the huge porticoed church of Saint-Sulpice. I had cabled my request for a reservation, but they had not received the message. Nevertheless, they had a cold little room for me, and there on the rickety table I laid out my unlined paper and fountain pen, earnest of serious work, no more farces. I undressed shivering and cried myself to sleep.

The next day's windy cloudy Paris was no improvement on the sad and empty city of the night. After a cup of bitter chicory coffee and a stale croissant I went to the bank on the Rue de la Paix to which my London bank had transferred the greater part of my funds. I left with my pockets full of dirty francs, watching without pleasure the stream of Red Cross motors, noting that great hotels had been turned into hospitals, hearing a shattering crump that could only be Big Bertha.

"Big Bertha," an Englishman said to me in a sad bar on the Boulevard Saint-Germain. "Saw a shell explode on the street yesterday. The thing to do is not to run down into the Métro with the rest of the shitscared bastards. If it comes for you, bow it a welcome. Who the hell wants to live anyway?" And he gloomily downed a small glass of something purplish. He then peered at me, pushing his glass toward the barman for a refill. "Know you, don't I? Were with Norman back there on that literary rag, that right? Douglas, that is. Ran away after he got picked up. Buggering little boys, that is. He's here, living off rotten chestnuts. You also in necessary but fearful exile? I'm Wade-Browne, by the way." He was lean and high and hollow-chested. "Clever idea, that filthy novel of yours full of tits, putting every bugger on the wrong track. Didn't take us knowing ones in, though." He chuckled sadly and dirtily. "Toomey. Let me see if I can recall Norman's limerick. Ah." And he recited:

> *"A notorious bugger called Toomey*
> *Has a heart that's excessively roomy.*
> *For shagging and shoving*
> *He substitutes loving.*
> *Prognosis: exceedingly gloomy."*

My hand trembled as it lifted the *ballon* of course *rouge*. I sipped and wet my tie. This man could not yet know of my bereavement. His friend Douglas had a fair idea, though, of my temperament. Even those of my own fleshly persuasion

were prepared to find *love* absurd. Such gigglers, shagging and shoving where
they could, were surely damned. But why not also the oiled cheap Casanovas,
chalking up shopgirl conquests? Perhaps they too, but not so damned as this
boy-shagging Douglas. I had only just arrived in Paris; already I knew I had to
get out. Douglas defiled it, already defiled as it was.

Wade-Browne watched me, leering. Then, by way of a sad sneer, he re-
lapsed into his initial gloom. "The problem is," he said, "to make the negative
fatalistic wait on the positively suicidal. I mean, in a war people don't take guns
and knives to themselves. Suicide rate's very low in wartime. A sought-out
blighty one's different. Self-mutilation in the trenches indicates a powerful desire to survive. I'd never do myself in, not with Big Bertha banging away. But
getting in the way of the shells is bloody difficult."

"Why," I said, "do you want to die?"

"Ah, got a tongue in your arse, sorry, head, eh? Why, you ask. Well, give me
a good reason for living. Go on, you do that."

"Certain physical sensations. The beauty of the earth and of art."

"Oh Jesus, such shit."

I said no more. I was not going to mention love.

"Western civilization has the right idea," he said. "Blowing itself up." Big
Bertha crumped again, northeast of us. The barman crossed himself, then
shrugged as to say: An inherited superstition, a mere reflex, forgive it. I decided
I had better move south. I was a free man, wasn't I? I had a right to flee from
dark and danger and deprivation and move to the woods of mimosa. My pockets were full of dirty francs. I could arrange for a drawing account on a branch
of the Banque Nationale when I got to where I was going. I would go and pack
at once. I nodded coldly at Wade-Browne, then drank up. He called something
obscene and whining after me as I left.

In the street I saw Maynard Keynes with a briefcase under his arm. He was
grinning manically at an official-looking Frenchman who spoke rapidly but
deferentially, as though this big, confident and clever-looking man had already
been created a milord. Keynes evidently wanted to get away from him. He
waved at me as though I were the one man he had come to Paris to see, then
strode toward me, throwing back fluent commercial French with a Cambridge
neigh to the other, a dapper and bowing hat-doffer. Big Bertha crumped somewhere across the river. Keynes and I knew each other, having been fellow guests
at at least three Bloomsbury parties. Morgan Foster had been kind to me and
had even made tentative gestures in the direction of the possibility of our
perhaps conceivably becoming perhaps *friends*. But, though I liked Morgan well
enough, I did not greatly care for his smell, which, incredibly, considering his
agnosticism, was not unlike that of stale holy water in a church stoup. Keynes
was at that time, as all Bloomsbury knew, trying to turn himself into a heterosexual with a ballet dancer. He now pumped my hand and leered at me, as if he

knew why I had left London. He seemed to consider that his own presence required an explanation.

"Buying pictures cheap for the government. The prices are down to nothing, what with Big Bertha and all the panic. I could," he said, "put you in the way of something. A Georges Rouault, dirt cheap, absolutely."

"Why me?"

"Why not you?" He then surveyed me with an eye closed and his bowler-hatted head on one side, not grinning. "You look bruised and lonely. You look like a man who needs a picture to look at. Come to the Ritz and see. Absolutely rock-bottom dirt cheap."

nineteen

It was not, and never is, possible to ignore the square porticoed bulk of the church of Saint-Sulpice. As I approached the Hôtel Récamier with a Rouault under my arm, ready to pack, pay, search for a cab and get to the Gare de Lyon, I had the sensation of a small bomb bursting in my heart. Was I not free not only in the vague sense that is conveyed by odd pictures of oneself drinking at café tables under palm trees, but also in the particular sense of being liberated from fleshly desire? Rodney was dead and I wanted no other lover; wanting no other lover, I did not require physical embraces. Should the itch of the flesh ever come in a depersonalized form, I had only to conjure an image of giggling Norman Douglas handling little dirty boys in order to dispel it. Partly magnetized by the solidity of the church itself, partly thrown toward it by the bursting bomb of hope, I mounted the steps and walked into the stale religious gloom animated by sinners come to confess. It was Saturday, traditional day for the scraping of the pan. I joined the seated bourgeoisie, half of them black-banded, awaiting shrift from Father H. Chabrier. The man next to me, who smelt of cloves, was openly reading a copy of *Le Rire*, or rather taking in a drawing of a skirt-dancer. He was like one who relishes the last drink before closing time.

Confessing in French was like confessing to my mother. I could see only Father Chabrier's hands beyond the grille, gnarled pale hands that sometimes beat time to his words with a rolled copy of a daily paper.

". . . Very nearly two years, hence I missed my Easter duty. Also mass on Sundays and feast days. Also my morning and night prayers."

"*Oui oui oui.*" He was impatient, he wanted sins of commission.

"Sins of impurity, Father."

"*Avec des femmes?*"

"With men, Father."

"Aaaaaah."

I had trouble with the word *love*. In French, in all its forms and their derivatives, it seemed frivolous or cynical or grossly physical.

"Do you sincerely repent of those sins?"

"I cannot very well repent of love, *mon père.*"

"You must repent of it, you must."

"How can I repent of what God ordains that we do? *Agape, diligentia.* I will not say *l'amour.* I loved a man, and he is now dead. What have I done wrong?"

"There was the physical in it, as you have said. That was a deadly sin."

"But that was tenderness, the expression of *agape*—"

"Do not use that word *agape* to me, *agape* means Christian love, that is blasphemous." He sighed, groaned, then smote the grille thrice irritably with his newspaper baton. "You have committed deadly sin, do you sincerely repent of that sin?"

"Whatever it is or was, I firmly resolve not to do it again. Will that suffice?"

"Resolution is only part of it. There must be penitence. Are you sincerely penitent?"

"You ask me to repent of love?"

"*L'amour* expressly forbidden, *l'amour* filthy and obscene."

"If that love was truly filthy and obscene, then I repent of it. Will that do?"

He was not going to be tricked. If there was to be any casuistry, it was for him, a priest of the Church, to perpetrate. He said: "There are without doubt many waiting outside. I do not think you have sufficiently prepared yourself. You must examine your conscience more thoroughly than you evidently have so far done. Come and see me again on Monday. My *horaire* is fixed to the door, you will see the times when I am here. Go now and pray to be made penitent." And he crashed down his baton in a final beat, like his namesake on the last chord of, say, the *Marche Joyeuse.*

So, then, I was to go south unshriven. None could say I had not done my best. When I left the confessional the waiting sinners looked up at me with vague interest. They had perhaps heard the bang of the rolled newspaper. A young girl in black looked up in disquiet and reproach: *le père* Chabrier was in a bad mood, and all my fault. As I walked to my hotel, Rouault also unshriven,

I felt myself to be gently fingered by the savants of the Enlightenment. Tap tap, they tapped. Do more than write farces and sensational fiction. Construct something in which to believe. Love and beauty are not enough.

twenty

As some of my readers will know, I wrote a little book called *Moving South*. I had originally thought of the title *Austral*, an austere and learned reaction to abominations like *Jig a Jig Tray Bon*, but filthy Norman Douglas in a manner preempted it with his *South Wind*. It is part travel book, part highly selective autobiography, part record of my reading *en route* and *en voyage*, part trite philosophical essay, ending with an Affirmation of Life, meaning sun, sea, wine, bad peasant cooking. I started it in the Gare de Lyon, during the long wait for the train to pull out, continued it at Orléans, Saint-Étienne, at Toulouse, at Marseilles.

Spring came, and the war rolled destructively toward its end. The new battle of Arras. The new German offensive. The British naval raid on Zeebrugge and Ostend. The appointment of Foch as commander-in-chief of the allied armies. The sinking of the *Vindictive* in Ostend harbor. The last German offensive. The successful attack of British Dominion forces at Amiens. The end of the Turkish army at Megiddo. By that time, summer had gone and I was basking in the Cagliari autumn. I had obtained an Italian visa at Nice, spent some weeks in Florence, taken a boat from Leghorn to Corsica, jumped across the narrow Strait of Bonifacio into Sardinia, then traveled slowly by train down the west coast to Cagliari. The Bulgarians signed an armistice, the last general offensive in the west began, the Germans accepted President Wilson's Fourteen Points, the Italians massively advanced, the Turks surrendered, the Austrians accepted the Italian terms. Bell-clashes and vinous rejoicing on the Via Roma while I sat, friendless, chaste, unloved, at an outside table of the Café Roma, with a bottle of black cold local wine. On November 9, the day of the Kaiser's flight and abdication, I was writing in my hotel room on the Largo Carlo-Felice:

I do not want to use terms like good and evil. If such terms possess a meaning, it must be only in a general context of theology. Right and wrong will do for me, variable in meaning though they are. It has been right to hate the

Germans; soon it will be right to love them. It was wrong to eat overmuch bread; soon it will be wrong to deprive the wheatmen of their golden profits. I know that many have been talking of an evil war, as though God had abdicated like Kaiser Wilhelm and the Devil presided over his own Revolution, but can one say more than that the war was both wrong and right? It was right to spring to arms to the defense of the little nations, wrong to condemn so many to death and mutilation. Men do what has to be done in order that some great basic principle of movement may be fulfilled. History is movement and movement is life. Who, except Hegel or Marx, would be so bold as to affirm that the movement of history is toward the better and may end with the establishment of the satisfactory and unchangeable? All we know is that men move, men change, and that the sufferings they undergo—and will themselves to undergo—are both wrong and right. As for good, do not tell me that God is good. If God exists, he is indifferent to men, and if he is indifferent, then he may as well not exist. Good is what I find in the taste of an apple, in the curdling of the clouds over the sea here at Cagliari, in the benison of the sun in the morning, new bread, coffee, friendship, love.

Oh my God, I can say now, and shudder.

On November 11 I wrote my final words:

We have all suffered, in one way or another, and now many of us will unreasonably expect a reward for having borne up so bravely. We have taken our medicine, and father will buy us a bag of sweets. The truth is that father will buy us nothing. The truth is that father does not exist, either as unpredictable Jehovah, beneficent Nature, or omnipotent State. We must look for our own sweets and not be disappointed if they are hard to find. For strictly we deserve nothing. We wanted this war. If we had not wanted it we would not have had it. Whatever we want we shall always have, but we ought always to calculate whether we can afford to pay for it. Ask little, expect less: let that be the pokerwork slogan we hang above our beds this eleventh day of the eleventh month of 1918. The little and the less are sufficiently satisfying. Seek the good.

I was young, a very young and immature man who believed it was a fine thing to be a writer. Sufficiently satisfying, indeed. Satisfactorily satisfactory. These things are almost as shameful in old age as fleshly sin or spiritual meanness, and they spring out of the same fault, which we may term unawareness. If I could write so blatant a tautology, I could write also of the goodness of evil or the badness of good, and probably, somewhere or other, did.

I had finished my little book, then, and I went out to celebrate a double completion. The bells clanged and whirred, and men and women in native costume and in the drabber garbs which aped the bourgeois modes of Milan strolled happily in the evening *passeggiata* or drank at the outside café tables in the mild autumn air. I climbed a corkscrew street down which a late loaded donkey slithered, whoaed by his master, mustached, fierce-eyed as a warrior, with his sock-cap twisted in the Phrygian mode. I entered a little wineshop and was welcomed, the Englishman, his war ended only a few days later than theirs. I drank too much of a colorless spirit that smelt of old sheepdog, brought, winking, by the fat proprietor from a back room: something strong, special, reserved. I sang:

> *"You wore a tunic,*
> *A dirty khaki tunic,*
> *While I wore civilian clothes."*

Even though nobody there knew English, I perverted the words of the parody to the truth. I had come through, better men than I had been slaughtered or maimed. And here I was, speaking bad Italian on behalf of my victorious nation. My fellow drinkers were in the bright stockings, bunched-up clout-trunks, flop-caps, stiff red jackets of rural Sardinia, or else in the baggy trousers and clumsy boots of workers of the town.

> *"Oh the moon shines bright on Charlie*
> *Chaplin,*
> *His boots are cracking*
> *For want of blacking."*

They all knew Charlie Chaplin. I believed that writers were fine people and the legislators of the world and so on, but I was already desperately out of date. The future belonged to the universal eye, to be tricked and overfed with crude images; it did not belong to the imagination. The last thing I clearly remember of that evening was a young man doing a very competent imitation of Charlie running from the cops and braking on one foot as he turned a corner. And then I was waking up in my hotel room at four in the morning, queasy and dry-mouthed, with a naked woman next to me.

Feeling warm flesh there, I thought at first it was Rodney. Then my hand caught the protrusion of a female breast. I was in bed with my mother, Hortense was in bed with me. Wait, I was in Sardinia. The woman snored. There was not enough light from outside the window for me to see what or who, how young or old. A church bell told four. I began to retch. I got out of bed hastily. I too was naked. On the table over there there should be mineral water. I could, I knew, find it in the dark. I retched. I must get to the *gabinetto* two doors down the corridor, but not naked. My dressing gown hung behind the door; I got it on.

I came back shaky to drink off the half-full bottle of mineral water. I shivered. It was a cold night and dawn was a long way off. I took off my dressing gown and got back into bed. My bedfellow stirred and muttered something about, or to, somebody called Pietro. I was lying on my back to her left, she was turned away from me. She then supinated briskly and struck my chest with the length of a hard forearm. The bed was narrow. She rasped out a single harsh snore that woke her. She smacked her lips. I could almost hear her eyeballs rolling, trying to pierce the dark as she wondered where she was. A distant cock crowed viciously at some sudden light somewhere, an immature cock with an ill-learnt *cocorico*. She knew where she was. Then she was on her left side, breathing on me. I could hear the swishing of her eyelids. I expected garlic and the foul accumulations of the night, but she smelt of apples. I pretended sleep and feigned slow sleeper's breaths, spiced now and then with a snort. Her right hand was on my penis. She tweaked my nose with her left. I acted the part of a man waking.

"Eh what who." And then: *"Chi?"*

"Francesca."

I was damned if I could remember any Francesca. If one got drunk enough one could commit murder and know nothing about it. I remembered once in London surfacing from somewhere or nowhere to find myself in a strange bed-sitter full of affable strangers, sitting on a divan-bed genteelly eating a kipper. What had happened in that little wineshop up the hill? The Englishman, one of a notoriously tepid race, taunted rollickingly with his stiffness, or lack of it, forced to prove his virility by taking off a girl notoriously loose, knowing that the virility would not have to be proved to the hilt? Or a prostitute picked or picking up on the Via Roma afterwards? You fall, you drunk, I take you ome. I cautiously felt Francesca's face with two fingers, a young smooth face with a frame of wild hair that smelt faintly scorched. She took my hand and firmly put it to her clitoris.

I was technically a virgin. I had spilled seed in sleep or with other males but never with a woman. I knew what men did with women but now for the first time (November 12, 1918) was drawn from duty not desire, far far from desire, to enact what I had learnt in sniggering school urinals and later, some-what modified, from bar talk and books. The sexual stimulation of an invisible but very warm and solid female body I performed coldly and with distaste. I tried to turn myself into a character in one of my novels, initiating the act in joy, which the Germans call *Lust*, but I could not. I was disgusted with the hypocrisy the trade committed me to, since the time for homosexual fiction was not yet, and might never be yet. I would continue to write about male and female reeling and writhing and fainting in coils, but it would always be a foul lie for me, also disgusting. I was damned if I was going to carry over a simulated tropism from the desk, where it was necessary, to the bed, where it was not. I removed my hand but not, it seemed, prematurely. She grasped my penis with the intention of guiding it toward herself, but there was nothing to guide except an inch or so of flaccid indifference. She laughed. I turned from her and mumbled into the pillow: *"Via via, non posso. Via via via. Voglio dormire."* She laughed.

She did not seem to require any light. A farm girl perhaps, not used to light that the Lord had not said let there be. I heard a rustle and a clop of shoes. Like a cat. But she laughed all the time. Enough to make a cat laugh. *Charley's Aunt* had preempted that slogan. It could not be used of the comedies of Kenneth M. Toomey. *"Soldi?"* I said, still into the pillow. But she laughed at that too. She had probably been paid in advance. I remembered nothing. Before she opened the door she said something rapid and derisive that might have been a Sardinian proverb about men not able to get it up. Then she was off. I felt terrible. Thank God I was leaving. She would know me all right, the Englishman who had sung about Charlie Chaplin. She would bring her friends to see me. Sitting at a café table I would be pointed out and giggled at. Let them do what the hell they wished. I was not staying, but I would go in my own good time. Where, though? To a place where I could find an English-language typist and a reliable postal service. I had a book to send to England. Had this sort of thing ever happened to Norman Douglas? He was probably an omnifutuant swine who could do it with anything. Watch this tautology, Toomey. That is what *omnifutuant* means. Live for style.

I sat at an outside café table next day going over my manuscript with a thick blunt pencil. Nobody laughed at me, but I had the feeling that I was looked at occasionally with grim wonder: a genuine English homosexual, regard. It may, of course, have been my lonely literary fussiness—tutting and striking things out. The tables were full except for mine, which had two empty chairs. None wished to take them. My loneliness was a visible property. Then a bulky shadow blotted the sun out. I looked up. My God, they were sending a priest after me. A bulky priest, his black rusty. A layman was with him. He flashed a handsome mouth at me, indicated the free chairs and said, *"Possiamo?"*

"Si accomodino."

They sat, and the cleric wrinkled a little at my foreign vowels. They talked quietly to each other in what I took to be the Milanese dialect. It was a busy noontime and they had trouble in getting a waiter. The layman clicked and clicked his fingers, then smiled at me as in deprecation of a vulgar but needful gesture. He looked down frankly at a page of my manuscript. "English?" he said.

"Yes, it's English."

"No, no, you. You are English? Or American?"

"English will do. British really. *Britannico*."

The waiter came, upright, fierce, mustached, a warrior. He took an order for vermouth from them, from me the same again. Coffee. Cognac. I was trying to cure my hangover. The priest drank and said, with comic tartness: "We end a long war and we celebrate by drinking wormwood."

"Such excellent English," I said. No flattery was necessary. The accent was faintly American; there was none of the interpolation of a linking vowel that so many Italians use to protect themselves from the bruising of our final consonants. I had taken this man to be a parish priest of no particular distinction, though I might have asked myself what a Milanese was doing in Cagliari. The layman was very ready to answer all the questions I had not yet asked.

He said, "Our mother, you understand, was born in the United States. In New Jersey, though Italian. Our father met her when he was in America on business. He brought her back to Milan, or near to it. The place of the famous cheese, Gorgonzola. She insisted very much that we should learn English. It was the language of the future, she said. I have been staying here to work at my music. My brother has come for a holiday. We have both been in the war, but he was in the war longer than myself." There it was, then, all: no picking and guessing and holding back, as with British table acquaintances.

"I am an English, or British, writer. I have published certain books. I have had certain stupid comedies presented in the London theater. I have just completed a little book. I am sitting here correcting it. I have not been in the war. My heart was said to be unreliable."

"You knew these comedies were stupid when you wrote them?" the priest asked. "Or have you since discovered they are stupid? Or have others told you they are stupid?"

"When I say stupid, I mean not of the highest artistic excellence. The comedies were intended as devices to promote laughter, in a bad time. They succeeded in promoting laughter."

"Then you should not have said that they were stupid."

"Would your name be a famous name?" his brother asked.

"I think not," I said, "outside London theatrical and literary circles. It is," I said humbly, "Kenneth Toomey."

They both tried out that name: *tuuuumi*. They liked it, though they did not know it. It fitted an Italian mouth very nicely. The layman said, "I am Domenico Campanati, a composer of music." He waited with small hope. No, I hadn't heard of him. "My brother is Don Carlo Campanati." It was not expected that I, or anyone, should have heard of him.

I said, "I have not yet seen my latest work for the stage. You say you are a composer of music. I should think you would despise the music of this work, which is a musical comedy. I have not, of course, heard the music," I added. I looked at Don Carlo and waited.

"If the music is good, why should he despise it? If you have not heard the music, then how can you know that it is not good?"

I was beginning to enjoy this in a bad-tooth-biting way. I said, "The story of this musical comedy is excessively stupid." Don Carlo shook his head amiably, as at a student slow but worth the teacher's perseverance. "It is the story of a young man," I began, "who cannot say *I love you.*" And I blurted it all out. They listened with attention, Domenico Campanati smiling, Don Carlo with Stagyrite seriousness. At the end Domenico gave a happy little gurgle apt for such a nugacity, but Don Carlo said:

"There is nothing stupid there. There is a profound truth embedded in a play of words. For love is great, and the professing of love is not to be done lightly."

I bowed my head. I said, "I should be honored if you would have lunch with me. At the *ristorante* of my *albergo.*" I invited them a microsecond or so before knowing why. It was Domenico, of course, handsome, *simpatico*, an artist. My glands were sniffing around. The brothers looked at each other and Don Carlo was the first to say they would be honored. He also said, as I drained my coffee and then my cognac:

"I presume you will take your luncheon backwards. You will end, after the soup, with a glass of wormwood." We got up and Don Carlo looked critically at the money I had left on the table. "That is too much. A *mancia* of two lire. The waiter will be dissatisfied with those who leave a smaller but more rational *mancia.*"

"You disapprove of generosity? Perhaps they will call me Don Quixote *della mancia.*" Neither of them thought that funny. I have frequently used that quip with Italians, but it has never been considered funny. We set off through the noon crowd toward the Largo Carlo-Felice. The weather was mild still, but Don Carlo wore a heavy black cloak. With my manuscript flapping under my arm in the breeze, I peered warily about for girls who would laugh and point the finger at me. But none did.

Don Carlo said, "Your eyes are busy. You are not a married man?" His own sharp black eyes missed nothing. He turned them to me, along with a nose that was a complicated structure of wide hairy nostrils, great firm wings, a number of hillocks on the shallow slopes, a zigzagging nose gristle. I smiled guiltily and shook my head. He was fat and came up to my chin; about five years my senior, I thought. His brother was younger than I and almost as tall. He had what I took to be the family eyes, black and wideset, but without sharpness: he was a dreamer, one of my own breed. His black oiled hair was long, as a musician's was expected to be in those days. He wore a suit from a good Milanese tailor, sober dark blue but the lapels assertive as his ears, ready to catch whatever sounds were going. I divined that there was money in the family. I guessed that his music was being subsidized by family money.

I said, as we walked, "What music are you composing?"

"An opera in one act. La Scala needs such things. Why should *Cavalleria Rusticana* always have to go with *I Pagliacci?*"

"Yes. Cavnpag we say in London."

"Why should the whole of Puccini's *Trittico* have to be done when they wish only to do *Gianni Schicchi?*"

"You have a good libretto?"

He raised his shoulders to bury his neck, dug his elbows into his ribs, fanned out his fingers. "It is by Ruggero Ricciardelli. You know him? No. A young poet who worships D'Annunzio. There are too many words. There is not enough happening. There is too much standing around and doing nothing. You understand me?"

"Perhaps," I said, "you would permit me to look at it."

"Would you, would you?" He was ready to wreathe himself about me in gratitude. "You say you have written for the theater, yes? Music comedy, you said. Meaning a kind of operetta, yes? Well, why not in my little opera new things, very American? Ragtime, jazz. I hear and see very clearly a mixed quartet drinking cocktails and the music becoming more and more *ubriaca*."

"Drunk, yes. Why not?"

Don Carlo rumbled "Drunk," prolonging the vowel into a Milanese *ah*. "Not too drunk, *fratello mio*."

I said, ready to be knocked down again, "Art and morality have little to say to each other. We do not go to the play or the opera to be taught what is bad and what is good."

"That is not what the Church tells us. But you are English and do not belong to the Church."

"My family is a Catholic family. My mother is French. She converted my father."

"Nevertheless," Don Carlo said, "I do not think you belong to the Church." And that was that. We had arrived at the hotel and we entered its restaurant, *trattoria* really, and Don Carlo went in first, bowed at, leading the way to a table as though the meal were on him. The place was not full. There was an old man patiently feeding soup to a little girl. There was a party of flashy young men, already on the cheese course and loud with wine. Our tablecloth was clean but threadbare, the glasses cloudy, the forks bent. Black cold wine was brought in two terra-cotta pitchers. The waiter looked hard at me, though without malice. He knew. Don Carlo poured. "Let us drink," he said, "to the end of war."

"You mean all war?" I said. "Or just the one of which the armistice was signed yesterday?"

He drank deep and poured himself more. "There will always be wars. A war to end war, that is, to use your beloved word, a stupidity." This was hardly fair; I had not used that word at all. "My brother there," he said, "got himself out of it quickly. He gave himself no opportunity to learn certain things."

"Got yourself out of it how?" I asked Domenico. For blatant buggery in the trenches. I thumped that unworthy thought away.

"A nervous condition," Domenico said. "Before Caporetto." He said no more.

Don Carlo said, "I was a chaplain. I gave the comforts of the Church to the Austrians as well as to the Italians. It was an Italian anarchist who shot at me. There is humor for you." He did not smile.

"Shot at you? Wounded you?"

"In a fleshy part. It did no harm. Ah." The soup came in a large chipped blue-striped white tureen. It reeked of cabbage but, as Don Carlo was quick to show with a questing ladle, contained also bits of celery, potato (very expensive in Cagliari), broccoli, even stringy meat. He served himself and broke thick coarse gray bread into it. He spooned it noisily, sighed with content, pointed his dripping spoon at me, saying, "What I learned was less of the badness of war than of the goodness of men."

I had not, for some reason, expected this. I looked at Domenico to see if he agreed. He sipped soup delicately. "But," I said, "think of the thousands and millions dead or mutilated. The starvation, the atrocities, children shattered and their mothers raped."

"You say you were not in the war?" asked Domenico.

"Heart. As I said. No, not in it."

Don Carlo snorted over his raised spoonful of brewis. He said, "My brother was in the artillery. He knows what I say is true. The death of the body. Man is a living soul who must be tested in suffering and death. He too saw the goodness of men. Then he got himself out quickly."

"You too," I said. "You were not in at the end."

"I was called to Rome." Don Carlo glared at me as though it were not, which it was not, any of my business. "There were other things. There were plenty of other chaplains ready to be shot at."

"Some men were good," Domenico said with caution. "You can always find good men. In the war there were many men, so of course there were many good men." I chewed that over with a bit of cabbage. It seemed reasonable enough. Don Carlo took more soup, bread, wine. He said, "*I fini e i mezzi*. The war has been a means of bringing out men's goodness. Self-sacrifice, courage, love of comrades."

"So let us at once start another war?"

He rolled his head in good humor. "No. The devil has his work to do. God permits him to do his work. But of course you will not believe in the devil." The waiter brought fish in one hand and tried to take the tureen away with the other. Don Carlo put out burly arms and grasped it by its rim: there was still half a plateful there. The fish was a kind of mackerel cooked with head and tail on, swimming in oil, adorned with lemon slices. Don Carlo took his soup fast, so as not to be cheated of his fair share of the fish. Taking more than his fair share, but he was welcome to it, he had leisure to say, "It is all in your English Bible. In Genesis. The fallen Lucifer was permitted to implant the spirit of evil in the souls of men. Where is evil? Not in God's creation. There is a great mystery but the mystery sometimes becomes less of a mystery. For the devil brings war, and out of the war comes goodness. You must believe in the goodness of men, Mr. Mr.—"

"Tuuuumi," his brother said. And then, "He is like me. He has no time for theology. We leave all that to you, Carlo. We work at our art." I could not resist giving him a smile of excessive intimacy. He smiled back. Don Carlo seemed pleased to be granted a temporary manumission from instructing the heathen. He finished his fish, soaking up the oil with bread, and asked for more bread when the main course came. This was a mixed roast of kid, chicken and what was possibly veal. There was a big boiled oiled cauliflower which Don Carlo at once, as though performing a sacrifice, chopped into three unequal portions. Also a whole gray loaf cut in thick wedges. Don Carlo ate with strong crushing teeth. My father would admire those. My poor father, ignorant of my sins as my womenfolk were not. I had hardly written. I was traveling abroad, I had said, and would be incommunicado for some time. Now I must start thinking of arranging a little holiday in the warm south for my sister Hortense, perhaps also for my brother Tom when he should be demobbed. I had no desire to go home again, but I could import temporary fractions of my home to wherever I was, warm and monied. The musical stupidity was doing well, that I knew. I had a mind to spend the winter in Nice. Sardinia could, so I had heard, be, though blue, bleak from December to March.

Domenico agreed: bleakish. He had been here for quiet, in the house of Guglielmi between Cagliari and Mandas. Guglielmi was in Naples now, fiddling. I had never heard of Guglielmi. "I must," Domenico said, "be in Catania for *Natale*, Christmas that is. There is to be a concert in the Opera House. They are to play my little partita for string orchestra. I had thought of trying to finish my opera in Pasi's house, outside Taormina. He has a Steinway." We musicians and writers, always on the move. "Finish," he said, his large black eyes melting like jammed fruit as he looked at me, "or start again? You said you would look at the libretto."

"I'm no da Ponte," I said. "I can only work in English."

"Why not?" he said, his eyes reflecting a new vista. "I had not thought of that. Why not in English?"

"Free men," Don Carlo said. "Free to say yes or no or go where you wish to go. I, who may say neither yes nor no, must go back to Milan."

"The boy?" asked Domenico.

"The boy will be all right. The devils are cast out."

"What's this," I said, "about devils?"

For reply Don Carlo worked away at the nibbled-looking chunk of *pecorino sardo*, the strong cheese which comes, among all Mediterranean cheeses, closest in flavor to an English cheese. A new crock of cold black wine was put on the table. I wondered whether to raise the theological issue of gluttony, but I knew what the answer would be. Eating your fill was not gluttony; it was a good, nay a necessity. As for eating beyond your fill, that was the devil's work and it contrived a kind of purgation along with the temporary agony, both salutary things. "Milan, but for a brief stay only. I must get my French ready for Paris. L'Institut Catholique on the rue d'Assas. La Catho, they call it. The History of the Church," Don Carlo said, pointing his bulky nose at me like a weapon. "I will teach that."

twenty-one

The libretto, as far as I could tell with my small Italian, was wordy but sound. There are very few plots available to the librettist—or to the novelist for that matter—and Ricciardelli's was the one that found its best expression in *Romeo and Juliet*. The title was Pirandello-like: *I Poveri Ricchi*. The Corvi are rich and the Gufi are poor. Gianni Gufo loves Rosalba Corvo. The Corvi forbid marriage. Old Man Corvo loses his money, and Old Man Gufo is left a fortune by a forgotten uncle in America. Now the Gufi forbid marriage. Old Man Corvo nevertheless gets drunk with Old Man Gufo and the two become friendly. Corvo offers to invest Gufo's fortune for him, and Gufo says yes. Corvo's scheme fails, and both families are now poor. The boy and girl may marry with everybody's half-hearted blessing. But Gianni and Rosalba are now so accustomed to clandestine trysts that they lose interest in each other when they are free to kiss in the open. So the two families (and this was stolen from Rostand) pretend a great enmity which they no longer feel and the lovers love each other again. Telegrams arrive speaking of restored fortunes for both families. Embraces, bells, wine, curtain. This story had to be put across in seventy minutes, with the terrace of the Corvo house overlooking a piazza full of choral market stallholders. Ricciardelli's lyrics and recitative were far too wordy and over-brimmed with poetic color: leave color to the music. Domenico needed a greater variety of forms—trios, quartets, quintets as well as duets—and he needed the pithiness which an admirer of D'Annunzio could not easily provide. Indeed, he needed what I was not—a new da Ponte.

I worked not in Nice but in Monaco, in the Condamine on the rue Grimaldi. I had a bare and airy top-floor apartment rented, on a six months' lease, from a M. Guizot, who was visiting Valparaiso. When I had finished the first draft I telegraphed Domenico in, or just outside, Taormina. He came. I hired a piano, a tinny Gaveau. He stayed. We ended with two versions of the libretto, one in Tuscan, the other in a kind of American with the title *The Richer the Poorer*. I learned a lot of Italian. He learned something about English prosody. He began to dream of doing something popular for the New York stage. He had no strongly individual musical style but could imitate anybody. This opera was mainly in the style of late Puccini, with acerbities stolen from Stravinsky. It had a ragtime sequence and a drunken duet. A drunken quartet would not fit into the narrative pattern, but the finale was loud and vinous.

While Domenico warbled and struck chords on the wretched Gaveau in the long bare salon, I worked on my novel two rooms away. This was *The Wounded*, about the legless man coming back from the war (poor Rodney) and nobly trying to make his betrothed marry another, a whole man. But his be-trothed is blinded in a car accident and the whole man who has fancied her no longer does so. So the two maimed marry and live happily and beget limbed and sighted children. This sounds worse than it really is, though, pace Don Carlo Campanati, it is still pretty stupid. What I was trying to do at that time was, in a sense, Shakespearean. I was taking a story that could not fail to be popular, especially when adapted to the screen, as *The Wounded* was in 1925, and attempting to elevate it through wit, allusion and irony to something like art.

And all during this time I lived a loveless life. Domenico, without my telling him, divined quickly what and how I was and regretted that he could not help. He took the train to Ventimiglia once a week, sometimes twice, and came back looking rested. I for my part bitterly masturbated, sometimes seeing, as I ap-proached climax, the figure of Don Carlo spooning in soup and shaking his head sadly. I tried to purge some of the rage of my loneliness in housework and cooking, though Domenico was a better cook than I and an old woman came in to clean three times a week. Friends, we were friends, he said, as well as brothers in art, but—ah, that kind of love seemed to him, if I would forgive his saying so, an abomination.

When Don Carlo came from Paris to stay with us for two days, I looked guiltily at him, as though his image had been a real presence. He had come, he said, when he had done panting from the long climb to the top story, to play roulette.

"Is that," I asked, getting him a whisky with a little water, "permitted? To a priest, that is?"

"The first shareholders of the Casino," he said, "were the bishop of Monaco and Cardinal Pecci. And you know what Cardinal Pecci became."

"Pope Leo the Thirteenth," Domenico said.

"We must exorcise the puritan in you," Don Carlo said, roguishly wagging his whisky at me without spilling a drop. "You think there is something irreligious about gambling. But it is only the opposing of one free will to another—"

"Talking of exorcism," I said. "Domenico promised that you would tell me the whole story. About this boy in Sardinia possessed by devils or whatever they were—"

"Domenico has no right to promise anything on my behalf. It's of no interest to you, who would not believe it anyway."

"What right have you to say what I believe and what I do not?" I asked, and that made him grunt as at a light blow struck at an ailing liver.

He said, "It is a thing I do. Indeed, any priest. But some do it better than others. Some take a chance."

"What do you mean—a chance?"

"You bring me back to what I was trying to say. One free will against another—that of the player, that of the little white ball on the big wheel—"

"You mean that figuratively? You mean an inanimate object can really have free will? What *do* you mean?"

"I am rebuked. You must soften the rebuke with more whisky." I took his empty glass. "I mean," he said, while I poured, "that what cannot be predicted looks very much like free will. I meant no more than that. I need," he said to his brother, "a necktie. I must go in as one of the laity. I must not scandalize the faithful. It is bad enough," chuckling, "to scandalize the faithless."

"Me? You mean me?" I said, giving him his fresh whisky.

"Why not you? You are not of the Church. You are not one of the faithful. Ergo you are one of the faithless. Does that annoy you?"

"I would," I said sadly, "be one of the faithful if I could. If the faith itself were more reasonable. I was in the faith, I know all about it."

"Nobody knows all about it," Don Carlo said.

"It's easy for you," I said, somewhat loudly. "You've put off the needs of the flesh. You've been gelded for the love of God."

"Gelded? A rare word, I think."

"Castrated, deballocked, deprived of the use of your *coglioni*."

"Not deprived," he said in no gelding's voice. "Not not deprived. We choose what we wish, but nobody may choose deprivation. I will take a bath now."

He took a very loud splashing bath, singing what sounded like highly secular songs in a coarse dialect. He shouted, in the same dialect, what sounded like
a complaint about the lack of a bath towel. "I'll take it," I said to Domenico,
who was scoring what looked like a semiquaver run for the strings at the round
center table. I got a towel from the corridor cupboard and took it to Don Carlo.
He stood in the swimming bathroom, squeezing a blackhead on his chin. His
eyes flashed from the mirror at my entrance. He was naked, of course, big-
bellied but also big-ballocked, with roadworker's arms and shoulders, very hairy
everywhere. He took the towel without thanks, began to dry himself, balls and
belly first, and said:

"If all goes well, it will be dinner at the Hôtel de Paris. But some light
nourishment is called for before we go. Bread. Salami. Cheese. Wine."

"Certainly, Father."

"What is your father?" he asked sternly.

"A dentist."

"In England?"

"In the town of Battle in East Sussex. The name celebrates the disaster of
Senlac, when the Anglo-Saxons lost to the invading Normans."

He dried his shoulders, exposing his balls and what the Romans called
dumpennente without shame. "And when are you going home?"

"I have no intention of going home. Not yet."

"It is not now the invading Normans," he said. "It is what some call the
intangible visitation. You have read the newspapers?"

"You mean influenza?"

"The Anglo-Saxons are being invaded worse than most. It is a cold country.
February is a cold month there. A long war ends and a long winter follows.
Paris suffers too. I lost three students this week. I hope you do not have to go
home."

I shivered, as though the influenza were being conjured here in mild safe
Monaco by this naked priest. "Why did you mention my father?" I said. "Have
you some occult vision of his succumbing to the—?"

"*Occult*," he bawled. "Do not use that word to me." And he pushed me out
of the bathroom.

"*Occult*," I bawled back through the shut door. "It only means hidden. It
only means concealed." But he was singing again.

I was sulky and vaguely fearful as we walked together up the road which
separated the Condamine from the Casino. But I was maliciously glad too that
Don Carlo was puffing and wheezing from the steep climb. Also the February
sea wind was stiff, and he had to hold on hard, grumbling, to his black trilby,
while Domenico and I wore sporty caps that could not be buffeted off. We were
in country day wear, though of course with stiff collars, while Don Carlo was in
wrinkled alpaca and an overtight shirt of his brother's, the tie rich but not

modest. He looked like a cynical undertaker. He was panting hard when we reached the Casino, while Domenico and I, with breath to spare for the crescendo, were singing a chorus from our opera:

> *"Money isn't everything—*
> *It's only board and bed,*
> *The only thing distinguishing*
> *Being living, being dead*
> *(So I've heard said)."*

Domenico liked those *ings* and had stressed them in the orchestration with triangle and glockenspiel.

But there was no grumbling when Don Carlo began to play. Domenico and I staked our few francs at roulette and promptly lost them, but Don Carlo was rapt in the miracle of winning. We were, of course, in the "kitchen," not one of the *salles privées* for the rich and distinguished. It was the depressed postwar time and there were not many playing. We had heard that the Société des Bains de Mer was being saved from bankruptcy only by the pumping in by Sir Basil Zaharoff of thousands out of his armament millions. We had seen him and his Spanish mistress, the Duquesa de Marquena y Villafranca, getting out of a huge polished car outside the Hôtel de Paris. He wanted to take over the principality and install himself as its ruler; his fat mistress longed to be elevated to princess. He never came into the gaming rooms; he did not believe in gambling.

"Messieurs, faites vos jeux."

And there was Don Carlo playing consistently *à cheval*, greedily wanting a return of seventeen times his stake. He got it too, twice. The plaques were piling up. Then he went into an anthology of other possible stakings: *en plein*, which should have brought him thirty-five times his money but didn't; *transversale*—I think it was 25, 26, 27—and there he won, eleven times his stake. *Carré? Quatre premiers?* He shrugged at losing: you only got an eightfold return. He went back to horseback, his stake on the line between 19 and 22. By God, it came up. Then he put three hundred francs on 16, *en plein*. He lost. Muttering something to himself, he tried a *sixain*, putting his plaque on the line dividing 7, 8, 9 and 10, 11, 12. It came up—five times the stake. He shrugged. He returned to that damned intractable *en plein*—16. He approached it cautiously, with a fifty-franc stake. He lost. *"Basta, Carlo,"* his brother said. Don Carlo frowned, grunted, then seemed *sotto voce* to curse. He reverted to putting three hundred francs, the "kitchen" upper limit, on 16 once more: the curse was on his timidity. The croupier spun the *cylindre.*

"Les jeux sont faits, rien ne va plus."

There were about ten round the table. Domenico and I dared not, of course, breathe. A middle-aged man with only three fingers on his left hand and on his right eye a black patch kept his singular gaze on Don Carlo's face, as though his study were gamblers' reactions to their own self-imposed hells. A silver-haired beldam seemed ready, blue at the lips, to suffer cardiac arrest on Don Carlo's behalf. "Oh my God." That was myself. Don Carlo looked sternly at me and my vain name-taking. Then he looked at the wheel, where the ball was just rolling to rest.

On 16. He went: "Ah."

"The luck," I said infelicitously, "of the devil." He did not seem to hear. He hugged his chips to his bosom, then threw one, in the incense-splashing swipe of the asperges at high mass, at the croupier. The croupier, who had never, to my knowledge, seen him in his life before, said: *"Merci, mon père."* Don Carlo sketched an unabashed blessing and moved away from the table.

"That's wise," I said.

"Trente-et-quarante," he said.

"No, Carlo, no. *Basta."*

"Roulette," Don Carlo said, "is really for children. Trente-et-quarante is for men. Tonight I feel myself to have," and he frowned at me humorously, "the devil's luck."

So we watched him while he sat at the trente-et-quarante table with untrustworthy-looking Milanese and Genoese who had come over the border for the weekend. He quipped with them in various dialects while the seals of the six new packs were broken. Trente-et-quarante is simpler than roulette, since it deals not in specific numbers but in *pair, impair, couleur* and *inverse,* but the stakes are double those of roulette: it is the serious gambler's game. Don Carlos staked *à cheval* most of the time. He seemed to know more about it than anybody there, including the *chef de partie,* and, stacking his winner's plaques in two high piles, he delivered a little lecture or sermon on the mathematical probabilities of recurrences—card rows to the value of 40 coming up only four times, as compared with thirteen times for a row of 31 and so on. He aspersed gratuities at the croupiers, then got up sighing with content as from a heavy meal. But the heavy meal was to come; he had promised us that.

Before cashing his chips he hesitated, looking back at the gaming salon with, in his eyes, the signs of a lust not sure yet whether it was satisfied. "Two things I have not done," he said. "The *finales sept* and the *tiers du cylindre sud-est.* In both cases *par cent,* I think. I think I shall do them now."

"Basta, Carlo."

"What in the name of God—"

"You are too ready," he told me, "with your casual use of the holy name of the Lord God. The *finales sept par cent* is one hundred francs on 7 and 17 and 27. The other one is one hundred francs *à cheval* on the numbers on the southeast segment of the wheel—"

"Where did you learn all these things?" I asked. "Is it a regular part of theological instruction in Italy?"

"Have you read," he counter-asked, "but I know you have not so there is no point in asking, the books of Blaise Pascal?"

"I know the *Pensées*. I glanced at the *Provincial Letters*. You have no right to assume to assume—"

"The holy and learned Pascal was first to use the word *roulette*. He was much concerned with the mysteries of chance. He also invented the calculating machine and the public omnibus and the watch on the wrist. The mystery of numbers and of the starry heavens. Who are you to sneer and scoff and re-buke?"

"I'm not sneering and scoffing and . . . I merely asked—"

"You would do well to think about the need for harmless solace in a world full of diabolic temptation. I will *not* play the *finales* and the *tierce*." As though it were all my fault that he was thus deprived of further harmless solace, he sulkily cashed his plaques. He was given a lot of big notes, some of which he dropped and Domenico picked up. Then he began to waddle out. Domenico shrugged at me. We followed.

Despite postwar shortages, the ornate but airy restaurant of the Hôtel de Paris was able to offer us the following:

Saumon Fumé de Hollande
Velouté de Homard au Paprika
Tourte de Ris-de-Veau Brillat-Savarin
Selle d'Agneau de Lait Polignac
Pommes Dauphin   Petits Pois Fine-Fleur
Sorbet au Clicquot
Poularde Soufflée Impériale
Salade Aïda
Crêpes Flambées au Grand Mariner
Coffret de Friandises
Corbeille de Fruits   Café   Liqueurs

I had expected little more than a choice of ornate renderings of the flesh of the pigeons that, wounded by palsied trigger-fingers in the famous Monte Carlo pigeon-shoot, wandering trustingly pecking round the outdoor tables of the Café de Paris opposite, were picked up as easily as kittens. But this was God's plenty and I said so. Don Carlo, after two seconds of consideration, accepted the term. It cost a lot, but Don Carlo had the money. For drink we began with cham-pagne cocktails, went on to a good Chablis and a fine Chambertin, took a refreshing Blanquette de Limoux with the dessert, and ended with an acceptable

Armagnac in flutes not balloons. Don Carlo ate with sweating concentration but, when we arrived at the sorbet, spared time to take in the charming *belle époque* décor. I said to him:

"This décor of the *belle époque*. You find it charming?"

He said, as I'd expected, "There is a vagueness about these expressions. Who says that epoch was beautiful? Beauty is one of the attributes of the divinity. And charming, I do not know what is meant by charming."

"Alluring. Pretty. Pleasing. Ocularly seductive. Unprofound but sensuously satisfying. Tasteful and delicate. Like that lady behind you."

He grunted, turning, munching the bread that was still on his breadplate and which he had forbidden the waiter to clear, to look at an animated woman in a chain-stitch-embroidered dress of very fine black pure silk chiffon. Ocularly unseduced, he turned round again. "A frivolous people," he said.

"The French?" I said, joyously. "All the French? The French in myself? My mother? And what do you mean by frivolous?"

He wagged his bit of bread at me. "Remember," he said, "that language is one of our trials and sorrows. We are forced, by the very nature of language, to generalize. If we did not generalize we would have nothing to say except such as," wagging it still, "this bread is a piece of bread."

"*Tautologia,*" Domenico said.

"Is language then," I said, "of diabolic provenance?"

"No," he said, and this time he munched. "Read Genesis, and you will see that God made Adam call things by name, and that was the birth of language. When Adam and Eve fell, then language became corrupted. Out of that corruption I say that the French are a frivolous people." And he swallowed his bread. There was nothing more to eat on the table. Don Carlo called for the bill. It was a big one. The table swarmed with paper money.

"This décor of the *belle époque*," I said. "You find it charming?"

His response was unexpected. He bellowed at me, so that heads turned: "*Adiuro ergo te, draco nequissime, in nomine Agni immaculati—*"

"*Basta, Carlo.*"

Don Carlo grinned at me without mirth but with a sketch of menace appropriate to the words of exorcism he had uttered. "That is excessive," he said. "That goes too far. I address a little demon only, and I will call it a demon of frivolity. We will burn him out of you yet. We will have you back before you are finished. We will have you *home*." For the first time ever on hearing that word my eyes pricked, and the charming décor dissolved momentarily in colored water. "Now," he said, "ask me again about the décor of the beautiful epoch." I said nothing, though my lips and tongue formed *We?* There was no bread in my mouth but I swallowed as if there were. Don Carlo was, I was learning, formidable. He drew from a side jacket pocket a big cheap watch that ticked at me across the table. "Seven o'clock mass at Sainte Dévote," he said. "You know Father Rougier?" he asked of his brother.

"*Lo conosco.*"

"I will say mass in my best Parisian Latin," he said to me. I had forgotten it was Sunday tomorrow, but the days of the week had long ceased for me to have individual flavors; they all tasted of the same loneliness and frivolity, which I termed work. So then, it was after ten and we must walk downhill from Carlo's mount to Carlo's lodging, that he might go to bed and be well rested for his early mass. In the vestibule of the Hôtel de Paris Don Carlo smiled at the bronze equestrian statue of Louis XIV and then, with neither malice nor menace, at me. The effigy had been there only about twelve years, but the raised knee of the horse had been so often touched for luck that it shone golden. Don Carlo rubbed it affectionately. Then he turned to the greeting of a British voice.

"The Don and the Monte. I knew sometime you two would meet. How are you, *caro Carlo, Carlo querido?*"

"*Muy bien.*" And Don Carlo shook hands with a pale-haired English smiler with a cricketer's body, got up in the uniform of an Anglican bishop, complete with gaiters. Domenico was introduced. I too.

"The writer? The playwright? Well, quite an honor. Saw one of your things when I was back. A real scream." This man was the Bishop of Gibraltar. The pale hair was parted on the right, which in those days was called the girl's side, and a lock fell engagingly over the left very blue eye. Looking back on him now I see a fusion of Messrs. Auden and Isherwood, homosexual writers like myself. Most of the bishop's strong brown teeth were on show as he shook hands manlily. The Bishop of Gibraltar's diocese extended to the Côte d'Azur, and one of the earlier episcopal duties had been to warn the sunning British of the dangers to their souls of gambling. As I was almost at once to see, those days were over. What puzzled and a little shocked me was the amicality subsisting between an Anglican and a Catholic prelate. "I saw your brother in the Windy City," the bishop said to Don Carlo. "We had dinner. We played."

"Craps?" asked, to my further shock, Don Carlo.

"The Idaho variety."

"What a good idea. You have, ha, *i dadi*?" He rerubbed the raised bronze pastern.

"*Los dados? Cierto.*"

"*Basta.*" Domenico was visibly tired from eating. I was weary too, but did not dare, for fear of exorcism, to protest. So we all went up to the episcopal suite on the third floor, and in the drawing room, full of *belle époque* charm, his lordship served whisky and brought out the dice in a cup of Florentine leather. Don Carlo lugged forth his big cheap watch and placed it on the table, where it beat aggressively.

The bishop said, "Fasting from midnight, of course. The blessed mutter of the, as the poet has it. Browning, is it not?" he asked me.

"Chicago," I said, nodding. "Why, if I may ask with a writer's professional cheek, Chicago?"

"Anglican matters," the bishop said, shaking the dice. "An episcopal conference. I say no more. Come on, seven, eleven." He threw a total of 12 and then of 9 and then of 7 and lost. Don Carlo burlily cast, muttering a prayer, and got 11, fifteen to one. It was all between the two clerics: Domenico and I were hopeless. But, ever the enquiring novelist, I stayed to drink and listen. The bishop, presiding over an Anglican enclave at the foot of a fiercely Catholic peninsula, had a special social if not theological relationship with, ha ha, the sons of the Scarlet Woman. Big Eight: even money. Hardways: seven to one. Baby wants a new pair of shoes. Roll dem bones. This was madness. They talked about colleagues: men with reversed collars were all in the same business despite the electrified fence of the Reformation. The third Campanati brother, Raffaele, was an importer into the United States of Milanese foodstuffs. He had trouble, there was a kind of Neapolitan brigandage in Chicago, different from other American cities where the Sicilians were the dealers in monopoly and violence, which they termed protection. Craps: seven to one.

The bishop said, "The big word came up, as you may suppose."

"*Ecumenico?*" Big Six: even money.

"Early days," the bishop said. I didn't understand. The word was new to me, who had done little Greek. But I began to understand, from fragmentary allusions, how it was that Don Carlo and the Bishop of Gibraltar knew each other, indeed were a sort of friends. Nothing to do with religion, though to do with Rome. His lordship liked autumn holidays in Rome. Don Carlo, in Rome for a task of translation of a very knotty document for the Holy Father's own benefit (English to Italian that was, about capital and labor or something), got to playing bridge with his lordship, not at the time more than a dean. Auction, of course, contract not yet having come in. The bishop proposed a session of contract, though, for the next day, after he had preached to the British and Don Carlo had eaten a long breakfast after his blessed mutter at Sainte Dévote. Contract was the coming version; it would supplant auction totally; had I read the article in *The Times* by the Reverend Causley, D.D.? Did I, for that matter, play? A little auction. You will soon pick up contract. No, I said, alas, I had some writing to do.

At one minute to midnight Don Carlo was served a stiff whisky. He finished it as, all eyes on synchronized watches, the hour came up. Like going into battle, the bishop said. Over the top into Sunday, and the best of luck. "It's a battle, yes," Don Carlo said. "It's all a battle." And he looked at me as though I were a white-feathered malingerer. I nearly made some excuse about my heart.

twenty-two

Not my father but my mother. I read and reread the telegram as the Sunday day train crawled toward Paris. Don Carlo was not with me: he was going to take the late sleeper. *Gravely ill come immediately.* I could not make the curt summons mean anything other than that she would be dead by the time I got to Battle. *It's* a battle, *all* a battle, rattled the wheels. I dined late at the restaurant of the Gare de Lyon, surrounded by charming décor of the *belle époque.* I tried to push guilt back down my throat with boluses of lukewarm gigot unsharpened by mint sauce. My hand trembled and I spilt coffee on my tie. The killer influenza was a neutral life force going about its proper business, or else an agent of Don Carlo's devil, or more probably a punishment from the other shop for our not having punished ourselves enough with a punitive war. It was not, then, my fault that my mother was dying or already dead. Death is never the point; the point is the peacefulness of the death. My mother would grieve about my apostasy, a pervertedness she would regard as within the realm of choice, the shamefulness of an exile which she would interpret as Wildean or, if she knew of the ghastly man, Douglasian. I had let her down. There would be a deathbed message for me, possibly a letter, a dying mother's plea for a promise that could not be fulfilled. I hoped, of course, that she was already gone. I did not want dying eyes aghast on me, pleading, modulating into a horror that I must, as it were, pin above my perverted bed.

I took a taxi to the Gare du Nord and then the boat train to Calais. The sole other occupant of the compartment was an old man indecently drunk who mumbled incoherently about the sins of the *intellectuels.* Did I consider myself to be an *intellectuel? Non, monsieur, je suis dentiste.* The dentists too, he said, were a sort of intellectuals. Hope lay only in the common people who could not cure their own toothache. France would fall before twenty years were done, and it would be because of the defection of the *intellectuels.* Home, country, loyalty: such terms were not to be analyzed or questioned. Unreasoning faith, that was what was wanted. *Conspuez les intellectuels.*

The bar of the cross-channel steamer was open. I drank cognac to defy the cruelty of the February Manche whooshing and battering. There was a man drinking light ale who, he said, was going to write a little book about the pet animals of famous people. He did not tell me his name and I did not tell him mine, for fear he might not know it. Dogs, he said, chiefly. Prince Rupert's Boy, for instance, dead at Marston Moor, his death rejoiced in by the Cromwellians, who believed he was an evil spirit. Charles Lamb's Dash, who first belonged to

Thomas Hood. King Richard II's Math, who forsook his master at Flint Castle and attached himself to the usurper Bolingbroke. Flush. Mrs. Browning's spaniel, scared of the big spiders under the bed of her filthy room. Flush.

There was no means of getting direct from Dover to Hastings, so I took the train to Victoria. Somebody had left a Sunday newspaper in the compartment, and there was a silly quip in a silly Sunday chat column about Peace opening the window and in flew Enza. Flu deaths reaching alarming figures. Black jazz bands. The pivotal pig. Short skirts oo la la for nightclub wear. An article about a certain Ernest Allworthy, Labour Boss of New Zealand. E.A. controlled N.Z., it said. The influence of wartime matiness on the postwar relationship between maid and mistress. The influence of wartime shortages on postwar culinary ingenuity. The influence of Hugh Walpole on the younger postwar novelists. *Say It, Cecil* was still running.

The black sky wept bitterly over London. I had forgotten English weather. I had nearly forgotten to bring my waterproof. I got to Charing Cross and caught a foredawn train to Hastings, stopping at Battle. I slept and nearly overslept my station, but a railman's voice yelled "Battle" through the rain. I squelched in the Monday dark, soaked and alone, to my father's surgery and house, my former home. On the High Street I had a very strange physical sensation. It was as though my shoes were full of nothing but air but where my heart should be there was nothing at all. I was giving out breath but taking none in to replace it. A rapid pen wrote in fire all down my left arm from shoulder to wrist. I staggered to rest against the window of a shut shop, a family butcher's. So this was the cardiac trouble that had kept me out of the war. It was, I could sense even in my panic, going to be a useful solvent of various kinds of guilt. My heart then resumed the vigorous thumping it had, like a drum in an orchestral score, followed some direction to intermit. The scrawled signature of pain in my left arm vanished, as though written in disappearing ink. My shoes refilled with flesh and bone and spelt out toes again. Air rushed, as into a pierced vacuum tin, back in lungs that groaned relief. I trembled for a cigarette, a ship's bar Gold Flake, and lighted it with a Swan vesta. I drew in the lovely smoke, feeling madly how good life had become. I was twenty-eight, a young man, an established writer, and life lay all before me. I splashed jauntily to my father's house.

The blinds were drawn and the curtains closed, but light escaped from the chinks. Light in the hallway, in all the front rooms, including the surgery. I knocked many times. The knock, I knew, was heard but was being for the moment ignored. There was something very urgent going on there. She was dying, it was the actual point of death, and there I was waiting outside in the rain. I was interrupting death, knocking. I nearly ran away, I would come back later at a time more convenient. Then I could hear my sister coming, sobbing my name. The door fumbled open and she was in my wet raincoated arms, crying: "Ken, oh Ken, it was just now, she heard the knock and she knew it was you, and she tried to live a minute longer but she couldn't, oh it was terrible."

"It was just now?"

"Poor poor Mother, she suffered, Ken, it was terrible."

So it was all over. No, I didn't want to see her, she wasn't there any more, it was just a dead body. Oh Ken, Ken. My father came leaden downstairs, dry-eyed, with no greeting for me except a bitter look as at a bad son. And there was my brother Tom, demobbed, still short-haired, in a suit too big for him. His grief was being expressed in a coughing fit. I embraced him and at the same time thumped him on the back. They were all in crumpled day clothes. Up all night. She suffered. Extreme unction at seven in the evening and she had seemed (and even to restore health if God sees it to be expedient) to recover a little. But then the final slide downhill. Brown, the doctor, had done all he could. People were dying of flu like flies all over England. There was a Mrs. Levenson round the corner who did laying-out jobs. A busy woman these days. It was too early to call on her. It was too early for anything except the making of a pot of tea. We all sat round the kitchen table, drinking it, Hortense and Tom and I smoking my ship's Gold Flake. Tom coughed. With the coming of the wet dawn we were already adjusting ourselves to a motherless or wifeless future. Or so I thought. There was a question I had to ask.

"No, no letter," my father said harshly. "It came too suddenly for her to think of writing letters. But she made it very clear what I have to say to you."

"Look, I couldn't, not even for her. A man's soul. It's his own—I couldn't go through a lie, not even for her."

"A man's soul. It's not just the soul, is it?"

"What do you mean?"

"No, not now. Not with the children here. And her lying there upstairs."

"She's not lying upstairs," said Tom. "She's in purgatory or somewhere. One lot of suffering and you're straight into another lot. Christ, is there anything but suffering?"

"You too?" I asked.

"Him too," said my father, "as far as *that's* concerned. I say it's the war, I say it will pass. We expected peace and look what we get. But we'll all get over it."

Hortense went to the cupboard for biscuits. "There's a lot of God-hating going on just now," she said, slim, pretty, her ankle-length pale green smart if crumpled, the boat-shaped neckline elegant, a woman now. "I can't think that God's so stupid as to be surprised. But Mother didn't hate, oh no." She sobbed fiercely and then crammed half a Garibaldi biscuit into her mouth.

"Not disbelief," Tom said. "There has to be a God, that stands to reason. Just hate. But we'll get over it. As *he* says." The *he* sounded hostile, certainly unfilial. And then: "Children, he says. One child turned into a sort of expert on poison gas. The other seduced by her art teacher."

"No, no, no," Hortense said. "He tried, that's all. What they call irony," she said to me. "Mother didn't like my German nuns so she had me go to the French school at Bexhill. But that's all over now."

"So," Tom said, "the children know all about you, Ken. We're not shocked. We belong to the new unshockable generation."

"You condone it," said my father. "An unnatural generation."

"Your bloody *natural* generation started the war," Tom said.

"You will not speak to me like that, Tom."

"Oh, for God's sake," I said. "This is no way to behave."

"I think we all ought to get some rest," said my father. "I think I'll go and lie down for an hour."

"Oh, come, Dad," Hortense said, "why don't you tell Ken all about Mrs. Scott?"

"Lydia Scott," said my father, "has been a good friend."

"Mrs. Scott," Hortense said, "is to be the second Mrs. Toomey."

"I never said that," my father said weakly.

"A patient?" I asked. I didn't wait for an answer. "Is this true? Mother hardly cold in her— No, no clichés. I see. It's been going on for some time, has it?"

"There are some things a man needs," Tom said, and I could tell he was quoting my father. My father glared at him.

"The privacy of a dental surgery," Hortense said. "A little trouble with that impacted wisdom tooth."

"How dare you," my father trembled. "You are not to, it is—"

"A widow?" I asked.

"A war widow," Hortense said, both hands about her teacup. "The gallant Major Scott caught it early. On the Marne or the Somme or somewhere."

"I will not have—"

"Why not, why not?" I said. "Some men need marriage."

"There are certain decencies," Tom said primly.

"Oh, for God's sake, come off it, Tom," I said. "Life has to continue, resume, whatever the word is."

"Whatever life is."

"I'm going to lie down in the spare room," my father said. And he got up wearily. "Your room," he amended to me. "It *was* your room."

"I see," I said. "So this is the end of the family."

"I didn't say that," irritably. "Hortense, you'd better go and get Mrs. Levenson. Tom, ring up Brown. There has to be a certificate of . . . of . . ."

"Death death death death," Tom said, with an intonation suggesting the Westminster chimes.

116

"You're a coldhearted lot," my father said.

"Oh yes, cold," cried Hortense and burst into loud sobbing. My father made a sketch of holding out comforting arms, then shook his head and shuffled off. "Sorry," said Hortense, wiping her eyes on a tea towel.

"Well," I said. "Will he be all right?"

"Some things a man needs," Tom repeated bitterly. "That's what he said when I caught them at it."

"*Caught* them?"

"Kissing, that's all. I'm sure Mother knew all about it. She wasn't well, you know. It wasn't just this bloody epidemic."

"Sex," I said, "can be a damned nuisance. As I know. As I shall continue to know. And now what?"

"I'm not staying," Hortense said. "I don't want a stepmother. I'll get a job somewhere."

"You're under age," I said. "And what kind of job can you do?"

"I can take one of these six-week courses in Pitman's and typing. Ah," she then said. "Do you need a secretary?"

"I think," I said, "you'd both better come back with me. Get away from this climate. Think things over."

"I've thought things over," Tom said. "I'm all right. Thrown into it in a way. Well, it was your name that did it. Any relation to the playwright wallah? Yes, I said. Let's see what you can do, they said. I just stood there and said any damned thing that came into my head. About Henry the Eighth and his wives. They thought it was funny."

"What is all this?"

"The show's called *Rob All My Comrades*. Or *Run Albert, Matron's Coming*. One can be the kind of sequel to the other. Or the two can run at the same time, two different troupes."

"It's what they call the RAMC," Hortense said. "The Royal Army Medical—"

"Look, I may have been a scrimshanking civilian—"

"Like the Roosters," Tom said. "And that Australian troupe called Les Girls. They reckon there'll be a lot of scrimshanking civilians who'll flock to see an army concert party. Old soldiers too. Professionally done, of course. Highest possible standards. The man we have, Jack Blades, QMS as was, he was in that sort of thing before the war. March twenty-first we start the tour. Summer we have a choice of seaside engagements."

"And you just stand there and talk?"

"Well, there are sketches. Choruses. I'm what's known as a Light Comedian." Yes, that was about it. I looked at him, thin, fair, frail, voice light and pitched well forward. My brother Tom the Light Comedian. "Tom Toomey, Tommy Toomey, which do you think?" he asked.

"Oh, the second one, without a doubt."

"That's what they all think."

"Well," I said, handing round the Gold Flake again, "who would have thought it? Two of us in the theater. Mother wanted something a bit more dignified in the French manner. I always got the impression she felt that tooth drawing was not quite a real vocation. Medicine for you, law for me. And now look at us."

"Marriage," Hortense said. "That's the French idea. You know, there's even a dowry tucked away in the District Bank on the High Street. Mother could never get that out of her head, that there had to be a dowry. Mademoiselle Chaton said that the days of free love were upon us."

"At this school in Bexhill?"

"Poor Mother. She thought it must be all right if it was French. And there they were, saying there was no God and we all had to be free. Have you read any D. H. Lawrence?"

"Free love," I said with weight, "is precluded by the facts of biology. I refer, of course, to heterosexual love."

"And now," Tom said, "tell us all about homosexual love."

"It was a shock?"

"Of course it was a shock. And it was a shock to know that our innocent sister here knew already and wasn't shocked."

There was a groan from upstairs. "Oh my God." The Gold Flake almost fell from my fingers. "She's—" And then I remembered that our father was up there, starting to fade out of our lives.

Hortense said, "I'd better go and get Mrs. Levenson."

I said earlier that Tom smoked three cigarettes in his entire career. The first was in the school urinal when he was fourteen. The other two were from my ship's bar Gold Flake packet on this occasion of our mother's death and the breakup of the family.

twenty-three

Hortense went back with me to Monaco. It was only when the train was nearing Nice and she was gold-flushed with excitement at her first view of the Côte d'Azur that I began to wonder at the propriety of having her stay in an apartment where a susceptible Italian artist sometimes made our morning coffee naked and occasionally micturated without shutting the toilet door. I had thought of Tom and Hortense visiting together and two brothers protecting her from possible southern lust, not necessarily Domenico's. Besides, Domenico was always on the verge of going to Milan to see Merlini about *I Poveri Ricchi*. The vocal score was finished and had been copied by a professional copyist in Cannes named Pécriaux, with the text in English and Tuscan set in beautiful print script under the vocal lines, the alternative ties and additional notes made necessary by the bilinguality done with exquisite spider penwork. There was no need for him to stay in my apartment, to whose upkeep he contributed little, in order to get the orchestration completed. In a day or two, he kept saying, he would be off to Milan. But he delayed, perhaps because, like most artists, he feared the consigning of his art to the coldness of the mere entrepreneur, feared too the possible confirmation of his own doubts about its value, even its competence, when it became orphaned, undressed and prodded by institutional strangers. We were cozy, the two of us, mothers at different stages of gestation, our art babies not yet ready to confront the exterior light and air. He diverted himself once a week, sometimes twice, in a *casino* at Ventimiglia, but, as the train drew into Monte Carlo station, I could foresee very lucidly his response to the presence of a lovely Anglo-French girl here, on the spot, on holiday, wanting diversion of her own.

I had foreseen accurately. The great melting eyes of admiration, quick to grow moist when he heard our bad news—mother dead, your mother dead, *O Dio mio*, for an Italian, hearing of another's mother dead has a terribly vivid image of the death of his own, may God not permit the day of that eventuality to dawn—and then the hands caressing the sheets drawn from the corridor linen cupboard to deck her bed, dinner tonight at the Vesuvio, on me, my mother's check has arrived (*madre, madre, O Dio mio*), then lasagne and pepper steaks, *cassata*, Bardolino and grappa. "Your brother," he said, eyes glistening in candleshine, "is my brother also."

"That's nice," Hortense smiled, glowing with wine from her charming low brow to her crossover V neckline. "What Sister Gertrude called *Kunstbrüder*. Brothers in art, you know. You two boys working away together at your art." She was only a girl but she had this pert and affectionate disdain which women, who produce real children, often show for men who give themselves airs about their child surrogates, broken-backed books and limping sonatas.

"My real brothers," he said, "laugh at my music."

"Italians laughing at music? Goodness, I thought Italians were the first people in the world for loving music."

"The Italians," Domenico said, "are mostly stone deaf."

"Tone deaf."

"What I said."

"Stone deaf, you said."

"Very well, both, tone and stone. They cannot hear music unless it is very loud. They cannot like it unless it is very sexual." Daring that word, very, in 1919, from a man to a girl he had met only three hours before. "I mean love duets. *La Bohème. Butterfly.*" And he gave out, wretchedly, with a bit of Pinkerton at the end of Act One.

"Composers can't sing," she said. "Tone and stone, you'd think. Sister Agnes used to do an imitation of Beethoven singing *Küsse gab sie uns und Reben, einen Freund geprüft im Tod.*" But she sang it herself very sweetly before doing a harsh monotoned growl, frowning, underlip thrust out.

"You should hear Carlo sing mass," Domenico said. "Like a dog." And he looked with a dog's adoration at Hortense, a known gambit which she was too young to know, unless that art master— I must ask her about that art master.

"Can you dance?" Hortense asked.

"Oh, I can do all the latest dances," Domenico said in feigned boasting. "The Bunny Hug and the Turkey Trot and the Castle Walk."

"Everybody's doing it," sang Hortense with the same sweetness as for the "Ode to Joy."

"Doing it, doing it," sang Domenico. "*Addition, s'il vous plaît,*" pulling out a wad of francs with the kind of bored automatism of one who always pays the bills, which was not true.

There was dancing going on at the Louisiane, not far from the Casino. "Ah, the famous Casino," Hortense said, as we got out of the cab.

"That word," Domenico said, with the hint of a leer, "is not a word used politely in Italy. A *casino*, you see, is a little house."

"A little house in Ventimiglia," I said brutally, "for example," prematurely perhaps warningly, a warning itself being a kind of encouragement. Domenico flashed a warning of his own back, though with leering warmth in it, being encouraged.

"You mean a *bordel*," Hortense said in her clear innocent girl's voice. "I see," looking at the rococo prettiness of the façade. "So that's what it is really. I read in *The Illustrated London News* I think it was about Mata Hari there and the other one, La Belle whoever it was, covered in jewels and nothing else. So the gambling is just a thing, you know, a whatsit."

"Pretext," I said. "No, not true. A difference between French and Italian usage."

"My holy brother has been very lucky in there," Domenico said. "A French kind of *casino* is permitted to a holy man."

I did not like this sort of talk. I must get Domenico on that damned train to Milan very soon. And Hortense wouldn't like that, released from cold England to the smile of southern teeth, wooed southernly by an Italian musician of good looks and family whose brother was a priest, meaning he wouldn't go too far, her spoilsport own brother as gloomy protector of her honor and him a homosexual anyway, what right had he and so on. We went downstairs into the Louisiane.

"Goodness," Hortense said, "a genuine nig to make it authentic." But the black man in the little band was, from his features, only authentically Senegalese; he played his cornet like a colonial army bugler. The saxophonist, pianist, banjoist and drummer were whites. They played from sheet music, commercial or diluted ragtime not real jazz. The banjoist was singing, in Frenchified American, an old song by W. C. Handy called "The St. Louis Blues":

> *"I love dat gal like a schoolboy loves his*
> *pie,*
> *Like a Kentucky colonel loves his mint*
> *an' rye,*
> *I'll love ma baby till de day I die."*

"Let's dance," Hortense said to Domenico, and it was left to me to order three beers. The décor of the place was black and white, as if the artist had studied the illustrations in Wyndham Lewis's 1915 *Blast*, and the motif seemed to be of stylized Manhattan skyscrapers ready to topple. The Modern Age, Jazz Age, we were into it now. There was a loud American with two local girls, a beefy man who proclaimed himself as hailing from Cincinnati, Ohio, round at the ends and high in the middle, probably left over from his country's Expeditionary Force, in some racket or other to do perhaps with sides of army beef, spending freely. He shouted at the band to play "The Darktown Strutters' Ball" and they did. He sang:

> *"Remember when we get there honey,*
> *The twosteps I'm goin' to have 'em all."*

He decided he would cut in on Domenico and Hortense but Domenico was not having that. Hortense said, "You sit down like a good little boy."

"Eo," the man from Cincinnati said, "gud leedle bawee."

"All right," I said, "cut it out."

He was three tables away and feigned not to have fully caught my rebuke. He aped a deaf old man, beefy hand cupped at ear, and said, "You make some remark, my friend?"

"I asked you to cut it out."

"Thought that's what you said," he said, and he tottered over to me. "Hog's piss," he said of the three beers on the table, making a gesture of being ready to smash them to the floor. "Garsong," he called, "whisky tooty sweety for this main sewer." The waiter did not respond. "Frogs," the man said to me, knocking one chair over but sitting on another. "Spilled good red blood for the bastards, drove the Krauts out of fucking Frogland and what you get?"

"Watch the language," I said. "My sister's not used to it."

"Sister, you got a sister?" He swerved round to look at Hortense then back again to me, achieving with some difficulty a maître d'hôtel's bunched finger *spécialité de la maison* kiss. "You sure have," he said. "Cute little can there, see it shimmy, aaaaaoooo," doing a dog howl. "British?" he said. "You British sure were a long time getting the Hun on the run, I'll say, I'll tell the world, aaaaaoooo, garsong, whisky tooty sweety," and, in his beefy swerve, he sent a full beer glass crashing. It was then that Domenico left Hortense on the floor and came over smiling with his good Italian mouth. He now disclosed something I had not suspected in him, though I knew it to be an aspect of Italian gang protectionism, namely neat professional, as it were musical, violence. Meaning that in a swift clean and economical rhythm he slashed the Ohio man with his ringed right hand thrice on his beef face, in a single measure of slowish mazurka time. This surprised Cincinnatian, whose town was named for Lucius Quinctius Cincinnatus, a Roman general of great and simple virtue, looked up at Domenico open-mouthed, an aitch of bursting red on cheeks and upper lip.

"Now," said Domenico, "we leave." And to the bald mustached manager, troubled, coming to see what the trouble was: "*Ce monsieur américain va payer.*" Then we were off, and Hortense's eyes shone in delight and, for Domenico, admiration. This was better than dreary cold old England, and she'd not been here yet for much more than half a day. She wanted to go dancing somewhere else, where perhaps there might be other rude Americans to be slashed by Domenico, but I said no, home. But then, just outside a bar called the Palac (which might have been an English word in adventitious apocope or else the Serbo-Croat for Thumb), I was given my own chance to put down brutishness. A young fair-haired man was being sick on the pavement and two Monegascan policemen were bullying him to stop vomiting in public or else come with them, vomiting or not, to the lockup. The young man said, very English, "I've said I'm sorry, damn it, look, one can't really stop this sort of thing, something I ate, fish or something, oh dear, I have to again," and he did. While doing it he was punched on the shoulder by one of the constables, and the other laughed. I was over there at once with my good maternal French, abashing them. How dare they, did they not know who this was, a personal friend of His Serene Highness, and so on.

"Where do you live?" I asked the young man.

"A village in Berkshire, you may not know it. As for stay, here that is, hotel up the hill there, the Immoral, Balmoral that is, little joke, very moral place really, oh my God here we go again." So I held his head. The policemen went through the gestures of saying I was in charge, get him off the street, look at all that defilement of the pavement of the playground of the rich, disgusting (they did a kind of long-skirt-lifting mime), does the place no kind of good, then they saluted me and marched off. "Awfully sorry about all this," the young man said. "My name's Curry," holding up his hand for shaking while, perhaps under the stimulus of his own name, he got more up and then, splash, down.

"Look," Hortense said, "while you're being the Good Samaritan, can't Domenico and I go dancing somewhere else and see you there?"

"See you in the bar of the Hôtel de Paris," I said. Not home this time, oh dear me no, not those two together alone going home, oh no. So off they went, her arm in his. A handsome couple, much of a height. "Better?" I said to the young Curry. "Ready to try walking up the hill? Take deep breaths, go on, really deep."

"You're really being most awfully decent. It was some damned fish I ate, *loup* or something, wolf that means, wolfing a wolf, oh my God." But there seemed little more to come up. He stood upright and sniffed in briskly sea air. "Better, I think. That *loup* is still around though, flying through the ozone, I can smell it, a bloody werewolf, I say, what's the French for werewolf?"

"*Loup garou.* Those police, look, are still looking. Can you walk more or less straight?" I took his left elbow and trembled. The first male flesh, or bone at least, I had handled since, ah God. "You needn't just blame the *loup* for my benefit," I said. "You've ingested more than *loup* tonight."

"Looooo garooooo. I say, I like that. Very well, right turn, quick whatsit." And off we went. "My name," he said, "is, no, better not say it, damned unfortunate name sometimes, can't stand the stuff, Indian muck."

"I know it. It's to do with leather."

"Ah, know it, do you? Interesting. Don't know yours though." He was weak-ishly handsome, very blond, thin, supple, smart in gray serge unspotted by vomit, a neat vomiter, not like, say, a Glaswegian at Hogmanay. "Ought to know yours really." I told him. "Ah, I like that. Rhymes with roomy, gloomy. To do with tombs, is it? Tomby. Grave, gravy. Oh my dear God." He heaved emptily.

"Deep breaths. See, we're there."

The little vestibule lounge was quite empty. He flopped, done, spent, soft, supple, edible, on a soft settee. I sat down more stiffly, saying, "You're here alone?"

"Orphan," he said. "Only got aunts and things who don't give a Chinese damn. Just jumped twenty-one so that's all right as far as administration of things goes." He drunkenly thumbed his nose at someone unseen.

"Half an orphan, me," I said. "Just buried my mother. Flu, you know."

"Mine," he said boastfully, "was seen off in the second month of the war. In the VAD, matron. Bomb on base hospital near Mauberge. The old man was luckier. Amazing luck till Amiens, less than a year back. Sir James. That makes yours humbly and sincerely Sir Richard." He puffed himself up and then collapsed into tired limp thinness again.

"Ah, baronet."

"Sir Dick, Bart. Got a handle to it. I say, I've a mouth like a whatsit. Uncleaned parrot cage. Could do with some Perrier or Evian or something. *Eau minerale*," he called to the solitary man at the desk, writing. "You got any of that?" The man shrugged, pecked toward the vestibule clock, put an arm out at a closed bar, locked cupboards, then wrote again. "Ah well, got some upstairs, a drop," Sir Richard Curry Bart said, "in my gloomy room." The sight of writing, my rimesakes, then the memory of my name made him then turn with some small vigor toward me and say, "I say, you said Toomey. Are you Toomey who writes things? *That* Toomey?"

"I've written things, yes. Kenneth M. Toomey, playwright, novelist, that sort of nonsense, yes."

"Well, *that* Toomey and no stuck-up big Iyamity, the Good Samaritan and all that rot, I say, that was kind, I shall remember that."

"You're staying long?"

"Thought of going to Barcelona. I say, I read one of your things, all about her heavy hair and heavy breasts and their lips were glued in a, ugh, I can taste that damned loo garoo."

"It tastes that way to me too," I said. "What the public wants. The law doesn't allow some of us to be honest, if you know what I mean." He knew all right. Bright green eyes though a little bloodshot appraised me under a fallen blond lock. "That dare not speak its name, if you know what I mean." Oh, he knew all right.

"Live here, do you?" he said. "Marine villa and chauffeur and apéritifs on the terrace?"

"Nothing like that. Not a bit like that, not yet. I say, why don't you get a decent night's sleep and perhaps we could have a bit of a chat tomorrow if you feel like it. Have lunch if you want. Get a decent lunch here, do you?"

"A bit gloomy, the dining room downstairs. Quiet, though. See you about oneish if you like, make up our minds about it. No loo garou, though. What do I call you besides Mr. Toomey?"

"Oh, Ken will do very well. They all call me Ken."

"When a new planet swam into his, right, Ken it is, Ken. I have a small bottle of, upstairs, not such a good idea, no, I can see that. Bedfordshire, sir, my old man used to say. Home's in Berkshire, great big bloody house, roomy, gloomy, coming up all the time now those aren't they, tomby, yes, you could say that. Tomorrow, then." And he got up. We shook hands, I gripping his warmly, his yielding, limp, boneless. Then I remembered that Hortense and Domenico were in the Hôtel de Paris bar waiting, and that he, hot on seduction, would be getting her drunk. So I didn't see Sir Dick to the lift.

Hortense was drinking crème de menthe frappée and laughing too much. Domenico was telling her some story that made her laugh. As far as I knew, Domenico knew no funny stories. When I went up to them they turned from each other, together on the red velvet banquette, to grin at me with what I would have termed in those days affectionate derision. Or, if you wish, the derision of conspiratorial heterosexuality, two young people who found each other attractive—no, wait, that *young* is vague and dangerous: Hortense was a child, Domenico an unattached man, hence by definition a womanizer, Latin also, also not of my persuasion—and were encouraged to be bold by their shared knowledge of my sexual aberrancy, an ambulant dirty joke forced upon them; nothing like a dirty joke to foster intimacy. And of course I saw what I was doing and saw why my position was hopeless: proposing an affair in a hotel bedroom and thus taking time off from guarding Hortense from possible indeed probable indeed certain importunacy from Domenico. "Pouring in oil and wine," Hortense said crudely. Then she hiccuped like a character in a French comic paper: *hips*. Domenico was delighted to bang her on the back. She separated her back from the banquette so that he could bang it better.

"You're not used to it, Hortense," I said kindly. "Let's go—" I could not say *home*.

"You. The Good *hips* Samarit *hips*. Dancing's the thing for. Let's *hips* go back to that place."

"Bed for you, dear. And for me. It's been a long day for both of us."

"Dance of the sheets, I see, *hips*. What *do* men do together?"

"That's quite enough, Hortense. Drink your drink and we'll go." And then, as she hipsed and hipsed, "Nine sips and hold your breath."

Domenico counted gravely nine crotchets in Italian. "*Brava,*" when she emerged gasping.

She filled her lungs in much the same rhythm as Sir Richard Curry Bart had. "Good. Gone. *Hips*. Damn." But she got up to go, and Domenico obeyed me too in mock meekness, making himself sib and coeval to Hortense, submissive to frowning elder brother, something incestuous in it. "*Hips*. Bloody thing."

"Hortense, language."

So we walked back down the hill, sea lights flashing on our left. *Hips*. She recovered with the three-story climb. My bedroom was between Domenico's and hers, and I lay awake for a time, listening for padding feet and whispers. But I heard nothing except Domenico's light snores and Hortense's crying "*Maman*" once in her sleep and then sobbing.

twenty-four

My old-fashioned inlocoparental fears for Hortense's honor were, you will say out of the future which is your enlightened present, absurd as well as hypocritical. They were also, if Domenico were to be considered the sole candidate or ingrate for battering at that honor, proved, temporarily at least I thought, needless by his receipt of a letter from Merlini in Milan. A letter I brought with his coffee the following morning, being up early to resume my moral watch. Idiot, considering that I proposed going off duty in the mufti of my own lust at the most sensitive time of the day. However. Merlini urgently wanted at least the vocal score of *I Poveri Ricchi*. It was proposed to open the autumn season at the Teatro alla Scala with the first two little operas of Puccini's *Trittico*. There had been serious consideration of making up the weight with Bayer's *Die Puppenfee*, last performed on February 9, 1893, after the *prima rappresentazione* of Verdi's *Falstaff*, but an examination of the score had confirmed the legend of its mediocrity. So, though there was no firm promise, here might be Domenico's big chance. The letter made Domenico fandango barechested about the apartment, kissing Hortense in joy and also, though with less conviction, myself. He remembered at one point that I was part-librettist and went into a mist-eyed routine about what dressing-gowned uncrapulous Hortense called *Kunstbruderschaft*. But soon it was all his dawn again.

Hortense and I went with him to the station just before noon. He would be back, he had left most of his clothes, his luggage being mostly the full vocal and half-completed orchestral scores, he would send news. He kissed us both again, in the same degrees as before, before climbing aboard the stopping train to Ventimiglia. Extravagant Tuscan waves from him, prim Anglo-French ones from us. Hortense and I looked at each other when he had gone.

She said, "It's all right, you know. I'm not a Henry James heroine, all eager to be seduced by the glamorous south."

"I see. Which particular heroine were you thinking of?"

"Oh, that one in the little book he gave you, Maisie or Tilly or somebody, he's a terrible old bore. The one with the long loving scrawl from your alas temporarily infirm but still fundamentally gay friend and master. Is it too early for lunch?"

"Well, now," I said. "Today I have a luncheon appointment. Do you mind terribly? A young actor who happens to be on holiday here. Why don't you make yourself a snack and we'll have a big dinner tonight, the two of us, and talk about the future. In Èze, perhaps. The place where Nietzsche was. He wrote part of *Also Sprach Zarathustra* there."

"And that makes the food good, does it? Sister Gertrude was always going on about the *Übermensch*. The *Menschlein* you met last night, is it? The willowy blond one you succored?"

"What's that word?"

"Helped, assisted in his vomity torment, held the suffering head of."

"I recognized him, you see. He was going to be in one of my things, but then he wasn't. I knew his father too," I added. "Sir James Curry. Dead now. He's a double orphan now, poor boy."

"You needn't give me all that," she said. "I could see you positively dithering to take his willowy form in your arms. All right, get on with it. But please do stop being the big moral disapproving elder brother with me, that's all. Ugh." And then, "What *do* men do together?"

"Pretty men I mean pretty well what men and women do together. Except there's an obvious difference. A matter of equipment, you might say."

"And it's wrong, isn't it? It's what Sister Magda would call a sin against biology. It has to be wrong, it's not natural." We were walking down rue Grimaldi in March sunlight.

"To some of us," I said, "the natural thing seems unnatural."

"And that's obviously wrong, isn't it? Diseased, isn't it?"

"So Michelangelo's diseased, is he?" I had said that before to her. No, of course, it had been our mother. But, of course, there *was* something diseased about the extravagant musculature of the David and the Sistine *Last Judgment*. "It's the way some of us are," I said as I'd undoubtedly said before, "the way we're made."

"I don't believe it, nobody's made that way. God wouldn't allow it."

"Ah, bringing in God again. Got over the God-hating, have we?"

"You ought to see a psychowhatsit," she said.

"I thought the Church didn't hold with amateur soul surgery."

"You're not in the Church. Only the biologically pure can be in the Church. All right, forget it." We had arrived at the front door of the apartment house opposite the Société Marsellaise de Crédit. On this door there was a smirking cowled monk's head knocker, perhaps a pun on the name of the principality. I gave her the keys.

"I'll be back about three or four," I said. "You'll find cold ham and salad and things in that sort of cooler thing."

She looked evilly at me and then sadly smiled, saying, right hand on my left cheek, "Poor old Kenny Penny."

What happened that afternoon after lunch in the single bedroom of the Immoral or Amoral, as Sir Dick Bart indifferently called it, need not be described here. It was satisfying to deprived glands and, indeed, emotions. But the term *love*, despite the warning implicit in that filthy limerick of filthy Norman Douglas (whom Dick had once met and been drunkenly fingered by briefly and

whom he called Abnorman Fuckless), threatened to mean more than merely
lust and gratitude. I love you, my lovely and lovable boy, signifying desire to
possess dog-in-the-mangerishly (Who is this man you're having dinner with?
Who was that one you smiled at on the Boulevard des Moulins? Who are these
people who invited you aboard their yacht? Yes yes, I know I'm taking my
sister to Èze or Antibes or Cannes, but that is duty, not pleasure. I *have* to
know where you are, and so on). Yet Dick was amusing as well as capriciously
accommodating, though he made too many jokes about his name. Coming to
the hotel on the third day of our liaison I found an enraging note awaiting me:
"Off with the Pettimans. Pizzle in sauce piquante not on the menu today." On
the fourth afternoon he pouted and said, "I expected a little gift, you know,
something nice and useless, you know, from Cartier's." But, though I now had
it to give, he would never demand money, like that little whore Val, for the
private printing of his poems. He had plenty of money of his own and he did
not write poems. He did not do anything. Some time in the early autumn, he
said, he would cease his wandering over Europe and go back to the *tomby*
house in Berkshire, there to consider putting the greenhouses in order and, my
dear, start learning something, seriously, you know, really seriously, about orchids, lovely ballock-shaped things.

Hortense, as I had half anticipated, developed her own routines. There were
no real facilities for seabathing at Monaco, though the organization that ran us
was called the Société des Bains de Mer, so she took to traveling by train
further up the coast, to Beaulieu or Menton, where there was sand as well as
rocks, and lunching off a *pan bagnat* and a *ballon blanc*, playing tennis back in
the principality in the late afternoon with some nice harmless English people
(right out of the court, what, thought I was playing cricket haha) who had a
bookish seventeen-year-old pimpled son, and dining with me in the evening,
least I could do, sometimes a film show at the Prince after, Lon Chaney,
Charlot.

"Off to Barcelona," Dick said, showing me half-packed bags. "Call in at
Avignon on the way." This was the tenth day, or eleventh.

"You said not yet. You said not till April."

"Change my shirt, can't I, gentleman's privilege. Nothing to stop you coming,
is there? Rather have you as a traveling companion than that nasty toothy
Boogie character."

"Who is this? What is all this? What has been going on?"

"Free as the pure and limpid, you always say. Unencumbered like a whatsit.
My pens and paper and aha sacred talent and a monastic cell with a chained
richardtionary. Live anywhere. So we go to Barcelona and Avignon on the way.
Sous les ponts de. Chase each other round the papal palace."

"But there's my sister, damn it."

"Yes, always hearing about her, aren't we, believe when I see."

"She exists all right, damn it. I can't leave her all alone."

"Well, isn't there this wopera character you told me about? He'll look after her, won't he? Sing to her, very oily."

"He's not here, thank God he's not. But you can't leave a girl of eighteen on her own."

"Put it in, would he, as soon as look. Man, woman, dog, throw them all on a bed. All right, no hurry for Avignon. Today I have a fancy for a bit of rough. Nice, you know, the old port. Funny, just saw that sort of written on the wall, like meeny meeny tickle your arse. My father, you know, after dinner. The old port, very nice. Still, Nice could be nice, very."

"What is all this? What are you after? Sailors? Fights? You want to be thrashed and flayed?"

"Highly yellowdramatic. No, just see, look. Hurtling bottles knocking one's body off the table, got that the wrong way round, oh I don't know though. Torn clothes and filthy language. Make a change."

"I think it's a rotten idea."

"Oh, listen to the transmuter of experience into deathless words. Read that somewhere, they didn't mean you, dear. Miss Mouse, writing about what he won't do, living by poxy, proxy that is."

"Has somebody been talking to you about me?"

"Oh, all self self self, as ever. None of my *friends* has even heard of you, dear. Come, a cab to the *gare* and a puffpuff to Nice."

"I have to be back by seven. Hortense expects me."

"Hortense? So that's her name. Oh yes, of course, half frog, the two of you. Chance for you to show off with the lingo wherever we end up at. Rare argot. Speaks it like a native. Monsieur is veritably formidable. Come on then."

So, despite my unease, we went. In the old port we drank cognac mildly in two cafés decorated with nets and anchors. It was the wrong time for whatever action Dick expected, it was the time for sleep after a heavy luncheon. Then, in Le Crampon, I was proved, to Dick's delight, wrong. There were roistering *matelots*, and they were not French but British. Tars, my dear. Their caps, thrust back to haloes, said HMS BELLEROPHON. The Bully Ruffian, out there in the harbor. Spring cruise. There was a horned gramophone on the counter, protected by a sour bulldoggy woman with frizzed ginger hair and bare mottled arms thick as thighs. Some of the tars danced. It was a wartime tune, from *The Bing Boys*: Notherlildrink notherlildrink notherlildrink wondousanyharm. It began to run down, to sailors' cries and groans. Naw lal droooonk. The *patronne* rewound muscularly. A Liverpool tar, brown as a nut, black hair knotty, then began to paw her, saying, "Summat nice, love. A bacon butty. No bub without grub." She hit out at him without anger. There was a strong hogo of sick and urine, and the flow from under the WC door showed the apparatus was blocked.

"*Ce monsieur-ci*," Dick said, with governess clarity, "*voudrait quelque chose à manger. Un petit sandwich, par exemple.*" The *patronne* gave out with a hoarse gobful of *Niçois*. "Just trying," Dick smiled to the sailor, "to get you that little something." A worn bald man in a filthy apron appeared yawning, showing gold and a caked tongue, just emerging from his siesta. "*Deux absinthes,*" ordered Dick.

"Water with mine," I said.

"Nonsense. Sacrilege. Makes the heart grow fonder," he smirked at the sailor. He tossed it off. "There," he said. "Toss it off, that's the way."

"We've all done it," the tar said, "but there's some as won't admit it. You two lads live here then?"

A lone petty officer sat glazed at a soaked table. "Bloody did for the bastard," he said, several times.

"Dancin with *im*," another *matelot* said, impelled by his partner's boisterous whirl toward us. His partner crashed to the wall, under a picture of Pierrot and Pierrette all sprinkled with artificial gold dust. *Im* was Dick.

"Charmed," Dick said, and swallowed his third.

"Toss off, that's right, when you can't get owt else."

"Watch it, please," I said, still on my first.

"Old fusspot." And, in the arms of the dancing *matelot*, a young man with a simian brow but honest eyes, he one-stepped willowily. The record had been turned over. If yoooo war the ownly garl in the waaaarld.

"You two lads live here then?"

"Did him proper, the bastard."

I hate to remember, and why should I remember, when I cannot remember a miracle? Your distrust of me should have begun a long time ago. Dick, I cannot forget, insisted on mixing a modified Hangman's Blood in, pulled from its nail on the wall, a metal chamber pot with the head of a *sale Boche* painted inside, *sale bouche* screaming mutely to be muted in. Cognac, whisky from Indochina with slant-eyed bonny Scot on the etiquette, white rum, genuine near-black Nelson's blood, gin, port, some of that sticky muck there like plumjuice, need a bottle of Guinness really, never mind, some of that pissy belch water will have to do.

"Really a sir, is he, your mate, like what he said?" breathed rummily on me a *matelot* called Tish.

"Smooth," said the sir, handing it round in tumblers, "you have to admit the smoothness of it." Dancing went on still, one dancer delicately gnawing his partner's throat, oh do do that it's nice. Dusking sea air outside when the land breeze burst open the door. Then we were battened in again to snug smelly dark with bulbous paper lampshades aswing. Oh, smooth all right, right.

"Princer Wales smokes that, did you know?" said the scowse whom they called Wet Nelly, one of the fighting Starkeys really he is though from the

Dingle, they has a fight afore they goes to bed. "Won many a bet on that, wack. Baby's Bottom it's called. You can buy it in shops."

The *patronne* wanted to know who was paying. Sir will pay. He unclawed a cram of bills onto the swimming zinc countertop. "For God's sake, careful." I scooped up most, thrust it into my own right jacket pocket, haggled about change.

"Better," swaying Dick said, "with an absinthe in it. Reinforce that whatsit. Put one in next time. Smooth, though."

"Who's absent when she's at home?"

"*Sang de bourreau*," Dick told patroness and own-rolled-caporal-puffing filthy-aproned barman. "Put that on list of genuine *délices étrangers*."

"*Étrangères*," I could not help correcting, pedantic fool. "Feminine in plural."

"What you say about lemonade in Bootle? You potty, wack?"

A no-lipped *matelot* with milky eyes had been watching me for some time from round the bend of the bar. He now came up and spoke in my ear with bitter sincerity. "You look to me like," he said, "a bastard that's fair crying out to be done, you fucker."

I drank nervously.

"Fair swaller on him," said a boy fair as an angel whom the others called Porky. The working class always looks best in uniform.

"The working class," I began to say.

In a quiet fury, "Fair begging for it, I know his fucking type, jimmy-the-fucking-one voice on the bastard." I thought we had better be going.

"Be going."

"It's his sister," announced Dick. "He shags his sister before dinner. Gives him an appetite."

"Nothing lower than that," Tish or somebody said. "Dad and daughter, that's different, stands to reason. Fuck a bugger that shags his sister which is his own flesh and blood."

"A joke," I said. "Crude, but still a joke."

"It's no bleeding joke, you bastard," gritted the one with milky eyes, his neck muscles knotty with the intensity of his speech. "That's why you've got to get done."

"Oh, this is nonsense. Dick," I called, "we're going." And I drank a random glass from among many. It was not thirst, it was a gesture of the nerves. Dick did not hear, or listen. He was dancing with a sulky-lipped bullock they called Sparks, and this Sparks was thrusting at Dick in rhythm. Lat the grite big warld keep tarning. I wondered whether to have a heart attack, but that organ beat strongly, well fueled by the muck I was toping or stuping. For I ownly knaow that I lav yew sao.

"You'll get done yet, you fucker."

"Oh, for Christ's sake," and oversqueezed my glass, which broke. Blood on my fingers. "Damn and bugger it."

"Porky'll suck that off for you. A real little bloodsucker is Porky here," Tish said. But Porky was a sweating angel, very pale.

"Damn and damn." I did my own sucking. The gramophone ran down and no one rewound. The big fat frizzed bitch was going on at me about the broken glass. Fahnd saaaam waaaan laaaaaak yaaaaaaaaow.

"I want to throw," retched Porky. "I got to."

"Come, dear," Dick said. "Daddy will holdum head for um." And he put an arm tenderly about Porky. Porky sicked spittle. "All right, madame, you fat unsavory cow. All will be taken care of." And he staggered Porky toward the door.

"What he is," said Tish, "is like a gentleman. Stands to reason, him being a sir." The door opened to a black wind. Sparks shut it with his arse. Dick and Porky were out there. I was going to go too.

"You're staying here, fucker," the milky-eyed one said. "You've got to get done."

"You and whose navy?" I quoted vulgarly from one of my own stupid plays.

"Summat to say about it?" somebody said, flushed face an inch from mine. "Got it in for the fucking Andrew?"

"I'm getting out of here," and I marveled at myself as I grabbed the rump of the smashed glass from the runny zinc and swiveled it from one to another of the blue swayers like a flashlamp.

"Ah, playing dirty. Right, here it comes." But the proffered fist with its tattooed LOVE AND DUTY with blue flowers could not really connect, drink having drained strength from the arm beyond it. The door opened again and to a windier blackness two genuine *matelots* came in, French, pomponned caps with MAZARIN on them.

"Parleyvoo wee wee. Jigajig traybon." Of course, my original play title. I dropped the tumbler stump on the filthy wet floor and, for some reason, ground it growling with my heel among the un-ground-out fag-ends. Then I shouldered and pushed out. "Come back, fucker, to get fucked."

"Dick," I called to the sidestreet. There was only one lamp, dimmish, near a Byrrh poster. I ran inland and came to an alleyway. I heard groaning, then a splash. The thin moon emerged to show Dick, sober and vigorous, holding the doubled-up sailor up with strong clasping arms round his middle. The sailor's trousers were right down, hobbling his ankles. Dick was buggering away deep and cheerfully in brutal Norman Douglas style.

"Just one second, dear," Dick smiled, "then he's all yours. Not all that tight, surprising really. Relaxation consequent on nausea and so on." And still he ground away. Then he shuddered, lips apart, as on unsugared lemon juice as he spattered. "Delicious. So mindless. There, come on, angelface, get it all up for daddy." The two voidings were one. I had an erection. I was bitterly ashamed. Then there were voices calling.

"Porky. Fucking Porky."

"Fucked Porky, really," Dick said, releasing him into his own vomit. "All right, dear," buttoning up, "he's all yours." And Dick ran with long expert strides into the blackness of the alley as the moon buttoned itself into its fly of cloud. It was as if he knew the damned place blind. The boy lay heaving, terribly besmirched, bare arse to the sky. A great gust blew the cloud tatters off the moon. Then Porky's mates were there.

twenty-five

The important thing, I explained as well as I could from my bloated mouth, was to get a message to my sister. No, we had no telephone. A telegram. But the post offices were closed and there was no night telephonic service. The plainclothes sergeant by my bed in the Hôpital Saint-Roch said a message could be telephoned to the Monaco police and it would then be delivered by hand. For God's sake, please, no mention of what's happened, don't want the poor young recently orphaned girl highly nervous panicking, say met by chance my publisher on his yacht staying on his yacht discussing book. Be back Saturday. The hovering sister shook a grim gray head at that *samedi*. Amend to *lundi*. Ah, said the plainclothes sergeant, so monsieur was a man of letters as well as a foreign visitor. That made the whole thing worse. And what was monsieur doing in that particular part of the old port, notoriously low and perilous, no place for, especially lettered, foreign visitors? Ah, I said, but surely in order for man of letters conducting examination of cultural or vivental spectrum of great southern marine city. Monsieur is writing a report on the criminal elements of Nice? Monsieur is doing a dangerous thing. See what monsieur has permitted himself to be led into. No, no, I said, my métier is that of romancier, I am a writer of fiction. Fiction, pronounced the sergeant, is written from the imagination, it is invention, it requires no meddling with the dangerous exterior world. The sergeant was a young plump man smelling of overgarlicked ratatouille, his celluloid collar overtight, eased with irritable fingers when he was not penciling in his little notebook. Could monsieur remember more than he had already re-membered, which was not, if he might be permitted to say so, much? Monsieur could not, monsieur said. Set upon suddenly by thieves when pursuing noise of a cat in pain apparently, we others English are given to love of animals, fought back, was vindictively torn and thumped. And also, the sergeant reminded, anally violated, though not severely, more in a token manner. Were monsieur's assailants francophone? Oh yes, most certainly francophone, though with a strong Algerian accent. Ah, monsieur knows Algiers, he has been conducting similar researches into the unsavory moeurs of the backstreets of that city? No, a guess really.

Contusions mostly, a tooth loose, but the behavior of the heart not well liked by either palpating Dr. Durand or stethoscoping Dr. Castelli. Found un-conscious near pool of vomit partially unclothed, light rain beginning to needle body already chilled. Patrolling police, following scream of pain, not mon-sieur's, disclosed with questing lantern. Evidence of intake of alcohol, whether excess or not not easily judicable, but no matter anyway. Police would continue investigations. No need, I said too eagerly, you'll never find them, besides, I've learnt my lesson. Ah, monsieur has learnt his lesson, is it not? Monsieur should occupy himself with being man of letters and not go carousing in unsavory lousehaunts of old port. Snap shut notebook, last irritable fingering of overtight celluloid collar, a sort of noose, metaphor of the stringency of duty. Message would at once be sent to monsieur's sister. Back God willing *lundi prochain*.

The heart had settled grudgingly to a steady enough rhythm by Friday evening. Though bruised and wretched, I wanted to be out of there. The ward was full of mostly old men who wanted to treat me as an official representative of a Britain that, in the war just won, had behaved treacherously to France. *Il n'y a qu'un ennemi*, kept nodding a dithering grayhead. You mean, I said, that we treacherously would not allow you with impunity to overcharge us for horse provender and the use of filthy troop trains to drive the Hun off your soil not ours? The Germans are at least Europeans, some other old fool said. I could walk, and I was going to walk out. Dr. Durand had, I discovered, his account at the Banque Nationale de Paris, my bank too. Would he sell me a check form? You also BNP, monsieur? He would sell me two check forms, one for settling my bill here; the check poundage could be added to my bill. I was permitted to entrust to a male ward orderly, squat with Eskimo hair, a message to the manager of the Banque Nationale de Paris on the Place Masséna, re-questing him to telephone my branch in Monte Carlo and, thus reasssured as to funds, kindly cash enclosed, seal cash in envelope and give to bearer. The bearer brought me this cash and I overtipped him. Then I asked him to buy me the cheapest possible impermeable at the nearest men's clothing store. Yes, I know it is not raining, but these filthy and torn garments, regard, must be concealed from the common eye.

This Saturday was March 29, 1919, day of the total eclipse of the sun which Einstein had predicted. I can remember a sudden darkness and feeling no surprise, as if it were natural enough for the sun to be occluded by my guilt and shame. I was so awash with shame and guilt that I could hardly think. Dick? Sir Richard Curry Bart? Was there had there ever been such a person? The name of that ghastly bistro was what? Thudding fists and ripping nails, spit and foul words clear enough in memory but not the inflicting of pain. I resented nobody except myself. But was this just or logical, seeing that I was made as I was? But who had made me as I was, since, as that German up at Èze had affirmed, there was no longer a God? Had I so made myself? When and how? What, anyway, was the solution save gelding? Brow bruised, left eye black, lips blubbered, hands in pockets of cheap raincoat, I limped from the station down rue Grimaldi, earning the odd look of curiosity. I had my keys still, their chain secured to my trousertop, though I had little else. I opened the main door and panted, near dropping, up to the top story. I opened the flat door quietly and knew at once that Domenico was back: his own impermeable, not cheap, hung on the hallstand. I knew, as you know, what was happening.

But it seemed already to have happened. When I opened the door of Hortense's bedroom I found them both sitting up naked in bed calmly smoking. My first instinct was to snatch that cigarette out of the wicked girl's hand. It was the smoking naked that was so intolerable. But I stood there, nodding, taking all the blame. I heard a dog yelp bitterly out on the street. The dog was being run over by an automobile, and that too was my fault. These two in bed were at first too shocked by my appearance to be abashed at being caught post flagrantem. "What have they done to you?" cried Hortense.

"What has he . . ." I began, but I knew the answer. "You dirty swine, you bastard," I told Domenico. "My own sister."

"Many women," Hortense said, her pert breasts still blazing from the bed, "are the sisters of somebody. Out, both," she ordered. "I want to get dressed."

"Get your clothes on," I said to Domenico. "You're going to be hit."

"You couldn't hit an underdone custard," she said. "Who's done this to you? Your nonexistent publisher on his nonexistent yacht? Or that willowy blond little puffball? Out, both of you."

I went into the salon and poured myself whisky. Domenico was soon after me, on bare feet, in shirt and trousers like a man surprised in seduction, which was what he was. "I cried," he said. "She comforted me."

"You cried so she could comfort you, you mean, swine."

"It was the bad news I brought back from Milan. They will not do the opera."

"Serve you bloody well right, you bloody filthy leering little Don Giovanni."

He was ready to cry again at this reference to an opera that had been done often and would be done often again, in Milan too.

"Pack your traps," I said. "Out. I don't want to see you ever again. Or," I added not really relevantly, "that greedy gambling hypocrite of a brother of yours. Defiling me and my house and my sister. Go on. I'd throw you out if I had the strength but you see how I am. The whole world's rotten."

"And what if it is love, what if she said love and I said it too? And another thing, it is the English that are the hypocrites."

"Don't give me that about love." I spilled whisky with my shaking. "I will not hear that word again, do you hear? Not from any man's lips and much less from yours. Go on, I won't look at you. You don't exist except as filth for the *poubelle* of the world. Out of the place for which I and I only pay the rent." Then Hortense came in with her honey-colored hair in a blue ribbon and wearing a wool and silk dress with pleated sides and bishop sleeves and artificial cherries on the left lapel.

She said, "I'll have a drink too." But I barred the drinks table from her like an innocent she would defile, saying:

"Oh yes, of course, sex and cigarettes and whisky. Be the big authentic fallen woman, you a mere kid of eighteen. God, the shame of it." But it was all, I was more and more aware, my fault.

"I do not," she said in a very sharp governess tone, "wish to hear from you anything at all in the moral line. You are not qualified to judge others. *Normal* others." The cheap novelist in me wanted, in a way, to forgo judgment and ask questions about what it was like to be deflowered by an urgent Tuscan: I might as well get some professional advantage out of what was all my fault, and of course heterosexual Nature's, and of course theirs.

"It is a kind of jealousy," said Domenico, "and it is very sad."

"Deflowerer," I tried to snarl. "*Defloratore*." That sounded too mild. Domenico seemed to think so too.

He suggested "*Stupratore*." And then, artbrothers, we looked at each other with the promise of unwilling warmth, working again, happy innocent days, on the opera Milan did not want.

"You bloody men," came the clear sweet voice of fallen Hortense, "with your bloody deflowering." She saw that the expletive was a genuine unpurposed, though redundant, adjective of description and she blushed. "Treating a hymen as though it were a whatsit a commodity. In any case, it was the French school that did it." I was bewildered—of poetry? Painting? Phenomenology? "Mother wouldn't have me taught by German nuns and that was the result. Domenico, go and get some clothes on. *More* clothes, I mean."

"And then I go?"

"Oh yes, you bloody go all right," I said. "I'm in charge here."

"And," he said, wary dog-eyes on Hortense, "you come with me?" I could tell from the belated teeth clamping his tongue that he had put himself into a situation of near avowal totally unwonted, but Hortense was quick with:

"No, Domenico, me *not* with you. You want me to live in sin, as they call it? And you with a brother a priest? Are you proposing marriage? No, of course not, you oleaginous little Don Giovanni—"

"Just what I called him," I muttered inaccurately into my whisky.

"I am not," also muttered Domenico. "The time is not. It is my art."

"Go on, sing it," I jeered, "like flaming Tosca."

"I will strike you," Domenico cried, bunching his fists. "I have had enough of your English hypocrisy."

"Oh," said Hortense in a kind of resignation, "they're all hypocrites. The French too. Burbling about the beauties of Monet."

"So the art master got there, did he?" I said, the whisky partly at fault, crudely.

"You nasty thing," Hortense hissed. "It was a horse. It was the riding we were made to do. There's nobody more English than some of the French. *Un cheval*," she added, "not *ein Pferd*." It would, she led me to believe, have been all right with Sister Gertrude demonstrating, black habit tucked up, hallooing like a Valkyrie. "As for the other, yes and no. The door opened, you see." And then, irrelevantly I thought, "You crude and unpleasant homosexual."

"Poor Mother," I said.

"Mother?" Domenico cried, not having well understood, perhaps even holding an image of a horse covering poor Hortense. "You mean you are already, that it, he—"

"Our mother, fool," Hortense cried back. "The French could do no wrong. She had no opinion about the Italians." That was well said. Then: "Go on, get out, Domenico. Go for a walk or a swim or seduce somebody or something. My brother and I have to talk."

"If you mean he's to come back," I said, "you're mad and also wicked. Have I not made myself clear? Out and out now and forever. And yes, talk, by God, I'm going to do the talking."

"I am sick at heart," Domenico said, hands limp at his sides. His intonation suggested an aria, perhaps from the *Principe di Danimarca* of Enrico Garitta, which I had not seen. "I will go to a hotel. I will come for my things tomorrow. I am too sick to pack now."

"Everything out this minute," I said. And then, not wanting Domenico to make an operatic scena out of filling his suitcases: "Tomorrow. At nine o'clock. Hortense will not be here."

"Ah, sending me away too, are you? Back home to Dad and the second Mrs. Toomey? That's what we have to talk about."

"I meant you would not be available to be seen and cajoled and perhaps also even . . . Ugh."

"Terrible, isn't it, a man and a woman together? At least I'm not all beaten about, rough sailors I suppose it was, friends of that bloody blond tulip, and look at the state of your clothes. Change them now. We've got to talk seriously. Dad sent a letter."

"To you?"

"To you."

"How dare you interfere with my mail. Have you been opening other things too? I won't have this, Hortense, you've gone too far, you need a really stern hand, the sooner you—" The sooner you what? Go back to the German nuns? Learn the disciplines of a seducible London stenographer? Marry?

"Oh, don't talk silly. It came three days ago. I knew it must be urgent."

"Where is it? I demand to see it."

"Get it, then. On your desk. On your way to changing your disgusting clothes. Ugh, blood and other things."

"I'm not leaving you alone with that bastard over there."

"I will not be called a bastard, you English hypocrite." And Domenico padded out, groaning his fancied wrongs.

"Can I have that drink now?" she said quietly, sitting in the armchair, as heavily as her frailty would allow. But no, women are not frail.

"Whisky?" I said almost humbly. "What does he say?" getting it for her, a single finger. "If it's an upsetting letter I don't particularly want to read it."

"Did you a favor then really, didn't I? Thanks." She sipped then coughed. Not all that grown-up. "The second Mrs. Toomey isn't going to be the one I thought. It's another patient, Doris something, and she's only in her twenties. Dad's selling the practice. He's going to Canada. So you see my situation. He sees it too, in his long-winded way. Oh, read it."

"Later. I see." I poured more for myself. "He has to have you, though. You're still under age."

"I don't want to go to Canada. I don't want a stepmother a few years older than myself. I don't want to stay with you."

"I can see," I said, "why you wouldn't want to stay with me. Unnatural goings on. And me going on about morality. On the other hand I don't have any duty to you, you know. Except what—family affection dictates." I would not say *love*.

"You bloody bore. You real horrible hypocrite."

Domenico, going off down the corridor parallel to, but at no point visible from, the long salon, must have heard that with approval. He sang a strangled *"Ciao, Orténsia"* as he turned left into the hallway, visible from the part of the salon where she and I sat through the arch with its twisty columns, opened the flat door and went out quietly. He could be heard going down the marbled stairway on sad punching feet.

"Operatic," Hortense said, "in everything. It's in the language, way of life. Sex, too. Religion, of course. England could never take to it. Still," she said, "I'm going to marry him."

"I'll go and change," I said. I switched off thought and feeling, though I could not switch off physical pain, as I stripped off my defiled clothes and put on a silk shirt and tennis trousers. Thus dressed as for games I came back to ask her to repeat what she had said. She repeated it. "You mean," I said quietly and tiredly, "that you love him? That you let him do what he did because you love him? I never heard such wretched and wicked and adolescent nonsense. You don't know what love is. You don't know anything of the world. He's practically the first man you've ever been in contact with. Social, I mean, apart from the other wretched and evil thing."

She ignored all that, swinging one crossed white-silk-stockinged leg. "It's not worthwhile, you know, trying to explain things to you. You're dense as well as homosexual. Marriage and love are not the same thing. Mother used to make that clear to me when we had our little talks. How can you ever know about the one big whatdoyoucall destined love when there are so many millions and millions of the other sex in the world, that's what she used to say, and it was very sensible. You don't go looking or waiting. Too much world and too little time. You take what you can get if you're at all keen on marriage. I mean somebody physically all right and talented enough and with enough money. Domenico seems all right. I mean, I've seen him naked, for instance."

"This is terrible."

"Oh yes, terrible. There's money in that family. With the right sort of encouragement Domenico can make a name. That opera thing you did together, he played some of it for me on that rotten old piano there, weeping while he played. Then I took him to bed."

I sat on the hard chair facing her, my hands clasped between my knees, bent forward, looking at the lemon-colored rug between tufts of which a minute intact cylinder of cigarette ash rested. I said without expression, "He arrived sad. They had rejected his opera, mine too incidentally. This *this* they have rejected, he cried, and sat down at the piano and sang you one of his brilliant arias. So you felt sorry for him and kissed him and took him to bed. He was willing, I don't doubt, but, I should imagine, also surprised."

"Well, yes," she said, smiling with reluctant admiration at the exactness of the reconstruction. "Just like that. Of course, you're a novelist, of course. I forget that sometimes. Most of the time you're so stupid."

"We were converging on you. He and I. But his train got in first. Such a pity."

"No no no no. He arrived the day before yesterday. I took him to bed then, but since then he's been taking *me* to bed. As broad as it's long, really."

"What is as broad as it's long?"

I could not understand for a moment why she railed at me. "You obscene horrible vulgar and tasteless horror." I looked bewildered. "Sorry," she said. "Perhaps I don't always do you justice. Perhaps I think too much about men being naturally coarse. Domenico isn't coarse, though. He'll be all right. He needs bossing and so on. I'll get that talent of his working. That was always Mother's regret, you know, that she hadn't married a man of talent."

"He was a talented dentist." And then I shook myself and said, "I have never in my life heard such madness."

She ignored that, of course. "I've no talent," she said. "Except perhaps for choosing the right father for my children. That's woman's responsibility now. Replenish the stock. All boys. Too many women in the world."

"This is very old-fashioned. And stupidly biological. As if you only knew about marriage from its its its—"

"In terms of its primary function," she said crisply, impatiently. "To breed good children. Haven't you read Bernard Shaw?"

"Back to the *Übermensch*," I mocked bitterly.

"Sister Gertrude made us read him in German. She said he was better in German. English wasn't his real language, she said."

"And when," I still mocked bitterly, "is this *Ehe* or *Ehestand* or *Eheschliessung* to take place?"

"The *Eheschliessung*," she said, "will be in Italy, I suppose. At that cheese place. With his brother officiating. And my elder brother gives me away. In," with her own bitterness, "the absence of a father."

"And when Domenico comes tomorrow morning to collect his clothes," I said, "he will be informed that he is to marry you and breed supermen for the new age, and he'll be overjoyed and leap in the air and cry *che miracolo* or *meraviglioso* or something."

"No," she said, ignoring my sarcasm, "not quite like that. But it'll be a relief for him, really. It's always a relief for a man not to have to go chasing women any more. For a time, anyway. Anyway, he's not to know yet what he's got to do. I've got to be cool and just friendly as though nothing happened, and then he'll wonder why and be worried and eager, men are such fools, and then he'll be down on his knees, you'll see, or rather you won't see."

"You know so little of the world," I said, "so very little."

"I know," she flashed, "a million times more about what goes on between a man and a woman than you'll ever know." She made a vulgar gesture with her fingers, the vulgar child, one of the new breed, coarsened by war. "So put that in your pipe or up it."

"All right," I said with patience. "I know certain biological facts, even if not out of direct experience. I know that when a male and female copulate, if you know the word—"

"You and your prissy stupidities. That's what's so diabolic about you and your lot. Pleasure without danger of conception or joy of it for that matter. I know what *your* bloody copulation if that's what it really is is all about. Pollution, that's what Sister Berthe called all sexual acts where you spill your seed, disgusting, the sin of Onan. With a man and woman it's a matter of taking a chance."

"Oh, no, it's not, it's not that at all, it's not by any means that. Do you mean you took a chance with that filthy smirking Domenico creature?"

"I used toothpaste, if you want to know. A girl at school used it. Domenico, and he's less of a filthy creature than you are, you homo, he remarked on the taste of the peppermint."

"Oh my God, oh my dear God, oh Jesus Christ, oh sacred Father in Heaven—"

"Hypocrite. You're a damned hypocrite, he was right, a bloody hypocrite is what you are, Ken Toomey."

"Oh my dear God." Then the doorbell rang. We looked at each other. "That's the doorbell," I said.

"Well, answer it, then. It's *your* doorbell."

"Who do you think it might be?"

"The Prince of Wales, Charlie Chaplin and Horatio Bottomley. Idiot," and she got smartly up and went out to the door. She had nobody to be afraid of, such as a new avenging boatload of sailors or the plainclothes sexual police. I heard her opening the door and then, the voice of one surprised but quickly recovering, going "Oh" twice. The other voice was male and breathy and pleading and scared. I had not thought, I genuinely had not considered that that filthy Domenico would return so soon. Hortense entered the salon demurely and said, "He's got this telegram." She handed it to me. Domenico was still, I assumed, cowering by the door. The telegram said: ARRIVO LUNEDI GIORNI CINQUE MISSIONE DELICATA NIZZA CARLO. Typical of a damned priest, assuming that other people's lives could never be so disrupted as to render their homes unavailable for damned priestly intrusion. Still, this somehow. It was rather.

I said, "Let's have him in." I heard no acerbity in my voice, I heard rather the effect on the vowels of the incipient lip-spreading of a smile. So Domenico was brought in. Eyes round and rolling, sweat on his cheeks, hands and arms most eloquent, he babbled a recitative: Was in the café across the street and the telegram man saw me and he said it was for me he knows me you see and he was glad not to have to climb the stairs with it. Was in the café or rather at a table outside taking a small cognac for my sorrow when he gave it to me. The, this, telegram from my brother. My brother Carlo has something to do in Nice. *Missione delicata*, I know what he means, it was also that that time in Sardinia. So as before he expects to stay here, so what can I do? On Monday he comes, the day after tomorrow which is Sunday, so what can I do?

Of course, I have to eliminate later knowledge from this scene, an image of His Holiness the Pope snoring away dead out but, by his sacred presence, thwarting the fornicatory designs of his brother. It was just fat Carlo who was going to snore, but he was a priest and a formidable spiritual entity, and I knew that Domenico feared him. "No problem," I said. "He can have my bedroom and I can sleep on this sofa here. Or I can go to a hotel, no problem." Domenico and Hortense both looked at me with care and suspicion, what the hell was I up to as if they didn't know. "Domenico, Hortense," I said, even wagging two fingers, "you have been naughty children. But in the eyes of God we are all naughty children."

"Hypocrite," Hortense said unemphatically. Domenico gulped and gave her a most hypocritical glance of reproach.

"You are still my brother," I said, "though an erring one, just as Hortense remains, though also erring, my sister. Don Carlo, I give you my solemn word, shall know nothing of the reprehensible things that have transpired here. He will, however, I trust, be unable to fail to observe the evidence of a certain warmth between you. He will, I doubt not, be a help to all of us."

"Oh yes, the warmth," Domenico said, not really understanding me at all, and sidling an inch or two nearer Hortense, who said, still, or even more, unemphatically:

"Bloody bloody bloody. Homosexual prig, setting yourself up as as as . . ."

"This is not generous, Orténsia," Domenico said, still sidling.

twenty-six

"I never," Dr. Henry Havelock Ellis told me, "prescribe castration. But, of course, I never prescribe anything these days. Like you, I call myself a man of letters."

This was on Sunday, March 30, 1919. That I have admitted to a large vagueness about past events, and yet am able so often to assume the exact chronicler, need in no wise be a puzzle to the reader who looks for consistency in his author. Photostats of my diaries and notebooks arrived from the United States about three months after my eighty-first birthday, and I found therein days and weeks of my life pretty fully recorded, though there are considerable lacunae. That the shameful events beginning at the time of my return from England to Monaco with Hortense, and culminating on March 29, 1919, were as I have set them down, you may accept without question, though the truth of the dialogues is rarely a verbatim one. About meeting Havelock Ellis at the Hôtel de Paris the day after I am unsure, but it was certainly in that year and almost certainly in the principality. The meeting and the things he said are wholly pertinent to this phase of my narrative, such as it is, so I expect the reader to expand his concept of truth to accommodate what follows.

Ellis was then about sixty with scant white hair and a great white beard, quite the prophet. He had practiced as a physician but had given up medicine to devote himself to literature. Many of us had been grateful for his Mermaid Series of the Elizabethan Dramatists, published in the late 1880s. It was in connection with an erroneous statement Ellis had made about the origins of Elizabethan act division that I first came into personal contact with him. I forget where he had given his public lecture about Sackville and Norton and the Inns of Court and *Gorboduc* and *Locrine*, but I remember vividly a kind of proletarian hogo (beer, black tobacco and inerasable grime) haloing it, so presume it was part of some London County Council extension series for self-improving workers. Ellis said that the Elizabethan dramatists got their five acts from Seneca, along with much else, and I counter-affirmed that they got them from Terence and Plautus, Seneca's brief closet tragedies following Greek procedure in admitting no act division. Ellis had to admit that he had not thought much about the matter, and later that I was right, but the fallacy he propounded on that occasion was taken up by T. S. Eliot and eternized in one of the magazine reviews he collected and called essays. I corrected Eliot in the dining room of the Russell Hotel in, I think, the late 1930s (he fed himself with crumbs of Wensleydale the while), but the error has survived his death. There was a lot of the dilettante about Eliot. The first volume of Ellis's *Studies in the Psychology of Sex* (1897–1928) was the occasion of scandal and state prosecution, and to many of my generation Ellis was a martyr-hero.

He had acquired, he said, a taste for beer in Australia when a teacher there, and he was drinking it in the bar of the Hôtel de Paris when I encountered him that Sunday at noon. He had various curious mannerisms. He would screw up his face so as to exclude the passage of air through his nostrils, at the same time snoring faintly and rapidly; he showed his teeth, which were not good, in unexpected and irrelevant as it were demonstration snarls; he swilled his mouth with beer before gulping it audibly; and he plucked at his crotch as if to extract music from it.

"Homosexuality," he told me. "This friend of mine at Roquebrune is a homosexual of long standing. I think there is little that can be done about it, and I fail to see why it should be regarded as morbid. It is the law that is morbid, but the law will in time be changed. What is your problem?"

"The etiology of it—"

"You cannot very well say that. Dear Sigmund in Vienna has rejected altogether the grossly physical Helmholtzism on which all his generation was raised. He will have it that neuroses and hysterias and what the world calls, if it knows the term, sexual aberrations and inversions and so on have no physical cause though they may have physical symptoms. The so-called aberration of homo-sexuality has nothing whatever to do with an irregular endowment of hormones or whatnot. No one is born homosexual. No one is born heterosexual either. But everyone is born sexual. This sexuality is first fixed, inevitably, on the mother, source of oral and other gratifications."

This was dry and cold and un-Elizabethan discourse, and it was far too loud. There was an English family of father, mother and two puppyish daughters seated nearby at a table, and they were taking it all in. Ellis suddenly roared with laughter, plucked a couple of harp chords from his tweeded crotch, and cried:

"Freud the Jewish scientist will end up a Christian Scientist if he is not careful. Eh? Eh?" He then snarled brown and yellow at the room, which was filling up at this apéritif hour, and said, "Most of the people here are hetero-sexual. Though, of course, we must not leave out of account the fact that the Côte d'Azur is a refuge for those of the opposed persuasion. Like, I presume that is your reason for being here, yourself." He then looked, it seemed, ap-praisingly at the bartender and said, *"Encore un bock."*

"Forgive me," I said. "All this is of the greatest interest, but—"

He was quick to understand. "Too loud, eh?" he said too loudly. "Yes, a foul fault. It comes of my going deaf." Then he began to whisper quite as audibly as he had declaimed. "Everyone, as I said, is born sexual. There are stages of infantile development which lead, in the majority of cases, to a dec-laration of heterosexual tropism. Now the homosexual is made out of an in-ordinate Oedipal situation. But his homosexuality is not a neurosis or psychosis. Only his attitude to it, which means his attitude to society's attitude to it, can produce a condition in which it is in order to talk of an etiology. Do I make myself clear?"

All too clear, all too too clear.

He downed his bock and said, to my relief, "Let us walk a little. It seems to be a gorgeous day."

We walked only about the square bounded by the hotel, the Casino, the Café de Paris and the little park. It was indeed a gorgeous spring day, a day for the heterosexual flirtations of literary tradition. I said:

"My father. The mildest of men, the kindest, as I well remember. I was never afraid of him. Despised him a little, perhaps, for not being firm enough with me, leaving all that to my mother. Despise him now for another thing, but let that pass." Then I suddenly caught a memory, shrill as the flapping seagull over the Casino, of myself screaming, held down, unable to get away, while my father approached me grimly with forceps. No, not his dental chair. Myself in bed with my mother, her arm about me, and my father coming into the bedroom grinning in (it must have been) mock ferocity with the kitchen tongs in his fist (impos-sible) and gripped in the tongs a monstrous brown and bloody molar. "Biggest

I've ever seen," he seemed to leer, thrusting the tooth toward my hidden genitals. "Remember this, boy, remember to look after your pegs." There was a fire (why?) blazing in the bedroom grate, and he untonged the molar and let it drop among the coals. Then he waved the tongs at me, making a dull metallic castanetting, and went out singing. Was that what they called the primal scene, or something?

"Despise?" said Havelock Ellis. "Nothing to do with it. I say," hands suddenly clasped behind him, swiveling his whole body to get a better look, "that's an awfully pretty girl." She was too, about eighteen, smooth olive, coming from mass with her mother, a blancmange-colored missal in her hand. As though he had merely done a conventional homage to old man's lechery, he dismissed his admiration and turned back to me, saying, "Put it this way. Your father owned your mother and was very ready to deballock you for being his rival in love, and you conceived the fearful assumption that your father owned all women. That's what dear Sigmund teaches. It will do as well as any other theory. Like false etymology, you know. Tell some ignoramus that Mary Queen of Scots liked to eat marmalade when she was ill, and so they called the stuff *Marie est malade*. Or that Alexander loved roasted eggs, and when he came in from battle they yelled *All eggs under the grate*, hence his historic title. Nonsense, but it fills in a sort of gap in the brain. Like the Freudian mythology. It doesn't *have* to be rational, you know, indeed it can't be. But your father scared you off all women, and that's why you are what you say you are. So forget it. Enjoy yourself, life's short." Though in full view of a group of, from their twang, New Englanders, he arpeggiated a chord on his crotch.

"And how," I asked, "am I suppose to feel about my sister?"

"Sister, eh? Younger than you? Interesting business, having a sister. Sigmund had a hell of a row with one of those errant disciples of his, the one that started up on his own with a theory about everything stemming from the birth trauma, Otto Somebody, something in it probably, a row about homosexuality and incest. The sister, one of them said, I don't know whether it was this Otto or the great old bugger himself, she's outside the net. The father doesn't own her as he owns the mother. She's not a sex object, not during that phase, if you see what he's getting at, whichever one it was. Did you read my introduction to *'Tis Pity She's a Whore?*"

"I read the play in the Mermaid Series. I don't remember an introduction."

"Never mind. Now I come to think of it, I didn't write one. Meant to, perhaps. It doesn't matter. Anyway, the only way out of homosexuality is incest."

"Or castration."

"I never prescribe castration. But, of course, I never prescribe anything these days. Like you, I call myself a man of letters." He made a terrible face and leered terribly: "Sororal incest." We were standing on the periphery of the terrace of the Café de Paris. Ellis looked at the apéritif-takers as if they were a zoo, then said clearly to a laden waiter, *"L'inceste avec la soeur."* The waiter shrugged, as to say it was not on the tariff. "That flashes on the conscious level, like sheet lightning on the marine horizon. To be watched, the occasion of the fall avoided. Out of the frying pan into the other thing. Though that can lead to the seeking of sister substitutes, sororal surrogates and so forth. Interesting. You ought to write a play about it. No, surely it was done by Philip Massinger. Perhaps not. A novel, a bigger form, no room in a play really." I did write a novel, in 1934. Half of one, anyway. But I knew I'd never get away with it, not in an age when the editor James Douglas, who called Aldous Huxley The Man Who Hates God, poor Aldous the God-drunk, declared he would rather give his children prussic acid than let them read *The Well of Loneliness.* My working title had been *She Hath No Breasts.*

"Which is the greater sin?" I asked. I was asking the wrong man. The right man to ask was arriving from Paris the following day. He would probably deny the existence of either of them, except as items in some hypothetical list worked out a priori by the Angelic Doctor, who had been so fat that they had to cut a half-disk out of his dining table. *Copulatio cum aure porcelli*, copulation with a pig's ear, is to be regarded in no different wise from the same act performed *in natibus equi*, in a horse's arse (A, 3, xiv), this being pollution and the unlawful spending of the seed which is intended for generation and the peopling of the heavenly kingdom with saved souls. Incest wasteth no seed so may be accounted the lesser sin, but see Ambrosius Fracastor, Bibellius, Virgilius Polydor Upyourarse, et cetera, et cetera.

"Sin? Sin?" cried Ellis at a small dog. "Oh my God, sin quotha."

It comes clear in memory now, but I cannot understand why I had walked painfully up from the Condamine to Monte Carlo, prepared to show my bruises to strangers who would think: "He was in a roughhouse with jolly jack-tars, the dirty bugger, serves him right." Had I come to look for that little traitor Curry at the Balmoral? Certainly not. Anyway, he had left. Hortense and Domenico, the hypocrites, had gone to late mass at Sainte Dévote. Why had I not stayed in the bed I must the next day give up to Don Carlo, catching up on the sleep I had missed during a long night given over to listening for sounds of padding fornicatory feet (watch this, Toomey; oh, to hell with watching things all the time)? Had I wanted my sister to be defiled and did I now wish her to be married? Masochism, sexual identification with my artbrother Domenico? Did I wish them both to be uneasy about my apparent change of heart? What was going on? I have practiced the craft of fiction for many years, but I know less than I ever knew about the tortuosities of the human soul.

Havelock Ellis now looked toward the little hill street between the Casino and the Hôtel de Paris and, at the sight of a man coming up it, opened eyes and mouth wide with joy. This man, about fifty, clad in what seemed to be a suit of alpaca that shimmered purply in the intense light, now began to trot toward Ellis, grinning like a gridiron. Ellis met him halfway with speed, though not trotting. "My dear, my dear." This would be the homosexual from Roquebrune. I found out later that Ellis's wife was unabashedly lesbian and he himself quite impotent. There they were, Ellis and this man, embracing each other, the man going "What? What? Eh?" in the patrician manner. Then they went into the Hôtel de Paris, embraced. Ellis had forgotten me already, the rude thing. I did not exist. And it was he who had brought me out into the square, leaving me now standing aimless and feeling a fool under the sun and gulls.

But lo, here they are coming up that same hill street to have luncheon with me at the Hôtel de Paris—Hortense in appropriate off-white cotton with flowered sidebow at the waist, wide wrapover collar, glass bead necklace, deep-crowned narrow-brimmed hat with wide silk band, and Domenico in decent gray, wearing a curl-brimmed trilby of the kind that Puccini, one of his masters, favored. They have come out of mass and look sober and demure, the sinners. What is the nature of the luncheon—celebratory, penitential?

"The ceremony," I said over the coffee, "will, I presume, take place in Gorgonzola." Domenico, who was drinking his coffee, spluttered. He had not expected this. I had deliberately kept, during the meal, to the topic of my and Domenico's little opera. Milan's rejection of it, I said, was not the end of the world. My theatrical contacts in London did not include operatic ones, but I was sure that I could get my agent to get Sir Hilary Beauclerk at Covent Garden to consider its production. Domenico had at first been suspicious, but I was affable and charming, despite my half-closed eye and bruises; I was being a *gentleman*, a breed that Domenico had read about if not previously met. "The marriage ceremony," I amplified.

Hortense said, "Look, Domenico, this is not my idea, you know that. This is him being pompous and heavy and in loco parentis and bloody hypocritical."

"With your brother," I said, "performing that ceremony. I suppose that Hortense must go with you soon to meet the family. This is something that we can work out with Don Carlo when he comes tomorrow. I take it that your family is living in the modern age, with all its social liberties, just as you are. I take it that there will be no antiquated nonsense about a dowry or a marriage settlement. You love each other, enough, no more, no less. Don't you," I said with sudden ferocity, "love each other?"

"You're a nasty filthy pig," said Hortense.

"Don't," I snarled. "How dare you address me in that manner. You're not too old to be smacked. On your bare bottom too." At a table some five meters away Ellis's friend from Roquebrune was fluting at Ellis some Jacobean lines which I recognized:

> *"Kiss me. If ever aftertimes should hear*
> *Of our fast-knit affections, though perhaps*
> *The laws of conscience and of civil use*
> *May justly blame us, yet when they but know*
> *Our loves, that love will wipe away that rigour,*
> *Which would in other insects be abhorr'd."*

Then he giggled.

"Yes yes," growled Ellis, too loud, a bit tipsy, "vocal metathesis. Scared of the word. I shall never forget the occasion, the bloody fool. Like 'Good Hamlet, cast thy coloured nightie off.' But that was only in rehearsal, got it out of her system."

"That play," I said to Hortense. She did not seem to know the keyword of the title for all her sophistication, sophistication meaning defilement. "Cognate with German *Hure*. Sister Gertrude may perhaps have used the word in some admonitory context or other."

"Yes," Domenico now said, having drunk his coffee and wiped thoroughly his lips with his napkin. "We love each other." And he put his hairy paw out toward Hortense's thin wrist across the table.

twenty-seven

Don Carlo's telegram had said he was coming for five days, but in fact he stayed well over a week. He had been gaining a reputation, I gathered, in the field of exorcism, and there was a tough job of exorcism to perform just outside Nice. The Bishop of Nice had requested his services, and so he had been granted a week's leave of absence from the Catho in Paris. A bit irregular, apparently, but Don Carlo was said by His Grace to be the best man in Europe at fighting the devil, and this was meant very literally. The devil was no metaphor to some of these churchmen but a palpable entity, or rather a well-structured army of entities (hence the name Legion, as in British Legion), with the Son of the Morning as generalissimo in charge of Belial and Beelzebub and Mephistopheles, as well as a large number of NCOs and privates eager to fight the bad fight and gain promotion. A lot of nonsense I thought at the time, but Don Carlo was ready to march in armed with the Rituale Romanum and, so to speak, knock hell out of these minor devils that had camped in the bodies of the innocent. He never had any doubt about the externality of evil, and this is what made him so formidable. Man was God's creation, and therefore perfect. The devil got in in the Garden of Eden and taught man how to be evil, and he was still doing it. Why didn't God annihilate the devil, then, and all his works? Because of free will. He had permitted the Revolt of the Angels because of free will. A divine bestowal by no manner of means nor in any wise to be rescinded. But let us hear the words of Don Carlo himself. The tough process of exorcism at which he daily labored (I imagined him with coat off and sleeves rolled up) had got into the columns of *Nice-Matin*. The victim of the attentions of some minor but limpet-like devils who had, apparently, names like Chouchou, Ranran, and Piquemonsieur, was a boy of eight, son of a railway worker who talked to a reporter in a bistro. Don Carlo believed, not without cause, that the press could do with its own exorcism and he refused to speak to its representatives. Instead he spoke to the world at large, or such of it as it was represented at eleven o'clock mass the following Sunday at Sainte Dévote. He gave a sermon in very reasonable, though Milan-accented, French, taking as his text the ninth verse of the fifth chapter of the Gospel according to Saint Mark, the one about our name being Legion and us being many. He said:

"A mere five months ago we came to the end of an excruciating, debilitating, murderous, thoroughly evil war. When I use that word *evil* I do not do so in the way of the politician or the journalist. For they use it loosely and vaguely, as a mere synonym for painful or undesirable. We have all heard phrases like 'the evils of capitalism' or 'the evil of slum landlordism' and we have permitted the term to take on a purely secular meaning. But *mal, male*, evil properly means an absolute force that has run riot in the world almost since the day of its creation and will only be quelled at the Day of Judgment. This force, being absolute, is not man-made. It is the monopoly of spiritual beings, creatures of God, high and majestic and beautiful servants of the Almighty who, under a leader, the most beautiful of them all, one whose name was Bringer of Light, rejected God's dominion, conceived rebellion, declined to serve, and were thrown from the empyrean into dark and empty space. They arrested what would have been an endless fall, for space knows no limits, by willing into existence a new abode of their own, which we call Hell, and substituting for the principle of eternal good the opposed principle of eternal evil.

"Now how do we define this evil? Very simply. As a principle, an essence designed to counter God's good and, through a series of acts of war, eventually to defeat it. Blind angels, misled in their sinful pride, hopelessly setting themselves up against the ever powerful, their own Creator, Him who could, with a snort from His divine nostrils, puff their being out like a candleflame! But God is defined as the Creator, not as the Annihilator, nor is it in His nature to destroy what He has created. Why then, the ignorant may ask, did He not quell that act of rebellion in its initiatory spark, choke the avowal of disobedience in the very throat of him who enunciated it? Because He gave to His creatures the awful and mysterious benison of freedom of choice. It may be said that God, being omniscient as well as omnipotent, foreknew from the very beginning that the act of angelic rebellion would be conceived and fulfilled, and that this foreknowledge must, of necessity, be a denial of the freedom of the creature. But this is a shameful and all too human imposition on the nature of the Godhead of a limitation which leaves out of account the illimitable fervor of His love. He loves His creatures so well that He grants them the gift of His own essence—utter freedom. To foreknow would be to abrogate that gift, for what can be foreseen is predestined, and where there is predestination there is no freedom of will. No, God, in His terrible love, denied Himself foreknowledge, imposed upon Himself a kind of human ignorance which we may take as the very seed of his eventual incarnation in human form. With the ghastly cataclysm of the Fall of the Angels God begins already to assume the potentialities of the Redeemer.

"Redeemer of whom or what? Not of Lucifer and his wickedness. There there is no turning back. Evil has been chosen and may not now be unchosen. But, out of a mysterious and awful divine necessity, God is drawn to the making of man. When I speak of the making of man I do not necessarily ask you to conceive of a literal forging of a being of flesh and bone from the dust. I will leave it to the literalists of America to deny the possibility of a long process of creation which we may even term evolution. Take it, anyway, that, at some point in the long workings of time, the creature called man emerges, flesh, blood, bone, into whom His Creator breathes a soul, and the essence of this soul is the endowment of freedom of choice, the pledge of His love. And what is the nature of this choice? It is a choice between the kingdom of good and the kingdom of evil. Indeed, we may say, as certain Church Fathers have said, Theodosius among them, that evil is a necessity, since if there were only good there would be only good to choose, and that would be no choice. So God makes man and gives man the divine *liberum arbitrium*, and behold there are two kingdoms for him to choose between, that eternal and luminous one of the Divine Lord's own making, and the noisome stinking pit of pain and horror that is the abode of God's Enemy.

"Let me make it clear to you, brethren, that as good is beyond man's making, being an eternal essence revealed to him for his choosing, so is evil, that deadly opposite, similarly beyond his making. It is the work of another eternal, leader of the Legion of the lost and damned, who seeks to strike at the Almighty through striking at His dearest creation. To speak of the evil works of man is possible only in an extreme looseness of thought and phraseology. To employ a convenient image, we may say that man plays on a keyboard the melody of evil, but he is not its composer. No, there is a deadly genius behind him, invisible but revealed through his works, and these works have a common property, a signature, a recognizable essence. As God is the Creator, so the Enemy of God, and of man, is the Destroyer. Evil is destruction, but we must consider now briefly the nature of this destruction.

"To destroy, as we know, is not in the human dispensation necessarily an action to be deplored or condemned. A decayed building may be razed to the ground that a fairer building may be erected on its site. An epoch of tyranny may be destroyed in order that an age of freedom may take its place. But note that these modes of destruction are of a special kind: they destroy what is already recognized as destructive. The decayed building is a danger to its inhabitants, more, it is ugly and displeasing to the sight. Ugliness is a recognizable attribute of the bad. The tyrant is a destroyer, and to destroy the destroyer and his works is the first step in the building of an era of good, of which beauty is a recognizable attribute. The nature of diabolic destruction is wholly different. It seeks to strike at the good and the beautiful, seeing in these things reflections of the divine. It strikes also at the true, the third of the blessed trinity of God's attributes. The devil's works of destruction may be recognized by their wantonness, by their apparent meaninglessness. They serve no end, other than that of spitting in the face of the Creator. We have seen, in the war that ended but five months ago, an unexampled panorama of destruction, with the meaningless loss of millions of lives, the infliction of wanton cruelty, the sowing of the seed of disease and destitution, the crushing of great cities, the poisoning of the air and the earth. And there are some who speak of the waste, the madness, the human dementia, the inexplicability of man's seeking to destroy himself. But may we speak of waste, when so many men, and women too, were driven to acts of heroism, love and self-sacrifice that could never have been persuaded to emerge out of an era of peace and torpor? May we speak of madness when the devil manifests such care and cunning in his setting up of the occasions of the massive enactment of evil, making the bad cause appear the good? May we speak of the inexplicable, when Holy Scripture and the teachings of Holy Church make it all too clear that the prevalence of evil is one of the two abiding facts of our lives, the other being the prevalence of good?

"Dear brothers and sisters in Christ, I have spoken of a great evil and I will speak now briefly of a lesser one—though I would stress, had I the time and, indeed, had I the expository skill and the eloquence, that we may not properly make quantitative judgments on the devil's work, since every act whether great or small that he perpetrates is an abomination, is an attempted defilement of God's goodness and majesty. Let him slaughter a myriad of the flower of the world's manhood, let him enter the being of an innocent child, and he must call forth from us an equal voice of protest in the name of the All Highest. I, the humblest and weakest of God's servants, have been engaged these last days on one of the regular duties ordained to the priesthood, commanded to His disciples by Our Lord Jesus Christ, I mean the driving out of evil spirits. I have been engaged in the quelling of small and dirty agents of the Father of Lies, filthy but formidable creatures and yet cowardly, striking in their cowardice at the innocent and defenseless. They settled, as arbitrarily as a swarm of bees, on the person of a small boy, the son of a good and humble Catholic family, and sought, by driving this poor child to madness, to destroy one of God's perfect creatures. There they were, their voices many but their theme the common one of whining blasphemy and obscenity, snarling back at God's minister, spitting at the holy cross, howling down the holy words of exorcism. But at the end they fled screaming and, praise be to God and His Blessed Son, the innocent was restored to his innocence, and there will be forever in that humble family a lively sense of God's greatness and of the final impotence of evil.

"I say these things to you, brethren, that you may be newly made aware of the struggle that God, in His ineffable wisdom, has decreed shall be the lot of our days. The struggle takes many forms but at bottom we must recognize the one enemy, the army whose name is Legion and whose warriors are many. Let me now make clear to you the true meaning of a very terrible word that you use and hear used every day of your lives, that you have shouted at you by prelates like myself, but which you perhaps have never sufficiently pondered upon. The word is *péché, peccato,* sin. I ask you to distinguish very carefully between that word *sin* and that other word *evil.* For sin is a thing that human souls can commit, but evil is the already existent entity that, through the act that we term a sin, a human soul may voluntarily embrace. Holy Church teaches that the capacity for sin derives from that first sin committed by our first parents when they listened to the seductive voice of the Father of Evil and ate of the forbidden fruit in the Garden of Eden. We have inherited this capacity for sin from them as we have inherited the other features of the Adamic, or human, identity. Now sin we may define as a transgression made possible by our ingrained capacity for confusing the truly or divinely good with what the fallen Son of the Morning represents as a higher good. Of course, there is no higher good than God's good, but, in our blindness, in the fleshly net that exalts mere appetite, in the credulity of our fallen state—a state we must blame on the fact that evil had already been brought into being by the devil—we may all too often succumb to the diabolic skill and cunning, accepting the ugly as beautiful, the false as true, and the evil as good. Now I say to you this: do not mourn that this should be so but rather rejoice in the struggle to perceive the truly and beautifully good, in the great and divine gift of freedom to pursue the struggle.

"Man was made by God in His own image. God made man without flaw, but also free to become flawed. Yet the flaws are reversible, the return to perfection is possible. If we call ourselves, sometimes with great justice, 'miserable sinners,' we must remember that we have willed ourselves to be so, that this is not the state which the Divine Creator has imposed upon us, that this is the working of free will. But that free will which enables us to sin is the most glorious gift of the Heavenly Father. We must learn to join that will to His, and not to that of the Adversary. This is, in a word, the meaning of our human life. The urge to sin is in us, but sin presupposes the prior existence of evil, and that evil is not in us but in the Powers of Darkness that harry us. Rejoice because God is in you. Rejoice in the war that God ordains. 'Our name is Legion, and we are many.' Yes, but the armies of divine grace are infinitely greater, flash in armor a million times more shining than the sun, brandish weapons of ineffable terror. Do not be afraid. Even from the most noisome evil the most radiant good may spring. We have fought the beast at Ephesus and elsewhere, and we shall fight him again and all his progeny, great and small. He shall not prevail. God is good and so is His world, so are His children. Rejoice and be exceedingly glad in the name of the Father, and of the Son, and of the Holy Ghost. Amen."

Don Carlo, who occupied the master bedroom while I—on my own unresisted insistence—slept on a couch in the salon, considered himself in charge of the household and as good as commanded me to attend the mass at which this sermon was preached. So, with a kind of sour good humor, I attended, along with my prospective brother-in-law. Hortense, of whom Don Carlo deeply approved as a good pretty innocent Catholic girl, went to an earlier mass, so that she might have ready for fasting Don Carlo a large English Sunday dinner of roast beef and Yorkshire pudding with Colman's mustard. She was a good hand with a Yorkshire pudding: it rose high on one side of the baking tin and was crisp brown without, gold feathery within. Don Carlo ate with the relish that he must have brought to the exorcising of Chouchou, Ranran and Piquemonsieur.

twenty-eight

"He can show nothing of his sentiments," Signora Campanati said, "but I know he is happy." She referred to her husband, who sat in a wheelchair, five years paralyzed. He was the still center of a lively open-air wedding party.

I have moved now to the summer of 1919, and soon I can be done with that first of the postwar years. In this summer Alcock and Brown achieved the first direct flight over the Atlantic and the interned German fleet was scuttled at Scapa Flow. On June 28 a Treaty of Peace with Germany was signed at Versailles and, the day after, Domenico and my sister were joined by Don Carlo in the bonds of holy matrimony in the chapel of the home of the Campanati family just outside Gorgonzola, a small town east of Milan. My and her father, whose permission for the marriage had had to be sought, sent a brief cable from Battle expressing no objection. He left the job of giving away the bride to me.

I had now left Monaco and moved to Paris, where I had an apartment on the rue Bonaparte. Hortense and Domenico, more he than she, talked of coming to live in Paris after a honeymoon in Rome and a spell at Gorgonzola again, where they had now been for a couple of months. All of us in Paris, then, Carlo at the Catho, me breathing in the oxygen of literary modernism, Domenico, as he said, making a name with the new jazzy spices of *Les Six*, perhaps studying under Nadia Boulanger or Martinú, certainly, for the fun and money of it, playing jazz piano with *nègre* saxophonists in night *boîtes*. Paris was the only place, he said.

As for Gorgonzola, this place, as the reader will know, originated a famous cheese, and it was the manufacture and foreign sale of this cheese that had made the Campanati family rich. Everyone knows the cheese but few the town, so that to set down the name is to evoke an oxymoron of savory taste and foul aroma rather than merely to indicate a locality. I traveled by wagon-lit from the Gare de Lyon to Milan, had luncheon (*riso al burro, vitello*, a bottle of Vighinzano) with Elio Spagnol, who had published two of my books, spent the night at the Excelsior Gallia on the Piazza Duca d'Aosta, and was driven in a hired open coupé the following morning to the Villa Campanati by way of Cernusco sul Nuviglio and Cassina de' Pecchi. The driver, who was well-fed and scornful of peasants, spoke of the tribulations of postwar Italy, which he blamed mostly on the British, and found his only hope in a communist revolution. It was a beautiful day, and the larks, unshot at, were permitted to ascend. He had a weak r-sound, rhotacismus as it is called, a speech peculiarity not popularly associated with the Italians but common in Lombardy. *'Ivoluzione. 'Ibellione. Lo spi'ito 'ivoluziona'io.* It made his tumbrils roll as though with muffled wheels. It was a beautiful day, heady with magnolia and cedar. "Capitalists," he said when we arrived at the high walls of the Villa Campanati. "Those walls will be down, you will see." On the gateposts were the huge stone balls, left and right, which the English used to call infangthief and outfangthief. "Their heads will be placed here," the driver promised. He haggled bitterly over the fare. It was a beautiful day, and the breeze that blew in from the town brought no whiff of its specialty.

"But I know he is happy." My chair at the great open square table on the great lawn was next to hers. The house behind us was a queer architectural mixture. It was basically a small mansion completed, I gathered, in the year when, at Bosworth Field, the English ceased to have English rulers, and formerly in the possession of a cadet branch of the Borromeo family. The eccentric

Principe Dragone had raved there, riddled with syphilis, till his violent suicide in the 1880s, and the property had been put up for sale. The Campanati family had taken over the house complete with certain artistic treasures, including a *Venere e Cupido* of Annibale Carracci, an *Annunciazione* of Bernardino de' Conti, and a *Maddalena Penitente* of Antonio Boltraffio. A large library of rare erotica was said to be bricked up in the cellars and an obscene stone satyr by, I think, Tallone had been permitted to go on cavorting among the cypresses. The family chapel, where my sister's wedding was solemnized, lay at the back of the house, across a wide courtyard, and it had four holy pictures by Lanzetti as well as a swooning Christ (eventually claimed by the Borromeo family: you may see it in the Palazzo Borromeo on Lago Maggiore) attributed to Zenale. I Campanati had added two undistinguished wings to the original structure, big stucco boxes full of hotel-style bedrooms, rather American, foreshadowing indeed the flavor of a Holiday Inn. On the ground floor of the left, or east, wing was the suite of the paralyzed head of the family, with a sort of subsuite for the resident nurse, a Miss Fordham, an American.

"Happy," Signora Campanati said, a lady in her early sixties, Italo-American, her family from Leghorn, with a slight venerean strabismus that made Hortense, who, as you will remember, had the same charming ocular abnormality, seem more her daughter than her newly created daughter-in-law. She was slim and smart in the American manner. Strictly, it was the responsibility of the bride's family to provide the marriage feast, but, despite my offer of a catered banquet (I had the money, the royalties were not ineptly named that year), the Campanati family had insisted on taking charge of everything. There was a kind of relief in the air, even among the servants, that Domenico was being made to settle down at last.

He and Hortense had spent some time with me in Paris, she to see about her wedding dress and trousseau. The dress was made by the rising house of Worth and was very modern, that is to say it had a tubular bodice, low waist, gathered skirt that only just covered the knees, shirttype sleeves, flared lace oversleeves, low U-shaped neckline, and a fine chiffon veil with embroidered edges. It was in Paris that she said, while Domenico was meeting the composer Germain Tailleferre somewhere, that she would never forgive me.

"For what?" I said in honest astonishment. We were having lunch at a restaurant that has now long disappeared, the Pélléas et Mélisande on the rue Buffon, south of the Jardin des Plantes, and I had just cut into my *steak au poivre*. "For what, for God's sake?"

"For your vulgarity. It was a beastly and vulgar thing to do, forcing things like that. It made me feel unclean, and Domenico too. It was not up to you to start saying when's it going to be and get on with it, make an honest woman out of my sister you cad and all that sort of thing."

"But you said you wanted to marry him."

"In my own good time. It was up to me to make up his mind for him, and there you go with your nasty heavy-handed hypocrisy and bless you my children and the rest of the filth."

"I don't understand, I just don't. I just wanted you to get settled with the man you say you love and—"

"Shuffle me off, a burden to you, and get on with your nasty pansy life. Besides, I'm not sure whether I do love him now."

"Oh, that's common, just before marriage, the realization of till death do us part and so on. And," I said, "I will not have you using expressions like that about my life, the one you used then. My life is my own life."

"And mine's mine, or was till you decided to take it over."

"You're a girl, you're under age."

"That's only what the law says, and the law's an ass. Now I feel caught and trapped and hemmed in and not free any more. And it's all your fault."

"It is not my fault. You took him to bed and then said you were going to have him and—"

"Those are English people over there. They're listening. Keep your voice low."

"You started all this. Look," and I put knife and fork down, "you don't have to, you know. There's many a marriage been called off even at the altar."

"Oh, I'll go through with it." And she picked at her endive salad. "I'll be very very happy," she said bitterly.

"The way you feel, or think you do. It's not uncommon, you know."

"You know all about it, of course."

"I know a bit about life. I have to. I'm a writer."

She pushed the salad aside and joined her hands as though about to say grace.

"He scares me," she said.

"Domenico? Oh, that's imp—"

"Not Domenico. Carlo. There's something creepy about the way he looks at me. As though he can see what's going on in my mind. He looks at me, then he sort of grins and nods."

"Yes, I've seen that. But he's just nodding with satisfaction. He approves of you. Domenico's been a bit of a wild one, as you know. Now he's going to settle down."

"Yes, that's it, everything's going to be fine for Domenico, it's always what everybody else wants, nobody thinks of me. And then Carlo starts talking of the children we're going to have, and he sort of sees them as though they were already there. Every good Catholic family, he says, gives somebody to God. What does he mean? Anyway, I feel all shut in, and I can't get out, ever. I'll never forgive you for this."

"This is the most absolute nonsense."

"It's not nonsense, and you know it's not. I mean, what's happened to us, to our family? We don't exist any more, and there are the Campanati, with the Church behind them, flourishing like a like a—"

"Vineyard?"

"No. Yes. Oh, alive, and not falling to bits despite the old man being near death, and there am I being swallowed up by them."

"You can walk out," I said, "now."

"You know I can't. That damned Carlo won't let me. Oh, perhaps it *is* nonsense."

"More than perhaps," I said, and I went on eating my *steak au poivre,* though not with much appetite. And then, with Signora Campanati next to me, I was eating a slice of the wedding cake, a most brilliant rococo edifice of many tiers, infested, as with flies, by fat-arsed *putti* or cherubim, designed and built by architectural confectioners in Milan. I was also drinking a glass of Dom Perignon, which helped it down. The paralytic head was fed some crumbs of the cake by Nurse Fordham. Hortense was somewhat drunk, which was in order, but not so drunk as Domenico, who flashed extravagant joy, though with an Italic leer in it, at uncles, aunts, cousins, school friends, monsignori, retainers, operatives of the *caseificio,* nuns. Among the nuns was the sole daughter of the family, Luigia, Suor Umiltà, a big mustached girl in her middle twenties, openly and without visible effect steadily tippling. Carlo gave a long ribald speech in dialect and sank a half-liter of bubbly in one applauded go. Signora Campanati's forced smile told me that this was not the way of the family: they were staid moneymaking people, speakers of a language called Italian, meaning a neutralization for national use of the Tuscan dialect, with all its nuances of culture and rule, while Carlo, as a kind of pastoral duty, would perform the stage act of one marrying the speech of earth to that of heaven. Another thing: Carlo was physically gross in comparison with that pared and elegant family. In a flash I saw him as a changeling, a goblin baby dumped in a Campanati pram. He was certainly unlike his elder brother Raffaele.

Raffaele was in Italy not because of the wedding but because, at this time of the year, he always left Chicago and came home. He looked like what he was, an international businessman, but there was an aura of refinement and even piety over him, as if the impulses that had made, respectively, Carlo a priest and Domenico a musician had been arrested and frozen into the intriguing inconsistencies of a personality which, I understood, was ironlike in its concern with commercial success. He was about thirty-eight and already a widower. His wife had been an Anglo-Saxon Catholic from St. Louis, dead of septicemia after her third, aborted, attempt at providing a Campanati heir. He had not remarried and said he would live and die a widower. The line was to be continued through Domenico and my sister, hence the importance of this occasion.

"He can show nothing of his sentiments," Signora Campanati said, "but I know he is happy." Meaning, again, her husband, a desiccated parody of Raffaele, dumb, bewildered, but theoretically under the necessity of being happy that the family was not to die out.

"Our happiness," Raffaele was telling the guests in Italian. He was as richly black-haired and mustached as King C. Gillette on the safety razor blade label. Also as handsome, in the old stiff way of the turn of the century—statuesque, stern, with no connotation of the flirt or masher. He was naturally chaste, so I had been told, and his appetites were, in comparison with those of Carlo, very frugal. He had eaten little and drunk less. He, I and his father were the only totally sober males present. "*La nostra felicità*," he said gravely.

The happy couple were to leave for Rome on that evening's sleeper. They could dine on the train, if they still had appetite, and might conceivably attempt formal consummation on one of the narrow bunks. But they had already anticipated that, the hypocrites, and would probably wait for the following afternoon, the shutters closed on the large Roman heat in the Hotel Raphael on the Largo Febo near the Piazza Navona. None of my or anybody's business.

Nor was I myself, I considered, having done my duty, or my father's, anybody's business but my own. I, the free writer. I intended to get away along with the other guests and spend another night in the Excelsior Gallia in Milan. I had left my bag there. A Dottor Magnago was very ready to give me a lift in his chauffeured limousine, no problem, not out of his way at all. Then, the next day, I would have a brief look at the islands of the Lago Maggiore, going from one to another in pleasure steamers, and catch the Lyon-bound train at Ascona. But it was Raffaele who insisted that they would all take it hard if I did not spend the night at the Villa Campanati: a room had been prepared in the west wing; toilet articles had been laid out. "We must have," he said, "a talk."

"About what?"

"A talk." We were all down at the big open gates in the first of the evening, delicious with lemon and magnolia, a peach-colored moon hung aloft. The car had arrived that would take the happy couple to the railway station. I kissed the bride in her gray going-away dress with crossover straps at low waist and neck, light satin coat over it open to the balm of the evening.

I whispered, "Everything will be all right, you'll see. We'll meet in Paris. Am I forgiven now?" Not, of course, that there was anything to forgive. She was grasped at once by Carlo, who hugged her till she howled, and then I had to kiss, though on the cheeks, a Domenico ready for tomorrow's shave. Kisses and cries and blessings and a nightingale in the cypresses.

Old Campanati had been wheeled to the gates. His nurse grabbed his right arm, limp as a piece of rope, and waved it at the departing couple. "They're off now, sweetie," she said. Like a dog being made to wave he looked the other way. Signora Campanati alternately wiped her sniffs and waved with a cambric handkerchief. Ribald Milanese advice was shouted at Domenico by his coevals, one

of whom made a vulgar gesture with a clenched fist. Waves and waves and cries
and a couple of frail showers of flower petals from, to my mild surprise, the nuns.

"Good luck to you both," Sister Humility called in English.

In England or Ireland the wedding party would have gone on all night and
finished, certainly in Ireland, with a brawl. Here it ended with the departure of
the bride and groom. There was family dinner, cold, rightly. A platter of left-
over meats and an *insalata mista*. Estate red wine in bottles without labels. We
ate, Suor Umiltà, Signora Campanati, Carlo, Raffaele, myself, in an aggressively
antique dining room that smelled of damp. Over the sideboard was an *Ultima
Cena* by Giulio Procaccini. The electrolier had many dead bulbs. Carlo ate as
though he had fasted all day. When coffee was brought he asked for the estate
liqueur, a grappa with a powerful reek of unwashed sheepdog. Nothing was said
about the absence of Nurse Fordham. I presumed, having fed her charge with
something from a feeding bottle, she cooked something American for herself in
her own kitchen. We all spoke English—it was as easy for them as Italian.
Raffaele said to me:

"Where in Paris?"

"Me or them?" He looked at me sternly and silently. I was in his view being
frivolous. "Well," I said humbly, "I promised to help there. Find a studio or
something. And if Carlo too hears of anything—" Strange, we were a sort of
relatives now. "I have a large second bedroom they can use while we're looking.
If, that is, nothing satisfactory has been found by the time that . . . Domenico
said something about a grand piano. I mean, there's no terrible hurry, is there?"

"Domenico," his mother said, "is anxious to start earning money. It is difficult with music, as we all know."

"No hurry there either, is there?" I said, perhaps insolently. "At least," while
they looked at me and said nothing, "I understood that all that was realized, the
difficulty, I mean, of Domenico's earning his living as a composer of serious
music. He says he is still learning his craft. He talks of taking lessons in
orchestration. He talks also of playing the piano in nightclubs. For the experience, that is. He believes ragtime and jazz and so on have something to give to
serious music. Ravel thinks so too," I said defiantly, "also Stravinsky."

"A player of jazz music in nightclubs," Raffaele said. "Married to the sister
of a writer of novels. How things change, how life changes."

"You made," I said boldly, "both those trades sound unseemly. Your tone, if
you'll forgive me, was somewhat disparaging. Any trade that brings harmless
solace is a respectable trade. Remember also, please, that Domenico and I first
became, well, friends, through collaboration on an opera. It was intended for
La Scala. I take it you will not be disparaging about La Scala."

"It was rejected by La Scala," Raffaele said, and his look implied that that
had been the fault of the libretto, something dirty in it perhaps.

"It may not be rejected by Covent Garden."

"That is where you have your English opera. I know." He made the shrug that used to be made by Germans and Italians when music and England were mentioned in the same breath.

"A theater surrounded by vegetables," Suor Umiltà said. Nun though she was, she knew the great world.

"That too," I said, now my hand was in, "sounds disparaging."

"Asparaging and cabbaging," Carlo struck in. "Come, come, let us have less gloom and more rejoicing." He meant Raffaele, whose fine eyes seemed to see a melancholy future for somebody or everybody in the bowl of oranges set out on a bed of their own leaves that stood in the middle of the table. "Change," Carlo said. "You say *change* as if it were not the essential property of living things. What would this family have been if it had not opened itself to the world? You fear the world of jazz and novels and Anglo-Saxons will swallow us up? No, it is we who swallow up them. You fear the loss of family dignity? We never had dignity, meaning we were always on the side of change and life. Take our poor father. He plucked our dear mother like an orange from East Nassau or wherever it was—"

"East Orange." His mother smiled sadly.

"Very good, like a nassau from East Orange then. He brought America into the family and with it the language of America. And now we have English blood and French blood coming in. If Raffaele would marry a black girl—"

"Enough," Raffaele said. "There are some jokes that ought not to be made."

"I say blood," Carlo went on, "but all blood is the same. Well, no, there is hot blood and cold blood. Cold blood like Kenneth's here, and hot blood for the Mediterranean—" It was the first time he had used my first name: I was really in the family now. "Well, no, we are all septentrional here, all a bit cool. What is Mother? Genova and the Alto Adige. Coolest of them all."

"I thought," I said, "all Italo-Americans came from the south. Calabria or Sicily. I had assumed Sicily."

"We want nothing to do with Sicily," Raffaele said. "It's the Sicilians who are ruining the United States. Chicago is mostly Neapolitans, who are bad enough, but at least the Sicilians are kept out. New York," he said, and shuddered.

"Change change," Carlo cried. "There you are, Raffaele, a real Chicago man, though you know by right and tradition you should be here in poor Father's seat. But change told you that the future lay in American big business—"

"I've thought much about that," Raffaele said. "But Zio Gianni does well here. Besides, our product is becoming a very small part of the whole. *Panettoni.* Canned *pomodori*—"

"Zio Gianni?" I asked. "Was he the one who sang the song with the comic stutter in it?"

"Stutter? Oh, *balbuzie*. No, that was old Sambon," Carlo said, "the manager. Uncle Jack, as you would call him perhaps, is in agony with his stomach and could not come. He ate something bad in Padova. Outside his own region he cannot eat. You will see him tomorrow or the day after perhaps."

"I'm leaving tomorrow," I said. "I have a book to finish."

"I must leave now," Suor Umiltà said. "Till ten o'clock only I was given." Her convent, I understood, was at Melzo, no great distance. "No, nobody rise." Her English was less idiomatic than that of the others. She kissed her mother and brothers and then kissed me, saying, "You have given dear Domenico a wife," which was not strictly true. Then, "Can you remember where my bicycle was put?" Carlo remembered.

When she had left, Carlo said, "A book? A novel?"

"Yes. Twenty pages or so still to do. About a blind girl and a crippled man who marry and produce lovely children." Unwisely I added, "Not very good, a lot of nonsense really."

"There you go," Carlo cried. "Why do you write these things if they are a lot of nonsense?"

"They start off," I said, "by being promising and even exciting. Then I become conscious of my own ineptitude, the streak of sentimentality in me that is ineradicable, the poverty of the style and my inability to improve it. Yet I cannot destroy what I have done, because that would be to destroy what to me are still living creatures. Moreover, I have a living to earn and readers who are less fastidious than myself. So, in a kind of hopelessness, I complete the book, send it away, try to forget, hope I will do better next time."

"Pray too, perhaps?" their mother said.

"In a way," I said cautiously. "In a way pray, yes."

"But," Raffaele said, "if the book were an immoral book and one that would make scandal, you would still think it possible to pray to write the book better?"

"Oh," I smiled, "I can't accept that a work of fiction should be either immoral or moral. It should merely show the world as it is and have no moral bias. It is for the reader to see in the book the nature of the motives of human actions and perhaps learn something too of the motives behind the social forces which judge those actions and which, I take it, we call a system of morality."

"There is divine morality," Raffaele said, "and that is the only morality which is important." He was entering Carlo's field, but Carlo was busy sucking an orange as a weasel might suck a brain. "I think it is possible and I think it is in fact not uncommon to have books which deny divine morality and are dangerous books to put into people's hands."

"I don't think my books are of that type. The novels I've written are morally rather conventional. I mean, I present wrongdoing but the wrongdoing is always rather conventionally punished. Nobody," I said, "gets away with anything in my novels. That worries me sometimes. I mean, the world is not like that. You remember the novel Miss Prism writes in *The Importance of Being Earnest*.

The good end well, she says, and the bad end badly. That is why it is called fiction."

"I don't know it," Raffaele said. "Who is it by?"

"Oscar Wilde. It was he, by the way, who said that there is only one kind of immorality in fiction, and that is when you write badly."

"That is nonsense," Carlo said, taking another orange. "You cannot make moral judgments on things, only on actions."

"But writing is a kind of action," I said. "You would make a moral judgment on a carpenter who made bad chairs."

"Only if he sold them as good chairs."

"Oscar Wilde," Raffaele said darkly. "You would call yourself a disciple of Oscar Wilde?"

"Oh no," I smiled. "Very much a writer of the Victorian era. We must write like writers of the twentieth century, and now like people who have experienced the terrible cataclysm of the war. We cannot go back."

Carlo ceased sucking and got up. "I will," he said, "take some oranges with me." He scooped an armful. "For if I wake in the night. But it has been a very full day. I think I shall sleep like a dog."

"It has been a very full day," his mother agreed, also rising. "But a happy one." She kissed her sons and then, not to my surprise, kissed me. "You will find your room ready," she said. "Raffaele will show you which one. Your sister is the most delightful of girls," she added. "I am very happy."

"If," Raffaele said to me, "you would come into the library for a moment."

"You look at me as my father used to look. When I had a bad school report."

"It is something to do with a report."

"Dear dear dear. You make me very apprehensive."

The library was notable for a number of bad busts of Italian authors— Foscolo, Monti, Niccolini, Pindemonte, all of whom, blind and as it were smelling toward the light, seemed interchangeable. There were leatherbound books, all, as in a library in an English country house, unreadable, but there were not all that many, Italy not really possessing all that much literature. But there was a very fine Florentine terrestrial globe or *mappamondo*, and near it we sat in club chairs, I spinning the globe backwards, Raffaele pouring whisky from a square decanter he released, with a key, from an English tantalus. I took the initiative in glass-clinking. "To the happy couple," I brindized.

"I hope so. I hope it will work out well. I do not know your sister, you see, I do not know your family. But Domenico has made his choice."

"And Hortense has made hers."

"Yes, yes, I should think so. You know a man named Liveright?"

"Why yes, my New York publisher. I mean, we correspond. I've never met him."

"I belong to a club in Chicago, it is called the Mercury Club, for business-men, you understand, Mercury is said to be the god of businessmen."

"Also of thieves."

He did not find that funny. "This publisher Liveright was the guest of a business friend of mine. At the Mercury Club. If I may say so, since he is your publisher, he did not seem to be a man of great morality. He is out to make money. He is as ready to make it out of scandal as out of piety or devotion or serious instruction. This he calls being a good businessman. Not *good*, I told him, prosperous perhaps but not good."

"He has a Calvinistic background. I don't think he'd see the difference."

"No? I talked about your work and he seemed surprised that I knew it. I said only that I had seen a book of yours without reading it. At least, I read the first page. I remembered the name Liveright because the first page seemed to be a discussion about what one of the characters called the good life."

"That would be *Before the Hemlock*," I said. "No, wait, a different title in America. *Dash Down Yon Cup*, not a good title. The one about Socrates. I'm sorry you found it unreadable."

"No no no no, please. I find most novels unreadable. I am not perhaps what you would call a reading man. But I knew of your name, of course, because of Domenico and his falling in love, as my mother put it in her letter."

"You make it sound ungenuine. They're in love all right. But, forgive me, I wish you'd come to the point."

"Liveright kindly sent me a folder of articles about your work. There was one article about uncleanness and obscenity and I think the word was sensuality. I have the folder in a drawer in that desk there. Perhaps I should get it out." But he seemed tired, a very full day.

"That would be my first novel," I said. "*Once Departed*. I think the Ameri-cans called it *Return No More*. It's a nuisance, having these different titles."

"Liveright also said something about you having to leave England and not daring to go back. Because of some scandal or other. Is that true?"

"Look, Raffaele, if I may call you that, all this is my business. To deny what Liveright alleges would be an admission that it's your business as well. I see I must change my American publisher."

"It is the business of the family into which your sister marries. You become a kind of relative. Let me tell you. There was a British actress on Broadway. The name is in that folder. A widow apparently, her husband dead of influenza. She said that her husband had begun to live an irregular life some time before he died. There was a party at which Liveright was present. He was going to publish the play this lady was acting in. The lady became violent and abusive about the part she alleged that you played in her husband's estrangement from her. She spoke of your sexual irregularities. When I asked if you were a disciple of Oscar Wilde I meant it not only in the sense of literature. We call this thing a disease and sometimes the English disease. I spent two years at a school in England called Orpington School. It is in these schools that the disease often first appears."

"Homosexuality is the term," I said. "It is not a disease. The world's attitude to it is probably morbid, but it is a condition that exists widely and is often found allied to artistic ability. Sometimes great artistic genius. Your Michelangelo, for instance."

"Michelangelo caused no scandal."

"And, you might add, he had no sister to marry into the Campanati family."

"Whether we call it a disease or an attribute of the artistic temperament, it is still a sin."

"You mean the homosexual act or the homosexual condition?"

"One makes the other so I see no difference."

"In that case you've no right to talk about sin. Sins are the products of free will. Your brother Carlo made that very clear to us all in the sermon he gave at Sainte Dévote in Monaco in the spring. I did not choose to be homosexual. Because the Church condemns it, illogically I would say, I find myself out of the Church. But all this is my business."

"I do not think so. I was seriously prepared to advise Domenico against this marriage, even last week when all was ready, but I saw that might be unjust. Moreover, Domenico is old enough to go his own way. I certainly could not forbid it. Still, the family must be protected, and I have become the head of the family. I have a duty to ask you not to bring scandal on the family."

I kept down my heat. "Also a duty to ask my father to watch his step in Battle, at the same time querying his right as a very recent widower to marry a young girl whose antecedents none of us know. You have a duty also to go to whatever theater my brother Tom is performing in and persuade him to keep his act clean."

"Now you are talking stupidly. You are a writer and have the opportunity to incite publicly to scandal. There is also the matter of your private life. This has become public even as far away as New York."

I still stayed outwardly cold. "So what does the head of the Campanati family wish me to do? To seek some other career? To dissimulate my true nature? To drown myself in the Lago Maggiore?" Then the heat broke through. "I never in my life heard such sanctimonious impertinence. I'm a free man and I'll do what I damned well please. Within," so as not to appear totally anarchic and thus to some extent justify his view of me, "the limits imposed by my own nature and by the laws of society and literary ethics. The Campanati family," I added, sneering, "*una famiglia catissima, religiosissima, purissima, santissima.* With your brother Domenico shagging everything that offered and likely to do so again, despite the state of holy matrimony."

"I do not know that word. And I do not think I will have you speaking in this manner."

"My sister, I may add, wished to make a man of your brother. She recognized a talent that had to be encouraged. Oh yes, she loves him as well, whatever *love* means. He's prepared to work for a living, or so he says, instead of writing music as a cheese-subsidized hobby, and you twitch your *naso raffinatissimo* at the prospect of his discoursing harmless twaddle on a broken-down piano. Your holy brother Carlo, a waddling banner for the deadly sin of gluttony—at least he's realistic and charitable and has no time for the first deadly sin. The pride," I said, "of a putrefier of lactic solids. A pride that stinks like the commodity itself."

He drank his whisky in one irritable gulp and stood up. "Perhaps this was not the best time for talk. It has been a long day. Perhaps I have not spoken to you with the right discretion."

"The theme is clear." I also got up but did not finish my whisky. "Clear as a bell. I'll sleep in Milan tonight."

"No no no no no. Your room is prepared. I will show you where it is. Perhaps we both need a good night's sleep. You are more upset than I expected. I don't think, however, that you understand my position. Surrounded by corruption, by immorality. Chicago is a most vicious city and it will grow worse. I am sensitive to these things, they become . . . a physical oppression. If you are angry, I apologize for making you so."

"I suppose I'll have to walk back to Milan. Perhaps I can pick up some filthy little Milanese boy on the way. Ready to hire out his *culo* for a couple of *centesimi*."

"There is no need to be disgusting."

"Oh yes there is. Pharisee. I thank thee God that thou hast made me pure. I never did much care for your putrid specialty. I'm getting out of here."

And so I did, walking to the town under the honeyed moon and finding a garage with a Daimler that had probably been left behind by the defeated Austrians, the bonnet dented and what looked like bulletholes in the rear offside door, the driver an Old Bill type who blamed the British for dragging Italy into the war and thus implementing her present distress. Still, he took me to my hotel, shaking with rage and contempt as I was, and charged me exorbitantly. The Milan Metro did not at that time exist.

I did not, the following day, make my proposed trip to Lago Maggiore. It was necessary for me to take a taxi from the hotel to the Stazione Garibaldi, there to catch a train for Arona on the western shore of the lake. But there were militant workers on the streets with portraits of Lenin and slogans about liberty. A knot of five had knocked down a *carabiniere* and were kicking his bloody body to death. When my taxi approached this same knot it seemed to them that I must be a bloodsucking Milanese industralist who had to be dragged out and given to brisk revolutionary justice. Some window smashers joined them, jeering but with their claws out. Good Northern Italian faces, terribly distorted by politics. My driver was not on their side. He rushed at them, bumping sickeningly over the *carabiniere*'s body, and they howled and stumbled and fell and rose and chased us. I felt approaching a cardiac spasm of the kind I had last known in Battle on the High Street in the rain, walking to confront the news of my mother's dying immediately on my knocking at the door. The attack missed its trajectory, seeming, in my temporary delirium, to crack at the window behind me. But what hit the window was a lump of lead piping. The driver rushed me and my bag circuitously without my telling him to the main railway station. He knew I was a foreigner; let me get back to foreign parts and not witness any more of Italy's shame. There were troops, armed, in the station yard.

"Hypnotized, that's what they are," he said, when I paid him. "But what can you expect? Drunk with what's happened in Russia. Bolshevism as the answer to the whole damned mess-up. Gutless politicians and gutless police. But they won't win, they can't. The patriots of the Trentino won't let them, and I'm one, by the mother of Jesus Christ. You heard of the Sansepolcrista? No, you're a foreigner. They'll remember the Piazza San Sepolcro, I can tell you, and what's been decided there. Last March, it was."

March 10, to be exact. In a room lent by a Milanese Jew overlooking that square of the Holy Sepulcher. Borrowing the black shirts of D'Annunzio's *arditi* and calling themselves the Fasci Italiani di Combattimento. They would stop red thugs killing policemen in the streets.

twenty-nine

Robert panted, "It will do you no harm, you will like it, you will see." And he gently undid the boy's shirt and drew it over his crisply curled head, casting it to the floor, where it lay limp as the boy's own body. "Ralph, Ralph," murmured Robert as he caressed the young warm flesh, running a hand ever and again over the thin but muscular arms with their delicate flue, the smoothness of the taut belly, the silkiness of the back, the delicate moving contours of the breast, where the tiny nipples had already begun to respond to the moist fervor of Robert's kisses. It was while his mouth held his in passionate prolongation that

Robert blindly tore at the buttons of the boy's trousers. He whispered, "See, Ralph my darling, we must be the same, naked as the day when we were born, and rightly so since we are both at this moment being reborn. The whole world will seem to have changed, you will see, it is the beginning of a life for both of us." The world outside, the alien world of disgust and hate, impinged in the clash of the Angelus bell, but, yes, it was the bell of the Annunciation, the Angel of the Lord, an impending miracle. His questing hand was aware of the boy's own nascent excitement, the silken sheath about the iron of tumescence, and he smoothed with a shaking hand the royalty of the scepter and the twinned orbs. Then: "It must be now," he gasped, "it is the moment, do not move, Ralph my love." Thus, newly locked in a kiss, Robert found the *antrum amoris* and eased his body up to engage it with his own palpitant rod, now grown and glorified to a mace of regal authority. The boy cried out, and it seemed not to Robert to be a cry of pain, rather a call or crow of acceptance. Encouraged, Robert gently eased his throbbing burden into the timid heat of the sacred fissure, soothing with gentle words, words of love, while the angelic bell pounded and pulsed without. And then the promise loomed, the declaration of the Angel of the Lord, and the rhythm of ancient drums pulsed in imperceptible gradations of acceleration under a choral utterance that was emitted from the silver throats of all the Angels of the Lord, filling the universe to the remotest crevices where lurked, like shy sea beasts, stars not yet named, galaxies uncharted. And then the madness followed, the drought of a demented hoarseness of arcane and terrible incantations, the rasp of words ineffable, prayers to gods long thrust under earth or set to gather the dust of eons in caverns remote and hallowed only by mouths themselves long filled with dust, for the rancorous hordes of those who flaunted the banners of Galilee had smitten and broken and flattened the ancient empire of Faz and Khlaroth.

And then, O miracle of miracles, the drought was overtaken by the bursting of the dam, by the flooding of the whole desiccated earth, and Robert's voice rose like a trumpet in the ecstasy of his spending. A love nameless, unspeakable, spoke the name over and over again, "Ralph Ralph my beloved," and the lips that were agape in a wordless prayer of gratitude now closed about the head and flower of the boy's Aaronic baston, mouthed softly as about a grape to effect and yet delay its bursting, and Ralph writhed and groaned and the words were strange. *Solitam . . . Minotauro . . . pro caris corpus . . .* Latin, the memory of some old lesson, of some ancient attempt at seduction in that Jesuit school library he had spoken of: the supposition flashed in Robert's cooling brain. Then, with the speed of incontinent youth, Ralph gushed his burden out, sweet and acrid and copious, and Robert gulped greedily of the milk of love. Then they lay a space, wordless both, the thunder of their twin hearts subsiding, Robert's head couched on the boy's loins, Ralph's right hand smoothing his lover's wet and tangled hair.

They did not, when they walked to the café around the corner, do so as lovers, hands entwined or even touching. They walked discreetly an arm's breadth from each other, as though to admit room for a third, silent, invisible, whose presence they sensed but whose identity they lacked words to define. Then they sat at an outside table, Robert with his absinthe and small bottle of Perrier, Ralph with his pressed citron. August Paris breathed exhaustion about them. A bearded Franciscan went by, swinging his breviary in rhythm with his jaunty step. "Sin," smiled Ralph. "He would say sin."

"Did it feel like sin?"

"It was enjoyable enough to be called sin. No, enjoyable is a stupid word. It can't be described. It can only be done again."

"What would you like to eat for lunch?"

"Meat. Red meat." And Ralph smiled knowingly. He put out his freckled hand to touch Robert's, brown, lean, unfreckled, and then drew it back guiltily.

"States and churches alike," said Robert, "must forbid pleasure. Pleasure renders the partaker indifferent to the power of both. I would like you to look at this," he then said. "It won't take long. A little thing I started to write." He had taken from the inside pocket of his jacket a page or two of his neat script, the ink purple, the deletions fastidiously ruled, the insertions enclosed in delicate boxes sharply arrowed.

Ralph said, "You read it to me. There's nobody around who speaks English. Indeed, there's nobody around." So Robert read slowly and clearly:

"In the beginning God created heaven and earth. And the lights in the sky and the thundering sea and the beasts of earth and air and water. And he created a man named Adam and set him in a fair garden and said to him: 'Adam, you are the crown of My creation. Your duty to Me is to be happy, but you must work for your happiness, discovering that it is in work that happiness lies. Your work will be pleasant work, that of tending this garden wherein all manner of pleasant fruits and roots have been planted by My Divine Hand for your delectation and sustenance. And you shall overlook the lives of the beasts, that none may prey wantonly on another. And this must be so that death may not come to the garden, for it is a garden wherein immortality must flourish like the rose.' And Adam said, 'I do not know these words, death and immortality. What do they mean?' And God replied, 'Immortality means that each day will be followed by another day and there will be no end to it. But death means that you would not be able to say: *This I will do tomorrow*; for the existence of death means the doubting of the existence of tomorrow. Do you understand?' Adam in his innocence said that he did not understand, but God said it was no matter, the less he understood the better. 'There is,' God said, 'a tree that I have planted in the middle of the garden and this tree is called the Tree of Knowledge. To eat of that tree is the surest way to understand death, for its fruit brings death. Touch it not. You know that to touch it is forbidden, but the beasts do not and I may in no wise make them understand that to eat of its fallen fruit is to court death and the means of death. But it shall be part of your work to keep the beasts away from the fruit of the tree, but therein you shall not wholly succeed, for there are beasts subtler than Adam, and the subtlest of these beasts is the crawling snake of the meadow. No fence shall keep it from the tree or its fruit, but I, your God and Maker, abide by this, since it is I Myself that have implanted the subtlety in the brain of the serpent. To work now, for the day is come, and you shall, when the dark descends, cease from your work and eat of the fruit unforbidden and drink of the water of the crystal stream that runs through the garden, and then you shall compose yourself to rest.'

"So Adam toiled and ate and drank and slept, and day followed night and night followed day and Adam was content but for one thing, and that was his loneliness. For the Lord God had given him the blessed power of speech, but this gift he had not granted to the beasts. Yet sometimes the serpent, that coiled in a kind of love about Adam's body, seemed to understand his words but could not himself reply to them. One evening, when God was walking in the cool of the garden, Adam spoke boldly and said, 'Lord, I am lonely.' The Lord exclaimed at that and said, 'Lonely? How can you be lonely that have My love, that were created to ease My own loneliness, for in you I see the lineaments of Myself and in your voice hear something of My own voice.' But Adam said, 'Lord, I would that You created one like to myself, endowed like myself with speech, one that could tend the garden with me and, at day's end, eat and drink and rest in companionship, two of one kind, the one like to the other.' And God said, 'It is right that I made you, Adam, for you conceive of things whereof I do not conceive, and in this are you become an arm of Myself, Who am Lord of all conception and creation. It shall be as you ask. Eat, drink, retire to rest, and when you wake with the sun you shall find lying beside you one like to yourself who shall be as a companion to you, and his name shall be Yedid, whose meaning is friend.'

"And it was as God said. For while Adam slept God took of the dust of the earth and breathed life into it, and when Adam awoke there lay by him one like unto himself, who spoke his speech and answered to the name Yedid. And in joy Adam was impelled to grasp his companion in love and kiss him with the kiss of his mouth. God saw this and wondered, for Adam had learned that fullness of heart for another that He, the Lord God, felt for Adam but which Adam, who sensed doubtless that his love for God must ever be the love of the created for the creator, could conceive in no fullness. But, thought God, through love of Adam for Yedid and of Yedid for Adam both might be brought to a greater love for their maker. So He was well content. And He watched them entwined in love at day's end or the beginning of the morning and granted them all the joy he could in their embraces. For out of the closeness of their locked lovingness sprang from the bodies of both a substance of joy, gushing like a fountain, of the color of opals, and where it lay on the earth flowers sprung. And all this the serpent too watched, and watched in envy, for he was alone and there was none other of his kind for converse or the joy of love. Thus it was, out of this envy, that the serpent one morning, while Yedid lay still asleep but Adam newly awakened, used words for the first time. And Adam heard the words in wonder.

"The words were these: 'You could in no wise keep me from the fruit of the forbidden tree, fallen or still on the branch, for I am subtle and slender and no way is barred to me. So I have eaten of the fruit and delicious was the taste, yet more delicious was the fruit of the fruit, for this was the fruit of knowledge. Lo, I speak as you speak, and this gift came from the first bite of the fruit, and of the last bite came a most bitter taste and yet delicious, for I saw that in another mouth the taste would be ecstatic and I rejoiced through my imagination in that ecstasy. But the bitterness was the taste of myself, who may see but not act, who may conceive but not create, who may dream of power but not encompass it. The power is for you and for your companion Yedid. Why should you be set in this garden as a mere day laborer, forced to the contentment of food and sleep and the embraces of love, when God who made you rejoices in the abundance of power and knowledge? Knowledge is there for you to taste, and with that knowledge power, and what is God's love that it should deny you a fruit which lies to your hand or dangles in temptation level with your lips? You see a thing, and yet that thing is denied you. What manner of love is this? I have eaten of the fruit and I am transformed and, subtle as I was, am rendered yet more subtle. Eat now, make your breakfast of the fruit, and bid Yedid do likewise.' Then the serpent glided away and left Adam to his thoughts which, when Yedid awoke, he was quick to share with him.

"So it came to pass that both plucked the fruit of the tree and ate, and at once they were furnished with thoughts, and with the means of expressing them, that were able to see God as a thought and, in consequence, see as a thought that which was not God, namely His negation or enemy. This in their eyes diminished their Lord and Creator and they doubted of His power. But this power struck at them. God, Who knew all, knew of their disobedience and was angry, and the expression of His anger was terrible to behold and feel and hear. For the earth shook, so that the beasts ran around with growls and shrieks of fear, and the sky erupted in lightnings and thunders and torrents of seething rain, so that Adam and Yedid prostrated themselves in their terror, but Yedid spoke loud, for the thunder and tremors were deafening, into Adam's ear, crying: 'Is He become the other one? Is He become the one that is His opposite? Is He transformed into the enemy?'

"But then the terror of earth and sky subsided, and God appeared in wan sunlight to Adam and his friend, in the guise of an old man, and He spoke, though in the wavering tones of an ancient, most terrible words. 'Cursed,' he said, 'both of ye, and I repent Me that I made man.' But Adam, with the boldness imparted by the eating of the fruit of the Tree of Knowledge, replied, 'The creator may not repent of his creation. The creator may not wish to be a destroyer.' And God said, 'True, but I may destroy at the same time as I sustain My creation, but in a manner that no eating of the fruit of the tree may reveal to you, for you are still man and hence less than God. From Adam and from Yedid I take the gift of immortality, for both shall die when you are become like to this guise under which I appear to you. You shall grow old and you shall lie at length without life, prey to the sharp-toothed beasts and the birds of the air that will learn to feed on carrion. But though Adam and Yedid may die, the race of man shall continue, and it will be through the coupling of Adam and Yedid.' And Yedid, in his curiosity, asked, 'How shall this thing be, Lord?'

"The Lord replied not in words but in the action of His hand, for He touched Yedid, and Yedid changed. He ceased to be like unto his companion Adam, for his breasts swelled and his belly and hips grew gross, and his sceptered pride was shrunken to nothing as likewise were the twin orbs of his manhood, and he shrieked aloud and covered his loins and cried, 'I am smitten, I am split asunder,' and Adam heard his voice in fear, for it was not the voice he knew, it was a higher voice, closer to the trilling of the birds of the air than to the growl of the beasts of the wood. And the Lord God said, 'Henceforth you are not man but woman, and your name shall no longer be Yedid but Hawwah, which means life, for from your loins life will come and the breed of man shall be sustained. For into where My hand has smitten you the milk of passion shall flow, and from out of where My hand has cleft you the new life shall emerge, for the milk of your embraces shall hold the seed of generation, and from your breasts shall pour the waters of sustention, yet account this transformation no miracle but a curse. For your love shall be a curse, and your bringing forth shall be accomplished in pain. Now get ye hence, both, and take on the burden of life that becomes death and quit the garden of immortality. And the beasts of earth and the birds of the sky and the fishes of the deep shall be tainted with your curse, for immortality shall henceforth be an attribute of the heaven of the spirit and the body shall decay and return to the dust whereof it was fashioned.'

"So Adam and Hawwah went forth in sorrow, and the curse yet holds on the generations of man, save for the blessed. For the blessed remake in their lives the innocence of Adam and Yedid, and their embraces call back the joys of Eden."

Ralph said nothing for a while, then he nodded, saying, "Why shouldn't that be as true as the other story?"

"This," said Robert, "is made true by the sheer act of writing it. Shall we eat something now?"

After their luncheon of red meat and redder wine the two lovers returned to their Eden on the fifth floor of 15 bis, rue St. André des Arts. In the midst of their writhing sweat-soaked embraces Ralph said, "So the beasts become our brothers."

"What do you mean?"

"This." And the boy took his lover like a beast, thrusting his empurpled royal greatness into the antrum, without tenderness, with no cooings of love, rather with grunts and howls, his unpared nails drawing blood from breast and belly, and the sky opened for both of them, disclosing in blinding radiance the lineaments of a benedicent numen.

thirty

"Benedicent numen my arse," Ford Madox Ford pronounced. He breathed out, with the smoke of his caporal, a mephitic hogo that soured the wine in its glasses. That halitosis, however, had to be excused, indeed reverenced: it was the olfactory equivalent of a missing limb, since Captain Ford had breathed in lung-rotting gas, a volunteer infantryman contemned by some of the London literary for his patriotism, a good soldier among despicable scrimshankers. "Not *my* arse," he then said. He then said, "It won't do, will it?"

"Do you mean content, or do you mean style?"

"You can't separate them, as you ought to know. Joe Conrad's sea smells of *Roget's Thesaurus*, as I was always telling him, but he wouldn't listen. Your act of buggery here smells of unfrocked priests. Or untrousered, if you like." He delivered another whiff of phosgene rot. "If by content you mean the general subject matter, seducing a boy and then justifying it by rewriting the Book of Genesis—well, that's nasty enough, but there you have my view as a heterosexual, not as an editor. As an editor, I think your style reeks of dirty shirts and sweaty socks. You may be making your living by writing books, but don't start calling those books literature."

"And what is literature?"

"Oh my dear fellow. Ask Ezra over there. Words charged with meaning, he'll tell you. Make it new, he'll say."

Ezra Pound was, I think, dancing with Sylvia Beach, or it may have been Adrienne Monnier. And you may as well have Ernest Hemingway shadowboxing his way round the periphery. Ford had just lumbered about the floor with a little Irish girl, frizzed auburn, who came up to his breast pocket and so missed the greater part of his panting effluvium. The Irish girl called herself a painter. The band consisted of a black cornetist named Truc Vanderbilt, a drummer with an artificial left arm who came from Marseilles, a consumptive violinist, and my brother-in-law Domenico. The place was the Bal Guizot on the Boulevard des Capucines.

The passage from my novella *A Way Back to Eden*, which Ford had been pretending to read (he read nothing through, ever, unless it was in French; he would just pick out the odd trope and never forget it: *ah yes Benedicent Numen Toomey*) and you have just read, may seem, from its position here, to represent a fiercely resentful reaction to Raffaele's sanctimony, but it was written four years later than that day of the wedding and was rather an attempt to cash in on the new candor which the Paris expatriates, particularly Jim Joyce, were dishing out in the sacred name of modernism. Ford Madox Ford was starting a new magazine called *transatlantic review* (the lower-case initial letters were modish, the Charvet cravat of modernism), and I had a transient itch to be taken seriously by the littérateurs as opposed to my lower-middle-class readers in Camden Town. I had half expected Ford's verdict, but I was bitter.

I said, "You seem to be implying that there's something wrong with making a living out of writing books. I call literature verbal communication. I'm communicating verbally with a largish readership. You'd give such teeth as you have left to be able to do that."

"Not at the price one has to pay, my dear fellow."

"The price of clarity, intelligibility?"

"The price of cliché, half-truth, compromise, timidity."

"There's nothing timid about this," I said, taking from his limp podgy hand the typescript of Chapter Three of *A Way Back to Eden* and waving it at him like a notice of distraint on his goods. "This has never been done before. Don't start telling me about compromise. You can't run a magazine without consulting your financial backers. Don't sneer about timidity. You just wouldn't have the nerve to publish it."

"Call my lack of courage aesthetic fastidiousness. I wouldn't have the nerve to publish a newly discovered draft of a suppressed chapter of *Uncle Tom's Cabin*. Or a Manx rhapsody from Hall Caine. Empurpled royal greatness, indeed. Benedicent numen."

"What's that about Newman?" The music had stopped and Ezra Pound was back at the table. Hemingway was engaged on another lap of shadowboxing. The band was getting up to take its break and Domenico was being rebuked by the cornetist for something, failure to keep time probably. Pound frowned, a bearded but moody poet of great energy. He had substituted for his native Idaho accent a kind of eclectic British English with a rolled Scotch r. "There are not," he said, "many prose writers as good as Newman." He gulped wine.

"Better," Ford blasted at me with his breath. "Perhaps that's what you meant. The empurpled royal greatness of the prose of the benedicent cardinal." He wheezed what was meant to be laughter. "You really have to think these things out first," he told me. "Harmonics, purposed ambiguities. You see how absurd it is having a sainted British cardinal beaming down on a pair of bug-gers." There were no ladies at the table. Sylvia Beach and Adrienne Monnier were on their feet near the bandstand, arguing hotly with, I think, Larbaud. I sulked briefly then perked up. It was envy, these people were envious, even Pound was envious. I had made money out of writing—*Windfalls of the Storm* was in its seventh printing. Anyway, Domenico had arrived at the table. He sat down, at his ease with literary men; his brother-in-law was a literary man. Mineral water was brought for him, stronger drink was forbidden the musicians till closing time. The *patron* had lively memories of a drunken Algerian trom-bonist who had, the night he was fired, used his instrument offensively.

Domenico said to Pound, "You saw Antheil?"

"It will go in, he says. It's the right length." Ford, having a dirty mind, wheezed briefly. Domenico beamed. He looked very much the Latin Quarter Parisian these days, thin, shabby, unshorn, the garret musician straight out of Murger. He and Hortense had a two-room apartment overlooking a timberyard in the Quartier des Gobelins. They were young strugglers, no more money coming in from Gorgonzola, but that was the way she wanted it. He played the piano and copied band parts in a neat hand. He did orchestrations for Paul Trentini-Patetta, the light opera man. He kept on with his composition. He had, I knew, written a fantasia for four player-pianos, six differently pitched Javanese gongs, and a wind machine. This was a kind of belated futurism, stale Marinetti, and it chimed, in its cracked bell way, in with what the American George Antheil was making modish—airplane symphonies and factory cha-connes and the rest of the Bolshevik nonsense. These two, Ford and Pound, thought more highly of Domenico than they did of me. Domenico was *modern*. He played jazz in a real jazz band with a genuine Negro cornetist. This sedu-lously dissonant fantasia of his was going into a concert that Antheil was organizing. The craze-hungry with money would be there—Harry and Caresse Crosby, Lady Gertrude (Binky) Carfax, the Principessa Cacciaguerra. So Domenico beamed. Those days when we had concocted a tuneful and witty one-act post-Puccinian diversion were over. My failure to get the thing done at Covent Garden did not depress him in the least. He was into the avant-garde now. Lessons from Nadia Boulanger? She could teach him nothing about the harmonics of the internal combustion engine. Martinů? He had actually seen a key signature in one of Martinů's scores, terribly *vieux jeu*. He was going to write a concerto for railway engine and orchestra, the orchestra to be accom-modated in drawn coal trucks. Harry Crosby would back that. Then would follow a quartet for Cunard liners, unbacked by Nancy Cunard.

I said to him, "A word with you. At the bar."

He got up shrugging. At the bar were a couple of bored *poules*. It was early yet. The place would fill up with Americans at about two in the morning. The décor of the bar was martini-glass aluminum templates tacked to a steel-blue ground on which clouds of genuine duck down floated. Boris the Russian prince served me a cognac. "She says," I said, "that she's not coming back. Not until she gets a written apology. And if I were you I'd add some flowers."

"I cannot afford flowers and you know it. Bitch."

"You mean myself or my sister? If the latter, don't dare to use that expression again."

"Her place is with her husband. I have my rights."

"She also has rights. Including the right not to be struck in the face wantonly, cruelly, peevishly and repeatedly."

"You know why it was so."

"I know why it was so. And I know," I said more kindly, "that it will happen again unless you both go to see a doctor, a specialist in these matters. There are simple tests. There are cures."

Domenico groaned. He looked furtively around. The *patron* would be in his office at this hour, eating a tray supper brought in from Les Hespérides, a restaurant on the rue de Sèze. "*Vite, Boris,*" he said. Boris gave him a sly cognac. Domenico downed it, returned the glass, the glass was washed, all over. The *patron*, perhaps having once got into the line of fire of Captain Ford, did not go around smelling breaths. To the table of Ford and Pound, I now saw, Hemingway had come, sweating heavily. Adrienne Monnier and Sylvia Beach were also there. John Quinn, a stern American lawyer, attired as for court, entered and looked around him with distaste. Ford and Sylvia Beach waved. Quinn approached them. Pound did frantic fingerclicking for a waiter. I saw what was going on. Quinn had money and was a great buyer of literary holographs. They were going to try to get Quinn drunk.

"It cannot be me," Domenico said. "Carlo says it cannot."

"That's because there are no sterile men in the Bible," I said, "only barren women. Does he propose praying over Hortense to drive out the demons of fruitlessness? Fruitless, totally. Go to a doctor, both." But I knew that Domenico did not desire a child, a son of course, out of pure philoprogenitiveness. There was a lump of Gorgonzola money involved in the production of an heir.

"I'll give you fifty francs," I said, "to buy some flowers. You should be able to get some good ones with that." He sulked. "Look," I said, "I'll write the note of apology for you. All you have to do is to sign it."

He smiled at me with his mouth only. "You are on my side. Why should that be?"

"Male solidarity," I lied. "No man likes to be accused of sterility. Besides, I want her out of my place. Damn it, I'm not her mother, heaven rest her. I'm a strictly male establishment."

"What is she doing now?"

"Sitting there, waiting for that letter of apology." This was not strictly true. She was still in bed, moaning in hangover. I should have been stronger and not let her go the previous night to the Four Arts Ball at the Porte d'Auteuil. Domenico certainly would not have let her. But what could I do? She was twenty-two now, a responsible married woman. Harry and Caresse Crosby, American playfolk, both with beautiful parchment skin and quivering mouths, had seen her lunching with me the day before at L'Alouette on the rue du Faubourg St. Antoine. Me they knew vaguely and vaguely respected as a writer who earned money. They did not know my work but they assumed, since I was living in Paris, it must be fashionably unintelligible except for the sex scenes. They cooed over Hortense's beauty, which was now considerable. That skin, they raved, that hair. She *must* come to the Four Arts Ball. How, I wondered, did Harry Crosby think he was going to be admitted, he was not a student. It was different, of course, for girls. He would get in all right, said Harry Crosby. He would pose as one painting a nude for the Prix de Rome. The motif this year was Roman and senatorial. Bedsheet togas, bodies painted bloody with Caesar's blood, fantastic Medusa coiffures for the girls. I did not like the idea at all. Hortense did, very much. Her eyes grew large, mirroring twice a fat woman nearby who gorged on June strawberries and Chantilly. What could I do?

She had been dumped, this noon after, outside the main door of my apartment building on the rue Bonaparte, red-painted and naked except for a long pale blue man's shirt, with a note attached to a string of Woolworth pearls around her neck: Pour M. Toumy. The concierge quacked long and loud in disgust. I got Hortense up to my flat and fed her strong coffee which did not only not stay down but, the black wave meeting the breakwater of her uvula, came whooshing out unswallowed.

At five o'clock, the hour for my China tea and petits fours, she was blind but articulate, aspirin bouncing off her centers of pain like little rubber balls, in occasional agonies of eructation as effervescent salts chewed at her acid. A supper party first at 19 rue de Lille, where the Crosbys lived. Sackcloth over the walls and chairs and bookshelves. "Stripped like a destroyer for action," Crosby had said. Eighty guests, students and girls. A champagne punch made of forty bottles of brut, five each of gin, whisky and cointreau. Canapés by Rumpelmayer, mostly trampled into the carpet. Harry, Caresse, Mai de Geetere (*who?*) all in the bath together. Harry took a sack with ten live snakes in it to the Porte d'Auteuil. He opened the sack and dropped them from their party loge onto the stripped dancers. Screams, but at the end of the affair a fat black girl was seen suckling one of the serpents. There were some pigeons ritually slaughtered to the opening words of the mass in default of appropriate pagan Latin. Real though thin blood dripping onto the writhing bodies of a couple coupling. Copulation? Oh yes. What did you . . . ? Do you remember anything more? Oh Christ I remember a lot but don't remember everything. She remembered waking up that morning in the Crosby bed with five other people. It was a gramophone woke me up. A man no one seemed to know playing it, dressed only in that pale blue shirt there. Tell me more. *I want to know what happened.* Oh Christ let me sleep.

"Waiting for that letter of apology."

He nodded and then shook his head as if to shake the nod away, left the bar and went back to the dais and the reassembling musicians. Domenico nodded in time to the four-in delivered by the drummer with the false arm, then did a four-bar intro and then they were playing "The Darktown Strutters' Ball." That took me back a bit, all of four years, Domenico and Hortense and I and then that damnable Curry boy. I had been good since, comparatively. Creating lovers on paper. Buying the occasional thighs of a complaisant Senegalese. No commitments, no talking of love except on paper. Lonely as hell, except for my art, such as it was. Adrienne Monnier was trying to persuade John Quinn to dance, but he wouldn't or couldn't. A great big golden woman in royal blue. *"Son frère,"* Boris said, *"est prêtre."* I said I knew.

If Carlo had ever spoken to his brother about the divine mystery of fatherhood, I doubt if Domenico listened or, listening, believed. I had been only a week before to the Catho (I was thinking vaguely of making my next hero an unfrocked priest) to hear Carlo give a very lucid lecture about certain heresies that had had to be uprooted from the Early Church. "Procrustes, Varius, Torquatus and others could not wholly accept the doctrine of the Virgin Birth. They argued over the true meaning of *parthenos*, which they said did not necessarily denote a lack of sexual experience. Saint Vitellius"—or somebody; there were so many of these early saints with names like Roman senators—"delivered a sermon at Antioch in which he said that there are a myriad myriad mothers but only one true father, our Father in heaven. The act of begetting is a creative act as miraculous as the making of the firmament: the divine seed passes from God to woman, but usually God employs a human male as the intermediary seminiferent. There is no necessity for God to do this, and, as a manifestation of his creative monopoly, he fructified the Virgin Mary directly— in the person of the Holy Spirit, whose primary function is that of God the Creator showing himself in human history—so that the birth of his Blessed Son might blazon the true nature of paternity. Human law wisely mirrors theological truth in that it stresses the frivolous impertinence of any human claim to fatherhood by regarding paternity as a state of its nature unprovable. The awful truth, as Tertullian wisely said, is, as so often, enshrined in the speech of the common people. It is a wise child that knows its own father, and, of course, vice versa. Any questions?"

I have a strong recollection of leaving the Bal Guizot (Hemingway drunkenly making an unfriendly Pavian gesture at me, or it may have been one from Oak Park; Quinn very sober, face averted from Ford's breath as if he were confessing Ford) and almost immediately encountering Jim Joyce and Wyndham Lewis at an outdoor table of a café not far from the rue Auber. Joyce liked sometimes to drink in the onomastic vicinity of minor operatic composers. But if this was late June, time of the Four Arts Ball, and the year was 1923, Joyce ought to have been in Bognor Regis listening to the gulls cry "Three quarks for Muster Mark!" This quark was later to be the name given to any of three hypothetical subatomic particles having electric charges of magnitude one-third or two-thirds that of the electron, proposed as the fundamental units of matter. We writers, building greater than we know. I will abide by my recollection in defiance of biographical fact and affirm that I went to sit at his table in June night air that carried the prickle of the charge of a coming storm. Joyce was drunk. He had an empty Sweet Afton packet in his hand, the cigarettes themselves lying on the ground virginal and wasted in a sort of quincunx pattern. Things tended to form into patterns for Joyce, but he could not see the fallen cigarettes at all, not merely because of drunkenness but because of his deteriorating ophthalmic condition, the consequence of adolescent malnutrition and various kinds of self-abuse. Wyndham Lewis was sober and got up to look like an anarchist, though he resembled rather an undertaker. God, was the whole literary world in Paris in those days? Let us bring on Thomas Stearns Eliot so that I may tell him (out of a discovery made in the thirties) that he had no right to be ignorant of, and hence misuse in his *The Waste Land*, the constitution of the Tarot pack. A novelist could never get away with that sort of inattention to detail. But no, I did not meet Eliot till the time of the Spanish Civil War. Did I perhaps tell Lewis to inform Eliot that he had been stupid with his Man with Three Staves, "authentic member" indeed? Joyce said, in his querulous tenor:

"Is that Toomey there?"

He had not read me but he had heard doubtless that I was a mere popular novelist and not to be feared as a literary rival. I think he rather admired me for having made money out of a trade which he himself could pursue only with lavish subventions. I had put on successful plays, whereas his *Exiles* had failed; he recognized that playmaking was more skilled craft than inspired art. He prized my story about being seduced by George Russell in 1904, though he had made me swear to keep it to myself: he feared the impairment of the structure of a book which was supposed to possess the primary virtue of strict adherence to historical truth. Finally, I think he envied me my maternal French, and he sometimes tried to persuade me to spend the rest of my life as chief of the Joyce-translated-into-French synod.

"This is Toomey. Your servant, Lewis." Lewis snarled something back. I put a cigarette in Joyce's mouth and his lips took it with greed like the lips of a diabetic in coma being fed with a sugar lump. I lighted it, and he drew on the scorched tobacco as if only the sensation of labial heat could inform him that he was smoking. A waiter came and I ordered coffee and cognac. Lewis frowned at the waiter and did a squint and lip thrust in Joyce's direction to show that Joyce had had enough of the potable urine in the near empty bottle before him. The typescript of Chapter Three of *A Way Back to Eden*, jolted up by my brief walk, protruded from my inside pocket. Lewis, as if he knew what was in it, seemed to sneer. Well, damn it, for all its crudities it was genuine narrative: something happened in it, for God's sake. Lewis's *Tarr*, out five years back, was all solid bodies that could be moved only with a crane; Joyce was all wordflow. I felt a certain contempt for them both; I said, "A fictional situation. A young man and woman, married, desperately desire a child but fail to produce one. Is it he who is sterile or is it she? He, to whom fertility is an aspect of virility, is reluctant for either to undergo a scientific test. Best to avoid the truth and berate his wife for barrenness. She, more realistic, resolves the issue by becoming impregnated by an unknown man at a party in the dark, an uncharacteristic vitiation of her virtue motivated by love of her husband. A child is born. The husband dare not suspect the truth. Continue the story from there."

"Very piquant," Lewis said. "You come to us for help with the writing of one of your novelettes."

"Och, you're a double-dyed snob, Lewis," Joyce said thickly. "What," to me, "do you call an earwig in your part of the world?"

"An eeriwiggle," I said.

"Eire wiggle," Joyce said in blind smoking joy. "Write it down on this cigarette packet. You err and then you wiggle out of it. Och," he said, "I was never much good at continuing stories. You end there where you said, Toomey. The chief thing is to get a child born." Joyce was, for all his verbal obsessions, often very direct, especially about money. But he had a short story mind. Worse, he didn't like movement if he could avoid it, so that he and Lewis were artistically more akin than either would admit. Novels as still life or sculpture for the one, for the other as massive arias with a lot of ornamentation. "Stertility," he said with sober excitement. "A stertile baron or bassinet of fruitfuit condominya. Shaun. Take that down, Lewis, there's a dear fellow." He could not see the sudden shaft of levin. But, a count after, he heard the thunder. "Oh Jesus," he said, "I can't stand the bloody stuff. Get me a taxi, I have to get hoooome. Oh Jesus Mary and Joseph," as the rumble renewed. Rain began to needle. I got up to look for a cab. Poor fearful Joyce. "Oh blessed Sacred Heart of Jesus keep us from harm." I would, I decided, get Harry Crosby to publish *A Way Back to Eden*. He was always going on about starting the Black Sun Press. Stertile thunder tonitruated terribly. "Oh Lord forgive us our bloody sins." Rain now pelted. It was hard work finding a taxi.

thirty-one

I went into the bathroom, and there was my sister Hortense taking, reasonably enough, a bath. Still, the vaysay was also in this room and I wished desperately to use it. She looked rosy and well, though languid, and her clean brown eyes knifed me as she grabbed a towel to cover her breasts.

"Ridiculous," I said. "You're my sister, I believe."

"You should knock."

"You should lock the door. Anyway, this *pudeur* of yours is a lot of nonsense. *D'ailleurs, je veux pisser.*"

"I'm getting out now. There's no more hot water. Go on, go." It was an old-fashioned bath with lion paws. The plumbing, in the French manner, tried to hide its inefficiency with boastful noise. I saw myself in the washstand mirror, the writer at thirty-three, with the same eyes as Hortense, our mother's eyes, though mine closer set and overwatchful, the brow creased a little in the pain of control of a brimming bladder, the strawy hair sleek with Clovis brilliantine, the guardsman's mustache. "Go," I said.

"May I do this? My back will be turned to you." I pounded my stream, saying loudly, "I want to know what happened last night. And this morning. I want to know who dumped you on my doorstep in that shameful condition."

"Hurry up. This water's freezing."

"Get out of it then, idiot. Wrap yourself in a towel. I don't want to see your nudity. I've no incestuous designs."

She sat shortly after, rosy-footed, in a pair of my black Charvet pajamas, sipping warm milk. This was in the salon, on the seventeenth-century sofa, product of Provence, *garniture en tapisserie au point polychrome de l'époque*. I sat opposite her in a matching *fauteuil*. I had taken the apartment unfurnished and had made it elegant with a bowlegged commode, its marquetry of the *époque Régence*, richly ornamented with gilded bronze; a North Italian *crédence* of walnut with angel's heads, flowery urns, roses; other things. My twentieth-century paintings were in the dining room. Here my pictures of the School of Barbizon—Daubigny, Troyon and Veyrassat—did not quite fit, but there was time enough, there would be money enough. "Do you not worry," I asked, "about the possibility of the hotheaded Domenico's hearing about your participation in the Four Arts Ball?"

"Don't talk in that stupid pedantic way. Reserve it for your stupid readers. He'll only find out if you tell him. Besides, I did nothing wrong."

"This morning you arrived here naked, in a condition of not caring whether anybody saw you naked or not. That's what makes your pudency of just now so hypocritical."

"I was drunk. Anybody can be drunk. I was sober when I woke up and then they started mixing Hangman's Blood. That brought the drunkenness back again. And both these Crosbys said oh what a sweet little girl where did you come from, so they didn't remember. Nobody knew who I was. Then I said I wanted a taxi and they said where to and I said here. Toomey, they said, Toomey, seem to know the name, oh that pederastic purveyor of shopgirl vomit."

"You're making this up."

"Oh, no. I remember very clearly that bit. It's last night I can't remember. And if I can't remember then it never happened is what I say. So you shut up about it and tomorrow I'm going back to Domenico and cooking *angelotti* or *capelli d'angeli* or whatever they are. I never realized there were so many differ-ent kinds of bloody pasta."

"I don't like this swearing, Hortense. And it's no use your saying if I don't remember then it never happened. Supposing you killed somebody and didn't remember, that somebody would still be dead."

My doorbell rang. "Oh Christ, Domenico," she started.

"It's only eleven," I said. "He's still playing. And if you did nothing wrong and nobody remembers what are you worrying about, you foolish child? I know who it is," I said, and got up to open the door. It was Carlo, accompanied by Father O'Shaughnessy and Père Leclercq, temporary professors both of the Catho, Moral Law the one, the Sacraments or something the other. They had come to play bridge.

"A marital quarrel," nodded Carlo, and, in mock-Irish learned doubtless from O'Shaughnessy, "and ye in your night attire flaunting yourself before the holy priests of the Church itself."

"Not bad," O'Shaughnessy conceded, a wiry little man with red hair from the County Athlone, destined, one would have thought, to be curate of a pub rather than one of souls. He and Carlo and Leclercq had been coming here now once a week for the last three months. They had never once been invited. Carlo had brought them in one night, himself uninvited, had handed round the whisky and picked two new packs of cards out of the pocket of his clerical raincoat. He always took charge, of time as well as place. Père Leclercq, from the Midi, liked gin mixed with a little altar wine, or *alt*, as O'Shaughnessy termed it, and a bottle of this, a sort of sugary British port surrogate with Jesus Christ crucified on the label, had been presented to my drinks cupboard by Leclercq himself, myself to provide the gin. Leclercq was too handsome to be a French priest; he had the sort of physique and golden god glow (whence in the Midi? Goths, Visigoths, transient crusaders?) which go with, say, the Director of the Chaplains' Department in the British Army. He would have made, but for his faith, a good bishop of Gibraltar. He had been keen on *le sport* in his time, *le tennis, le rugby, la boxe*. He was not yet running to fat (why do we?) despite the gin and *alt*. They were, all three of them, very good bridgemen. "Sure, I'll teach him proper English in God's good time," O'Shaughnessy leprechaunishly twinkled at me. "Shall we then?" and he pulled the folded green baize card table from behind the *époque Régence commode*. Leclercq got chairs.

Carlo said to Hortense, with a heavy jocular fingerwag, "Too much of this quarreling, Orténsia. You need that place of yours crawling with babies." He made them sound curiously unsavory.

Hortense struck back. "Are you speaking as his brother or as a bloody priest of the Church?" Leclercq, who spoke little English, responded to the tone with bland puzzlement, wetting with his lips the while a Monte Cristo he had taken, uninvited of course, from the humidor. But O'Shaughnessy was delighted.

"That's the way, girl. You give it him hot and strong. Bloody bloody bloody." His psychology was good: she blushed. Carlo remained goodhumored. He was really terribly ugly, fatter than when I last showed him, his big complicated nose a cornucopia of hairs unplucked. His head hair though was fast receding. Those were very gross fingers for the pincering of the host. His clerical suit was crumpled and spotted. Formidable, however, always formidable.

He said, "Mother sends her affection."

"How are things there?" I asked. "How's everybody responding to Mussolini?"

"There's a man," Carlo said to Hortense, "you can say bloody at all you will. Because he is a bloody atheistical *farabutto* with his bloody blackshirts that don't show the dirt. Full of devils and perhaps the big one himself. And nothing inside him to fight back at them. The devil taking possession of bloody Italy."

"But now," I said, "you've nothing to fear from bloody atheistical communism."

"You do not use Beelzebub," he cried, "to drive out Beelzebub. Let us pray, I mean play," he said more gently. "Orténsia, you seem to be very tired, *cara*. Your brother perhaps has been taking you to the Four Arts Ball." It was meant as a joke, but I got a sudden novelist's vision of Carlo disguised as a saxophonist in one of the two bands, seeing it all, including Hortense yielding (now

182

where did that detail come from?) to a young pared man wearing drooped Icarus wings. Hortense, not blushing, said:

"Poked about by Dr. Belmont. At his *centre gynécologique*. A very tiring experience."

"Aaaaaah," Carlo went. "You will have good news for us all?" He was already at the card table, flicking a new pack skrirr skrirr with powerful gambler's fingers. He had a stock of packs, a gift, for some shady reason, from the manufacturer Rouach et Fils. Or perhaps he had just waddled in and said: "Give me those."

"Life is more than that," Hortense said. "A woman is not a childbearing machine. There is the whole of life to be lived. *Je vous quitte, messieurs*," pertly. "I leave you to your fun." And, with no other valediction but "I won't forget my night prayers," she padded on her lovely rosy feet to the spare bedroom.

"A delightful wilful girl," O'Shaughnessy said, "and very close to the Almighty, I should think. Is there any Irish in either of you?" I served him Irish, saying nothing. Gin and *alt.* Scotch, scotch. O'Shaughnessy raised his Irish whimsically to Carlo, bowing as he did so. "Your health, Monsignore."

"Monsignore?" I said.

"Not yet, not yet," grumbled Carlo, dealing.

Nineteen twenty-two would seem in the far future to have been a momentous year for literature, what with productions like *Ulysses* and *The Waste Land*, though not of course my own *Windfalls of the Storm*. That it had been a big year in the sphere of public enactments was, to some, already evident. Mussolini had marched on Rome, or rather his henchman had marched and he had rolled into Termini in a wagon-lit. Pope Benedict XV, that great pacific prelate to whom neither the Germans nor the Allies would listen, Giacomo Della Chiesa, James of the Church, lawyer and diplomat, hopeless with money, his prodigality of aid to the needy having put the Vatican in the red, had died and been succeeded by Pius XI, Achille Ratti from Desio near Milan, Archbishop of Milan for a year, a friend, I gathered, of the Campanati family. "Monsignore?" I should have expected that there would be something for Carlo in the new dispensation.

"The supervision of the spreading of the word," O'Shaughnessy announced as though it were the title of a brief. "The imparting of efficiency to the propagation of the faith. Three diamonds. He'll lose some weight now perhaps."

"Four spades," Carlo said. "I told everybody that the war would seem like a childhood memory of a country outing compared to what would come afterwards. Well, here it is, the diabolic forces more vigorous than ever. Ah, let us play our game."

But we did not play it, chiefly because I was playing like a fool. "You make it too simple," I said, throwing down my cards. "God and the devil stuff. Childish."

"Very well," Carlo bellowed, fanning me with his cards as though the flames were getting at me. "You look at last year—nineteen twenty-two. Stalin elected to the general secretaryship of the central committee of the Communist Party and talking about making the central control commission clean up the country. Purges, he talks of. Look," he turned to O'Shaughnessy, "at your Four Courts being blown up in Dublin and killing everywhere. Greeks," he turned to Leclercq for symmetry's sake, "being massacred by the Turks." We were talking, by the way, in French, except for certain proper nouns. "Nineteen twenty-three and the villains are settled in, grinning. Villainy is very simple, Kenneth *caro*. And the weapons for quelling it are very simple too. The first thing is to stop the flames spreading." He fanned me again. "That is my task."

"The Volstead Act," Leclercq said. "Evil also."

"Evil breeding more evil," Carlo agreed. To me, "I have something for you. From Raffaele." He pulled out a fat wallet whose leather had been nourished, in the manner of Tartar horsemen, by greasy fingers. He looked, grumbling, through its contents. O'Shaughnessy was very red and wagging a nicotined finger at Leclercq. His French became very Irish:

"Don't you call a thing evil that will be the occasion of less of the damnable thing that happened to my sister Eileen in Baltimore. Black men drunk on cheap gin molesting white women."

"They will still get their cheap gin," Leclercq said. "Gin or whisky or cognac that will blind them and give them paralysis and even kill them."

"The Volstead Act was right, the Volstead Act was needed."

"Something from Raffaele to me? Another rebuke for writing filthy novels?"

"He read your new one. He said it was wholesome and not at all filthy. He talks about a change of heart. *Ecco*." He gave me a folded newspaper cutting.

"So," said Leclercq. "Have it in Ireland too. Have it here. Let us empty those bottles into the vaysay."

"It's different with us. We're civilized. We have self-control. A thing like the thing that happened to my poor sister Eileen would not have happened in Westmeath."

"All men are the same. All men have the same rights. To get drunk. To molest women. To repent."

"Wine," bawled Carlo, "you miss the point. The falsification of doctrine. They are saying that Christ turned unfermented fruit juice into his own precious blood—"

I read. It was a brief article written by Raffaele and published in some newspaper. I was presumably to read it in order that my pride in being a professional author should be mitigated by the reminder that anybody could write if he had something to write about. "The law is evil and cannot be enforced in the great centers of population. Scotch whisky being shipped to the British islands of the West Indies and to the French islands of St. Pierre and Miquelon off the Canadian mainland is being smuggled into the United States by means of swift motorboats. The whole of the eastern coastline of the United States is insusceptible to adequate policing. The expected rivalry between bootleg gangs seeking rule over city territories is already being expressed in murder which the police are too corrupt to wish to investigate. I condemn this lawlessness and anarchy, but first I condemn the United States Government and all of the blind Rechabite persuasion of such as Congressman Volstead . . ."

"Yes," I said. "He's right, but he'll get himself into trouble. Why do you want me to read this?"

"He writes well, yes?"

"Well enough. Grammatically, clearly. And so?"

"He wants you to write. You have a name, he says, in the United States, you are known. Articles, he says. You are right about the trouble. He has names and facts. He has contacted the Federal Bureau of Investigation but so far they do little. There is need for great airing of the question. To shame the Congress and the President and the people. Articles, perhaps even stories. You will be safe, you see. He not so safe. He was shy of writing to you direct. He asks me to ask you."

"Carlo," I said, "this is not my trade. I practice an art, such as it is. I'm unskilled in propaganda. Besides, there seems to be a lot of fear in America. Land of free speech but, so I hear, the consequences of free speech can be lethal. Editorial offices set on fire. Editors with meat axes in their bellies. I can write, but there's no guarantee that I'll be published."

"Propaganda," Carlo mused an instant, his scarlet lower lip thrust out. "What is this I hear about your writing propaganda for the children of Sodom? Domenico mentioned seeing something of yours on that desk there."

"I write no such thing," I said, flushed somewhat. "I'm a teller of tales. Domenico had no right—" When could that have been? But publication, the making public, began with the rolling of the paper into the typewriter. I had given up the pen, a more private instrument. Domenico coming in one evening to say he had a solution for one of Joyce's problems. Joyce had said to me something about *insect* and *incest*. The dread word could not be uttered even in a dream, hence the metathesis. But there was something superficial there, whimsical, a mere snigger. There had to be another justification. A musical one? I had suggested. Domenico told me one was available. Joyce's hero HCE resolved into a musical theme, H being the German for B natural. The SEC of *insect* was, again in German, E flat E natural C. The two three-note themes went together in perfect harmony. CES would not do. (Joyce had been delighted.) And I had gone to the toilet and Domenico had read part of Chapter Two.

"All words are propaganda," Carlo said. "Propagandize for a good cause. The sodomites are always with us, happy with their self-elected devils." Innocent, always. "You can speak out and help a man who has become your brother. He must fight with caution. He says the situation will get worse."

I looked at him. "What does Raffaele import, besides dry goods? Chianti, Strega, Sambuca, grappa?"

"The liquor trade has been liquidated. But that is not his main concern. Will you think about doing what he says?"

"No harm in thinking," I said, thinking the foolish laws of the United States to be no business of mine. They had chosen independence a century and a half back and could now stew in their own Californian grape juice. I had my own things to do.

"Let us," Carlo cried, "have a few hands of poker. I cannot concentrate on bridge. That freak in the tournament at Juan-les-Pins," he said in sudden English to O'Shaughnessy. Then he went on rapidly about the proper defense to North's bid of seven hearts, West ruffing the conventional club lead. Then he was overruffed and lost his trump trick. To be expected. A formidable man, the new monsignore.

"*Formidable*," Père Leclercq said, meaning, of course, something different, the flavor of the Romeo and Juliet I had just lighted for him. Or something. I cannot be expected to remember everything.

thirty-two

On the first day of spring 1924 my sister Hortense, in the nursing home run by the Petites Soeurs de la Passion, gave birth to *jumeaux*, *gemelli*, twins. Joy and wonder. Especially since they were, like William and Anne Shakespeare's own pair, a girl and a boy. Two girls would have looked like deliberate Anglo-Saxon insolence to the Campanati family. Two boys might have involved disputes about seniority. A boy and a girl, splendid, both doing well, mother too, genetically artistic, so neat, like an Easter gift box of a red and a white of the same *cru*. The twins seemed to me when I saw them plausibly Anglo-Franco-Italian.

No black or yellow blood there, which was a relief. Hortense, sitting up in early spring rainlight in her turquoise bedjacket, looked me in the eye and I looked her back in the eye. "No more," she said.

"I thought you were all for repopulating the world."

"This is enough."

"Call them Hamnet and Judith. No, perhaps Harry and Caresse."

"You nasty filthy sterile disgusting pig."

"My fertility has never been, nor will it ever be, tested. It doesn't worry me in the least. I am not Domenico."

"Go on, get out of here."

"You used to like me, Hortense. You used to admire me. There was a time when I could honestly say that I believed you adored me."

"Don't make me laugh," she scowled. "Get out or I'll get the nuns to throw you out." I wondered whether to take away with me the huge bunch of mimosa I had brought and give it to the first poor old woman I saw on the rue des Minimes. But Hortense was, after all, my sister.

The twins were christened in the Madeleine, which was the parish church of Hortense and Domenico, since they had now moved to the rue Tronchet. The names chosen were John and Ann, simple names that did not lose their identity when put into French or even Italian: Giovanni would quickly become Gianni, and that sounded like Johnny in American English. Indeed, the boy was destined to be Johnny Campanati when he was taken to California. Those poor children, I think, looking back, one of them to suffer directly and terribly, the other vicariously; but I must not anticipate. I must be like God, giving them the illusion of free will, allowing their future in the spring of 1924 to be as velvety blank as the fine bond which the author, all too soon, will commence to defile with his pen.

Nineteen twenty-four was a good year for Domenico. He rode on the wave of the success of George Gershwin's *Rhapsody in Blue*, first performed that year, being commissioned to compose for the pianist Albert Poupon, who had heard his ridiculous fantasia the previous October, a jazzy concerto with saxophones and wa-wa trumpets and the rest of the nonsense. This work was considered by Vladimir Jankelevitch (*Ravel*; Éditions du Seuil, 1958) to be a sleeping influence on Maurice Ravel, who produced his own jazzy concerto seven years later. This year Ravel had his *L'Enfant et les Sortilèges* presented (libretto by Colette Willy, a very catty woman with a considerable sensual appetite), and there was talk of preceding it with my and Domenico's *Les Pauvres Riches*, but Ravel's friend Ducrateron got in instead with his banal and now forgotten *Le Violon d'Ingres* (which was actually about Ingres and his violin, as though putting all your eggs in one basket meant literally that). Domenico did not repine since, as I have already indicated, he considered that he had traveled beyond that early rubbish, though I observed that he was not above using one or two of its themes for his jazzy concerto. He and Hortense and *i gemelli* were in a much bigger apartment than before, and he had an old Broadwood grand bought at the auction of the effects of poor Edouard Hecquet.

The year began and continued well for me too, though (and my stomach shudders at the prospect of having to set it all down) it ended in agony. It was the year of the British Empire Exhibition at Wembley. This was presided over by the Prince of Wales (whose sculpted effigy in New Zealand butter was one of the attractions of the show) and opened by his father on Shakespeare's birthday. There were Palaces of Art and Industry and Engineering, and this last was six times the size of Trafalgar Square. There was a model coal mine and cigarette factory and printing works, and there were pavilions dedicated to the industrial achievements of the dominions and colonies. There was also the Queen's Doll's House, which had tiny books in its library, distinguished auctorial holographs, myself unincluded as not yet sufficiently distinguished. Kings and queens came to visit the exhibition, and I seem to remember that it was in June that the nominal ruler of Italy and his consort were there, thus being absent from Rome on the occasion of the brutal murder of Giacomo Matteotti, the great progressive and bitter foe of Italy's true new ruler, by fascist thugs. That stupidly overt criminal act might have been the end of Mussolini, but Britain, along with other nations fearful of bolshevism, showed stupid cordiality to him, and Austen Chamberlain was in the Holy City later in the year to praise the ghastly régime.

On May 25 (the day of the deposition of George II, King of the Hellenes, and the declaration of a Greek Republic), my new play, *The Tumult and the Shouting*, opened at the Prince of Wales Theatre in London. This was a tongue-in-cheek piece whose popular success Jim Joyce would have given his left eye (not much use to him, admittedly) to emulate. It was appropriate to the spirit of imperial enthusiasm that abounded and was seen by many visitors to London, but you will not find it in the three volumes called *Toomey's Theatre*. The plot dealt with a young anarchic firebrand, only son of a retired colonial official who suffered terribly from sandfly fever, and he began the first act by screaming against British imperial oppression and shouting the necessity of declaring the Universal Republic of Man. His father, dithering in a febrile bout theatrically highly effective, told him to get out of their Swiss Cottage home if that was the way he felt. I will, I will. He slammed the door, and the quavering father regretted his dismissive heat. The young firebrand did some screaming about human liberty at a public meeting and was beaten up by fascists (I had modeled these on the Italian blackshirts whom I had seen in the European illustrated papers; they anticipated Sir Oswald Ernald Mosley's cornerboys by some seven years). Picked up broken and bloody by a kindly Hindu doctor and nursed back to health by him, he was gently instructed in the virtues of British imperialism and told that from it was already emerging the international commonweal he desiderated. He also fell in love with a dusky beauty, a quadroon from Trinidad, whom the Indian doctor had adopted, and declared his wish to marry her. She ended the play with a speech in which she expressed regret that the time for the mingling of the bloods was, despite the precedent of her own parentage, not yet, though some day it would come. Some day, she said, the brotherhood of all who lived under the British flag would be more than a pious (sanctimonious really) aspiration. For now it was necessary to defer to the prejudices of the unenlightened, thinking particularly of the cross of others' stupidity and ignorance that the offspring of a mixed union, such as herself, still had to bear. The reformed firebrand nodded and nodded, taking on the appearance of a wiser, older, more patriarchal man with a sandfly fever dither, and kissed the sensible quadroon gently on the brow as the curtain went slowly down and the applause started. It is strange now to reflect that both colored parts were taken by uncolored players colored for the occasion, these being Phil Kemble (who still, incidentally, wanted to play Pitt) and Rosemary Fanshawe. We have come a long way since then.

Rudyard Kipling, with his bossy American wife, came to the first night. After all, the title was taken from his own "Recessional" and he had a right to a couple of free tickets and a free drink in the first interval in the manager's office. His wife watched closely as Ferguson, manager, poured Kipling whisky. "Plenty of wawder," she said. When Ferguson offered a refill she said, "No, Ruddy." Kipling began to sing, unexpectedly, from Gay's and Handel's *Acis and Galatea*: "Oh ruddier than the cherry oh sweeter than the berry." "See what I mean?" Mrs. Kipling said sternly to a piece of the wall between myself and her husband.

Kipling said to me, "You young men, you never see what it's all about. The insincerity comes through." His intonation had a lilt which suggested a Welsh background; one did not dare think of it as babu, chichi, a long-learnt gesture of solidarity with the Indian anglophones. The mustache was gray but the heavy eyebrows still black. He had been sunning in Hastings perhaps and was browner than an Englishman should be. His spectacles were as thick as bottle-bottoms, and the eyes swam fierce and enlarged. "A bad play," he pronounced, "so far. But that won't worry you. I wouldn't have come if we hadn't been in town already. *That damned tattoo*," he cried.

"Now, Ruddy."

"You weren't there, Toomey?" No. "The most crude pantomime of my little poem about Gunga Din, with a burnt-corked *bishti* doling out drops of *pawnee* to the wounded under fire and then being shot by whooping tribesmen. He knifejacked up before dying and then saluted. The cheers of the *kuchnays*. Oh my God. And the music. What *was* that music, Carrie?"

" 'Nimrod,' " said Ferguson, who had read the reviews. "Elgar. Sir Edward. From the *Enigma Variations*."

"Oh yes, poor Elgar."

"Poor?" Mrs. Kipling exclaimed. "You should have no sympathy for the man. He ruined your big steamers." I did not understand and showed it. " 'Oh where are you going to all you big steamers?' " clarified Mrs. Kipling. "His setting. Elgar's setting. The music he put to the words."

"We were in the royal box," Kipling told me, "with George and Mary and young David puffing away at his gaspers. Elgar at one end, the wife and I at the other, separated by a large wedge of whatwhatwhat nobility."

"Stop that, Ruddy."

"*Kuchnays* with coronets. We exchanged glances of shame. We're both long past that tawdry expansionism. Elgar and those damnable words. Land of grope and whoredom."

"Ruddy, that is not amusing."

"I'll have another drop of that."

"The bell has gone, Ruddy. We must return to our seats."

"Must we? Got to, have we? You want us to, Toomey? Ah, well. Elgar," he suddenly chortled. "Hippism and microscopy, given up music as a mug's game. And me?"

"Guilt, symbolism and technology," I said, or perhaps did not. I say it now anyway.

"Not bad," Kipling said. "Is there a toilet anywhere near here? Bladder not as good as it was."

"Show Mr. Kipling," Mrs. Kipling ordered me, "to the nearest facility."

The second bell was trilling as Kipling pounded away. "Saw the other Toomey," he gasped. Micturition seemed to take a lot out of him. "Any relation?"

"My brother."

The public had not yet tired of *Rob All My Comrades* at the Cambridge, but the khaki element was giving way to mufti, and in the second act the entire cast was in evening dress. There were also real girls instead of hairylegged transvestites. The title was taking on a bolshevik flavor, and it changed to *Friends, Just Friends* for its next edition. Tommy Toomey's turn was military enough. He was a hawhawing subaltern giving his platoon a lecture on the Empire. Occasionally he would cough and say, "No good, I shall have to give 'em up, what." This catchphrase caught on widely among the million or so British scratchers of carborundum pyrites when Tom did this and other turns on 2LO the following year. The Prince of Wales was to use it while trying an Argentine gasper at the British Exhibition in Buenos Aires. The catchphrase ceased to be funny when Tom's cough was revealed as clearly unvolitional and could no longer be interpreted, to use the new jargon, as a suprasegmental prosodic trope. The damned irony of it, as I have already, I think, said. But Tom was well enough and coming into his success in 1924. He was very amusing with his mixed-up story of Clive of India and the Black Hole of Calcutta (No, Jones 69, I do *not* mean B Company's latrines). He was too good for the show.

We had a late supper one night at Scott's, top of the Haymarket. His lady friend came too, a girl with a blue-black bob and kohled eyes, Estella something, a small actress, an artist's model, anything that offered. She knew exactly what she wanted as we took our seats in the crowded smoky restaurant: potted shrimps, lobster Mornay, a carafe of house Chablis. How we all smoked in those days—Gold Flake, Black Cat, Three Castles, Crumbs of Comfort. All except Tom, who merely coughed. He had *goujons frits*, I coulibiac of salmon. Estella read books. She had read one or two of mine. She thought little of them. Sentimental, she said. Contrived. Old-fashioned.

"All right, Stell, enough," Tom smiled. "This is just biting the hand that feeds you."

"Oh, *his* treat, is it? Well, I mean, compared with Huxley. *Antic Hay*, that's marvelous, isn't it, Tommy, marvelous."

"I only read the papers. Gags, you know," he said to me in apology. "Topicalities. I try to keep the act up to date. You know, so they built a statue of Clive in ghee but it didn't last long."

" 'There was a young man of East Anglia whose loins were a tangle of ganglia.' That's in *Antic Hay*, that's marvelous."

"What are ganglia?" Tom asked.

"It won't do," I said. "There's no other rhyme. Anybody can *start* a limerick—"

"Now you're jealous." She drank Chablis and left a coating of chewed white bolus on the rim. "Aldous is marvelous."

"You know him?"

"We all know him. He's our voice. Postwar disillusionment, you know, marvelous."

"An overtall gangler with glass eyes, mooning after Nancy Cunard. Marvelous, yes."

"Good God," she said, not listening, "there's a coincidence." A young man, very upright, with a trimmed golden beard and, just behind him, a more sluttish version of Estella, overrouged and dirty looking and wobbling on heels like stilts, had just come in, laughing loudly. "That's Heseltine," Estella said. "Or Peter Warlock, his other self. He's in two books, isn't that marvelous, *Women in Love* and this Aldous one." There seemed to be others in Heseltine's company. Heseltine clapped his hands for a table. The place, as I said, was crowded. He lalled mockingly the coda of the finale of Brahms's First Symphony. There had been a Henry Wood Promenade Concert at the Queen's Hall.

Every eye was on him, he glowed. The others in his company seemed to include Val Wrigley, my former lover. I nearly choked on a fishbone as I looked at him. What seven years can do. He had become what used to be known as a *queen*, his hair henna and his gestures elegantly petulant. To my horrible shock Estella waved at him with vigor, rattling the tortoiseshell bangles on her arm. "Val, Val, Val, there's room here."

"Oh no," both Tom and I murmured. She said to me very eagerly:

"The most marvelous poet. If you don't know him you ought to. They did his thing tonight. Do congratulate him."

"What thing?" I frowned. And there Val was, a little tipsy, his eyes not quite in focus, recognizing me all right, bowing derisively to the *cher maître*. She said, all in one breath:

"Couldn't be there Val how did it go I'm sure it was marvelous."

"The words," Val said, "were inaudible. They were the mere vehicle for his gush and flood and bangs. Well, old thing," to me, "sorry I can't stay. You flourish like the rose from the look of you." He sibilated fiercely, spittle rode the smoky air. "My place is with," and he made the name preposterous, "*Bernard*."

"What is this, what's been happening?"

"Bernard van Dieren, you see him? That dim thing with the gray face in napless velvet. *Amoretto Two*, it was called. Words mine, and the scrapes and blowings and chucked fire-irons and hurled dustbin lids all *his*, my dear. His hour of triumph, just look at that beautifully assumed modesty. Come and see me, will you, old thing?"

"Where?"

Estella pouted at the evidence of Val's and my knowing each other and raised a finger at the ancient waiter who trundled the dessert trolley about. With that finger she pointed at what she wanted, with the corresponding one of the other hand she twined a black curl. The waiter mumbled as with distaste at all the chromatic sweetness in his charge and piled her plate with caramel cream, trifle and chocolate mousse with Chantilly, setting finally on top of the mess like a cloacal overflow the sugary buttocks of a meringue. "Oh, I'll be at the Neptune tomorrow night. Most nights actually. Sort of club call it. Dean Street. Lateish."

Sort of club call it. I could guess what kind. "Lateish, yes. I have *royalty* coming tomorrow night. The Clarences, you know." Val was coloring me. I was overstressing and alveolizing, making all preposterous.

"Up in the world, aren't we? Remember Baron's Court and the ragout de bully? So *gray*, just like dear summoning Bernard, and quite as inesculent. I see they actually have a *seat* for me. I must go and be scolded." Heseltine, or Warlock, was roaring something obscene about towsing. Val went, undulant, hands gracefully molding figurines symbolizing regret, grimacing. Then he turned deliberately back to look on Estella, nose wrinkled. "Don't know you, do I? No, thought not." And he went, undulant and so on. The poor silly girl blushed strawberry above her mess.

"Marvelous poet, eh?" I said cruelly. "I discovered him. Some damned thing about a thrush in the heart of Ealing." I would not go. Yes, I would. I was curious. I wanted to see the world into which, had I not exiled myself, I might have fallen. And I wished to bitch at Val, over whose desertion I had once wept. To Tom I said, "You still write to him, Father I mean? I gave it up, so did Hortense. Well, I did drop a note about his being a double granddad, Hortense wouldn't even do that. No reply."

"Well, it's to her I write actually. Doris, our stepmother. I knew her, you know. Who would have dreamt? I didn't actually—you know, but I might have done had I not been so *chaste*." There was a Val-type intonation on that word, but Tom was, of course, now a professional stageman. "She said that Father doesn't particularly like being a grandfather, it's as though Hortense did it to spite him. She says he's well but tired, and we know what's causing the tiredness, don't we? Very advanced, she says he says, the dental work. He's had to get himself up to date, and that's tiring too. American style. They call themselves stomachologists or something. I don't see the connection."

"Stomatologists. Stoma. The mouth. Don't you remember Father Dwyer? Too much stomulia going on here, me boyos."

"He left just after you did. There was no more Greek then."

"I want some coffee," Estella said truculently, "and a crème de menthe." Warlock or Heseltine could be heard clearly reciting what seemed to be a poem by Lawrence in a high parsonical voice. "Of course," she said, "you're both RCs, aren't you?"

"John Milton," I told her, "wrote something about Roman Catholic being one of the Pope's bulls. Particular universal. You see that? And would you perhaps like some coffee? With a liqueur? Perhaps a crème de menthe or something?"

"I already said I wanted precisely those two things. Nobody reads Milton any more. He's *vieux jeu*."

"What terrible French vowels you have." I smiled. "And, for that matter, what terrible manners. Both could be put right, you know."

"All right, Ken," my brother said. "Let it go, please. Don't let's spoil the evening."

"It's the priests who cause that, isn't it?" Estella said. "They make you scared to death of going with a girl because that's the sin of fornication, so you do the other thing."

"What other thing?" I smiled still.

"Please, Ken," Tom said. "All right, Stell, enough."

"Either nothing or the other thing. Tommy ought to be a priest himself. And we can all see what you are."

I looked at Tom, who was blushing furiously. It seemed to me that our whole family was in something of a sexual mess. To Estella I said, "Dr. Freud would be most interested. And your dear gangling ganglionic Aldous. You ought to write an article about it. A new theory of homosexuality."

"*Please*, Ken," and Tom started to cough. He coughed bitterly. "Damned smoke," he gasped, then drank off a glass of water. "Let's get the bill and get out of here."

"I want my coffee," Estella said with governess clarity, "and," with an exaggeratedly correct French accent, "some crème de menthe."

"Somewhere else," Tom still gasped. "Cáfe Royal."

I put a couple of pound notes on the table. "I have to go back to the hotel. A little rewriting. Rudyard Kipling told me I'd got some of my Indian facts wrong." This was a lie.

"Kipling?" Estella said and put out a white tongue tip in a vomiting gesture. "Oh me Gawd. Wen yiou've eard ve heast a-cawwin." Her cockney was very accurate. She leaned back dangling her creamy spoon like a pendulum, and said, "Pansies for thoughts."

"What is that meant to mean?"

"Oh, go, Ken, for God's sake." Tom, white from his coughing, waved my two pound notes at a distant waiter.

"Going," I said, and I went. I had to pass Warlock-Heseltine's table. He, with what looked like potato purée on his beard, was loudly ridiculing the opening of *The Rainbow*: "'For heaven and earth was teeming about them, and how should this cease?' Mark the Nottinghamshire miner's grammar, my bullies." Val twiddled his fingers at me and sweetly mouthed *Tomorrow*. It struck me that I had no friends.

The next day I went to see my literary agent, Jack Birkbeck, whose office was on Maddox Street. The weather had turned chilly and he had his gasfire alight. "I envy you," he said, "getting away from all this. We haven't had a decent summer since the war."

I knew his proleptic modes of speech and understood that he meant something other than my going back to the same chill June in Paris. He was about thirty and totally, one could say obscenely, bald; he had achieved, I understood, this state while only twenty and still at Cambridge and dreaming of becoming a great novelist. He had blistered meaty lips and a pronounced diastema, the top incisors inclining left and right, the consequence of thumbsucking as a child. The interdental gap accommodated a cigarette like a Panglossian holder; he tended, as now, to forget it was there, going *damn and blast* when his lips scorched. He wore a brown suit peppered with blue dots, suitable for the country. I waited. He threw papers around on his desk. "Famous Lasky," he said, "Paramount Pictures, you know, want to buy *The Wounded.*"

"Ah. How much?"

"Oh, a thousand or so, quids that is. For Gibson Gowland. You know him? He's on at Leicester Square, one of these places. Now the next thing is a travel book. Becoming very popular with the world opening up again. Scribner's man Jeffreys was here, we had lunch, he paid of course, he was keen on that. That would be jest fahn ah gayess. He insisted on taking me to the Lucullus, Wembley. The British Empire, he was very struck with the British Empire. India, Ceylon, the Federated Malay States. Now then, here's my idea. You do that, and you also do some so to speak travel stories. Memsahibs committing adultery, planters' wives murdering their Chinese lovers, district officers going down with DTs."

"A rather limited image of the British Empire."

"Well, out east, you know. Eard the heast a-cawwin. You know *Collier's*? I don't mean those dirty poetic men in D. H. Lawrence, I mean the magazine. Thought you did. One thousand dollars per story. They'll arrange a contract for twenty stories, half and half for foreign rights, then perhaps another twenty if all goes well. Really short ones, two and a half of their pages with a big illustration—you know the sort of thing, the memsahib in her camisole threatening a leering muscular coolie with a broken gin bottle. Anyway, it's two birds. You end up with two books, one throwing harsh tropical light on the other. Toomey's East. *Damn and blast.*" That was the cigarette.

"Fifteen hundred dollars," I said. "Short stories are hard work."

"Well, you'll have the book as well. Forty stories, about ninety thousand words all told, a fair size. Anyway, I'll do what I can. So you get yourself some nice tropical gear, including two nice white dinner jackets, American fashion but you could introduce it east of whatsit, and don't bother about a solar topee because those are *out*. I can get expenses out of Scribner's. Or perhaps they and Secker might share. Treat me to some lunch, I think I deserve it."

I took him back to Claridge's, where I was staying, and there was steak and kidney pudding that day, welcome enough in the June cold, no salad weather. A bottle of purple Pommard. Strawberry flan with Devonshire cream. Brandy and coffee and a dish of friandises, all of which Jack Birkbeck ate. Like most literary agents, he had a good appetite. "I don't have anybody coming till five," he said. "We ought to go and see that picture with Gibson Gowland in it. Zasu Pitts. Done by Stroheim, an Austrian. It's called *Greed,*" he said, taking the last two friandises.

"I have to bow to the Clarences. That means sleep and a bath and slow dressing over a cocktail."

"Sleep, yes. Bit heavy, wasn't it, the pudding? Well, you might as well get used to the tropical ziz, as they call it. All right, no movie. A Corona Corona perhaps and some more coffee and another drop of Rémy Martin." And then, as he tried to fit the cigar into the interdental holder and failed, "Why Paris?"

"What do you mean why Paris?"

"You're the sort of writer who ought to be here. Paris is for the international gang that laughs at commas and doesn't write *fuck* with asterisks. It's not you."

"You sound to me as though you're quoting somebody."

"You don't read reviews, do you? Don't blame you really. Well, I wasn't exactly quoting. There was a long article in *The Times Lit Supp*. Paraphrasing call it."

"About me?"

"Nawwwwww, not about you. You're not the type. About what he called the Paris Expatriate School. Anon, of course, but everyone knows it was Robert Lynd, lit ed of the *News Chron*, or some other stay-at-home ess aitch one teabag. There was a sort of tail-end dig at Toomey pathetically trying to be in the Paris fashion with his stream of consciousness and a whole paragraph of upper case with no punctuation."

"Well, he seems to have read *Windfalls* anyway, that's something. Those were meant to be parodic and there wasn't much of it. The great unerudite public didn't complain."

"You need this travel. You need the big winds blowing on you. Did you go to Proust's funeral?"

"I wasn't invited."

"Ingrown stuff, a big incestuous whatsit. That's what he left behind."

"Ganglion?" A strange word, that, meaning either a bundle of nerves or a cystic lesion like a tumor. But to be a bundle of nerves was to be diseased. "Anglia or ganglia, take your choice, is that what you mean? Remember the British heritage and don't mess about with foreign muck. Tour the Empire and come back to London and meet Arnold Bennett for lunch at the club. I don't know what I want, Jack."

"You want to take a P and O from Southampton. I'll ring up Cockspur Street for you if you like. Sooner the better."

"Give me a day or two to think about it."

I slept more heavily than was proper for a siesta. I dreamt that I was putting on a new play whose title was something like *Spicy Garlic Smells*. There was genuine tropical foliage on the stage and I was there, naked, being made love to by a great naked black African under very hot spots and floods. The audience catcalled and I seemed to see Tom's girl friend Estella standing up in the stalls leading the jeers. Royalty was present in the royal box, and royalty, disgusted, stood up and then left. The little pit band started to play the National Anthem. I woke up dry and sweating and rang at once for tea.

The Tumult and the Shouting went well that evening, and the Duke and

Duchess of Clarence graciously congratulated us all, though the Duke seemed to think I was Jerry Comrie, who played the sandfly-fevered father. "Keep it up," he told Jerry, "very powerful, some of it, some damned good lines." Then I walked down Shaftesbury Avenue in tails and light overcoat, turned into Dean Street and looked among the filthy and sleazy for the Neptune Club. It was between a Continental news agent and a condom shop with the Works of Aristotle (the obstetrical monk, on the Stagyrite) on show. The club had an ordinary shop front with the glass mauve opaque. A shopbell tingled when I opened the door. A doorthing said, Yes dear? "I'm a guest of Mr. Wrigley." Who, dear? Oh, *him*. Oh yes, like a worm, we know, don't we?

It was pretty horrible inside. There was a marine motif of nets and ropes in paper cutouts all over the duckegg-blue walls. The bar, over which presided a very muscular man with a sort of corpse maquillage, the club owner, stern, addressed as Paul or Paulie or Pauliballs, had been carpentered into the likeness of a dead-white jollyboat. A boy with lank black hair played the cottage piano nonstop, while another boy fed him cigarettes. "Lady Be Good." "Felix Kept on Walking." "Stardust." No, not "Stardust" that year. And there sat Val, watching the dancing. Tom's coughing of the previous night had reminded me that Val was supposed to be tubercular. He did not seem so now. "How," I asked, "is the chest these days?" We were served light ale.

"Money, you mean? Queer way of putting it. Oh, the other thing. The *chest*." And he pressed his chest with five spread fingers, trying to raise, but not succeeding, a cough. "Oh that was the Keatsian thing I used to be, old thing, used to frighten me sometimes, then I got sent off to this place in Switzerland, Aargau, Argovie, you know it? Very expensive, all that cold bright air, drink it in, do you good."

"Who paid for it?"

"Well, we know who didn't, don't we, old thing? Not your fault, of course. Still, we've both come a long way since then."

"I didn't know there was any money in poetry."

"Oh, there's not. It's the sidelines. Reviewing. I worked on Nancy Cunard's thing for a bit, *Ivory and Ebony*, then she kicked me off and put a nig in charge. Not much ivory left in it by the time she'd finished. I've done a couple of children's books, you know."

"I didn't. So you're all right then, independent and so on?"

"Yes," he sibilated, looking at me none too warmly. "Not *kept*, if that's what you mean. I've been felicitated on the authoritative virility of my verse. Dear Jack Squire, silly old fart. See, look, admire." He was wearing a kind of poacher's jacket over a cream silk shirt, tastefully teased out crimson neckerchief, and peagreen flannel trousers. From a big side pocket he pulled a thin book. Valentine Wrigley. Faber and, highly reputable. The title: *A Feast of Cinders*.

"This is not for—"

"*No*, it is *not* for. *Nothing* to do with *Cinderella* at the *ball*. Look, admire, take in."

A glance or gander of this gandy dancer,
Ganef gannet of mind I mean,
Takes in seasky's immensities,
Black wingtips hid, see crass beak pincer
Thoughtfish, gulp, in a wavewhite preen
On rock rests nor questions what rock is.

"A long way from the thrush in the heart of Ealing."

"Oh, *that*." A boy had started to sing If I were the only girl in the world and you were the only and two other boys were spitefully spoiling the act.

"What's *she* doing?"

"*She* is" (pause) "*hinging*."

"You're staying in London long?" Val asked. "Are you considering even coming as it were," he asked, "home?"

"Well," I said, "I have to confess that I wonder why I'm in Paris. But if I lived in London I'd have to wonder why I was here."

"It's where your language is spoken, dear, your mother tongue."

Mother tongue. It sounded curiously and bitchily physical in Val's mouth. Mother putting out her tongue for a purpose for some reason obscene. "My father tongue," I corrected. "My mother was French." And then, the mention of my mother taking me back to myself wiping tears for Val and catching a train for Battle. "I take it you're not suggesting—"

"I am suggesting *nothing*. I am certainly not suggesting a ménage, if that's what you had in your mind. I've become quite the little Don Giovanni, you know, tikin moi fan where ah fahnds it as dear old terrible Ruddy Kipling says. Oh, look, he's actually done it. I never thought he would."

I could not at first believe my eyes. There wheeled into this club a ridiculously young archbishop in full archiepiscopal robes, ring agleam smirkingly held out for kissing, genuine crosier in hand. The pianist began to play "Whiter Than the Whitewash on the Wall." The club members were admiring and abusive but not astonished. They campily genuflected and osculated. *Lovely* material. Must have cost a *fortune*. Oh, *do* hear my confession. What do we *call* you?

"Autocephalous," Val explained. "No, cephalous not syphilis. You've heard of autocephalous churches, surely you have. Anybody can start one, apparently. Consequence of our break with Rome, or something." The *Rome* grasseyé, petulant, very nasal. I said, marveling at the young mock prelate, crosier in one hand, bottle of Bass's barley wine in the other, no glass, that I just could not, that I had never seen, that the world was full of surprises. "Oh, it is, dear. And don't think that he doesn't *believe*, because he does. The trouble is that anybody who *believes* can't wait till he's got the finery, not theatrical, oh no, the real thing, and then he's the head of his own church, the tail too, and no body in the middle. There's talk of an autocephalous ecclesiastical conference in Whitby I think it is."

"I must send you something," I said grimly. "A rewrite of part of the Book of Genesis I did. His Grace there might like it."

"If it's *mockery*," Val said with severity, "he *won't*. He's very devout. He'd like to convert all these naughty boys here to what he calls the way, the truth, the life. God is not mocked. As a man rose, so shall he seep."

The archbishop raised his bottle of Bass's barley wine like a little trumpet— for some reason it seemed right, drinking straight from that bottle with its red triangle on the label; a glass would have been vulgarly secular—and the pianist, fresh cigarette apuff, began to play "Abide with Me." We cannot dance to that, Cyril. Play "Felix" again.

> *Felix*
> *Kept on walking kept on walking still*
> *With his hands behind him*
> *You will always find him*

A man in full Scots day dress came in, the tartan Stuart. He brought three sailors with him, already drunk. Oh my God, sailors. They were all from Liverpool and they responded complicatedly to the sight of a high prelate in full robes drinking from a bottle at the bar. One of them, full of guilt at something, tried to get out again; another said fucking mockery I'll do the bastard. The archbishop, prepared for the buffetings of the world, raised his crosier in threat. His bottle finished, he lifted two fingers in general benediction, then went out. Fucking mockery. He's fucking real, Curly, there's no fucking law that says he can't have a jar. The three sailors, trying to focus, gazed around and saw me with a white bow tie on. Fucking posh, all got up in his fucking soup and fish.

I said, "It's been nice seeing you again, Val. Now I really must go. I have a little rewriting to do." My intention had been to enjoy making Val snivel somewhat over his eight-year-old, or nearly, treachery. It was clear he would not snivel. "Kipling, no less, found fault with some of my Indian allusions."

"Again?" And he looked at me coldly over his light ale.

"What do you mean, again?"

"That was your excuse for getting away last night, according to that little bitch Estella."

"Whom you alleged you did not know."

"Oh, she deserves it, old thing, real little campfollower, all artiness and no brains, no art, no heart either for that matter. I read her some Felicia Dorothea

Hemans and said it was Tom Eliot, oh how maaaaaahvelous, stupid cow. Which reminds me that your brother can be very witty. He took that line of Landor's, you know, Nature I loved and next to Nature Art, and Art, you know, said Tommy, was the butcher's boy. It's the way he does it, timing. He is, as you ought to know, a real little saint."

"Tom?"

"There was this Estella, a real drab, being given syph and gon and gleet by Augustus John, and Tommy has her living with him in that place of his in Earl's Court and going to a doctor, nothing wrong with her actually but there might well have been, and he never touches her, you know. Naturally chaste. Very generous, your Tommy or Tom. Don't like *Tom* much. We all know what a tom is, don't we? All right, off you go then, you've not changed much, I was going to give you a copy of my poems, signed here and now in a fine flowing hand, but I won't. Ah, trouble."

The sailors were causing it. The man in the Stuart tartan kilt was trying to control them. He did not seem to be a Scot. He had a Levantine accent: You stob dad boyce you my guists rimimber. Well you stop that bastard saying what he just said about me having a fucking red nose will you I won't have no fucker touching my fucking nose without he's given permission. Paul or Pauliballs came from behind the bar to protect his cottage piano, which two of the tars proposed turning on its side. Glass was being crunched into the coconut matting. Most of the club members looked on with shining eyes, trouble their element. "We'll have the police here soon," Val said happily. "They're always watching. They had poor old Paulkins on running a disorderly house once, not here, somewhere off the Edgware Road, innocent as the day, just like this. Always on the move."

"Talking about moving," I said, getting up, light ale unfinished. Val grasped my coatbelt and pulled me down again. Indeed, there was no clear exit at the moment. Pauliballs had the two piano-moving tars well held by their bunched-up sailor collars (intended originally, of course, to protect the jacket under from the tarry pigtail) and was jolting them to the door, telling the kilted Levantine that he could consider his membership void. Fuck fuck you fucking. The other sailor had released a mealy coil of vomit onto the piano keyboard. The pianist and his cigarette-feeder got him for that. Dirty thing.

"Yes, out of course when there's trouble," Val said. "No *Ballad of Reading Gaol* for you, old thing. Respected author in full evening dress has embarrassing brush with the sex police. Toomey taken with filthy tars. Can't have that, can we, dear?"

"Got it in for me, haven't you?" I said. "You walk out and seek the big meat, no time for a struggling writer, and the little treacherous bitch bitches. Not that I care, of course."

"Of course. Best of both worlds, isn't it, dear? You didn't join in the petition, oh no. Five hundred names, but not yours. You scuttled ratlike, but you wouldn't waft the precious clean Toomey name across the Channel, oh no."

"What's this? I don't know anything about—"

"Oh, come off it. Copper in disguise as a rent and poor innocent Kevin takes him home and does nothing except give him a drink and the other bastard bursts in. Oh, you know it, who doesn't? The gloating of the beefy bulldog clean-living popular press. *The Times* too, hypocrites. You got a letter, don't deny it."

"I," I said, "get a lot of letters. I don't read them all."

"How's it all going to be changed? You scuttled, shitting your trousers, we know all about it. Anyway, she's in Australia now."

"That was a long time ago. That was during the war. Besides, we all have to look after ourselves. You were quick enough to do that, leaving me heart-broken—"

Val did a comic doghowl. Then, in a schoolmistressly way, he said, "We have to look after each other. Unless, of course, we're prosperous novelists in exile in places where the laws aren't quite so draconian. There have to be some *real* martyrs, not put-up ones like poor little Kevin Rattigan with the stammer and the cough. A martyr is a witness."

"I'm working over there." I didn't like the quaver of apology but I couldn't control it. "I've written this thing. The first time ever in English fiction—"

"Published in Paris, of course. In *Arsehole International* or some other coterie rag. Under a pseudonym, of course."

"That's not fair."

"Oh, you smell. Go on, off then. Tell the coppers watching across the street about the filth of everybody here. Boys dancing together, constable. I'd made a mistake, officer, I thought it was somewhere different. Just come from bowing to royalty, sergeant. Distinguished playwright. Look into it, duty to the clean-living public. Still stands thine ancient sacrifice. Oh, go on, *get out*."

thirty-three

I was not the only one moving east. There was Carlo too, Monsignor Campanati, roving commissioner for the faith on heathen soil. But his east would be more comprehensive than mine. I was limiting myself to the Malay Archipelago and bits, perhaps, of Polynesia. India was too much, and Kipling had, for the moment, said all that was necessary, but no, there was Morgan Forster or would be. I was to make money out of my trip, while Carlo was, among other things, to explain to the far-flung priests and nuns why no money was available in the Vatican coffers for the further propagation of the faith. Schools, hospitals and so on. Penny catechisms. While dandling his nephew, and mine, on his fat knee, he told me with exasperation of the state of the Vatican finances, while I dandled my and his niece on my bony one. This was in the apartment of Domenico and Hortense. Hortense was reading André Gide or some similar nonsense, and Domenico, scoring paper on piano music stand and pencil like cutlass in teeth, played over and over the same three bars of his slow movement. It was like strong blue peppermint.

"Benedict was bad enough," Carlo said in French (why French? Probably because we were in Paris), "but Pius is the world's great idiot in matters of money. I will tell you." He told off point after point on the child's downy head, ear to ear, occiput to brow, while the child gazed like a drunk at the wonder of its own fingers. "The day after he took office he gave—I will put it in American dollars—$26,000 to the German cardinals because they suffered from the devaluation of the mark. Then he handed over $62,500 to that French sanatorium. Then $156,250 to the Russians. Then $9,375 to the poor of Rome, who probably got drunk on it. Then $50,000 to the victims of that fire in Smyrna—"

"How do you remember these figures? So exactly, I mean."

He stared at me as if I was mad. "Because those are the sums he gave away. Every *centesimo* counts. Then another $81,250 for the Germans, $21,875 to the Viennese, $20,000 for the Japanese earthquake. Something will have to be done. That madman must be forced to see sense."

"Pius?"

"No no no no no." He was irritable today, much to do, off to Rome before off east, the family news not good. He jolted little John or Gianni and the child frowned briefly as at the memory of something similar in the womb. "The brat of the atheistical blacksmith. Benito after Benito Juárez, Amilcare after Amilcare Cipriani, Andrea after Andrea Costa. A revolutionary, an anarchist and a socialist. The three devils within." Out of hindsight I am able to see the whole Lateran business shaping behind Carlo's inkblack eyes. "The Godless animal must be put to work like the ox he is. Good out of evil." He turned to Domenico, whose fine teeth gripped his pencil to snapping while he tested, ear down like a mechanic's to a car engine, the oxymoronic sonority his haired fingers held. "Stop that one moment," Carlo cried, still in French. Domenico cut the chord off, but its harmonics lingered like the memory of a toothache. "Did you too receive a letter from Mother?"

"No, no letter. You know it is only to you she writes."

"Well, there is not much more time, she says."

"*Povero babbo.*"

"You say poor, but he has been virtually dead for ten years and more. When he is truly dead his soul will go to purgatory and then be with God. Now his soul is howling silently for release along the uninhabited corridors of his brain." That was well put, perhaps something Carlo was getting ready for a tactless panegyric. "You had better get over there so as to be present at the end and to make all the funerary arrangements."

"I am the youngest. It should be Raffaele. I am not a priest. It should be you."

"By the time Raffaele arrived it would be all over. He cannot leave his work to bite his nails and wait. For me I must be on the train to Rome tonight and in Tunis in one week." He looked sternly at me and said, "Kuala Lumpur?"

"No, that's not anywhere near Tunis. It's in the Federated Malay States."

"I know I know. Will you be in Kuala Lumpur?"

"I presume so. Quite when I have no idea at present. I have drawn up no timetable. I am to wander, observe, meditate, write as the spirit moves."

"The spirit." Carlo shrugged away certain theological implications and gave little Johnny another jolt. "I," he said, "will be celebrating Christmas midnight mass in the Church of Saint Francis Xavier in Kuala Lumpur. A promise made to Father Chang."

"That's a fair way ahead." Today was August 4, tenth anniversary of the start of the Great War. Work had delayed my setting off, but it would not be long now. London, then Southampton, the P and O 20,000-ton passenger ship SS *Cathay* first class, Gibraltar, Port Said, Aden, Bombay, Colombo, Singapore. "Who," and also Hong Kong for whoever wanted it, "is Father Chang?"

"His first name is Anselm. He was formerly Chang Li Po. I met him in Rome. He is a fine bridge player. He conducts the bridge column in, I think it is called, *The Straits Times.* Under the pseudonym Philip le Bel. The Grand Inquisitor of France." He looked at me as if I, an indifferent player, ought to be holily tortured. "So," he said, "we shall meet. A tropical Christmas," in English.

"And a tropical Christmas to you too." This damnable facetiousness. It was very hot in cold Europe. We were both, though independently, to travel toward truly great heat, and I wondered how fat Carlo would get on in it. Probably very well, sweating buckets.

"There you go again," Hortense said, looking up, excusably, from her Gide, "silly little jokes." But she was nicer to me now, otherwise I would not have been there, dandling a little niece who watched, with slowheaded interest, the flight of a fly. "I don't want to go to Gorgonzola," she told Domenico. "It will be terrible traveling in this heat with the *gemelli.*"

"Ah, but you must," Carlo delivered. "Mother has not yet seen them. It will be a comfort. Life goes on, doubly we could say. Life confronts death and does the *marameo* at it." He sternly demonstrated the *marameo* or long bacon, in the two-handed version, juggling little Gianni perilously on his knee. He grabbed him swiftly as he began to cry. His sister, in a demonstration of twillies, began to cry simultaneously. They were defiling their clouts or napkins. Hortense came for them. "More," demanded Carlo, surrendering his twin and rising. "You must have many more." I surrendered mine and also rose. I saw that Carlo had been sitting on a copy of *Le Figaro*.

"Ah no," Hortense said, a twin howling on each breast. "No more. My duty is done." She took them off. Their nurse, Sophie, was on a week's holiday somewhere.

"A full quiver," Carlo told his crotchet-penciling brother in English. "A quiver full." He liked the phrase. Bow, bow, quiver, shiver, quaver. I was looking at the newspaper, which Carlo's weight had turned into a kind of shallow bowl.

I said, "Good God, Joseph Conrad is dead." Neither Campanati cared. I got a swift and complex image of the austere agony of a white man's soul in the midst of heat, humidity and pullulation. "India, Carlo. Are you going to tell them there about the virtues of multiplying? A child every year and little to eat. A Tamil girl starts at the age of nine and goes on till she drops. Girls old at thirty and breeding like flies or dying of septic midwifery." I had been reading something, not Conrad. A world full of howling kids with wet bemerded bottoms. I was aloof, not breeding, a harbinger of a new rational age in which breeding would be no virtue.

"Souls for God's kingdom," Carlo said. "God will take care of the ratio between the world's population and the food supplies of the world. Today we celebrate the tenth anniversary of the outbreak of a war which reduced the population of Europe by some millions. Out of evil good. Famines, earthquakes. Everyone has a right to be born. No one has a right to live."

"This is terrible," I said, he who had been made to opt for sterility and was, presumably, drawn into Carlo's network of checks and balances, along with wars and earthquakes.

"You think it terrible? There are many things that people say are terrible. They are mostly things that are decreed by the laws of nature, which are God's laws, or by the laws of the Church, which are also God's. A child every year, you say. God foresees all, ensuring that children are not born according to the pattern of cats or ants or rabbits. Hortense and Domenico had to wait five years. He saw that the wait was expedient. And now they may not have to wait so long. The seed flows blessed or unblessed, but man must always assume that it is blessed. And if it does not flow, if it is withheld by holy celibacy, in marriage or out of it, then the term *blessed* or *unblessed* has no application. You understand?"

"Why are you telling me all this? I do not, if I may say so, find it pertinent to my situation."

"I worry sometimes about your situation," Carlo said, shaking his head over a page of Domenico's score. "Do you really mean that diminuendo there?" he asked the composer, who both shrugged and nodded at the same time. Oh my God, he knew far too much about everything except common sense, which is not the same as Aristotelian logic, and homosexuality. They ought, I thought even then, to turn the ugly greedy bastard into a saint. "I wonder," he addressed me, still looking at the music askance, "often what your situation is. Do not you, Domenico?" Domenico said, with a sort of guilty loyalty:

"He does not much care for women, marriage, children. God has said that he shall be lonely. You too, Carlo. In a way. You and Kenneth are in a way like each other." I could not see that. I said nothing. An artist myself, I knew better than to scoff, even inwardly, at another artist's insights.

"It sometimes seems to me," Carlo said, wagging the music at me and creating a small pleasant breeze in the flybuzzing heat of the apartment, "that we will have you back only when you are ready to engage life. Even in sin to engage it. Do you understand my meaning?"

"I must," I said, "have a word with Hortense." She was in the shaded bedroom where a small electric fan sang and staidly wimbledoned. The naked twins punched and kicked as they were fitted with fresh clouts. "I brought," I said, "the spare key. If you have occasion. I mean, is everything all right?" She looked at me coolly but not with hostility, a safety pin between her lips. She removed it to say:

"Everything's all right. Except that I have to find something to do. I thought of learning to sculpt."

I nodded in sympathy. "Being a wife and mother. I understand. Who will teach you?"

"Sidonie Rosenthal."

"Ah." I knew her, a high thin blond woman in her late thirties, a heavy smoker with irritable but clever hands, with a studio just off the rue de Baby-lone. She had recently entered a metallic phase: high thin men fashioned out of bolted steel. "Do be careful," I said. "I mean, don't hurt yourself." And then, astonishing myself, "You, Hortense, are the only one I love. Do please re-member that. You know I mean it." And I kissed her on the cheek, smelling her faint sweet toilet water, as she bent to pin a clout. Then she unbent, placed her hands on my forearms, this tall lovely young woman who was my sister, and kissed me lightly on the lips. I felt a beneficent current cool me and, for some reason, I caught a brief cinema image of Moses coming down with the tablets of the law. "I'll be back," I said, "in the New Year. If he ever wants to hit you, interpose a twin."

And so, fairly soon, off. Planters and government officers and their wives going back off leave, leaving regretfully a European summer: the sun back there was no gift wrapped in two layers of cold, it was an irksome and daily aspect of duty. Children imperiously yelling *"Ayah!"* or *"Amah!"* Kenneth M. Toomey at the captain's table.

A curry was always served as a first course at luncheon in the first-class dining saloon. The passenger three or four places distant from myself regularly ordered the curry with nothing to follow except a jug of milk and some sugar. He ate the curry with bread, then poured the milk and sugar into the rice dish and spooned that up as a dessert. "Sir Albert Kenworthy," the steward told me. "Needn't tell you what he's worth. Always does that, always has done."

The point was: could you make a short story of it? Probably not. Ever since embarkation at Southampton I had been taking notes. I had even been writing stories, typing them straight off on my portable Corona in my Bibby, or L-shaped, cabin. The first was a free fantasy, ready to be mailed by the time we reached Gibraltar, based on the couple in the double cabin next door. He was a fat beersoaker who planted tea near Jaffna, she a high thin blond not unlike Sidonie Rosenthal, though dried up and with a tropical pallor. He snored to wake up the whole corridor. Presumably back on the plantation they had separate rooms, perhaps even separate bungalows. Here she could not sleep, and she was not the only one. I lay awake analyzing the snore, timing periodicity, separating out the snorts and the squeaks, noting the lip shudder, the choke, the groan that occurred in irregular spasms. In my story I made her get up one moonlit night in the Bay of Biscay and lean on the taffrail in her summer frock, pondering her marriage, Philip such a good man except for that snore, and they had tried everything, cotton reels tied to his back, a strip of sticky plaster on his mouth to force him to breathe through his nose, but nothing any good. Then she meets the man from the next cabin, also kept awake by poor Philip, and they commit adultery in his narrow bunk, her very first time but all really Philip's fault, and Philip snores away out of rhythm with their transports. When they get back to Jaffna she insists Philip and she share the same bed again. It is her guilt, she must suffer, but this time, walking sleepless in her negligee under the Ceylon moon, she commits adultery with a big blueblack Tamil, the bookkeeper of the plantation. Overcome with remorse, self-deprived of sleep, foreseeing the impossibility of her position henceforth, she tells Philip she must go home, can't stand the climate any more. He never sees her again. He takes into his bed, on fraternal urging, the sister of the Tamil bookkeeper, a snorer who can outsnore even him, and they live happily ever after. You may know the story: "The Watch of Night." (*Henry IV, Part II*, IV. v. 28. Philip and Helen Biggin. Look it up at your leisure.)

There was a fair amount of shipboard fornication, though none for me. Below decks, I understood, there were riotous midnight parties with stokers in party frocks. The leader of the ship's orchestra and the chief barman in first class were, I could tell, seasoned buggers. The unreasonable prohibitions of land were at sea all suspended. Are navies, marine or fighting, a cultural product of sexual inversion? I sat around with pink gin, the notetaker. My typewriter could be heard during the hours of the siesta. Some of the passengers knew who I was. Going to put us in your next book, Mr. Toomey? They spoke better than they knew. Mrs. Killigrew, whose husband played bridge all the time, discovered a passion for a man whose face was covered with warts. Why was this? In a story you had to find a reason, but real life gets on very well without even Freudian motivations. I asked Sir Albert Kenworthy about the rice business, had to, excused myself as a pathologically curious writer. He was good-humored over his big cigar, said he liked rice cooked that way, salted, unsugared, the sugar added after. Had never cared for rice pudding. Got your main course and your dessert at one and the same time, no waiting. Got lunch over quickly. But why did he wish to get lunch over quickly? This I did not ask.

I had a copy of *R. O. Winstedt's English-Malay Dictionary*, second edition, Singapore, 1920, and I tried to learn five words a day. Open at any page. Demon. Black earth spirit, *awang hitam, jin hitam, hantu hitam*. Muslim demons. *Shaitan, iblis, afrit, ifrit, jin kafir*. No way to learn the language, a tin miner from Ipoh told me. You can't go into a bar and ask for a *hantu hitam*. Though perhaps you could in time. Good name for a black velvet.

At Gibraltar embarked the Bishop of Gibraltar. He was in the bar before dinner as we eased our way away from the Detached Mole with hoots and moans, the great rock to starboard under a sumptuous sky of mauve and gamboge and smashed eggs, the sun's upper tip burning Willis's Farm. He was elegant in lightweight episcopal evening dress, gaitered, his silver shoebuckles ashine. "Toomey," he greeted. "It was at Monte, as I remember, with Carlo. Craps, eh?" A blear-eyed lay drinker, still sweaty from his shore trip, looked at him, not sure whether he had heard right. "I heard of the alliance of your families. A good thing, we need such alliances. What will it be, gin and something?"

"May I," I said, when my stiff pink gin came, "say something about bless thee Bottom?"

The blear-eyed drinker shook his head sadly while the bishop laughed boyishly. "Jolly good, thou art translated. Bombay. One hellhole of a diocese. Pullulation, what will Carlo think when he sees it? A remarkable man. News came of him via Tangier. Legends quickly accrete around him. He is said to have played poker with *sa majesté* and been able to hand over ten thousand francs to the discalced Carmelites of Rabat or somewhere. He won a sheep-eating contest in Colomb-Béchar. Needless to say, I don't believe any of these stories."

His lordship was the life and soul of the captain's table. He could cap

Captain Ferguson's tales of typhoons with horrors of his own, shamelessly lifted from Conrad. He spoke of rat stew on a China freighter, delicious enough if you did not know what it was, like small rabbits, and clean enough, you know, really, none of your sewer chaps, all fat and sleek with the finest grain. He organized a ship's concert the night before we reached Port Said and showed his skill as a light comedian. "A female passenger," he recounted, "on her first evening out of Southampton asked a steward in the first-class bar where the ladies' heads were situated. The steward responded: Portside, madam. Gracious, she exclaimed, don't we stop at Gibraltar? Now I have pleasure in calling on Kenneth Toomey, renowned author and playwright, to sing for us 'Une Petite Spécialité Called L'Amour.'" I could not well deny knowing this song, since I had written the words. It came in that wartime horror, Say It, Cecil. So there I was, Miss Frisby vamping the accompaniment.

> "All the city sparrows
> Are chirping at the sun,
> Market stalls and barrows
> Say morning has begun.
> Light as bright as taffy
> Is sugaring the day
> While you sip your caffy
> Au lait.
> Bite upon your croissant
> And smile upon your love,
> Hear the larks en passant
> Above.
> Paris may be wicked,
> But one thing's pure—
> They make it every day
> In their own Parisian way:
> It's a p'tite spécialité
> Called l'amour."

Then Miss Pauline Higgins of the mottled limbs like underboiled spotted dick danced to "Narcissus" and an asthmatic district officer did card tricks. What a good lot of people they all were, I was betrayed by their applause and too many pink gins into thinking, the red-jowled sustainers of a great empire and their ladies, quaffers and yarners and players of deck games. And this imperial bishop, being shifted along three diagonals across the great board of the great game, was as damned good a chap as there damned well were.

Ah, how I fear this needless clarity of memory. I see it so sharply, the cardroom at three in the morning. His lordship led the nine of clubs and discarded the six of hearts. So Collins the planter threw an eight of hearts and I unblocked the ten of diamonds. His lordship, not too sure about the position of the queen of hearts, led the queen of spades from the dummy. I won with the king of hearts and led the eight of diamonds. His lordship won with the dummy's ace of diamonds and continued spades. I won with the ace of spades and led the seven of diamonds to Collins's nine, squeezing his lordship in the major suits. His lordship knew that Collins still held the nine of spades so had to discard the nine of hearts. I won the next trick with the ace of hearts, but his lordship scored the last trick with dummy's knave of hearts. A bloody damned well-played contract.

At Port Said with the heat really starting the gullygully man came aboard and performed a trick straight out of the Old Testament. He had a drugged snake that was locked into a sleep of absolute straightness, an olive-hued cane with snakehead handle. He threw it to the deck of the lounge and it coiled out of its trance and wriggled. Gullygullygullygullygully. "As for miracles," the bishop said that evening as we drank Stella beer in a shore café where a fleshy Greek belly dancer performed, "when we reach the stage we must some day reach, they will be the first of the discardables. Optionals for the superstitious, of course, no harm in a bit of superstition, like that bloodlike stuff that melts in Naples under the auspices of Saint Januarius. The Eucharist—Carlo and I had a long argument about that in Rome or somewhere. That's where Rome and Canterbury don't see eye to eye, but there must be a way out somewhere—"

The belly dancer oozed toward our table, her cuplike navel apout. The Bishop of Gibraltar gravely tried to insert a British sixpence in it but she grabbed it and said, "Ejcharisto."

"What," I asked, "is going on precisely? A unification of the Christian churches?"

"It will take a long time." This, remember, was late August 1924. "A hell of a time. But there are a few of us—I mean, it was I who proposed a kind of subterranean doctrine that could be called plain substantiation. I don't know why I'm telling you all this. Not much of a religious man, are you?"

"Either," I said, "it's really the flesh and blood or it's not." She now had her complicatedly working bottom toward us, charming an embarrassed table of beef-red laughers.

"A kind of modification," he said vaguely. "Metaphysical, epistemological. It will all have to be thought out."

We were easing through the Suez Canal the following day, Sunday, and the Bishop of Gibraltar held a well-attended morning service on deck. The final hymn sung was "For Those in Peril on the Sea," which was bawled without irony or smiles, though our only peril seemed to be that of grazing the canal embankments. You could see a town clock on one side and one on the other, and they showed the same time. When we entered the Red Sea the heat really raged.

The bishop, in deck-game vest and shorts, sweated under lank hair, an empty pipe between his yellowing teeth, and he pointed to the grim pentateuchs of red rocks and the arid texts of bitter custardpowder desert. He removed his pipe and it nearly tumbled to the deck from his sweaty butterfingers. He pocketed it and pointed again at the fearsome aridity in the grinding churning heat. Women went by positively wilting, underwear straps visible beneath frocks that sweat had rendered transparent. My dear, I'm positively wilting, my dear. Soon be in Aden, my love, demiparadise. "Islam," the Bishop of Gebel-al-Tarik said. "A desert faith, sworn enemy of Christendom, though they have Jesus as a prophet, Nabi Isa or Esa. The inveterate foe. Though can we say that now when a newer foe has arisen, that of Soviet materialism? Once the Christians fought the Muslims, and then the Christians fought each other. Faith is hard to sustain unless it is either beleaguered or dreams the imperial dream. So what fight do we fight now? Are those who accept the dominion of the spirit, Christian, Muslim, Buddhist, Hindu, to unite against its despoilers? God versus Notgod? I must go to my game of quoits."

Halfway between Aden and Bombay there was a dance, evening dress not fancy (that would come the night before Singapore), and the bishop to applause performed a demonstration tango with a Mrs. Foxe. During "Felix Kept On Walking" a typhoon struck. I found myself toiling uphill with my partner, a little girl, Linda something, astonished at the behavior of the chandelier which, with a tinkly warning, agitated all its tentacles to starboard. People passed me downhill as I climbed, bright silks and tuxedos and one woman tumbling to show peach camiknickers. Then the tilting floor recovered and the yelling-and-screaming-no-longer dancers sought the bijou bulkheads, the bandstand, tables before we tilted the other way. Spray and then slogging knouts of water hit the windows or lights like snarling disaffected at a mansion of the rich and frivolous. The Bishop of Gibraltar had somehow got to the bandstand and was clinging, as to a rock, to the fixed grand piano, shouting *Courage courage* or some similar word. The violinist-saxophonist and drummer were packing up, the pianist swigging from a bottle. The ship seemed to labor forward a space without rocking, rolling in a slow and brief rutting movement, then plunged like an otter, then emerged, it seemed, shaking itself, and I and little Linda sat on the bandstand's edge, my arm round a piano leg, she with her arms about me. Could that singing of "For Those in Peril on the Sea" work proleptically, cash paid into the musical bank against an eventually like this? Ship's dancing officers, ready to leave discipline and encouragement to the man of God, this being an act of God, embraced their temporary girl friends, some of them married women, comforting. Then everything steadied, and the bishop, as in a child cyclist's no-hands gesture, raised arms of supplication or praise to heaven. The ship lurched again and he went sickeningly over, embarrassingly, drunk at the altar, cracking his head on the bandstand's sharp selvage. This was shocking, a senior officer of God struck by brutal agents of his own master. He was out and bleeding, and the orchestra leader, who had, I saw, a Craven A between his lips, bent down to inspect the damage.

Ready tars appeared with ropes that they anchored to pillars, gnarled un- afraid men smoked like kippers, their bare horny feet holding the deck, or posh dainty floor, like suckers, except where there was broken glass which, with their own digital wisdom, they avoided without the prompting of their owners. The frightened passengers were encouraged to get up and grip the ropes like tug-o'- war teams and, in a temporary settling, move out to other ropes and their cabins. The ship's doctor was busy elsewhere, but two orderlies came in with a stretcher for the Bishop of Gibraltar. "Right out, Jack," the orchestra leader said through his Craven A smoke. "Poor bugger's concussed."

I went to the sick bay the following morning, when the Indian Ocean was as quiet again as a bluefleeced lamb, and the Bishop of Gibraltar was conscious after a long blackout, though exhibiting the classic symptoms of concussion— irritability, a tendency to drop off without warning, patches of lost memory. "Who the hell are you?" he asked.

"Never mind. How are you, how are they going to get you ashore, how's your control of your limbs?"

"I can't remember the Athanasian Creed." He began to cry.

"It begins *Quicunque vult,* doesn't it?"

"That's Latin, the damned thing's in English, I can't remember it, a damned fool I'm going to look to the Indians."

"Ah, you've not forgotten that anyway. Tomorrow morning we reach Bom- bay. The Athanasian Creed will all come back, you'll see, you'll be right as rain in a couple of days."

"What's rain to do with it? Is it the season of the rains? Have the rains come? Falleth alike on the just and on the unjust. Why did God strike me down?"

"That wasn't God, that was Mother Nature."

"God rides on the storm. There's a hymn about that, Isaac somebodyorother. You'd better hear my confession."

"No, no, you know I can't. Besides, you people don't have concussion. I mean, you don't—"

His bandaged head fell sideways and he began to snore. Poor devil. His poor church. Deck games and tangos. When we arrived at Bombay in great gray humidity, there was a welcoming party of brown clergymen, girls in saris, choirboys singing a hymn unidentifiable as to either words or tune, and an old white man in glossy alpaca who seemed to be the retiring bishop. There were wreaths of frangipani wilting in the damp heat. The quondam Bishop of Gibral- tar tottered but was much better. Indian bearers took his baggage ashore which included, as far as I could tell through the crush, a full-size crucifix perhaps used as a hatstand, and he fussed over everything, waving a walking stick. A

Dravidian photographer enlivened the grayness with flashes, and a Eurasian in a topee from *The Indian Express* (Bombay) asked questions. But the bishop, looking like a haji with his head bandage, spoke words to all in a forward-placed professional baritone. "Struck," he said, "by God's hand but fast recovering, though I cannot remember the Athanasian Creed, I am happy to be with you." Laughter and applause. "Good old bish," one of the Malayan planters said. "We will march forward together in our fight against vicious materialism." Applause and laughter. "All who believe in God, *quicunque vult,* are one body. First things first. May the creeds sink their differences and unite in the face of the threat of a common enemy." This, in early September 1924, was the first public statement ever made, I believe, in favor of an ecumenical movement. God works in a mysterious way His wonders to perform. He somethings His footsteps in the sea and rides upon the. This should have been a historic moment. The retiring bishop got his successor ashore as quickly as he could. Laughter and applause. A couple of Buddhist monks in daffodil robes came aboard later to ensure a continuing religious presence, but they were sailing to Colombo in steerage. We missed the Bishop of Gibraltar, now of Bombay.

Of Colombo I remember one thing only. The local madrigal society gave a concert in the Mount Lavinia Hotel, and a local baritone interspersed some solos, among which was that aria of Gay and Handel, "O Ruddier Than the Cherry." Instead of "Or kidlings bright and merry" he sang "Or kiplings." No one seemed to notice. It is possible that there was an inverted d in his copy. He accepted perhaps without question that there was a class of things called kiplings. I have been haunted by this all my life. Colombo and the collective nightmare of rooks in the great raintree over the hotel and a Handel aria with kiplings in it.

And so at last Singapore came up from the sea in the night, greeted by revelers in fancy dress. I was Julius Caesar, all things to all men, my mustache having been removed distractedly by the ship's barber while I dozed. Disembarkment at noon the following day. My dear, the heat. Life in a slow oven. Someone had chalked, as in welcome, a gross caricature of buggery on the wall of one of the godowns. Singapore duly smelt of boiling dishrags and cat piss. I stayed at the Raffles Hotel which Willie Maugham, under their later notepaper heading, was to laud as breathing all the mystery of the Fabled East. The mystery lay perhaps in the provenance of the meat for the curries. The lounge was as big and bare as a football stadium, ringing with the frustrated thirsty crying "Boy!" The boys or waiters were ancient soured Chinese wandering unheeding forlornly under the ceiling *kipas* or fans. I picked up one tale from a bank manager. Forbes, his young assistant, had had to get to work each morning by way of the Botanical Gardens, which were full of monkeys. He got into the habit of bringing a loaf of Chinese bread with him and throwing bits of it to them, who pranced and gibbered about him, bolting without gratitude. They grew used to his coming and soon took Forbes's bounty as their due. One night he took home a Malay prostitute from the Park of Happiness, was vigorous with her at dawn and then overslept. He had no time to get a loaf for the monkeys. The monkeys were enraged when they saw Forbes breadless and they tore him to pieces. Literally. The entire monkey population of the Botanical Gardens tore Forbes to pieces. You may know the story I made of this, "A Matter of Gratitude."

I took the night train to Kuala Lumpur, the muddy estuary, and stayed at the station hotel for three days. I picked up the materials for "The Smoking Sikh," "Little Eleanor," and "Without a Tie" (the tale of a man who tried to get into the Selangor Club without a tie). Then I went to Ipoh, the tin town, chief city of the state of Perak (whose name means silver, or tin), and there a visit to Kuala Kangsar was recommended to me, the royal town at the junction of the rivers Perak and Kangsar. Picturesque, I was told, with a fine mosque and *istana* where I must make my number, meaning sign the book. Also there was the Malay College, a public school on English lines for the sons of the Malay aristocracy. There was also a peaceful rest house where they served the best damn cup of tea in the entire FMS. From now on for a time my story must seem to be a Tale of Horror and Imagination, but it is all true. In Kuala Kangsar I met, if I may be permitted the novelettish locution, my love.

thirty-four

"Full house," I said, showing two kings and three nines, and then my heart behaved strangely. It bounced at my ribs as though dangled and my arms swiftly filled with air. The air was evidently being drawn off from my lungs. I gasped, tried to stand, then went over. I saw the weave of the fallen rattan chair like some mysterious page of the codex of the dead and then I was out. I came to in, so the planter Fothergill was to tell me, three minutes flat and felt well again though weak. I tried to rise but they said stay there. Greene the planter said he was going to telephone Doc Shawcross. The Chinese boy said it because very hot very hot for new *tuan*. I was, then, on the floor of the Idris Club, saying at least let me have my drink there, so Booth the planter allowed me a sip or two of my Booth's gin *pahit* or *merah*, meaning bitter or pink (red really), holding my shoulders like Hardy Nelson's. The *kipas* spun above my eyes, but the boy, Boo Eng, fanned me with an ancient copy of *The Illustrated London News*. I'm all right, really. You wait, *tuan doktor* he come. You all right, old chap? Really all right? You have to get used to this climate, the humidity causes the trouble not the heat. So I was allowed to sit. You do look all right now but that seemed to me to be rather nasty.

Doc Shawcross found me sipping brandy and ginger ale. "Well," he said, "what's this I hear?" He was a young man in white shirt and shorts and white long stockings, very brown and pared, I could tell, by duty and heat and an athletic or certainly ascetic mode of living, unlike the planters, who were all paunched. The tropical egg, the French called it. "Toomey?" he said. "Kenneth Toomey? But I read you. I've some of your books at home. Well well, we can't allow anything to happen to Kenneth Toomey." He said that with evident sincerity.

"Heart," I said. "It happens very very occasionally. Five years I think it is since it last happened. I'm perfectly all right now."

"Watch the drink. Cut down on the smoking." With his doctor's eyes he had noted my stained index finger. "Don't eat too much. First few months in the tropics and you eat like a horse, I know. Then follows anorexia. Hard to say which is worse. Where are you staying? How long are you staying?"

"Rest house. How long I don't know. I've been writing. This is a good town for writing. Peaceful."

"A drink, doc?" Fothergill offered.

"A *suku*. Plenty of water." A *suku* was a quarter of whisky as a *stengah* was a half. Doc Shawcross had a plain honest face with a high narrow forehead, his hair closecropped sunbleached wheat color. The eyes were a speckled hazel. No sexual heat came out of him. A cool man, cool as his trade. About twenty-nine. "I'll have to give you a bit of a going-over, won't I? A bit rough, our rest house. I thought you might be staying with the DO." Meaning the District Officer, an unliterary man with, I was told, a secret sex life that precluded hospitality. Near the end of his tour, they said, and he wouldn't be coming back. "Or the Sultan, for that matter. Pearce could have fixed that." Pearce was a very old Australian who had married one of the Perak princesses and, a widower now, lived in a sort of gazebo in the grounds of the *istana*. "Anyway, why not move in with me? The doctor's house on Bukit Chandan," meaning Sandalwood Hill, "designed for a married doctor with a full quiver," ah, "but this doctor's by way of being a bachelor."

"That's awfully kind."

"That's a good idea, doc," Booth said. "He can take a trishaw down to the club. Arrange a two-buck weekly contract with one of those bastards. Same time every day." They liked me, I think, or they wanted me to put them in a book, even libelously, no matter, being put into a book was the important thing.

"Come now if you like. My boy can fetch your *barang* from the rest house. Tea should just be about ready."

"That's awfully kind."

"A good idea, doc," Fothergill said, a scrawny bonykneed man with a paunch like a disease though it was only Anchor beer in the evening, Tiger beer in the morning.

"That's really most awfully kind. But I have some packing to do. And must pay the bill."

"Don't you bother about all that," Greene the planter said, a man with appropriately latexlike chins. "That can all be fixed up without any trouble. Those lazy sods at the rest house can do a bit of work for a change, and they won't pinch anything, more than their job's worth. So you go off with the doc and get a bit of a rest and perhaps we'll have a hand or two of something this evening." All these planters were in Kuala Kangsar for the day and most of the night, drove back to their estates near dawn, Rambutan and Pisang and Gutta Percha, all off the main Ipoh road.

"This is really most terribly kind."

So I was taken up Bukit Chandan by Doc Shawcross in his little Ford car. He had a bungalow newly painted green and white by the Public Works Department in a fenced garden cool with bougainvillea, banyan, flame-of-the-forest and wild orchid. He had a great raintree, a papaya tree and two pomelos, as well as three flaring-red pepper bushes, and the gardener or *orang kebun* was at work with a hoe or *chungkol* while a copperhammer bird attended to its distant plumbing. Doc Shawcross parked the Ford in the porch, and we went onto the verandah toward the tinkle of teacups. No, one teacup and saucer, the standard blue of the British community. Yusof the *kuki*, a very muscular Malay with gentle manners, ran off with pleasure to get more crockery and make more sandwiches (corned beef pounded with paprika, paprika being a wonderful reviver in the late afternoon), and Doc Shawcross and I sat creaking on the rattan chairs. Purple clouds were being pulled with haste, like a blanket over pudic nudity, over the duckegg sky, and the view of golf course, mosque, *istana* and distant jungle was fine but glum. "At this time every day, prompt at teatime," he told me, "we get this douche." And gentle rain came down as gentle Yusof reappeared with sandwiches and Tiptree's cherry jam. "*Terima kaseh*, Yusof." Meaning thank you, meaning literally received with love. Then the rain eased and stopped and jungle smells sidled in to growl at the scent of grass refreshed, and the clouds were gone and the sky clear again.

"This," I said, "is all one needs. I hope," I added, "you'll call me Kenneth or Ken."

"Philip, me. When a new planet swims into his. I read a fair amount of poetry. The romantics, you know. I need a bit of beauty in this job. Ugliness, ah—perhaps you'll come round to the hospital tomorrow morning. Run a few quick tests on you. Blood pressure, that sort of thing. Show you what I mean by ugliness, if you can take it. But you can, you're a writer, I've read your things, said that already, haven't I?" He poured me more tea. "You could write here, couldn't you? Very quiet." Very quiet indeed, for the birds of Malaya have no song. There are Christmas Day chirpings from tiny yellowbeaked sparrows, and the other calls are mere noises devised for the benefit of the Chinese, for the copperhammer bird reminds of the virtues of hard work, and the fever bird gives them something to gamble with, for one can never predict whether its descending chromatics will add up to three notes or to four. Thousands of dollars, I'd been told, laid on that. "Yusof," Philip said, *"minta jalan sama Mat kebun ka-rest house dan bawa barang tuan ini ka-sini."* Meaning that Yusof and Mat the gardener were to go and fetch my stuff from the rest house. "You feel like a little lie-down? I have to go back to the hospital. I'll show you your room anyway."

The room was at the back of the house with an uninterrupted view of the jungle. Simple PWD furniture, a bed with a rolled-up mosquito net, a ceiling fan, a bathroom leading off. "This is really most terribly." There was a plain deal desk and before it, ready, a Windsor chair. I foresaw Yusof padding in with ladyfingers or something in a jamjar.

"I'll get Mas, she's the *amah*, to bring sheets. Nice name, don't you think, Mas, it means gold. I've been asked out to dinner tonight, I'll chuck if you like, we could spend a quiet evening at home." *Home.* I felt the promise of the prick of tears at the word, sentimental, noble, nostalgic, yearning, what the hell does it matter? "Or perhaps you'd like to come. He'd take it as an honor, two white men instead of one. A Tamil. Mahalingam is the name. That means great ah generative organ—"

"Goes further, doesn't it, religious, holy symbol of life and so on. Well, yes, why not, thanks, I'm here to learn. Dinner with a Tamil. I thought the Tamils did the rough work out here."

"Not all. I have one in the lab, a good lad, Madras degree. Mahalingam's new, in charge of the waterworks, sent from Penang, at the last club meeting we argued about inviting him to join, but it *is* a white man's club, except for the Malays of course, and the nature of a club is exclusivity. I mean, *we're* not allowed to join the Chinese Club or the Indian. Seems reasonable, really. Now I really must go and do my evening round."

"Perhaps if I just sat on the verandah for a bit."

"You do that. Awfully glad to have you, you know that."

"Oh no, it's I who am awfully delighted, really."

So I sat on the verandah and did nothing except gaze onto the golf course, which was full of natural hazards, and the bulbous mosque and the honey-colored *istana* as the sun made its cautious approach toward plunging plummet-like for the rush of stars and the stride of night, delightful, very much at peace.

I heard the squeak of the wheels of two or three trishaws bringing my *barang* and the soft voices of Mat the gardener and Yusof the cook. Then Yusof came and said, *"Saya buka barang, tuan?"* And he made the gesture of opening bags. *Terimah kaseh,* received with love and two dollar bills which Yusof tucked into the waist of his sarong.

I showered and dressed in gray flannel trousers, white silk shirt and a gold and blue striped tie. The living room was long with a dining alcove, primrose cushions on the sturdy bamboo armchairs, ceiling fans spinning gently at their bottom notch, a bookcase with photographs on it. The women in his life: a plain sister and a handsome mother. His father evidently a doctor too, a smiling snap of him with black bag entering a car. The arms of the University of Manchester on a tobacco jar: Virgil's serpent *arduus ad solem.* A student group, Philip smiling uneasily in the back row, with a scowling professor impatient in the front middle. The books very ordinary, and I make no exception of the one or two of mine that were there, RLS, *The Jungle Book,* Hall Caine, Marie Corelli, the Keats and Shelley in one volume a fourth-form prize, medical texts including Manson-Barr's *Tropical Medicine.* A decent ordinary colonial medical officer, hardworked but comfortable, not overpaid, one of the white leeches to be later vilified by the forces of disaffection, living in a standard pattern colonial bungalow which he called home.

Yusof switched on the lights and drew the curtains of cream and leafgreen and said, *"Tuan mahu minum?"* Yes, a drink would be welcome. He brought me a whisky and soda, cold but without ice. Received with love. *"Tuan datang,"* he said, hearing the Ford before I did. And then there was a weak brandy and ginger ale for Philip as we sat in the delightful languor of a tropical early evening.

I said, "A lonely life would you consider it?"

"Plenty of patients, not much time to feel lonely really, the local planters are decent enough chaps, the odd drink, the odd curry tiffin, the wives are mostly a great pain, was it Kipling who said the fall of the Empire would be due to the memsahibs?"

"It sounds as though it might be somebody from the outside, an American perhaps. How long have you been here and why?"

"Coming to the end of my first tour. Due for leave after Christmas. Why? Oh, I don't know really. The call of the East. Adventure." He said it with an ironic intonation. "I read a book by Conrad. *Youth.* It's there somewhere."

"Conrad's dead, did you know that?"

"I didn't, no, we get the news two months late. Dead, is he? I used to have this dream about being called in to save the life of a great man. I've only saved little men, and not too many of those. I take it you'll be writing about the East now. And then some medical student will read you and say ah adventure and go for an interview in Great Smith Street. A big responsibility."

"So it's not like Conrad?"

"Conrad left out the hookworm and the malaria and the yaws."

"What are yaws?"

"Yaws is not are. You'll see yaws tomorrow. We've got a yaws ward. Tropical paradise, that's a lot of nonsense. Bacilli and spirochetes like the hot damp. Vicious mosquitoes, snakebite. The Malays are mad, they won't report a snakebite, superstitious, then they die smiling, the bite's supposed to bring good luck. Straight to paradise, perhaps, sherbet and houris forever and ever. Then there's *amok* and *latah* and the Chinese have this peculiar disease they call *shook jong*, *koro* among the Buginese. Paradise indeed. And we can't do a thing for them, can't get into their minds. The Eastern mind, the West can't touch it, they say only Karl Marx can get into an Eastern mind because he's down to rockbottom, more rice and kill the bosses. I don't know, I know nothing about anything."

"What are those things, *mah jong* and the other ones?"

"*Shook*, not *mah*. The patient gets the idea that his penis is shrinking and retreating into his abdomen. He gets scared. He ties it to his leg with a bit of string or even tries to anchor it with a pin or a *li teng hok*, that's a special double-bladed knife that jewelers use. Did you ever hear anything like it in your life? Then he dies of anxiety. You can't do a thing. It's all to do with sex, but it's no use bringing Freud into it. *Amok* means running amuck. It's nearly always Malays. They get a grievance and then they brood on it and are very sullen. They kill the man who causes the grievance and anybody else who happens to be around, many as possible. And then the *amok* johnny gets killed himself, if he's lucky. *Latah*—that's infinite suggestiveness. They'll imitate anything. There was one old lady in Taiping, heard a bicycle bell and started to imitate a cyclist pedaling and she just couldn't stop, died of exhaustion. Tell an *orang latah* that his mattress is his wife and he'll start trying to give it a baby. Conrad missed all that."

"The three diseases of modern literature," I said. "D. H. Lawrence for that penis thing, *latah* is it for James Joyce, amuck for this young Hemingway character. Bang bang, punch punch, but it's really the death urge."

"Don't know any of those chaps. You'll have to teach me what to read. Send for books from Singapore, that's what some of them do. Look, we'd better think about leaving. Quick shower, change." He was still in his working shorts. "You look very cool and smart, if I may so say. I like the tie. Shan't be a jiffy."

We set off under a big full moon, bigger than you see in the north, for Mahalingam's bungalow, which was off the Taiping road, easy to find since it was in the grounds of his waterworks. It was warm and damp and I wriggled to detach my damp shirt from my damp back. "How are you feeling?" Philip asked. All right, I said. "Don't eat too much of what he offers. Cold grease, you know. Things looking like toads in warm syrup. Chilies, give you the squitters. Gallons of Beehive brandy, just to show how well off he is. Get offended if you refuse, white man scorning their hospitality sort of thing. Say you've been ill, telling no lie after all, but you just had to come. Knew some delightful Tamils in Ceylon or somewhere. Touchy as hell, some of these people. When I first came here I tried to be matey, you know, sitting at tables with them in drinking shops, chewing the fat. Then one day one of them said to me, Bengali he was, you know, Dr. Shawcross, I despise you. That gave me a shock, I can tell you, but I said why? Because, he said, you lower yourself by drinking with people like me. Oh my God." Flying beetles kept crashing into the windscreen, leaving a deposit like a fingerful of cream and jam. "Look, a flying fox." A *burong hantu* or ghost bird or white owl swooped into the headlights, beaked something green and squirming, then swooped up back into the dark. What looked like a small brown bear hared across the road from jungle to jungle. "Yes, a *beruang* it's called. A bit like bruin, coincidence of course. Wonderful country for animal life, but the beasts get sick too. Scabby old tigers, monkey corpses falling from the coconut trees like coconuts. A big dead python, long as a street, lying in a monsoon drain, a whole menagerie gnawing it."

"Will you come back after you leave?"

"Oh, I'll be back. Somebody's got to do the job. Here we are." He turned left between huge open metal meshed gates, his headlights catching a big board like a language lesson, three alphabets and a platoon of Chinese ideograms. *Pejabat Ayer*, Department of Water. The works lay some way away, moonlit, gray as a prison. Then there was a headlit garden obscene with blooms as if to advertise the virtues of water. Mahalingam, I took it to be, was out there quick-eared in the porch of the bungalow, ready to greet.

"The more the merrier, as you say. Too many cooks spoil the broth, but many hands make light work." It was as if one dicton automatically primed others, relevance being irrelevant. "The name again? Mr. Toomey, very nice in the mouth. A writer? The pen is mightier than the sword, as you say. You must tell me the name of your book and I will get it from the town library." We were now into his living room which, not being in a Class 1 residence, had no ceiling fan. The air was close and complicatedly spiced. "Sit, sit, sitting is as cheap as standing." The standard pattern PWD furniture was a link with *home*; otherwise I was adrift in a world that was not merely exotic but disinterestedly malevolent. I could smell the richness of it. The dining table in the alcove was already set for two and there were blue soup plates containing cold heavy sauced dishes in nursery jelly colors. A desperately smirking youth with bare feet, shirt and dhoti stood by the table, bowing and bowing. "My eldest son," Mahalingam said. "A fool." And he gave Tamil orders for the laying of another place, hitting out at the lad with both hands. The lad ran to a door and opened it, and the jungle noise of females escaped from cast-iron purdah. He ran back with a plate and cutlery, forgetting to shut the door. Mahalingam slammed it and then his son. He bubbled what seemed a disproportionate quantity of Tamil at him.

A smoking Sikh taxidriver in the FMS Bar in Ipoh had told me the fable of the origin of the Tamil tongue. One day the Lord God created all the languages of the world, a tiring and sweaty business. The task done, the Lord God doffed his robe and entered a cold bath his number one boy had drawn for him. Cleansing himself, the Lord God felt a timid tap on his shoulder blade. It was a little Tamil complaining in dumb show that he had not been given a language. "No more languages left," said the Lord God. "You'd better take this." And the Lord God subaqueously farted: worrabarrahotwarrerborrel. And lo, Tamil had come into existence.

Mahalingam was probably about forty-five. In honor of the white visit he was dressed as for tennis with a striped tie very similar to my own. The costume made his blackness peculiarly aggressive. It was really a deep purple with shades of burnt gold under the eyes. Once you got as black as you possibly could you became other colors. In build he was not unlike Carlo Campanati but with a vaster paunch. His feet were bare and his toes prehensile: they seemed always to be about their own work, trying to pick up crumbs and fluff and delicately hammer stray insects. In full face the flatness of his color obliterated all features except the eyes that appeared to have no irises and the forty or so great teeth that champed Tamil and English alike with relish. With a table lamp on him or in profile you saw wholly Aryan features, though wide, spread, big, the nostrils splayed and the mouth corners striving to reach the jaws. A rank but somehow attractive smell oozed with his sweat as he handed me a stiff whisky with ice. He had a Frigidaire, not, like Philip, a mere old-time icebox: it squatted like a disregarded relative in this living room, family photographs glued all over its door, and it hummed and choked as in senility, though it was new.

"That is as you like it, Mr. Toomey, if that is the name, it is what you will or else much ado about nothing?"

"If you had perhaps a little soda water—"

I had said a terrible thing. Mahalingam turned flailing on the boy, who cowered and whimpered. Then he drove him out of the house by the front door, crying his rage. Once he was driven out the boy seemed, from the tinkle, to have money thrown at him. Too quickly, it seemed to me, we heard the noise of a car starting then starting off with, surely, impossible speed. Philip frowned.

"You too have sons, Mr. Toomey, or are you living in a state of unwedded bliss?" I was given no time to answer. "So you have written a book, well, you will find much to write about here, a hotbed of vice, intolerance and ignorance, and also superstition. The doctor here will tell you it is so."

"Oh, come," Philip said. "People are much the same everywhere. In India, too, surely," he added with caution.

"In India, yes, and so I left India. What, Mr. Toomey, do you seek out of life?"

A very straight question. "To enjoy it. To fix the phenomena of human society in words."

"That is very interesting. You think it can be done with words?"

"The right words, yes. If one can find the right words."

"Do you believe in life after death, Mr. Toomey, or are you like your compatriot Prince Hamlet in dubiety since peoples do not come back from undiscovered bourn?"

"I'm not a Dane," I said, "but since Hamlet's Danishness is very nominal I'll accept that— Sorry, not really relevant. Oh, I was brought up to believe in it but now I'm not really sure."

"The personalities of the dead do not in your opinion survive and are not susceptible to be brought back to world of the living by express conjuration?"

On that last phrase the noise of a car swiftly slowing and then grinding to its stop purred and growled in. "Impossible," Philip said. But then the dhotied boy appeared with six bottles of soda water, Frazer and Neave, Singapore, under his arm and in his grip. Mahalingam grasped one rudely, snarling, untopped it with a chop of the side of the hand against the arm of his chair, then poured into my glass as it were insolently, as though pissing into it, railing at his son as the bubbles overflowed onto the floor. I felt I had to get out of here. I might have to simulate a heart seizure, but Mahalingam's son would be terribly blamed for that. This son now let in more jungle female noise for five seconds and then was standing by the dining table with a bowl of what seemed to be saffroned rice, beseeching, smirking, agonizing, he would be blamed if the rice got cold.

"At the table," Mahalingam said, "we will continue interesting conversations."

It is always easier to eat things if you know what they are called or, better, if you know what they are made of. There was no cosmological structure in Mahalingam's meal, at least none that could make sense to a Western mind. To begin with what looked like beef rissoles in a black sauce and find them to be piercingly sweet cakes in honey was disconcerting. I mean, a Western banquet recapitulates the history of the earth from primal broth through sea beasts to land predators and flying creatures and ends with evidence of human culture in cheese and artful puddings. Mahalingam's dinner was all brutal surprises. In a sense it was fortunate he did not name anything, saying, for instance, "That curry you are now eating, Mr. Toomey, you are thinking is made of bats, not aha the cricket variety, we have already eaten crickets, and you are nearly right, for it is flying foxes carefully prepared with nourishing parasite life still clinging to body." When Philip or I had downed a spoonful of colored rice, the wretched boy was there with his dish to refill the plate, so that the torture would never be finished. The sweat poured off all of us, and though the liquid loss was more than made good with Beehive brandy and water, the salt loss was not, since there was not one single item in the meal that had salt in it, nor was there salt on the table.

"There is," Mahalingam was saying, "no death in sense of disappearance forever. Do we not eat the dead? They become a part of ourselves and so go on living. Souls of the dead take other living forms, so my poor mother, long dead in Madras of tertiary fevers, may be in that flying beetle there, or else long eaten by her son in form of beef or sheep or pig."

"You accept," I said, "transmigration, but you are not a Hindu or anything else er er of a known orthodoxy?" The Beehive brandy.

"I am what I am, Mr. Toomey," he said like God, "and have been diligent student of many mysteries. I take what I need from all, but I say religion is mysteries at bottom, and such are not made clear, of very nature, to ordinary peoples. There are holy of holies which man of exceptional intelligence must spend his life seeking and attaining. You may say my religion is personal and electric."

"Surely you mean eclectic?"

"I mean what I mean," he said loudly. "Because you are an Englishman does not mean you have monopoly of the language."

"I do beg your pardon. I misunderstood. I see now what you mean. I thought perhaps you had meant to say eclectic, which is from the Greek *eklegein*, meaning to choose or single out. That you had chosen from the religions of the East, or perhaps of the world, those elements which pleased you best. I do sincerely apologize."

"Your apology," he said generously, "is acceptable. What you say is an acceptable summing up of what I believe. Is your mother living, Mr. Toomey?" he seemed to threaten.

I was happy to be able to say she was dead, like Mahalingam's own, else he might have ranted of white injustice. "Of influenza. There was a terrible epidemic at the end of the war, as you know."

"It took my father and my sister," Philip said. "Within the same week."

"Terrible terrible," Mahalingam smiled, "the consequences of human beings meddling with due processes of nature and upsetting delicate equilibrium of the universe. Now, Mr. Toomey, do you see picture behind me on the wall, above my head as it will be, I think?" I saw it, I had seen it already. It was a framed pictorial chart, in the nursery colors of Mahalingam's own banquet, of a selection of punishments being meted out to brown sinners by what I took to be gods in the forms of elephant- and tiger-headed multibrachiate beings in red underpants. The punished too were in red underpants, and they seemed not to be complaining at being sawn through the middle, decapitated with scissors, and having thick rods thrust down their throats. It was like a page in the colored cartoon supplement of an American Sunday newspaper, though far cruder. It seemed to have no iconic significance in Mahalingam's domestic décor, just something bought for a couple of pice and put on the wall since something had to be done with it, waste not want not; the colors were pretty.

"Yes?" I said, and lowered my gaze to Mahalingam's smiling teeth in time to see him change for a split second into my sorrowing mother and then become himself again. I did not like this at all. I looked at my wristwatch.

"You are thinking, Mr. Toomey, you would like to return to congenial company of European gentlemen, having spent long enough in the household of peoples of exterior race and customs."

"Not at all," I said with guilt. "Dr. Shawcross here ordered me an early bedtime. I've not been too well."

"Collapsed this afternoon," Philip confirmed. "A kind of cardiac seizure. Giving him a thorough examination tomorrow. It may be the heat, of course, he's not used to it. I told him he ought not to come here this evening, but he insisted. Didn't you, ah Ken?"

"I have had," I said carefully, "previous delightful hospitality from gentlemen in Southern India. I wanted to come. I'm glad I came. I think we've both had a most refreshing evening." That word *refreshing*, with its remoter connotations of freshets and bursting water in general, acted on my bowels. "If I could," I said, "make use of your ah." I got up. Mahalingam crashed into his son, being too far away to hit him but making hitting gestures, and the boy bowed and bowed at me, indicating that he would show, would take, do please come, sir. I followed him out of the room and down a dark corridor. He pushed open a door, bowing me toward a Turkish toilet or terrible crouchhole. "What's your name?" I asked. *"Siapa nama?"* He bowed and bowed, gesturing, please now, while it is still there, my father may make it suddenly disappear and blame me for it. I crouched, and he seemed ready to watch me, but I waved him away. He shut the door on me but I heard no departing feet. There was no electric light in the toilet, but a great lamp on the periphery of the waterworks I assumed it to be shone in through the high window and was abetted by the moon. I squirted liters from my anus and found a roll of brown PWD paper. There fell from within the cardboard cylinder what looked like a wickless candle-end. It was wax but also hairy. Was there not something in the Book of Revelations? I dropped it as though it burned. And the moon was as sackcloth of hair and the light of a candle shall shine no more? Nonsense.

"Well," Mahalingam smiled at the front door, "I look forward to reciprocation of hospitality," meaning he was inviting himself back. "Different races must mix together and learn from each other. That also is part of my eccentric religion." For no reason he hit out at his son, who smiled and smiled and bowed and bowed.

"It was pretty terrible," Philip said when we were a good way down the road. "Rank mutton fat. Things rolled in dirty paws. Where the hell did he get that soda water from? He bought it somewhere, but where? There's no *kedai* within seven miles. Out and back like a bat out of hell. I can't think of the word, but that boy reminds me of something, one of those dug-up dead they have in the West Indies, working in the plantations, what do you call them—"

"A zombie. *Zumbi*, a Congo word, it comes in Conrad, I think." I didn't mention seeing Mahalingam turn briefly into my mother. "Have you had medical dealings with any of the family yet?"

"No, but I will have. He'll get his money's worth so to speak out of the department. And more. Paid for in advance with all that horrible muck."

"The whisky was all right. The soda too."

"Look there," and he slowed. In a scrub clearing at the foot of Bukit Chandan, two old Malay women in sarongs knotted just under their armpits were fixing candles into clay sconces. One struck a match. The candles, alight, did not flicker. There was not a belch of wind. The other woman placed, with a reverent gesture, a bunch of horn bananas on a tump of earth. "A *keramat* or shrine," Philip said. "A brother and sister disappeared from near that spot about two years ago. They either ran from home or were grabbed for debt slavery, nasty business, father can't pay his debts, children work for the creditors. According to the locals they ascended into heaven like the Prophet himself. But they come back for bananas and they catch the whiff of supplication, you might say. It's the monkeys that eat the bananas, but nobody ever thinks of that. The place is loaded with superstition."

"Colonialism. The enforced spread of the rule of reason," I said without conviction. Of course, they were right to be superstitious. "But who is going to spread it among the colonizers?"

"I can taste that honey and rancid fat and sliced bull's pizzle thing. Home, home," speeding toward it as to a pocket of health and sanity, "home."

thirty-five

Dawn and half-naked Yusof with bedside tea and a little bunch of *pisang mas*, tiny golden bananas like a cricket glove, he raising arms with no hair in the pits to bunch the mosquito net up onto its frame, smiling "*Selamat pagi, tuan.*" The tropical day as an allegory of life, starting in coolness and cleanliness and Edenic beauty and too soon continuing with sweat and the feel of grubbiness and the shirt and shorts already defiled. It was very brief, the innocent watching of the sun lift onto the lovely green land from the verandah with toast and more tea. And then a Berlioz orchestra of brassy heat and a humidity in which hostile spores rode and danced and the colonial work of vainly trying to turn a wilderness into a garden until the convalescence of evening. Philip and I were in his hospital or *rumah sakit* (house for the ill) by eight, and it felt already like noon. He nuzzled me with his stethoscope and took my pulse and then obliterated it with the pneumatic armlet of his sphygmomanometer. Then he went hmm.

"Tachycardia," he at length said.

"Yes, I've heard the word before. Overactivity of the thyroid gland or something. But it doesn't explain the passing out, does it?"

"I don't think it's serious. You have to live with it. Just as you have to live with being a writer. The two probably have something to do with each other. You shouldn't smoke or drink or make love for that matter, but you will. This condition isn't going to kill you. If you avoid overexcitement you'll probably live to a very ripe old age."

"Good," I said with indifference.

"Now we're going to look at the yaws. You'd better wear one of those white coats. A visiting *tuan doktor*."

The yaws cases were in a long bungalow building across a lawn. "I suppose it's a kind of moral question," Philip said as we walked over. "What I mean is you have a spirochete, just as in syphilis, but you don't have to brood guiltily at having been involved in dirty sex. The virus clings to dirt, true, but that's just dirty anything, walls, floors. Get an open wound, any kind of skin lesion, and you're away. Frambesia is the posh name. You'll see why."

"*Framboises*? Raspberries?"

"You'll see why. The local name is *purru*. That goes well too. Purulent. Only a coincidence, of course."

Two tiny nurses, one Malay, the other Chinese, piquant in crisp white, greeted us at the ward entrance. "*Tuan Doktor* Toomey," Philip said.

"Oh my God."

"Precisely. Or rather not precisely. How can you believe in a God, looking at this gang of innocents?"

Innocent Malays mostly, mostly smiling with hand-to-breast gestures of courteous greeting. *Tabek, tuan.* A monstrous raspberry grew from a youth's ankle, glistening as it oozed, a primary chancre. A boy of six or seven was warted all over with secondary yaws. Tertiary ulceration on a forearm, crab yaws on a pair of Chinese feet. "The women," Philip said, "are behind that curtain thing."

"Oh Jesus Christ."

"Goundou. Tumors have eaten his eyes. The hard palate's gone too. Bone lesions. You can touch if you like. All that skin's healthy. It's just the deformity that puts you off. He can go out now, nothing more we can do. But nobody wants him, he's cursed, he has no eyes. Gangosa or ulcerous rhinopharyngitis. The smell was insupportable, but that's all over. God in his infinite mercy has done with him. No eyes, palate, nose. Otherwise he's all right."

"I think I'll have to—"

"Courage, sir, you're a writer, fearless recorder of God's creation. That one's not too bad, is it? Deformed phalanges, tibial periosteal nodes, dried-up ulcers. Nobody dies, you know. It's not like flu. That's Madura foot, white mycetoma. Shouldn't be in here really, but we haven't room for a separate fungus ward. Here's a nice long word for you—chromoblastomycosis. Like a boat covered with barnacles. But it doesn't touch the sole, look."

"I really will have to—"

"Can't blame you. Let's go and have some coffee. With a nip of Beehive if you like." Out on the lawn I retched emptily. "I suppose I shouldn't," Philip said. "It wasn't fair. But I couldn't have you going back burbling about paradise. Tell England, as they say."

"What did you mean," I asked, back in his office, "about it not touching the soul?"

"The? Oh, I see what you mean. We can't grind our spiritual essence into the ground, but we do the next best thing. We shove it as low down as we can, walk on it."

"Oh, I see what you mean." And I gulped at the syrupy Chinese coffee a Malay peon had brought. There was a private enterprise coffee stall just within the hospital gates. Curry puffs, pao, Rough Rider cigarettes. Such simple amenities were everywhere—in school playgrounds, outside mosques, probably in prisons. "Have I seen the worst?"

"There are less spectacular things. Dysentery, hookworm, malaria and its painful consequence the quinine abscess, trypanosomiasis, ulcerating granuloma of the pudenda—that's pretty spectacular, put you off the act of love forever."

"Has it," I asked, "done that to you?"

"I'll tell you," he said, somewhat fiercely, "I haven't been with a woman since I was a student in Manchester. Of course, it's the big thing for medicals to be screaming womanizers, big and tough, bonechoppers, assault the staff nurse when matron's not looking, dances at Shorrocks's and a quick ram in a dark entry. I did my share. But then I saw the sexual act as a snare, a hairy net. A confidence trick, sort of. I've grown scared of the body. Oh, not as a dysfunctioning organism to be cured, if it can be, but as a bloody trap. I'm not explaining myself well."

"Well enough. What you mean is you *have* been put off the act of love. Ulcerating whateveritis of the pudenda."

"When the urge strikes, and it doesn't often, I go and take a look at Asma binte Ismail's pudenda, with her little sister there waving a paper *kipas* to keep the flying ants off. I can do without it and I have to do without it. The whole bloody East is caught in the trap. Breeding kids so they can have yaws, inedible raspberries. Leprosy. This," he said, as the door opened and a white-coated Chinese entered, "is Dr. Lim. Mr. Toomey the English writer disguised as a doctor. You can take that off now, Ken."

Dr. Lim and I shook hands. "My cousin," he said, "is also Ken, though he prefers the full name Kenneth. I am John, which was not a good idea, because all Chinese are John to white men and it is a kind of insult. But Englishmen are John Bull, so I do not see the insult." He said to Philip, "We have a case of meningitis just admitted. A Malay girl."

"Oh God, that means the whole damned family. Crammed together in an attap hut. I'd better— What do you want to do, Ken? Have you seen enough?"

"If I can pick up a trishaw I think I'll go home."

"Home?" He seemed startled. "Oh, you mean back to the *rumah*. I mean, I'm flattered you should think it such. I can send you back there in the ambulance, but that might scare the wits out of Yusof. Plenty of trishaws out there, if you don't really mind poor man's transport."

So a pair of brown muscular Malay legs pedaled me back, for fifty cents, to the house on Bukit Chandan. The *amah*, Mas, was sweeping out my bedroom with broom in one hand, the Malay manner, a girl with various kinds of blood in her, about four foot ten, charming, probably proud of her gold incisor. "Soon ready," she said in English. "Must make clean."

"How well you speak."

"Little bit here, little bit there. Malaya many language."

How badly I wrote. I took the completed page out of my typewriter two hours later, read it with disgust, and then caught an image of all the badly written pages of the world since the burning of the library of Alexandria, all the bad and useless books cramming the shelves of the world, diseased books, books with yaws and suppurating pudenda being born to clutter and to trap, offering an unreal reality, lies. There was a better and simpler reality in the mere act of sitting here, cool under the ceiling fan in a bare swept room, the windows open to sun and green and birds without song, knowing that Philip would be home soon for tiffin and that *home* was the finest word in the world, no trap or confidence trick, the ultimate unanalyzable, basic as the scent of an English flower.

"*Tuan mahu minum?*" Yusof in sports shirt and sarong was there.

"*Minta stengah, Yusof.*" *Minta* meaning I would be grateful for, be so good as to give me, I beg you to do me the favor of kindly granting me the pleasure of. And then: received with love. A cool whisky and water and a cigarette. The page I had written was tolerable, and the readers of the world asked no more. They would not be pleased with exactness of language: mort meaning the note sounded by the horn to announce the death of the deer; mortmain meaning ownership of land in perpetuity; morphalaxis and morphosis and morula and the morris chair. A Chinese came into the room, and that was enough, slant eyes and bilious complexion. They did not want the exact and only Chinese with gangosa or a Madura foot. We do not wish to frighten our neighbors with exactness. We do not wish to drive them from home.

"A hard morning?" We sat at the dining table under the gentle fan. Canned tomato soup and cold local chicken and a potato salad, sliced papaya to follow. Beer, bitter coffee.

"Like all the rest. The Malay kid with meningitis was in the spotted fever stage, and the local *bomoh* or *pawang* said the body was writing its own special language, all red dots, saying it was nothing to worry about. She'll be dead in a week. Blind, deaf and then dead. It won't matter much. The mother's six months pregnant and it may be a boy next time. Praise be to Allah."

"You don't like God much, do you?"

"When I use the name I mean the other bastard. He didn't fall, he rose. Our theology has been written upside down. Have some more of this papaya. Not that it has much taste."

"But it's delicious. Could I perhaps have a little sherry on it?"

"Of course." He reached for the bottle of Amontillado on the sideboard and laughed. "The man before me, O'Toole, he had a Chinese *kuki*. Drank like a fish, brandy mostly, O'Toole had to keep his bottles locked up. Except the sherry, which he kept in the icebox. Well, he found the level of the sherry going down a little day by day, so O'Toole thought he'd have some sport with his *kuki*, so he peed in the bottle day by day, just enough to restore the loss. But the loss continued so eventually he tackled his *kuki* and accused him of getting at the bottle. The *kuki* denied it, said he didn't like sherry, too weak, not like good old brandy. Well, asked O'Toole, what's been happening to it then? Oh, said the *kuki*, every day I put just a little in the soup." Before I could fabricate a hearty laugh, he said, "Do you think we ought to have Mahalingam here for dinner?"

I was touched. It was already *we*. "I have a feeling that you ought not to let Mahalingam past your door. Why not invite him to a Chinese restaurant or something?"

"That wouldn't be at all the same. That would be evading the duty of reciprocal hospitality. We'll have to have him, but not yet. Put it off for a bit. All life is putting off. Well, not entirely. I have an operation this afternoon, an appendectomy. Perhaps you'd like to see it? Very crude, of course. Old John Lim with the chloroform pad and me with the knives and forks and the needle and thread."

"Thanks, but I think I'll write. I *can* write here. I think you'll have quite a job getting rid of me."

"Stay as long as you like. It's nice having someone to come back to."

"It's nice having someone coming back. Well, *someone* isn't quite the exact pronoun, is it?"

"No, it isn't. What would you like to do tonight? I have my *munshi* coming just after dinner, twice a week, laid down in the rules, the government pays. But that's only for an hour. We could go to the Royal Electric Cinema."

"What's a *munshi*?"

"A *guru*, a teacher. Syed Osman has me translating the *Hikayat Abdullah*. Into English, then back into Malay, then we compare. It's the exams, you see. We have to take these exams, and if we fail they invoke the efficiency bar. That means no increase in salary. I'm afraid I cheat with the old *Hikayat*. There's a translation of the whole thing in *The Journal of South East Asian Studies*. I pinched the appropriate number from the club library. Put it back of course when I'm done, if I ever am."

"What is it?" I recognized myself, somewhat sadly, as being a bookish man, ears pricking at the mention of a book unknown in an unknown language, any book, any language. Novelfodder, playfodder.

"It's this *munshi* that Sir Stamford Raffles had. He wrote his life story, but most of it's about Raffles. A white empire builder seen from the viewpoint of one of the natives." Novelfodder. I felt stirring a known excitement. "He thought the world of old Raffles, and quite right too. He built Singapore with his bare hands."

"May I see? The translation, I mean."

"Of course."

That afternoon I read the brief autobiography, lying on the bed under the gentle fan. I tingled cautiously. A novel about Raffles, an East India Company clerk who got Java out of the hands of the French during the Napoleonic wars, ruled it like an angel, then grabbed Sumatra, then negotiated the purchase of a lump of swampy land called Singapore. And what did he get out of it? Nothing except fever, shipwreck and an early death. The story to be told by this hypochondriac Muslim Abdullah. I could see my novel done, printed, bound, about a hundred thousand words, displayed in bookshops, rapturously praised or jealously attacked. *King of the Lion City*, by Kenneth M. Toomey. No, *Man of the Eastern Seas*. I held my novel in the fingers of my imagination, flicking, reading: "The fever bit badly tonight. The candles flapped in the first warning gust of the monsoon. His hand shook as he sanded the last page of his report to the EIC in London. A house lizard scuttled up the wall cheeping." My God, what a genius I had then, was about to have then. And, of course, besides, I clearly saw, the writing of a novel about that old Malaya necessitated staying here and staying put. Odd trips to museums somewhere, Penang, Malacca, but the writing done here, in this bare room, *tuan mahu minum*, a queer case of propro this morning at the *rumah sakit*, home. You could write short stories anywhere, a novel required a base. No, *Flames in the Eastern Sky*. No, *He Built an Island*. "I, who am called Abdullah and am by trade a *munshi* or teacher of language, sit here pen in hand remembering. The ink dries on my penpoint but tears remoisten it. I am remembering my old master, an *orang puteh* or white man from a far cold island, one who was father and mother to me but has abandoned me to a loneliness which only memory can sweeten." By God, I would do it. Novel in the morning, short stories in the afternoon. I must go halves with the rent and the provisions. *Lion City*, that was it. I saw the jacket illustration: a handsome weary man in Regency costume brooding over a plan with a Chinese overseer, a background of coolies hacking at the mangroves. By God, the book was ready except for the writing of it. I deserved a light sleep till Philip's return and teatime.

thirty-six

"The point is," the District Officer said, "that people are talking." He stood in the corner by the magazine table, which had been pushed right to the wall to make more room for the dancers. The ceiling fan just above, whirring at top speed, was leafing rapidly through an old *Tatler*. The gramophone was playing a waltz:

*What'll I do
When you
Are far away
And I am blue
What'll I do?*

There were a lot of unplayable records: the heat had turned those unprotected by the icebox into shallow soup plates. The club secretary had been heartily blamed for this and had resigned. He said orders had been given to Ah Wong, number one boy, but these had been ignored or ill understood. Still, there was a tango, "*La Paloma*," and a couple of one-steps, including "Felix," and some Irving Berlin waltzes. And Greene the planter could bash out the odd tune on the tropicalized piano. All the wives were here tonight, uniformly shingled by the town hairdresser Fook Onn, wearing new flowery frocks from Whiteaway's in Ipoh. They spun in the arms of black-tied sweating men, one of whom was Dr. Philip Shawcross, neat, spare and grave. He grinned gravely as he passed and the District Officer frowned. The District Officer was not a dancing man but he drank enough to slake a dancer's thirst: his tenth or so unwatered pink gin had just been handed to him by Boo Eng.

"Who," I asked, "is talking, and what precisely is being talked about?"

"It's unusual to say the least. You shouldn't be here by rights. Kuala Kangsar is a place for visitors to, well, visit. I didn't want to have you into the office about this. You're not a colonial officer, you're outside my jurisdiction. Still, you're sharing government accommodation with the District MO, and that sort of drags you into the, sort of, a bit. When I say people are talking I mean they're making sort of sly remarks about two men living together."

"There are plenty of them, aren't there? Symes and Warrington in the Malay College, those two in Drains and Irrit Irrigation. Bachelors sharing, there's a lot of it."

"Well, if you want me to come out straight with it, there's the matter of your reputation—"

"Literary reputation?" I said, swallowing.

"Well, look, I don't know much about the kind of world you live in back home except that it's a bit, you know, well, we're pretty conventional here, have to be. They say you're a well-known author, must be true, found your name in *Who's Who* and so on, afraid I don't know your stuff, don't have much time for reading, but, well, this man passing through, whatsisname, the MP—"

"Colin Garside?"

"That's the one, he said something, look, this is rather embarrassing—"

"You started it. What do you have to say?" The DO, Porson, was a man of fifty, wholly uncharming, with only one mobile eye, the other perhaps glass, crooked brown incisors that fanged his lower lip even when his mouth was shut, and dandruff on his collar.

"You've been here well over two months, that's a hell of a lot of time for a mere distinguished visitor. When are you moving on, shall we say?"

"Blunt, very. I'm writing a novel. About Sir Stamford Raffles. Malaya's the place to write it in. Philip Shawcross has kindly given me a quiet place to work. The rest house here is *not* quiet. I pay for my keep. If you like, I'll write to the Colonial Secretary, I know him slightly, get formal permission. The Sultan is delighted I'm here, or so he says. One of his daughters is at the London School of Economics. She saw a play of mine."

"You know the Malay expression *kaum nabi Lot?*"

"Yes. Strangely enough, I heard it used of you. Tribe of the prophet Lot. It should really mean those who are *against* sodomy, but the Koran probably got it wrong. I think you ought to confront Philip Shawcross with the term. He's nothing to lose. His tour's nearly over. He'll carve you up with a scalpel."

"I've said my say." And he loudly called, "Boy, gin *merah*."

"You've more than said it. It strikes me that you've made a very slanderous accusation. Cloaked in a piece of periphrastic Malay."

"It strikes me," and his voice began to trill deeply as in a gargle of blood, "that you're no different yourself with your saying that you first heard that used about me."

"The slander's not mine, if it *is* slander. It's what one of the girls in Taiping said. At the Gates of Heaven cabaret. A girl from Kelantan called Mek Hitam."

"And I'm only saying what people say. The same as you. So I suggest we drop the whole business."

"It was you who started it."

"I was merely doing my duty." Boo Eng brought his gin *merah*. Received without love. The waltz ended and the dancers clapped the recorded dance band. "Informing you about the general feeling."

"Which you'll now do your best to exacerbate. It makes me feel unclean. It makes me want to leave. With an unfinished book. A book that will not now be dedicated to the friendly community of Kuala Kangsar. Because of the unfriendly attitude of its District Officer."

Greene sat down at the tropicalized upright among backslaps and good mans and began to play "If You Were the Only." I went over to Mrs. Renshaw, wife of the headmaster of Malay College, and asked her to dance. Her back was damp, our joined hands were damp. A dance was a very damp occasion. The French chalk on the floor had become a tenuous light gray mud. "When are you coming over to dinner?" she asked. She was a pretty little woman from the Black Country with a translucent wart on her brow that her damp coiffure no longer masked.

"When you invite us."

"Inseparable, aren't you? I've already asked Phil Shawcross but he said something about you working like a fury."

"That's true. A novel about Raffles." The DO was now at the bar talking grimly to Grieves, physical training instructor at the college. Grieves looked at me. What was being arranged? A serenade on Bukit Chandan, the word *homo* set to the Westminster chimes? A rugger club roughing up of a rich visitor here on the cheap, a member of the *kaum nabi Oskar*?

Her eyes showed her brain churning from raffles to gentleman crook to the founder of Singapore. "Oh, *that* Raffles. That's going back a bit, isn't it? There won't be any of us in it."

"Why not? You'd look beautiful in a Regency ballgown. And I have a very villainous Malay who looks a bit like the District Officer."

"Oh Mr. Toomey, you authors." How many had she met? Our dancing tour of the room had brought us to the street door open for the heat. A lot of the townfolk were there, tolerantly observing our fun, chewing wads of *sireh*.

Mahalingam was there, agitated. He grasped my sleeve. "If You Were the Only" ended with sung rugger club harmony. Claps and cheers. "Good evening, Mr. Mahalingam," Mrs. Renshaw said queenlily. The tone of condescension was not willed, it never was, it was the unconscious product of long cultural transmission, never to be eradicated. Mahalingam seemed to make a distracted forelocktugging gesture.

He said, "It is Dr. Shawcross I want. Where is Dr. Shawcross?"

He was at the far end of the room. A fat planter was demonstrating to him the agonies of some disease of the joints. Mrs. Renshaw was grabbed by Symes the English teacher for "Felix." "Some trouble, Mr. Mahalingam?" I asked.

"My son. He will not wake up. We have tried everything."

I threaded through the dancers and got Philip. As we threaded together, I heard someone whistle "Here Comes the Bride." "Your son?" Philip said. "The one we saw? The one you call a fool?" That was nasty but a mere natural emanation of situational authority. "I'll come."

"Shall I come too?" I asked.

"Nothing you can do. I'll see you back home. Had enough of this anyway." So I went over to the bar. I would have one more drink and then pick up a trishaw. The DO was no longer there, was perhaps micturating out his load of gin *merah*, but Grieves greeted me cheerfully though with shifty eyes.

"Still pushing the pen? A deathless masterpiece born in the suburbs of KK? Have a drink."

"Have one with me. Nothing deathless, just practicing my trade. No pen, I use a typewriter. *Dua stengah*," I asked Ah Wong.

"Speak the lingo, eh? Good for you. Nothing like knowing the lingo."

"A few words, no more. Just enough to get around. Cheers."

"Chahs." There was a certain difference in our accents, but it was surely unseemly of Grieves, a Liverpudlian I gathered, to mock the difference. He turned on his barstool to grin at the sight of Mrs. Hardcastle, whose husband was down with gyppy tummy or something, whispering something hotly to Grieves's colleague Warrington as they trod the floor in steps uncoordinated. "Looks as though Jack Warrington's getting in there," he said. "He's left it pretty late. Could have had it a year back."

"Dissatisfied colonial wives," I said. "Yes, I've heard about the phenomenon."

"Heard about it, have you? The onlooker seeing most of the game. Of course, a lot depends on what game you play." I ignored that; I even smiled pleasantly. Fothergill the planter came up. He had removed his jacket and also his black tie; he was wiping face, neck and a good deal of his chest with a glass cloth from behind the bar. He ordered a pint of lime juice with a quadruple gin in it, saying:

"I don't know why we're such bloody idiots. Sweating cobs, as they say in your part of the world," to Grieves. To me, "Don't see much of you, never even got my revenge."

"Revenge? Oh, poker. I've been working. Evenings I came in here you weren't there, simple as that."

"A lot depends," Grieves said, "as I said." The DO appeared from the yard at the back where the jakes or *jamban* was, raised two fingers at everybody in grim and qualified blessing, then was off. "He's done well," Grieves said. "He's kept it quiet."

"Kept what quiet?" Fothergill said. "Oh, that. He just has them in and then out. A buck a time, fifty cents for infants. A good clean thrust before dinner, gives him an appetite."

"Like Norman Douglas," I said, perhaps unwisely.

"Don't think I know him," Fothergill said. "If you mean old Potch Douglas, he was very clean-living, know that for a fact." He downed half of his pint gin and lime with gulps like labor contractions.

"A bit of brown," Grieves said. "No harm in it if he keeps it quiet. But bugger a man that sets up house and home with his own kind. Lets the side down."

"I take it," I said boldly, "you're referring to homosexual relationships. As opposed, shall I say, to impersonal bouts of sodomy."

"Homo," Grieves said, "meaning a man. Man and man. *Homo homo* it would be in the glorious Malay lingo. Yes, something like that. Two more of these," he said to Ah Wong. "*Dua stengah lagi.*"

"A common error," I said. "The homo bit doesn't mean man. It's not Latin, it's Greek. Meaning the same. Sex between members of the same sex," very ineptly put.

"Well, we haven't all had the benefit of a classical education." Grieves smiled pleasantly at me, signing sightlessly for two *stengahs* in his club book. "Not like Norman Douglas and the rest of the Greeks. Take this in your right hand, remembering the ancient Greek wisdom about a bird never flying on one wing." The gramophone was playing "What'll I Do" again, but not many were now dancing. Exhaustion was quick to set in here: pallid wives suffering from anorexia and tropical discontent were dragging their husbands home, as they called it. I sipped my *stengah*, positively the last one, must go home too.

"You know Norman Douglas?"

"I've been to the isle of Capri, ignorant as I am. Last trip UKwards, picked up an Eyetie boat at Suez. Quite an education."

"But," I said, "the point is that Douglas is a buck-a-time man, just like your DO."

"Look," said Symes the English teacher from the Malay College, "let's have no talking about a man behind his back." Symes was fattish, pale, without eyebrows. I noticed that there were quite a number at the bar now and that I was hedged in. "Especially," he added, putting it straight, "from guests of the community. If," he added, softening it, "you don't strenuously object to my saying so." He had probably read some of my books and didn't like them much. After all, he taught English literature.

"Mr. Toomey," Grieves said, "was giving us a classical education. Explaining the difference between home oh and hommo."

"Right," I said. I drank up. "I know when I'm not wanted."

"Oh, but you are," Symes said. "Very much wanted. I mean, the Upper Fifth would be honored if you'd give them a little talk about *The Mill on the Floss.* Keeping it simple of course. George Eliot, Victorian master, or should it be mistress? Afraid of admitting what sex she was. Those were bad times for a woman."

"All writers," I said, "are like Kipling's jollies. A sort of a blooming ermophrodite."

"I like that," Grieves said sincerely. "I like that very much." Nobody was attending to the gramophone. It wound down. Wokkle aaah dawwwwwww.

"Soldier and sailor too," I explained. "I really must be going."

"Oh, come on," Fothergill said. "Push the boat out, talking of sailors. *Satu empat jalan.*"

"One two road," Symes translated. "*Daftar dua bintang papan.* List to star board. Talking of sailors. *Stengah* for me."

"Talking of sailors," Greene said, "what did you do in the war, Toomey?"

"Faced the terrors of Europe," I said lightly.

"Meaning," Greene said, "you weren't stuck out in the glamorous East chewing bananas. Nasty, very nasty."

"Heart," I said. "Heart trouble. As you saw."

"No need to defend yourself," Symes said softly. "You're not on trial or anything."

"As we saw," Greene agreed. "Doc Shawcross to the rescue. Well, let's toast a beautiful friendship."

"Do doctors have to learn Greek?" Grieves asked with an extravagantly puzzled look. "Or is it just Latin?" He shrugged excessively, then drank. Others drank, I drank off. I signed. Off.

"Thanks for a pleasant evening." They would not let me get through. "Please," I said.

"All the ladies have completely disappeared," Grieves said in feigned surprise. "All men together, situation normal, more or less. You," he said to the planter Booth, "are by way of being our new secretary. Is there a club rule that forbids debagging?"

"Cut it out," Fothergill said. "We're not at school now."

"Not," Symes said with mock prissiness, "before the natives. The DO," less mock, "would not be pleased."

"Ah, come on," Grieves Liverpudlianly whined, "you don't know the DO like I do. It only means that Mr. Toomey will parade in his shorts. Nothing indecent."

I was glad to find myself feeling contempt. I was gladder when it moved to rage. "You and your bloody infantile games," I said to Grieves. I was surprised to see myself picking up Fothergill's empty pint glass by the butt. I opposed its mouth to that of Grieves. But wait, it had first to be cracked, jagged, to threaten to draw blood. The stern planter's hand of Booth grasped it, wrested it away before I could smash it on the bar-counter's edge. The number one boy Ah Wong, who must have been near seventy, crooned something, the fulfillment of some Taoist prophecy.

Booth said, "The club rules certainly forbid violence or attempted violence between or to or from members, temporary or otherwise. I think we have a quorum. Will anybody put the motion?"

"I can go, can I?" I said, shaking with indignation.

"You not only can," Symes said.

I could not find a trishaw. I walked to cool off, to heat up, up Bukit Chandan. Philip was not yet back. Yusof was in bed. I helped myself to a neat slug of Beehive brandy, shuddering with anger. I was dithering out another tumblerful when the Ford shook into the porch. "The bloody club," I told Philip as he came in. "The bloody bastards."

"What's happened? Give me some of that. No, not that much. Christ, you're shivering."

"They hinted, they leered, the bloody DO as good as spelt it out. They want to believe we're carrying on a homosexual relationship. Gives them a smug little thrill, the dirty-minded bastards."

"Oh no." He sat in an armchair, I paced the Siamese carpet unsteadily. "Well, I suppose they were bound to, sooner or later. I just didn't think about it. The DO doesn't have much room to talk from what I hear. A homosexual relationship, eh? Well well well. Pure as the driven. We ought to have imported a couple of bints from the bazaar, that would have shut them. Looks as if I shan't want to come back here."

"The trouble is. You remember that MP who came that time, Garside, the cocktail party at the *istana*? He did a bit of smearing, apparently. Bachelor writer living abroad, stories, actors, Oscar Wilde—"

"Are you?" Philip looked at me pale. "Have you? I never even . . . It didn't cross my . . . Good God, my blessed innocence."

"Ours. Ours. Whatever word I use will probably be wrong. We've just been here together. We didn't have to put it into words. I was never so happy in my life. And I'm not leaving you, I'm not going to lose you."

"No," Philip said very blankly. "We didn't have to put it into words. And we never talked about the future. What are we going to do?"

"When does your leave start?"

"Beginning of January. I get three months on full pay. Then back here, things as they were, Yusof on full pay too, caretaking. Pity. We'd just got things running nicely. Definitive thesis on yaws I thought, next tour, setting up of federal yaws clinic. Oh well, Ipoh, Penang, Kota Bharu, on the Beach of Passionate Love as they call it." He laughed without moisture. "Passionate love, well well."

"We have to be together," I said. "But first I have to get out. I need to, anyway. I have to see Malacca. I thought of going up to Bangkok. Then I come home."

"Where's home?"

"You know damned well where home is. Where it will always be. Where did you propose spending your love, I mean leave?"

"In a town I've never before visited, Adelaide, South Australia. My mother and stepfather are there. I haven't yet met my stepfather. A man who's gone partners with another man in a big sports store, the Aussies being keen on sport. Of the name of Black, which is a good plain no-nonsense unequivocal undescriptive kind of name, my mother's now, she being a very fair woman, very fair to herself, why not, why languish lifelong in widow's weeds?"

"You don't approve?"

"Oh, it's not up to me to have any opinion. Anyway, there's nowhere else to go."

"I proposed the same general direction for myself, though further. I similarly have a stepparent unknown in the Empire, Canada as a matter of fact. No one in the world can plan all the way. We must think for the moment of a particular ship moving where?"

"The SS *Lord Howe*, Singapore to Fremantle. Early January. Yes, we go together. We go everywhere together now. That's just something we know, isn't it? Is it wrong, I wonder? Are we depriving potential sexual partners of their right to a less, what's the term, Platonic bliss?"

"It's not wrong, not from any point of view. This I know. I can leave now, I think, feeling, you know, for the first time—"

"Secure, yes, secure, yes, secure. And that ought to make us both frightened. It's dangerous to feel secure, what with the big dirty Lord of Insecurity hovering. Don't go too far. Not without me. You need Malacca for this Raffles book?"

"The look and feel of Malacca. I suppose I could get it all out of reading and imagination. But I feel I have to see Malacca."

"Malacca, then. Stay at the rest house. I need to know exactly where you are."

"Tomorrow, I thought."

"Not tomorrow. Mahalingam's coming to dinner tomorrow."

"Why for God's sake why?"

"He was miserable, and no wonder. It's not the zombie son who's sick, it's the youngest, aged eight, the Benjamin, Jaganathan, the same as Juggernaut, a juggernaut's driving over him, poor little sod." Philip sounded drunk, it was the drunkenness of a sober elation for the first time articulated. "Tuberculous meningitis. Bad hygiene, bad feeding, a background of measles and whooping cough. They've left it late, trying to cure the vomiting with some bloody Indian confection and the constipation with castor oil. Now there's not much I can do. Mahalingam says he'll pay anything, anything, sell his daughters into concubinage, anything. I told him I couldn't do more than my best. 'My friend,' he said, 'my dear dear friend.' So he comes to dinner. And now we, tired out, much put upon, traduced, maligned, buggered about generally, go to bed."

"Anyway, we know."

"Yes yes, we know now, thank God we know."

Mahalingam, in white tie and off-white suit, looking like a photographic negative of a European, came an hour early. The zombie son brought him in the phantom car: we heard objurgatory Tamil and metallic slaps before it sped off, too fast to be possible. "I have ordered the fool," Mahalingam told us, "to return for me in four hours' time." Oh Christ. "A very nice class of quarters," he admired grudgingly, "with ceiling fans and ornaments I take to be personal. This is your dead father, I see, and one of these two European ladies is your dead sister, the youngest of the two I must take it to be, the other is your living mother. Living, yes? Ah yes, it is *your* mother that is dead, Mr. Tombey."

A very necrological beginning to the evening. "Toomey."

"That is the name I said. And this is you, Dr. Shawcross, standing at the wicket with bat awaiting delivery of ball. That is good, that makes you look young and well and content with life."

"I've changed a bit since then."

"To die," Mahalingam said, "to sleep, no more." Sitting down, accepting a watered whisky, he kicked off his shoes and allowed his large purple toes to touchtype the matting. "My dear son appeared better today, he seemed in much less pain, you thought so too, Dr. Shawcross, I know. We may hope now."

"We may always hope," Philip said.

"If anything happens to him, if anything happens . . ."

We waited. "Yes, Mr. Mahalingam?" Philip said.

"I do not properly know what I would do. Because he is the youngest and the best and also the last, because there will not be any more unless I rid myself of my present wife and marry a younger one, which it is not according to my eclectic religion to do. You were wrong, Mr. Toomey, to say electric, I think you were having a joke with me. For the son in the middle is not intelligent and the eldest son is a great fool, and in little Jaganathan rests all my hope, so we must hope. And also pray," he said fiercely to me alone. "Pray pray."

"I promise you," I said, "I will do that. And not only for your own son, but for all children in pain and danger. Including the daughter of Mr. Lee the grocer who, I understand, was admitted also last night."

"With what disease?" Mahalingam asked Philip jealously.

"A condition of the lower intestine. The prognosis is good," Philip said unwisely.

"Intestines," Mahalingam sneered. "A girl. Chinese. A race of peoples that think themselves to be very clever." Yusof came from the kitchen into the dining alcove bearing a big partitioned dish of *sambals*, for we were to have a chicken curry. "Your boy," Mahalingam confirmed to both of us. "How much do you pay him?"

"The usual," Philip said. "He is well looked after." Mahalingam then loudly told Yusof in the special Malay of Tamils, the possessive morpheme *punya* used, for some reason, as a noun emphasizer, that he must be a good boy, loyal to his good master, undrunken, industrious and honest, not bringing dirty girls from the bazaar into his quarters, otherwise he, Mahalingam son of Sundralingam *punya*, would be on to him *punya* with visitations *punya* of various evil spirits, including the *hantu hitam* or black ghost *punya*. Yusof said nothing but looked toward Philip as if to know how seriously he must take all this, and Philip returned him a slight apologetic shrug.

"They are superstitious peoples. Ghosts and spirits with floating lower intestines frighten them and make them do their work. They are stupid to believe such things can be seen when they cannot. For a spirit is of its spiritual nature invisible. It is serious study and not materials for superstition."

"You know much about it, Mr. Mahalingam?" I asked.

"It is a very curious thing, Mr. Toomey, and says much perhaps of ultimate constitution of the universe that invisible powers can rarely be employed to work good things. We cannot call spirits down to heal my poor little Jaganathan, who must be left to the mercy of human skills of Dr. Shawcross. But the spirits of destruction are ever eager to obey the call of even the unskilled caller upon them. This is a great mystery."

"You mean it's an evil world?" I asked.

"I did not say that, Mr. Toomey. I spoke of mystery. Destruction and creation are together with Siva and his wife Kali in mythology of Hindus. Evil and good are not words to be employed lightly. When we speak of good things we mean good for ourselves, which may not be good for eternal beings. But we are weak and ignorant and must live our human lives, and love of our own flesh and blood may be stupidity and foolishness in world of the eternal beings, but still to us it is real. He must, he must," with violence, "he must be made hale and hearty and safe and sound again."

"I know," Philip said, "you have an eccentric that is eclectic religion, whatever it is, but there are orthodox Hindus who say all life is sacred. This means the mycobacterium tuberculosis and the spirochete as well as the worms and insects that Indian laborers here so laboriously remove from their shovels. Western medicine seeks to kill these organisms. Is this a blasphemy?"

"We must," I said, "draw the line somewhere."

Mahalingam shook his head sadly and much. "I can speak only of love and loss and human misery. My dear son is in your hands, Dr. Shawcross, and I wonder why at this moment we are sitting here with our whisky and in expectation of by the aroma a curry when we, meaning your good self, should be watching over him with the eyes of eagles. Though I recognize the necessity of brief relaxation from work and sorrow, yes yes, but still I wonder. Still, I am now in your house and that is a blessing of itself. It is a balance and a control of things," he added obscurely.

"He's sleeping," Philip said wearily. "I telephoned Dr. Lim a little while ago," he lied. "He is sleeping peacefully. His pulse is near to normal though his temperature is still high. We can do nothing more for the moment."

"Yes yes yes, I see that. In my house both you gentlemen have observed many photographs of friends and colleagues fixed to the door of electric and also, Mr. Toomey, eccentric icebox. As I now know you are a friend, Dr. Shawcross, I beg a little little favor, and that is of a photograph of yourself to join them. The one of yourself in batting posture at wicket should serve well and be deeply cherished. I ask only the picture, not the frame."

"Well," Philip said, embarrassed, "this is a request that— Well, I suppose so. If I want to look at myself I suppose I can always look in the mirror."

"*Makan sudah siap*," Yusof announced. The curry and the rice steamed on the table.

"We must eat, yes, eat," Mahalingam sighed, getting up quickly and first. "My deep thanks," he said, going to the little display of photographs and, with remarkably nimble fingers for such great puddings of hands, freeing cricketing Philip from the staples at the back of the frame. "Now I know I have you with me all the time." The sort of thing I should have said and done, having a period of absence from home ahead of me, but Philip and I were British and not much, except about animals, given to sentimentality.

thirty-seven

The following morning we were both still exhausted after four hours and more of Mahalingam. Mahalingam's anxiety about his Benjamin had expressed itself in large appetite and atavistic table manners, a session of unashamed weeping, a phase of profound and anxious dyspepsia which Philip had to treat with a solution of baking soda inducing resonant relief, a request that we should all go and spend the night around little Jaganathan's bed, temporary anger at our unwillingness to comply, a maudlin assurance that despite everything we would always be his friends unless we harmed him in which eventuality he would demonstrate that he could be a proper pig, a desire to threaten over the telephone the nursing staff with direst consequences in the case of deterioration of the patient's condition, a long pseudophilosophical disquisition on the joys and agonies of paternity, a number of regurgitations of ill-digested school Shakespeare, a cadenza of ancient proverbs, a detailed account of his, Mahalingam's, career as a public servant, a Timonesque diatribe against an ungrateful Madras, vitriolic brief lives of treacherous friends and colleagues, and an embarrassing and most explicit catalogue of copulatory postures. It was no wonder that Mahalingam was heavily on Philip's mind: his first act on waking was to telephone the hospital and enquire as to the Benjamin's condition. The juggernaut had been apparently deflected from its crushing course, for Philip said "Good" and even tiredly smiled. "Call the father, will you?" he said. "Yes, at the waterworks. Thanks." He sat down to tea and toast and segments of pomelo on the verandah saying, "It looks as though the diagnosis was wrong. A sort of colitis, Lim thinks, just like the Lee kid. Constipation, so the mother stuffs him with aperients. Pain, so she pours in the laudanum. No wonder they couldn't get him to wake up. I've had meningitis a bit too much on my mind lately perhaps. Anyway, temperature's down and pulse near normal. That's a load off. Don't much like the look of the weather." Coiling clouds that seemed loaded with machine oil rolled as in slow pain. You could almost wring the air of humidity. "Monsoon time coming, though, have to expect it. Hits the lower part of the town badly when the rains start. The river overflows and some of them have to drag their bedding and *kualis* and umbrellas onto the roof. Crocodiles snap at them. I had an old Chinese year before last with an arm bitten off at the elbow. Snakes nest in the trees. Last year wasn't too bad. We may be lucky again. Anyway, thank God we're on a hill." He looked at me in a new way, appropriate to a joint avowal that Mahalingam had temporarily driven out. "You're off today then?"

"Noon train to Kuala Lumpur. Then Malacca."

"How long, do you think?"

"Well, look at it this way. I've written the novel pretty well backwards, one way of doing it. I have to have a couple of chapters with Raffles lamenting the silting up of the Malacca harbor and the general decay of the town. I need some Malaccan Portuguese phrases. I want the feel of the place. A week, no more."

"Watch out for those rains. The railway lines get flooded." He spat out pomelo seeds and said, "I have to confess it's a bit of a relief. About this lad of Mahalingam's, I mean."

"I know what your worry was," I said. "Mahalingam could be a very nasty customer. Nasty in a very Eastern way."

"Five dollars for a quiet assassination. The *orang kapak kechil*, you know, Malays with little axes. They'll do anybody in and ask no questions. Lies and no witnesses. Though it would probably be that eldest of his, the zombie. I'm damned sure he's permanently drugged with something. The Old Man of the Mountains and the hashish eaters. *Assassinus*, assassin. Speech centers not working, acute motor responses, great speed. Could be some other narcotic. We'll never get to the bottom of the blasted East." Yusof came to say *telefon, tuan.* "That'll be the man himself, oozing with gratitude, slobbering down the mouthpiece so I'll get my ear wet." He went off. By the time I had finished my first cigarette of the morning he was back grimacing. "He wants to give me a big dinner. He's going to fill the whole *rumah sakit* with flowers. He's kissing my photograph, he says. I don't think I want you to go, Ken. My enemies are his enemies, he says, and who would I like to be seen off first."

"The District Officer."

"Oh, be serious. He scares me, blast him. I tried to get out of the dinner invitation, but he said it was no mark of a friend to wish to repudiate gratitude, or something."

"I won't go."

"He knows you're going, I told him. He proposes taking you to the station in a hired Daimler with the KL Police Band playing. Flowers, flowers and flowers."

"Be serious."

"He thinks your benign presence has been as much a help as my scientific skill. Oh, he'll cool down as the day warms. Perhaps I ought to lend him one of your books and tell him you'll give him an oral examination on it when you get back. That may quieten him a bit. Of course you must go. I can easily put off that dinner till next week. I was only joking."

At twenty minutes to noon Philip took time off from the hospital to drive me to the station. Mahalingam had arranged no enflowered Daimler. When the train for Kuala Lumpur came in, Philip and I realized that there was no repertoire of valedictory gestures that accorded with our relationship. No handshake, no Italianate embrace in the manner of Domenico Campanati. Just friendly cool banalities. Don't work too hard, take it easy, enjoy yourself, I'll be back. Waves as the train moved, waves and waves. The sky boiled and writhed over the jungle. A jungle reek wafted in on no discernible wind. I rang the compartment bell until a white-coated Chinese came. I ordered whisky and water. A departed passenger had left a copy of yesterday's *Straits Times*. Bridge column by Philip le Bel. Who was that? Father Chan, Chang. Ruffed and loses his trump trick. Make contact by telephone perhaps, anticipatory greetings to Carlo Campanati. No hurry. There was a curious story from Negri Sembilan in the middle pages. A Malay, Mohamed Noor, had fallen in love with a certain Aminah binte Lot. She rejected him for another, Haji Redzwan. Mohamed Noor sought revenge through services of local *pawang* or sorcerer. He employed sympathetic magic. Mohamed Noor made a crude drawing of the girl's face. This was hung from a clothesline in a scrub clearing. Spells were directed at the portrait and hand drums were beaten, scents of noxious herbs alight arose to inspissate the air beneath the hanging image. The girl took sick, wasted. Haji Redzwan discovered the sorcery but, despite the grace (which, reporter said, his name meant) bestowed by pilgrimage to Mecca, felt himself powerless to oppose Muslim cantrips to pagan spells. Nevertheless he intervened during eighth night of sorcery, gained possession of portrait, drew the incantations by a most heroic act of will onto himself. The girl recovered and he wasted. His uncle called in the police. No action could be taken against the *pawang* or the spurned lover, no crime being provable under prosaic secular laws which took no cognizance of attempted homicide by witchcraft. When the Muslim authorities stepped in, a plethora of suborned witnesses swore that this man was no *pawang* and the girl merely needed a course of Iron Jelloids and Brand's Chicken Essence, green sickness or something like. All ended happily, recovered haji now married to his love and living in her *kampong*, following Negri Sembilan matriarchal law or *adat perpatuan*, he teaching Koran in village school. I would use that story. I would write it up, with suitable literary embroidery, when I got back to Philip. Money for jam or old rope.

Alone in the Straits Settlement of Malacca (which, like Singapore and Penang, came directly under the British crown in those days, while the other, federated, states enjoyed a simulacrum of autonomy under British-advised native rulers), I saw clearly how much I needed Philip, and I marveled at the mystery of a particular nonphysical love apparently driving out generalized physical desire. The thought of embracing Philip—an abomination. But I had assumed that, like bowel movements and thirst, which are irrelevant to the soul, the libido would stir impersonally as the cells protected by the *tunica albuginea* would inexorably produce seed. But when, each morning, beautifully made half-naked Yusof performed his balletic act of raising and stowing the mosquito net, I felt no distracted urge, no waking chordee rose. Perhaps the sight of yaws had traumatized me. Here in Malacca the atmosphere of prolonged convalescence after the illness of a turbulent history conduced to the maintenance of sexual calm.

Wandering the town, crossing the bridge over the Malacca river which separated the native and the European quarters, or halves, surveying the ruins of the ancient cathedral, reading in the graveyard HIC JACET DOMINUS PETRUS SOCIETATIS JESU SECUNDUS EPISCOPUS JAPONENSIS OBIIT AD FRETUM SINGAPURAE MENSE FEBRUARIS ANNO 1598, made drowsy by the drowsiness of the Malayo-Portuguese, I knew that, if Philip had been with me, he would have illuminated nothing with briskness of wit or aptness of image. There was no scintillancy in his brain or speech. I could remember no occasion in Kuala Kangsar, sitting at dinner or after, lazing through the bazaar, walking by the riverbank, or on motor trips to Ipoh or Sungei Siput or Taiping, or venturing timidly into the suburbs of the jungle, when he was able to enclose an image or happening within the filigree cage of temperament or individual vision. There was nothing remarkable in Philip's body or brain; I had to resurrect and dust off a concept long discarded by the humanists whom I believed I had joined, namely the *spiritus* of the theologians, the entity you could define only negatively and yet love positively, more, love ardently, with and to the final fire. So, however reluctantly, a man may be brought back to God. There is no free will, we must accept, with love, the imposed pattern.

"Stay at the rest house, I need to know exactly where you are." So the telephone could link us, the clumsy crackling colonial trunk lines of those days, singsong Chinese operatrix in Kuala Kangsar calling to Ipoh sister, KL sister, then sister in the Malacca exchange? Not really, since there would be nothing to say except "I miss you," which would redden us both with its sentimentality. It was enough for Philip to picture me in a known setting, even though unvisited by him, since all rest houses were the same, tea from blue cups in the morning, the ghostly overdarned mosquito net at night. And I, following in memory his daily routine, could see him more clearly than he me. But one night I tried to call him at home and was told by the singsong voice that the line was down outside Ipoh, winds and heavy rain, that men were with difficulty trying to heal the cut and it might be two days. I was thus rebuked for my sentimentality by the monsoon itself, which was now on its way to Malacca.

I had, after five days, my Stamford Raffles surveying the silted harbor and dreaming of a new port. He read the tombstone of Father Peter, S.J., second bishop of Japan, dead in Singapore Straits in 1598. Singapore, what was that? A mangrove island that nobody wanted. He noted, with his characteristic scholar's interest, the Portuguese showing the Malays how to number, not name, the days of the week, except for Sunday, *domingo, hari minggu.* He meditated on Saint Francis Xaxier, who turned half-baked Muslims into half-baked Catholics but personally directed the firing of the fleet of the Achinese invaders. A sense of the Malayan past was what the novel needed, and it was all here in the sleepy Malacca which Chinese millionaires chose for their retirement.

I awoke in the middle of the night to the first heavy rains and knew I had better get back. I awoke to a watery dawn and a single thump of the heart that bounced me on the comfortless mattress. Philip speaking loudly the name *Ken*. There was trouble. There was very large trouble. Before breakfast I asked the number one boy to get me the Kuala Kangsar number. He tried. No can do. Line still down. I chafed, packing, at the thought of the long journey ahead, the furious sky, tree trunks blocking the line, the line itself drowned. In the rest house *jamban* there was the odor of something other than the last occupant's gases, worse than fecal, inorganic and malevolent. Someone had, since my last use of it, penciled on the whitewashed wall a crude picture of an animal head sprouting human toes and fingers. The effluvium rose to it. I tried to shake my head clear of visions. A hotbed of vice, intolerance and ignorance, also superstition. The doctor here will tell you so. Saint Francis Xavier fired the Achinese raiding ships. I saw him in white robe and rosary girdle, superhumanly high, alone on the summit of Mount Ophir, his arms out as though blessing but really ready to drop on the agreed signal to fire.

I was mostly alone in my compartment traveling to Kuala Lumpur. At brief stops named for rivers which were themselves named for animals, quacking Chinese with ducks in baskets, Bengalis in dhotis with portable strongboxes, Malays with nothing but a mouthful of *sireh* got on, got off. A ginger Englishman in his twenties, a junior government official from his disdain, shared the last miles with me, saying nothing, making no gesture of kinship in a strange land, reading *The Four Just Men* by Edgar Wallace. The rain raved and the train rocked in tempest but, cleaving an unending sheet of water like a ship, it ploughed on to the federal capital. Kuala Lumpur station was colored with all the faces of the East but always the same pair of feet sandaled or bare in multiplicate, the platform a gray stone shore of these scuttling crabs, their reek of damp rising to the burnt smell of soaked tar hair. I entered the long crowded refreshment room that was steamily rank and pushed my way to the counter. The rain slanting to the southwest was mercilessly deafening on the roof. The telephone, local calls free, was at the end of the bar under a tradesman's calendar showing a smirking geisha, the Chinese year and the Islamic year and their unreadable lunar months and, staunch and shaky as reason, December 1924. I ordered brandy and asked for the telephone directory. Two sallow planters drank Tiger and talked of cricket at the Oval. Cut to square leg and damn near put out the square-leg umpire's eye for him. So many Changs in the book. I looked up St. Francis Xavier's Church, Batu Road. There was a presbytery number. One moment please. "Father Chang?"

"This is Father Chang speaking." There was nothing Chinese in the voice, which had the slack falling disdainful tune of an Anglican rector's.

"My name is Toomey. I am a friend, well, more of a relative really, by marriage that is, of—"

"Your name is? This rain, you know, is very discouraging."

On the train north I was alone as far as Kampar. My message had gone some way toward purging a lover's apprehension. Wordsworth riding to Lucy. I got out the typescript of the first third of *Lion City* and made ink corrections and improvements, though the Bakelite barrel slid on sweat. That Penang dinner party, candles flapping sometimes to extinction in the wind of the punkahs. Miss Drury's pale lips reddened with curry sauce. A rill of perspiration starting at Miss Denham's left ear and coursing toward her décolletage. Directoire dresses. I inked in a wart on the cheek of wheezing Major Farquhar and penciled a few lines under the eyes of old Mrs. Saunderson who knew Sanskrit. Candlelight drowned in the rummers of watered claret. Live, you swine, come to life. "I observe from the recently arrived *Times*, and stap my vitals what a time, ha, it takes to get here, that Mr. Raffles's friend Tom Moore has published a new volume."—"Some tale of the fabled East? Oh, how I adored *Lalla Rookh!*" At Kampar a Scotch mining engineer got on, very garrulous. More than twenty years in the country and ye canna get to the bottom of the mentality of the folk. He was beautifully and brownly bald. Soothingly rational for a time with his Calvinistic engines, he ended with the mystery of divine election, the inscrutability of God's will. Aye, I've seen things here I'd not credit were possible. I lost ma faith here in mechanical cause and effect. A Malay mechanic will first pray to the *semangat* or divine soul of an unfunctioning engine, then threaten it, only at the last bring out the spanner. First things first. Well, here's Ipoh but our true location is the rain, the rain's the reality, the rest but a shadow. Good night, it was pleasant conversing with ye.

Kuala Kangsar was a lake that swilled into the compartment when I opened the door, but there was a rehabilitation or temporary remission in the heavens, the clouds not oppressive and a full moon underfoot. I splashed to a Malay rowboat and for one Straits dollar was pulled to rising land where the keel ground on a new shore. There were no trishaws about, I had to sweat on soaked feet up Bukit Chandan. Philip's Ford was in the porch, and foolishly I thanked God. Yusof came out, knotting his sarong. *Tuan sakit, tuan. Tuan di-rumah sakit.* I could not breathe, my heart knocked thrice to be let out. Yusof was grave and this was a sign of hope. Had he been laughing I would have known the worst, for laughter is the wise Eastern response to the inhumanity of death. I changed socks, shoes and trousers and, when I came back to the living room, Yusof had a whisky and water ready for me. I rested and drank and smoked a cigarette. I gave Yusof one and he puffed it with grace. I did not have enough Malay to elicit anything like a story. *Anak orang Tamil mati?* Yes, *mati*, the child of the Tamil man was dead. *Tahi Adam*, Yusof sneered, emboldened by his cigarette, but he looked swiftly behind him as though the obscenity could perhaps just possibly conjure its referent. Adam's shit, the brown man despising the black. And *tuan*? *Tuan*, so far as I could make out, was very tired and was sleeping at the hospital. The death of the child had struck him to the *hati* or liver. Things might not yet after all be so bad. *Tuan* has been working too hard. *Tuan* is a good man. True, Yusof. I was ready to walk to the hospital.

I collapsed in Philip's office onto the rattan armchair. Dr. Lim, dozing on the examination couch, came to startled. I added the main overhead light to the dim desk one and took the brandy out of the medicaments cupboard, being, by extension, at home here, then I swigged from the bottle sitting down again. "Nobody," Dr. Lim said, "could make contact with you. He asked for you until it was not possible to ask. Today a telegram was sent but I do not think it will arrive. But you are here nevertheless."

"I knew something was wrong. The child died, I take it?"

"The child was already far gone. What looked like improvement was rehabilitation, I mean temporary remission. It is what comes at the end of the illness. The nurses should have known. I should have remembered. Mr. Mahalingam was very angry and made threats. Dr. Shawcross blamed Mr. Mahalingam for not bringing in his son much earlier. Mr. Mahalingam had to be thrown out of the hospital."

"And Philip?" I swallowed and swallowed, then swallowed more brandy.

"He was depressed. He was already tired. An hour of very painful dyspepsia and also the symptoms of colic. Then much diarrhea. Then collapse. The diarrhea goes on during the coma. It cannot go on much longer. There is little left in his intestines although I have set up an oral drip of glucose solution."

"What are you doing for him?" I could hardly get the words out.

"Dr. Howes is coming from Ipoh. It is a coma. All we can do is to expect him to emerge from the coma. But I have seen nothing like it before. It is the face that is so strange."

"The face?"

"Are you willing to come and see?" He spoke the last three words with the exact intonation of the Chinese *kan i kan*, look one look. It did not sound like a question.

"I *must*." But I did not want to. I wanted Philip to walk in here, tousled and yawning, seem to have slept for days, feeling a hell of a lot better, ah a little note from Mahalingam admitting criminal remissness, how did things go in Malacca, Ken?

Philip was in a private first-class officer's room with the overhead light full on him. He was in plain gray pajamas and lying under a single sheet with his hands joined loosely over it at the crotch. A cannula was fixed to his mouth and the cannula fitted to a rubber tube and the rubber tube fitted to an inverted bottle of colorless fluid fixed with clamps to the bedhead.

"You see?"

"Oh my God." The face was set in a rictus of amusement, sardonic, meaning either grinning like a dog or sourfaced after the eating of an astringent plant of Sardinia, what art historians call the archaic smile, meaning that the lips were engaged in mirth while the eyes were aloof from it. The eyes were open, the upper lids well up, but they looked at nothing. "Philip," I called. "Phil. It's me, Ken, I'm back." There was no response.

"Pulse is very slow but very regular," Dr. Lim said. "Temperature much subnormal. Breathing regular also, but faint."

A Chinese nurse came in, showed sad teeth at me, spoke brief Hokkien to Dr. Lim.

"What do you really think?" I asked Dr. Lim.

"He is not near death, if that is what you mean. It is just a very deep sleep, but it is unnerving to see the face. Our Malay nurses will not go near him. If one tries to recompose the face into into—"

"Something," I said bitterly, "more in keeping with the state of being ill—"

"You could say that, yes. The face does not change. Ah." He sniffed the air near Philip. "I think the bowels have moved again." And he said something in Hokkien to the nurse, without doubt about changing a diaper, as though Philip were little John or Ann.

"He is not left?" I asked.

"No, no, somebody is always near. I sleep in the office. Let us go back to the office. We can do nothing here just standing by his bed."

"He might hear my voice, might respond."

"He will do neither. Dr. Howes is a doctor of much experience. He is very old. He will give a name to this. He will know what is to be done."

"Why don't you go home, John, if I may call you John? You look worn out. Get a decent night's sleep." Though the night was far gone. "I'll stay here, look in every half-hour, summon help when help seems in order. You can trust me. Philip's my friend."

"My friend also." And then, "Too conscientious, too conscientious." That long word, so un-Chinese, attacked him like the foreign invader it was. "Conscientious." We were back in the office. He sat down on the examination couch and began to sob dryly. The inscrutable Oriental. It is the British who are the inscrutable ones. None could tell my feelings. You, reader, cannot tell them.

I said, sitting also, "Tell me, John. Do you think Mahalingam has done this?"

He looked up, a black lock fallen over his eye an ideogram of his feelings. "I know what you mean. I was born in Penang. I am a British Chinese of the Straits Settlements. I was told many tales as a child and saw some strange things too. Then my education was very Western. I took my medical degree in Scotland, in Edinburgh. Such things were driven out of my mind, especially in Scotland. I was told of cause and effect and sickness as dysfunction to be

explained and rectified. I did a brief course in psychiatry and learned of hysterical illness. I try to think that this may be Philip's and that his unconscious mind
may be spoken to. I do not want to believe what you think may be possible. But
I may have to believe it."

"I'm not," I said, "committed to science as you are. I'm a mere novelist. I
will believe anything. Once I ceased to see the world as very mysterious I would
no longer wish to write. Many things came together in my mind when I was
traveling back. I read once in a book that there are certain men who must be
avoided. You must not entrust them with anything of yours. You must not even
allow them into your house. To give them even a glass of water may be dangerous. They will take hairs off your comb or your fingernail clippings if they can
get them. They are after power over you. I used to think this was very thrilling
and absurd but now I find it not absurd and not thrilling. I feel that I am
walking into a boy's book and being subjected to the laws of extravagant fiction.
This may be a punishment on me for having built my career on fantasy. But my
punishment is an indirect one, and I am being selfish in mentioning it. Because I
am not innocent, and it is the innocent always who are set upon. This doctor
from Ipoh will do no good. He needs a priest."

Dr. Lim stared at me, black Chinese eyes, pupil and iris one, the slight
strabismus of exhaustion, Hortense's, her venerean brand much exaggerated
when she was. "Philip is not Catholic. He is not anything. You mean the Last
Sacraments?"

"You and I have been brought up on the same catechism. *And even to
restore health where God deems it to be expedient.* Well, I'd clutch at that too.
But that was not what I had in mind."

"I know," he said, "what you have in mind."

The road between Ipoh and Kuala Kangsar was mostly flooded. The rain
resumed and the medical books in Philip's office were covered with a faint
mold. When Dr. Howes arrived he told us irritably of a stalled car five miles out
of Ipoh, his *sais* swimming to a police post and getting a police launch, what
you've got me here for had better be good. He was over seventy, his face a map
of rivers, thin except for the colonial egg, overworked in Ipoh, why the hell
couldn't Kuala Kangsar look after itself, damn it all in Ipoh we have *real*
illnesses. But he was impressed by the sardonic mask of Philip, the coma
without excitatory trauma, the continued though scanty action of the bowels.
He sniffed at a sample of the stool. "Christ," he said, "what's been going on
here?" Lim and I looked at each other and kept to ourselves the inadmissible
etiology. Then Howes said, "Has somebody been getting at him?"

"You mean," John Lim said cautiously, "one of the local—"

"Look here, Lim, you were born here. You know what goes on. We don't
know it all and we never will. If Manson-Barr can't explain *amok* or *latah* or
that other thing, the shrinking penis one, he's not likely to be able to explain a

thing like this. They're scared of putting it in their bloody tomes, unscientific. Has it ever struck you that some of us expats just daren't go home? I mean, I'll die here, unretired. We start to reminisce and the sweet pink innocents tap their foreheads when we turn our backs. He is crazed by the spell of far Arabia, they have stolen his bloody wits away as the poet puts it. What's been going on here?" he said again.

I told him. He looked me all over while I spoke and the effect was of a dog sniffing, what the hell was I, what the hell was I doing in this Godforsaken hole back of beyond, East Jesus. "So," I said, "we have it out with him."

"Are you out of your mind? He won't admit it, they never do. He'll have a damned good laugh and then complain about molestation. Now I'll tell you what's going to happen. Our young friend here is going to wake up tomorrow or the next day screaming for eggs and bacon and a nice iced slice of papaya. Punished enough, see. The long rest won't do him any harm, look at it that way. Keep on with the glucose, watch dehydration. Anything else for me to look at while I'm here?"

Philip did not wake up the next day or the day after that or even the week after or the week after that. The Chinese nurses set up in the vestibule of the main hospital building a Christmas display of fierce olive-green leaves viciously spiked, bloodily berried, a mockery of holly, surrounded with little wax candles, *lilin-lilin* as they were prettily called. These blew out whenever the door opened to the monsoon, but, with Eastern patience, the nurses were quick to light them again. To the door of the emaciated grinning Philip odd scrawled hieroglyphs and pictograms were affixed by furtive hobbling patients. The club secretary called on me to say sorry about that stupid misunderstanding, everybody was drunk that was the trouble, welcome back any time, general vote that Mr. Toomey should dress up as Santa Claus for the kiddies, season of good will and mellow fruitfulness. The members, he added, greatly mourned Doc Shawcross. Hoped his successor would be as good. They assumed he was as bad as dead, a dire shadow on the Christmas drinking. Two days before Christmas Monsignor Carlo Campanati arrived.

thirty-eight

He entered the house carrying a little bag, dressed in dirty tropical white with a black armband. Oh my God, no, devilish precognition, he has just come from there having that thing ready in his bag putting it on in the trishaw. He saw me staring at it aghast. "My father," he said. "At last. A time for rejoicing. He is freed from that ridiculous contraption called a human brain and his soul has begun its pilgrimage toward the All High." Yusof came in to gape at him, fat man in white skirt. *"Ni hau ma?"* Carlo greeted.

"Ah no, he is Malay. *Selamat pagi. Minta stengah.*" Openmouthed, Yusof went to the bottles like a sleepwalker.

"How did you? How did . . . I mean, thank God you're here—"

"You in trouble, is it? You look very very ill."

"It's not me, not. I mean, the roads are flooded and the trains have stopped running. I gave up hope."

"Despair and presumption," Carlo said, sitting. "The two sins against the Holy Ghost. It is hard to steer between them, but that is what life is all about. Scylla and Charybdis. I have come from Kuala Lumpur," he said with pride, "and this is the first time I touch land. I took a coastal steamer at Kapar and sailed north to Terong and then was brought by police launch down your river, or rather two conjoined, since you are an estuary. Great winds and devastating waves. But I think the rain will ease off," he said, in the manner of one who has organized a parish fête. He took the *stengah* from Yusof with an Italianate *terima kaseh*. Yusof stared in disbelief: it was the first time, I could tell, he had ever heard a white man trill the r. *"Siapa nama?"* Carlo asked. Yusof told him. *"Nama yang chantek sa-kali,"* Carlo said, a pretty name. *"Nama bapa nabi Isa."* Name of father of prophet Jesus, not quite accurate but it would do said Carlo's smile and shrug. He was uglier than ever and seemed to have lost no weight. He was clearly as much at home in the British Orient as in Gorgonzola. He drank off his drink and said, "Tell me what you want me for here, not of course that it is not delightful to see you again under any circumstances." I told him. "I see," he said. "Let us go."

Philip's car was still outside. I did not, as the reader will have divined already, drive, but Carlo got Yusof to crank the engine and, when it sparked and throbbed, he drove off with the assurance you will always find in priests, me pointing the way. I sat next to him nursing the book he had handed me: *Rituale Romanum Pauli V Pontificis Maximi Jussu Editum et a Benedicto XIV auctum et castigatum.* Published *Ratisbonae, Neo Eboraci et Cincinnatii*, MDCCCLXXXI. Cincinnati? Those years ago when Domenico had drawn blood in a nightclub. Everything ties up ultimately. Signatures of reality. Strange to see New York drawn into the net of a dead, no of course living, empire. It had never before quite struck me that the Roman Empire was still there, organized and ruled from the exorcised and sanctified site of Roman martyrs. An officer of the Empire was here, ready to smite the jujus of the heathen. And now I broke down for the first time, saying ghastly terrible evil, such a good man, my dear friend, what the swine has done to him, you must save him, you must. And Carlo, eyes on the colonial road, said courage courage courage.

John Lim was there, not sure of Carlo's rank, taking his hand and looking for a ring to kiss but finding none. The Chinese nurses sketched charming genuflections, the Malay nurses crossed their fingers covertly. "Where is he?" Carlo asked. Then he saw him, and I hid my eyes in my palms while John Lim gave me courage courage pats on the shoulder. It had taken no more than the thin arms of one Chinese nurse to lift Philip onto a water bed: he was raw on the back and rump, I knew, with suppurating bedsores. Carlo saw the sardonic rictus and nodded at it as to an old acquaintance. He sniffed the air fiercely. He did a conjurer's pass over the staring eyes. He noted a minute escape of breath from the gray lips. "Baptized?" he asked me.

"Into the Church of England."

"A genuine if misguided Christian communion," Carlo conceded. "How is your Latin? Were you ever an altar boy? Can you recite these responses?"

"Try." And he made crosses everywhere in the air, rumbling from the Rituale Romanum, while John Lim and I looked on, half-expecting that at least that rictus would loosen. The waves of Latin beat at the body, but the poor eroding flesh was a rock to it.

"*Omnipotens Domine, Verborum Dei Patris, Christe Jesu, Deus et Dominus universae creaturae . . .*" I knew it was hopeless; what the hell did these Eastern spirits know or care about *Christe Jesu*? Carlo pronounced his own Amen then nudged me roughly, and I recited my lines over his bulky shoulder, smelling his sweat and my own. He made the sign of the cross on Philip's uncaring head, saying firmly: "*Ecce crucem Domini, fugite partes adversae.*"

"*Vicit leo de tribu Juda,*" I said, "*radix David.*"

"*Domine, exaudi orationem meam.*"

"*Et clamor,*" I said, thinking: They don't understand Latin, it's gibberish to them, "*ad te veniat.*"

"*Dominus vobiscum.*"

"*Et cum spiritu tuo.*"

Then Carlo said, "Leave me now. Rest. I will be some time." So I closed the door gently as he thundered: "*Exorcizo te, immundissime spiritus, omnis incursio adversarii, omne phantasma, omnis legio . . .*" I had heard such words before, in the restaurant of the Hôtel de Paris, Monte Carlo. A heavy win in the Casino, then a heavy dinner, then exorcising words: how could I take them seriously?

John Lim and I looked at each other outside the door. He shrugged and said, "It can do no harm." There was weak sunlight at day's end. It had not rained since noon. The watered green and orange and magenta sunset shed mock Parsifal benediction. "I must go home," John Lim said. "I have not been home for three days. Telephone me if."

Carlo came into the office two hours and more later. I had been dozing on the examination couch, the desk lamp on. Carlo said, with his usual vigor unabated, "We have to see this man."

"How is Philip?"

"The same, no apparent change. But in him you see only the effects of demonic action. The face still grins, he is very weak. Tonight we confront the demon. What is the English term—warlock? Warlock." Scott's Restaurant that night, everything being prepared. "Witchcraft." He smacked this word with relish. "Very Anglo-Saxon. You perform an act of violence to the mouth when you utter it. *Stregoneria.* We have to visit the *stregone.*"

"It's a—" I nearly said game, toy, piece of Gothic fiction. "He'll feign ignorance. He'll threaten us with the police. He'll throw us out. He'll be malevolent because he lost his son. You won't board that malevolence. I'll have to offer myself—" But the words were wrong. I was not a Malay about to beg a village *pawang* to deflect his aim. I belonged to the world of reason. This magic nonsense could be explained away in terms of suggestibility. Carlo did not belong to the world of reason. I had no faith in him after all.

He said, "I've not eaten for many hours. Is there something to eat?"

"Outside." Outside the little stalls had returned to the open, selling *mee* and *sateh* hot. They had not given up during the worst days of the monsoon; they had sold cold *pau* and bananas in the hospital colonnade and the ambulance garage. Now they had their fires going under clouds and a watered moon; their wares tasted of smoke and lamp oil. Carlo ate ten or twelve skewerloads of goatmeat kebab dipped in chili sauce and, proficient with chopsticks, a couple of bowls of *mee*, swilling it down with warm bottled orange crush. *"Mo-liao hai yao ho chia-fei,"* he said to the vendor, but the old man understood only Hokkien. His son, who was learning Kuoyü at school, translated, and Carlo and I were given thick Camp coffee and condensed milk. "How did you learn all that?"

"It has to be learned," he said. "You must always be able to speak to people. There are people who say it was God's curse to confound the speech of men, but I do not see that. That there are many different kinds of flower is no curse, so why for many different languages? Finish that and we will go."

I felt very sick as we approached the waterworks. Nightlife was active, and heavy flying bodies hurled themselves at the windscreen, leaving smears of lime and brown blood. A *burong hantu* poised a long instant on the radiator cap with a squirming bat in its beak. Carlo steered boldly through deep or shallow lakes in the road. "You are dubious," he said. "You have been corrupted by the rule of reason. Reason, you must remember, is a human invention, and we are not now dealing with human matters. To me everything is very simple, but that does not mean I think there will be easy victory. For your part, you must go in there with diffidence and humility. You will find that you will know what things to say. I will wait outside. You will say among other things that you have an

Italian friend who wishes to understand the meaning of a piece of Tamil he has been given. He will let me in. Or if he will not let me in he will let you out, and then I will come in."

"If he lets me in in the first place."

But the great gate to the waterworks was open and the indoor lights of the house were on. Carlo stopped the car some way beyond the gate in a puddle on the side of the road. We both got out, Carlo armed with his Rituale Romanum, myself weak with sickness and dubiety. I shook to the door and knocked. I heard feet coming at once, hurrying as though I were expected. I turned an instant to see Carlo's dirty white slide behind the bulk of a raintree. The door opened and the eldest, now elder, son was there, bowing and grinning. "Your father," I said. "I wish to see your—" Then Mahalingam appeared, black gross bareness to the waist, a Malay sarong knotted at it.

He said, "Mr. Toomey." He said it flat, he merely stated who I was. And then: "I suppose you would wish to come in."

"I've been away," I babbled, going into that remembered smell of spicy malevolence. "I was horrified to hear of the death of your . . . I have no doubt everything was done that could be done. I think you would feel that to be so. That nobody is to blame, that one must weep and then cease to weep and start to forget, that life must go on."

He did not ask me to sit. "Who sent you?" he said.

"Nobody sent me. I come to you having seen the dreadful effect of Dr. Shaw-cross's own despair at his failure. He is very ill. Perhaps you did not know that." Mahalingam said nothing. "Perhaps you have wondered why Dr. Shawcross has not been to see you. In the friendship for which you seemed once to be very eager."

I was aware of the idiot boy behind me, breathing through his mouth with a slight rasp. "Let us have no words about friendship," Mahalingam said. "There was no friendship in Dr. Shawcross's speech to me after the death of my child. He blamed me for neglect. He said it was all my fault. He did not confess that it was the fault of himself and his own peoples and was stupidity or negligence or worse. The child of that ignorant Chinese was better and is now at home. My own child died through stupidity or negligence or worse. The child of a black Indian, nothing. The wicked telephone call that gave me hope, and this whole house was happy, and then the wicked killing of a father's happiness and relief. Do not talk to me of friendship, Mr. Toomey. If you are unhappy now I am sorry for you, since you did no wrong so far as I know. But if your friend is a sick man it is his own fault. That he fell sick is a sign of justice and he knew of the justice, and there is no more to say."

"He will die," I said, "and I must be reconciled to it. Life must go on. I will have sad duties to perform, the duties of friendship you understand. His possessions must be sent to his mother in Australia. There is a photograph of him playing cricket that she will want." Carlo was right when he said that I would know what things to say. "You took that photograph as a token of friendship. If that friendship no longer exists, then the token is no longer required by you. I would be glad if you would give it to me so that I may send it with his other effects to his mother."

"I do not have the photograph," Mahalingam said. "In my anger I destroyed it."

"How did you destroy it?" I asked, very bold now, perhaps too bold. "Or should I say, how are you destroying it?" The idiot boy's breath behind me seemed closer.

"I do not understand your meaning. If you have said all you wanted to say, then it is time for you to go. You understand that I do not feel obliged to make you the honors of hospitality as before."

"I understand," I said. "But there is one small request that you will be able to fulfill. It has nothing to do with myself or my poor friend. I have an Italian visitor who wishes you to help him with a small matter of your Tamil language. He brought me here in his car this evening. He is waiting outside. I know that, in your grief, you may not feel disposed to grant the small service he asks— which is the translation into English of some words in Tamil he has received in a letter—but he is a kind man who likes the Tamil people and he would appreciate it. Life must go on," I added.

"An Italian man? What is an Italian man doing in the Malay State of Perak?"

"He is in the rubber business."

Mahalingam seemed faintly amused. "Let us then see this Italian man in the rubber business. Tell him he may come into my house."

So, the idiot boy behind me, I went to the door and called, and Carlo's dirty white ploughed briskly through the dark and into the squares of thrown light. "Carlo," I said as he came in smiling, "this is Mr. Mahalingam. Mr. Mahalingam, this is my friend Monsignor Campanati."

"Not," Mahalingam grinned, "in the rubber business."

"Ah, no," Carlo countergrinned. He took—

You will see my problem here. If this were fiction, I should have no trouble in imposing on you a suspension of disbelief, but it is not fiction and I require your belief. And yet there is a sense in which all reminiscence is fiction, though the creativity of memory is not in the service of the art which is itself in the service of a deeper than factual truth. Memory lies, yet how far we can never be sure. I can do no more than transcribe memory.

He took from within the breast of his half-buttoned soutane a finely made evidently heavy metal cross. "*This* business," he said. Mahalingam barked something to the idiot boy. Carlo seemed ready for the boy's response, which was a catlike snarl and a catlike hurling himself at Carlo's off-white bulk. Carlo upped with his cross and banged the boy's head with its flat and then, with a quick wrist-twist, struck him laterally with the edge of the crosspiece just under the ear. I had never thought to see that barbarous instrument of punition so used. It was very quick and Mahalingam was very surprised. Carlo then used his cross with an ice pick thrust of some force on the boy's skull. The boy went down foaming and out. "Ah," Carlo went as the boy lay there. And now Mahalingam made for Carlo, gurgling deep and dirty Tamil. "If," Carlo said, "I place my cross flat on your forehead it will burn your forehead and the fire will then pierce your brain. This you know." His Rituale Romanum in one hand and his cross in the other, he said to me: "In my pocket there on the left you will find a rubber container. The rubber business, it is not altogether a lie. It contains holy water. Take it out and squeeze some holy water onto this gentleman's face. Holy water can do him no harm." I fumbled as directed and found a rubber bulb, pear-shaped, nozzled, and I spurted at Mahalingam's eyes, difficult since Mahalingam, roaring, wove with fat arms at Carlo, Carlo getting in odd cracks with his cross, so that I had to dance about seeking a way in. When the fluid sprang at Mahalingam's left eye and reached it there was a very unholy gust of ammonia. Mahalingam yelled and cupped, yelling. I got the other. He yelled louder and doublecupped. There was, I was sure, a whole seraglio beyond the kitchen door, but the door did not open. Male business, the noise perhaps nothing new. This did not seem to me to be exorcism as I had read about it, but Carlo's technique appeared reasonable: after all, you had to get some degree of attention out of your subject. Carlo womanishly raised his soutane and delivered to Mahalingam a great kick in the belly. Mahalingam rolled on the floor.

"Good," said Carlo. "It is the boy I must deal with." And he opened his book at page 366. Crossing and crossing with his right hand, book in left, he growled out the liturgy. ". . . *Audi ergo, et time, satana, inimice fidei, hostis generis humani, mortis adductor, vitae raptor, justitiae declinator, malorum radix, fomes vitiorum, seductor hominum, proditor gentium, incitator invidiae, origo avaritiae, causa discordiae, excitator dolorum . . .*" It was not so foreign, after all. Tamil had a large Sanskrit lexis; Sanskrit was an elder sister of Latin. "*Quid stas, et resistis, cum scias, Christum Dominum vias tuas perdere?*" From the boy's body came a succession of frightful odors—rotting meat, overripe durian, stopped-up drains. His mouth opened to emit a high screech like car brakes. He farted in a slow brief rhythm, there was then a noise like the opening of bowels. "Not pleasant," Carlo commented. The boy's limbs thrust and thrust like pistons. A long coil of some substance like porridge worked in rhythm out of his mouth. "*Recede ergo in nomine Patris † et Filii † et Spiritus † sancti . . .*" The porridge lay on the boy's shirt and dhoti and spread, thinning. "That," Carlo said, "will have to be burned." The boy lay very still, as if exhausted. "Now you, sir," Carlo said to Mahalingam. Mahalingam, groaning, blind, tried to rise. "You know the situation," Carlo said. "We will not talk of Jesus Christ and the devil. We will just say that you and I are on different sides, as in a game of football, but you have been doing all the kicking and what you have been kicking is a human soul. You must cease to do this, do you understand?" To keep Mahalingam on the floor Carlo did another womanish lift of his kirtle and kicked him again in the belly. Mahalingam groaned and stayed where he was. Carlo looked up and saw the framed prospectus of Hindu hell pains in cartoon colors and said, "Very crude." He detached it partly from the wall with a finger and thumb at its lower right-hand corner. Something slid from behind it and planed to the floor. "Look at that," Carlo said to me. "Though perhaps you will not wish to."

It was a fair-sized piece of cartridge paper. On it had been copied in careful enlargement the image of Philip at the wicket. At least the stance was identical, but there were terrible changes. Philip's face held a sardonic rictus under the cricket cap. His gloved hands grasped his own penis, grotesquely enlarged, and forced it to spray downward an equivocal fluid. The cricketing flannels were bunched about his ankles, the legs were thin and hairless. A black humanoid clutched him about the thighs and seemed to be buggering him. "Do not try to destroy it," Carlo cried. "If you ever require evidence—" Mahalingam, moaning bitterly and then starting to curse again, lifted himself in pain to a standard pattern PWD dining chair. "What is your rank?" Carlo asked him.

"Temple master, ough. What have you done to my boy? Are you not satisfied with killing ough one?" He squinted painfully.

"There is not the time now," Carlo said, "to determine precisely the nature of what you call your boy. When he wakes we shall know if we are here to know. Or if you allow him to wake. Call off your dogs from the other, this is an order of the higher powers."

"*Uccidiamolo*," I said.

Carlo shook his head many times very sadly. "That cannot be done. You do not fight him that way. He will only call off his dogs alive." Mahalingam staggered over to the sideboard by the dining table, grasped the bottle of whisky, unscrewed it shakily, drank.

He said, "Too late, *padre*, as I must call you. Nature will have its way. Get out of my house before I harm you both."

"You will not harm either of us," and Carlo carefully kicked his shin. Mahalingam howled. "*Magister templi, magistrum verissimum cognosces.*" He held his cross out to Mahalingam, Mahalingam promptly spat on it. Carlo seemed delighted. "Good, no hypocrisy. You do not dissemble your hatred. Remember me. In various forms we will have other meetings. Ah." The boy on the floor had awakened. He saw in horror and wonder his defilement. He flicked his eyes from one to another of us in bewilderment, then painfully levered himself up. Mahalingam howled Tamil at him. The boy did not seem to understand. Mahalingam made hitting movements of recovered burliness. The boy responded with a kind of animal wonder. Then he was aware of physical pain. He put his hand to the crown of his head and brought it back to look at dried blood. He did not seem to know what it was. "Give him what money you have," Carlo said to me. "He will remember where he has to go. Wherever he goes will be better than this place." I had seventy-odd Straits dollars in my pocket, nearly eight pounds. The boy took the notes unwillingly but he seemed to know what they were. "*Pergi-lah,*" Carlo ordered. Without salaams the boy hurried out in his defiled dhoti. Mahalingam squinted at his departure, scowling, but said nothing. "A very ordinary boy," Carlo said. "Perhaps a good boy."

"About Philip," I said. Carlo shook his head, though not sadly. "Are we going to let this bastard kill him?"

"You will not call me bastard," Mahalingam cried.

"No, not bastard," Carlo agreed. "There have been some good bastards. Servant of the father of abominations say, of the seducer of men and betrayer of nations, creator of discord and of pain. Also dirty, smeared with abominations, glorying in filth and disease. Let us leave him to seethe and boil in his wickedness."

"Can you do nothing more?"

"If you know where his *gabinetto* is," Carlo said, "that filthy drawing you have between your fingers can be thrown down it and washed into the waters. The waters will not be corrupted. He has done his worst."

I began to sob. Mahalingam looked at me with interest.

On the way back Carlo said to me, "He is going to die, and you will now start cursing me because I could not effect a miracle. Our friend the *stregone* was right when he said that Nature will have her, its way. That it is too late. I was needed before, long before. Blame circumstances, the bad weather, nobody's fault."

"He wins. The black bastard wins."

"What do you mean, *wins*? It's a long war. We know who will win at the end. Was I expected to reduce the *stregone* to empty skin and bone and then pump him full of the Holy Ghost? That would be a long battle and even then I might lose it. God gave his creatures free will, all of his creatures. Tonight surely you saw a small victory."

"But Philip dies."

"This is a man you seem to love. What do you love in him? You know the answer to that. What you love in him is not going to die. You have pure cleansed spirit there, I have already cared for him as I would for a son of the Church. What I say of him now is what I have said already of my father. It is better that he die and move on to eternal life. You lose him, you think. You have lost nothing. A bodily presence, a voice, the gestures of friendship." Carlo looked at his right arm and found his black brassard missing. "I must have lost it in my agitation," he said. "It does not matter. It was a hypocritical thing. Listen. You are to go to the house, I will take you there if you can remind me where it is. I will go to the hospital. I do not think it can be long now." I made noises of rage, hatred, frustration, loss. "Stop that," he cried. "Rejoice. For God's sake try to rejoice."

thirty-nine

The cemetery of Kuala Kangsar is almost filled with graves of British soldiers who fell in the Perak wars. Philip was interred there, though in the presence of neither Carlo nor myself. With the sinking of the waters and the end of the rains Carlo had gone back by train to Kuala Lumpur, two days too late for his midnight mass. I left for Singapore, very numb and thin, handing over the task of packing Philip's effects to the department of the District Officer. I was, on Carlo's instructions, to ignore the sentimental appurtenances of the terrestrial life, books and photographs and a tobacco jar with the arms of the University of Manchester. The real presence was now in purgatory, along with others of the invincibly ignorant (though that was all to change, Carlo said, there was only one communion, as the vincibly ignorant would in time be taught). I loved a soul, he kept saying, even as the train pulled out, and if the soul did not die neither did love. All was for the best, I would see. I never did wholly see.

I traveled with eleven other passengers on the SS *Archippus*, a merchant vessel that called at innumerable ports of the Dutch East Indies and ended up at Darwin. I tapped away at *Lion City* in my cabin, came late to meals, posing for self-protection as a man of sorrows. The town of Darwin was wretchedly dull, but it suited my state. Life, bottom heavy like a kangaroo, was concentrated in the southern territories; up here in the north only the telegraph station sent dry hints of the existence of a world of action. It tapped, and I tapped on my verandah at the rest house that called itself a hotel, sending away my greasy beefsteaks hardly bitten. I swam in the tepid treacle of the Arafura Sea, which was patrolled by an armada of Portuguese men-of-war. On the coast tree ferns and pandanus palms. Inland termite menhirs seventeen feet high. The kooka-burras did not laugh, for, it was said, there was nothing to laugh at. In Perth and Adelaide they roared their heads off. I would not be staying in Adelaide: I did not wish to break down in the presence of the wife of a man who ran a sports store. I walked south of Darwin to the fringe of the forest, seeing cycads, baobabs, a tree all pink and white blooms. I approached the tree, and it at once broke and flashed and whirred into a hundredfold flock of galah birds, white-bellied, orange-crested, their wings of the hue of the tea rose. Nature, which had taken away, began to give again.

I heard there was a man called Ted Collins ready to emigrate to Alice Springs. He had bought an old Ford truck that was to be laden mainly with petrol cans. I met the man and said I wished to move south, adding to myself: cautiously approaching life again. Go halves on juice and provisions, he said. It was a thousand-mile journey, a week's travel with luck. He was a burnt taciturn man made mournful by working as a carpenter in Darwin. He seemed to foresee bright lights in Alice. He was to show himself dourly expert at firelighting in the desert wastes, in the termite territory of abandoned cattle stations, cooking soggy bugger-on-the-coals with powerful tea in a billy. He said little. Three hours out of Darwin he said:

"It's all bloody well cut off. Like God had snipped it off with a bloody pair of scissors."

"It was cut off two hundred million years ago," I said. "Mammals that lay eggs. Marsupials. You don't find them anywhere else."

"Look at that bloody lot there," he said. It was a locust swarm of budgerigars moving south to nip fresh forest buds, having eaten as much as they could in the north. They flew at our speed: thirty-five miles an hour. Collins accelerated. "Bloody birds," he said. "Bloody animals hopping about. Bloody abos."

"If you don't like it why don't you leave?"

"Stuck with it, ain't I? My granddad did that for me. Australian, ain't I? We've all got to take what we're given. It's in the bloody Bible, that is."

"Bugger the bloody Bible."

He was shocked. "You don't want to say that. I had an uncle said that and he was struck. Look at that bloody lot there." This time it was fruit bats in a flock, a squadron of little angels of black death to southern orchards, on their, distance no object, way.

"Is there *anything* you like?" I asked when we were sitting at sundown by the cooling truck and he was watching the billy boil. He looked up at me with suspicion, saw I was sincere, said:

"I like something nicely made. I like something nicely mortised and tenoned and a good polish on it. Then the bloody white ants get to it and chew it up. They do it from the inside, so that it looks all right from the outside till you lay your hands on it. It's the mockery I can't bloody well stand." Then he looked at me with some cunning and said, "What is it you do for a living?"

"Did nobody tell you back in Darwin?" I inserted the tab of a can of bully into the nick of the opener, turned, heard the fairy sigh of the death of the vacuum, turned with more vigor. "Books, Mr. Collins. Books are what I do for a living. I write books."

"What kind of books? Tecs? Buffalobills? Dizabils?"

"What are dizabils in the name of God!"

"Where they have these girls in their dizabils and he lays his hot hands on her trembling with passion. What you might call dirty books."

"My books are very clean, I think. Good clean stories."

"And you're going to write one of those about bloody Darwin? Nothing goes on in Darwin, mate, clean or dirty. You must be mad. Money, you make money out of it? You're carrying money now?"

"I have what is called a letter of credit. I take it to a bank and get cash on it." The corned beef flopped onto a tin plate and squatted there in its thin robe of fat. "Why do you want to know, Mr. Collins?"

"I've not charged you anything except tucker and juice for the truck. And it's me does the work of driving to bloody Alice."

"You'd be doing that anyway. Do you want money? I don't have much cash. I have to get from Alice to Adelaide, remember. Besides, there was no talk about money before we started."

"If you write stories for a living then you have to tell me bloody stories. That's only right."

"Are you serious?"

"Too true I'm bloody serious, mate. Starting tomorrow. Give you time to think them up."

"Dizabil stories?" The skysign of the Southern Cross flashed on.

"The lot. Tecs and nedkellies. And dizabil ones too."

So from Birdum to Daly Waters I told him the story of Beowulf and Grendel, which he pronounced kid's stuff. From Daly to Newcastle Waters he got *The Miller's Tale* and from Elliot to Powell Creek the putting the devil in hell story from the *Decameron*. From Powell Creek to Tennant Creek I told him *The Pardoner's Tale*. This impressed him. "Serve the bastards right," he delivered, and he asked for the tale again. All this was doing me good. From Tennant Creek to the Devil's Marbles just before Wauchope I gave him the plot of *Doctor Faustus*, and he said it shows no bugger ought to go buggering about with what goes against Nature. From Wauchope to Barrow Creek I summarized *Hamlet*, and he said it was a bit bloody farfetched. From Barrow Creek to Tea Tree Well Store it was *Paradise Lost*, but he was suspicious about my alleged authorship, saying that his old dad had told him something similar when he was a saucepan lid. From Tea Tree Well Store to Aileron I gave him *Robinson Crusoe*, but then he stopped the truck in the fierce heat to give me fair warning. He'd read that story in the papers somewhere, he said, and there'd been an abo on walkabout in Arnhem Land that some bloke had called Man Friday. Pinching was pinching, he said, whether it was yarns or money, and I might get away with that with the ignorant, but there were some you couldn't put upon with no amount of codology. So from Aileron to the start of the Macdonnell Ranges and the distant smoke of Alice Springs I appeased him with *The Turn of the Screw*. As we drove into Alice he summarized my storytelling gifts and short-comings, saying that a story was like a table, a matter of good carpentry, and that if I kept on with things like that one about the three jokers meeting death under a tree I might get on all right and make a bit of a name. So we shook hands and parted over a last pint of pig's ear after a steak with a couple of fried eggs on in dusty Alice, and I took the Port Augusta line to Adelaide, hell of a bloody journey. Then I took the slow chug to Melbourne, where all the talk was of the fierce drought and the fire that had erupted to the north of the city, eucalyptus going up with a stink of an explosion in a coughsweet factory, and a cliff-face throwing back the hot wind onto a clump and setting it off with spontaneous combustion.

The most soothing and at the same time humbling thing I saw in New South Wales was in Professor Hocksly's aviary, where a bowerbird had set up a tunnel of twigs through which to chase possible mates, decorating the Gaudí-like struc-ture with blue and purple flowers and feathers and stolen laundry bluebags, and I saw him painting the damned thing with a twig in his beak which he dipped into blue and purple berry juice. So much for the spiritual pretensions of art. Staying a week in Sydney at Phillips's Hotel in King's Cross I gained weight and a small beer paunch. I could even bring myself to watch a cricket match. There was no evil in this vast blue air, I thought, and then I read in the *Bulletin* about some mad joker breaking into the little kangaroo and koala zoo in the suburbs and slaughtering seven adult leapers and three joeys. I sailed to Auckland and there, in a bookshop, was recognized. I was persuaded into giving a talk to the local literary ladies on The Novelist's Life and said yes, travel is useful, one meets people, hears things, gets ideas. And your love life, Mr. Toomey? asked a big half-Maori lady. That was when I had to walk out.

From Auckland I sailed in the SS *Celsus*, a ship of the Pacific Line bound for San Francisco, calling at Fiji, Tonga, the Marquesas, north over a dead waste humanized by two tropics and an equator to Hawaii and, after two days in Honolulu, the final haul to the American mainland. A day before reaching Honolulu I finished *Lion City* and celebrated by swimming in the tepid syrup of waters watched over by Diamond Head, a Chinese meal after, many beakers of rum and pineapple and passion fruit, self-pitying to bed. I would get my novel professionally typed with two carbons in San Francisco and then hand over a copy to Joe Phelps, my agent on Madison Avenue. I had also a fair sheaf of short stories for *Collier's*. Life going on, justification by works. In the ship's small library I made a remarkable discovery. I found an Austrian author named Jakob Strehler in, of course, translation. The whole of his seven-volume novel sequence under the general title *Father's Day* (*Vatertag*) was there. It was my excitement at the discovery, my conviction that here was perhaps the greatest novelist of the age, that led me not long after to buy the books in German, along with the big Cassell dictionary and the crib of the English version, no translation ever possessing the power to convey the total force of the original, and thus to gain such knowledge of what I had looked down upon as a glottal fishboneclearing soulful sobbing sausagemachine of a language as I possess. Thus, though now remembering that first reading in William Meldrum's somewhat pedestrian rendering, it is the German titles of the constituent volumes that come most readily to mind: *Dreimal Schweinekohl; Nur Töchter; Wir Sassen zu Dritt; Hinter den Bergen; Wie Er Sich Sah; Arbeit Geteilt; Woran Sie Sich Nicht Erinnern Will.* Why were these novels (*Three Helpings of Pork and Cabbage, Over the Mountains* and so on) sitting there in the stiff brown binding of the line, a gold anchor stamped on the front cover? Because, I gathered from the dogsbody officer who did library duty, the author's wife had once sailed this way and, at San Francisco, had bought the Scribner's edition of *Father's Day* and presented it to the ship in token of a pleasant voyage. What the wife of a Viennese author had been doing in these parts was a question not yet to be asked.

The reader will at least know of Jakob Strehler, since he was in 1935 awarded the Nobel Prize for Literature, and he will feel inclined to a sneer of superiority at my simple-minded excitement of nearly ten years earlier (it was now March 1925). But Strehler was not well known in those days outside the literary circles of Vienna and Berlin, and the difficult originality of his structure and style did not commend him to the kind of reader who would pick up, say, a Toomey in the expectation of easy thrills, crude chronology, and comfortingly flaccid language. The reader will forgive me perhaps if I summarize Strehler's content and quality. The *Vater* of *Vatertag* is the Austro-Hungarian Emperor presiding over a Central Europe that is undemocratic and infested with police spies but is also charming, comic and creative. The Bürger family is involved with the fringes of the arts—music-hall double-bass-playing, cabaret singing, street conjuring, score copying, walking on in operas—and it spreads from Vienna to Trieste in its desperate concern with making a living. Its tattered bohemianism is able easily to accommodate small criminal activities like fencing stolen goods, forging, thieving church candlesticks and prostitution. It has no moral sense at all. But it survives in a bumbling talentless way and enjoys life. It makes the acquaintance of most of the great artists of the Empire, from Metastasio to Richard Strauss, but always in some shady connection. We hear the rumble of the threat of the fall of the ramshackle structure of Magyars, Teutons and Slavs, but the great talk of the coming of the modern age and the anachronism of empire provokes a cynical response. If the work has a moral it may be summed up as *For God's sake leave us alone.* It denies the possibility of progress. The life of the individual is brief and we have to make the most of it.

Wine is always good, but if the *Wienerschnitzel* is badly cooked you must throw it in the waiter's face. The Bürger family is loud, quarrelsome, always *sympatisch*. Uncle Otto is an *Ueberfalstaff* and the dark-haired Gretel is a foul-mouthed siren who can make the Emperor himself ejaculate spontaneously. The book is dedicated to the greater glory of life.

The narrator is a member of the family, Fritz, a survivor of the Great War (Strehler wrote all seven volumes in Hainburg an der Donau between 1915 and 1920) who has found a cache of wine in an abandoned castle near Bratislava or Pressburg and relates in increasing drunkenness the Bürger annals. His memory is faulty; he has no sense of history and allows the epochs to melt into the one imperial day he calls the *Vatertag*. To him people are more solid than institutions and even architecture: if one of the Bürger family leans heavily against a museum wall the wall is quite likely to crumble. All the towns and cities are fluid as though built of wine; frontiers both temporal and spatial are shakily drawn as with a wine-dipped finger. We meet Mozart and Rilke at the performance of a new Strauss waltz (Johann, Josef or Richard? One is unsure. The orchestra is certainly Richardian) at the Congress of Vienna. Mozart faints with the stress of the harmonics of the brass. Sigmund Freud fights on horseback, cigar in not yet cancerous mouth, at the battle of Poysdorf. All the battles are hilarious. The language of the narrator is full of rare slang and Slav loan-words and neologisms. We have here a great but difficult comic masterpiece, as mad and as sane as Rabelais, and it stands out in stark contrast to the delicate simplicity of Strehler's other novels, bittersweet tales of love in Austrian villages, except for the great *Moses* tetralogy (1930–35), which applies the technique of *Vatertag* to Jewish history. I say no more for the moment about Strehler, except that my chance discovery of him in the Pacific was a potent tonic and speeded my convalescence. The great life-enhancer reconciled me to the world again.

It was while I was standing at the cable car terminus not far from Fisherman's Wharf, where I had lunched on oysters, and looking across the bay at Alcatraz, that I had a visitation of the kind I was always inventing for novels and was often persuaded by editors to cut out as being crude and naif in symbolism and sentimental in effect. A butterfly rested a moment on my right hand and, though the air was moist enough, sipped at my sweat as though we were in the Australian desert. The wings, shuddering minimally in the spring breeze from the sea, were decorated with the Greek *phi*. I was being told that everything was all right, there was no death and so on.

I made the transcontinental train journey from San Francisco. Traveling men, ten-cent cigars, cuspidors. Business pretty bad in the South. That so, pretty bad, eh? Yeah, not hardly up to snuff. This genman here says business pretty bad in the South. That so? The great heartland of the lavish willful continent flowed past and the ghost of Walt Whitman (those who went down doing their duty) flew in in disguise as a flying bug which a stogie-chewer caught twixt paws and clapped to dayth. Pretty bad, I'll say, yep. Yes *sir*. We all take the special blue plate. Horrible hooch in pocket flasks, hip oil.

In spring Manhattan I put up at the Plaza. Central Park a glorious froth of green, flowering cullens and bryants, thanatopsis. Boom boom went the city like siege guns. You could sniff prosperity like pyorrhea along with the bad whisky and cloves. Must call my father in Toronto but no hurry. Nothing really to say. I went to see Joe Phelps on Madison Avenue, a courteous sharp Yankee who had majored in European History at Princeton, anglophile, his suits made in London, had been a second or third aide to Pershing. His hair was parted dead in the middle and held down with the same brilliantine that Valentino used. His eyes were the color of sloe gin. He and Jack Birkbeck in London shared commission in a way they had worked out secretly to their own satisfaction. Jack had got the *Collier's* story contract for me in London though *Collier's* was a New York magazine; Joe would hold this sheaf of stories in a metal drawer and dole out one at a time to the fiction editor, like pocket money to a child or an alcoholic. I now handed him the cardboard box containing *Lion City* and he weighed it on one palm as if it were a block of metal yet to be assayed. He did not believe that people actually *read* books, though they would often go glassily through magazine writings up to the point where it said *Continued Page 176*. On the other hand people would buy books if they were so long that they seemed like a leisure investment for retirement. He had studied a little literature and knew its limitations. The movies and the theater interested him more. Money interested him most.

He said, "How soon can you have a play for the Keepers ready?"

"Cuypers?"

"Tim, Rod and Alice Keeper, the intolerable trio."

"Oh, those." Two genuine brothers and a genuine sister of genuine original New Amsterdam stock who specialized in triangular *drames* or comedies specially commissioned. Noel Coward had written *Liberty Measles* for them and Willie Maugham *A Pig in a Poke*. The fact that the audience knew the Keepers were genuine sibs made their adulterous stage caperings both wholesome and alarming. All in the family meant this was really playacting, no offstage funny business, but it also carried a delicious whiff of incest.

"Strangely enough, I had an idea. I didn't have them specifically in mind, but, yes, I'll think about it."

"Don't think too long. I promised, you know how it is, no use half-promising, there'd be something for them by the end of April. Not necessarily you, you couldn't be found, where in hell have you been since Christmas, never mind, you're here now, get down to it. The Keepers close in Chicago in May, Lonsdale's *Cash on Demand*, go and see them, it's a riot. Do something with a lot of British style, you know wit, you can't lose. Big money."

"Talking about money," I said. My American earnings were all lodged with Joe, untouched by me as yet. He looked after my special account in his own bank, accumulating feebly at five percent. I suspected he cautiously played the market with it. I lived comfortably enough off my European and British Empire royalties. He said, without having to look it up:

"Sixty-five thousand three hundred ninety-two dollars forty-one cents. It's a crying shame."

"What is?"

"Let me put all that in Haigh Purdue's hands. Old Tiger like me. He's on the Street, Gillespie Spurr and Purdue. He'll treble it in a year. Radio, for instance, Radio is going to be fireworks, they're only just lighting the fuse."

"Fireworks make a nice show, but not for long. Joe, I don't like the smell of this boom of yours. It's hysterical, just like Prohibition. Boom and bootleg— aspects of the same disease. Stocks anyway are too much of an abstraction for my innocent brain. Leave the money where it is."

"Real estate," he said. "You can never go wrong on real estate. What do you say to a nice little piece of property in Manhattan, not three minutes' walk from here? Upper East Side, Seventy-sixth Street. Twenty thousand."

"An apartment?"

"Three bed, two bath, living room long as a rink. Tenth floor, spectacular view. It's Bernard Lamaria's, you know, the writer, *Friends and Fiends* and the other thing. He moved out last Thursday. He hasn't put it into a realtor's hands yet. Furniture still in, all good stuff, let that go for, say, another three thousand. His wife wanted to move to Great Neck, Long Island, mother left her a house, a bit Babbitty but nice. Great Neck's where they all are now, Lillian Russell, George M. Cohan, Flo Ziegfeld himself. A place for big parties. Can't see any big literature coming out of it. Still. Half an hour from Broadway by the Long Island Express. Anyhow, I'm not trying to sell you Great Neck. Not trying to sell you anything. Just saying it'd be nice for you to have a little place to come to when you come."

"I don't come often." I wondered how much this Lamaria was really asking. Land of the quick buck. "The Plaza suits me well enough."

"Buy, you can always sell, why let it lie idle? Real estate's a skyrocket. Anyhow, you have this play to write, right. Nice little bar Bernie made too, his own hands, maple, real leather on the stools. I saw some bareknuckle-boxing prints in Stolz's, Forty-third Street, a dozen, going for a song. Look swell on the wall behind the bar. Can put you in touch with a very good bootlegger, the best." I could see in Joe's sloeginny eyes that he could already see this bar stocked and me installed, pie-eyed, writing. In his innocence he believed writers could only write drunk.

"I could at least take a look at it."

"Sure you could. We'll go for lunch now. Baxter's, real English steak and kidney pie, just like home for you. Then we can go round, I have the keys here. Get the whole thing tied up nice and legal with Max Lorimer, he's just around the corner. Yours in ten minutes, move in tomorrow. You won't regret it, Ken, believe me." How many bucks would this mean in Joe's pocket? You could never have too much.

I did not regret it, not really. It was to be a slow business getting rid of the smell of this Lamaria, the writer: razamatazz wallpaper and imitation antiques and carpeting like a lake of oatmeal. Smell of his wife rather, and literally too: terpineol and cinnnamic aldehyde and chlorostyrolene strongly lingering after the death of the synthetic flower scent. I set up my typewriter and wrote my play, sustained by ham and eggs I cooked myself, real Booth's gin, Chesterfield cigarettes and views of the towery city. You will find the play in my collection *Toomey's Theatre*; it is entitled *Double Bedlam*. It is the first really experimental play I ever wrote, but the straightforward laughs were a sauce palatable enough for the audiences to swallow the tricks like oysters. Three characters and only three: Richard and Marion Trelawney, man and wife, and the amorous intruder John Strode. Four scenes, two acts. Scene 1 is Elizabethan, with the agony of cuckoldry; Scene 2 is Restoration with the cuckold, who is about his own more ambitious cuckolding, complaisant. Long intermission. Scene 3 is Victorian-Shavian, with the characters prepared at length to establish a *ménage à trois* on a purely rational basis, which, they eventually see, is only possible because all three have through Shavian rationality become sexless. In the final scene, Manhattan, 1925, the three are living together, but the wife is temporarily away, ostensibly with her mother. Trelawney and Strode receive a telegram to say she has been killed in a road accident. Husband and lover cry on each other's shoulder, united in a common devotion which, they start to realize, was always a little conventional, even insincere. They discover that it is really each other they love—nothing homosexual, of course, purely a matter of compatible character and shared tastes, the shared taste for Marion being perhaps, after all these years, the least important. The telegram proves to be mistaken: other car, other people, same accident (collision). Marion arrives home very much alive. But she confesses, shaken, penitent through narrow escape from death, that she was with her lover of three years' standing. Never again, she says; she will be faithful ever after to Richard and Jack. But they say: Get out, we do not wish to forgive. Curtain on pipe-smoking sodality *à deux*.

It was in late May that I took my four typescript copies of the comedy in first draft form to Chicago. There was, as I have earlier recalled, an exhibition of the Monets and Manets and Renoirs of Mrs. Potter Palmer, but I was not there primarily to look at it. I did indeed stay at the Palmer House, a hotel with a vestibule like a cathedral though, then anyway, unlike a cathedral unlicensed for drink. The Keepers were there, we met on a Sunday. They were vigorous people who looked younger than they were, startlingly alike all three, their sexuality, I was nearly sure, turned in on each other, Dutchly blond, with large thirsts for the best bootleg scotch. I read my play to them and, with certain reservations, they approved. Alice's eyes, dollblue like her brothers', flashed onto the cornices of their drawing-room images of herself in a striking variety of décolletages. Trelawney, though, they didn't much like the name Trelawney. Cornish, wasn't it? It was an unnecessary and unpursued bit of regional color. And there was *Trelawney of the Wells,* wasn't there? Tim Keeper turned to the back pages of the *Chicago Tribune,* obituaries, in memoriams, your prayers are asked for (the Chicago newspapers were nearly all necrology in those gangster days), looking for a more plausible name. "Allenby, Aubrey, Bertorelli, Boehme, Brancati, Bucer, Caliente, Campanati, Campion, Ciano. How about Campion, that hits some kind of a note, Campion sounds fine."

"Did you say Campanati?" I asked.

"Campion. Poet, priest, musician, martyr, something." Searching for suitable vehicles they had become a pretty well-read family.

"Let me see." Your prayers are asked for the recovery of in critical condition at Chisholm General Hospital, Michigan Avenue. Now, having remembered so much, often accurately, but memory as a human faculty is subject to human limitations, we are condemned to invent so much of the past, I must prepare to remember, as accurately as is at all humanly possible, the thing I was enjoined by His Grace of Malta to remember.

"How," I asked Carlo, "did you manage it? I mean, here you are."

"Here you are also." He looked quite the American priest in his celluloid dog collar, artificial silk black dickey, St. Louis-cut clerical suit. We stood in the private room at the Chisholm, looking down from either side of the bed with pity and anger on bandaged and unconscious Raffaele. There was little to be seen of either face or body. The signs of breathing were barely visible. By grace of Captain Robertson and Drs. Rous and Turner blood in a 3.8 percent sodium citrate solution to prevent coagulation had been pumped into arteries of Raffaele; the Great War had, as Carlo was always ready to affirm, brought its blessings. But. "I," Carlo said, "was here already. At least in New York." Self-reproach, for the first time in my hearing, came into his voice. "Perhaps it would have been better if I had not been in America. We spoke on the telephone. I said perhaps what should not have been said."

"What happened?" I could see something terrible had happened. Head, chest, belly, surely one leg was shorter than . . . "Who did it?"

"The Chicago police say he was suspended in some place of frozen meat storage with a meat hook under his chin. That was after he had been hit many times on the head and brought back to consciousness again. He was struck in the body with an axe used for breaking ice. His left foot and ankle were chopped off with a different kind of axe. It is bloodier than what happened to your friend in Malaya but it is the same devils. I am, you see, no more able to do anything for my brother than I was for your friend."

"Good God," I said, seeing it all. Fellow Italians, the language of contempt Italian, though a southern dialect, Neapolitan, the tongue of the *guapi* or wops. Fine teeth and animal eyes, the muscles of brainless immigrants, instruments of a brain at the top, the Big Head.

"You say good God but you do not mean it. You think we have a bad God who allows things like this to be done to the innocent."

"Where was he found?"

"At the corner of a street where there was a big store of frozen meat. There is a lot of frozen meat in this city. Wind and slaughterhouses. He did what he thought was right. You did not help and I tried to make him a hero. But it would have happened anyway."

"I did not—" Of course, I had not used such writing skill and popular authority as I had in the showing up of evil, even at a safe distance. It had been Raffaele's own fault that I had not helped, his righteousness had found too easy a target in myself: it had smelt too much of sanctimony. "You tried to make him—"

"Oh, Raffaele was hesitating about giving to the Federal Bureau some information that he had. I said he must never be afraid. Some man in that Bureau has been corrupt, that is sure, but who will be hard to discover. He has destroyed that information for gangster money, he has said where the information came from. It was about the death of a mother and child. Even corrupt Chicago and the corrupt Bureau must take notice of that kind of information, so one would think. Raffaele was dining with another man in a restaurant. He was dragged out, nobody prevented it, they would all go on eating I should suppose. I am inclined to go to the Big Head or the Castrated Chicken and speak the words of commination. Whether I go or not, he is hard to find, he will get the words. They are all very superstitious."

"That won't help Raffaele." I spoke with bitterness, and Carlo could tell I was not thinking of Raffaele. "What do the doctors say?"

"There is a condition of brain damage. There is a condition of *cancrena*."

"Gangrene?" The ghastliest word, I had often thought, in the English language; it insolently connoted life.

"They do not give him much more time. I have prayed, yesterday I gave him extreme unction. We can still pray, but it must be only for his soul." Carlo's heavy shoulders moved as though he were about to sob, but his eyes were dry and hard. His body seemed to be trying to initiate a human act which his head rejected. He would not weep at the prospect of bereavement; he would merely stiffen himself in the continued fight against the dark powers. But he said, "Poor Mother. In less than six months. First Father, then her eldest son. You must go and see her. I believe she has confidence in you. You will find things to say to her that Domenico is too selfish or stupid to think of. He is only a musician." Carlo was always full of surprises. He was planting me confidently into the family. Why, there was not even a term in the languages of the West which expressed my relationship to the Campanati. I was nobody's brother-in-law. Carlo was turning me into a son of his mother, a very Christlike act. "I," he said, "cannot go back yet to Italy. There are things to do in America."

"You surely haven't finished your world tour?"

"Oh, it is all a matter of money. You cannot propagate the faith without money. The Vatican has much to learn about the power of money." I stared at him: was he perhaps, the lucky gambler, playing the stock markets with the scanty papal funds? "There are other things too, one other thing. I have meetings, here, in Boston, in St. Louis. Some day you will hear of it, there is no hurry." He did not seem to wonder what I was doing here in Chicago. It was just an aspect of my writer's freedom.

I said, "I'm going back to Europe next week. I've been writing a play. I was asked to stay to discuss changes. I think it's best to go back to Paris and stay away from actors and producers. One final version, let them take it or leave it. *Quod scripsi scripsi.*"

"Has it ever struck you," he asked, "that Pilate has the lines that people remember best? You must write a play about him sometime. Everything he says and does is for the theater. There is one sect of the Eastern Church which believes he was converted to Christ and they revere him as a saint. A character of extreme interest. Do not forget to go to see Mother as soon as you get to Europe. I shall have to write, but I do not really know how to. You must talk to her, tell her all. Poor Mother. I do not think she will be much longer in that big house. There is much selling to do. I must see to the selling." Our eyes had hardly moved once during these exchanges from Raffaele stretched and bandaged on that narrow bed of enameled metal, the enamel chipped here and there to blackness as by agonized fingers of previous occupants. A nurse came in, a sturdy girl with a complexion from the Illinois wheatlands.

"You have to go now, Father. There's things to be done to the patient."

"There is nothing more any of you can do except fight for your city and your country. To kill the madness. There is no point in cleaning him and changing his dressings. But thank you for everything you have done."

"You're welcome." Madness? City? Country? She frowned, puzzled.

"Tonight," he said. "We will come back tonight." We left the little room as the nurse began to uncover sheeted Raffaele. Carlo's ear caught something as soon as we opened the door. "Do you hear?" he said. "A scream of pain. Do not blame that on God." We were in the cheerless vestibule outside the doors of the public ward to which Raffaele's room was an annex. The doors were kneed open by a nurse carrying a covered kidney bowl and at the same time blowing blond hair from her eyes. The cry came out loudly now. Carlo pushed into the public ward with his nose pointed forward as on the scent of pain. I followed doubtfully, ready to say "Let's go, Carlo, none of this is our business." The anonymous sick who filled the ward stared at the bulky frowning priest striding in, the elegant layman in summer pearl gray following, smiling in embarrass- ment and apology. They stared with the dull hope of diversion or with weak fear (perhaps an end coming not previously intimated) or with feeble resent- ment of our health or of our appearance of official standing undefined and suspicious. There was a flowered bedscreen at the end of the ward. The cry was renewed piercingly from behind it. Carlo thrust his way into the screened space from the end wall side. I followed reluctant, though seeing it as a way of hiding from the eyes of the watching wardful of sick.

The child was about six years old, a boy, Caucasian as they said here. His eyes were open and the pupils dilated, but he did not seem to see anything or take in even the light that came through the breeze-made gaps at the sides of the brown blind on the partly open window behind him. His head with its rumpled black hair rolled on a sweaty pillow and he picked at his face with idiot fingers. I saw, remembering Kuala Kangsar, the depressive stage of tuberculous menin- gitis. The child screamed again, but the scream could mean nothing since there was no pain in this phase of the disease. The lungs and larynx still remembered the former paroxysms of skull-splitting headache, however, and screamed at the truth that such pain, though past, should be possible. The third stage would bring coma, convulsions, blindness and deafness, emaciation, death in a fit or death from exhaustion but certainly death. *"Poverino,"* Carlo muttered and touched the child's forehead. Then he touched temple and temple in a kind of rhythm that matched the pulse of the words his lips nearly soundlessly formed. The child's eyes shut in great weariness and his arms slowly fell to his sides in the boneless languor of fatigue. Carlo touched with his own spittle the child's forehead and sternum and shoulders. The cry stopped now. Carlo looked at me fiercely though said softly, "We must do what we can where we can." And then again, *"Poverino."*

I was the only witness of this act. For the moment the act meant nothing.

Carlo seemed to bring sleep to an ailing child through the fierce gentle compassion of his presence, the compassion itself perhaps no more than a desperate nervous response to two epiphanies of priestly impotence, devils uncast out, devils permitted to encompass two innocent deaths. We must do what we can where we can. He had given the sleepless sleep. The noise of pain had been stopped.

We came out of the screened space to see a ward sister approaching in a sort of guilty anger. The ward had been left untended a while and she knew it. Patients had said two guys in there, a priest one of them sister, you better get up there see what's goin' on. Behind the sister came clattering food trolleys wheeled in by ward maids, a couple of nurses checking diet sheets: this explained the untendedness. The sister was fiftyish and tough, Scandinavian cheeks and a stocky body. "You a relative of that patient?" she said to me. Carlo gave me no chance to answer.

He said, "I am, as you see, a priest. Visiting my brother Mr. Campanati in the end room there. I heard a cry of pain. I came to say a prayer. This," he added, oversimplifying, "is another brother. We're leaving now." She frowned less than before but still frowned, probably Lutheran.

"Not a relative," she said, concentrating on me. "I thought not. That poor child has no relatives. Okay, I guess praying can do no harm, but do nothing without permission from me is the regulation here."

"Tuberculous meningitis," I said for want of something to say. She looked at me with the small resentment that nurses, if not doctors, always show at evidence of medical knowledge in the lay. "The second phase," I added boldly. And then, "Poor child."

"One of the kids at the Saint Nicholas Orphanage. A saint. I guess a Catholic prayer was okay then."

"Okay," Carlo said, making it sound like an amen.

We went out onto Michigan Avenue. Friday noon, sunny but, as so often here, windy. "Shall we," I said, "go and eat some fish somewhere?"

"Their lake fish is good," he said. "The Indians called this lake Gitche Gumee," looking at me as if he were a tailor. "You seem better. You have more flesh on you. No, I must eat with some other people now. Nun's cooking, never of the best. But tonight we will have dinner together and then come in to witness the end of poor Raffaele." He made it sound a treat, like going to the movies. "The swine," he said, but in an unrancorous sacerdotal manner. "The, to borrow your word that time, bastards. But they will see in God's time. Where?"

"At the Palmer House. I'll see you in the lobby at seven."

"Good." And he walked off with the casualness of a man who knows his city. I waved for a taxi.

I slept that afternoon after a grilled steak and iced water, and I woke shaking after a bad dream. I was standing by Philip's deathbed in the *rumah sakit* of Kuala Kangsar and Philip suddenly blinked, then came out of his coma, then leered at me with a face that was not his. *Get you all before we're finished,* he said. *So long, old thing.* Then he settled that face into a gargoyle of horrible cunning and died leering at me. I fought my way out of the monsoon flood yelling. The shirt and underpants I had slept in were covered in sweat, and my civilized muscles had checked at the moment of waking a bowel loose as after eating chilies. I went to void and then bathe. I knew that my reaction to Philip's death, long delayed, was soon to overtake me in some kind of breakdown. I thought of the purge of writing it all out, making a book or a story or a confession a surrogate for the illness. But I knew this could not be done, now or ever. My facile craft did not go deep enough.

Carlo arrived at the Palmer House Hotel clutching two bottles of, I assumed from their common label of Christ on the cross, altar wine. He bore them into the dining room and plonked them firmly onto the table we were allotted. Then the maître d'hôtel expressed disquiet. He seemed, from his accent, German Swiss.

"Is there hard liquor in those bottles, sir? The law does not allow . . ."

"The law," Carlo said, "does not allow a priest to be in possession of the wine he must use on the blessed altar? This seems to be a very bad law."

"Everybody thinks the law is crazy, sir, but we must obey the law. You may have that, true, in your possession, but not here to drink. This is a hotel not a church. I know," he added with sad humor, "it looks like a church in the lobby."

"Priests do their work where they must do it. On a hilltop or in a field or even in the catacombs. Or even at a restaurant table. If I propose to say mass now are you going to tell me that there is a hotel regulation which forbids it? If there is such a rule, I beg to be allowed to see it."

The maître d'hôtel was unhappy and looked round for the manager, who was not there. He was a short man in middle age with a crest of ginger hair and too much blood in him. The other diners, who were drinking Coca-Cola and fruit juice and, God help them, rich full cream dairy milk, gazed with interest at our table. Carlo relented and told one of his easy lies. "The juice of the grape only. I am a Baptist minister. Is the juice of the grape also forbidden? If not, kindly fetch a *tire-bouchon* and arrange for our order to be taken."

So we ate lobster and lake trout and strawberry shortcake. And we drank what, protected by the image of Christ crucified, turned out to be a good if warmish Chablis. Carlo said during dinner what I myself had, more briefly, said to my agent. "A country that denies itself the solace of wine in theory but is drunk in fact. Blood and hooch, as they call it. And also very prosperous, but that cannot last. If you are buying, buy quickly and sell quickly. This country has gotten the devil in it." When coffee was brought he took from an inside pocket what looked like a missal but proved to be a liquor flask. He shamelessly glugged cognac into our cups. Then he offered me a horrible Burmese cheroot, which I refused. He puffed away, saying to the hovering German Swiss, "Is this too forbidden? Are all harmless pleasures banned by the law?" Then, to me, "We will go to see poor Raffaele." Quite cheerfully. So we went.

Raffaele's face was covered with a bedsheet. A doctor in a white coat was there, along with a nurse, Spanish-looking this time, and a gum-chewing orderly. The doctor, a decent-faced Anglo-Saxon of about my own age, was filling in a form clipped to a clipboard.

"When?" Carlo asked.

"You are . . . it says here Monsig-," the doctor read off, "-nore Campaneighty. His brother, right. About fifteen minutes ago. We did all we could. We're moving him off to the morgue now. You'll need to register the death at City Hall. Miss Cavafy in the main office can give you a list of names of morticians." This was the first time I had heard the term, a commodious and dignified one. "At nine tomorrow."

"You," Carlo said to me, "can attend to that business." I bowed in acceptance of my punishment.

"Okay, Ted, here's Larry." Another orderly, not gum-chewing, his face arranged in decent gravity, had just come in. The doctor handed him an official bit of paper and Larry, thrusting it into the breast pocket of his soiled white coat, nodded.

Carlo said, "One moment." Then he muttered over his dead brother and blessed him. I bowed again and stayed bowed. Then, "He may go now." So the bed was creakingly wheeled out, the Spanish-looking nurse holding open the door. The end of Raffaele, brutally murdered by mobsters of the Camorra. Then: "The child in the bed at the end of the long ward."

"What about the child?"

"The child with what my other brother here says is meningitis."

"Oh, you another Mr. Campaneighty? How do you do, sir, and my sincere condolences in your grief. You were right. Tuberculous meningitis. Ah. Was it you two gentlemen who were in there today? Sister said something about a priest. Well, that child's doing just fine. Taking nourishment. Seeing and hearing. Paralysis going from the lower limbs. There's always some unknown factor. The disease travels the road and we expect it to move on to the end of it. Then something sidetracks it. Especially in kids, you can never tell with some kids. Pardon me now, I've my round to do. Nice seeing you two gentlemen. We did all we could, but you know how things are. He was lucky to be brought in here alive. Well, you know what I mean." And he went nodding pleasantly, leaving us to a totally empty room.

"You see," Carlo said. I did not know what I was supposed to be seeing. "You'll ask yourself the question why that child. A child whose name I don't even know and don't want to know. But the mystery of God's will is beyond us."

That, then, was the miracle. Raffaele Campanati, on whom no miracle could be worked, had been a prominent and respected citizen of Chicago, a devout Catholic who deserved the requiem mass that was held for his soul in the cathedral the following Thursday. The archbishop himself presided, and Carlo delivered what began as a panegyric and ended as an anathema. There was a full congregation, and concentrated at the back were a number of southern Italians unshaven that day in token of mourning. Carlo kept his eyes mostly on those as he tolled out ringing English words from his diaphragm. His brother, a man whose dedication to virtue and to justice was exemplary but regarded by the stupid and the wicked as a sort of imbecilic weakness, an infantile inability to come to terms with the sophisticated world of affairs. Because he was just he was to be seen as a quixotic madman, because he was virtuous he was to be taken for a eunuch, because he was magnanimous he was to be gulled and derided. Because he was Christlike he had to be barbarously tortured, mutilated, left to die like a dog in a ditch.

Carlo said, "Yet when the value of the estate he leaves, the amassment of personalty and realty, shall come to be computed, it will be seen that the building of wealth is not incompatible with the prosecution of the Christian virtues. There are many here today in this great modern temple of the Lord who have come not out of the piety of friendship or respect but following sickening forms of hypocritical convention, and among these are some that are soiled, bemerded, stinking with wealth amassed unjustly, wealth made out of torture and murder and the exploitation of human frailty, a precarious wealth as insubstantial as fairy gold, demon gold rather, that will crumble into dust at the dawn of the recovery of sanity and virtue by a great nation temporarily demented, an angelic land to its immigrants that is now set upon by the devils of greed, stupidity and madness. Men in this city who now consider themselves powerful and prosperous shall find themselves peering for crusts in the gutter, but the wealth of Raffaele Campanati will survive, the just reward of justice.

"He accrued this wealth in a land he loved and a city he loved, and he sustained his love even when both land and city became most unlovable. He cried out for justice when justice was ground under the heel of those whose duty was the maintenance of justice. He saw great wrongs done and he tried to bring those great wrongs into the light of day that all men might look upon them. But the forces of civic justice were intimidated by the threats of cornerboys and hooligans grown into great men. The law became what it is—a bitter joke at which only the devil laughs. You have here a city made filthy and cruel and corrupt. You have a country that ignored the word of the New Law of the Christ that came to save men and accepted in blindness the eccentric rules of the sect of Rechab. Christ our Savior manifests himself in wine, but the wine casks were adjudged wicked and smashed, and the elixir of the sun flowed into the sewers. But the law of the abhorrence of the vacuum is man's law as well as Nature's, and it was only through the breaking of the state's laws that men could find again the solace that God had always deemed a wholesome and holy solace from the day that Noah grounded his ark on Ararat. Yet break one law of the state because, rightly, you consider it demented and you must inevitably be drawn to breaking others, and those others may not be demented. Now there is no law, only anarchy. You all drink blood along with your liquor.

"The words I will now speak I will speak in a language known to many here. It is not my language, though I know it. It has become in this city the language of wrong, of violence, of corruption, of death. A curse lies on the language. Listen." Then Carlo crashed into what I recognized as the Neapolitan dialect, a speech distinguished by ah-sounds made at the back of the mouth which make it seem to the English ear vaguely aristocratic, though it is the tongue of poverty and crime. Listening, I heard the tones of malediction and I seemed to hear a litany of names. The unshaven at the back listened with total understanding, but the understanding was unexpressed in any decipherable response of shame, fear or resentment. Heavy eyelids came down over inkblack eyes and then up again. The owners of the names, if they were present, did not twitch in the reflex that even a sleeping dog will show when its name is spoken. Then Carlo said in English, "I have been granted archiepiscopal permission to end with the liturgy that calls on the demons that infest the wicked to obey the word of the Lord and depart. I select from that liturgy the following." And then, in Latin delivered with what seemed still to be a Neapolitan accent, Carlo howled out the words I had already heard in Kuala Kangsar, ordering the most unclean spirit, every incursion of the adversary, every phantom, every legion to, in the name of our Lord Jesus Christ, pull up its roots and quit the plasm of God. "*Recede ergo in nomine Patris et Filii et Spiritus sancti: da locum Spiritui sancto,*" crossing and crossing and crossing in the air. There had to be a response among that silent sullen gang of the swarthy unshaven, there had to be, and there was. A short plump man with immense shoulders stood up gurgling, hand to throat, hand toward the vaulted roof. Then both hands became occupied with breaking open his stiff collar, baring his chest for better breathing. The rasp in his tubes was audible all over, many turned mildly shocked to look. The man's neighbors, as if fearful of contagion, kept their hands to themselves and their haunches glued to their pews, lids slowly going up and down in a diversity of rhythms over black indifferent eyes. Then the man collapsed to his knees, which thudded on the oak kneeler, and his upper body drooped limp on the backrest of the pew in front, which was, at that point, conveniently empty. It was a posture of terrible penitence but it meant only that he was unconscious. Fainting, after all, was not unusual in a long mass like this. It was left to four Irish-looking sidesmen to lug him off, eyes shut, mouth gaping for air. Carlo finished his Latin, glared at the entire congregation, made a last sign of the cross, then bulkily got down. The mass for the soul of Raffaele Campanati was resumed.

forty-one

We sat on the lawn where, six years previously, there had been a marriage feast. An *ombrellone* against the fierce sun languidly flirted its decorative fringe in the almost no breeze. The pole of the *ombrellone* was stuck in the center of a round white enameled iron table on which were Sambuca, grappa and empty coffee cups. The widow Campanati, pale but not looking her sixty-odd years, sat in black silk on a chair that matched the table; so did I, in white silk shirt and gray flannels. She had eaten a, so to speak, defiantly hearty lunch; I little. It was not the pain of bereavement she had been defying, it was the emotional consequences of a visit from a trio of blackshirts. They had come that morning while I was still on my way from Milan. They had heard that Professor Gaetano Salvemini was staying at the house, and Salvemini was an enemy of the regime. He had written that Mussolini was a bloated bullfrog and that the sole fascist achievement so far was the contrivance of a brutal cure for constipation, and much else in the same spirit. Salvemini had indeed visited the widow Campanati the previous week, but he was not there now. The blackshirts, without warrant, had insisted on searching the house for incriminating documents. They had found nothing but had been insolent and one of them had ostentatiously pissed against the wall. The widow Campanati would be glad to be leaving Italy. She was going to take a small house in Chiasso in Switzerland, a brief train ride away. It would be like being in an Italian town but without the blackshirts.

"Look," I said, "what do I call you?"

"Concetta," she said. "Very Italian, very Catholic. I don't think there's an equivalent in English. The boys used to call me Connie, much more of an American name." The American tonalities were now more evident than they had been six years earlier. The American look was stronger too. What was or is the American look? The mouth more generous, less cautious than you find in Europeans, the eyes too. Her white hair was fashionably shingled. The skin was moist. A milk diet perhaps. The chin was firm. "Concetta Auronzo, that's what

I was. It still says that on my U.S. passport. I kept it and I keep on renewing it. Cheating, according to the Italian government. But they've never known. My mother said, 'Concetta, we've come out of the Old World into the New. Don't lose the advantage. Don't let the Old World swallow you up again.' "

"What," I said, "can you do in a place like Chiasso?"

"Live out my days. I might travel a little. Visit the States and put flowers on poor Raffaele's grave." But she said that perkily, as if Raffaele had been a dog known back in New Jersey. Still, as hearing that tone and wanting to correct it, she added, "Poor boy. Poor *good* boy. You didn't get on too well with poor Raffaele. But I'm glad you were there at the end. Perhaps he knew."

"I admired him. The trouble was that he couldn't accept that a writer like me has to touch pitch and be defiled. It seemed a rather sinful trade to him, writing. He was a very upright man."

"Oh yes, very upright. And look where it got him, poor boy." She had not been told all the details of where it had got him. It had been made to sound like a clean death. "I gather they were all there, all in black, mountains of lilies. The hypocrisy. My own people, Italo-Americans. Catholics, good sons of the Holy Apostolic Catholic Church." She said it bitterly and seemed to shrink from some inner image, as of a big black spider lowering itself from an *ombrellone*.

I said, "Carlo said you'd turn from God for a time. That was to be expected, he said. He talked about divine mysteries and so on."

"Divine mysteries, all nonsense," she said. "There are bad men and good men, it's as simple as that. Greed and malevolence face moderation and decency. Carlo always wants to bring theology into things, blame everything on the devil."

"That's his trade."

"Yes, his trade. Evil's necessary to his trade. Without evil he'd have nothing to do. So go on, let's have more evil." I gave her a Gold Flake and lighted it for her with Ali's Maltese cross gift, no, with a Swan vesta. She puffed it like a girl with her hair newly up, daringly, at some dance, not inhaling, wetting the end so that the paper dissolved on her lips and she had to throw it away after three puffs. She ground it out on the brown grass with a firm high heel. "You won't be shocked," she said. "Your own Catholicism," she added.

"What about it?"

"Carlo says you've lost your faith and he'll have you back one of these days. When he has time to work on you. He seems very busy making money at the moment. For the Holy Apostolic et cetera."

"For the propagation of the faith among the Hindus and Muslims and Taoists. And the black benighted Africans. Carlo, as you know better than any, is a very remarkable man. But he'll never get me back in the Church. Perhaps when we're both old men together. But not *nel mezzo del cammino*." I had just celebrated my thirty-fifth birthday. A little dinner at Fouquet's with Hortense and Domenico, Hortense's left cheek heavily made up to hide the purple of a slap, she and Domenico having had a blazing row about something.

"*God make me pure,*" Concetta quoted, "*but not yet.* Saint Augustine, apostle to the Chicago Neapolitans." I could see now why she could be the sort of person whom Gaetano Salvemini might want to visit. And then, "May they all rot in hell." Very American, the l-sound very dark. "Bleeding statues and ignorance and superstition and violence and villainy. Scared of the thunder. The Catholic Church can accommodate anything." It was a passage of bitterness, but like something in an aria, the fulfillment of some obligatory form. I waited for it to pass. She said, with affection only slightly bitter, "Carlo believes that good always wins. In the long run. Well, that long run's just a little bit too long." It was a long *long*, American. "What I've heard called a desperate optimism." And then, somewhat defiantly, as if I might not wish to believe her, "I've read books, you know. I've tried to keep up with my two religious children. I go on reading books. I've read yours. I've even checked the Italian translations with the originals. They're not too good in Italian."

"They're not too good in English. But I go on trying to make them better."

She said, "There's a limit to the amount of improvement you can make in anything. Despite what Carlo believes. I think what Carlo believes may not be quite orthodox. But orthodoxy may be a matter of strength of will. Carlo thinks you can will anything. Oh, with a bit of grace and prayer as side dishes. You've evidently," in a teasing tone, "not willed yourself to be Shakespeare."

"Nor did Shakespeare," I said. "You've hit the root of the trouble as regards my faith. I should be going with you to Switzerland. Money breeds and watches tick, and it's nothing to do with free will. I was predestined to be Kenneth M. Toomey, indifferent and overrewarded scribbler."

"And predestined to lose your faith?" She was smiling. "That's a little hard, I'd say. God willing you not to believe in him."

"Oh, I believe in him all right, whatever he is. The enigmatic Jehovah of the Old Testament. You don't know whether he's good or bad but he's there all right. Giving us a hard time when he bothers about us at all."

"To do with sex, isn't it?" and she gave me a straight gaze. "I read this novel of Aldous Huxley's. The best thing about it was the quotation on the—what's it called?"

"The epigraph?"

"That's the word. *Created sick, commanded to be sound.* Look, I don't mean you're sick. Poor Raffaele talked about sickness, though poor Carlo can't believe it really exists."

"It exists all right. If there's only one kind of soundness, then I suppose I'm sick. But I don't feel sick. This postwar world's learning to separate the act of sex from the act of generation. The Church says that's a sin. But it's deliberately chosen, a healthy act of wicked free will. If it's a sin then I'm predisposed to sin. The Church and I can't agree on it. So I'm out of the Church. Very simple and very unfair."

"You've talked with Carlo about this?"

"He'd only bring up the sin of Sodom. *Kaum nabi Lot.*" Then the tears came. I forced them back into their ducts.

"Carlo wrote about— No, I won't mention it. Love between men. He could see that all right. That's Malay or Arabic or something you were saying, isn't it? Yes, he wrote about that. Bereavement, bereavement. What a world it is. Do you want to take a siesta?" Forced back, the tears revolted and had their own way.

"Sorry. Sorry sorry sorry." So I shook and shook on the white iron chair, eyes in hands, feeling her hand tapping my shoulder in dry sympathy. After all, she needed sympathy too.

She said, "The agency in Milan was pretty quick getting somebody. Some big art professor from Philadelphia on what he called a sabbatical, meaning a Sunday one year long. A wife and seven children and he moves in at the end of the month. Then we don't know what. Sell the place? Italy's crammed with unsalable *palazzi.* Is there any odd picture you want to look after for me in Paris? I can't make up my mind about putting them up for auction. I suppose London would be the place, Christie's or somebody. I guess I must wait till Carlo gets back."

"Sorry sorry sorry."

"That's all right, you get it out of your system." I could tell my sorrow was a bore to her and she couldn't be blamed. "You take that siesta. I've some letters to write."

In my cool room with the shutters shut and the thin shives of air and light coming through the slats, I cried myself to sleep in an overloud self-pitying transport. I heard briefly a couple of servant voices in the corridor muttering about it, not displeased probably with, at last, some noisy manifestation of grief, the *vedova* Campanati having been unnaturally quiet through two bereavements and those close together. I dreamed the dream I ought to have expected: a fusion of Raffaele and Philip devoured by something in the Australian wastes. Waking in terror I was aghast to find myself grotesquely engorged and pumping out seed onto the white top sheet. I saw, in the forewaking instant, the metal lettering of the King's Cross hotel on its white façade, and heard a voice saying *O ye of little faith.* And then the flood of semen.

There were just the two of us at dinner. *Zuppa di verdura,* veal fillets, a *zabaglione,* a very cold *spumante* to drink. She said, "That one, for instance," meaning the Tommaso Rodari above the sideboard (had it been there last time? I thought not) of Lot and his daughters. *Nabi Lot,* having fled the incinerated Sodomites, ready now to be made drunk and incestuous. Was there a delicate malice here? I thought not, judging from her eyes, serious but not sad. "Or something else, take your choice."

"Too great a responsibility," I said. "Thanks all the same. Won't your sabbatical professor expect to be surrounded by Great Italian Art, no extra charge?" Then, aghast again, I found a fresh engorgement beginning, hidden for now by the white damask: what the hell was going on? I said quickly, "October the seventeenth. Domenico's concerto, a great event. Will you be coming to Paris? You could stay at my place, plenty of room."

"That concerto," she said, her slight venerean strabismus glinting, as her daughter-in-law's so often did, in faint mockery. "He put all that scribble between himself and his own father's funeral. Rubbing things out and penciling things in and hitting out at poor Hortense, the great artist not to be diverted from his great art even by a death in the family. Is it good, this concerto?"

"I've only heard fragments. Besides, I'm no judge. Will you come?" A dangerous question with this throbbing engorgement under the tablecloth. But then old Rosetta, who had not so far entered the dining room, came in with coffee and a harsh look for me, my incontinence of the siesta perhaps already discovered. The engorgement, embarrassed, receded.

"All right, I'll be there. Though I'm no judge either. There's no music on either side of the family. Well, that's not altogether true. His father was a great frequenter of the backstage of La Scala. When there was an opera with a ballet in it. He never cared much for Puccini or Wagner, not enough legs." I couldn't help smiling at this tartness: she acted neither the widow nor the mother in the right Mediterranean tradition. "Raffaele," she said firmly, "my husband that is, not my son, developed paralysis out of a condition of syphilis."

"Good God, I'd no idea." I even spilled my coffee.

"No reflection on the *belle ballerine* of La Scala. Good clean girls, many of them. But Milan has other girls, not so good, not so clean, not to mention the other cities where a businessman goes on business. Raffaele was considerate enough to develop his condition fairly late in life, when he could do no real harm at home. He went to mass every Sunday, of course. He'd committed no sin. He'd merely done what a good son of the Church was expected to do. Perhaps you wonder why I'm telling you this."

"I can see," I said, aware of a total flaccidity now, "that you'd want to tell it some day to somebody."

"Domenico has a lot of his father's temperament. But I think he has shown more, what's the word, prudence." She smiled, quite without bitterness. "*Prudenza*. That, incidentally, was the name of one of Raffaele's longer lasting mistresses. My husband, I mean, of course. Domenico at least has not begotten *bastardini* in the neighboring villages. So far as we know. Your dear sister," she drank her coffee unshakily, "has taken on something of a handful. But I'm glad about the twins. The twins are adorable. Domenico doesn't seem to think so. He thinks Hortense should regulate their crying and screaming more efficiently. They get in the way of his composing *concerti* and so on. The twins," she said, "have a lot of their mother in them, but not much of their father. To look at, I mean. I think," she said, and she gazed at me directly, "Hortense is a very good girl, but not too good a girl."

"I don't," I said, "think I know altogether what you mean."

"Oh come now. A girl of fire and spirit and perhaps talent. I understand she has taken to art, sculpture I think. She will not be browbeaten by Domenico the great musician. I should think she hits back. All this is very good for Domenico. Shall we go and walk in the garden a little? There's a fine moon and we may hear a nightingale." Her intonation on that last word had the faint mockery she had given to *concerto*: something showoff and male and sexual and lacking in fundamental substance of a nutritious character. Gilt and ginger, not bread. The talk about Hortense had, not shamefully for this was clearly a pathological condition, brought the engorgement back. I thought of iced water and felt a sufficient slackening. I was able to get up from the table.

The moon was like a round of Breton butter with fromatical veins and a nightingale gushed ridiculous cadenzas. The fig trees proffered limp mittens and the oleanders were rich with heartless daisies. "You'll be sorry to leave this?" I said.

She did not answer that. She said, "Hortense cried when she spoke of her mother. She cried more when she spoke of her father. She talked of betrayal, a silly thing to do I think. You can't be loyal to the dead."

"It was the speed of it that upset her. Or ere those shoes were cold. Funeral baked meats and so on. He's really the dead one, I suppose. I telephoned him from New York. He seemed quite the stranger. There was nothing to say. He sounded disappointed because I wasn't a potential patient. Parenthood is probably a lot of nonsense."

"Unless," she said, always ready like Carlo with some little shock of truth, "it's a willed relationship. I'm glad to have Hortense as a daughter. There's nothing stupider than that in-law thing that's tacked on. Very cold, like somebody forced onto you by the state. The Italian's better—*nuora*. And you, of course, ought to be a son since you're her brother. But I don't think you need anybody."

"I need somebody," I said fiercely, and then, "Forget that. It will give you the wrong kind of image." And then, "Female Friend. That has a fine Augustan ring. It sounds like a better than family, better than sexual relationship. You remember Cyrano—just before he dies, what he says to Roxane. I can't remember the French. *I've had one friend in a silken gown in my life.*" And then, "Do, if you wish, consider my place in Paris as another home. There's room enough there. And," I added, "you won't find little naked Thorvaldsen shepherd boys disporting themselves, whatever that means. Heterosexuals aren't always expected to be in action, why we others?" She smiled as we strolled under the moonwashed quercus, or it may have been a cypress. I said, fiercely as before, "I need somebody. I found somebody. I lost somebody. We're the same as the ones blessed by Church and biology. Do you see that? Do you?" And in mockery the devil at the base of my belly began to rear.

"Carlo," she said, "told me all about Malaya. You expected him to work a miracle, he said."

"Did he tell you everything?"

"His letters are like preparatory notes for letters. He said something about God making the decisions. He mentioned an unknown child in that Chicago hospital. I," she said, "don't believe in miracles. I shall have leisure now to decide what precisely I do believe in. But I shall keep the façade up. I have two very holy children." She turned back toward the house so I did too. "I'll take you up on that kind offer," she said. "Thank you. Chiasso may turn out to be just that little bit dull."

I swathed my ithyphallus in hand towels that night, noting that the sheets had been, ostentatiously, tucked in in hospital style at the corners, changed. I woke six times to find seed pumping out, no less lavishly at the sixth than at the first. Shaken, but not notably weaker, I went to see a doctor in Milan, Ennio Einaudi, a first cousin of my Italian publisher. I may say here that I had not come to this region solely to see the widow Campanati. With the fascist restriction on the exportation of the lira I had to collect my royalties in cash and spend the cash within the borders of the Italian homeland, the new empire not having yet been built. It was from this period that I began to make use of the services of a Roman dentist, except, of course, during the war that was still fourteen years off. Dr. Einaudi, a bearded man in his fifties, said that I was suffering from spermatorrhea, an ailment pretty rare in Italy, associable, according to the textbooks anyway, with guilt, overwork, depression and, if I understood him aright, loneliness. When the sexual urge came, he said, I must take advantage of it. He himself, to judge from the loud and many voices of children wafting in with the cheesy scent of *riso al burro* when the door opened from his living quarters, was a man who had always taken advantage of it. I said nothing of my homosexuality but, following his prescription, picked up a ready dark thin Sicilian immigrant in the shadow of the Duomo and was led by him to a complaisant filthy *albergo* for the afternoon. So there I was back again with bugs, sweat, open vowels and brutal shoving. I was visited with no reproving vision of Carlo or Raffaele the younger or poor well-loved Philip, though my mother peered in briefly at the window without seeming to recognize me. It was a therapeutic act performed in far from aseptic surroundings. The condition began to ease and eased further in Paris, relieved with Algerians or chilled out with memories of them, some of them. I evaded the expected breakdown.

October the seventeenth, the Salle Gareau. A fair audience, mostly there to hear Albert Poupon, but Hortense and myself and Concetta Campanati were joined by Antheil and Pound and, for some reason, the Misses Stein and Toklas, for the calming and encouragement of sweating Domenico. The Conservatoire Orchestra under Gabriel Pierné (best remembered now for his little piece about little fauns) began with two of Debussy's *Nocturnes—Nuages* and *Fêtes, Sirènes* requiring a female chorus that was always a nuisance to rehearse and, anyway, put up the cost—and then Poupon waddled on to applause extravagantly acknowledged. He was like a prosperous provincial grocer whose pastime was dancing, bald with an old-time walrus mustache, a carnation nodding in his buttonhole. He spent an excruciating two minutes adjusting his piano seat, cracked all his fingers in a manner that suggested he was counting the tempo for Pierné, then smashed out the opening solo two measures. The orchestra, wind machine and sizzle cymbal and xylophone and all, clonked and squealed and shouted five simultaneous themes in five different keys, each of them, considered separately, as banal as the others. So there it was, Domenico's piano concerto, first movement, *allegro con anima*, polytonally up to date and yet strangely old-fashioned with its corny jazz riffs on wa-wa trumpets and glissading trombones. Domenico watched and listened with a kind of incredulous awe: God, what a genius he unexpectedly had. The second subject on solo piano with accompanying muted divided strings playing chords like a representation of brave suffering was a kind of blues tune with flattened third and seventh: I was sure that Domenico could never have sold it to Tin Pan Alley. The development section was brief because Domenico did not know how to develop, and the coda, when it came at last, bore an embarrassing resemblance to "Onward Christian Soldiers," though well peppered and vinegared with discords. The slow movement seemed to be made up of some of the Puccinian themes of *I Poveri Ricchi* but was notable for its left-hand arabesques, grotesquely mocking, Domenico clearly being ashamed of an outmoded romantic lyrical gift which was really all he possessed. The concluding *moto perpetuo* was tricks and fireworks, farts and shrieks, and a fugato which Domenico was insufficiently skilled in counterpoint to make into more than a tasteless joke on someone insufficiently skilled in counterpoint. Thuds, bellows, a tune like "Some of These Days," a sidedrum crescendo, contrary glissades on black and white keys, highheld dissonance on trumpets and horns tremolando, the chromatic scale played synchronically fortissimo, and it was all over. Acclamation (*c'est de la musique moderne, mon pote*), Poupon graciously pointing to Domenico in the audience, making him stand, bow, sweat, look modest, smirk, then sit. We all clapped hard except Domenico's mother, who tapped gently

three left-hand fingers on right palm. Interval. The second half was to consist of
Beethoven's Seventh. Domenico's friends, not wishing to see their loyalty impaired, did not propose staying for that. I must say again what I have already
represented myself as saying, namely that I was, am, no judge of music. On the
other hand, I was convinced that Domenico had a musical future, but it was not
yet possible to suggest in what direction it might lie, this being only 1925.

"So," I said to Concetta as we took a nightcap of brandy and soda under my
rosy floorlamps' blessing, "that was it. Domenico's triumph. You too must be
very proud."

"Don't mock." She was elegant in Worth black wool with pearls. "Leave the
mockery to Domenico. Did he tell you about his next proposal?"

"He told me nothing."

"The money that Raffaele left him. He says he's going to use some of it to
buy time to write a Requiem. In memoriam his *caro fratello*. Negro spirituals
for some reason. A *Dies Irae* with police whistles and Chicago typewriters as
they're called."

"Did he say that?"

"He said it must combine the extravagantly modern and the austerely traditional. Large orchestra with saxophones. Double chorus and little boys in the
organ loft. For heaven's sake try to put him off doing it."

"Carlo's the man for that. He combines in one person all the needful kinds of
authority—spiritual, familial, artistic. He also has a very thick fist. But I don't
think we need worry. Domenico's no Verdi. The energy of that work tonight
seemed to me factitious. More noise than drive."

"A pity he got so much praise. From that wild man—what's his name,
Anthill?"

"George Antheil. He calls himself the bad boy of music."

"And that fat Jewish woman. And her sort of satellite. I fear for poor
Hortense when they get into bed tonight. If she shows any tepidity he'll get to
work with his own thick fist."

"She can always brain him with her bust of André Gide. Very solid art."

"I didn't know," Concetta said, picking up a copy of *Woran Sie Sich Nicht
Erinnern Will* from the floor by her chair, "that you read German."

"I'm learning. I have to learn. Strehler's quite incredible. I've done something
I never dreamed I'd do—well, not since my Henry James days—sent him a
gushing schoolgirl letter, in English of course. No reply as yet. Perhaps he gets
lots of them. Do you know his work? If not you must. He's absolutely—"

"*Doch als uns der Fliegenpilz seine Wirkung entzog, als kein Glück mehr
nachdämmern wollte*," she read, with a light tripping accent that evoked nothing of the Teutonic North, "*als wir uns . . .*"

"But," I said, amazed, "really, I never cease to be—"

"My Alto Adige inheritance," she said. "This looks good."

forty-two

It was 1928, and Hortense's two and only children were now talkative human beings, spouting to their uncle or *tonton* or *zio* Ken the kind of macaronics to be expected in trilingual infants, using *strap* to mean rip, calling the moon the *lun* and the watertaps *robinettes*. The conventional sexual differentials of dress and hair style had been imposed on them; otherwise, when not in the bath, they were the same child in duplicate. *"Soyez sages,"* Hortense bade them, dressed for the journey, the taxi already, as Eliot had taught us to say, throbbing waiting. She and I were going to London for our brother Tom's wedding. He was marrying the girl you have already briefly met, the stupid one who had been rude to me four years before in Scott's, her name Estella. The twins' nurse, a new one from Gattières on the Var, forty-odd, her eyes disillusioned and the hue of Var mud, sallow, stockings always wrinkled about her rustic ankles, a big cachou sucker, unhappily named Désirée, assured her mistress that they would be *sages*. Domenico would be *sage* too, at least in his own household. He seemed sincerely sorry that Hortense should be going off, even if for only a day or so. His eyes were moist as he embraced her. He was handsome as ever, though graying in the way known as distinguished, but plumpness was, in the Italian manner, beginning to overtake him. I too was graying but remained thin as though steadily devoured by the worms of various kinds of guilt—at my sexual aberrancy, mediocre money-making prose, failure of faith. Hortense had never, approaching her thirties, looked more beautiful or more elegant. She was in short-skirted pale green linen with darker green and white spotted contrast trimmings, horizontal tucks in her flared skirt and on the arms of the jacket, underblouse buttoned to the waist, hat with wide brim bound with spotted silk bowed with fringed ends, soft wooled coat with collar fur-trimmed, fur-trimmed too the two-tier flared sleeves. Her heels were high and brought her up almost to my own height. I was, as always, proud to be seen with her.

Domenico had not, of course, composed that threatened Requiem. He had made money out of a graduated series of piano exercises for the young in the style of Bartók's *Mikrokosmos*, called breezily *C'est Notre Monde, les Enfants!* He had written other things too. He was working on a set of polytonal quartets for various combinations. It bothered him that he had reached the limit of discord. A chord made out of the entire chromatic scale was, after all, as far as one could go if one did not use the microtones of Hába already prefigured in a song by Gerard Manley Hopkins. Little did he know that his true world was preparing to open for him.

"Tesoro, tesoro!" The bust that Hortense had sculpted of Domenico and

which showed the real sullenness beneath the Milanese charm gazed with sullen blind eyes at the parting. We left to the sound of the twins demanding *cadeaux* from *Londres*, wherever that was. We were driven to Orly and there we boarded the once-a-day Imperial Airways biplane for Croydon. Those were the good flying times, with the ground and Channel almost palpable beneath, the natural chill of the lower air, the comfortless cane chairs antiphonally creaking to the engine's roar, and the coffee served from thermos flasks. There was an airline bus that took us from Croydon to the West End terminal, and then it was a brief taxi ride to Claridge's. As Hortense and I sat in the living room of our suite, sipping dry martinis and looking out on the Dutch façades of Brook Street, a former time was recalled to us, wartime London, my early stage success, bedtime cocoa, an artificial limb, a radiant schoolgirl innocently fascinated by the great banned book of sex. And, talking of banned books, here it all was in the *Evening Standard*—Radclyffe Hall's *The Well of Loneliness* on trial. Hortense read aloud the words of the presiding magistrate:

" 'The book's greatest offense is its failure to suggest that anyone with the horrible tendencies described is in the least degree blameworthy. All the characters are presented as attractive people and put forward with admiration.' " She looked up. "It says that there are forty witnesses, and that he refuses to listen to any of them. Why aren't you one of the witnesses, Ken?"

"There wouldn't be much point, would there, if he refuses to listen." She frowned. "Sorry. I was asked. A lot of writers were asked. But I couldn't read the damned thing. It's so badly written. Have *you* read it?"

"There was a copy lying around in the studio. I didn't know what it was about or else I would have."

"It's about lesbianism."

"I know that now, stupid. What do they *do*?"

I couldn't help smiling. She'd asked that identical question all those years ago in a London living room not unlike this, though then about the brothers, not sisters, of deviancy. "They don't seem to do very much except be in love with each other. No torrid descriptions of cunnilingus and the thrust of dildos, if that's what you expect."

"Why do you make everything sound so cold and horrid?" And then, "There's a woman here called Rebecca West. Do you know her?"

"A very fine writer. She used to be H. G. Wells's mistress. That isn't her real name. It's the name of a character in Ibsen. She used to be an actress, you see. What does she say?"

" 'Everyone who knows Miss Radclyffe Hall wants to stand by her. But they are finding it far from easy to stand by *The Well of Loneliness*, for the simple reason that it is, in a way that is particularly inconvenient in the present circumstances, not a very good book.' "

"That's precisely what I would have said. But I thought it best to say nothing."

"And if some man had written a bad book about men doing it would you have thought it best to say nothing?"

"The only defense you can raise in law is literary value, which they take, wrongly of course, to mean the same as moral value. You know, like *Paradise Lost*. It strikes me as wrong to pretend a book's good when it isn't."

"But that's not the point, is it? The point is surely that people should write what they want to write. Just as people should sculpt what they want to sculpt. Suppose I want to sculpt what you in your nasty cold way would call the male sexual organs—"

"Nothing to stop you so long as you don't exhibit it publicly. But I should have thought there were more comely things to sculpt. Look, I don't see why bad artists— I mean artists who are obviously incompetent, as Radclyffe Hall is—why they should be presented hypocritically as good artists just because they're supposed to be advancing the frontiers of freedom of expression or, you know what I mean, demonstrating that there should be no limit on subject matter. I didn't want to put myself in a false position, nor did Rebecca West."

"I think you were being a bloody coward."

"Hortense, you really must not speak to me like that."

"Because in court they might have said: Are you homosexual, Mr. Toomey, like the author of this book?"

"They daren't ask that sort of question. A question like that would be struck from the record. A man's sexuality is his own business."

"Not according to the law it isn't, as you know perfectly well. What would you do if somebody wrote a great blazing masterpiece about being a male homosexual and the law got on to it and said it was abominable and horrible and so on?"

"I'd raise hell about the right to publish. And a lot of others would too, regardless of their sexual position. And then there'd be such an outcry in the press and in Parliament that there'd be changes in the law of obscenity."

"But you wouldn't say: I'm homosexual myself and I can whatsit confirm or affirm or something the truth of this writer's depiction of homosexuality."

"Not in the present state of public opinion."

"Meaning you have a nice middle-class public and you'd be scared of losing it?"

"There's a limit to what a man, or woman for that matter, ought to be willing to undergo."

"Oh God, that's sickening. That's really sickmaking. Did Jesus Christ think there was a limit?"

"Jesus Christ was in every way exceptional, Hortense. Your brother-in-law Carlo would say you were being blasphemous."

"Oh, to hell with Carlo, the fat pig, fatter than ever since he's been living in fat Rome, the fat spaghettiguzzler. I don't see the difference between standing up for your belief in the right to make love to who you want and the other thing."

"What other thing?"

"Being the Son of God and bringing in the Kingdom of Heaven and the rest of it. That was thought to be bloody blasphemous and obscene by those old Jews on the Hedron or whatever it was."

"Sanhedrin. Christ was preaching supernatural doctrine. A homosexual is supposed to be infranatural."

"All right, that means that both of them go against Nature, whatever Nature is. You're getting on for forty, Ken Toomey, and you're settling down into bloody smugness. You ought to be out there in the streets of London pleading for the rights of the unnatural." She saw the comic in that and had to grin.

I said, "I've done a book, you know that, a short one. I wanted Ford to publish it. Under a pseudonym, of course."

"Oh, of course. Mustn't lose that fat smug middle-class readership, must we? Pour me another of these."

I got up and took both our glasses to the frosted jug on the sideboard. "It's the thing that counts, not the name. It's going to be done next year on a private press. Part of it, anyway. Your friends the Crosbys—"

"They're not my friends. They don't know me and I don't know them."

"All right, not your friends. But they're going to do it. It's a start. It's something in print that the magistrates can't pounce on. So don't keep on at me about being smug and middle class."

"Yes, you can have anything in dirty Paris. You wouldn't dare to risk it here in London under your own name."

"I wouldn't stand a chance. Not yet. The time will come." And then, giving her her glass recharged with gin and a smell of vermouth, I said, "Adultery, for instance. Would you stand up for a book on the joys of adultery?"

She took it and sipped. "Adultery," she said, "is only sleeping with people you're not married to. It may be wrong but it's not unnatural. Why do you say that? What have you got on your cold low mind?"

"Oh, nothing really. Just wondering. It was mentioning the Crosbys that put it into my head."

"I tell you I don't know the Crosbys. Or rather I knew them for a few hours and they were drunk and disgusting. What you're really saying is how are things between you and Domenico. And I say it's none of your concern, Ken Toomey."

"Sorry. Mere fraternal interest, no more." And then: "Are things all right? Really all right? I mean, apart from that nasty temper of his which he excuses on the grounds of artistic temperament, the bloody idiot, and his tendency to acts of violence on his own wife and his somewhat indiscreet sleeping around."

Hortense pulled in her lips and looked evilly at me, holding her martini glass as if ready to throw its contents in my face. There was not much liquid left so she sensibly drained it instead. Then she got up and tried to do her own refill. I took her glass as before and served us both down to the last trickle of the jug. She said, rather reasonably, "Most marriages are the same. It's a question of knowing what to shut your eyes to."

"Both of you, you mean?"

"I," she said with adorable iciness, "have been faithful. For the last five years I have been entirely and absolutely faithful. Fidelity, marital fidelity, if you know the phrase."

"But five years ago you were not faithful."

"And you know why not, not that it's any of your business."

"I see. That Arts Ball business wasn't the only lapse?"

"Lapse, what do you mean, lapse? That was a kind of, there used to be a name for it—"

"Saturnalia. Ritual license. I see. But the other things were sober, deliberate, perpetrated in full awareness?"

"I hate you when you talk like that, you damned prig, like a bloody judge or a bloody Jesuit. It's all over now, anyway."

"Does Domenico still not suspect that his seed is infertile?"

"How ghastly you make things sound. Of course not, fool. We've both agreed that we don't want any more children, and to hell with fat Carlo. He thinks I've been fitted with a thing."

"Domenico's a bloody idiot."

"Whatever Domenico is or isn't, Domenico happens to be the man I married. And that's that. Now shut up about Domenico. I've told you more already than I should have done. Let the whole business alone now, will you. I want my dinner and then we have to see this stupid film."

"You don't have to see it. Nor do I, for that matter."

"Don't talk wet, I *have* to see it. I have to see how bad it is."

"How do you know it's bad?"

"The book's bad, isn't it?"

I sighed. "Poor little girl, enclosed by mediocre art. My books, Domenico's music."

"Shut up about Domenico."

The film, the third to be based on a book of mine, was an adaptation of the novel *Wasting in Despair*. It had been made by the German company Universum-Film-Aktiengesellschaft, acronym UFA, one of the least sinister of the truncations in which the language of the German State was soon horribly to specialize. Arnold Fanck was the director and Leni (Helene Bertha Amalie) Riefenstahl, later to be Adolf Hitler's Egeria, played the female lead. Fanck was mad about mountains and made, with the occasional collaboration of

Pabst, a large number of mountain films. Leni Riefenstahl was a better dancer than actress. My novel was about a young man falling in love with a ballerina and, rejected by her, going off to the Swiss Alps to ski and forget. The plot was, is, perhaps, preposterous, involving the ballerina's turning up with her dance troupe in Zürich, a meeting, a last lover's plea, his expressed intention of skiing off in a terrible blizzard or something and hoping that he will die. She, relenting, alarmed, follows him and is revealed as an expert skier. Blizzards, avalanches, love on an icy ledge, happy ending. The German title was, I think, *Bergensliebe* and the English one certainly *A Mountain of Love*. It was one of the last of the silent films. As Hortense and I taxied to Leicester Square, we passed posters of Al Jolson in *The Jazz Singer*, a blacked-up silly face with naughty eyes and dilated nostrils and white-lipped smirk. Cinema musicians had been picketing the cinema where it was being shown: there was hardly any talk on the cartwheel Vitaphone sound disk but there was plenty of music.

Bergensliebe was, when the Nazis controlled the German cinema, converted into a sound film, not a difficult task: there was not much conversation in it. The ballet sequences needed music exactly synchronized to the choreography, and the mountain scenes required something Wagnerian, not a couple of tremolando fiddles and a pounded piano, which was all we got at Leicester Square. *A Mountain of Love* was not, and even Hortense had to admit this, altogether a stupid film. It was psychologically crude but technically expert, and there was a peculiar fascination in the orts of Expressionismus that tarted up the kitschy tale and made it suggest that it might be an allegory of something else, such as the sickness, say, of the Weimar Republic. Makeup was dead white, gestures were like slowing piston rods, a head waiter hovered like frowning Wotan, there was a Fritz Lang nightmare with the word *SCHICKSAL* in Gothic script in an art nouveau setting. All the time I was aware of the inadequacy of the musical accompaniment, to be made more than good by the Nazis: always that Délibes *Pizzicato* for the dancing, starting and ending too late; the *Midsummer Night's Dream* Overture for the mountains; Elgar's *Salut d'Amour* for *die Liebe*. And then, of course, I knew where Domenico's musical *Schicksal* lay. How to get him to embrace it? Time enough.

Hortense and I had a drink in a Leicester Square pub when it was over, brandy and soda without ice, ice then being an exoticism in the British catering trade. I said, "That's where Domenico's musical destiny lies. In providing music for the talkies."

She looked all over my face as though searching for comedones of sarcasm. She must have found the trace of a sneer at my mouthcorners, for she said, "That's right, bring him down to the level of the Toomey brothers. Shopgirl novels and musichall monologues and music for the talkies."

"I can see further ahead than you, Hortense," I said, or make myself say out of hindsight. "The new art's in its infancy. *The Jazz Singer* is nothing." We'd seen it, though not together, on the Champs-Élysées. The orchestral score had been, I thought, well tailored to the action, but it was a potpourri of popular opera tunes, mostly from *I Pagliacci*, nothing original. There would surely soon be a need for a kind of music specially composed, plastic, anonymous, the humble furniture of action. Poor Erik Satie had produced what he called *musique d'ameublement*, disregardable background for talk at a morning champagne party. The guests had stopped talking to listen when the music started. Satie danced round crying *"Parlez parlez!"* The father of many modern or future things, that dapper man with no underwear and a filthy attic bedroom. "Great composers will be glad to compose for the films, you'll see. Gaumont or Pathé or somebody are already making the first French talkies. We must get Domenico into that."

"He'll talk about desecration."

"You must drop this highbrow business, both of you. Artists must serve as much of the great public as they can. What's wrong with the kind of thing Tom's doing? He makes people laugh. I'd give anything to be able to make people laugh."

"Your books make *me* laugh," she said grimly.

Tom's marriage took place the following afternoon in a church in Soho patronized by Catholic stage performers. Sarah Bernhardt had stumped to mass there during a phase of superstition, and Coquelin had dramatically taken the host on his tongue. The last Sunday mass was at noon, since Catholic actors, sword swallowers and trick cyclists needed a long lie after the rigors of Saturday night. Many British stage people were of Catholic family: families that had not yielded to the Reformation had, when not burned, hanged or beheaded, been deprived of the opportunities of commercial and social advancement which were the birthright of British Protestants. Unable to become lawyers, surgeons and professors of Greek, many old Catholics had taken to the only profession for which documentary qualifications were not needful and established family stage traditions, especially in the recusant North. Catholics were now emancipated, though the hierarchy was unrepresented in the House of Lords, but the tradition held. Perhaps there was even something in transfused Catholic blood. That would explain Tom and, for I after all sporadically wrote for the stage, myself. Most stage homosexuals were, I thought, of the Reformed Church.

I was not best man. That office had been given to a low comedian colleague of Tom's, Ernie Callaghan, who, one could see, was badly tempted to go into a ring-not-here-not-there-surely-I-put-the-damned-thing-in-this-pocket routine at the altar. I recognized many moderately famous faces in the congregation, and somebody had brought a brace of well-comported performing dogs. The priest appeared to be cast for the role: a man who, I was later told, had got no further than third murderer and discovered a late clerical vocation. The demands and responses of the ceremony rang clear, the timing was good. Estella wore a short-skirted wedding dress with shirt-type sleeves and flared lace over-sleeves, a low U neckline, a chiffon veil with embroidery on the edge, soft kid shoes with straps over the instep. Late in the ceremony Augustus John and Peter Warlock (or Philip Heseltine) came in drunk but were ejected by two strong men later, jocularly, identified for me as Cough and Spit the Flemish Twins. Warlock was heard crying that he wanted to play an old chantey called "Rumbelow" on the organ. There was no time for more than a little champagne in a hired upper room of the Wheatsheaf. Tom, and certain others, were per-forming that evening: there would be a *real* party on the stage of the Palladium after the second house. Tom was last turn of the first half.

Estella, our sister-in-law, sat with Hortense and me in one of the stage left boxes. "They were *gorgeous*," she told us, meaning the Framboise silver coffee set, my gift, and Hortense's, some genuine Sèvres oversize dinner plates. You could send things from Paris in those days without danger of breakage or pilfering. "I *love* that sort of thing," Estella said. She seemed to have forgotten me; Hortense, of course, she had never met. She had transferred her old arty enthusiasms to the Catholic Church, for her conversion to which there had been lengthy preparation from, of all people, that Fr. Frobisher of Farm Street who had damned me. She wished to be known as Stella Maris, she was devoted to the Little Flower, she observed the First Fridays, she prayed to Saint Anthony of Padua for the recovery of lost things, she *loved* fasting, it was so good for the figure, and would fast, regardless of the Church ordinances, at the drop of a hat. When the Palladium orchestra blasted with excessive noise and speed into *The Entry of the Gladiators*, she took rosary beads from her purse and, with a faint superior smile, began to tell a decade. I had heard about Joe Framley, the beery conductor. The orchestra had begun to rehearse that piece at a good lively tempo but he had cracked down with his baton and yelled, "This is not a fucking funeral march." Hence the ripping and tearing now.

When, after Estella's fifteenth or so decade, Tommy Toomey came on, neat and slight in tails, there was affectionate applause from the audience. They knew he had been married that afternoon, for there was a picture and a brief story in the *Evening Standard*, the bride looking lovely and pious. Instead of rushing straight into the blisses of matrimony he had come here to couple with his public. Fidelity. Duty. Tommy was well and smiling. He had put on a little weight, the old cough, fruit of an innate bronchial weakness exacerbated by being a gas corporal at Boyce Barracks, was hardly to be noticed. That light voice, expertly forward placed, filled the fine vulgar auditorium with the melody of mock patrician speech. There had been a good deal in the news about a trade agreement between Great Britain and Denmark, so Tom retold the story of *Hamlet* in terms of dairy exports. Hamlet, he said, was really christened Ham Omelette. Claudius, his wicked uncle, was a very bad Danish egg. He owed his name to the fact that he was regularly clawed by his wife. "Clawed," said his subjects. "Better 'e than us." So he was called Clawed e us. His queen had formerly been known as Gert. It was rude to go on calling her Gert, she said at the coronation breakfast (eggs and bacon), so she was called Gertrude. Rosencrantz and Guildenstern were two pawnbrokers who had gone broke but had now become pawns in the paws of the king and queen. Polonius was a Polish import. The Danes had enough sausages of their own, so Ham Omelette carved him up behind the arras. Arras, I said arras. Ophelia was proud of her egg-smooth skin and was always inviting people to touch it: "Oh, feel 'ere," she would say. Ham Omelette duly felt and said something about a nice piece of crackling and then found himself trapped in a long engagement. It was so long that Ophelia went mad and sang the most filthy songs. Ham Omelette felt depressed and contemplated suicide. The second law of the Danish State (where Ham Omelette had discovered something rotten: a load of eggs intended for shipment to England) was divided into 2A and 2B—2A said you mustn't kill other people; 2B said you mustn't kill yourself. "2B or not 2B," brooded Ham Omelette. And so on. Infantile really, prep school stuff, but Tom's manner acknowledged it as such. The consistently weak jokes couldn't be ridiculed because Tom's ridicule got in first. At the end he sang, and I got a little round as brother and lyricist, my old song about love and Paris:

> *"Find a cozy* table
> *Inside a* restaurant,
> *Somewhere* formidable
> *Where you'll be* très contents.
> *Let your lady fair know*
> *That she is all you see,*
> *Prime her with a Pernod*
> *Or three.*
> *Watch her crack a lobster*
> *And strip it to the buff,*
> *Rough as when a mobster*
> *Gets tough.*
> *Keep the wine cascading*
> *And you'll ensure*
> Une p'tite spécialité *called* l'amour . . ."

Prolonging the ultimate *l'amour*, he made a courtly signal which brought dimming up a cozy pink spot on his bride. She, queenly as the Star of the Sea, rose to the clapping, rosary firmly gripped. Then the curtains closed to Tom's tabs music ("It's Tommy This and Tommy That"—old Rud Kipling and Sir Charles Villiers Stanford), the house lights came up, and the audience went off for a bad-tempered struggle at the bar.

The party we had after the show was, for a time, the best kind of party it was possible to imagine. The bare stage was French-chalked, the orchestra came onstage and played the latest Charlestons and fox-trots. There was also the Black Bottom:

> *They say that when that river bottom's covered*
> *with ooze*
> *They start to squirm*
> *Couples dance and that's the rhythm they use*
> *Just like a worm*

The dancing was lively because there were so many professional dancers, such as the girls of the Palladium chorus, probably far more seductive in their short skirts and fancy garters than in their former spangled nearnakedness. Low comedians recited from *Othello* and *Measure for Measure*, a Dantesquely ravaged old laddie actor performed a cakewalk. There was bottled beer as well as whisky and champagne, and there were hearty vulgar pork pies with a thick dark crust. Ernie Callaghan recited "Little Orphant Annie," making little orphan Estella cry. But she recovered to sing the Bach-Gounod *Ave Maria* very badly, though the company applauded with the admirable insincerity of stage folk. Tom gave us, movingly, the final stanzas of Spenser's *Epithalamion*. Dick Bradshaw got me into a corner by the bank of dimmers and said the time was ripe for a big patriotic musical. The country needed confidence in its own *Schicksal*, what with the General Strike still strong in memory and trade suffering from the dumping of the Japanese. There was a lot of unemployment in the profession and it was going to get worse: you could cram a stage with crowds at thirty bob a head and glad of the money. The story of the quarter century in song, laughter and a bloody good cry. Tell Noel Coward, I said; ask him. In time for the cutting of the cake (the Palladium in sugar with an embracing sugar couple on its crown), my old lover Val appeared.

Val was now Soho's favorite drunken poet and growing fat. He brought with him an overhandsome young man in royal robes who was introduced as the exiled king of Bohemia. This man had a stage sword in a stage scabbard and, for five bob or a triple whisky, he would willingly dub anyone knight or dame. Val was already a multiple Sir Valentine. Val recognized Hortense at once. "All that time ago, dear," he said, "during that *destructive* war when we were all fighting for our honor, I thought to myself ah there is *real* beauty that will burgeon and blossom and I was *not wrong*. To think," he said, squinting without favor at me, "that you and this foul weed should have sprung from the same compost." He munched cake.

"You should have brought your archbishop pal as well," I said. "Exiled kings are ten a penny." I nibbled icing.

"I know," Val spattered saliva at me, "your cynicism, dear. The sentimental sneerer steeped in pusillanimity. My *archbishop pal* as you vulgarly term him *is dead*. He was kicked to the ground and booted while he lay in a puddle. By, I might add, drunken Irishmen on a Saturday night. A rib was broken. He caught pneumonia lying there. He did not recover." He swallowed cake.

"So that's one autocephalous church out of the way," I said. "Plenty more, I suppose. Plenty of theatrical costumiers on Charing Cross Road."

"He's filthy, isn't he?" Val said, evilly slit eyes on me, to Hortense. "All that sentimental scum for a public surface, while underneath is the most adamantine heartlessness."

"You're talking about my brother," Hortense said.

"Yes," Val went, with comic splayed nostrils and a manic glitter, "that's who I'm talking about, dear. The death of love and Toomey is its tomb."

"Don't give me that," I said, "about the death of love."

"Corned beef and slobber," Val said with unerring memory. "Tripe and onions. Ah, here's Jenny." A woman of four and a half feet in a liver-colored costume and a cloche right over her eyes like a guardsman's peak, somewhat humpbacked, about my age but with lines like overflow channels for gravy scored from mouth to chin, stood there looking up at me, sipping what I assumed was neat whisky. "This," Val said, "is the great Toomey. This is his exquisite sister."

"Ah yes, exquisite," she said eagerly. "Jenny Tarleton," she said, imprisoning Hortense's hand for too long. "Literary agent," she clarified. "Val here's mine." She ate no cake.

"You mean," I said, "you sell Val's verse to the highest bidder? Things are looking up."

"Verse," she said, letting the hand go with reluctance, "is coming back to the theater. We're done with the well-made play."

"So now," I said, "you're going to have badly made ones? Tarleton," I said, "is a great theatrical name. Dick Tarleton, cirrhotic leader of the Queen's Men. There's a picture of him somewhere with his little drum, prancing. Any relation?"

"Never heard of him. You were not to the fore in the *Well of Loneliness* case."

"A bad book."

"What's badness to do with it?"

"Just what I said," Hortense struck in. "It's a question of the right to say what you want to say, well or badly."

"I disagree," I said, and to Val, "Plays in verse, eh? Back to the glory of Stephen Phillips and prolix theeandthouery. What dost thou have in thy mind? Empedocles? Cyrus the Great? Tintinnabulus the Tyrant?" I palatalized the t's campily.

"Yes yes, how exquisitely you put it," Jenny Tarleton was saying to Hortense. "The right, as you say, to say, to do. Yes, exquisite."

"Or," I said, inspired, "how about a nice falsification of English history? An archbishop martyred for his homocephalous church, four butch knights sticking it in."

"You're so awful," Val said indulgently, "that one can't take you as one should. Just a tease, so out of date with everything. Not heard of Brecht, for instance? Stuck there in Paris, where it's all coming to an end. Berlin is the town of the future, you old fart. Brecht. Wystan Auden and I were entranced."

"Who's he?"

"There you are, what do I tell you? Nose always in the air among the pink-candy cumulus of your appalling fiction, never to the ground, sniffing."

"I thought it was ear not nose you had to have. Sorry," I said to two dancers who bumped into my back.

"To be at least honest," Hortense was saying.

"I could not conceivably agree more with you than I do. Without honesty where are we? We must stand up for things, true, exquisitely so." I caught Estella's voice saying ginnily to someone:

"I wish I'd discovered virginity, you know, while I was still a virgin. But we're chaste, you know, we're going to have lots of it. I love chastity."

"She'll be a good wife," Val said. "No plying awye. Not at any rate till she gets all that ordure out of her system."

"What do you know about good wives," I said, "apart from Louisa M. Alcott? What do you know about bloody chastity?" Tears came to my eyes then left.

"You could have stood up for that nice sincere little woman," Val began to scold. "You could still do it. There's Bascombe over there of the Evening Standard. Give him something now while he can still see straight. He's very accurate. Poor dear Radclyffe." He evidently did not know her, no one who knew her called her by that name. "Well, we're going to fight, we're going to lobby. And we can do without the help of the great bloody Toomey."

"What is this? What are you talking about?"

"Hortense here," Jenny Tarleton said, "if I may call her Hortense, which I'm sure I may, exquisite little name, I knew there was French blood there as soon as I saw you, something to do with the cut of the wrists and, yes, the ankles, Hortense will love to be there, won't you, little angel?"

"Where?" Hortense asked, not now too happy about the right to lesbic self-expression.

"Westminster," Jenny Tarleton hissed, as if it were a snakepit, "where people are supposed to look after our liberties but never do. The time is exquisitely ripe. Tomorrow at two with our banners."

"What is to be engrossed on these banners?" I asked.

"They have already been *engrossed*, as you put it," Val said, "with your little property conveyer's mind. There will be at least three hundred of us. London will see the terms *gayboy* and *gaygirl*. They will become part of everybody's vocabulary."

"Christ," I said, "those are prison words."

"Yes," Val said, "precisely. And the other words belong to the teminology of such as Krafft-Ebing. We must make our choice."

"Mass martyrdom," I said. "The new English martyrs."

"They can't martyr us all," Jenny Tarleton said. "Nor can our petition be rejected. Five hundred signatures."

"What exactly," asked Hortense, "are you petitioning for?"

"Well," Jenny Tarleton said, frustrated in seeking for Hortense's hands, which were both now behind Hortense's back, raising her voice above "The Post Horn Gallop" and the hunting whoops and tallyhos, "we demand *all* the freedoms—association, action, expression. We are *not* criminals."

"How," Val said, "did Christianity get started? We've already had our crucifixions and we have our saints."

"It's not the same thing," I said.

"Isn't it? Aren't we proclaiming," cried Val, "a new view of God? God made us what we are and he had his reasons. I don't see the difference."

I smiled, though with no smear of triumph, at Hortense. "You," I said, "were saying something similar this very afternoon."

"I'm sure she was," Jenny Tarleton cooed. "She has an attuned mind. I could feel its exquisite vibrations as soon as I saw her. You'll be there, angel, won't you? There'll be plenty and plenty to look after you."

"We're flying back tomorrow, aren't we, Ken?"

"The day after," I said. "I've some people to see tomorrow. Will you excuse me now?" I said generally. "I must have a word with my brother."

There was now tangoing for the nearly sober and dervish-style whirling for the drunk. Tom had his arm about his bride; both were leaning against the stage-right knobbed and voluted column of the proscenium arch. Tom was nodding, and Estella looked vacant, at something an old woman in black, somebody's dresser perhaps, was telling them. "All she craved was a bit of affection and love but he had to be poured into bed every night he come home. There's a warning for everybody in that." Seeing me coming she repeated "For everybody" and went off for more drink.

"Much happiness again, dear brother," I said in a stage tone. "Dear Estella," I added.

"I don't think we've been introduced."

"Oh, come off it, Stell. If she can put up with the life," Tom said. "Well, she has already. Manchester next week, the old Palace. Not much of a honeymoon, is it, Stell?"

"You're looking fit," I said. "That cough seems to have gone."

"Stell found me a remarkable cough medicine, Dr. Gregg's. She gave me the whole bottle when I was near dead with bronchitis. I passed out for three days, marvelous dreams. When I woke up I was as clear as a bell. Astonishing little girl, aren't you? Who's that woman there trying to embrace Hortense? Ah, that's stopped her." Hortense had hit out. Jenny Tarleton seemed very surprised. Ernie Callaghan grabbed Hortense and was tangoing with her in long flat-footed strides. The band was playing "Jealousy."

"Hortense," I said, "has taken to sculpture."

"Why do you say that?" Estella said. "I don't see the connection."

"Muscle," I said. "She's good with a hammer and chisel."

"I think I know you," Estella said. "You're a friend of Peter Warlock's."

"Much happiness," I said again. "Not much more I can say really, is there? I'm glad you've taken the plunge."

"What a horrid thing to say," Estella said. "Does she do religious sculptures and things?"

"She's going to do a Madonna and Child, she says."

"Do you believe in chastity? I think chastity's marvelous."

"Not too much chastity," Tom said.

"All you can get," I said sincerely. The King of Bohemia was zigzagging toward us, sword ready for accolade.

"Well," I said to Hortense, when we were taking a late-night pot of tea in our drawing room, both, having drunk so much, being thirsty, "do we go and support the petitioners?"

"That was a horrible little woman. I had to hit her, you know. Clawing and fumbling like that. But I can't help feeling a bit sorry for her."

"Lesbians," I said, stretching my legs on a limegreen pouffe, "are said to know far more about giving sexual satisfaction than men. They have patience, for one thing. They're not in a hurry to get it all done. Like," I guessed, "Domenico."

"You have this great gift for making everything sound horrid. And what do you know about Domenico?"

"Men are like that. With women, anyway. Poor Tom. I don't think there's much sex in poor Tom. What's known as a white marriage. Do we go tomorrow?"

"You put me in an awkward position, don't you? I mean, about freedom and so on. You *must* go, of course. You must be in the forefront and to hell with the consequences."

"Such as a truncheon or a police horse's hoof. I don't really believe, Hortense," I said, getting up with energy to pour myself more tea. "I really don't think it's right to be the way we are, those of us that are, I mean. I don't glory in it. It's not right and it's against Nature. It's a curse. That silly girl was going on about chastity tonight. I found chastity and I felt no frustration. I found a way out."

"I've heard all about that, what happened in the Federated Malay States." She pronounced *Malay* with two *ays* and a stress on the first syllable. "That seemed to me to be unnatural."

"Like Jesus Christ? Like priests?"

"Now it's you who's being blasphemous. Get on the telephone to the Vatican or wherever fat Carlo is. He'll tell you what to do. He'll talk about free will and standing by your brothers in adversity."

"He'll talk about free will used evilly, as you damned well know. What I talk about is predestination and not liking what's been predestined. But I agree with one thing—it's nothing to do with the state or the secular law. Damn it, we'll both go. But we'll both run away if there's trouble. This martyrdom is all nonsense."

"Run away, oh no."

"Run away or else get an eye kicked out or your crowning glory pulled off along with your scalp. We both have duties elsewhere."

"I do. Do you?"

"I may," I said, "one day write a good book. Perhaps all the tripe I'm doing is a preparation for that. *Schicksal.*"

"Sister Gertrude, Rude Gert, Tom is silly really but you have to laugh, was always going on about *Schicksal*. I know all about *Schicksal*. It's nonsense. And now I'm going to bed." She went with no good-night kiss for her elder brother, locking her bedroom door with a loud click of the bolt. Stupid girl, what did she expect? My rushing in to peep at her naked? Somnambulistic incestuous rape?

Dreams have been too often my surrogate for experience. I sank to sleep before being able to finish my last cigarette. Almost at once I heard Big Ben's thirteen tons clang the hour of two and then clang it again, then again, a kind of chuckling grinding between the repeated messages, something wrong with the works. I was standing naked facing the public entrance in Old Palace Yard: the door was open but nobody was within. The Yorkshire magnesian limestone of the Houses of Parliament was visibly corroding in the acid rain of London: knobs and nuts of black petrous matter dropped and feebly plashed in the puddles. "Now," I cried, and I turned. I faced a horde of sexual aberrants at their worst, hissing, camping, simpering, Val nowhere to be seen. Oh do fetch the bobbies, the little darlings. We do so want to be done. Bits of corroded stone were picked up and thrown at me, weakish, girlish. Hortense appeared in underwear from within the building, coming through the Norman Porch and high-heeling down the stairs with a clatter. Domenico, dressed as a fascist, cried "*Disgraziata*" and hurled a hefty missile, gray lead tortured into a cricket ball. This caught Hortense in the right eye. Blood spurted and then the eye itself stared out dead on the end of its stalk. There were cheers. That will spoil her beauty, disgraceful little bitch. Her scream seemed to be a waking not a dream one. It woke me as if it were in my bed. I knifejacked to sitting, shaking and sweating. The rain was teeming, and Brook Street was full of drowned quivering lamps. I relighted that discarded cigarette.

And now, as so often happened, my brain in a fever took over the datum of the dream and enriched and expanded it. Norman Douglas spoke pedantically on behalf of the buggers. "We have this right, you see, to shove it up. On a road in Capri I found a postman who had fallen off his bicycle, you see, unconscious, somewhat concussed. He lay in exactly the right position. I buggered him with athletic swiftness: he would come to and feel none the worse." The Home Secretary nodded sympathetically while the rain wept onto him in Old Palace Yard. "I mean, minors. I mean, there'd be little in it for us if you restricted the act to consenting males over, say, eighteen. Boys are so pliable, so exquisitely sodomizable. You do see that, don't you, old man?" The Home Secretary nodded as to say, Of course, old public school man myself, old boy. I saw a lot of known faces, Pearson, Tyrwit, Lewis, Charlton, James, all most reasonable, claiming the legal right to maul and suck and bugger. I put myself in the gathering and said, also most reasonable, that it was nothing to do with law: you were still left with the ethics and theology of the thing. What we had a right to desire was love, and nothing hindered that right. Oh nonsense, he's such a bore. As for theology, isn't there that apocryphal book of the Bible in which heterosexuality is represented as the primal curse?

That was my own invention, which was to appear the following year as a superbly printed little pamphlet from the Black Sun Press. Am I now, knowing what happened to this publication, knowing how it is in use at this moment as a text read aloud at homosexual marriages, indulging in the false insights of pretended prophecy? I have already, by reproducing that text earlier in these memoirs, avowed authorship, and it is for the first time in print. I have provided a kind of theological justification for homosexuals to whom instinct is not enough. Why did I do this? Reaction, partly, against the sanctimonious rebukes of Raffaele Campanati; the surrogation of a fury of lust unappeased; the fulfillment of the right of even the bad artist to see how far imagination can take him; submission to a rational demon. Shakespeare could have done it, and better, had he been called upon. Write me, O writer, a justification of Jew-baiting and death camps, put it in the invented mouth of an invented zealot, make it convince. The artist's pride: he must see if he can do it. What is the point of the dialectic of fiction or drama unless the evil is as cogent as the good?

"There is," Norman Douglas said with a Scots twang, "the question of sterile seed. Its spending in the *vas naturale mulieris* is as much of a pollution as its spurting in male mouths and around male thighs and buttocks. I mean, old man, if you're holding to the strict Aristotelian view. Yes, I know, if you know you're sterile, which is perhaps a good reason for not wishing to know. You speak truth in that mock biblical thing of yours: the primal function of the flow was the expression of joy and it remains so. What, are we to be chained, like beasts, to biology?"

The rain was still heavy as Hortense and I sat facing each other over the breakfast brought to our suite: kippers, kidneys, eggs, toast, strong Claridge's tea. I said, "It won't happen. They're not the sort of people who'll face the rain."

"It'll stop," she said. "It's too heavy not to." Both her eyes burnt cool and steady at me: that dream had not been a melodramatization of her catching ocular cold from a draught or bumping her brow on a darkling visit to the bathroom. But the rain continued as we went out into the West End on our different missions: she to buy toys for the twins, I to visit my diastematic agent. They wouldn't face the rain, which mewled consistently all day. The *Evening Standard* proved me wrong. A procession of men, young and not so, carrying slogans blurred by the wet—*We are as God made us*—*Justice for the Gay*—got mixed up on Bridge Street with a hundred or so unemployed from the North, the destination of both groups the House of Commons. The unemployed, outraged by the frivolity and, yes, indecency of the deviant demonstrators, initiated violence to which some of the others responded, though many ran away. The police, apparently, looked on for a time before intervening. There were no serious injuries except for a young man who was blinded by a stone in the left eye. Representatives of both groups were permitted, under police escort, to present signed petitions, the one to the Member for Warrington, Lancs, the other to the Home Secretary. Having delivered his document, the leader of the deviant demonstration, a poet well-known in Soho, Valentine Wrigley, shouted obscene slogans in the outer corridors of the House of Commons. The police had remonstrated kindly but he had knocked a portcullised cap off a constable's head. He had been taken in charge.

"They don't," I said to Hortense over tea, "really want the big gesture. They don't really want a change. They want to be naughty and they want to be noticed, no more. For their activities to be proscribed by law is meat and drink to them. And they call themselves early Christians. They want the titillation of acknowledged wickedness. There's no mention of any women being there. So much for your Miss Tarleton."

"Not mine."

The Well of Loneliness was not to be republished in Great Britain for another twenty-one years. It remained and remains a bad book. At the trial in the United States in 1929, the New York judge rendered the same judgment as the London magistrate, but his verdict was unanimously reversed by a higher court. You could no longer prosecute a book on its subject matter alone. There was never much point in moral activism in Great Britain, it was always a matter of waiting for the Americans to move. The colonies still worked for the old mother bitch.

forty-three

A decade ends in zero, not nine, and the twentieth century will still be going on (or, if this book survives its epoch, was still going on), though very wearily, in the year 2000. Still, the switchover to a new ten is dramatic and feels like a beginning. In 1929 we were ten years away from a new war and eleven years beyond the end of an old one. An age was beginning in one sense; in another it was ending in spectacular style. There was, for instance, the Lateran Treaty which Monsignor Carlo Campanati, collaborating behind the scenes with Pietro Cardinal Gasparri, did so much to implement.

It was February 11, a wet day in Rome, and the Angelus was clanging and throbbing. The noon gun fired from the Gianicolo as Cardinal Gasparri, accompanied by Monsignor Campanati, drove into the Piazza Laterana. Into the Palazzo Laterano strode Benito Mussolini and his aides. On a long table, gift to the papacy of the people of the Philippines, the papers lay waiting, along with polished silver inkwells, blotters clean as a baptized infant soul, a beautiful gold pen.

Cardinal Gasparri said in greeting to the Duce, "This is the feast of Our Lady of Lourdes. Auspicious, auspicious."

"Is this Our Lady of Lourdes the same as all the other Our Ladies?" the bullfrog atheist asked.

"That is unworthy," Monsignor Campanati said.

"I've had just about enough of you," the Duce said surlily. "I'll be glad when this is over."

"It is also," Cardinal Gasparri said, "the seventh anniversary of the crowning of His Holiness."

"Yes yes," the Duce said. "By a retrospective act that coronation is converted into a purely spiritual ceremony. That is what the Italian State is paying for."

"I was reading the other day," Monsignor Campanati said, "your pamphlet entitled *God Does Not Exist*. Is that still your view?"

"Irrelevant," the Duce scowled. "I've had enough of you, I say. I want you packed off to America or somewhere. Your Eminence," he said to Cardinal Gasparri, "your assistant here is well aware of my church marriage and the baptism of my children. He knows that I've repaired your churches damaged in the war, I've had crucifixes put up by law in schools and public offices. I've been bullied enough by this underling, with all respect to his holy cloth. I would remind you to remind him that I am the secular head of the Italian State."

"You must," Cardinal Gasparri told Monsignor Campanati mildly, "not bully the secular head of the Italian State."

"I apologize," Monsignor Campanati said humbly. "It was and is no more than the affectionate bullying of a father. I am delighted that the Duce, as he calls himself, has at least represented himself as having seen the light, though I have the duty in God of continuing to question his sincerity. I have heard that he still talks of a priest-ridden people and alludes to a marriage of convenience between Church and State. Look now where he has put his left hand; it is Godless superstition. We will not through magic drain away his potency."

The Duce hurriedly withdrew his left hand from his crotch and thrust it into the bosom of his morning coat. He had instinctively been making the apotropaic gesture against the sacerdotal evil eye. "Let us get this business over," he grumbled. "Where do I sign?"

"Here," Cardinal Gasparri said, pointing with a heavily laden ring finger. "And here. And here." So the Duce attacked the documents as though they were an enemy and trampled his signature across them. He then stood upright and said:

"Is there more?"

"No more. Praise be to God, the Lateran Treaty is concluded."

"Initiated, one might more properly say," Monsignor Campanati said. "Will not the Duce also say *praise be to God?*"

"I will say thank God it is done," the Duce said. "Listen to me, Monsignore. I wish now to be left alone. I will go my own way. I do not want the catechism wagged at me and spies reporting on whether or not I have been to mass. A man's soul is his own."

"God's," Monsignor Campanati said. "God's. Still, at least you talk of a soul, and that is something."

"Shall champagne be served?" Cardinal Gasparri asked. "Very well, no champagne. No no, that pen is yours. It is all chaste gold. A gift from His Holiness." The Duce, still scowling, handed the pen to an aide. The aide wiped the ink off on a corner of a blotter and then stowed the pen in his top pocket.

"Do not forget ever," the Duce said, "and bid His Holiness not to forget, that this idea was mine. Tell your flocks that it was mine. We want no falsification of history."

"I," Monsignor Campanati said, "first put the idea to Moscon, and Moscon put it to Dragone, and then it climbed the long ladder to you. As you say, let us have no falsification."

"Well, then," the Duce said.

"Well, then," Cardinal Gasparri said, and he proffered his hand. The Duce took it. He did not take the hand of Monsignor Campanati, since that was not proffered. The Duce about turned and marched out, his aides following. Monsignor Campanati and Cardinal Gasparri looked at each other.

Monsignor Campanati said, "He is too stupid to realize yet what this will mean to him. He is established solid. They will make a little god out of him. They will cherish his very snotty handkerchiefs as holy relics. Women will offer themselves like sacrificial virgins. His picture will be everywhere. The Church, God help us all, has sanctified his castor oil and rubber truncheons."

"It's you who are always saying that good can use evil. I believe that too. The point is that he won't last. We will. Let's go to lunch."

I have put together the above out of what Carlo later told me. The significance of this event in Rome on a wet February day perhaps requires elucidation. During the Risorgimento the Papal States, which were rich secular territories covering some seventeen thousand square miles, including all of the city of Rome, much land north of the Tiber, much south of the Po, champaign, river and township extending from the Tyrrhenian Sea to the Adriatic, the papally ruled population more than three million strong, were rudely wrenched away by the forces of reform. Mussolini's new order, needing if not the vocal support of the Church at least a silence that could be interpreted as complicity, offered a settlement to compensate for the loss of its temporal power. The Lateran Treaty provided for the setting up of Vatican City as an independent sovereign state. Three basilicas—San Giovanni Laterano, Santa Maria Maggiore and San Paolo—and all their subsidiary messuages—were declared extraterritorial and rendered immune from state property taxes. The same applied to the Pope's summer residence at Castel Gandolfo as well as a number of other odd edifices within the city of Rome. In return, the Vatican recognized the existence of the Italian State and the permanent secular occupation of what was still, ineptly, termed the Holy City. But it insisted that, if the state left the Church alone, the canon law of the Church should nevertheless suffuse the laws of the secular commonalty. Thus, the state could not grant divorces and, if you were married in a church, that was deemed to satisfy the requirements of the civil authorities.

There were really three separate agreements unified in the Lateran Treaty. There was the Lateran Pact, which created the new state of Vatican City. There was the Financial Convention, under the terms of which Italy gave the Vatican the equivalent of some ninety million dollars—part in cash, part in government bonds—and agreed to pay the stipends of parish priests. And there was the Concordat, which exempted the clergy from paying taxes and gave the Vatican financial control of a number of so-called ecclesiastical corporations all over Italy. The Concordat also banned the Protestant Bible and the holding of evangelical meetings, even in private homes. Catholicism was the official religion of the Italian State. Religion had to be taught in schools, and educational establishments under a Catholic aegis gained preference over lay or state institutions. February 11, the day of the signing, became a national holiday. On June 7, 1929, the day of the ratification of the Treaty, the Pope created a Special Administration of the Holy See and put Bernardino Nogara, who was related to the Archbishop of Udine, in charge of it. Carlo was never too happy about this; he believed he could have managed all those millions far better himself. Nogara, he said, was not a holy man. He was a liar and a hypocrite. Lay as he was, he lacked ecclesiastic scruple. He fell into the trap of allowing Vatican money to serve dubious secular enterprises.

"Money is money," I told Carlo, "whoever manages it. It's neither dirty nor clean. Even Judas's money was blessedly above or beneath the taint of treachery. Like an animal. And, like an animal, it must be permitted to breed. That is the law of Nature."

Nogara bred money out of Italgas, which he bought from Rinaldo Panzarasa when his group of companies was foundering. Soon Italgas, with the Vatican as the controlling stockholder, was hissing and flaring in the buildings of thirty-six Italian cities. Including brothels. The Vatican swallowed La Società Italiana della Viscosa, La Supertessile, La Società Meridionale Industrie Tessili and La Cisaraion, and put them all, as CISA-Viscosa, under the control of another unholy man, Baron Francesco Maria Odesso. But Nogara was the brain, skilled at persuading the Duce, who knew nothing about economics nor, indeed, much about anything except gaseous oratory and the administration of murder (though he had written a novel at least as good as any of mine, *The Cardinal's Mistress*), that a Vatican-owned bank was really a kind of church, its transactions blessed by the Paraclete, and that it was one of the ecclesiastical corporations to which, under the provisions of Clauses 29, 30, and 31 of the Concordat, tax concessions must be granted. Nogara even, after the economic crash of late 1929, made Mussolini accept the transference of the much depreciated securities held by three banks in which the Vatican had invested lavishly—the Banco di Roma, the Banco dello Spirito Santo and the Sardinian Land Credit—into the government's holding company for dud enterprises, the Istituto di Ricostruzione Industriale, not at the current market rate but at the original worth of the holdings. The Vatican got $632,000,000 out of that, and the Italian treasury wrote off the loss.

But, in a way, Carlo was right. In 1935 Italy invaded Ethiopia and a munitions plant controlled by Nogara supplied arms to the invaders. Money could, after all, become dirty. Still, all in all, generally considered, not to put too fine a point on it, Carlo's initial concern about an impoverished Vatican that could not subsidize the propagation of The Word had been the match that had, after slow smoldering, ignited the great blaze of wealth. The speed with which the Vatican grew rich was positively obscene, as unnatural as a swift-motion nature film showing a mustard seed turn into a tree, with birds dwelling in the branches thereof. He had wanted money to bring light to the heathen and, by God, he had got it. Not that he himself was now in charge of the mechanics or maintenance of the spread of the faith. Mussolini's words about wanting to see him packed off to America, though of no import within the Vatican, bore fruit perhaps merely because they were uttered. The Holy See had to dispatch ambassadors abroad, like any other independent state, and, though Carlo was not yet ready to head a legation, he would be, it was recognized, very useful as an aide in a country whose language he spoke, literally, as a mother tongue. So, in the early thirties, he was sent to Washington under an archbishop who spoke American like a street organ-grinder. (Carlo was, unkindly, sometimes to be called his monkey.)

For, while he was still in Italy, Carlo would not let Mussolini alone, and his enmity was not in accord with the amicability of the Vatican. Mussolini was called, by the more naif of the clergy, a man sent from God. His Holiness himself once spoke, when the guard was off his tongue, of the divine provenance of the Duce. Carlo, Monsignor Campanati as he still was and would still be for a long time, never missed an opportunity of abusing the pyknic atheist, as he termed him. The Lateran Treaty had been signed and could not be (nor would the Duce, now a saint, wish it to be) revoked. The Church was safe from the fascists, and Carlo was of the Church. He was untouchable, though he lodged with me a document to be opened in the event of his sudden death, in which, whether death was caused by double pneumonia or by overeating, the black-shirts were unequivocally to be blamed.

I was, on one of my visits to Rome to see my dentist, dining with him one evening at da Piperno, a Jewish restaurant next to the house of the Cenci, well known for its artichokes and a dessert called grandfather's ballocks. There were two middle-ranking fascists near our table, and they recognized Carlo. Da Piperno was much patronized by fascists. They had not yet been taught by Germany that the Jews ought to be persecuted. Indeed, there were fascists among the Jews. The Jews had killed Christ and made money, but they had been in Italy longer than the Christians. They tolerated the Pope as a Roman, but Christ was a kind of foreigner. Up on the Gianicolo the Jewish stallholders sold metal replicas of St. Peter's and Romulus and Remus and jawjutting pictures of the Duce. They were all right, and da Piperno was one of the best restaurants in Rome. One of the middle-ranking fascists snarled at Carlo and said, "You'd be wise to stop it."

"Have we been introduced?" Carlo put down the skeleton of a grilled sole he had been sucking the flesh off and turned to them very amiably.

"No nonsense. You know who we are and we know who you are. We know what you've been saying and we warn you to stop it."

"About the Duce and your stinking regime? Let me, as your father in God, warn you not to meddle in matters you are not well qualified to understand. You may know all about truncheons and castor oil—a very good aperient, incidentally, if taken in moderation—but you know nothing about theology. May I now proceed with my dinner?" And he got back to sucking sole bones. The one who had not spoken grasped Carlo rudely by the shoulder in order to make him turn round to listen to abuse. Carlo sighed, put down the skeleton, wiped his fingers on his napkin, then, with an athleticism surprising in one of his fatness, so twisted himself that he was freed from the fascist grasp. He then gripped the wrist of the grasper and held on to it till he produced a little yelp of pain. Then he let it go. He said to both of them: "I love Benito Mussolini probably more than you do. Indeed, you would cut his throat tomorrow if you could get a thousand lire out of it. I love him because he is a human soul, and I regret that his pure humanity, which issued from the hand of a God in whom he does not believe, has been so foully sullied by the devils of greed and power which have clearly taken possession of him. I would like to purge him of those devils, but, in his perversity, he is happy to be possessed."

"Devils," sneered the one who had spoken, an oily-haired handsome man in early middle age. "Get back to your dusty books, priest, and leave the modern age alone. Devils, indeed. We're done with your superstitions." And the other, who had a wine stain on his black shirt, laughed sillily.

Carlo put on a shocked look. "Indeed? You call strict Catholic teaching superstitious? And you and your leader so anxious to get on the right side of the Church and hang crucifixes even in knockingshops? Perhaps, of course," he said more loudly, "you do not always agree with the Duce's enactments."

A man with a bib on halted the delivery of a forkful to look at the two fascists. The younger of the two, the shouldergrasper, said, *"Mussolini ha sempre ragione."* It was one of the comforting slogans of the regime. Carlo was delighted to hear it.

He said, "Right, for instance, in paying the wages of the priests of the Church so that they may perform their priestly duties? One of which duties, I may add, is the casting out of devils."

"Mussolini ha sempre ragione." The oily-haired one clicked his fingers for the bill. "We want no more of your priest's nonsense."

"Untrained minds," Carlo said with pity. "Hiding behind party shibboleths that protect you from the human duty of thinking for yourselves. Your dirty regime is a disgrace to a great country, mother of art and intellect. Go on, find an answer to that. It isn't enough to say Mussolini is always right."

"Look," I said in English, "there's going to be trouble. Stop it, Carlo, enough."

The Italians never, under any regime, an aspect of a natural wisdom that big words like patriotism and duty have never altogether been able to expunge, seek more than a minimal amount of trouble. Carlo, of course, was not entirely Italian. So the oily-haired one merely sneered again and said:

"Perhaps you'd like the bolsheviks here. They'd soon stop your shitty talk about devils."

"Well," Carlo said, very reasonably, "there's more sense in Marx than in Mussolini. At least Marx got down to some solid thinking. And a dialectic process implies movement and progression to an ideal goal, which could, with charity, be interpreted as a kind of Christian thinking. Don't understand me, do you? Don't understand a word." The two were up now, having paid the bill, and their secular black glowered down at Carlo's spiritual. Black, I thought: it doesn't show the dirt. "Well, of course, we're all supposed to rejoice in the imperial goal," Carlo said. "The revival of the Roman Empire, which means squeezing the juice out of a lot of poor innocent Africans. A travesty, like everything else dreamed up by that Godless hypocritical bullfrog of yours. Now get out and let me get on with my dinner."

"You'll hear more about this," the oily-haired one growled.

"I do hope so," Carlo said. Then the other one, before leaving, jolted the table edge with his hip and made our second bottle of Acitrezza wobble. I thrust out to save it but it toppled and began to glug out onto the floor. The bottle had been nearly full; it was a good wine and not cheap.

I said, in my English way, "Oh, really—*Rovinoso*," I added, "*e molto scortese.*"

"*Non mi frega un cazzo.*" And they left with a lipfart apiece and an ironical salute. Carlo watched them go amiably and said:

"One moment." He got up.

"Don't do anything foolish," I warned.

"One moment." He was out. The tiny square that car-driving patrons used as a carpark was enclosed, apart from the restaurant, by the façade of the disgraced Cenci house and its deconsecrated chapel. I got out there to find the oily-haired fascist doubled up from, I assumed, Carlo's kick in the testicles. At the other Carlo was lashing out vigorously with his fists. It was a soft little man whose courage was all in his shirt. When he saw another man coming, a lithe enough looking Englishman whose wine he had spilled, he went off down the sloping alleyway excreting naughty words. The doubled-up man made many groaning threats from what seemed to be a posture of devotion to Carlo's cloth. Then, still bowed, his hands a cage about his scrotum, he followed, cursing, his friend. "They will do nothing," Carlo said. "Nobody will believe they were attacked by a prelate. Or if they do it will be accounted a great disgrace." I could see Mussolini's point about protecting your testicles in a priestly presence. "Let us," Carlo said appropriately, "now go and eat grandfather's balls." This was a sweet dish: cream enclosed in light pastry and plunged briefly into hot fat, little orchidaceous gobbets served with plum jam. It was clear from this kind of behavior that Carlo would be better off in America.

But we were all destined for America. Domenico, as I foretold, was to find his true métier in writing music for the talking films, and the talking films were to lure me as a scenarist. We were both minor artists, and here was minor art in excelsis or in mediocre. In 1929 Paris seemed full of alltalking allsinging alldancing American movies, advertised on posters showing stylized tophatted highkickers, cooled by the rare sorbet of heavily nasal straight drama (those early sonic techniques appeared to favor the nasal moan). But the straight drama always had to have a theme song, even if it were not possible to have words in it. Phonograph records were helpful promotion, and films were helpful to phonograph records, the symbiosis began early. Thus, there was J. M. Barrie's *Half an Hour* turned into *The Doctor's Secret* with Ruth Chatterton ("*I was the woman in question.*"—"*Ah, mum's the word, dear lady*"), and the song without words was called "Half an Hour." The singing film was recognized at that time as the primary form. Neither playwright nor novelist felt, as yet, challenged by a medium essentially frivolous.

On the Champs-Élysées in the autumn, just before the Wall Street crash, *The Fox Movietone Follies of 1929* was playing almost next door to the Pathé film *La Fille du Pendu*, with Jean-Luc Carel and Claudine Pellegrin, directed by Georges Legras, music by Domenico Campanati. I remember almost nothing of it, but a residual image remains with me of the quality of the music—blurred, distorted in the tutti, too much (obligatory at the time) oleaginous saxophone. I had recommended Domenico for the job, and, after initial demurrals, he had delighted in the brutal exigencies that the cutter's craft imposed upon the score. Any measure had to be able to flow into any other measure: any musical sentence, however truncated by the scissors, had to make sense. You could have Stravinsky dissonance and you could have post-Puccini slush. Anything, really, went so long as it more or less fitted. The theme song of the film—a rather grim film about a girl blighted by her father's execution for murder—was something sung in a cabaret, and it kept recurring in contexts of irony. It was called *"Il était une fois,"* words by Roger Le Coq, and it made Domenico a lot of money.

I remember the American neighbor of this film rather well, at least the songs in it. "Breakaway," for example:

> *Write a little note*
> *On your toes*
> *Don't forget to dot the i*
> *Look at what you wrote*
> *Goodness knows*
> *It's easy as pie*

> *Let's do the Breakaway*
> *Get hot and shake away . . .*

And so on. What is the human memory playing at, that it can hold such inanities and forget great lines by Goethe?

I will say little of the Wall Street crash, which Carlo, when he had been playing the markets for the Church, using of his goodness some of the estate of poor Raffaele, had sharply foreseen. It was based on overconfidence, lack of prescience, stupidity. The American expatriates in Paris, sustained by American dividends, now had to scrape together enough to get home on. The light of literary experiment went dim, except for Jim Joyce, who toiled on at his mad work in progress. Whining Americans, cadging drinks in bars where they had once flashed generous dollars, became a bit of a bore. Franklin Dowd shot himself in a room in the Georges V for which he had not the money to pay. Silver-haired Hastin Newsom, who had sold his bank to live the life of Riley (whoever Riley was; he too probably crashed with Wall Street), threw himself from the top platform of the Eiffel Tower. Police were eventually installed up there to listen for American accents. Joe, my New York agent, was discovered, as I had suspected, to have parlayed the money of his clients and lost all in Radio mostly. He left his office at midday, typist still clacking, and went off to Nuevo Laredo in Mexico. Withdrawing, on Carlo's advice, my American earnings to Paris, I had forestalled my own segmental crash and lost only about fifteen thousand dollars. Harry Crosby, who had published my biblical pastiche in February under the title of *Fall for Lovers, auctor ignotus,* killed himself and his girl friend Josephine in a Boston hotel bedroom on December 10, thus, in identifying his own talentless gaudy extravagance with the age, achieving the work of art he knew was, despite all contrary evidence, in him. e.e. cummings wrote an elegy:

> *2 boston*
> *Dolls; found*
> *with*
> *Holes in each other*
>
> *'s lullaby and*
> *other lulla wise by UnBroken*
> *LULLAlullabyBY*
>
>   *the She-in-him with*
> *the He-in-her (&*
> *both all hopped*
>   *up) prettily*

then which did
lie
Down, honestly

now who go (BANG (BANG

Whatever else went bang bang, the talking films did not. Domenico wrote a very workmanlike score for *Bourrée Italienne,* all mandolins and tenors and tarantellas, and impressed Wouk and Heilbutt of MGM, who caught the film in Montreal. There were to be a lot of desperately cheerful movies in the next few years, some of them set in sunny It, as Wouk termed it, always to be thought of as a desperately cheerful place. Domenico was put under contract, and his first two scores were for *The Kid from Naples,* which had a Roman setting, and *Mamma Mia,* which was about a poor family on Mulberry Street, New York, who won lottery money and went back to sunny It to show off. For my part, I stayed on in Paris which, lacking expatriate Americans, was duller than it used to be. Then I was summoned to Hollywood to write the screenplay for *Singapore!,* an adaptation of my novel about Sir Stamford Raffles. The Pacific and the Indian Ocean and the China Sea were regarded also as diverting locales, and a mint had been made out of *Clive of India,* with Ronald Colman.

"It is," Carlo said, "a kind of blasphemy. I don't see why the Muslims allow it."

"There aren't any Muslims here," I said. "Only Jews."

"How would they like it to be called the Garden of Jehovah?"

He meant the hotel where I was living on Sunset Boulevard. It had once been the residence of Alla Nazimova the film actress, as I explained to him, hence the name, the aitch being a legitimate addition for people who thought of Mohammed's God as an aspect of Oriental décor, like sherbet. "That swimming pool out there," Carlo said, "reminds me of something."

"It's the shape of the Black Sea. Alla Nazimova came from Yalta."

Carlo shook his head, rightly, at the madness of the place. It was a long way from Washington, whose madness, being political, was excusable. He lowered himself with care to a chair of molded cane as though he thought it might be an illusion. The hotel was divided into bungalows, and the bungalows into apartments. In the apartment next to mine was a former *New Yorker* humorist who laughed bitterly most of the night. I was earning fifteen hundred dollars a week to write scripts as slowly as possible. They turned out films fast here, but off the set there was a great quality of indolence. Carlo opened his briefcase, which bore in stamped gold the keys and tiara of Vatican City, and pulled out what seemed at first Hollywood-conditioned sight to be the longest film script ever written. "No," I said. "It's not possible." And then I had it in my hands and I saw what it was.

"Don't read it now," Carlo said. "Wait till you have plenty of leisure. This is the result of many long years of work and discussion. It's finished in one sense, in another sense it's a mere draft of shameful simplicity. The thing to do is to sow the ideas widely. Then when the time comes for turning the ideas into action the world of the believer will be ready." I saw the title page: *The True Reformation—A Blueprint for the Reorganization of Institutional Christianity with Some Notes on Techniques of Affiliation with Related Faiths.* "My own typing," Carlo said. "It could not be entrusted to any of our stenographers in Washington. They would blab, and there must be no blabbing. I must not be associated with it, nor must any of those who worked on it. It's highly secret."

"And yet you bring it to me?"

"You're different. You have nobody to blab to. Or rather it will not be worth your while to blab." He seemed to have taken a fancy to the word. "Blabbing about religion is not in your province. What is there to drink?"

He knew what there was to drink, for the bottles were all set out on the little bar, but few of the labels meant much to him. Southern Comfort, Old Grandad, Malone's Sour Mash. I had taken to native American beverages. There was now, of course, no Prohibition: all those deaths in vain, including Raffaele's. He found a bottle of Old Mortality, a rare scotch, and poured himself a slug. "Ice in the icebox," I said, pleonastically. He took his Old Mortality straight. "This is not," I said, flicking the typescript through, "really my cup of tea, is it?"

He had forgotten, or had perhaps never known, the idiom. He stared at me an instant as though perhaps I had become suffused with *Alice in Wonderland* through working on a film treatment of it. Then he saw. "It has to be published," he said. "It has to be a lay publication, anonymous or pseudonymous. No question of a nihil obstat or imprimatur. Perhaps you could publish it under your own name. The name doesn't matter. You have a known name and your publisher will publish it. You can keep the money or give it to the poor. The important thing is to sow the ideas. You could even make a kind of novel out of it, people sitting round a table in a garden discussing religion. I don't mind what you do with it so long as the ideas are sown. Sitting round a table, drinking a cup of tea," he added, "which will make it more of your cup of tea."

I put the kettle on. It was getting on for five o'clock. "Gallons and gallons of tea," I said, flipping through the opus: there must, I reckoned, be about a hundred and fifty thousand words here. It was, contrary to professional convention, single-spaced. It was fastened together, rather like a film script, in blue covers with no spine, three paper fasteners of a length I had never before seen, forked golden stilettos, perhaps a Holy See speciality, brochetting the margins. I spooned Orange Pekoe into the warmed pot. "The Bishop of Bombay quondam Gibraltar would be in on this."

"He became somewhat unreliable. I speak confidentially. He grew obsessed with the interpretation of the Athanasian Creed, an aspect of his Anglicanism. But some of his terminology is there. Dr. MacKendrick, a Calvinist who, now I come to remember, liked to drink his tea very black and with no sugar or lemon, was helpful with the structuring of the work. Like an engineer almost. Many people collaborated. None of them will blab. In the present state of affairs they dare not. They would be in trouble with their own sectarian leaders. With, so to say, their *Duci.*" His eyes softened as in the nostalgia of battle.

"Under my name?"

"It will do your reputation no harm. It will gain you a new reputation for seriousness. This evening you can start reading. I shall spend the evening quietly with Domenico and Hortense and my, our, dear nephew and niece. They grow big, though no longer in the same proportions because of sex. There's a radio program I like to listen to about two black men called Amos and Andy. They are not really black but they put on a black maquillage even for this radio program. That is a kind of seriousness."

"Have you already been round there?" I meant 151 South Doheny Drive in Beverly Hills, where Domenico and Hortense and the twins lived. "Because tonight there's this party on in Bel Air, we're all going, perhaps you might like to—" Tea was ready. I poured for myself. Carlo frowned to show he preferred scotch.

"They were not at home. The children at riding lessons and the parents working." Hortense had gotten the job of providing a bust in multiplicate, or rather in progressive phases of completion, for the new Marlene Dietrich film, which was about a sculptor falling in love with his model. "There was only this black servant of theirs who is a Baptist. I dropped my *grip* there. Grip because you grip it, a good word. A party? What kind of party? Film stars?" He had seen Hollywood films about Hollywood parties: that incest had started early; was narcissism a kind of incest?

"Oh yes, lots of film stars. It's the birthday of Daisy Apfelbaum, whom you'll know better as Astrid Storm."

"Ah." He tongued moist lips. "She was in *Ocean Bear.*"

"She loves religion of all kinds. You can talk to her about religion." I sipped tea and sighed. As for that thing there . . . "As for this thing here," I said, "you know you're asking the impossible."

"Pooh," shooing at me, "I have never known the impossible to be much trouble. You start off with the impossible, and that is a blank sheet on which the possible may be written. When people talk of things being easy or even difficult, it's then you have trouble. This is so impossible that you'll do it."

"Under my own name?" I said again.

"Any name. No name. It is the thing itself that counts." Like my biblical buggery piece. "But when there is no name readers will start guessing. My own Duce in Washington may start guessing that it is myself. A pseudonym, like of this film star we're seeing tonight? I never knew that, by the way. That might start guessing too. Your own name is perhaps best, and you can prefix a preface saying that in the present state of the world you've been forced to give much thought to these questions and here humbly as a layman you proffer the tentative results of your thinking. Something like that. *The True Reformation* by Kenneth M. Toomey. I can see it," he said, seeing it, another one harmlessly corrupted by America, "on the bestseller lists. A burning cross perhaps on the cover."

"Like the Ku Klux Klan? No, let's have a pretty frowning woman in décolletage, perhaps Daisy Apfelbaum would do it, and for a title something like *Give Me God*. Or *God Help Us*."

"Now you're going too far. Now I think you're joking. But I can see you are ready to think about it. What time is this birthday party?"

"Any time after eight."

"I go as I am? I brought no other clothes." I surveyed Carlo, who had gone to the bar for more neat Old Mortality. He was in, so far as I could judge, the same clerical suit he had worn at the time of his brother's death. It bagged, it was stained, it was terrible, a triumph of the deformation squad of the wardrobe department. It fitted his ugliness, which would be specially appreciated here in Hollywood and environs. This was cinematically Gothic, a skilled work of special makeup men long in the business.

"You look fine," I said.

He nodded, sat heavily, swallowed whisky raw with no grimace, then looked troubled. He said, "Mother."

"I beg your pardon?"

"Have you received word from our mother?" The *our* was certainly meant to include myself.

"A couple of postcards," I said. "One from Salzburg. One from Chiasso to show she was back there from Paris. She increasingly regards my Paris apartment as her home, but she seems to feel guilty at finding Paris so enjoyable. Chiasso is her penance."

"She has the money," Carlo said with satisfied gloom. "There is Cartier. There is Maxim. The fleshpots of Egypt. She visits Luigia from Chiasso. A short train journey only. Luigia writes to me in her sharp way, she will be in charge of that convent soon, you will see, that Mother is losing her faith."

"Ah."

"She has this idea that the fascists are really Catholic. She has read that this Hitler is an Austrian Catholic persecuting the Lutherans as well as the Jews. She says that Christianity is a kind of Jewish heresy. She has become friendly with her bank manager in Chiasso, and he is a Jew. She is reading the Old Testament."

"Is that wrong?"

"She says the reality of the relationship between God and man is to be found in the Old Testament. And that the New Testament is very dull reading. Of course, the Scriptures should never be entrusted to the laity. That's how all the trouble began, letting untrained minds feed on the Bible."

"Your mother has a very good mind. I shouldn't worry about her."

"I pray. I pray for you too." He drank off his Old Mortality. "I pray for the whole damned world. Can I lie down somewhere?"

"Do you pray lying down?"

"I pray in all positions. God has no interest in our physical postures. Now I want to sleep for an hour. Where?"

"There." And I pointed to the second bedroom. He lumbered toward it. He closed the door. I heard his bulk meet the bed. Then his snores began like a shofar.

I had for at least two months been working, with the unnecessary assistance of a young screenwriter named Al Greenfield, on the scenario of *Singapore!* I had reached a phase of onomastic deadlock with the producer and the head of the studio. They wanted me to change the name of the founder of Singapore. This was because there was another Raffles, far better known, a gentleman crook, and a film on this Raffles was being prepared by a rival studio. Why not Sir Thomas Stamford? But good God man, I said, you can't falsify history like that. It would be like, say, changing the name of Jefferson or Ben Franklin because a Franklin or Jefferson was in the news as a kidnapper or fornicator. It's not false what you said, Ken, it's the same guy but you just cut the ass end off of his name. But good God man. I would not yield. Riffles would be okay, it sounds like a kinda limey way of saying it anyways, said a brutal man with a cigar frayed at the mouth end. Reffle Roffle Riffold. Riffold Schmiffold, nothing doing. Raffles or nothing. The project had to be shelved for a while, no matter really, since Loretta Young was not yet available to play Lady Raffles, Riffles what the hell. I could foresee that the thing was going to be taken out of my hands, me get no screen credit, but what the hell, this was not my trade, I could buy and sell any one of the bastards. I was put on to King Arthur and his

Knights. My employers were vague about the subject but knew it was a swell one for a costume movie. Now I was going to cause trouble again, because I didn't want any of this Lancelot and Guinevere crap, I wanted an embattled Celtic Christian dux vainly defending the faith against the brutal Teutonic invaders. I wanted it to be made in England amid the smell of wet evergreens. In the West. Faith. Duty. At this time my eyes began to prick at these words: the script, I foreknew, would be full of them. I was reading Geoffrey of Monmouth from the Los Angeles Public Library, not *Idylls of the King*. I was not in the Writers' Building today; I was not writing, though I had been told solemnly that my job was writing, wear down one whole pencil to the butt every day prompt by five, okay? I had been setting up the whole thing in the projection room of my head, seeing it, hearing *faith* and *duty*.

But now the ram's horn of Carlo's snores called me to at least the skimming of his typescript, not really irrelevant to the job for which I was being paid, embattled Christianity. It seemed a curious work that, attempting impersonality, was yet full of various voices, as from a body set upon by demons whose name was Legion. There was a German theologian there going on about the *Abendmahl* or evening meal, cozy sauerkrautish name for the Eucharist. The Bishop of Bombay quondam Gibraltar juggled with terms like substantiation, consubstantiation, insubstantiation. There was a dour struggle with free will and predestination, Carlo himself confronting somebody Scotch or Swiss. What seemed to me at the time, me the renegade, heterodox and shocking, nobody more shockable than the renegade, was to become the orthodox and bland. Here was the terrible ecumenical strategy set out in clumsy single-space typing, and I, who considered myself to have lost my faith, was appalled.

The Pope of Rome was, in this scheme, to be more of an elder brother than a father, an amiable chairman of the interdenominational committee of the faith, holding office by historical right but asserting no divine authority. The faith was to be both broadened and loosened, and there seemed to be proposed a technique of what I could only call semantic jiggerypokery whereby age-old fundamental diversities of belief could be united. The doctrine of the *Abendmahl* or Lord's Supper or Eucharist, for instance, with some believing in the Real Presence, others in a sort of realish presence, yet others in a mere act of commemoration. Remember, said some voice or other, that Christ, Son of the Father, is not bound of necessity to descend to take possession of the bread and wine at the moment of consecration, despite his promise on the eve of his execution, and despite the fact that the consecrating priest has mystically assumed the office of Christ himself. The free will of the godhead is unpredictable, being free. Moreover, in what manner is Christ, according to the belief of the Unreformed Church, really present in the accidents of the ceremony? Not in the sense of susceptibility of physical analysis, not in the sense of spatial and temporal containment. The ceremony of the Eucharist, in whichever of its sectarian interpretations, is concerned with conjuring the presence of Christ in an essentially physical context, bread and wine being, as common and humble gifts of the God of Nature, physical elements which will serve well as analogues of human flesh and blood, as the ordainer of the sacrament implied when he, following his practice of divinely poetic utterance, asserted not analogy but identity. A personal contact with the divinely human essence of the Lord is effected when certain entities come together: the officiating priest, the worshiper, and the physical elements which connect them. With the utterance of the words "This is my body, this is my blood," the recipient of those elements undergoes an experience of a kind too overwhelming to be more than temporary and perhaps merely instantaneous: an imaginative, and hence spiritually valid, communion with the personality of Christ. Hence this sacrament is adjudged excellent and perhaps necessary for salvation.

The ceremony of supper with the Lord is the kernel of a larger ceremony (so I read on), but a ceremony of little meaning unless that kernel be there. What Catholics call the mass and others the communion service is a ritual extensible or reducible according to aesthetic or devotional taste: the sacramental nucleus of the ritual remains its unassailable essence. The outer, or decorative, elements should follow no central prescriptive ordinance and should, in fact, be freely developed out of the cultural traditions, or serve the cultural needs, of the community at worship. Then there was a good deal about, as an instance of this free adaptation, the African mass, in which dancing and chanting would be more appropriate, and probably far more pleasing to the Lord, than the imposition of organ voluntaries or Western hymns.

The ceremonies of the Truly Reformed Church should be, it followed, closer to the needs of the people than had been possible in the hieratic forms developed and imposed at a high level of authority. It went without saying that the vernacular should replace Latin, and, moreover, not solely at the level of a national language but down, so far as was feasible, to the level of a regional language or dialect. This would be a matter for diocesan decision, where applicable, or even parochial consensus, the form of the mass or Sacrament of Christ's Coming being, ultimately, except for that central and sacred kernel, a genuine emanation of local culture and the will of the people.

And so on. There was as yet no index, but I riffled through looking for the True Reformed view of sin. There seemed less emphasis on what was wrong than on what was right, or good, or holy. The big theme was Love or Charity. Homosexual love? Nonsense, love was above sex. Marriage and children? The sexual act, when sanctified by matrimony, was what it had always been—a source of pleasure made holy by its purpose: the peopling of God's kingdom with souls. Everybody seemed agreed on that, there seemed to be no resolution in compromise on sectarian dissonance. Birth control? Abortion? Abortion was murder, but there were highly exceptional cases where decisions might be made, after intense examination of conscience and ample prayer, at the episcopal level or its equivalent. Birth control was, since it diverted the copulatory act from its biological and spiritual purpose, always reprehensible. The intention in emitting semen must always be the act of conception, though frustration of this intention through the vagaries of Nature was beyond human will and therefore was beyond the sphere of moral judgment. The spending of semen to a purely pleasurable end was an abomination.

Carlo emitted, at the point of my reading that, a snore of particular vehemence. I looked bitterly at his closed door.

Despite the stern prohibitions, the treatise emphasized again and again the principle of *liberum arbitrium*. Man was defined by his capacity for moral choice, and the existence of evil in opposition to good was a guarantee of that capacity for free election. But if good, as one of the attributes of the Creator, was built into man as the crowning work of the Creator, evil was essentially external. It was when, through the wiles of a destructive force which it was logical to personify as the Evil One, an eternal being whom God could himself destroy only at the expense of denying the right of all his creatures to act through free will (for, with the rejection of the Manichean heresy, the Evil One must be accepted as God's creation), evil was presented, as it always was, as good, that man fell into sin. The responsibility for sin could not be placed wholly on the shoulders of the human sinner, and God, knowing the strength of his enemy, was infinitely merciful to the dupes of that enemy, but man was not free of the necessity to develop judgment, the capacity to recognize evil even when it masqueraded as the highest good. Why did God allow evil to exist? A question not to be asked. Without evil there could be no freedom of choice. But so pervasive is that original good, that it can even inhere in evil as a potential consequence. Dangerous words, dangerous, dangerous.

Dangerous this denial of original sin, though it was not expressed in so many words. You could blame yourself for lack of moral judgment, but not for the dynamic which animated your acts of evil. Original sin was original weakness, not being sufficiently clever, or Godlike, to spot the machinations of the fiend. I was not surprised to find, in one of the numerous appendices, a rehabilitation of the heretic Pelagius.

Somebody, probably Carlo himself, that expert in ecclesiastical history, set out the whole story. Pelagius, a British monk in Rome in the early fifth century, was deeply disturbed when he heard a bishop quote from Augustine's *Confessions*: "Thou commandest continence; grant what thou commandest and command what thou wilt." This seemed to Pelagius to be a denial of moral responsibility. At the same time a commentator on the epistles of Saint Paul, usually named Ambrosiaster, seemed to affirm that the transmission of Adam's sin was effected biologically, human souls being derived, like human bodies, from the parents. "In Adam all sinned as in one lump." Pelagius, upset by this, wrote his own Pauline commentary and asserted that there was no hereditary transmission of sin, since this would be a denial of free will. Man sinned by an elected imitation of Adam's sin, not through an inherent fault of human nature. In all sin, said Pelagius, there had to be personal assent. The consequence of Adam's sin was a mere bad example which his successors voluntarily embraced. Infants had to be baptized into the faith, but the baptism was not a device of absolution from inherited sin. All this caused a hell of a row. Jerome called Pelagius a fat dog weighed down with Scotch porridge, his brains thick and muddled, a stupid rather than sinful denier of elementary truths—the necessity of infant baptism as an expunger of hereditary sin, the saving power of God's grace, the comparative impotence of man as a free agent thinking himself capable, without that grace, of voluntarily embracing the good. Augustine, expectedly, went wild.

Pope Innocent I said: Heresy. Augustine was happy. Then came Pope Zosimus (417–18). Zosimus was rather pleased with Pelagius's emphasis, in a new book, on free will, as well as his lofty view of morality and papal authority. He told Augustine and the rest of the Africans that Pelagius must be adjudged orthodox. Augustine, expectedly, went wild. But Pelagius had, in Sicily (how these people got around), written a socialistic pamphlet denouncing the irresponsibility of the rich toward the poor and the sinfulness of the maintenance of governmental power by means of torture and wanton execution. Augustine drew the attention of the Emperor at Ravenna to this preaching of social revolution. On April 30, 418, an imperial edict banished Pelagius and his followers from Rome as a menace to peace. Zosimus had to bow to the ultimate secular authority. He formally condemned Pelagius as a heresiarch, and the Church ever since had endorsed that condemnation. But, Carlo (it had to be Carlo) seemed to say, the condemnation, being made under duress, had no true validity, and there were grounds for accepting (he was discreet and cautious here) the Pelagian thesis as more consonant with the True Reformed premise of the goodness and dignity of man than the Augustinian doctrine of his natural depravity.

I had got to that word *depravity* when Carlo came out with a snore that seemed devised by his unconscious to wake him. He emerged a minute later in his shirt, creased but clearly refreshed, lipsmacking, brighteyed, ready for the fray. I closed the typescript. I would read more of it later, but I felt compelled already to tell him that I couldn't, that he had better give it to somebody else, that it was not my cup of tea. Carlo nodded without displeasure, unlidded the pot to find tea still in it, though cold, and fed himself with the bitter amber fluid straight from the spout. With wet lips, "No hurry," he said. "Don't make a hasty decision. Read it with care."

"I think," I dared to say, "that this is a highly dangerous document."

He was delighted. "*Exactly*. Religion is the most dangerous thing in the world. It is not little girls in their communion frocks and silly holy pictures and the Children of Mary. It is," he said, "high explosive, dynamite, the," he smiled at the conceit, "splitting of the atom."

forty-five

I did not drive, I have never driven. I made use in Los Angeles of a studio car to take me to Culver City and back and taxis for excursions of pleasure. Carlo and I, then, traveled in a taxi to the party, and, because of the garrulity of the driver, were able to talk no more for the moment of the holy or unholy project. "Picked up this guy, British, Cary Grant, stingy as hell, you know what I mean, he give me a lousy dime on a five-dollar fare. But Ginger Rogers, she's a lady, yes sir, that ain't her real name, you know that?" And then, "You guys in motion picutres?" and so on. Carlo looked as at the world of fallen man on the endless suburbs that passed for a city—an eatery in the likeness of a sphinx (enter between its forepaws); another, for jumbo malts so thick you can't suck 'em through a straw, in the form of an elephant crouched as at the bidding of its mahout; gimcrack temples of various faiths; attap roofs of nutburger stands with Corinthian columns; loans loans loans; stores crammed with cut-price radios; a doughnuttery; homes like Swiss chalets, like Bavarian castles, minia- ture Blenheims, Strawberry Hills, Taj Mahals; a bank in the form of a tiny ocean liner; dusty trees on the boulevards (date palm, orange, oleander); bars with neon bottles endlessly pouring; colleges for stuntmen, beauticians, morti- cians, degrees in drummajoretteship. It was better at night, even under the sick lamps: the surgical exposure to the Californian sun made one's eyes prick with shame and pity. We arrived at an exclusive residential world of Aztec temples, Parthena, Loire châteaux. I tipped the driver a dollar. Picked up this guy, British, stingy as hell, he give me a lousy buck.

The Storm residence had a long driveway with gravel carparks already fast filling on either side, a driveway guarded by stone or plaster patriarchs in robes with open mouths that gave out soft organ music. It led to a façade roughly modeled on Borromini's (ha) San Carlo alle Quattro Fontane. Within, as I knew, the hall was a miniature Balthasar Neumann pilgrim church of Vier- zehnheiligen in which a cinema screen could be lowered over the reredos. Hidden elevators led up and down to rooms in Chinese or Byzantine or Colonial Spanish or Regency styles. If you saw the mansion from the back, you found something like Martino Lunghi the Younger's *SS Vincenzo ed Anastasio*. This, tonight, was floodlit from the commodious lawns where the party was being held, though there would be cardplaying, roulette, a new movie, and fornication indoors. Over the lawns shone seven artificial moons; the real, dimmer, moon was rising over the distant hills. A dance orchestra was playing on a raised platform under a Pier Luigi Nervi waffled ceiling. A singer sang through a microphone:

> *"I'll crash the moon*
> *To fetch a spoon*
> *Of precious lunar dust.*
> *I'll fly as high*
> *As heaven's eye.*
> *I'll even die*
> *If I must . . ."*

Popular songs were, at that time, going through a brief phase of literacy. Guests already drank, twirled, laughed, bitched, ate—men in white and silver and gold tuxedos; women in flame, royal purple, cerulean, mock virgin white, bosoms hoisted and teeth snow-capped, many famous, all vulgar. There was a smell of scorched meat, ginger and soy sauce. Fire flared for an instant as cognac was thrown over a Hawaiian pig roast. The dance floor was a polished silver disk by the heartshaped swimming pool. Searchlights played like lewd fat fingers on ravishing girls diving and ploughing the water, from which a loud scent of patchouli arose. Lorelei-like, these girls with perfect teeth tempted fat bald dressed men to jump in just as they were. Carlo seemed awed by all this. Faces he had known only in unnatural enlargement were now, however, reduced to accessibility: it was like a reversal of heaven. Still he murmured, "That, surely, is Joan Blondell. And that Clark Gable. And there is Norma Shearer. And there's Domenico. But where is Hortense?"

One could not first greet one's hostess. One could not find one's hostess. We went to the bar where Domenico, who now wore a corset on ceremonial occasions, was drinking, on the showing of the white flecks round his mouth, a Ramos fizz. He was still handsome, and the recession of his hairline had been disguised with careful blow-combing. It was without gray, and it glistened under the moons like a grilled steak. Drinking with him was a small Mexican starlet called, I think, Rita Morelos, hair like ink, not one straight line in her shape, her scarlet dress subtly slit to the thigh, eyes naughty and lips wet and apout. Domenico, who now called himself Nicky, did not appear to be pleased to see his brother. "I would not have thought," he said, "I mean, a priest."

"Is there some law?" frowned Carlos. "Where is your wife?"

"Hortense," Domenico said, pronouncing the name to rhyme with *hence*, "is looking after Johnny. He fell riding a pony. He twisted his ankle. There is a little pain. He woke up crying. She is staying with him. Anyway, she doesn't much like parties."

"You do, I see, you do. What's that drink, my child?" he said kindly to Rita Morelos. She was holding a glass long as a bottle on whose foam sat a miniature parasol. It was a Mai-Tai. Carlo asked for whisky.

> *"Anything at all*
> *I'll gladly do*
> *To prove a lasting*
> *Love for you.*
> *Each and every task*
> *Beneath the sun:*
> *You only have to ask—*
> *It's done . . ."*

Fitted out with a heavy rummer of scotch, Carlo was now ready to be introduced to the cinematic great. My situation in Hollywood was a comfortable one. I was glad to get money out of the industry but I did not really need it. I did not have to bow or yes or cringe. There was one writer there, I noticed, down on his luck: Godfrey (God) Thurston trying to ingratiate himself with a couple of stone-faced moguls. I was Kenneth M. Toomey, distinguished British novelist in distinguished early middle age, whose face was known from book jackets, whose sexual proclivities had not been declared (though all British were supposed to be fags: sour grapes because of our patrician accents and European elegance), who was known by as much as he knew and didn't give a damn anyway. So, at ease, I led Carlo from group to group, introducing him, for convenience, as my brother-in-law, high officer of the Apostolic Delegation to the United States. Some thought this to be a new religious sect and a wide-mouthed comedian named Joe E. Brown swore he knew some guy who had joined it: no nooky, no booze, take nothing dead into your system, right? But Edward G. Robinson, an actor of about Carlo's height though not as ugly, knew all about it, could catalog from memory the Vatican's art treasures, and gave, as a *bonne bouche*, a crisp summary of the Sabellian heresy. At length we met our hostess. Say what one would about the cynical craft of stellifaction, there had to be a *donnée*, and Astrid Storm did really possess a charm which ate Carlo like Venus's-flytrap. Transfixed by those great violet eyes, even when they looked away from him, he gulped and agreed when she uttered nonsense about the need of the Christian churches to be, you know, spiritualized by techniques of Mayan umbilical breathing.

After an hour I had already had enough. Somebody said to Domenico,

"Nick boy, I loved your last score, it was the greatest." And Domenico, seeming to be in a hurry to do something somewhere else, said, "Well, thanks, Dave." There was a woman of unearthly beauty who said nothing to her interlocutor but "Yah. A-a-a. Yah." A young blond man of magnificent physique which his tuxedo could not disguise, evidently desperate to be working again, dove from the high board fully clothed and entered the pool hardly raising a ripple. Nobody seemed to notice. A paid ribber came round to insult people.

Carlo said to me, "They tell me there's poker-playing in there," jerking his thumb at *SS Vincenzo ed Anastasio*.

"Very high stakes, Carlo. Can you afford it?"

"None of these people look like serious card players. Come in and tell me when you think we ought to leave."

"But you'll be going back with Domenico."

"I think not on second thoughts. I think we ought to discuss the book."

"But, Carlo, I have to go to work tomorrow morning."

"Four or five hours' discussion, then sleep. We'll discuss all the better for the little relaxation we're having. Our hostess is a charming woman. I regret," he said roguishly, "my vow of chastity."

"She's been four times divorced."

"American divorce," he said, "is serial polygamy. The Garden of Allah," and he waddled off.

I went back to the bar. A drunken man with a long head and no back to it looked at me narrowly and said, "You call yourself Toomey?"

"That's my name."

"It's not. You stole it from me, you bastard."

"Ah, you a Toomey too? There aren't all that many of us. Where does your family come from?"

"There's only one fucking Toomey and that's me. You're a fucking limey fag thief, you bastard." He picked up a Southern Comfort bottle from the bar and prepared to strike. Such a bore. Two dark-jowled men in black tuxedos, sixty-inch chests on them, rose like exhalations from the dry grass and bore this cursing other Toomey or pseudotoomey away complete with Southern Comfort. Then my eyes were drawn to the Pier Luigi Nervi bandstand. The orchestra had started playing "Happy Birthday," and the singer, an epicene willow-wand with a tow lock over his right eye, was singing it. "Happy birthday, dear Astrid . . ." The lights were on dear Astrid. She smiled like a piano concerto, not Domenico's. The brass fanfared in a massive cake on wheels, apparently self-driven, an exhaust farting bluely behind. It was far too beautiful to savage with a knife, but chefs with toques fell on it as though it were a white whale. Champagne was poured from methuselahs and dear Astrid's beauty and youth, unassailed by yet another year, were toasted. The cake was passed round in tiny nibbles. "Happy Birthday" was played as a creamy waltz, and men lined up to twirl Astrid in a few celebratory steps each. Very wholesome, but in dark corners of shrubbery low-voiced assignations were being initiated and quarrels smoldered. Teeth gleamed more in snarls than in smiles. But an unknown happy girl dove in in her Directoire gown and emerged with it pasted to her succulent body, and a tap dancer took over the dance floor and tap-danced, a man admirably pared to bone and a fixed smile, to the tune of "Sweet Sue."

There emerged from the façade of *SS Vincenzo ed Anastasio* what many took at first to be a comic duo. It was Carlo dragging out Domenico and both cursing each other in the Milanese of the streets, a tongue unknown to the Sicilian gorillas in tuxedos who, with their ears pricked to what should have been familiar but was not, were getting ready to move in there. But the fat dragger-out was clearly revealed as a priest, one who ought to know what he was doing. Domenico's coiffure was disarranged and recession showed. His feet were socked but unshod, and under his tuxedo a hairy chest wobbled. *In flagrante* was the term. Carlo, his face contorted to shame and rage, had no goodnight for anyone. He dragged and occasionally hit Domenico over the lawns toward the front of the house. I had, though discreetly, to follow. Toward the carpark. I knew Domenico's car, a Studebaker in lime and apple, but Domenico would, I knew, pretend not to know it. Dragged home, indeed, by his priestly brother, and he only (I assumed; what else was there to assume?) committing mandatory fornication. "There," I called, pointing, "is what I presume you're looking for. But what in the name of God has been happening?" Domenico twisted himself to spit at me and Carlo used his free hand to try the driver's door. Cars were not locked in this private carpark with its black, probably armed, attendants. And the ignition keys were left in so that these attendants could redistribute locations and facilitate egress. As now. A Plymouth huge as a rock was swung out of the path of the Studebaker.

"Get in there in the back," Carlo commanded. "Both of you." And he pushed Domenico in and me after him.

"Look," I protested, "I've done no wrong. I'm guiltless as the Pelagian snow." Carlo was not amused. "Damn it," I said, "this is none of my business. I'm going back to the party." But Carlo had slammed the door and was getting into the driver's seat. "You," I said to Domenico, "have presumably been doing something naughty."

"Go and say the same thing to your whore of a sister," Domenico growled. I could not resent that locution: a husband had more rights than a brother. The back of Carlo's neck said:

"You, Kenneth, remind me of the way. We are going back to the Garden of Allah. You, *fratello*, say no more. What you have to say I desire to see you saying. I need to look into your insolent and adulterous face." That was very Italian. Italians, like women, had to see the true meaning behind the spoken words. Or written. Italians did not write letters because there was no face in letters.

"It was not adultery," Domenico said in sulky pedantry. "She is not married."

"That Mexican *puttana*," Carlo corrected, "is a married woman. I follow these things. You will say she has been divorecd. There is no such thing as divorce. I do not have to tell you that. Now be quiet. You will have plenty of time to speak. Not about your fornication of which there is nothing more to say. About the thing you said and then said you did not say. *Stai zitto!*" he cried, though Domenico was taking a breath only to breathe. So there was a kind of grumbling silence as we passed facetious mansions and grandiloquent hash joints, though Carlo rumbled at the view as at a long scrawled signature of human depravity.

"Left here," I said. He obeyed, thoroughly expert with somebody else's, anybody's, car.

We arrived. *"La ilaha illu'lah,"* Carlo mocked. He parked by the Black Sea, between Constanta and Cetatea. We got out, and Carlo was now free to shove Domenico brutally toward my apartment. I unlocked and put lights on. Two scowling brothers were now fully illuminated, sweat and rumples and all.

"A drink?" I said.

Carlo said, "For me yes, for him nothing. Now," he truculently invited. "The thing you said."

"I said nothing except that you had no right." All this, by the way, was in English. "You call it sin and I say that everybody does it. It is the way here. And I say that whatever you call it a man is free to do what he wants. You had no right, you disgraced me, you made me look a fool."

"You looked a fool and also an animal lying on top of that woman. *Naked,*" as though that were a worse sin than fornication. "Your stupid *culo* working away." Carlo took his neat Old Mortality with no thanks and grimly mimed the movement.

"You had no right to burst in, you knew it was not the *gabinetto*. I was ready to come, blast you, *ready to come*, and you have the filthy stupidity to talk about sin." He then snarled some filthy Italian. Carlo drank with one hand and slapped at him, though missing, with the other.

"A lucky accident, little brother, that it was you and this *puttana* and not the *gabinetto*. I caught you in sin and your shame may lead to sincere repentance. I want to know what it was you said."

"I said you had no right."

"No right as what? As a priest of your Church? Or as your brother?"

"I said you had no right."

"I ask," I said, "by what right you call my sister a whore?"

"That," Carlo said, "is another thing. One thing at a time."

"I said you had no right."

"Why," I asked loudly, "is my sister a whore?"

"I will say nothing else until I too have a whisky like this drunken priest here." Carlo, of course, hit out at that, but Domenico dodged. I slopped a cheaper whisky into a tumbler and handed it to Domenico. Domenico drank thirstily, all the time dodging Carlo, who was trying to knock the glass out of his fist. "You will listen." Domenico was panting less from emotion than from the single swift draught. Carlo could not now take that drink away from him. He held on to the glass firmly, his knuckles creamed, any more hitting and he would counter with that. "It's not my habit," he said, "to fornicate and commit adultery. I am not like the other people here." Carlo combined a whoop and a sneer. "If you want to listen, listen. If not I will go home."

"Home," tolled Carlo. "You will not sleep in her bed or even in the same room. You defile her purity with just being there. You will keep away from her until you receive absolution and do penance. And, by God," Carlo fiercely promised, "it will be a long and hard penance. Many many many many decades of the rosary. You will never have done with saying them."

"You have no right. I have the right to go to my own priest."

"I know the man. I will tell him all. I will tell him what to give you."

"You have no right and you know you have no right." And then Domenico sneered. "Purity. Chastity. Fidelity. These fine big words that mean nothing. What I say now is: whose are those children? Who is the father of those two kids who call me dad?" Ah. "It's from the *orecchioni* I start to learn the truth."

"*Orecchioni?*" I did not know the word. Both Carlo and Domenico distractedly mimed big ears and big cheeks. "Swollen glands? Oh, mumps." I remembered. Johnny and Ann had had mumps. Domenico had been infected. It was a painful harmless ailment. There was a certain danger when male adults caught it. Hortense too had caught it but there was no danger for adult females.

"I go to the studio doctor," Domenico said, "because I do not like the shrinking of the balls. What he calls with his big words partial atrophy of the testicles. He neither likes it nor dislikes it. He says it happens in thirty percent of the cases. I tell him they are not his balls to like or dislike. They are my balls. And I do not like it. He says to give him some of my seed. So I go into another room to get some. It's not easy. He gives me a book of dirty pictures and that helps."

"Filthy," Carlo pronounced. "Pollution. Masturbation."

"Ah, *cazzo*," Domenico cried in disgust. "You know nothing about anything, stupid priest." Very fascist. "He takes my semen and he puts it under a microscope. This afternoon he gave me the results. He said there was nothing. He said," crescendo, "there was nothing there. He told me that there was the most perfect example of infertility he had ever seen. *Perfect* was the word he used. He said another thing. He said that it was very very very unusual for the disease of *orecchioni* to make a man infertile. He said that it was almost certain that I had been born like that. And then I told him I had two children, twins. And then he said very quickly, *too* quickly, very well then obviously it must be the *orecchioni* that are the cause, very rare but it does sometimes happen. But I can guess he's saying this to quieten my mind. But my mind is not quiet, very far from it. Now you see the doubt that comes into my mind."

"There must be no doubt," Carlo bellowed. The Manhattan humorist in the next apartment laughed. "For a man to doubt his wife, especially when his wife is a woman like Hortense, is not to be considered. How dare you ask who is the father of your children!"

"Staying the night with you," Domenico scowled at me. "How do I know where she spent the night? How do I know where she would go when she said she was spending the afternoon at the Louvre? I've seen her smile at men in Paris. You're her brother, I suppose you will protect her."

"There's nothing to protect," I said fiercely. "Hortense has been a good and faithful wife and also a much provoked wife if you wish to know the truth. You know your terrible tempers which you would call temperament as if you were Verdi or Puccini and your cowardice in lashing out at a woman."

"Oh, now it's she who does the lashing out," Domenico cried, "when I speak to her about the doctor and his damned microscope and his saying there are no spermatozoa swimming around. And I spoke reasonably, ready to forgive if she's done wrong, because after all it was a long time ago. She said how dare you how dare you louder even than Carlo here. Be honest, I said, dear Orténsia, be honest, I'll forgive you, I love these children whoever the father is or the fathers are, and then it's how dare you and she lashes out with her fists. And then she said go and ask your brother Carlo about the purpose of the act of marriage, the act of marriage is for producing children, how many children can you produce now, you infertile bastard, keep away from me in future."

"She's wrong," Carlo said, though weakly. "The Church doesn't penalize anybody because of the failure of Nature. When the sacrament of matrimony is entered on in good faith then the pleasures of matrimony are legitimate."

"Ah," Domenico said, "she wants different pleasures. We Italians are all innocent fools, not like the French and the English. I wondered about this friendship between her and my *fagotto*. Bassoon, if you like," he said to me. "In the studio orchestra. All this friendliness and how are you darling and little kisses when they meet."

"A male bassoonist?"

"No no no no no no, *stolto*, a woman bassoonist," as though it were self-evidently a female occupation blowing that long heavy thing. "Her name is Fran Lilienthal, a ridiculous name, but she's a good *fagottista*, she can reach high *mi bemolle*, E flat if you like. That is not the point," with ferocity as though somebody else had gotten him off it. "Hortense said to me several times that men know nothing about making love to a woman. Especially Italian men. I asked her what she knew of other men, and she said she talked enough with other women and learned plenty from them, and also she reads books. She says it requires a woman to understand a woman. So now I begin to think. There is a lot of this among the women of Hollywood." We were all still standing up, but now Carlo sat down. The whisky in his glass tried to stay where it was and splashed his black jacket. He ignored this, looking, frowning, up at his brother. "You know the word," Domenico said to me. "I think there's something wrong with your family."

"That's a stupid and cruel thing to say," with much heat. "Retract those words or I'll push them down your throat. Along with your silly crowned fornicating Latin lover teeth." The humorist next door clapped and went hooray.

"You're saying stupidities," Carlo said, "as you so often do. You're being insincere and sinfully so, as you so often are. You wish to commit adultery or at least fornication, so you find all the excuses you can. Your wife pushes you away, or so you like to think, then you dream up this abomination of perverseness. Women," he pronounced sagely, "are not the same as men. They kiss each other and embrace each other. I've seen this among young nuns even, novices. It's friendship, no more. Women are more emotional and more demonstrative than men, it is their nature. Women are incapable by their physical nature of committing the sin of Onan. But now you dream up this filthy calumny and because of a frustrated and bitterly broken love of Kenneth here, which you know all about, all, you say words he is right to want to ram down through your throat. You justify your sin of tonight. You will go on trying to justify similar sins. I know your nature. Now go down on your knees. Go on. *On your knees.*" He pointed to a suitable spot on the thinning rust carpet. "Beg forgiveness of God. *Now.*"

"Ah, *merda*," Domenico said, not kneeling. "You don't know anything about the real world and what sex is and the different kinds of sex and what sex does to people. But what you do know now is why I did what I did this evening. And you stopped me. You damned and fucking well stopped me. The worst crime in the whole of life, the worst sin, worse than murder. When a man is almost coming." He shuddered with genuine horror. "To stop a man at that point is a terrible terrible sin. It is you who should be down on your knees."

"Don't tell me what's sin and what isn't sin," Carlo said, getting up again, "and don't say filthy words to me, a priest and a monsignore. So, we have your sin sin sin, do you hear me, and we have your feeble motivations." He sounded a little like the head of the MGM script department. "But you have not repeated what I asked you to repeat. The thing you said when I was forcing you into your trousers in that disgusting bedroom with the naked *puttana* laughing and showing her brazen bare body. I want to hear that thing again. I can bear it. It was a terrible thing to say to a brother. It was a denial. But I can bear it."

"I said you had no right."

"No right as a priest or no right as an elder brother?"

"No right as either one. You always said we have free will and the right to choose what we do."

"Yes, and we have the right to stop a man choosing to harm himself. We have that right and I used that right. What was the thing you said?"

"It was you," Domenico spoke accusingly, "who said I must go home to see my father die and take care of all arrangements. There was important Church business for you and Raffaele had to stay in Chicago to be murdered by Al Capone."

"That is not a good thing to say. Speak sensibly."

"All this is true. I had to see my father die and then settle things for my mother. You talked a lot about my duty as a son."

"What is this singular possessiveness? *Our* father, *our* mother. It was not my fault if I could not be there. You did all our duties for us, very good, thank you, a good son and a good brother and all the rest of it. What has this to do with anything?"

"I had to go through documents, burn some, burn most of them, keep some, read all. Mother left it to me, she wanted no part of it, leave me to my grief she said, but she didn't seem to grieve much. That is a different story. My story now is that I found this old *certificato di adozione*." Carlo's sudden alertness was like a stick cracking over a knee. He said with little voice:

"*Tu?*"

"*No, tu.*" I had never seen Carlo, nor, I think, could anyone ever have, so suddenly shrunken and naked. He, the formidable, always full of surprises, had met a surprise of such monumental gravity that its nugget weighed more than his whole arsenal of faith and learning and superhuman confidence to deal with the world. The two kept to Italian, not Milanese.

Carlo said, "You have it? Mother has it? It is still there?"

"It was one of the things burned. She said it should have been burned long ago. She did not know it was still among the family documents. She said you must never never be told. She was very disturbed that I had seen it."

"Rightly so rightly so, you were bound to tell me sometime even if you had to wait a hundred years. You waited ten years. More. But you were bound to tell me. She was right to be disturbed." The humorist next door was laughing again. Carlo beat the wall with terribly earnest fists. The humorist gave a feeble horselaugh and then was silent, probably off to bed.

Domenico said, "I told you because I was angry. No man can be angrier than when he is put into that state. I could not otherwise have said it. So now we forget all about it. There are rights you do not have. But you're still my elder brother."

"What is known? Who am I?" A terrifying question, the question of Oedipus.

Domenico said, "You're Carlo Campanati. The certificate of adoption says your parents are unknown. Mother said that it all happened that time when Italy was taking Ethiopia. The man was in the army and he did not come back. The woman was on the estate for the pressing of the grapes. She had you and then she went off. My father, our father, had a dream of some kind. He woke from the dream and then he called in the advocate for the papers of adoption. He said you had to be of the family. It was a time, Mother said, when the doctors said it would not be wise to have more children, she had had a difficult time with Raffaele. But of course she had no difficult time with myself. Mother said you were a gift from God."

Carlo groaned terribly. I ventured to say, in English, "I can see nothing to worry about in all this. Why such knowledge should be withheld. Why such knowledge should cause unhappiness."

"You knew your mother," Carlo groaned. "All men know their mothers, even Jesus Christ. Not to know your mother. Not to know your father is not so important. This is a very profound shock."

"You were destined perhaps," Domenico said with characteristic stupidity, "to choose your mother, which not many men can do. I mean your mother the Church. But our mother is still your mother."

"It's not the same," went Carlo hollowly. "I did not issue from her womb. I am not flesh of her flesh. I will worry now hopelessly about my real mother, whom I can never know. Your two children know their mother, that's all that matters for them. And you come to me with your sinful doubts about your paternity, as if that mattered. I have no mother," and he groaned again.

"The Church," Domenico said, "the Church. You have your mother the Church."

"The truth is good," I said comfortingly and vaguely, "whatever the truth is. It is good," I clarified, "to know the truth. You are what you are, you are not changed. Your gifts? They come from God, and the parental channel of their transmission is of no importance."

"Kenneth is right there," Domenico said. "It's like my own gifts. Neither my father nor my mother had them. They come from the unknown. I won't say God, because I'm not sure about God. Talent or genius is a great mystery."

"What do you mean," Carlo asked, "not sure about God?" He had raised his muzzle at the noise of a straying sheep, sick collie dog though he was. "Tonight seems to be dedicated to your not being sure about anything. Except about my having no mother. What do you mean, not sure?"

"Talk to the *mafiosi* about God," Domenico said boldly. "They run the labor at the studios. They say who shall be in my orchestra and who not. You drag me from a bed where I only commit fornication, but these people kill. Why is it all the Catholics are bad men, tell me that? It's six months since I went to mass. I'll work out things for myself. *Your* mother not mine."

Carlo nodded. "You wouldn't say this if I were really your elder brother."

"I've known it for over ten years," Domenico said.

"Yes, but it's tonight you *really* know it. Tonight you say it. Go on, go away. I'll see you tomorrow."

"You won't see me tomorrow. I'm recording music all day. If the *mafiosi* allow me. Now I think I'll go back to what you interrupted." He insolently left without a goodnight.

Carlo said, "That bottle is finished. What other whisky do you have?"

"Scotch, you mean. White Label, Haig, Claymore—"

"Very good. It is many many years since I did this." He took a beer glass, half filled it with Claymore and looked at me tragically before drinking. "You must join me," he said. "A man cannot drink alone." The Studebaker could be heard zooming off from the Black Sea. "Well, let him. Let him be damned. Let the devils of pride and lust and stupidity devour him. He was always a fool. Come, drink with me."

"Vodka," I said. I did not propose to be incapable the next morning, I had a script conference at ten. In the icebox I kept a number of used liquor bottles filled with water. I went to it and chose a chill quart Kavkaz. Then I sat with Carlo, ready out of companionship to slur and dribble, grimacing with simulated distaste of raw spirit as I sipped the cool blessed and neutral.

Carlo took an hour to get through the Claymore. He said nothing for half of that time, though he made noises of self-pity and occasionally barked dialectal curses. Then he said, "Is it true what Domenico suspects?"

"This," I said, "is the confessional. Is that clearly understood?" He did not understand for a moment, but then he did and nodded.

"Sealed," he said. "Sealed, sealed."

"It's possible for someone to commit a sin out of love. If my sister sinned it was for Domenico's sake. Do you see that? She put her soul in jeopardy to protect his self-esteem. Remember, though, that you'd told Domenico that it was always the woman who was barren. One of the stupidities of the Old Testament. Hortense was driven to it. There's nothing to repent. Does she now go to hell?"

"Hortense," he said with care, "will not go to hell. If she goes to hell then that is where I would wish to be. I love Hortense. She is too good for that idiot who used to be a brother."

"Tell me," I said, "how do you get on? I mean, with your vow of abstinence. I mean, love. *Eros* not *agape*."

"I get on," he said in his innocence, "as you get on. You found love with chastity, the best kind. And you lost it. I did my best. The evil in the world, the evil. I have nobody. Even Christ had John. I suffer," he said, "from the pangs of lust. I'm a man like any other man, except perhaps you. Some men find chastity easy. I do not. I wonder sometimes whether when the time comes it will not be wise to permit marriage to the priesthood. Better than to burn, take bromides, quinine, bark at the flesh to get into its kennel."

"When what time comes?"

"When the Church is remade." Then Carlo got down seriously to his drinking. On the broaching of the dimple Haig he began to curse and spit blasphemies. Like Luther he seemed to see the devil in the corner of the living room, though he did not, in the absence of an inkwell, waste good whisky on him. The devil assumed the guise of a large rat, whose sleek fur and bright teeth Carlo admired extravagantly in various languages, including, I think, Aramaic. In the tones of an upper-class Englishman he said, "For the moment you are in the ascendancy, old boy, what, rather. I see your large clean fangs grinning at my temporary failure. *Salut, mon prince, votre* bloody *altesse.* You and I are alike in not possessing a mater, old boy. Even God forced himself into a filial situation. But will prevails, don't you know. There is never any failure of the will. We are what we make ourselves, old chap. Let's see you now as a serpent, your first disguise. Very good, that's really a most remarkable cobra hood, old fellow. I've never been much afraid of snakes, don't you know. The colonial experience, so to say, *mon brave.* But you bore me rather, you tire me somewhat. A little shut-eye is indicated, wouldn't you say? Rather."

It was certainly time. Carlo finished what he had in his glass, then he threw the glass in the corner. It did not break. Then he nodded at me quite soberly and went off to bed, sketching a blessing. He was soon roaring. He was up before me next morning; indeed, the aroma of the coffee he was brewing was what woke me. He remembered everything, especially his new stoical loneliness.

forty-six

King Arthur and Sir Bedivere stowed the Holy Grail safely under the rubble of the ruined chapel in the forest, and with it the rusting spear that had pierced Christ's side. Then they rode wearily to the hill where the remnant of their ragged army was gathered for the last battle. The sky boiled and seethed in eastward-driven coils of cloud, and the banner of the dragon fluttered, tattered, fingers in feeble *marameo* at the approaching enemy. Arthur spoke to his troops, and his weariness was evident from the slackness of his vocal cords, but the wind carried his words as far as the boys in the rear with what was left of the baggage train, and all listened hopelessly to his words. "We who are redeemed through Christ's blood, we who glorified the civilizing skills of the Roman with the good news from Galilee, we the ancient Celts to whom was vouchsafed the living faith to bear among the folk of the dark north, we face now annihilation at the hands of a ruthless and Godless enemy. Yet, though we die, the faith can in no wise perish. Our blood will smoke to the sun and it shall be as incense to the Father of all things. From the soil we nourish with our blood a new race of Christians shall arise. Be of good cheer, for the faith cannot die. Men, do your duty, as the Blessed One did his. Cannot you now hear the noise of the approaching Saxon hordes, merciless, pagan, feeders on the flesh and blood of Christian men? Face them without fear, sustained by the vision of the divine cross, hopeful of heaven. Christ died and rose and may not die again. Fare we forth to battle in faith and duty. Trumpeter, sound the charge." And with a main voice the wretched torn army raised its spears and gave praise to God and King Arthur.

Al Birnbaum liked none of this. Nor did Joe Svenson. Since they did not like it, neither did Chuck Gottlieb, nor Dick Rothenstein, nor Ed Kingfish. We sat together at a script conference in Al Birnbaum's office. We sat about a great beautiful empty mahogany desk disfigured only by coffee beakers. On the walls were signed photographs of great stars, all however contractual slaves to the studio, and their disdainful smirks were the celestial counterpart of the weary disappointment of the Ashkenazim and the Nordic pout of Joe Svenson. "I told you," I said, "I wasn't going to have any of that Lancelot and Guinevere nonsense. This is what the legend is really all about." They could not see anything in the legend, the children of the Diaspora, the lapsed Lutheran from Minnesota.

Al Birnbaum said, "A lot of Sunday school stuff." What did *he* know about Sunday schools? "Too much jabber about religion. We want a human story. This King Arthur sounds like a preacher."

"Just what I was going to say, Al," Ed Kingfish said.

"When is this all supposed to be going on?" Joe Svenson asked. "Shakespeare's time?"

"A lot earlier than Shakespeare," I said. "Earlier even than the Middle Ages. This is the beginning of the Dark Ages. About five hundred years after Christ. Celtic Christianity fighting for its life against the Anglo-Saxons. The Anglo-Saxons," I explained, "are what you'd call the British. But the British are really Celts. King Arthur's the last of the Celtic rulers of Britain. Then it was the Anglo-Saxons." Nobody seemed to understand that. Celts schmelts, they didn't want education, they wanted a human story.

Dick Rothenstein said, "I've run all the King Arthur movies I could get a hold of. It's not like what you say, Ken. It's this guy, sir something, and he goes off with the queen, and then King Arthur says, sir whosis, you fucked my wife."

"Did they say *fuck* in those days?" Joe Svenson asked.

"It's a very old word," I said. "Anglo-Saxon. Cognate with the German *ficken*. The same word, I should think, in Yiddish." This piece of speculation did me no good. All looked at me warily and with even less confidence than before. Al Birnbaum fanned cigar smoke away with my treatment, all it was good for. "My contract finishes in a fortnight," I said.

"A what?" Chuck Gottlieb said.

"Two weeks. It seems to me we've been at cross-purposes all the time. A waste of time and money, I'd say."

"Don't let me hear you say that, Ken," said Al Birnbaum earnestly. "Nothing's wasted. You've done fine work. Only thing is we can't use it. Not yet. The time's not yet. Some day they'll be saying fuck and showing it too. And this religious schlock, they'll be eating it. But it's human stories now and the Hays Office and the Catholic League of Decency. We'll have more coffee, Lydia," he said to the ugly woman, his wife's choice for a secretary, who looked in.

"So," I said, "I don't see much point in working that last fortnight or two weeks. Fortnight, by the way, means fourteen nights, which includes days of course. There's also sennight, seven nights, for a week. No extra charge for that information." They nodded in appreciation of my generosity.

Joe Svenson said, "Like in Shakespeare."

"You fix that with the contracts department, Ken, no trouble. I think you'll find a clause about reparations or some damn thing, penalty for breaking contract, Rob Schoenheit will explain. Where's your hurry, I'd say, take another look at this, knock out the religious megillah, *that* we don't need."

"Like a loch in kop," agreed Ed Kingfish.

"I've been invited to Germany," I said. "A film festival. They put sound to a movie based on one of my books. I'm collecting some royalties too. I don't know why I'm telling you all this," I added.

"They don't burn your books?" Dick Rothenstein said. "Like these books they burned in the book-burning?"

I felt ashamed. They did not burn my books. My books were rather popular in Nazi Germany. There were a fair number of unexportable marks to collect and spend on lederhosen and alpenstocks and whatnot. "There it is," I said humbly. "Next Thursday. I'm booked on the *Hindenburg*. From Lakehurst, New Jersey. So I break contract. I suppose one should always read contracts."

"Always read contracts," Joe Svenson said. "Not going through the small print, that way you can lose your ass."

"You want to watch those blimps," Ed Kingfish said. "Lose more than your ass in one of those gasbags. Like the *Shenandoah* and the *Akron*. My wife's cousin married into the U.S. Navy, this guy was on the *Akron* when it went down. Lose gas in bumpy weather. Like what happened to that British one, the *R one-oh* something. Lousy business that was, no offense, Ken. Bumped into a fucking French church."

More coffee had been brought in. Al Birnbaum sucked loudly at his beaker. Chuck Gottlieb said, "That would make a swell movie, an airship on fire in mid-Atlantic, thousands plunging to their doom."

"They only carry about a hundred," I said.

"A collision," Chuck Gottlieb said, starting to see it all. "A multiple collision."

"So, gentlemen," I said, "I reiterate my regret that things have not worked out as they might. Multiple collision of opinions and no resolution of differences. So, with your permission—"

"Only the box office has opinions," Joe Svenson said. "You remember that, Ken. The rest is strictly for the birds."

"For the can, Ken, right," Al Birnbaum said. "You see Rob Schoenheit, he'll spell out that small print."

I left the administration block and crossed a couple of lawns whose rotating irrigators wet my turnups. "Off of there, outa that, fella," cried an old man in a peaked cap. I walked, under the brassy Culver City sun, to the recording studio, where Domenico would at this hour be fitting atmospheric music to film. There was a blue light on forbidding ingress, but this soon went out and I went in. The musicians were taking their mandatory cigarette break, five minutes every hour. Horns and fiddles sat at rest. A jowled overseer, union man or *mafioso*, sat watchful in a tight blue suit, chewing a match. Domenico in shirtsleeves was penciling something into a full score. A little man with the deformed fingers of a professional copyist was emending a trumpet part. The producer of the film, dressed as for Waikiki beach, hovered.

I said to Domenico, "So there's no change?"

He penciled in *pp cresc f* and said, "Why should there be a change? We've tried change. The money will come through, she knows that. I'm not what she calls me, whatever I am."

"It's a terrible shame."

"A lot of things are a terrible shame. What has to be has to be."

"It's a terrible shame as far as Carlo's career is concerned, have you thought of that? His elder brother gets killed by gangsters in Chicago. His younger brother wants a divorce. His mother's disappeared." Three months and more had gone by since the night of Astrid Storm's birthday party. "Alternatively he's a foundling."

"A what?"

"Like Tom Jones. A bastard bundle left on a doorstep. They're not going to like any of this at the Vatican."

"We live our own lives," Domenico said.

The producer said, "Okay, let's get on with it."

The musicians stubbed out and reassembled. Lights dimmed except for the desk glowworms. On the cinema screen there appeared an ocean and on it in an open boat unshaven men in a desperate condition. It was gray foredawn, but then the sun started to come up. A seagull appeared flapping and provoked a slow suffusion of first bewilderment and then joy on the stubbled face of Clark Gable, quicker on the uptake than his fellows in distress. Across the screen there traveled a vertical bar, something to do with timing. It was a looped piece of film. "Land?" Gable said. Then the sequence started again. Domenico had just watched the first exposition. For the second he raised his stick. The strings undulated. Discordant lower brass symbolized the situation of the men in the boat. With the rising of the sun three muted trumpets and two oboes sketched a diffident flourish. When the seagull flapped in a flute performed an arabesque. It was a fraction of a second late, and the fault in the timing was, of course, the composer's. Domenico said, *Merda.*" Lights went up. Stopwatches clicked off. The flute was to ignore the written point of entry and respond merely to the baton.

"We got to have something, Nick," the producer said, "for that arm movement." Meaning one of the exhausted men in the boat whose right hand dropped from his neck in a final gesture of weariness.

"Why is his hand up there in the first place?"

"He thinks he's choking, Nick." So there was another cigarette break and Domenico had to write in a descending passage on the clarinet and a soft thud on the bass drum.

"No final message?" I said.

"Nothing," he frowned, dotting in his semiquavers.

"So," I said, "I too had better say goodbye." And I held out my hand. Domenico took it distractedly and flabbily. He was firm enough here on the rostrum, though, no doubt of that.

"We'll meet," he said. "It's a small world."

"Too small sometimes." And then, with a demotic gesture of valediction not very different from a U.S. Army salute, "*Addio.*" I did not think I would ever see him again. I left him to his plastic music and castaways and went off to look for studio transport back to the Garden of Allah.

Hortense and the twins and I flew from Los Angeles to New York a few days later. It was all over between them, through after over fifteen years of marriage, not a bad record by Hollywood standards. Whatever Domenico did about a divorce on grounds of incompatibility fully admitted by Hortense, Hortense would remain married. She was holding on to her faith as she was holding on to her British passport. But Domenico and the twins were American now, and the twins sounded American. They sat across the aisle from Hortense and me, bickering as kids will, working a jigsaw puzzle the hostess had given them. No, that one, stoopid. Here, dummy. Who're you calling dummy, stoopid? This hostess, a magnificent brainless Californian blonde, had served us a dinner of stewed chicken and canned lima beans with a salad of tasteless tomato slices as wide as saucers. I had brought along a bottle of Mumm and we were pensively sipping it from paper cups as we sailed through the dark over New Mexico. Transcontinental air transport was new and slow and we would not reach New York till morning. Hortense and the twins were to take over my Manhattan apartment. Hortense was to rent a studio in Greenwich Village, where rents were fairly low, and carry on with her sculpture. The twins were to go to an exclusive school on Park Avenue founded by a pedagogic theoretician who had written a book called *Thou Eye Among the Blind*. He accepted the doctrine of Plato's *Meno*. The twins would not learn much. You finished that puzzle already? My, you *are* clever. Yeah, we wanna nother. "So," I said to Hortense.

"So what?" She was lovelier than ever in her middle thirties, elegant in a cinnamon suit, skirt with knife pleats on the front panel, short knife pleats at the back, wide collar and revers, wide self fabric belt, tieneck blouse, tiny stylized bowler hat with bow brim and band. Her speech had been barely touched by America. She would never really fit in here, while Domenico, Nick Campaneighty, had become the totally acclimatized Californian. I had heard him say on the telephone: "How's about a little golfie?" and to a singer, male: "That was but beautiful, sweetheart." She felt she might have a future in New York, a town full of art and galleries to show it in. She would work hard at the metal artifacts which Sidonie Rosenthal had pioneered in Paris. Sex? The chastity imposed by marriage though broken still an unbreakable sacrament? I did not discuss that with her. If, as I thought possible, she had discovered lesbic pleasures, these wasted no seed and the sin, if it was a sin, was venial. Its representation in fiction might have been proscribed by the British State, but there seemed nothing offensive in the reality, unless it were practiced by such as that ghastly Tarleton woman. The thought of two comely naked woman pleasuring each other rather excited me.

"So nothing," I said. Anyway, Carlo, though drunk, had assured himself that Hortense would never go to hell. And I am, at this moment of reminiscing, concerned with confirming Carlo's sanctity. A saint should know.

She smiled faintly. We were back to nursery nonsense. The twins were playing a small hitting game. One held up a finger and the other had to strike it with a finger if he could, she could. Speed of reaction was the thing. But their reactions were slowing. They were growing sleepy. "Show me that letter again," Hortense asked. I showed it her. There was a postage stamp of the Third Reich on the envelope but no address on the letter itself. It was a brief letter and said that as the disease was considered incurable she was determined, if need be, to use her death to help others. The point was that she had nothing now to be frightened of and would use the time that was left, despite her growing tiredness, to give aid where aid was most needed. Nobody was to worry about her. She had had her life. "Brave," Hortense said, her lovely eyes moist. "She's so right. But she must have a lot of pain."

"She wrote to Carlo something about an artificial rectum. That stops irritation of the growth. Carlo said nothing to her about that *adozione* business. Not worth while saying anything now. My dear mother your loving son. Have you thought, when she goes Carlo will have only us?"

"There's his sister. Who'll go on believing she's really his sister."

"She's the sister of sisters, no, mother superior now. Carlo's in the world and we're in the world with him. He really only has us. That's what a marriage does, forms new constellations. And when the marriage ends the constellations remain."

"I still don't like Carlo much."

"Even though he recommended this separation? He didn't throw sanctity and duty at you. Just the opposite. Carlo thinks more highly of you than of anybody in the world."

"You talk of Carlo as though Carlo mattered."

Hindsight? I think not. I said, "Carlo is going to transform Christianity."

"And you think that matters?"

"It matters to those who are able to believe in it. Millions and millions. It might even matter to me."

"If what?"

"If the two Gods could fuse. The one who created me sick, the other one who commands me to be sound." I caught a bright image of Concetta Campanati that day in the garden, outside the town dedicated to the rotting of lactic solids. "The God of my nature and the God of orthodox morality. And if God, either one of them or both, could show that he's really going to beat the rat prince."

"The what?"

"The father of lies. Carlo saw him as a rat in the corner at the Garden of Allah. He addressed him as *mon prince*. And also as a fellow orphan."

"I don't believe in him."

"You don't have to. I saw him. In another Garden of Allah."

The glorious brainless Californian goddess leaned over us with a smile of exquisite and meaningless loveliness and said, "Aren't you two night owls going to get some sleep?" I could tell she thought Hortense and I were man and wife. Our kids had already dropped off. We must be now be approaching the northeastern tip of Kansas. Most were sleeping: the two bald executives of United Artists, the fat and kidding salesman, the new juvenile lead who, jaw dropped, looked moronic, his loins visibly rutting under the blanket, the dim others. Hortense returned the smile, meaningfully, and said:

"You're a very lovely girl."

"Well, gee, thanks, you two talent scouts?" And she did some comic primp-
ing. American women could not be trusted with their own beauty. They had
helped create a culture in which everything had to be exploited. Her beauty was
like the case of samples on the knee of the snoring traveling salesman. She gave
us blankets as if acting the part of an airline hostess giving blankets. Hortense
murmured the night prayer our mother had taught us in childhood, asking for
the *protection de Dieu* and her *ange gardien*, and then closed her eyes. How
alike they were now, she and the sleeping twins, long sooty lashes, the skin hue
that was the gift of a moist and temperate climate, the honey hair. I could not
sleep yet. I had a Dante with me, and it opened at the *Inferno*, Canto Sixteen.
Guido Guerra, Tegghiaio Aldobrandi, Jacopo Rusticucci, burning for the sin of
sodomy. It was not the best of somniferents. I closed the book and my eyes and
let a mood of nostalgia wash me: Hortense's night prayer, the rejected treatment of the Arthurian legend. The fight went on, with motherless Carlo in the
middle of it, and I had been thrust, by will, by endowment, to the fringe of the
field that was the whole universe. I wanted to fight, but I had no cause. And yet,
out of pity perhaps for the orphan, I had endued the armor of his cause: that
book on the reform of Christianity was going to come out next spring under my
name and under my title, *New Roads to God*, by Kenneth M. Toomey (Scribner's), with a partially disowning foreword: "These are the ideas of thoughtful
Christians who seek a universal faith, a definition of divine good to oppose to
the growth of evil in our time. Call me many things—the listener, the stenographer, the editor—but do not call me the originator of this tentative schema. All
I will say is that I am aware of the power of evil and conscious of the need for a
new summation of the good. It is in the hope that this book may clarify the
ideas of the bewildered man and woman of good will, desirous of faith but
unable to find it, that I temporarily put off the rags of the novelist and assume
the robe of the theologian." Ernest Hemingway had been in Scribner's office to
fight some lousy bastard who had said his *cojones* were prosthetic at the time
when I delivered the typescript to Perkins. Full of Spain and the baroque, a self-
confessed convert to Catholicism in wartime Milan, he was willing to scrawl a
few lines of commendation without, however, even reading one page of the
typescript. "This book is important. If we believe in man we must also believe
in God. This book shows you how to believe in God. It is a god damn wonderful book." The last sentence was to be omitted, as he had already used it of Jim
Joyce's *Ulysses*.

What was in my mind as I waited for sleep and the engines thundered their
ineffectual *berceuse* was the chapter, a brief one, about the Jews. There was a
sense, it said, in which Christians were also Jews, since they shared a common
book of divine provenance with them, spoke of Abraham as a father, revered
the prophets, exulted in the heroism of the warriors, saw in Moses the founder

of the covenant, recognized that the doctrines of Christ were based on the tenets of the Torah, and so on. That the Christians had moved on to a recognition that the Messiah had come to an obscure Roman province, and the Jews denied this, did not in any way invalidate their ancient beliefs. Christians, responsible for a long and shameful persecution of the Jews, must learn to recognize that they had a right to subsist as so many exotic islands in a Christian community, that their talents were special and a divine gift and their sometimes bigoted exclusiveness was justified by a history that was also ours. There must be a closing of ranks in the time of Godless pogroms and, ideally, Christians must be willing to fight for and with and die with and for the children of Israel. Plain speaking, and, so far as I could judge from her letters, Concetta Campanati's present acts endorsed it. But what was I, committed to nothing, a spectator on the fringe, going to do about the debasement, expropriation, enslavement, annihilation of the Jews?

I was going, if I could, to forget that what was happening in Germany had touched my masters in Culver City hardly at all. The Hays Office and the Catholic League of Decency would not permit the cinematic exploitation of the Nazi treatment of the Jews in all its obscenity. I must forget too that Ed Kingfish and Chuck Gottlieb and Al Birnbaum and the others had thrown out my dramatization of the desperate fight for Celtic Christianity with the coming to the kingdom of Arthur of the pagan hordes. I must forget that Rob Schoenheit had been unaccommodating about a breach of contract that was a mere harmless anticipation of the completion of contract and had set me back ten thousand dollars in what was really a gratuitous penalty. It was the Jews who read the small print; reading the writing on the wall was strictly for the Babylonians. An unworthy thought, and I escaped from it into sleep.

We all woke wretched and crumby to orange juice and carton cups of coffee and the dawn of early fall over the towers of Manhattan. "I dreamed about Daddy," little Ann said, not an auspicious start to the day. "I dreamed about horses," said Johnny. "I dreamed of nothing," their mother said. "What did you dream of, Uncle Ken?" Towers made all of polychrome ice cream and the sun was God's tongue licking it. "I dreamed," I said, "of talking turkeys. Their speech was gabble gebble gibble gobble gubble. Hence the expression you hear in Hollywood: let's talk turkey." So the kids talked it to each other. How magnificent this city they sometimes called Jew York, made for God's eye to look at. Jerusalem the golden, Babylon the great. The aircraft came down at the little field where hares raced. "See, Johnny, a rabbit." Soon we were in the black limousine of the airline racing through the Holland Tunnel, all white tiles. And then a checker cab to my apartment, which was to be my sister's home.

"It's all right," Hortense said, wandering through it. "Needs dusting though." Uncle Ken, what building's that one? Why can't we see the Empire State? Kids, you are now living in the Empire State. Huh? Children, you may now call yourselves New Yorkers. You are better off here than in California, a slack place full of indolence and oranges and an industry dedicated to mediocrity. This is the center of the world and the bastion of free enterprise. Tomorrow we shall go to the top of the Statue of Liberty. And then I said to myself: These are my loved ones, they are all I have. Here they are safe, I have given them a home. Tears of various provenances mingled in my eyes.

forty-seven

Nobody met me at Hamburg, but at Berlin a young man in a double-breasted jacket and no hat was waiting at the ticket barrier with a card which said "HERR TOOMEY!" The exclamation point offered a selection of nuances: I had actually got here, I was *Herr* not Mr., I was important. He introduced himself as Toni Quadflieg, of the Reichsfilmkammer or National Chamber of Film, and spoke English not too good. He was delighted with my German. Where had I learned to speak so good German? Through reading the novels of Jakob Strehler, the great Austrian writer and recent winner of the Nobel Prize. Toni Quadflieg was hesitant in his response. A Jew, I said, and hence undoubtedly consigned to the flames by your Jewless regime, but notwithstanding a great writer. Perhaps the German I speak is tainted by the fact that I learned it from a Jewish writer? No no, it is good German learned you it from whatever writer. There is a car for you to take you to the Hotel Adlon.

There was no doubt that, especially under the apple honey of the autumn sun, Berlin looked well under its Nazi masters. So clean, so well-fed, the very railway porters rejoicing in their non-unionized prosperity. The silver whistles of the *Schutzpolizei* shone, and the golden hair of *echt* Aryans, of whom I saw few, seemed newly shampooed for my arrival. The polished body of the Daimler that awaited me mirrored in jovial rotundity the citizens arriving at and leaving the *Bahnhof*. The chauffeur saluted with a military punctilio that the fit and cleanliness of his uniform abetted. Toni Quadflieg and I got in. He said, "You had a good flight?"

"Excellent. I can thoroughly recommend the *Hindenburg*. It is the only way to fly. Have you flown in the *Hindenburg*? It is a masterwork of German aeronautical engineering."

"Unfortunately have I in the *Hindenburg* not yet flown. It has fifteen main transverse frames, each of which a thirty-six-sided regular polygon is. Its passenger accommodation is on two decks inside the outside envelope organized. A control car and four engine gondolas are externally mounted. The outer fabric is with cellon with aluminum powder on the outside mixed the heat reflection to increase doped. On the underside is the fabric porous ventilation to assist."

"Such knowledge. I am overwhelmed." Nowhere on the streets so clean you could eat your dinner off them did I see wretches wearing the yellow David star into trucks being harried. That would all be round the back. I saw three genial men in black with swastika brassards chaffing two pretty girls, one of whom was pushing a pram that contained a new gift for the Führer. A caramel called TILL! was proclaimed on posters as smacking really good, this assertion by the picture of a blond boy smiling with distended cheek confirmed.

"I am for all kinds of machine passionate," Toni Quadflieg said. "That is why I in films am. Cameras and sound and lights. I am to technical perfection strongly dedicated."

"Good films," I said indiscreetly, "can be made with very mediocre technical resources. Do you not think that much depends on the sincerity, the feeling, the originality of vision?"

"Something depends, yes."

"What is the program?"

"The program, good. Tomorrow there will be visits to the UFA studio at Tempelhof, to the studios of Tobis, Johannisthal and Grünewald, to the Neubabelsberg installations, to the Froelich studios. In the evening there will be *Hitlerjunge Quex* at the Astoria Ufa-Palast on Windmühlenstrasse. This will be the true beginning of the festival. Then the following days there will be many films, with one day devoted to all the mountain films, of which yours is one."

"And what do I have to do? See everything?"

"There will be much paper material awaiting you at the hotel which will tell you everything you are required to know. It is your presence that is truly required."

"And this evening?"

"This evening a reception at the Propaganda Ministry. Food and drink and some words from Reichsminister Dr. Goebbels. This car will call for you at seven o'clock."

In the drawing room of my suite at the Adlon there were journalists already assembled drinking drinks. They were from the *Völkische Beobachter*, *Film-Kurier* and *Jugendfilm*. *Der Stürmer* was not, I think, represented. There was a woman interpreter supplied by the Press Bureau, handsome in a rust open jacket with fur trim over double-breasted waistcoat, long tight sleeves with fur cuffs, box-pleated skirt, rust felt hat with bow trim, rust shoes with buttoned canvas inserts. But I was able to answer the questions in German. Where had I learned to speak so good German? I told them. There was a brief silence which the interpreter, Fräulein Dahlke, broke into with an interesting point. Doctrines could not, in the nature of things, be enforced retrospectively. She herself had learned to play the piano with Mendelssohn's *Songs Without Words*. Was she to forget the fingering she had mastered from the *Frühlingslied*?

What did I think of the achievements of the cinema of the Third Reich? I knew little about them, they did not seem to export very well. What was my opinion of the products of Hollywood? I considered them mediocre. I had been working there, what had I been working on? A treatment of the Arthurian legend rejected by the studio. Messrs. Birnbaum, Gottlieb, Rothenstein, King-fish and Svenson had not wished to present the tragic essence of the legend but wished to concentrate on love and adultery. Did I consider the American cinema decadent? Ah no, to reach decadence you had first to be civilized, though Oscar Wilde had made an epigram . . . God forgive me, I was giving them precisely what they wanted. What were my impressions of the new Germany? Clean, efficient, ingenious. The ingenuity applied solely so far to the box of matches that was on the table along with a complimentary tin of Wahnfreud cigarettes. To save wood, these matches consisted only of phosphorus heads to be picked up with tiny tweezers: *streich* but no *holz*. What new book was I working on? A book was to come out in Britain and America next spring on the necessity of finding a faith in an age of great evil. The evil of bolshevism? Yes, that and other evils. The journalists seemed very pleased with the interview.

The car called for me at seven precisely: indeed I corrected my watch by its arrival. White-tied and tailed I sailed off to the Propagandaministerium through the bright night streets. Bannered swastikas flapped gently in the still air, illuminated. The trouble with that damned swastika was that it was a very satisfying symbol and very ancient. *Svasti* meant good luck in Sanskrit. Kipling had the swastika on the title pages of all his books. Medieval scribes filled in spaces with it and called it a fylfot. Whether or not you approved of the regime it represented, your heart could not help but lift when you saw its arrogance on the Berlin skyline.

There was arrogance within too, but not untasteful. The huge vestibule celebrated, in statuary and bas-relief, the Nazi arts: naked eyeless classical Nazis with lyres and Bach trumpets, a robed Nazi Cicero or perhaps Demosthenes declaiming Nazi truth, Nazi Athenians frozen in a Nazi saraband. And everywhere swastikas seemed to spin widdershins. I joined tailed and diamonded guests mounting the fine curved stairway to the *piano nobile*, gazed down upon less disdainfully than distractedly, eyes lost in the world of the *Ding an sich*, by a floodlighted portrait of the Führer. Dr. Joseph Paul Goebbels was at the top of the stairs to greet us, *Reichsleiter* and President of the Reichskulturkammer, he in tails, his lady in white and jewels. I had met her before, I

remembered, though she evidently did not. It had been when she was still the
wife of a certain Herr Friedländer, a rich Jew who had been forced by the Party
to endow her on her new marriage with half a million marks and also to give
her new husband as a wedding present the Friedländer *Schloss* at Schwann-
werder.

Goebbels greeted me with a Rhineland accent. I knew he had written failed
plays and blamed their failure on the Jews. He knew I had written successful
plays. "Will," I asked, "your Führer be present at the festival?"

"Alas, no."

"And he so great a film lover."

"He prefers his private showings. *Mutiny on the Bounty* and *The Hound of
the Baskervilles.*" He spoke the titles in Rhineland English. "Those are his
favorites still."

"His taste must be reformed."

"His taste will be reformed." Then Dr. Veit Harlan was announced. I passed
on into the huge brilliantly lighted reception room. The only uniforms were on
members of the Hitlerjugend, delectable boys with straight hair, probably performers in *Hitlerjunge Quex.* They carried the canapés round; gloved and
whiteclad elders brought chilled Sekt, a wine I have always preferred to champagne. An eating lady said to me:

"Monsieur Toumy?"

"Madame Durand, is it not? What, if I may ask, are you doing in this
galley?" She was, I remembered, something to do with Gaumont.

"Ah, what we have to learn." She was of luscious figure and her blond hair
was metallic. "And not only in the cadre of the cinema."

"You are sympathetic to this regime?"

"How can one not be? The young men, observe, so slim, so straight. It is
Wagner come to life." She ogled me insolently. "And your own tastes too, I
understand, would not find aversion in the prospect of such muscular embraces
as are there implied."

I felt sick. I still had in my right hand some *vol-au-vent* or something and
there was nowhere to put it. I put it boldly in Mme. Durand's mouth. She made
a silly gesture of delight. I said, "My tastes are my own affair. But, if you wish
to know, they are best satisfied in the world of the dark." I'm damned if I
remember what language I am supposed to be translating here. I have the
insane illusion of a Gallicized German or Teutonicized French. I incontinently
came out with: "The Mediterranean. Jews, Arabs, Phoenicians, Sicilians. Wine
and garlic and olives. All civilization springs thence. What are these Nords
trying to do? What have they ever done except crush the civilizations of the
Middle Sea?" I must have spoken loudly. A long gray man with his hair parted
on the right, a Scandinavian from his sobbing French, said:

"It is time for the North. For the North it is time." An American of delicate and hence dangerous culture came in with:

"Toomey, isn't it? Of course." He spoke the English of patrician Philadelphia. "Divisions, divisions. I have an image of pubic curls black as tar and glistening with sweat like tar." He was from his looks of Philadelphian *deutsch*, what they call Dutch, origin. "And then loins of pared thinness in the sun to which the North has an equal right, the mane like gold foil."

"What the hell are we talking about?" Had I been slipped an MF? Was this Sekt of an unprecedented fortitude? A white-coated servitor served me more. I took. Mme. Durand, who spoke little English, giggled. "Are we here to celebrate the death of the Mediterranean?"

"Our Italian friends over there," the Philadelphian said, "would not think so. Is it not rather to glorify a new spirit, a freshly made Europe, Alberich thrust underground and Siegfried phallically rampant?" He was certainly drunk.

"What the hell have you to do with Europe?"

"Tomorrow," he said, "the world." Mme. Durand giggled.

I said, "*Gaumont Gauleiterin.*" And then, "*Ou bien Pathé pathologue.*"

"*Dingue, dingue,*" she tinkerbelled. To a white table men in chef's toques brought great steaming dishes. "*Goulache,*" she slavered, going over there.

And not only goulash but a kind of rich soldier's stew with bobbing sausages, pork cutlets with mushrooms and radishes, beef in a sauce of spiced mugwort, wobbling pink pyramids of saffron custard, a cream cake in the shape of a fylfot, a Tower of Babel chocolate confection reeking like a barbershop of rum, berries of the German forests, cheese the hue of lemons or of leprosy, and, like a warning of heroic times in store, wedges of tough black bread. I ate nothing but drank thirstily of the ample Sekt, while the two hundred or so others spooned in hard, some of them sweating. A godling in mufti who I did not doubt was of the special SS intake in whom not even a filled tooth was acceptable said to me, accurately, "You do not eat."

"No, I do not eat. But I drink." And I drank, promptly to be refilled. "*Danke sehr.*"

"I too drink."

"That is good. To drink is very good. Of blood have you yet drunken?"

"It is English of a strange kind you speak. Of blood, no. It is the Jews that eat blood dry. It is in their religious cakes mixed." He seemed to be serious.

I spoke German to him, saying, "They say that under the microscope you can see the difference between the configurations of Jewish blood and Gentile blood."

"Aryan blood, yes."

"The term Aryan has a purely philological significance. It can be applied only to languages. There is in fact no difference whatsoever between Jewish blood and other blood. This I know. This you are forbidden to know."

"You are wrong."

"When I say that you are forbidden to know?"

"What you say of the blood. Be quiet now. The *Reichsminister* is to speak."

Goebbels, who had not been present during the feasting, now made an applauded entrance. He was no man to improvise a word or two of greeting; he had typewritten sheets of which copies had undoubtedly already been given to the press. He welcomed us in his Rhineland accent with its not yet expunged peasant tones. He called us friends in a double sense: of the art of the cinema, of the new Germany. Nay in a triple sense: of the art of the cinema of the new Germany. But some inner grace bade his deep-set simian eyes register an instant's doubt of the logical propriety of that conclusion. He then spoke of the cinema as the popular voice of the state, reaching audiences as yet uneducated in the understanding of the traditional arts. He seemed to consider that the guests of the Reichsfilmkammer had to pay for their guesthood by extolling in their own lands the excellence of the products of the German cinema that they were to see. Nay, more, in persuading cinema distributors in those lands to show those products, themselves a means of cleansing the world film market through their purity and excellence of the regrettable decadent ordures excreted by international Jewry. For the Third Reich spoke for sanity everywhere. The National Socialist philosophy had purified and made strong a Germany long corrupted by international ordure excretors; Germany by her example would yet save the world.

I had felt sick before and had been saved by Sekt. Now I was beginning to feel sick of the Sekt. I would, I knew, shortly have to vomit. The *Reichsminister* seemed to have three or four closely typed pages still to get through. I started gently to move toward one of the open windows. The aims of the artistic policy enunciated by the National Chamber of Film might, said Goebbels, be expressed under seven headings. Oh Christ. First, the articulation of the sense of racial pride, which might, without reprehensible arrogance, be construed as a just sense of racial superiority. Just, I thought, moving toward the breath of the autumn dark, like the Jews, just like the . . . This signified, Goebbels went on, not narrow German chauvinism but a pride in being of the great original Aryan race, once master of the heartland and to be so again. The Aryan destiny was enshrined in the immemorial Aryan myths, preserved without doubt in their purest form in the ancient tongue of the heartland. Second. But at this point I had made the open window. With relief the Sekt that seethed within me bore itself mouthward on waves of reverse peristalsis. Below me a great flag with a swastika flapped gently in the night breeze of autumn. It did not now lift my heart; it was not my heart that was lifting. I gave it, with gargoyling mouth, a liter or so of undigested Sekt. And then some strings of spittle. It was not, perhaps, as good as pissing on the flag, but, in retrospect, it takes on a mild quality of emblematic defiance. When I got back to listening to Goebbels he was onto point seven, which did not seem very different from point one.

I slept heavily that night and woke to heartburn about half past eight. I would not, I decided, that day visit the studios of Tobis and Johannisthal and Grünewald and Froelich and Neubabelsberg. If they wanted me to pay for my air trip and accommodation I would, a free *Mensch*. I would go to see Fritz Kalbus at Wehmayr Verlag and draw my royalties and go back to Paris. I rang room service and requested bicarbonate of soda and a cannikin of mocha and some dry toast. While I was belching heartily the front desk called to say that there was a lady downstairs for me. I assumed it was an escort with car sent by Toni Quadflieg, and I passed on my regrets that I was too ill to participate in the day's program. No no, it was a lady downstairs who wished to come upstairs, a friend of mine by the name of Fräulein Auronzo. *Auronzo* first rang no bell then set a whole belfry clanging. Of course. I might have known. Please send her up.

Concetta Campanati née Auronzo looked very thin and very old but very vigorous. It was a vigor of the will and not at all of the body, wherein, I could divine, the growth that ate her monopolized all vigor. We kissed each other. Coffee? She would have some, yes. She sat, no longer elegant but dressed as for hard work in mustard tweed and lisle stockings. "I thought," I said, "you might be in Berlin."

"I've been here only a week. Dresden, Leipzig, Magdeburg. I started off in Munich and then kept moving north. Here, I think, I shall finish."

"How did you—"

"The *Völkische Beobachter*. Haven't you seen it yet?" She took it, rolled to a baton, from a workmanlike brown satchel. "It says an interview here on arrival. You seem to have been attacking the American Jews. I don't believe it, of course. They twist everything. Here, read."

"No, I don't think I will. I'm sick enough already."

"Sick? But you've seen nothing yet. Nothing at all."

"What precisely have you been doing? You realize we've all worried. I mean, just going off, no address, very vague. Not that we don't. I mean, courage. Almost Hortense's last word before I left her in New York. She's separated from Domenico, by the way. She'd had enough. Even Carlo didn't talk about the sacred bonds of matrimony. But we won't talk about that. What precisely?"

She drank some coffee. It was mostly real coffee at that time, with only a whiff of pounded acorns. "They all seem a very long way away. Don't forget to give them all my dearest love. Even stupid Domenico. He's not bad, he's just stupid." And then, "There's no time to give you the whole story. It began in Chiasso with my bank manager, a Jew. A discussion about investments. We got friendly, he's a widower. He said this was no time to talk about *safe* money, not the way things were. If there was any spare money about, he said, it ought to be used to get Jews out of Germany. Big Jews, writers, scientists. The Nazis confiscate and then kindly let some of them out. But only on condition that they pay special imposts to the state. It's monstrous, a kind of dirty joke. They've already paid up. Now they have to find the money for this tax and the other tax. The taxes have horrible long names, sneering names. That's where the Davidsbündler comes in."

"The—" The name was familiar. I caught an image of Domenico playing something on his Paris piano. That was it, Schumann. The March of the David gang against the Philistines. But that had been just art. "Yes, yes, I see. Working from Switzerland?"

"The trouble is they have to have somewhere to go. And nobody wants them. Not unless they're very very big. Or have families somewhere. Nobody seems to like the Jews. Somebody said that all Hitler's done is to do what other people only talk about doing. I'd like to make the Jews crawl, somebody says, and that's that. But Hitler actually does it. Only it isn't crawling. There are these work camps and worse. Trucks coming to decent respectable Jewish houses in the middle of the night and taking people off. Nothing in the newspapers. Nobody cares. No justice for the Jews, meaning they're literally outside the law. It's going to get worse. I saw Jewish heads smashed in Dresden. What can we do about the small Jews with no international reputation, the little clerks and the watch repairers?" Her face twisted a moment as with referred pain. But, of course, it was her own. She fumbled in her satchel and brought out a glass cylinder of tablets. "Could I have a little water?"

"Of course." Bringing her a glass, I said, "How is it? I mean, how are you?"

"The times's coming," she said, having swallowed, "to make an end of it. No, no," she said, seeing my jaw drop, "I'm still a kind of daughter of the Church. I wouldn't," with her old irony, "want to endanger my immortal soul. I'm not," she said, as though rebutting a proposal of my own, "going to die in one of their work camps which are really death camps. There's nothing wrong with dying spectacularly. Christ did it."

"Nobody," I said, "can touch you for anything. I take it you're armed with an American passport. I mean, you gave your name as Auronzo. Nobody could touch you as an Italian either. Surely the name Campanati means something. What do you mean—die spectac—"

"Campanati," she said, "is not too popular a name in the new bright lands of oppression. Carlo, I gather, has been what they term indiscreet."

"Carlo," I said, and nearly said: *who now knows all*, "has been speaking out, no more. A priest's duty he called it, his own voice not the official one of the Holy See. But the Pope has been speaking out too."

"The Pope is vague and full of generalities. Carlo has been bringing in blood and bones and talking of casting out the devil."

"How did you learn about this?"

"You can see the American papers in the consulates. One of these radio talks was reported in the *Washington Post*. Have you actually heard him?"

"He was very good. Guest on this weekly program run by Father Somebody. He didn't have him long. He stole Father Macwhatsisname's thunder. Look," I said, "I don't like this talk about dying."

"A lot of people are dying. I saw a Jewish girl of ten with her head smashed. That was outside Leipzig. These people are murderers. And they haven't really started yet."

"It's not only the Jews, is it?"

"Ah, no. Not only the Jews. Have you heard of the Brown Houses? No, of course not. Hedemannstrasse and Papenstrasse, the Ulap. God, the hypocrisy. Doctor Goebbels telling the International Penal and Prison Congress all about humane rehabilitation—here in Berlin."

"You seem very well informed, Concetta."

"I am. And you're going to be very well informed too. And you're going to inform anybody who's prepared to listen. You're the writer in the family."

I groaned inwardly. "I let poor Raffaele down, didn't I? Scribbling my shop-girl romances instead of attacking the gangsters. But what good could I have done?"

"People don't want to know. They have to be made to know. Whether they act on what they know is up to them. But they have to know."

The telephone buzzed. It was a discreet noise here in the Adlon, Venusberg not Valkyrie. Toni Quadflieg, querulous rather. Message about my crankhood received. But I was expected, he said, on the studio tour to be present. I wanted to blast obscenities but I kept calm. Crank, I said, crank crank. You will be well for *Hitlerjunge Quex* today evening? Crank crank, and I crashed down the handset.

Concetta said, "Why did you come?"

"Invited. All paid. Film based on book of mine. Royalties to be collected and spent. Curiosity."

"Who have you met?"

"Goebbels. French and American and Viking admirers of the regime. Film people. Mrs. Goebbels."

She nodded. "There'll be a lot of the big ones at this *Horst Wessel* premiere." She got up painfully and went over to the escritoire where the telephone was. Next to the telephone was a bulky folder with, on the cover, a film projector flashing a swastika onto a screen. The program. Film personalities. Synopses, cast lists. Very thorough and comprehensive. She brought the folder back to her chair; standing seemed to take a lot out of her. "Here it is. Thursday evening Eight o'clock. God, what an obscenity.

'Die Fahne hoch! Die Reihen dicht geschlossen
S.A. marschiert mit mutig festem Schritt.'

A ponce and a cornerboy and his dying word is *'Deutschland!'* Ken, don't go to that abomination."

"I have to see the worst, don't I?"

"Don't go. Leave this place. But take this stuff with you." She dropped the folder to the carpet, red turkey, and let its glossy unbound contents fan out. The stuff she meant was what she now took from her satchel, a buff quarto envelope, legal and solid, the size of an eighty-thousand-word typescript ready to be mailed. "It's all in here," she said.

"What's in here?" I took it.

"Disposition of things," she said vaguely. "Domenico will be disappointed, no money for him, a bit in trust for the twins, very little. The Davidsbündler gets the bulk of the estate, Dr. Nussbaum in Chiasso has everything organized. As for the other things, that's facts. One or two photographs, personal stories. If you still feel sick don't look yet. Don't open up till you get back. Back where?"

"Paris. But not for long. I thought of taking chambers in Albany. What is all this?"

"Whatever it is, publish. I'm egoistic enough to want to be remembered. Other names—there aren't any other names but there are a few helpers, quite a few. They have to go on living. I think you can be trusted."

"Concetta! How can you say that?" The hurt was sharp.

"It's a question of your trade. You deal too much with unreality. Don't make a novel out of all this."

"Novels can be more real than—"

"These are bad bad times. This is the worst century that history has ever known. And we're only a third of the way through it. There have to be martyrs and witnesses."

"They're the same thing, you know."

"You see what I mean," she said kindly. "A certain tendency to frivolity. I know that *martyr* means witness. You're too used to dealing with words." She suddenly writhed and I saw for the first time the evil of pain: that face, comely still despite age and disease, had ceased to be comely. "I have to use your— It may take quite a little— Jesus—" Shocked, I helped her toward the *Abort*. It was clear that she was past muscular control.

forty-eight

If I may anticipate, I did what had to be done with Concetta's material in 1937, in London, having taken over from Aldous and Maria Huxley Apartment E2 in Albany, Piccadilly, they, with their son Matthew and Gerald Heard, sailing into American exile on the *Normandie* on April 7 in that year. I had finished with Paris, which was animated by political broils and smelt of various kinds of corruption. Concetta's big buff envelope contained photographs of men and women recently emerged from places of torture and interrogation on Hedemannstrasse and Papenstrasse and other houses of correction, some facts about Buchenwald near Weimar, a concentration camp set up as early as 1934, and other well-attested evidence of atrocities mostly committed by the Schutzstaffel or SS as it was affectionately called by its members. In comparison with what was to be discovered later, Concetta's revelations of Nazi diabolism were fairly mild but, as Carlo was to point out to me, evil must never be measured quantitatively: to shove the face of a rabbi into his own shit and let him suffocate was evil enough. The millions we were to hear about later, Jews and Slavs and gypsies and Aryan defectors, still form a body of ghosts too vast to impinge in palpable horror on the imagination, and one of the photographs Concetta had obtained remained and remains for me a sufficient testimony to German Faustianism, or soul-selling for secular power. The face is that of a woman schoolteacher, a pure Teuton from Bitterfeld, who had taught some traditional humanist doctrine now heterodox and, betrayed by members of the Hitlerjugend in her class, been subjected to a brief course of rehabilitation. The face was virtually mouthless. A black toothless pulp under a broken nose would no longer be able to recite Goethe; an eye was missing and an ear had been cut off. This was merely what had been a face. For the body the photograph was not able to speak.

Concetta knew that the Nazi persecution of the Jews was only one aspect of the infamous philosophy of the satanic regime, but she had the foresight to envision it as the most spectacular of their achievements. The Crystal Night or night of the smashing, which inaugurated post factum the official mass pogrom, did not take place until November 9, 1938 (two days after Herschel Grynszpan killed an official of the German Embassy in Paris), and the threefold disposal of the Jews—(a) seize their property (b) exploit them as slaves (3) kill, despoil, process—had not yet been presented as a formula, nor had it begun to conflict with the wasteful Final Solution of which Heinrich Himmler (God forgive me; wait for the next chapter) was already dreaming. Concetta, as an Aryan, to use their sickening pseudoscientific cant, and as a Christian, already was well enough qualified to identify herself with millions who were in purely ideological conflict with the regime, a conflict very speedily resolved, but she elected to be considered Jewish and worked for the Jews as an adoptive sister or mother.

Her attempt to have herself accepted as a Jew by the very officials who were persecuting Jews was, on the evidence of the diary which formed a major part of the material she entrusted to me, more comic than heroic. In Hanover, by dint of loud German, the flashing of her Italian passport, and intimations of urgent messages from Rome, she had persuaded underlings at the SS headquarters to admit her to the presence of a certain Oberbannführer Hummel. At first properly polite to one who seemed to represent herself as a senior official of a sister party of villains, Hummel allowed his jaw to drop progressively as he heard what he took to be a kind of madness or, more probably, a dangerous trickery masquerading as madness. For she said that Judaism was not a matter of race, since there were no physiognomic or hematic indices which could distinguish Jews from, say, Germans; Judaism was a matter of faith and she, though born an American Italian Catholic, had decided to adopt the faith of Abraham and Moses. What did he, the Oberbannführer, propose to do about it? Nothing, he said: he had no authority as yet to persecute foreign nationals of the Jewish faith. Ah, she riposted, so it was only German Jews who had sinned against the light? No no, the Nazi ethnologists accepted that the Jews of the entire mondial Diaspora formed a homogeneous body infinitely dangerous to the cause of Aryan civilization, but Germany recognized the unfortunate limitations of its own purificatory or punitive authority. Limitations, she said, which will not last forever? No no, it was hoped not. So then Germany was to declare war in time on the Jews of other nations, which meant, of course, the entirety of those nations, since it would be unthinkable to segregate, in the more civilized nations, Jews from Gentiles? May I tell my friends in America that Germany is already contemplating war? No no no. (He was a very stupid Oberbannführer.) Good, she said, so I shall report your imperfect anti-Semitism to the appropriate authorities in Berlin. No no no. Very well, persecute me. As a Jew I demand to be persecuted. I shall sit outside in that corridor that smells of SS carbolic and await persecution. I have, of course, already informed the Berlin correspondents of the major American newspapers of my conversion. They will be interested to learn what you propose to do. Concetta was not exactly thrown out but she was persuaded to leave through threats of prosecution for trespass on private, or SS, property.

It was sad to have to report that Concetta did not meet, from the Jews she contacted in eastern Germany, the cooperation she had, in her capacity of willing helper, the right to expect. For many of the Jews mistrusted her posture of conversion, regarding it in some instances as a frivolous blasphemy. Like the Nazi theorists themselves, they considered that the Jews were a race different from other races and, moreover, a very special race, a chosen race on which

God, to show his exclusive affection, had willed suffering. In a sense, it sometimes seemed to her, the Nazis and the Jews had been made for each other: no
nut without a cracker, no cracker without a nut. A little old lady whose luggage
was too innocent to be inspected as she crossed the border at Basle, she had
been lucky enough to have her suitcase opened by the *Zoll* only twice, and on
those occasions she had not been carrying arms. She brought altogether something like thirty lightweight Webley-Wilkinsons and Smith and Wessons into
Germany from Switzerland, complete with ammunition. Her view was that,
when SS rank and file, drunk and euphoric, tried to break into decent Jewish
homes on a Saturday night, they should be resisted with the odd bullet and that
would soon cool them down. With the elder Jews this advocation of violence
was abominable, but some of the younger Jews actually wounded and even
killed various of their oppressors (a Sturmbannführer was found shot on a
rubbish heap in Finsterwalde), though the retribution was terrible. Concetta's
other schemes included the importation of SS uniforms with insignia of high
rank (made by a tailor in Zug), to be worn by young courageous Jews representing themselves as visiting brass and ready to deflect arrogantly acts of
persecution with alleged changes of policy in Berlin. All this, alas, was mere
play and dangerous play too. Totally harmless, pathetically so, were the little
pamphlets she had had prepared (one of them written, and very perfunctorily, by
the long exiled Hesse) and printed in Geneva—on Hitler's Jewish ancestry with
genealogical table, a plea from Himmler's dying Jewish mother to stop this
nonsense, a letter to the world from a dying Jewish child. Concetta did most
good with money, which rides over even the most perverse ideology. It may be
yet money that will save the world. But no man or woman was then able to
arrest a process which seemed as much willed by the destroyed as by the
destroyers.

I put together a little book called *A Heroine of Our Time*, which stated who
Concetta was (I did not blow the secret that Domenico had blurted that night in
the Garden of Allah), what she did, and how she died. My publishers on both
sides of the Atlantic demurred when the typescript and its accompanying photographs were presented to them. What the hell was I, a popular novelist and
playwright, playing at? I had already brought out a heavy book on religion, and
now here I was with a piece of hagiography which would please few and anger
many. Germany was a friendly nation, none of the allegations presented could
be proved, the photographs (which could be trick ones anyway and, anyway,
could not be shown to be of the provenance stated) were obscene and unpub-
lishable. It was not, you will remember, till the outbreak of war that the British
Government had the guts to publish, through His Majesty's Stationery Office, its
white paper on the Nazi treatment of German nationals. By then it was considered too late to bring out my book on Concetta, paper not being available
anyway, it all having been commandeered to print death certificates for the

entire British nation, soon to be destroyed, except presumably for its bureaucrats, by the Luftwaffe. I had fifty or so copies of *A Heroine of Our Time* printed at my own expense by a firm in Loughborough. It is now, as you may know, a collector's item.

That theological book, by the way, caused little stir and sold little. It was reviewed equally scathingly by the *Tablet* and the *Church Times* and was publicly burned as Godless in the town of Branchville, South Carolina. But *non importa*, Carlo said: the seed had been sown, nobody in the future would be able to say that the Christian world had not been warned. He made the message of salvation seem strangely ominous.

forty-nine

I got there late, but I got there. A boy called Heini was giving out tracts (title in closeup: *Hunger und Not in Sowjetrussland*). Cut to a café with a young Communist, walleyed, reading the latest issue of *Vorwärts*. Cut to a street: Communists, including walleyed one, have grabbed Heini's tracts and are throwing them into a canal. Cut to another street with Communists clawing down Nazi posters. Now begin chase sequence. Heini is chased by Communists, including walleyed one in the lead. He takes refuge in fairground resounding with calliope music. He looks for hiding place, finds it behind throbbing generator truck. Communists find him and Nazistically kick and beat him to death while trivial music continues in the background. Walleyed one delivers booted coup de grace. Before Heini dies he murmurs the opening line of the *"Marsch der Hitlerjugend"*: a heavenly choir takes it up, crescendo. Closing montage of marching Nazis, swastika banners, snarling Hitler, song continuing:

> *Unsre Fahne flattert uns voran*
> *In die Zukunft zieh'n wir Mann für Mann.*
> *Wir marschieren für Hitler durch Nacht und durch Rot,*
> *Mit der Fahne der Jugend für Freiheit und Brot . . .*

I got out *schnell* as *ENDE* came up and the audience started cheering. Tripe, filthy, tendentious, sickening. Thugs against thugs. I very badly needed a drink.

Just round the corner of Windmühlenstrasse, on, I seem to remember, Korngoldstrasse, there was a red-lighted cabaret sign: *Die Rote Gans*. A red neon goose goose-stepped endlessly on wheeled feet. I went down the steps toward stuffiness and Germanic jazz, Weillian, somehow already crammed with *Heimweh*. A sad elderly waiter showed me to a table and I ordered blond beer and schnapps. The place had not yet begun to fill up. A little man not unlike Goebbels was singing *"Wenn die Elisabeth nicht so schöne Beine hätt'* . . ." As I drank a few men in uniform came in, rank-and-file SS in black, perhaps fellow auditors of that damnable film. The management turned on the revolving kaleidoscopic lights and we were all fantasized into a Fritz Lang dream, though colored. I thought of Concetta and worried. When she had come that morning out of my bathroom, spent, a rind, tottering, she would not let me telephone the hotel doctor, arrange an ambulance, anything. A large tot of cognac and then she would go. I could ring for a taxi. But where was she staying? This surely I had to know. But she would not tell me. Brutally I said, "Someone will have to know sometime where you are. Someone will have to take you away." She still would not tell me: it was as if she had things so arranged that there would, when the time came, be no problem in locating her. I didn't like this. Nor, to be frank, did I wish to be involved. I had already been too much involved with the Campanati family. I had my own life to live, books to write. I looked troubled at the small dance floor. The band was playing *"Eine kleine Reise im Frühling."* Three couples were stiffly fox-trotting. The SS men were calling for Willi. "Willi, Willi," they called.

At the end of the fox-trot Willi appeared to applause. It was the little man not unlike Goebbels, now dressed as a nun. He went into a dirty routine in falsetto Berlin dialect, apparently holding off a dirty priest, he/she mincing about its being *Blutschande* or incest since he/she was a sister and he a father. Finally he sang *"Auf Wiedersehn"*:

> *"Und wenn du einsam bist,*
> *Einsam und alleine,*
> *O süsse denk' an mich,*
> *Dass ich auch einsam bin und weine . . ."*

And then he turned his back to the audience, disclosing a nun's habit split down the middle and protruding his bare arse at which time the trombone farted. Blackout and SS rapture. I now knew whom I had to get in touch with. But I would leave it till tomorrow morning, everybody at Melzo now surely being in bed.

I awoke fairly well and ordered coffee and boiled eggs, which appeared poured in a glass. My eyes shut I staggered with this obscenity to the toilet and flushed it down. The flushing down of the copy of *Der Stürmer* which had been sent up with an attached note from the editorial office (*Dritte Seite!*) took rather longer. On the third page was a foul cartoon showing Hollywood Jews trying to drag a Parsifalian King Arthur away from a vision of the Holy Grail and make him go to bed with an evidently syphilitic Jewish whore. Underneath my words about the decadence of the American film industry were cited in Gothic script. I breathed deeply for several minutes and then initiated the process of speaking to Suor Umiltà, or Luigia Campanati, now *madre superiore* at the convent in Melzo. I knew there was a telephone there but did not have the number. It was a matter of speaking to an underling in the office of the Archbishop of Milan, who took a long time going through the holy local *elenco telefonico* but at length came up with a *numero*. Then I had the very tedious job of getting through to it. At length I found myself speaking to Sister Humility. She did not at first know who I was. Then she descended from the plane of conventual administration with incidental holiness and listened and interjected pious expletives.

"So," I said, "I think you must come and at once. And I think it would be wise to come in, how would you put it, *vestiti laici.*" With Willi's performance still in my mind I had a notion that as a nun she might be defiled by this Godless regime, slit up the back with scissors.

"But she is where?"

"That I do not know, but I have a feeling that very soon we shall be in no doubt as to where she is and that arrangements will have to be made to transport her back to Italy."

"You mean," she said, "not alive."

"I mean very much not alive. If there is a problem of money for the journey—"

"There will be no problem. The problem is getting permission."

"Your own mother damn it your own mother."

"If you can arrange for hotel accommodation—"

"You will stay here at the Adlon. Take down that name. I will at once see to a room."

"I shall come," she said firmly, "as I am. I will not pretend to be what I am not. But it may be two or three days before I am able to leave."

"So long as you come. You're the only one of the family I can call on." And then, after reciprocal God's blessings, we ended our talk. I think it was in Italian.

I had no doubt that Concetta had some stratagem in mind to disrupt the premiere of the *Horst Wessel* film at the Capitole cinema. A bomb? She had warned me to keep away but had made this a very general caution, more moral than physical. Abominations, leave the stinking country. She evidently did not want my own martyrdom, since she had entrusted me with the materials of her testimony against the Hitlerian order. Therefore, probably no bomb. But no bomb anyway, since, with the announced attendance of many top Nazis (not Hitler, who would doubtless be watching *Mutiny on the Bounty* with cream-cakes and tea in his eyrie, or else, with and in the same, *The Hound of the Baskervilles*), there would be profound security and the place swept clean. What then? The faint shouting of a ridiculous old lady's slogans of enmity? A fire? Jews with guns? I saw that I would have to attend the, her word though she had not seen it, abomination. It was bound to be an abomination.

There had already been, in 1933, an *Urfilm* on Horst Wessel which, a week after a premiere attended by Goering, Wilhelm Furtwängler, members of the Sturmabteilung and much of the diplomatic corps, had been interdicted as both ambiguous and ideologically inadequate. Ambiguous, apparently, in that the communist enemy, when it had the jackboot in its teeth, excited a measure of sympathy. Ideologically inadequate in that the hero was dark-haired and of only medium height. There had been suspicions that the film would not really serve when it came to the editing phase, and the name of the hero had been changed to Hans Westmar, thus raising no real problems of postsynchronization. But everybody assumed, seeing the film, that Horst Wessel was meant, hence the ban. Three weeks after this ban a note in the *Hannoverische Volkszeitung*, probably written by Goebbels himself, asserted that the film could do no harm if it were clearly understood that Hans Westmar was not Horst Wessel but a quite different man named Hans Westmar. Still, the film was recognized as an inferior product and Goebbels had set his heart on the sponsoring of a masterwork of commemoration of the author of the official Nazi hymn. And here it was. No dubiety this time. The film was entitled *Horst Wessel*.

I knew I would not be able to stomach the entire masterwork, so I turned up as late as I decently could to the Capitole, which was patrolled like a fortress by armed *Schutzpolizei* and *Schutzstaffel*, *Schutz*, which sounds like *shoots*, meaning protection. There were some harmless people around clearly awaiting the egress of the great, but Concetta was not among them. I was dressed in drab street clothes since I had been told by Toni Quadflieg that it was, as it were, a fighting film and evening dress would not be appropriate. The top brass would be in uniform: Dr. Goebbels had suggested that perhaps I myself might like the loan of a uniform and afterwards be photographed in it. Ah no. Ah no and again no. Ah most certainly bloody well not. No bloody uniform. Drab street clothes. I showed my card at the entrance, went in, and was kindly made room for at the back by a little man who offered me a pepperment. *Danke sehr. Bitte sehr.* When the screen erupted into sunlit street violence I could see a plain decent face with pince-nez on and SS uniform beneath. He smiled diffidently at me. *Noch ein Stück Pfefferminze? Danke, nein.*

The film seemed to be a kind of purged adult version of *Hitlerjunge Quex*.

Purged, that is, in the sense that there was no dangerous dubiety: all the Germans were tall, fair and chivalrous, and all the Communists small, dark and violent. Horst Wessel, most brutally beaten up by the filthy swine, lies in a hospital bed. Cut to Communist Party HQ, where it is smally and darkly proposed to go to hospital and violently finish Horst Wessel off. Cut to SA HQ, where warning letter is received. Cut to hospital, with dark and small Communists breaking in and tall fair Nazis waiting for them. Nazis chivalrously do in Communists. Two SA keep guard outside the door of the sleeping Horst. His mother sits proudly sad by his bed. Horst opens his eyes and says: "The moment is coming." SA come in, prematurely one would think, with flowers. Later, alone with his mother, the hero dies. His last word is *"Deutschland!"* Not the end. Silent procession of weeping comrades in the hospital corridor. Funeral cortège with Nazi flag on coffin. The police protest (the year, after all, is 1929): *"Diese Fahne ist verboten!"* The flag stays where it is. Funeral ceremony, police and crowd violence. Funeral oration: "Lift up your flags! For the German Reich!" Horst Wessel is seen against dark cloudscape duly lifting his own flag. Night, torch procession. The *"Internationale"* sounds loud then faint, overborne by *"Horst Wessel Lied"*:

> Zum letzten Mal wird nun Appell geblasen,
> Zum Kampfe steh'n wir alle schon bereit.
> Bald flattern Hitlerfahnen über allen Strassen.
> Die Knechtschaft dauert nur noch kurze Zeit!

Workers raise clenched fists but, by miracle induced by Horst Wessel, now in heaven, they open them and stretch their arms in the Nazi salute. The stepfather of Horst's fiancée, Agnes, who bears strong resemblance to Stalin, also stretches arm in Nazi salute. Great cheering crowd. End. The man next to me offered another peppermint. *Danke sehr, nein.*

Outside in the vestibule I saw, I suppose, nearly everybody who counted in the Nazi Party. Goebbels was showered with congratulations, but the director of the film was nowhere to be seen. Hess, Heydrich, Streicher. Fat Goering. The actor, Paul Hörbiger, who had played Horst Wessel, quite clearly to me homosexual: impulses flashed between us in the garish swastikaflagged eaudecolognesprayed entrance hall. How did you like our film? asked the peppermint man with pince-nez. Technically of high standard, as Englishman I cannot feel for content as you gentlemen do. How well you speak our language. It have I from reading the novels of Strehler gelearnt. Him know I not. He is Jewish. Ah then, him know I not but him should I know already. We were moving out to the open air. Shining limousines waited in line. There was to be a good rough party meal served in an upper room of the Friedrich Schiller Hotel, nothing elaborate, mind, plenty to drink though. Crowds held back by SS and Schupos (*Weisst du was ein Schupo ist? Ein Schupo ist ein Polizist?* A children's rhyme somewhere in Strehler) cheered and heilhitlered the emerging dignitaries. The moon shone on them as once on Charlie Chaplin, but floodlights outbraved her wan dignity. Then I saw Concetta Campanati as little, harmless, very sick and hence heroic being here to honor country's leaders old lady in front rank to my right, framed by two bulky SS bodies. She was carrying her satchel and she raised her satchel to breast height and from the mouth of her satchel protruded the nozzle of a pistol too big for her with which she aimed at the genial shy short peppermint-chewing man whose eyes behind pince-nez were on the greeting crowd to his left and mine. *"Achtung!"* I cried and pushed him. Father forgive them for they know not what they do. He went flop into the back of little Goebbels who, in his turn, flopped into the back of Goering, too heavy to go down like a domino. Goering turned to bark, Goebbels to yap. The bullet, if bullet there was, hit nothing or nobody. I am damned sure there was no bullet. But I would never know whether there was a bullet or not. Explosion, yes, like a firework. The little old lady smiling, sheered away from by the rest of the crowd crying, like a Schoenberg chorus, in *Sprechgesang*, pointed her gun at Schupos and SS, making a spraying motion as, most pathetically, with a machine gun. A brave SS boy who could have been her grandson drew his Mauser and shot her down. There was a bullet there, no doubt of that, and then another and another, all very noisy. There was smoke and the reek of frying *Speck*. She went down more or less smiling. I kept away from her body, I had nothing to do with that body, that body was now for the SS morgue. Heinrich Himmler, the peppermint-sucker, slowly began to see that he owed his life to somebody, not a uniformed comrade but a visiting Englishman in a drab street suit. The body of Concetta Campanati was carried away by one SS man only in an easy fireman's lift, no staggering. Another took off her satchel. Passports would be found in there issued by two governments, both friendly. There would be two embassies to contact. For Suor Umiltà too. I would do no more. I would leave. The Reichs-filmkammer would not, surely, be so base after such service to the state as to demand reimbursement. The cancer, I thought, seeing the body carried to a police wagon, would still be blandly eating away, though puzzled by its own progressive loss of appetite and a change in the quality of the nutriment. I felt very sick. *"Wie kann ich,"* Heinrich Himmler was saying, hands on my elbows, hogo of peppermint breathed in blessing upon me, *"meine Dankbarkeit aussprechen?"* Or something like that: I recall only the shunting of the infinitive to the end. Kenneth M. Toomey, British novelist and savior of Reichsführer Heinrich Himmler. I would somehow have to get them to keep that quiet.

The town of Moneta is in Lombardy, not far from either the Swiss or the Tridentine border. It looks north to the Rhaetian Alps: St. Moritz is only a brief train ride away. It had, in the prewar year of my visit, a population of about seventy thousand, some engaged in the marketing of agricultural and viticultural produce, others in light industries such as the making of surgical corsets. There was also ironwork and ceramics. The bulk of the town lies west of the Torrente Melaro, stoutly bridged at three points in the names of Garibaldi, Cavour and Cesare Battisti, the bridges touching east of the river the fine Viale Milano and Via de Guicciardi, with the Piazzale Mottalini between them. There is a noble Prefettura and the best Ospedale Civile in the region. There is only one first-class restaurant, the Oca d'Oro, but admirable *trattorie* abound, the regional cuisine there presented being at its most characteristic in the winter, when excruciating winds knife down from the Rhaetians: thick bean soup, tripe stew with gnocchi, fat sausages from the grill, the black wine that is Moneta's pride. It is an episcopal seat, and the Duomo and the bishop's palace lie between the Via Trieste and the Via Trento, both of which are exactly set on geographical lines of latitude. The Duomo had its foundations laid in 1397, the style Gothic, but various interruptions such as civil war, invasion, famine and plague delayed completion of the work till about 1530. Jacopo della Quercia was bribed or blackmailed into coming from Siena and decorating the central portal with a Saint Ambrose presenting to the world with the open arms of a master of ceremonies Christ's final agony. The pillars of the door are embossed with bas-reliefs of the history of the faith from Adam and Eve up to Ambrose's conversion of Augustine. Within are frescoes by Giovanni da Modena (Saint Lawrence grilled) and (the Virgin giving suck) Lorenzo Costa. The bishop's palace is Renaissance work and cold in winter. I dined there with Carlo in early spring, when the cold was abating. He was, of course, Bishop of Moneta.

"Do you miss Washington?" I asked over the mixed fry of tiny fish.

He was not dressed at all episcopally. He was still feeling the cold after the central heating of Washington and wore a heavy fisherman's jersey. In the fireplace with its ornate proscenium (nude ladies stretching their arms toward the focus or *fuoco*) some green logs spat and the resin in them flared like bad temper. He frowned at the cold splendor of the room with its peeling frescoes of the codpieced chase. "I knew it couldn't last," he said. "Not with that bastard jealous of my English." He meant the Apostolic Delegate to the United States of America. "I knew what would happen when fat Bertoli died of a stroke." He meant the previous incumbent of this diocese. "Send him home, they said, give him a bit of pastoral experience. Not that I mind," he added. "I have to be home if I want to make Pope." A very American idiom. This was the first time he had mentioned that ambition, but it had been always implied in his hints about secret meetings to change Christianity, had been as good as articulated the day he handed me that typescript in the Garden of Allah. "When I'm Pope," he said, "I won't have to worry about the name they gave me. I'll be able to choose one of my own."

"It's not the Carlo you mean, I take it, it's the Campanati."

He brooded as Mario, his butler, took out the fish dish. "Not to know your mother. I tried, I asked around. The father doesn't matter, the father's always God. But not to know who your mother is or was. Was. She has to be dead."

"Look," I said, "it was better the way things worked out. You got an education. You got English as a mother tongue. That's going to make a difference when the time comes."

"Some of these bastards don't believe Catholicism exists outside of Italy."

"Why do you say bastard all the time?"

"Eh?" Mario brought in very pallid veal and served it. He was an old man, very bent, a skilled snufferup of impending dewdrops. He too felt the cold. "Oh, they say it a lot in Washington, especially in politics. It's a neutral word, like bugger in British English. Besides, I'm a bastard myself. I mean in the literal sense."

"You can't know that."

"I do know it. That's the one thing I found out sniffing around Gorgonzola." The phrase was apt. He saw it was apt. "The mites of gossip, the green mold of scandal. There were some old women bribed to forget all those years ago, but some of them remembered. But they didn't remember any surnames. Surnames are a kind of modern luxury in some parts of the world." And then, chewing without relish, he said, "What are those lines in *Oedipus Tyrannos*?"

I knew which ones he meant. And he meant not the original but my own translation, which I had made with the help of the Loeb crib. Ernest Milton had commissioned it, more of an adaptation than a translation, more in the manner of the new poetic drama that Auden and Eliot had been bringing in (that Tarleton bitch had been right) than in the old Gilbert Murray style. Carlo had seen it in New York with, sitting next to him, the quondam Bishop of Bombay, now Archbishop of Old York, down from visiting his sister in Toronto where, incidentally, he had received emergency dental treatment from an old shaky man named Toomey. I quoted:

> *"I must unlock this last door to the last room*
> *Where I myself am lodged. I must look on myself.*
> *At worst, I am the son of the goddess Fortune.*
> *Who would not have such a mother? I am*

> Kin to the seasons—four-legged spring,
> Summer upright in his pride, tottering winter.
> I rise and fall and rise and fall with the
> Rising and falling and rising year. This is my breed.
> I ask no other."

"That's it," he said. "But why all that rising and falling?"

"The riddle of the Sphinx," I explained, "integrated into the imagery. Four legs, two legs, three legs man with a stick. Four, two, three—a pattern of return, circular. You see that?"

"I don't," he said with apparent irrelevance, "believe in tragedy. It's not a Christian concept."

"You can't blame Sophocles for not being a Christian."

"This *vitello*," he said, "is horrible. I'm going to have some changes round here. The only good thing is the wine."

"The wine is good." We raised glasses grimly to each other.

"The tragic victim," he said. "They use the term very loosely. Especially in newspapers. Tragic victim of a road accident. Sacrificial victim. Christ is that, but he's also the victor. That's the big difference between *Oedipus* and the mass. Christian victims have to be victors as well." There was a big brass bell by his plate. It had the lion of Saint Mark writhing all about like a Chinese dragon. He raised it in the air like a town crier and tolled it with vigor. When Mario snuffled in like, I thought, a personification of winter, Carlo asked him what else there was to eat. *Pollo alla diavola. Patate arrosto.* Fetch them in and take this muck away. To me Carlo said, "I don't like failures."

"We're all failures."

"Damned nonsense. You're not a failure." How little he really knew. "Neither am I. Listen, I'm glad to be out of that family. All failures."

Shocked, I said, "Your sister is a kind of Saint Teresa. Your brother Raffaele died for the cause of civil decency and justice. Your mother was a witness for the victims of Nazi persecution. Domenico," I said, and then stopped.

"Domenico is a fool. A Godless fronicating idiot with a talent for spinning silly music for silly movies. Well, not all of them silly perhaps. That one with Astrid Storm, *The Passion and the Pity*, was not, but it was nearly ruined by Domenico's half-witted music. And I know all about my adoptive father, another fornicator and a syphilitic one, leaving the running of an ancestral cheese business to his brother who called himself my uncle Gianni. Luigia became a nun because she's sexually cold, couldn't bear the thought of the touch of a man, a negative vocation. The woman I called my mother committed suicide—"

"Look, I was there—"

"It was like those *amok* people in Malaya. Kill so that you can be killed. She didn't even kill."

"That," I said contritely, "was really my fault."

"Where's her victory? The SS turned her into a spoonful of ashes, Luigia brought her home in a jar. Stamped out of history, as though she'd never existed."

"There's this book I'm doing."

"Which no one," with prophetic accuracy, "will read. Raffaele let himself get hacked to pieces by the Chicago thugs. Another failure."

"So all the Christian martyrs were failures too?"

"That's different. They went into it singing, damn it. They shook the Roman Empire. Damn it, Raffaele was killed by Catholics, he only bore witness to a half-baked secular faith that he didn't even have the eloquence to articulate. He was a fool for getting on the wrong side of you, you could have been his voice."

"*Mea culpa, mea maxima culpa.*"

"Don't mock," he cried as the charred chicken and spuds came in. "The woman I called my mother said she was a Jew, but the Jews didn't want her. She knew cancer was going to kill her and she cheated it, which was undoubtedly not God's intention."

"I see. So the cancer was God's idea?"

"Ah no. Ah no. That comes from the other side. But you have to suffer it to the end. Christ could have lunged out and got a sword in his guts in Gethsemane. But he didn't. He didn't cheat. He went right through with it to the limit as the rest of us have to. And he had his victory."

"Concetta and Raffaele will have theirs. Their reward will be great in heaven."

"Ah no." He scraped some burnt skin off his *pollo alla diavola*. "They'll be lucky to get in. They both committed suicide."

"You're harder than you used to be. You used to have a lot of compassion."

"I brim with compassion," chewing and brimming grease. "I feel desperately sorry for them. But my compassion means nothing. It's God's compassion that counts. This chicken is pretty terrible." He forked a cube of potato, four faces golden, two black. "I know what's on your mind. You think I'm being suicidal too."

"I don't. You've shut up about the fascists."

"I speak my mind, but I'm not political. I don't condemn their filth as political filth. I just say that that bullfrog had better remember his Christian duties. And the rest of the thugs. There's nothing political about that."

"And the war in Spain?"

"There's wrong on both sides. I leave it to you English to call Franco a

Christian gentleman. The Church in Spain is wrong to side with the Falangists just because they make the Virgin Mary a captain general in their damned murderous army. The Church should get on with its job, which entails being persecuted. The Church is never a victim, remember that. The Church survives. And I," chewing comfortably, "intend to survive. Do you honestly think I could allow myself to die before that pyknic atheist? I'll live to see them all hanged or else die screaming in their guilty beds like Herod the Great. I," he showed his big fine teeth as he tore at his meat, "am not going to be a victim."

His ugliness was taking on a kind of beauty as he strode through middle age. His fat was solidity not flab. There was nothing of the victim about him. "Beware," I said, "of hubris."

He spat out a small bone and hubris with it. "I'm not pitting myself against God. God knows his servants. Listen," he said. "About the Campanati family. I may need it, and I may not. It depends on the general atmosphere when the time comes."

"Which will be when?"

"After the next one, probably Pacelli. I don't think Ratti has long to go now. Pacelli's been doing a lot of his work for him—*Mit brennender Sorge* is his, I'm sure. And perhaps *Divini Redemptoris*. One fist for the Nazis and the other for the Russians. But I think there's a way of beating the Communists at their own game. They'll try and take over here when Mussolini's had his throat cut. I'll be ready for them."

"I read all about that. Damn it all, it's in that book I foolishly put my name to. What do you mean about the general atmosphere?"

"Eh? Oh, that. It may be a good thing to have a mother who fought for the Jews and was shot by the SS. And a brother who was public-spirited in Chicago. And a sister who's a mother superior."

"And another brother who's a fornicator and doesn't go to mass and wants a divorce."

"I'll bring," he said, "that bastard to heel if necessary. I'll have him back with poor Hortense if need be, God's light shining on a reformed sinner."

"And if poor Hortense doesn't want him back?"

"Matrimony is an indissoluble sacrament."

"You're the bastard, Carlo. A bloody opportunist, that's what you are." He liked that. He beamed greasily then wiped grease and beam off with his napkin.

He said, "Or it may be better to be like Oedipus. Child of the goddess Fortune. Everything depends on how things will be at the time."

"Which, I ask again, will be when?"

"After Pacelli. I bet you a thousand dollars that Pacelli will call himself Pius XII. I give Pacelli till, oh, say the middle nineteen-fifties."

"And then you'll be Pius XIII?"

"Oh no, thirteen's unlucky. I'll be something else."

"What?"

"Ah," as Mario, having forgotten first to remove the meat dishes, brought the cheese in, no Gorgonzola there but nearly everything else, a stinking anthology of Italian caseation, "that must remain a secret." And then, carving himself a hunk of lactic decay, he said solemnly, "Death."

"It does smell like death, yes. The corpse of milk, Jim Joyce used to call it."

"No no no, I mean we're going through a time of death. Death's riding, the skeletal horseman. We must all watch our health—you, Hortense, me. We have to survive a bad time. You and Hortense are my family. You know that."

"Yes, I do." And then, "Poor Tom."

"I'm sorry," Carlo said cheesefully, "I never knew him. But I don't think we would have—"

"Got on?"

"You told me those jokes of his but I could never see them as very humorous. About Hamlet really being an omelette and so on."

"Tom," I said, "was a saint." Val Wrigley had said that, but he'd been right.

"What do you think you mean by a saint?"

"Tom was a man who did no harm to anyone, who brought a good deal of harmless pleasure into people's lives, who was chaste and charitable, who suffered pain uncomplainingly, who died saying God's will be done."

"He said that?"

"No, he made jokes. He made the doctors laugh and the nurses cry at his courage. He insisted on dying undoped. He wanted to meet God, he said, as he used to meet his audiences—smiling but bemerding himself with fear. He was too good, perhaps. His wife left him because of that. Women can't stand goodness. Some people said it was she who was the saint. Always going to mass and confession and saying her bloody rosary. Talking about the delights of chastity. And then she went off with a low comedian." Carlo frowned at the technicality. "Tom was what is known as a light comedian. Without a red nose. Not dirty. Not like George Robey who peels a banana and says one skin two skin three skin five skin." Carlo's blank face reminded me of the temperamental and cultural gap between us. He would not be a humorous pontiff.

"A saint," he said, "is something different from what you seem to think. I've known cats and dogs that were saints by your definition. A saint," he said, "has to modify the world in the direction of being more aware of the presence of God in it."

"Feeding an illusion," I said with some bitterness. "God's removed himself from the world. As we'll see. As we'll see more and more." Mario brought in a zabaglione in a blackened pan in one hand and two plates and two spoons in the other. He snuffled up a dewdrop loudly. Carlo shouted *No!* Mario dumped all down and got out quickly.

More gently Carlo said, "You're not ready yet. But you may be ready for the *noche oscura*. Have you read San Juan de la Cruz?"

"We're all ready for the *noche oscura*." And then I considered it was time to have the whole thing out. While spooning in the zabaglione. "Carlo," I said, "for some reason you refuse to understand my situation. The way I am. The sexual way I am."

"I've never seen evidence of this way you say you are despite the talk I have heard. You don't behave like a *finocchio*, you have no eye for seducible boys. I know sodomites, foul perverted sinners. I've seen in you only something which I'd regard as Christlike—the urge to love another man and thus rise to that higher sphere of love which stands above the commerce of Nature. An urge so holy that it had to be diabolically frustrated. I know of my failure there and I regret it, but I cannot be blamed. Perhaps the road to that kind of love had to be beset by physical temptations, but I cannot see those as at all like the dirty elected lusts of the city of Sodom. I think you will find that love again. I do not think," scraping up the last of the dry flakes of zabaglione from the pan, "that you and I will find it together. Our relationship is a fraternal one, very different. You must never hesitate to say to others that that is our relationship: the Bishop of Moneta is my brother, the Archbishop of Milan is my brother, the Holy Father of the faithful is my brother." He had it all worked out. "The love you seek may perhaps only be satisfied in the personality of Christ. It may be you who are destined for sainthood." He let his spoon clang into the pan like a promise of eventual bells. He wiped his fingers on his fisherman's jersey.

"Carlo," I said with some weariness, "*fratello*, God made me as a being desirous of spilling seed in forbidden places. God made me incapable of the ordinary philoprogenitive lusts of man."

"God did not make you so. We leave that kind of implantation to the devil. It does not come at birth, even Dr. Freud says that, a man who could be a very good Jewish theologian if he stopped inventing terms like id and so on. If the devil has done this to you, then it is as I said your duty and your glory to convert a desire for the flesh of your own sex into a desire purely spiritual. You must not yield."

"I haven't your sense of vocation. I need the release and comfort of the flesh. I'd hoped that the book I published on your behalf—how ironic, my sponsoring of a view my nature forbids me to hold— One of these days you'll have to change that dogma. There's plenty of seed in the world, too much. Onan committed no real sin. He was just ahead of his time."

"The devil, you see," he smiled, "lashing his tail like a cat. God's kingdom was built for an infinitude of souls. God's love of individual human souls is insatiable. With the frustration of the seed you enact the deadly sin of frustrating the satisfaction of the divine appetite."

"Moloch, Moloch," I groaned. "Feed him with newborn babies in a land lacking bread and water and hardly enough spittle for the desultory rite of baptism. No no no, Carlo, it won't do. Your logic ought to have priests and nuns leading the way in the thriving of uncondomed copulation."

"We," he said, not without complacency, "are different. We attest the divine paradox. We are barren only to be fertile. We proclaim the primary reality of the world of the spirit which has an infinitude of mansions for an infinitude of human souls. And you too are different. Your destiny is of the rarest kind. You will live to proclaim the love of Christ for man and man for Christ in a figure of earthly love." Preacher's rhetoric; it would have been better in Italian, which thrives on melodious meaninglessness.

I said, with the same weariness as before, "My destiny is to live in a state of desire both church and state condemn and to grow sourly rich in the purveying of a debased commodity. I've just finished a novel which, when I'd read it through in typescript, made me feel sick to my stomach. And yet it's what people want—the evocation of a past golden time when there was no Mussolini or Hitler or Franco, when goods were paid for with sovereigns, Elgar's Symphony Number One in A flat trumpeted *nobilmente* a massive hope in the future, and the romantic love of a shopgirl and a younger son of the aristocracy portended a healthful inflection but not destruction of the inherited social pattern. Comic servants and imperious duchesses. Hansom cabs and racing at Ascot. Fascists and democrats alike will love it. My destiny is to create a kind of underliterature that lacks all whiff of the subversive."

"Don't," Carlo said, "underestimate yourself." Mario brought in coffee and a box of Pártagas. Carlo spoke to him at some length in the Milanese dialect—close enough, I gathered, to that of Moneta—telling him that the dinner we'd just had was fit only for flushing down the *gabinetto* and that he'd bite everybody's balls off unless there was a speedy improvement in the *cucina* and much else in the same style. "I can," Carlo told me when Mario had gone, handing me the cigarbox and wax *fiammiferi*, "be like a peasant if and when required. I can be anything they damned well want." I was in my cold bed early that night. I had an early train to catch for Geneva. I was opening a bank account there, not at all liking the prospects for the rest of Europe in the spring of 1938. Hitler had just marched into Austria (not ridden: all the motor transport had broken down on the road to Vienna) and received in his hometown Linz a welcome of fruit and flowers. But Carlo was looking beyond Hitler and the rest of the predatory bastards.

fifty-one

Pope Pius XI died on February 10, 1939, and Eugenio Pacelli fulfilled Carlo's prophecy by being crowned, just over a month later, Pope Pius XII. There seemed already to be a vague sense hovering like cigarette smoke in Fleet Street that I was somehow connected with the Vatican, and I was asked by the *Daily Mail* to cover the obsequies, the attendance on the right smoke signal, and the coronation. I refused: I did not wish to hang about Rome with Sir Hugh Walpole, who was doing the same job for the Hearst organization, and be drawn by him into pursuing the *pedicabile* what time the Conclave decided the claims of the various *papabili*: it was not, despite Carlo's prognostication, all that easy going for Pacelli.

I stayed home and saw Great Britain recognize the government of General Franco, Hitler annex Bohemia and Moravia and proclaim a German protectorate, Lithuania cede Memel to the Reich, Italy seize Albania a week after the end of the Spanish Civil War. That there was going to be a Second World War few would then accept: we had had our scare the previous September, and now Chamberlain and Daladier would repeat the pattern of the Sudetenland in respect of the Polish Corridor and Hitler's final territorial demand. We were all learning to live with our shame, an aspect of the human condition.

On the day of Great Britain's signing of a defense agreement with Turkey I was sitting in my salon in E2, Albany, studying the studio portrait that Hirsch had done of me. Careful underlighting and airbrushwork made me look younger than I was. When I faced the shaving mirror each morning I saw a man of an undoubted forty-eight years, uneasy, unloved except by his readers, weary, tinted by good living, chin sagging, hair graying and thinning but superbly sculpted by my regular operative at Trumper's of Mayfair. The creature in the photograph was your popular novelist, unlined and with youth's dreaming eyes but wise with a hard-bought wisdom: a man you could trust but not too much, traveled, of sure taste in the arts, not terrifyingly overintellectual but well-read and sufficiently clever, sharp or compassionate as occasion required when giving in the mass press his views on modern woman, the intentions of the dictators, friendship, the importance of Faith, the status of William Somerset Maugham, the decadence of the French, the beauties of rural England. The portrait would serve perhaps for another decade in the promotion of my books. My agent would ensure that it got to isolationist America, falangist Spain, Nazi Germany, fascist Italy, imperialist Japan, and other countries where I fed an appetite for sedative fiction. My most sedative to date, meaning exciting with no hint of the subversive, would be out shortly: *A Time of Apples*. I had already told Carlo what it was about.

I put down the portrait sighing and reread the letter from my father's second wife. He was very ill, she said, with ailments appropriate to advanced age, nearly eighty now, that was to say pulmonary congestion, a growth in the prostate, cataract, what looked like Buerger's disease or thromboangiitis obliterans, oral ulcers, chronic dyspepsia, the approach of feeblemindedness. His second marriage had not been blessed with increase and he talked or rambled much now about the children he had not seen since the end of one world war and would not, unless we all (all!) made speedy tracks to Toronto, see again because of the impendence of another. He did not seem to have taken in that Tom was dead. He had a vague notion that somebody had turned him into a grandfather. He had one or two books of mine and had the idea that I lived with my British publisher. He did not know that his daughter dwelt a brief flight away and was making a name as a sculptress.

"No," I said aloud to my books and pictures and bibelots and Bokhara rugs. "No," to the English May sun and the distant comforting hum of the London traffic. Carlo had taught me that paternity was a fiction and that filial piety was due only to God and one's blessed mother, if one knew who she was; Carlo might be right, since he was going to be the next Pope. Fathers and sons: nonsense. And then the bell to the apartment discreetly sounded and Jack, an old warty porter, showed in the son of a very distinguished father.

This son bowed and clicked heels mockingly and said, *"Ein Brief für Sie,"* putting down his suitcases and tennis racquets. He took the letter from his inner jacket pocket with his left hand and handed it over with arm stretched and body forward inclined as from a posture of mock military attention. The letter was from Jakob Strehler and the printed letterhead said Albrechtsgasse 21, Wien. It was in German and penned in a kind of mockery of primary school calligraphy. Mockery, then, was in the blood. "Please sit down," I told the son in English, and he sat to mock military attention on one of the Louis Quinze chairs. I sat in a fauteuil facing him and read.

The great Strehler addressed me as his dear friend and said that I must not think he had been ungrateful for my frequent expressions of admiration, both in the reviews I had been good enough to send, safely received but, as he was aware, never acknowledged, and also in my letters, similarly unacknowledged. He was, he feared, no letter writer. He wrote only for fame and money, especially money. The situation in Austria, now a mere province of the Third Reich, was undoubtedly dangerous for such as himself, a Jew, a so-called intellectual, a democrat, a believer in free speech; nevertheless he proposed to stay on more or less in hiding, helped by the international reputation (though not the money, alas spent) bestowed through "the bounty of Sweden" as Yeats called it, helped too by his own comparative indifference to the future. His wife, as I might not know, had returned to her native New Zealand some years past, taking their daughter with her but leaving their son to his own, Strehler's, unhandy ministrations. For him Strehler feared, and him he assigned to such care as I, Toomey, was able to give him. He apologized for the unsolicited gift of a son, but he doubted not that the traditional hospitality of the British to refugees from oppression was well represented in me. He wished now he had read some of my books, but it was probably too late; besides he did not usually read his contemporaries.

Heinz, as he was called, had few talents except for pleasure, which included the good-natured or perhaps, to be cynical, advantage-seeking willingness to give pleasure to others so long as it cost nothing. It was through the good offices of one to whom he had given such pleasure, a high officer of the Austrian Nazi Party, that Heinz's egress had been able to be effected from the Reich, a Jew-hungry entity (*Judenshungrige Einrichtung*). I was to do with him please as I thought best. I was to tell the Anglo-Saxon literary world not to worry about the fate of Jakob Strehler. His works would outlast the thousand-year Reich. *Es ist,* as Bach affirmed in a chorale borrowed for a violin concerto by Strehler's friend Berg, *genug.* I was to receive Heinz as a piece of a broken father and as a token of appreciation of past kindnesses. *Ich danke Ihnen herzlich.* Jakob Strehler.

I took this letter reverently and placed it in a desk drawer, on top of another German letter of appreciation, though one brief as a bark, from Reichsführer Heinrich Himmler. Then I turned to look glumly at my present. "Welcome, Heinz," I said. "How old are you?"

"Twenty-three years."

"What do you propose to do here in England?"

"*Bitte?*"

"What do you wish in England to do?"

"Ah." He smiled lusciously as he melted with great speed out of his mock stiffness, entwined his legs with the bonelessness of Jim Joyce, leaned back in an odalisque pose, and searched his pockets for cigarettes. He came up with some Chesterfields, and he sent one flying to his lips with a nail flick on the base of the pack. "Give me fire," he said.

"A light, you mean, give me a light." I gave him fire from my gold Dunhill lighter and he rested, during the lighting process, his hand lightly on my firing wrist. The cigarette, too much nitrate in its paper, crackled. He said, walrussing smoke from his nostrils:

"I do what you wish that I do."

He disturbed me. He was so blatantly, almost commercially, epicene. Handsome, very, despite the thin mean mouth. It is hard to say what a Jew looks like, but Heinz would have served well as chief exhibit in some *Ausstellung* of male Nordic beauty. It was the New Zealand side of him probably, but it might have been abetted by a throwback to Crusader blood, the rescuers of the holy places being generous in the donation of their northern seed to Palestine. I lighted a cigarette of my own and we sat facing, puffing smoke at each other in unequivocal signals. He was a whore all right. I was crackling, like his Chesterfield, with conventional desire tainted with foreknowledge of disgust. I felt like at once sending him packing, tennis racquets and all, but I had a duty to a great man. "The great man your father," I said. "He must also leave Austria. What plans have been made? What friends does he have? Sigmund Freud is already in London, but it took time to arrange the payment of the *Reichsfluchtsteuer* and the other ridiculous taxes. I cannot believe that your father wishes to stay. Please tell me precisely what is the present position as regards your father." I spoke in German; his English, for one whose blood was half anglophone, was atrocious. In German he told me that his father had been lucky because of his Nobel Prize, but that the luck would not last. The day after *die Kristallnacht* of last November his father had had made a metal plaque and affixed it to a spot on the façade of the apartment building somewhat above the reach of SA hands painting *Jude*; the plaque said: "Jakob Strehler, Austrian Novelist, Honored in the Name of the World by the Academy of Sweden Which Awarded Him the Nobel Prize for Literature." The Reich did not want to offend Sweden, nor, as yet, was it altogether convinced that Jakob Strehler was an *echt* Jew. Strehler was not a Jewish name. There was the evidence of his own son, and here Heinz stretched and grinned complacently, a true piece of Aryan manhood if ever there was one, to contradict the cruder imputations. But the time would come, and Heinz did not seem greatly concerned about it. I said, "Let me show you your room."

"*Bitte?*"

"Your English is not very good. Perhaps you have had nobody to speak English with, to."

"My father, a little. Once I speaked it good."

"Well, you mean. You spoke it well."

"Once I spoke it very well."

"Good, that's very good."

I carried his bags, which he seemed to expect, but I left the racquets to him. He looked at himself before looking at the room: there was, just within, a cheval glass, a fine old spotty one I had picked up at the sale of Lady Huntingdon's Belgravia effects. Then he tested the bed, its sheets newly changed after a visit from the American producer Jack Rappaport, and bounced his arse on it for resilience. "Well," he said, "very well. So here I sleep." At least he did not ogle me from that position. Rather he ogled himself anew in the dressing-table mirror, admiring the sit of the fawn jacket with its skimpy Central European cut and the blue tie with its horrid design of golden leaping hares.

"We will go to the Café Royal and there drink a cocktail and then eat lunch and discuss your future."

"*Bitte?* Please?"

"*Deine Zukunft.*" He simpered at my unthinking use of the familiar form. Then he bounced up, opened one of his suitcases, and began to change his clothes. No *pudeur*, of course, no *Schamhaftigkeit*. I was expected to watch, so I watched. He encouraged me to note that he was not circumcised. The rest of the body was a hard golden almost textbook model of Aryan male comeliness. He put on what he must have thought of as his British suit: drab gray but still skimpy. He hummed *Trink, trink, Brüderlein, trink* as he redressed. That had been, at the time of the 1934 massacre, an SA favorite.

We were looked at knowingly in the Café Royal upstairs bar. Middle-aged Toomey, tastes often guessed at, tastes now blatantly advertised. Heinz drank three martinis and smacked his lips after sipping. I took him down to lunch and he tucked in to a large hors d'oeuvre, poached turbot, roast beef with horse-radish, Stilton, and a double helping of chocolate mousse. "*Das schmeckt gut,*" he said often, and once, "*Die gute Englische Kochkunst.*" We had two bottles of chilled Wachauer Schluck in memory of dead Austria. We talked. My father said that you would see to everything. He spoke of your becoming my *Pflege-vater* and of British papers of *Annahame* or adoption. Is your father mad? It is all too possible, to me he has always seemed mad. You do not like your father? I like him when he is away in the house near Gerasdorf and I am in Vienna or he is in Vienna and I am in the house near Gerasdorf, though I do not like the house near Gerasdorf, it is too far from Gerasdorf and besides there is nothing to do, not even in Gerasdorf. I should be glad of another father. Oh my God. No, I cannot be your father. If you can get work in England then a work permit can be arranged and you can be your own master, I can look into that, but you cannot, God help us, assume so serious and binding an enactment as adoption. Out of devotion to your father's work I will do everything possible for you, but there are, you understand, limits. He seemed to regard devotion to his father's work as a demented foible, not less demented for his having met it often and seen it sanctified by the Swedes, but he considered his father's work to be old-fashioned, boring and pretentious. Himself he preferred a good Jack London or a *Kriminalroman*. Or the cinema, he was mad about the cinema. How many cinemas gave there in London?

A well-known sodomite, James Agate the theater critic, came in and looked hard at Heinz, making signals with his puffed and englowed cigar spunk. Heinz twinkled at him and moved his shoulders. I told Heinz that the situation as regards employment might shortly ease for the incoming Jews, the trade unions relaxing their strictures. Jews? Jews? Heinz said he had no time for the Jews, a grasping and puffed-up race. Yids, sheenies. But damn it, man, you yourself are a Jew. Ah no, I am not because my mother was not, that was made very clear to me by a Jewish rabbi who visited my father, but the Nazis do not always understand what it is to be a Jew. God, man, your father is a Jew and a very distinguished one, isn't that enough to make you a Jew? Isn't the fact that you were liable to be persecuted as a Jew enough to make you feel solidarity with that suffering race? Never: me they would not persecute; me they wanted to feature on a poster persuading young men to join the army and serve the Fatherland. The Jews are getting now what has been coming to them for a long time. Oh my God.

What jobs have you had, what trade or profession were you reared in? I have done many things but I liked none of them. I worked once in an insurance office but they dismissed me on a false charge of peculation. I played the drums for a week in the orchestra of the Gestiefelte Kater or Puss In Boots cabaret. I acted a silent soldier in a play by Schiller or Schilling or somebody. I have had friends, both male and female, who have looked after me but they always ended the association by becoming unreasonable. My father sometimes gave me money, sometimes not. He gave me money for this journey but it was not enough, I spent much of it in Paris and what was left in Dover where I stayed last night. There was not much in Dover to spend money on but I spent it. I think a man in a *Bierstube* robbed me of some but I cannot well remember. The fact is that now I have no money.

We had coffee and cognac. Heinz asked for whipped cream with his coffee, an old Viennese self-indulgence, Oedipal, Freud had said in his autobiography, and when I took out my wallet to pay the bill he made whistling noises and *come boy to me* gestures as to a dog. He meant that he required some of the banknotes in that wallet. I sighed and gave him five pounds. His eagerness to be off to spend them was of the writhing kind of one merely anxious to spend a penny. You give me the key also? Ah no, ah no, no key. You ring the bell like everybody else. He made a *moue* or *schiefes Gesicht.* I went out with him through the stares of the lubricious and watched him hare off toward Piccadilly Circus.

I had an article to write for the *Daily Express* about women who painted their toenails and what this signified in terms of the decline of our civilization. I went out to dinner with John Boynton Priestley, the Yorkshire novelist. When I got back to Albany at just after ten Heinz had not yet returned. I put on pajamas and dressing gown and waited. I tried to read the literary essays of his great father and saw for the first time that their pomposity was a mockery of pomposity. I must not be pompous with young Heinz.

Well after midnight he came back, not too drunk though tieless. Two giggling girls were with him, slobbermouthed and coarse but not prostitutes, at least not yet: they had arrived that evening at King's Cross from Jack Priestley's county. They had met Heinz, whom they called Baked Beans, in a pub in Leicester Square and he'd stood them port and lemons and said they did not have to worry about where to spend the night, they understood him all right though he talked funny, but that was because he was a foreigner, he had this old man that was his friend and he had plenty of room in his posh place. I'm Elsie and this is Doreen, pleased to meet you. They wore low-cut summer frocks and artificial silk stockings, were inexpertly made up (caked powder, greasy lipstick) and had overdeveloped busts. Out, I said, out out, ladies, this is not a dosshouse. I was mean, that's what I was, where was they to go at this time of night, and Heinz said they was his friends, they had started to give him English lessons. That's right, Elsie or Doreen said, we had sausage and chips in one of them corner houses and he said he wants us to learn him to talk proper. Out, both of you, and I slippered sternly toward the telephone. Oh all right then if that's the way it is, but you're proper mean. And Doreen, or else Elsie, feinted a punch in my balls as I showed them out. Ta-ta, Baked Beans, see you tomorrow. Then I confronted Heinz, who muttered things at me with *Scheiss* in them.

What he seemed to wish to do, seeing my anger, was to increase that anger and convert it into lust. I would take him by force, something I could see he was used to. He needed, in fact, a good punitive buggering but he was not going to get it from me, at least not yet. I ordered him to his room, but he said he wanted to go out to a nightclub and would I give him some more *Pinke*. He had spent all of the five pounds, a lot of money in those days. To bed, sir, we're going to have a serious talk in the morning. He scheissed off, snarling. During the night I half woke to find him proposing to get into bed with me, hot and naked. I slapped out at him and he spoke words I could not understand, something that had been Primitive High German but had now turned to street dirt. He sulked and cursed back off to his room and I heard him fist his bed like an enemy before getting into it. This would not do.

He did not get up the next day till after eleven. He came yawning and tousled, also naked, into my study and said he wanted breakfast. Make it yourself: there, see, is the kitchen. And then, oh, let me do it, you're certain to break the crockery. So he sat with coffee and fried eggs, trousered and shirted but barefooted, while I spoke sternly to him. He must learn to behave. These apartments, which were once a single mansion owned by the Duke of York, whose second title was Albany, had been turned into bachelor chambers at the end of the eighteenth century and had accommodated great men like Lord Byron, Macaulay, George Canning and Bulwer-Lytton. They were very particular about whom they had here, and there were strict rules of decorum to be observed. Did he understand? *Ja ja.* He must not bring home drabs in the small hours, he must learn to behave like a gentleman. *Ja ja ja.* I would send him, I said, to the Berlitz School to learn English. Then I would see about finding him work somewhere. He pouted. Time was short for us all, he said prophetically, it was necessary to live a little before the bombs dropped and the poison gas circulated. Nonsense, I told him, there was not going to be any war. Here is a ten-shilling note, it is plenty of money. It will buy you lunch and dinner. Today

I myself lunch and dine with friends. Go to see the wonders of the National Gallery and the British Museum, take a boat to Greenwich, enjoy yourself quietly and soberly. And do not come home later than eleven tonight. Come home, moreover, unaccompanied.

He did not come home unaccompanied. He came, somewhat chastened, in the company of two plainclothesmen, both with mustaches. "This is the address he gave us, sir," said the one of senior rank. "The name he gave is this, sir. Is that right? And this name is yours, sir?" He had a bit of paper with that basic information on it.

I said, "You'd better sit down. I take it you're on duty, but I don't suppose you'd say no to a drink. I certainly won't." I began to pour whisky at once and lavishly into the Heinrich Wilhelm Stiegel glasses I had brought back from America.

"Soda for him, for me straight," the senior man said as they sat. "I take it you know what he was doing, sir?"

"I can guess. Don't ask any more questions for the moment. Let me tell you all." I told them.

"Doesn't look much to me like a Jew, sir," said the junior one. "More of a real Nazzy type. One of them storm troopers like you see on the newsreels."

"Just like that?" the other said. "Just dumped on you like that?"

"There are a lot of refugees that are going to be dumped on us," I said. "Hitler's going to slaughter all the Jews he can lay his hands on. We're going to have to make some adjustments. Morally, socially, everything."

"The fact is, sir," said the senior man, "that he was picked up by us on Goodge Street openly soliciting. The law's the law, and we can't make adjustments to use your words for them who don't know the law. They have to learn it, and that might mean the hard way. For him there it may have to mean deportation, sir. If he tries it again, that is, and he looks to me the type that will." Heinz sat deep in an armchair, sulkily and loudly smoking some ghastly brand of cigarette he had discovered somewhere that smelt like a Mexican twitchfire.

"You mean back to the Third Reich and the concentration camps."

"Our streets have got to be kept clean, sir," the junior said.

"That's Hitler's idea, too."

"We can't speak for him, sir," said the senior, "though there may be something in what he's doing. We can only speak for our job which is the law. Give him a good talking to in his own lingo, which he says you speak like a native. Why would that be, sir?"

"Suspicious, aren't you? Is there some law against an Englishman getting his German grammar book out and doing some hard study?"

"No offense, sir, I was just interested. I thought there might be some tie-up you didn't tell us about."

"I've told you the situation as clearly as I could. I take it you've never heard of Strehler, who got the Nobel Prize for Literature. I take it you've never heard of me."

"We don't have much time for reading, sir." To Heinz, "You were lucky tonight, young fellermelad. You won't be so lucky next time. Say that to him in his own language, would you, sir?" I said it. The two listened like phoneticians. "Very nicely put, if I may say so, sir, not that I understood a dickybird."

"Thank you for your forbearance and discretion. I'll make sure it doesn't happen again. Another whisky?"

"A short one for the road, sir. Plenty of soda in his."

There seemed no point that night in raving at Heinz. He was, anyway, somewhat shaken at the prospect of being sent back to the Nazis with a docket saying *Jude*. The following morning I took him to Harrod's and, in the appropriate department, bought for him a rucksack with steel frame, shorts, boots, sleeping bag, and a youth hostel membership card. I was going to turn him into a bloody *Wandervogel*. In Harrod's travel department I bought him a second-class one-way ticket to Glasgow. There was a nonstop train leaving King's Cross the following morning at 7:40 A.M. He could see the beauties of bonny Scotland and sleep in the heather and catch cold and die. I gave him lunch in Harrod's restaurant—steak and kidney pudding and plum duff, a meal sufficiently stultifying—and bought cold provisions in their food department for that night's dinner—a roast chicken, half a ham, potato salad, Mrs. Goodber's cherry cake, genuine Viennese *Schlagobers* for his coffee. I took him home and supervised his packing. He was still docile. He even said that he quite looked forward to seeing the beauties of *Schottland* and how much money was I going to give him? Ten pounds, I said, ten bloody pounds and no more, he must see how long he could last on ten quid. If he lasted as long as six weeks, then I would give him a reward of a fiver. I got him into bed at ten and quietly locked his door after ensuring that he first evacuated his body thoroughly. I set my alarm clock for 6:15 and dragged him out of bed and into a taxi and to the station. He looked very delectable as a backpacked blond *Wandervogel*. I saw him onto the train and waved him off with joy. *Gute Reise*.

There was peace for a week, peace so pure as almost to be palpable. Then I received a telephone call from Falkirk. It was the voice of a Presbyterian inspector of police, articulate under the burrs and very grave. A young man by the name of Strayler had been picked up trying to steal a bicycle. He gave your name and address, sir. At the moment he is in the lockup. He comes before the magistrate in the morning. He has no visible means of support. He says he was robbed of everything, money, rucksack, even, as is evident from his appearance, razor. Tomorrow he will get off with a caution as this seems to be his first offense and he is an ignorant foreigner. But what do you propose doing about him, sir? I said I would telegraph money for a ticket back to London, meanwhile keep him in a cell and feed him nothing but bread and water. Beat him if he causes trouble. Trouble, aye, do you hear him now? I heard Teutonic shouts and hangings a long way away. Dearly as we'd relish administering a wee bit of corporal punishment, sir, this is Scotland, not Nazzy Germany. He gave me the address of the police station.

I groaned in my very bowels. What was I to do with him? The only thing was to break Strehler's resolution to stay in Nazi Austria, indifferent to the future, ready to face the worst. God help us, none of us then realized in our innocence what the worst was. If Strehler had not yet been cuffed and trounced off to camp it was because there was no hurry: there were plenty of undistinguished Jews around to persecute first before insulting the Swedish Academy. I saw it as the only solution: the reunion of father and son on free soil, but a long way from Albany. Was I myself now to assume the burden of arranging for Strehler's asylum? The morning mail had a letter from a certain Professor Waldheim of the State University of Colorado, inviting me to come over and give a series of lectures and seminars on the contemporary European novel. Who better qualified to give them than the most distinguished contemporary European novelist of them all? I would write to Waldheim. There would be no difficulty about arranging for Strehler's temporary asylum in Britain, though the agony of getting the *Reichsfluchtsteuer* and the other punitive imposts paid and the man himself to see that his future lay with his son would be intense: the agony had better be shared. The P.E.N. organization must help, as also Strehler's British publisher.

I went to see Charlie Evans at Messrs. William Heinemann and discussed the situation with him. I was told, over a glass of warmish Amontillado, that Strehler was, of course, a highly prestigious author and Heinemann was honored to have him on the list, but unfortunately he did not sell anywhere near so well as Willie Maugham and Jack Priestley. There was probably something like thirty-five pounds due to him in royalties. I went to see the urbane secretary of P.E.N., who, over a glass of warmish South African sherry (Spanish sherry was out, definitely out, it stank of republican blood), told me of his admiration of Strehler's work and what a good idea it would be to get him out of that horrible fascist Germany, Hitler's no better than Franco, damn their four eyes, and the next general meeting of P.E.N. would discuss what could be done. I went back to Albany and the clear realization that it would all be up to me.

Heinz returned hangdog, in filthy shirt and shorts and with golden fuzz all over his chin. The Albany porters shook their heads when they saw him. They shook their heads when they saw me: my tenure would be cut short, no doubt about it, this was, despite Lord Byron, an establishment of long cherished respectability. Heinz cheered up in the bath, singing, with a slight Scottish accent, "The Umbrella Man":

> *"Toora lumma lumma*
> *Toora lumma lumma*
> *Tooraleye eh*
> *Any umber–ellas*
> *Any umber–ellas*
> *To mend to–day?"*

He came out shaven and suited and hungry.

"How the hell," I said, "did you manage to spend all that money so quickly?" Robbed by men he had thought good and decent. "Why did you try and steal a bicycle?" The only way to get back to London. I toyed deliriously with the notion of buying him a bicycle and sending him to Land's End on it. He was overjoyed to be back with me in London, he said. He desperately desired to see Walt Disney's *Snow White and the Seven Dwarfs.* Wearily I took him that evening. We had to join a long queue. A couple of files ahead was Val Wrigley with a nondescript boy.

Val waggled his fingers and stepped back to join us, saying first to the boy, "You have the money safe, Charles? It is *two* tickets you must ask for. I am *not* deserting you." And to me, "Well, whom have we here? Such handsomeness, bracing as a bath with pine essence in it, straight, I take it, from some health through joy camp among the conifers." Val was always very sharp and quick. He could even tell, something in the eyes and mouth and incurious ears perhaps, that Heinz probably did not understand much English. "Very toothsome, I must say."

"This is the son of the great Jakob Strehler. *Heinz, darf ich einen grossen Dichter vorstellen*—Valentine Wrigley." And then, hope and cunning beginning to boil within, "Here, Val, is your chance to do something for the cause of the oppressed."

"Jewish, is he? One would never have thought. Aryanly delicious." That damned misused word.

"I am not Jew."

"All right, dear, nobody's *forcing* you." And to me: "I know your hypocrisy, Kenneth Toomey, I haven't forgotten. Cause of the oppressed, indeed. Not one ounce of altruism in that aging carcass. I know you of old."

"Your own carcass doesn't look too good."

"No? Handsome is as handsome does. *Do* get him to say that in German. A most sinister language it's become, hasn't it? Sends shivers right through me." The queue moved forward. Heinz seemed much taken with Val's uninhibited admiration. *Ein grosser Dichter.* Handsome was as handsome did.

I said coarsely, "Untouched, I can assure you. And properly house-trained."

"Death of the libido? My dear, I saw Sigmund Freud with his daughter in a pub, would you believe it? That mouth looks terrible. He was quite bucked to hear somebody talking about the Oedipus complex. Speaks beautiful English, very slangy. Getting some splendid refugee specimens, aren't we?" And he twinklingly nudged Heinz.

I got Heinz briefly off my hands by giving him Val's address and sending him there with his racquets and suitcases. Before that I gave him money daily to spend most of his time with *Snow White and the Seven Dwarfs*, which he adored. He saw it seventeen times and it improved his English. "Magic mirror on the wall," he recited to the cheval glass, "who is fairest of them all?" He knew the answer to that. He could reel off the names of the dwarfs. He sang "With a Smile and a Song" in falsetto. Walt Disney did not wholly tame him but he quietened him down. Temporarily.

fifty-two

It was not until the third week of August that the mode of action for getting Jakob Strehler out of Nazi Austria presented itself. I will not disgust the reader with an account of the ménage Heinz and I conducted in a rented house on the outskirts of Herne Bay during the month of July. In that period Heinz was complaisant if often petulant, though he was soothed by the admiration of girls on the beach. There was also a dance hall he visited nightly. He only twice got into the hands of the police, and that was for drunken brawling. Talk of deportation for refugee delinquents was not now heard much, the Home Office adjusting itself to the steady incoming flood of the persecuted. Heinz seemed now to understand the British way of life and to settle down somewhat. Val Wrigley, unwilling for a whole month to admit to me his inability to control his enforced guest, sent him off to be a guest elsewhere. Heinz was even, for a time, a kind of prisoner in a kind of concentration camp. This was called a *Ferienslager* and was run by the Freie Deutsche Jugend; it was situated near Scunthorpe and its pleasures were imposed draconianly. It was, Heinz shuddered, full of Jews. The guards on the gates were Jewish and very tough. They would hit anyone trying to get out without a permit. Everyone had to stay in and learn strength through joy. Heinz once tried to swim away from the camp but strong Jewish lifeguards dragged him back to shore.

During the first two weeks of August, which we spent home in Albany (I had started a new novel), Heinz was well behaved but furtive and I feared the worst. He did not ask for money. He stayed in all the morning and read children's comic papers of the order of the *Rainbow* and *Chick's Own*, in which disyllables were divided for greater ease of comprehension with hyphens. I bought him a portable gramophone and English lessons on disc, but he preferred to listen to popular songs and learn the words. He sang in his bath:

> *"Two slippy people*
> *In dawn's early light*
> *And too much in laugh*
> *To say good night."*

He also sang "Blue Orchids" and "Skylark" and "Stay in My Arms, Cinderella." We ate lunch fairly amicably together, and then he would quietly go out. Where? To Hampton Court by river. To the cinema. Sausages and chips will I eat in a Lyon's Corner Haus. Have you finished the money I gave you? No, it gives a little left, thank you, perhaps tomorrow you will give. He would return, somewhat shifty but quiet and not too drunk, at about eleven.

Mrs. Ollerenshaw, who cleaned my apartment, said to me, "Are you sure it's all right me not cleaning his room, Mr. Toomey?"

"Not cleaning his—?"

"He keeps his door locked. He says he always cleaned his own room and changed the sheets too when he was living where he used to live. Least, that's what I think he says. He doesn't speak English like what you and me do."

"Sorry, I never thought about it. I've been concentrating on this— Locked now, is it?"

"Always locked, Mr. Toomey. You never know what young men get up to. I knew one that kept white mice in his bedroom, wouldn't let nobody in. Perhaps if you had a spare key we might take a look at what he's up to."

"I've no spare key. There was just that key always in the door."

"Well, it's in his pocket I'll wager." She had three or four knobby warts on her face with gray filaments waving from them. She was a decent hardworking woman, gray and dusty, glad of the used garments I gave her for her unemployed husband.

"I'll have a word with him when he gets back, Mrs. Ollerenshaw."

He did not get back that day. I received a telephone call from Savile Row police station. He had been picked up trying to steal a wristwatch from a jeweler's on Regent Street. Very angry I walked round and found Heinz indulging in loud plaintive *Sprechgesang* which nobody understood, though the jeweler, a speaker of Yiddish, caught one or two words. "It's the accent," he said, "I don't understand the accent." I spoke to the desk sergeant.

I said, "You must understand I have no legal responsibility. This is a refugee wished upon me by an Austrian Jew I haven't even met. Out of charity

I've done my best for him, but here my charity stops. The law must take its course."

"He didn't get away with it, sir. He'll only get a fine or a caution. If you've taken responsibility for him you'll have to go on taking it. Some mad ideas get into the brains of some of these coming over here from Germany and suchlike. It's the sense of being like free that does it. He's sorry for what he's done, you can see that. Nobody wants to be too hard on him. Perhaps Mr. Goldfarb here might like to forget all about it."

"This," I groaned from my stomach, "is going to happen again."

"Happened before, has it, sir?"

"Well," I wavered, "very nearly."

"Like the sergeant says," said Mr. Goldfarb, a kind shrewd man hooknosed like a *Stürmer* cartoon, "we forget all about it. But we don't forget all about it till tomorrow morning. Tomorrow morning I telephone perhaps to drop the charge. Let him spend the night thinking what our people go through over there and being thankful that the British people are decent."

"He's Jewish himself," I said.

"It takes all sorts," said Mr. Goldfarb.

Heinz's pockets had been emptied all over the desk. There was, among the coins, handkerchief and Durex, a single key. This I took. "That's the best way," I said to the sergeant. "Frighten him a little. Loud voices and bread and water."

"This isn't Nazzy Germany, sir."

Heinz's room was in a remarkable state. The windows were fast shut against the poison of fresh air, the stench of various brands of cigarette tobacco was nauseating, the bed was unmade and the sheets were filthy. The room was full of stolen goods. How he had sneaked these in without my seeing I did not know, for not all were pocketable. There were, for instance, two suitcases and a dispatch case, an ormolu clock, a portable radio, and a partly eaten wedding cake. In one of the drawers money was neatly stacked—I didn't count it: that would have taken a long time—and another drawer was loud with Ingersoll watches, all of which he must have conscientiously and regularly wound. In yet another drawer there were three British passports. I sat down heavily on the dirty bed and looked at them. And then the mad idea dawned. Heinz had found the only means of getting his father out. Unfortunately, all the passports had been stolen along with ladies' handbags—from, I presumed, Victoria Station: Mrs. Hilda Riceyman; Miss Flora Alberta Stokes; Dr. Julia Manning-Brown. Dr.—the great epicene title. Dr. Manning-Brown was a physician born in Leicester on April 9, 1881. She was five feet six inches tall and had hazel eyes and no special peculiarities. She looked as kindly at me as her passport photograph would allow: a plain though noblenosed woman with chin uplifted as in pride of profession or, perhaps, sex. Her passport had been issued by H.M. Consul

General in Nice. The official chop had been applied carelessly low to her portrait: its rim rose into the frame like the sun at first light. Jakob Strehler was, I knew, in his early sixties: he had been late in begetting Heinrich Mordecai Strehler, as that villain's own travel document, here too nesting, called him—a document rich in eagles and swastikas and compound words of great length. It was as though there had had to be a leisurely seeping into the seed conduit of familial depravity which, in the father's instance, had been cathartized only through the creative imagination. How tall Jakob Strehler was I did not know, but the Reich was a land of meters and no scrutinizing official would trouble to look for a conversion table. Hazel eyes? Everybody's eyes were hazel, except those of my dear sister Hortense. Hazel was a nut not a color. Strehler's new name would be Julian Manning-Brown: there was just space to insert the letter. The problem would be a photograph.

I had written stories about spiriting good people away from wicked places. Every fiction writer ought, once in his lifetime, to be forced to fulfill in fact what he had fashioned in fancy. I was to attempt a deed that would look well in my biography. I was also going to be rid of bloody Heinz. I looked at my watch: 5:05. All Heinz's stolen Ingersolls said the same. The office of William Heinemann, Ltd., would still be open. I was going to consult their publicity department.

All the photographs of Strehler that Fred Holden was able to show me over warmish Tio Pepe made him look blatantly the biblical prophet: the Nazis would not be subtle enough to discern the mockery. I took Fred Holden into my confidence. He said, Jesus, very risky. I said, What else honestly can one do to rescue a great man whose danger hour nears if, and then we'll never forgive ourselves, it hasn't struck already? Don't talk to the press when you bring him back, Fred Holden said, I want that story first. Let's see now. And he searched among the pictures that had been taken in Stockholm in 1935. Christ, that would do it with a bit of luck. Strehler in a group photograph with other prizemen: C. von Ossjetzky (Peace), H. Spemann (Medicine and Physiology), F. Joliot and his wife Irène Curie (Chemistry). Strehler looked gloomily into the camera lens, large schnapps in hand. Try it for size. I opened poor Dr. Manning-Brown's passport. Fred Holden called in his assistant, Christine, a girl in her element with scissors and paste. The photograph of the rightful owner was peeled off; it formed a template for the razorblading out of Strehler. Isn't this illegal? giggled Christine. Yes, I said, but very very moral. There's the matter of this bit of arc from the Foreign Office stamp, Fred Holden said. Let's see. On Strehler's pasted-in portrait he tried for size the rims of various tiny liqueur glasses: the publicity department had a fair hospitality allowance. The trouble is these things are round and that bloody thing's oval. Christine went out to the fusebox in the corridor and came back with what did the trick. Bless you, girl, you're a genius. We ended with the imprint, hammered home with the heel of Fred Holden's shoe, of half an inch of thick fuse wire. The passport might perhaps not pass a British immigration officer's inspection, but it was emigration I was concerned about. Get him on a Lufthansa plane, Wien–Milan. From then on everything would be all right.

The following morning at about eleven Heinz came furtively in, walking in a crouch, arms up ready to defend his beauty from my blows. He was frightened to find me in a fauteuil with *The Times*, relaxed and amiable. "Sit down, my boy," I said. "Make yourself comfortable. Listen to me carefully." He humbly begged permission to smoke. "Have one of mine," I said, and flicked my gold Dunhill lighter: I realized I was lucky to have it still. "You," I said, "are going to stay for a little while at the Marmion Hotel on Coventry Street. I've telephoned and made all arrangements. The bill will be sent to me. Certain other arrangements have been made too. The next time you are tempted into criminal activity of any kind you will be promptly sent back to the Reich, where my friend Heinrich Himmler, Reichsführer and head of the SS and the Gestapo, will have, with Teutonic efficiency, rendered all things ready for your reception. Do you understand me?" *Ja, ich versteh'.* "I myself have to go away for a week or so, and I shall be locking up this apartment. I shall be back at the beginning of September. I shall bring you a present." I did not, of course, specify the present. It was all too possible that Heinz, hearing that I was to spirit his father out, might hare off to the German Embassy and forewarn them. And then, with novelist's cunning: "Perhaps you find it boring here? Somewhat like that place you told me about near Vienna—what's it called?" Gerasdorf? Was I mad, was I joking? Gerasdorf was a pain in the *Arsch*: London was fine though beset with temptations. But Gerasdorf— Anyway, his father's country place was many kilometers from Gerasdorf, a fair tramp through a wood. "Do you have perhaps photographs of your father's house and your father and yourself perhaps standing in front of it? Knowing my old devotion to your father and my newer devotion to his son you will appreciate how much I cherish such tokens of a time of happiness for him and for yourself." Happiness? *Scheiss*. But I have such photographs in my room. He went toward it, feeling in his pockets for the key, then remembering that I had taken it. He looked at me with horror horror, then truculence: My room is my own, you have no scheissing right— "All right, Heinz, I know all. My felicitations on a very nice little lootheap. Don't worry, I won't talk. I'll put you in a book some day. I sincerely admire your criminal skills." The young fool then slid into a grin that became a smirk of complicity not without foundation: after all, was not sodomy a deadlier sin than theft? "Photos, Heinz."

Most of his Kodak snaps were of himself in narcissistic poses, but there were one or two of him swinging beaming from an apple tree branch or vaulting a fence some kilometers from Gerasdorf, the house behind him. I learned its features swiftly by heart: triple-gabled, with a front porch roofed conically and wooden-railed, a low machicolated garden wall, a walnut tree, an American red currant bush. "Lovely," I said. "Peaceful. South of Gerasdorf? Not too far from Vienna?" No, no, it was northeast of Gerasdorf, halfway to Seyring, another arsehole of a dump. "Ah well, some day you'll see it again and perhaps, who knows, I may see it with you." Never want to see the scheissing arschloch of a place as long as I ficking live. Excellent boy.

Some few days before I was able to get off to Vienna, via Paris and Berlin, the Germans signed a nonaggression pact with the Soviet Union. It was not a pact of friendship. Stalin was later to say: "The Soviet Government could not suddenly present to the public German-Soviet assurances of amicality (*druzhba*) after they had been covered with buckets of filth by the Nazi Government for six years." It was, I was assured by a Foreign Office acquaintance with whom I had a quick Pernod at Orly, not a bad thing: it limited German activity in Poland, which was a Russian sphere of influence. War? There'd be no war. The British Government could not take seriously an alliance with a country so far east and landlocked as to be less accessible than China. Things would arrange themselves. Chamberlain was talking of setting up a special international commission to discuss the problem of the Polish Corridor. There'd be another Munich, it was the only way. Rest easy. You have lovely flying weather.

I snapped some of the feathery cloudscape through a port window of the Lufthansa cabin as we approached Vienna. I had borrowed a small Kodak from an ample store of stolen cameras that Heinz had proudly shown me in his wardrobe. At Vienna airport there were amiable SS officers helping to glamorize the normally tedious process of getting through immigration control. Mr. Toomey, Mr. Toomey, I seem to know the name. What is your purpose in visiting the Reich, Mr. Toomey? I am an author with a new book coming out, its title, I think, *Es Herbstet*. What excellent German you speak, Mr. Toomey. Of course, I knew I knew the name. An author, yes. And at which hotel in Vienna will you be staying? I am not yet sure, I thought of breathing a little country air in an inn a brief train ride from Vienna, perhaps at Bad Vöslau. And how long will you be with us, Mr. Toomey? Again, I am not sure. My old friend Reichsführer Himmler spoke of perhaps coming to Vienna and combining a few festive evenings with a rigorous toothcombing of the local Schutzstaffel. I beg your pardon, Mr. Toomey, would you say that again please, perhaps your German is not so good after all. I took out, bloody fool, always going too far, my prized Himmler letter and handed it over. It was read with awe by all there; there was a temporary blockage of the immigration machine. The SS officer gave it back to me with reverence and some fear. He was a handsome dark young man with the rare distinction of irises of different colors, only one was hazel. He had a compassionate face, he would be compassionate while supervising human liquidation: this liquidates me more than it does you. I was heilhitlered and heelclicked to the freedom of beflagged Vienna. More than a bloody fool, I automatically heilhitlered back.

It was too late to go to Gerasdorf today. I got a taxi to the Messepalast Hotel on Mariahilferstrasse and booked in for the night. Before dinner I walked up Neubaugasse, turned into Burggasse, then, off Thaliastrasse, found Albrechtsgasse. Outside Number 21 there was a half-obliterated red *Jude* scrawl but no boastful plaque any more above the level of the painting fist. Swastika flags listless in the windless warm evening hung from windows of the two top stories. The bottom floor, which I presumed to have been Strehler's, had smashed windows and, so far as I could tell by ungainly jumping two or three times, deserted rooms. A cat negotiated broken glass delicately and came out onto a sill to stare at me astonished with garnet eyes. I went back to the hotel and, in its almost empty restaurant, ate some *Bouillon mit Ei* and *Tafelspitz* with dumplings, following it with *Sachertorte* and coffee that smelt like burnt barley and tasted like embittered Ovaltine. Then I strolled to an open-air café in the Michaelerplatz and drank *Gösser Bier*. An orchestra played Waldteufel. It also played, in honor of the new pact, the "Song of the Volga Boatmen." The laughing drinkers, pretty women and solid burgesses and slim men in uniform, relaxed, civilized, some of them joining facetiously in the *yo-oh heave-ho*, seemed an assurance that there would not be any war. *Bright is the river flowing forever*. A cool breeze blew in from the Danube.

The following morning I got a taxi to take me to Gerasdorf. The driver, a lean shifty man and much too curious, noted my suitcase and wanted to know where I thought I'd stay in Gerasdorf: no hotels there. Are you sure you don't want to go to Gänserndorf? You bring a foreigner—English?—the names might sound the same. It's a tidy way to Gänserndorf but I'll take you. Drop me in Gerasdorf, I have photographs to take. Why there? That's my bloody business. All right, no cause to get offended, I was only trying to help. It was glorious late summer weather, all plums and apples and beanfields and little children waving with sprays of cow parsley. Drop me here, I said. There was a *Stüberl* with vineleaves over the lintel. I paid him and he was sullen in his thanks. He was also slow in turning his vehicle to take the road back. He watched me as I sat at the table outside. It was as if he wished to see whether I found my first sip of the local white wine satisfactory. I nodded at him. He nodded back and was off.

The keeper of the *Stüberl* wanted to know what I was after in these parts. He was a robust man with a belly tight as a white cabbage and a mouthful of ruined teeth. I wanted to take some photographs, I said, patting my suitcase. My apparatus is all within. The beauties of rural Austria. I had been advised to come to Gerasdorf. Ah, said the man, you can begin by photographing my wife and myself under the vineleaves. He called Lise, Lise or some such name. A fat woman with fine teeth came out. *Küss' die Hund, mein Herr.* I snapped them. I will come back for more of your excellent wine when I have wandered a little. He watched me set off wandering, shaking his head. A mailman with a horn on a long lanyard and a thin letter sack wove to the *Stüberl* on his bicycle. Both watched me.

I took the road north toward Seyring. A village idiot appeared from behind a hedge and went gurrh at me, pulling burrs off his dirty trousers. After a mile or so of blank fields I came to a wood on my left. I entered its dapple of gloom and sudden sun and stumbled over mast and crackling twigs, hazelnuts falling on my shoulders occasionally like timid welcomes to rural Austria. There was a crow's nest high above and a crow croaked *caution caution*. Squirrels darted and a lizard on a fallen trunk huffed and puffed at me. Free of the wood and sweating heavily I came to an expanse of stubblefields. There was the house over there beyond three elms: three gables and a cone and a low machicolated wall. I was surprised as well as relieved to see it, even Heinz's photographs ought to have been delinquent. I marched through exploding stubble for over a mile. The house was in need of pointing and painting. The gate, swinging from one hinge, whined when I pushed it. A couple of apples, admirable cookers, thudded from their tree. As I reached for the tarnished knocker, which seemed to be the head of the Emperor Franz Josef, the door opened. Strehler had heard me coming. He carried a shotgun.

"*Ja?*" He looked like his Stockholm picture. He was about five feet eight, but he could always stoop. He was in baggy torn trousers, food-stained flannel shirt, waistcoat with two buttons missing, carpet slippers.

I said, in English, "Toomey. The British writer. To whom you sent your son." He replied in English:

"You should not be here. You should be looking after poor Heinz."

"You and Heinz are to be reunited. May I come in?"

"Reunited? You're mad. But come in."

A passage cut straight through the house from front to back. It was crammed with old trunks and suitcases, a large child's rocking horse, books, books, topcoats flung about anyhow, dust dancing in the light from the front door. Which he now closed and bolted. He led me to a room on the right. Inside it, by its far wall, an iron stairway spiraled up to the next story. A vast cracked window showed fields and sky and swallows rehearsing their exodus. In front of the window was a large teak table covered with open books and paper. Strehler was working on something. His study, then, full of the junk of travel in ivory and ebony, the dust bristling from flat surfaces like gray iron filings. On the walls framed photographs: a grinning woman in a cloche hat in a park with kiwis, the young Strehler coming into his fame, Heinz as a little boy holding a tabby cat by its tail, Sigmund Freud, Hermann Hesse. Stefan Zweig, Rainer Maria Rilke. "Rilke," I said. "The last time I saw him was in a café in Trieste. He cried."

"He often cried. But nobody heard him among the angelic orders. Sit on that chair there. It will not, I think, collapse." And he sat at his desk and looked at me frowning. "What was that word you used—*reunited*?"

"I have the means to get you to England with little trouble. I have a passport for you. Thank God you speak English. It's as an English physician that you must travel."

"Why a physician?"

"Because the most suitable passport of those stolen by your son Heinz belonged to a physician. It's as simple as that."

"Has he been stealing much?"

"Oh yes. Also soliciting on the streets. But he's not in jail yet. Except for the odd night in the lockup he's lived a very free and self-indulgent life. A remarkable young man. I hope you'll be glad to see him again."

He grinned. "Perhaps I should have read one or two of your books after all. You have this English quality—what may we call it? Sense of humor, tolerance, forbearance. There must be a single word but I don't know it. I shall not, of course, be at all glad to see him again. I thought that perhaps by now you would have packed him off to New Zealand to his mother."

"Strangely enough I hadn't thought of that. I thought only of the reuniting of father and son. I look forward to witnessing the first embraces, the first tears of *Gott sei dank*."

"There will be no embraces or tears. I stay here. Until they come for me. But I shall kill some of them first." He fondled the bolt of his rifle—Austrian, a Mannlicher-Schoenauer, 6.5-mm. caliber, as he was to tell me later.

"I see. And when do you think they'll be coming?"

"Soon, soon. Have you heard of a small reactionary man of letters named Johannes Braunthal? No, of course not, why should you. A critic of sorts and a sort of novelist. He has found his true—*Beruf*—how do you say it?—"

"Calling, vocation, métier. What excellent English you speak, by the way."

"Thank you. In the SS. A cruel little man like so many literary critics. He will make sure that I am put to lavatory cleaning or whatever Jewish intellectuals do in these camps of theirs."

"I think," I said, "you underestimate the intentions of these people as regards the Jews. I understand that there is serious talk in Berlin about the extermination of the entire race."

"They've talked a lot about that in Vienna too. They always have. Jew-hating is no monopoly of the Nazis. Still, grateful as I am for the trouble you seem to be taking on my behalf, I feel that I must stay here and wait for the worst. But first I shall kill Johannes Braunthal. I've always wanted to do that anyway."

"He probably knows this. Therefore he will not come himself. Besides, these people usually arrive in the middle of the night. They break in and point guns at your bed."

"I shall hear them break in. As for sleep, I sleep mostly in the front room in a hard chair, facing the window, my gun cocked—is that the word?—and ready."

"Do they know where you are?"

"Oh, they will find out. I may even send for them. You would be a very useful ah ah emissary. You see, I'm coming to the end of a piece of work. There too you could be useful. Take it back to the free world."

"What is it?"

"A curious thing. Have you heard of a Latin author called Frambosius? No, of course not, very minor like Braunthal. And also Austrian, the name being a *Deckname* or pseudonym, his true name Wilhelm Fahlrot of Klagenfurt. He died in 1427, he wrote in Latin. Oh, here is his book, you may see for yourself." And he handed me, as reverently as the SS man had handed me back my Himmler letter, a little book with rotting brown covers, duodecimo I supposed, the pages spotted as with liver disease, the content a poem of about a thousand lines, Latin hexameters, the title *Vindobona*.

"*Vindobona?*"

"Means Vienna. I do not know how good your Latin is. Mine has inevitably improved since I started to translate it into German. In rhyming verse. It is a remarkable prophecy. A horde of human-sized rats floods into Austria from the northern lands and sets up its government and culture in the capital. The haute cuisine is garbage and the music is squeaks, the chief pastime is leaping at the gentle or the infirm and tearing out their throats. Their flag is of four legs stylized on a black ground. Those who will grow whiskers and glue on long tails and walk like beasts are accepted into the community of rats. The king rat is called Adolphus."

"Good God."

"I have perhaps one hundred lines left to do. I have written already the long introduction. I think I can get it all finished before Braunthal and his ruffians come for me."

"You can finish it in London. In my study. I think you must make up your mind as to that. I'm not going back without you."

"Ah." And he smiled. "How will you take me back if I am not willing to go? I have a gun, you I think not. But I'll make a bargain with you. Stay here in the country air and let me finish my work. I have wine in the cellar and whisky in that tantalus over there which is wearing, you see, an old velvet tricorne. The water from my well is like wine. I have a sack of dried beans and a pan of them soaking. There are two hams, one of them from Westphalia. I have learned to make bread, more satisfying than the making of novels. There is a bed for you up that stair there and there are blankets. Three or four days give me. Then we can talk again. But you understand that my heart is set, if that is the right expression, on killing Johannes Braunthal."

The narrow world of the writer, the pettiness of his enmities. The *Anschluss* to Strehler meant little more than a chance to kill a critic. I said, "There are British and American critics I myself should like to kill. But that is a luxury. The necessity, an urgent one, is to get you out of here. I've a sense of responsibility to literature, pretentious as that must sound."

"And a desire to get poor Heinz off your hands. I cannot blame you altogether. Send him to Christchurch, New Zealand, a dour city which will quieten his exuberance. Go to the kitchen now and make us both some coffee. I have real coffee from a Brazilian admirer. Have you by chance brought some real British tea? Twining's? Or from Jackson's in Piccadilly? It was buying tea there that I first met Amelia, who became my wife. She was trying to force herself on John Middleton Murry and Katherine Mansfield, her compatriot. She taught me all my English. *Box of birds*—do you know the expression?"

"I regret I brought nothing except a passport. I mean, I had but one aim in mind. I thought that tomorrow we could be on the flight to Milan, be out of the Reich with all speed. Perhaps even tonight—"

"No, we must not rush matters." There was, yes, a tinge of the Oceanian in his speech. The voice was harsh and yet had a *wienerisch* singsong. He occasionally coughed phlegm into his mouth and swallowed it. The eyes were black and bold and devious. The dirty gray hair fanned or rayed. The skin was russet, the nose huge, the mouth full of crooked brown teeth. He had a Sherlock Holmes pipe on his desk and now he lighted it, dribbling. The smell was of a burning herb garden. "Make," he watered, "coffee and ham sandwiches. Let me continue with my work. The king rat Adolphus is enforcing the teaching of the rat language in human schools. It has a very limited vocabulary."

fifty-three

The red light went on, just as in Broadcasting House, Portland Place, W. 1, and the pleasant young official from the Propaganda Ministry said, "Welcome to the Third Reich, Mr. Toomey."

"You make it sound as if it were my first visit."

"Ah no, of course we know it is not. We know you as an old friend and, in addition, one whose books have been greatly loved by the German people. It is all a great pity, is it not, this misunderstanding that has come about between two great nations."

"Misunderstanding is always a great pity, especially when it turns into war."

The reader will already have divined what happened. I spent the first week of September, both relaxed and stimulated, in the house and garden of Jakob Strehler. The weather was gorgeous and the apples fell. We were quite removed from the outside world of terrible enactments, and I had all I needed except cigarettes from the Burlington Arcade. But Strehler had a pound of blond tobacco for rolling, as well as packets of *Pferd* papers, and he even showed me the craft of fixing a tube with one hand only. I had previously met only one man, except for film cowboys, expert in this knack, and that had been young Eric Blair at a P.E.N. meeting. He lost it, for some reason, when he became established as George Orwell. Strehler practiced the skill distractedly when looking over what he had just written. Like most pipemen he regarded cigarettes as palate cleansers between smokes.

He was nearly at the end of his translation of *Vindobona* when the forces of the Nazi State arrived. It was early morning and I was asleep on the sheetless bed in the loft above his study when he came and softly breathed black coffee and ham on me, shaking me gently, saying, "There are men coming through the wood." I was awake at once. He considerately rolled me a pipe opener.

I said, "For God's sake remember who you are. Do you have the passport in your pocket?"

"It will not work."

"It will and must. Two Englishmen staying in the country cottage of Strehler. Strehler's gone. We don't know where he is. It will be easy."

"These people will know me. Unfortunately Braunthal doesn't seem to be among them. I must demand that Braunthal make the arrest. I have all things, or rather one thing, ready for Braunthal."

I coughed over my cigarette while I pulled trousers on; I had slept in my shirt and underclothes. I put my feet bare into brogues, coughing: "It will and must work. Let me do the talking. I told you we should have been on that plane days ago."

"You lost your urgency."

"You made me lose it. We're both bloody fools. Still, everything's going to be all right." We were at ground level now. We went to the front room and saw through the window six men now crackling over the stubblefield.

"You see," Strehler said, "no Braunthal. I insist on having Braunthal."

"Shut up about Braunthal." There were two stocky civilians in trilby hats and raincoats, two revolvered Schupos, and a Wehrmacht *Unteroffizier* and private, both bearing rifles. "The SS doesn't seem to be represented at all."

"I think I know that one there, the one with his hands in his pockets. Saw him in the Gestapo place when I was trying to arrange things for poor Heinz. He knows me. *Verflucht* and *Scheiss* and so on. I had better open the door. Perhaps they would like coffee."

The small company seemed disconcerted when the door was opened and Strehler and I stood before it in the cool morning waiting. It was as though they had been invited to a breakfast and were late. Strehler took his turnip watch from his waistcoat pocket: 7:51 A.M. The uniformed part of the group began to double. They halted and waited till the civilians arrived. "Do come in," Strehler said. It was all German from now on. To my surprise it was myself who was to be arrested. Neither Strehler nor I was aware that Britain and France had declared war on Germany the previous Sunday. Today seemed to be the following Sunday. The war was officially well launched. We learned all this over coffee in the kitchen. The news that an Englishman with a camera was in the vicinity had been slow in getting through to the police in Vienna. But now I was under arrest. So, of course, was Strehler. Both police and military liked the solidity of Strehler's having proved his disloyalty to the Reich by harboring an enemy alien with a camera. He was also a Jew, of course, and should have long been sent to a work camp, but Jews were for herding into trucks in ghettos, not for picking up on specially made journeys to remote country residences. "I thought," Strehler said, "Braunthal would have been sent to get me."

"Look," I said in German to Strehler, "I'm terribly sorry about all this. You won't have time to finish that damned poem now."

The two Gestapo men sat on the edge of the kitchen table sipping good Brazilian coffee. The *Unteroffizier* and the private had their rifles trained on Strehler and myself. The Schupos stood at ease, their holsters still buttoned. The senior Gestapo man, the one whom Strehler knew and who knew Strehler, tried to work himself up into a righteous lather of philosophical patriotism by snarling, coffee safely finished, "Jewish shit, the only bastards in the Reich able to get real coffee while the rest of us have to drink muck made out of acorns."

"That," Strehler said gently, "is because you want guns instead. You can't have both guns and real coffee, apparently. Now I don't want guns, so I'm entitled to real coffee. You should by rights stick your fingers down your gorges and vomit it up as unpatriotic poison."

"Filthy Jewish shit," the senior man said, "shut your filthy gob before we shut it for you." He was a very ordinary looking man, shiny like a glazed bun; an unusually early shave in probably bad light had left him dotted with dried bloodclots. His companion was gray-faced, probably ulcerous; the hot coffee had made him wince, but he had finished it to the last drop. Both kept their hats on.

I said, "What do you suppose is going to happen to me?"

"You'll get shot as a spy and this Jewish bastard will be shot too. And another thing, it's not right for an English swine to talk good German like you do."

"He's got to speak good German if he's a spy," the other one said.

"I learned my German," I said, "through reading the work of Herr Doktor

Strehler here, the finest living novelist. I'm not a spy, by the way. I came here on a vacation and lost track of time. How is this war going, if there really is a war?"

"London's been bombed into a load of catshit. There's a war on all right, as you'll soon find out. The Führer will be in Piccadilly Platz before Christmas. Come on, time we were moving."

"I demand," Strehler said, "to see my old enemy Braunthal. If I can't kill him I can at least spit in his ugly face." He used the phrase from *Faust*, Part One: *shreckliches Gesicht*.

"Shut that filthy hole," the second Gestapo man cried in dyspeptic pain. "You're the one who'll get spat on and worse."

"It's a Circus," I said, "not a Platz." And it dawned on me that I might never see Piccadilly again.

I was permitted, under a military rifle and a Schupo pistol, to dress properly and pack my bag. Strehler was allowed to use the toilet, though with the door open. He sat there a long time reading one of the old copies of *Punch* he kept there in piles to beguile his costive waiting. The Gestapo snarled at him and went on about Jewish shit, but he said in a courtly manner that that was precisely what he could not conjure. Then he winked at me and I knew he was secreting the British passport inside the issue of June 20, 1934: at least that would not enter into the charge or charges of either of us. We were marched across fields and through the wood, with a soldier, Schupo and Gestapo man each, the seniors of all three arms being reserved to me, but Strehler's party well ahead. I was very lighthearted. This is often the way when the abandonment of personal responsibility is enforced: neither wronged innocence nor just guilt can seriously impair the sensation of freedom one has. That Strehler's heart was light I could tell from his trolling of the old song of the archpoet—*Mihi est propositum*—which came from the nationless Middle Ages when Germany was the Holy Roman Empire. I was seeing the last of him; he had produced great work which would outlast the Nazis; he had every right to be content, despite the proddings and the execrations. He even had *Vindobona* in his case, but I doubted if he would be allowed to finish its translation. For me, I had used what talent I had in the service of popular diversion; I had eaten and drunk well; I had attempted a worthy act even if I had botched it. If I were shot there might be a statue erected for me in some London square, as for Edith Cavell.

On the road there were an Opel Medium Truck Type S and a Porsche *Kübel* and a few interested villagers were being kept off by three or four soldiers under a *Feldwebel*. All this struck me as wasteful, but probably they knew best. I, being a dangerous English spy, was encircled by riflemen in the open truck, while Strehler was thrust into the back of the *Kübel*. The Gestapo as well as the two Schupos were traveling by courtesy of the army: there was a fluidity, or reduplication, of authority in the Nazi system which I have never well understood. Strehler and I waved goodbye to each other, and that was the last of him. He joined, I presumed, that anonymous Jewish force which was to be exploited to the brutal limit and then, in a cleansed Germany, to fertilize those large white asparagus which are still on sale in May in both the Berlins. But Strehler is alive, like Heine and Mendelssohn, and the Nazis are merely the stuff of television movies.

Strehler neglected on parting to mention poor Heinz, from now on to be both fatherless and fosterless. I did not mention him either, and yet he was much in my mind as the cause of my present trouble. Indeed, I was surrounded by a group of Heinzes on top of the Opel Medium Truck Type S, all with foreskins and fixed bayonets, their postures of military alertness no mockery, however.

To be quick about it, a combination of various authorities in Vienna was efficient to establish that I was no spy. My roll of film was developed and found blank except for a portrait of a bad-toothed innkeeper and his wife. Abwehr and SS and a rather charming chain-smoking professorial man in a double-breasted tunic of dovegray whom all deferred to got my situation typed out and indexed and sped on the wire to Berlin. I was Kenneth M. Toomey, distinguished British novelist who, believing there would be no war, had innocently come to rural Austria for a vacation and had been staying in all innocence with another even more distinguished novelist whose criminal Jewishness had somehow failed to register as it had failed to register with the Swedish Academy. No harm done. Regretfully I had to be sent off to an eventual camp for hapless enemy aliens of similar innocence; meanwhile I was to dwell under guard in what had formerly been a small nursing home for epileptics on the Stromstrasse.

My fellow internees included two Poles who, having learned something of the Nazi doctrine on the expendability of Slavs, feared for their lives in bad German. There was also a French newsreel team, their camera confiscated, who had been picked up entire in the Zillertaler Alpen. They snarled a good deal at myself as one of an untrustworthy nation that had dragged France into a useless war. Their deprived cameraman was muscular and aggressive. There was no one of my own nation to support me except an ancient Lancastrian toymaker who had worked all his life in Graz and wrongly assumed that he was a naturalized Austrian. "Bloody Frenchies," he said. "Couldn't rely on't' buggers in't' last lot and it'll be't' same in this. Only good Frenchie's a dead 'un." After two weeks I was told loudly by one of the guards that I had to pack in readiness to be moved off. This was a rainy morning in the dayroom, the French quarreling loudly over a poker game. They jeered and made throat-cutting gestures at me. "Bloody frogs," said the toymaker. "You watch yourself, mate. Don't stand no nonsense."

I was taken to the Viennese headquarters of the Reichspropagandaministerium and, in a beeswaxed office with swastikas and a portrait of the Führer as Parsifal, was introduced to Doktor Franz Eggenberger. He was a small swarthy man with hair on the backs of his hands like a sketch of fur gloves and he spoke excellent English whose rhythms had been arrested at the prep-school level. He had been educated, he told me, at a place named Hyderabad House near Bridport in Dorset, his father having been a great believer in the British ruling class educational system, cold baths and spare diet and Latin. "So here we are, old chap," he said, passing me a box of Stolz cigarettes. "Read one or two of your things. Rather liked them. Just had the great Joe Goebbels on the line."

"Ah."

"Seems to think the world of you. I think you'll be able to guess what he's after. A two-minute radio interview. In English, of course, since it's meant for British listeners. Nothing treasonable, from your angle I mean. Nothing too nasty from ours. A bargain, call it."

"You mean you're letting me go?"

"The idea is everybody suddenly turns their backs. A special exit permit to a neutral country. Plane to Milan was suggested, and then you're on your own. It seems a very civilized idea to me."

"We're not supposed to bargain with the enemy, are we?"

"Nobody's forcing you, of course."

"The question is: what will they say back home?"

"Well, you can't really expect us at this end to worry overmuch about that, can you? I mean, be reasonable. There *is* a war on, you know."

"I'll do it, God help me."

"Stout chap, thought you would. Joe Goebbels will be pleased."

So they put me up at the Josefstadt on Lederergasse and sent this pleasant young official to prepare me for the interview. He apologized for not liking my work: he had had Dr. L. C. Knights as a tutor for a year at Cambridge and had been taught a rather rigorous approach to literature. And so, on the rainy evening of September 29, I found myself saying:

"Misunderstanding is always a great pity, especially when it turns into war."

"How, Mr. Toomey, do you define the term *nation*?"

"Well, as I think I've already said in some of our private conversations, I think in terms of a certain continuity of culture—literature, of course, chiefly—"

"And literature's made out of language, isn't it?"

"Well, yes. In a sense you could say that England is the English language and Germany the German. You may, indeed, say that Luther was the creator of Germany as he was the creator of modern German."

"And Germany is wherever German is spoken, whether it be Austria or Danzig or the Sudetenland?"

"You could say that, yes."

"You were surprised on your holiday visit here to the Reich to hear that war had broken out between our two countries?"

"I was surprised to discover that after conceding the *Anschluss* and the Czechoslovak business both Britain and France felt so strongly about Poland, a country they were in no position to comfort or assist—"

"When you say England and France, Mr. Toomey, you mean, I presume, their political leaders?"

"Well, of course. To be loyal to the democratic system, if not to the elected leaders now in power, I feel compelled to register a vote of very little confidence in Mr. Chamberlain. This, I must emphasize, is not disloyalty. Unlike your own people, we British have the privilege of changing our leaders."

"That is perhaps because you have no real leader, Mr. Toomey. If you had one, you would not talk of changing him."

"There may be something in that. Democracy has its price. So, of course, does dictatorship."

"You regret this war then, Mr. Toomey?"

"I regret all wars with their wasteful expenditure of young lives. Young blood and high blood, as Ezra Pound once put it, fair cheeks and fine bodies. For an old bitch gone in the teeth—"

"For a botched civilization. I know the poem. It was a text for practical criticism when I was at Cambridge. You say in your book about religion, Mr. Toomey: 'Something gets into a man, some force beyond his control, something we must term diabolic and learn how to drive out.' Do you still believe that?"

"Yes, I do. I believe these destructive forces can be overcome if we try hard enough. *Exorcizo te, immundissime spiritus, omnis incursio adversarii, omne phantasma, omnis legio—*"

"What is that you are quoting, Mr. Toomey? It sounds very impressive."

"Oh, it's the old Rituale Romanum. I was thinking of my friend, almost my brother, Monsignor Campanati, Bishop of Moneta in Italy. He has always stoutly held to the view that man was created good and that evil is from the devil. I saw him once at work, driving out demons. I trust he is at work now, exorcising the demons of war that infest this world of ours. Meanwhile, the rest of us can at least pray that peace will soon come again."

"Amen to that, Mr. Toomey. If I may ask you a general question, what do you consider to be the finest thing in life?"

"Marcus Aurelius put it rather well, I think. He said, 'For us creatures, knowledge that heaven exists beatifies life—' "

"Very beautiful, Mr. Toomey."

" '—Or opens doors yielding noble actions. Zeal inspires sanctity.' "

"Have you a message for both the German and the British peoples?"

"Yes. May all your hearts in the long eras rolling relentlessly on teach innocence, not hate. Everyone—*everyone*—"

"Yes, Mr. Toomey?"

"Learn love."

"Thank you, Mr. Toomey."

The red light went out.

Next morning Dr. Eggenberger accompanied me to the airport in a polished Daimler. "Gorgeous weather," he said. "England should be looking lovely just now." In the departure zone he rasped at Lufthansa officials in what seemed very theatrical German. So might he have acted some cardboard jackbooted Prussian in an end-of-term comedy at Hyderabad House near Bridport. I half expected him to wink at me to show that the gross barking was just an act. He did not wink. It was his English that was the act. "Got everything? Passport, cash, traveler's checks?"

"Everything. And thanks for everything."

"Well," he said, "let's have you out of the bloody Reich." And in terrible earnest he took a smart pace back, raised his right arm in the ancient European salute, and cried: "Heil Hitler." Bridport was very far.

On the plane I sat next to an American journalist. "Europe," he jeered, "playing its little lethal games. This time you're really going to be out for the count." I had to be a European, not being an American, but he was incurious as to what sort of European—Icelandic, Latvian, Attic or Spartan, all one to him.

"Europe's not an entity. That's the mistake you Americans are always making. And it will go on resisting being an entity. That's why Hitler won't win."

"We'll be in at the end like last time to save all your asses." He then got stuck into a copy of *Time* with an American senator, unknown to Europe, on the cover: Idaho's George F. Schlitz or somebody. I saw Alps like ruined pastry below. We landed at Graz, then at laked Klagenfurt. The American got out. "See you, fella. Or maybe not." Then we sailed over the border at Tarvisio and I was safe. I celebrated with a doze until we got to Milan.

Once in the Federated Malay States, visiting a Chinese patient old and bed-rid with Philip, passing through the back room of the jeweler's shop above which that dried fish of an ancient dwelt, I saw in an otherwise empty bookcase a copy of *The Cloud of Unknowing. Bagaimana kitab ini datang di-sini?* I asked the Mah-Jongg players. How the hell did this get here? They did not know, nor did they care. And now, in the taxi that took me from Milan airfield to the Milan rail terminus, I found, equally baffling, a copy of Hobbes's *Leviathan*. It was, moreover, from the Molesworth edition of 1839–45, the only complete edition of Hobbes that, before Professor Howard Warrender got to work very recently, was, so I recently was told, available. I asked the driver what it was doing there, and he shrugged and said *Ta' tahu*, I mean *Non lo so.* I opened the volume, dog-eared, penciled over, bought at Brentano's in New York but by whom was not indicated on the flyleaf, and found myself looking at Part IV— *Of the Kingdom of Darknesse.* I read:

Besides these Soveraign Powers, Divine, *and* Humane, *of which I have hitherto discoursed, there is mention in Scripture of another Power, namely, that of* the Rulers of the Darknesse of this world, the Kingdome of Satan, *and* the Principality of Beelzebub over Daemons, *that is to say, over Phantasmes that appear in the Air: For which cause Satan is also called* the Prince of the Power of the Air: *and (because he ruleth in the darkness of this world)* The Prince of this world: *And in consequence hereunto, they who are under his Dominion, in opposition to the faithfull (who are the* Children of the Light*) are called the* Children of Darknesse . . .

And then he spoke of

a Confederacy of Deceivers, that to obtain dominion over men in this present world, endeavour by dark and erroneous Doctrines to extinguish in them the Light, both by Nature, and of the Gospell; and so to dis-prepare them for the Kingdome of God to come.

Looking up from the volume as we approached the station, I saw a poster advertising Mercurio light bulbs. The god Mercury, naked, helmeted or battle-bowlered, wings on heels, sped through the blue with a flaring light bulb in hand powered, one presumed, from his own body. Had the Christian image of the devil been contrived out of a mixture of Hermes and his hoofed son Pan? The Prince of the Power of the Air—how noble a title. Lucifer, the bringer of light. The rulers of the air could not also be the rulers of darkness. The air was where brightness fell from. (Yes, Toomey, leaving it dark.) It was God who sat in darkness fingering his beard, everybody's unwashed old clo' man. (Unworthy, Toomey: a light beyond light striking human souls as darkness.) He could not even look after his first chosen. Come on, Toomey, let's have William Blake: hell as energy and energy as eternal delight; John Milton of the devil's party without knowing it. Anything to empty certain words of meaning—words like, for instance, *England, home, duty.*

I was, of course, scared of going home. I had failed in my duty to England. I should have watched for the red light's glowing and then cried: *God's curse on Germany.* Then I would have been taken away and imprisoned for the duration, hero, patriot, best-selling author now to sell even better. I shook myself out of the taxi at the Milan terminus: I was going to my *fratello* in the episcopal palace at Moneta. The taxi driver had no objection to my taking away a book that was not his property and was, moreover, in an unintelligible language. I clicked open my suitcase and stowed Hobbes. I tipped the driver extravagantly. I bought a ticket to Moneta and, on the train, quietened my shaking by pondering the mystique or metaphysic or theology of war. Was war a natural product of historical wrongs or was it an allegory of some eternal opposition? It seemed to me that good and evil were probably as indefinable as right and wrong, and that the sole reality was the electricity of opposition. Alpha versus omega, and the two at pacific rest in a Creator who said he was both. He was the Creator of the Prince of the Power of the Air, but he must also be the Creator of an opposing prince whom we blasphemously called God. You were doomed to take sides, but did it matter which side you took? And then the words *home* and *duty* bellowed from a baby in the next compartment.

I told my story to Carlo as we sat over a flask of the local wine in his *salone*. But first I had had to be admitted by snuffling Mario and stand by while Carlo—formidably, nay beautifully hideous in a black gravy-stained cassock—delivered hard words to two middle-aged men in fascist uniform. Carlo seemed to have said something in a sermon displeasing to the local representatives of the regime. Something about the war and Italy's need to stay out of the war and initiate in the Italian soul if not elsewhere a fight for liberty. "There," boomed Carlo, as I came into the great vestibule with its pious pictures, "is an English-man. He is by way of being my brother. Nevertheless do your duty to the cause of fascism. He represents democracy, a free opposition, a free press and free speech. Fall upon him, tear him to tatters. Or bring your thugs to do it, we shall be ready for them." They glowered at me but at the same time made vague gestures of greeting. Mario held open the door, snuffling. They left mumbling and with salutes that looked more communist than fascist. Carlo said to me, "What are you doing here? I understood that England had locked her doors."

He listened to my story. "You did what you had to do," he said. "Whatever they do to you your conscience is clear." And then, "In comparison with Domenico you are as pure as snow."

"What has Domenico done?"

"Domenico has obtained a civil divorce in Reno or somewhere and has remarried. He has gone through a form of marriage with some film star I have never heard of. It is mere incidental news in a letter I received from our nephew. A fifteen-year-old boy stained and shamed with Domenico's filthy lust and defection. And his sister too. And Hortense having to go through lawyers to obtain what they call alimony. The name Campanati clings to me like the stink of old grease."

"It will cling to Hortense also."

"Along with the faith, the faith, faithful unto death." And there it was: the picture of the wide-eyed Roman at attention while Pompeii fell, my father's surgery, my pulling out of a bad tooth on Christmas morning. "The children will themselves be strong in the faith, thank God, but they need a father and they cannot have a father. It is you they need."

I groaned in my stomach, remembering that Heinz was awaiting me back in London, his *Pflegevater*. I began to curse the Nazis, softly but without inhibi-tion. Carlo listened sympathetically and nodded. He said, "This, I think, will be the last time we will see each other for some years. The sooner you return to England the better. Make your peace. Use your talents in propaganda. There are bigger ruffians at large now than ever there were in Chicago. I will tell you what I think is going to happen. The French will give in to the Germans and the Germans will overrun Europe. Mussolini will enter the war and gain such scraps from Hitler's table as he can. And then Italy will collapse and Britain invade Italy and Germany take over this poor benighted country. America will come in at the end as she came in in the last war. But before that we are going to have a terrible time." Carlo's prophecies were always pretty accurate. "I may not survive. I am not by nature a discreet man, though I have tried to practice discretion. You remember that time in the Garden of Allah, ridiculous blasphemy of a name, when we got drunk together? We shall get drunk together tonight, though on wine. Tomorrow you will need time to recover, though I shall not. Then the following day you may take the train from Milan to Ventimiglia and then the train from Ventimiglia to Paris. And then cross the Channel. The amenities of peace are still with us, but they will not be so much longer. It will be a long long time before we see each other again. If we ever do."

fifty-four

The body of grim men who faced me in the bare room on Ebury Street were not quite a tribunal, not quite a court of enquiry. They all wore civilian clothes, but they had military manners, except for one man who had police manners. There were represented, I supposed, Scotland Yard's Special Branch, one of the numerals of MI, and probably the Home Office. The chairman was named Major de la Warr and he had small features set in wide margins of flesh, two chins also, also a fat voice. There was a canned ham called Plumrose, and I tend, when I recall him, to catch an image of the coffin-shaped tin with a pink porker on it. A voice, in other words, both plummy and porky. All the men had what I took to be copies of my dossier, or rather a reduced version of it, since one of the policemen, whose rank I gathered was that of superintendent, seemed to have the definitive unabridged version before him. This, I noted, contained newspaper clippings and even photographs. Major de la Warr said, "You took your time getting back."

"I was lucky to get back at all."

"We'll come to that later. What were you doing in Italy?"

"Visiting Monsignor Campanati, the Bishop of Moneta. He's related to me by marriage." Everybody already knew this, or should have known it, but nobody liked it. A thin man with a stiff collar and black tie penciled rapid notes.

"Yes," Major de la Warr said. "All this Latin. Some nonsense about casting out devils."

"You know it's nonsense apparently," I said. "Certain prelates of the Church think differently."

"The Church of Rome."

"To which I belong." This only became true when I confronted the Church of England.

Major de la Warr said, "And what were you doing in Paris?"

"Seeing James Joyce. The Irish writer." I gave it them all. "A confirmed neutral in the last war, despite his British passport. Trained by Jesuits. Author of *Ulysses*, long banned for dirtiness. He'd promised me a copy of *Finnegans Wake*. Signed. A great experimental masterpiece. Confiscated by HM Customs for investigation. I assured them it was not in code. Damn it all, the publishers are Faber and Faber." Everybody made notes.

"What," the thin man asked, "were you doing in Austria in the first place?"

"I've already made it perfectly clear in writing that I was trying to arrange for the exodus of Jakob Strehler. The author. The Nobel prizewinner." Nobody seemed to have heard of him. I was angry and said, "I realize that literature doesn't come into the province of you gentlemen, but I submit that the name Jakob Strehler should not be altogether unknown to you. I was trying to perform a duty to international literature."

"Why," quacked a small man who kept spinning his spectacles round in a left fist that loosely grasped an earpiece, "did you not try to get him out earlier? After all, we were on the brink of war."

"His son had been sent to me. I decided that the son needed his father."

"So," still twirling, "it was not altogether a devotion to what you call international literature." Very shrewd, very nasty. "How were you proposing to get this Strehler fellow out?"

"I had a forged passport ready for him."

"British?" Major de la Warr asked.

"I'm afraid so. I mean, it was the only way."

"Where is the passport?" That was the man with the stiff collar.

"Hidden, I think, in the middle of a pile of old copies of *Punch* that Strehler used to read in his lavatory."

"Left there for some Nazi agent to use. I see." The same man. "How was the passport obtained in the first place?"

"Stolen. By the son of Strehler. He stole. He badly needed parental guidance." There was much penciling.

A man who smiled with the left side of his mouth and had made a cage of his fingers said, "Where is this Herr Strehler the younger now?"

"Interned, I gather. I left him in a hotel when I went to get his father. He got himself into some trouble undefined. The two men who came to tell me were not very communicative. But thank God I'm free of him."

"We have," Major de la Warr said, "copies of the transcript of your ah interview. It was picked up on what is insolently termed the Free British Radio. From Berlin. And yet you say you were in Vienna."

"I was most certainly in Vienna. Landline landline." Why I made a song of it I did not and do not know. Further notes were scribbled.

"You realize the gravity of giving comfort to the enemy?" Major de la Warr said. "You gave a lot of comfort. All very chummy. Old friend of the regime. You ah reviled the Prime Minister. You regretted the war. You spoke of the need for ah ah love."

"Your scrutinizers evidently failed to spot two cunningly prepared acrostics," I said. "Look at your transcripts. One of them, which I fitted into an alleged aphorism of Marcus Aurelius, says FUCK THE BLOODY NAZIS. The other is contained in my final statement. The one beginning 'May all your hearts' and ending 'Learn love.' I leave it to you gentlemen to work it out." They worked it out. The policeman with the fat dossier got it first:

"May Hitler rot in hell."

"Amen," I said. The board or tribunal or court, probably all men who started the day with *The Times* crossword, had to smile faintly at my ingenuity. "I should think the Nazis have probably worked it out too. They are no stupider than you gentlemen." I should not have said that. "And you talk about my giving comfort to the enemy."

"In effect," a bald brutal-looking man with an exquisite voice said, "you were uttering obscenities. You could have expressed your ah ah ah ah arcane detestation of the Nazis without using the language of the gutter."

"It has only become apparent to you now," I said, "that it was the language of the gutter. It is, however, the only language appropriate to the Nazis."

"I was thinking," the bald man said, "of some decent Englishwoman listening to your broadcast and detecting your coded message and having a sense of outraged modesty." He was serious, totally, totally serious.

The police officer said, "This was not your first visit to Nazi Germany."

"I was, as you will undoubtedly know, in Berlin for a film festival at which a film based on a novel of mine was presented."

"You saved the life of Heinrich Himmler according to one of our reports." There was a stir of grudging respect not horror. "From the bullet of a would-be assassin."

"My sister's mother-in-law in fact. She was suffering from terminal cancer and wished to die. She wished to take Heinrich Himmler with her. My salvatory act was instinctive, and I do not think I have to apologize for it. We then considered Germany a friendly power."

"What is this about your mother-in-law?" the thin man with the stiff collar asked incredulously.

"The mother in fact of Monsignor Campanati, Bishop of Moneta." They all sat back and had a good look at me. "She did much good and dangerous work on behalf of the German Jews."

"This Ezra Pound," the policeman said, "broadcasts from Rome radio on behalf of Mussolini. He has a lot to say about the badness of Great Britain. You quoted from him."

"He's considered a great poet. He wrote the poem I quoted just after the Great War."

"You consider," Major de la Warr asked, "that Great Britain is an ah old bitch gone in the teeth? That this is a ah ah botched civilization?"

"To some extent, yes. If Britain had had teeth to show against Hitler she would have shown them earlier. And, yes, our civilization is nothing to be proud of. Black and brown helots, an unbridgeable gap between the governing and the governed. Shall we say that some civilizations are more botched than others. Ours is botched, but there are some more botched. Take our ally France, for instance—"

"We don't want to hear about France," the bald man said. "Indeed," glancing along the line of his colleagues, "I don't think we want to hear any more about anything." Some grunted.

"I've only been answering questions," I said. "May I now ask a question— what do you propose doing with me?"

"I understand," Major de la Warr said, "that you were fairly prompt to make application to various government bodies to assist the war effort in whatever ways you could. In what ways," he asked, "could you?"

"I take it that I'm not eligible for the armed forces. I was not eligible in the previous conflict. A heart condition. And now I'm approaching fifty. But I can write. I have some experience in filmmaking. I can get on my feet and put words together."

"We have heard you," the man with the twirling spectacles now no longer twirling but on his nose said, "putting words together."

"You consider yourself trustworthy?" Major de la Warr asked. "Might you not indulge in subversive acrostics or anagrams or something?"

"You seem to be implying," warmly, "that I might really seek to give comfort to the enemy. There's a whiff of accusation of treason about. I think I ought to demand an apology."

"You're not a traitor," the bald brutal-looking man said. "You don't have the stuff of treason in you, I can see that. But you're naif and could be used by real traitors. You also put the saving of your own skin before duty to your country."

"So I should have refused to do the broadcast," hotly, "and then been interned for the duration? Five years, ten years, whatever it's going to be? What would you people have done?"

"We wouldn't have put ourselves in that situation in the first place," the man with the stiff collar said. The others grunted.

"No, you don't have a duty to international literature. What precisely are you proposing to do with me? Intern me as not exactly treasonable but as naively dangerous? Chop my bloody head off on Tower Hill just to get me out of the way?"

The man who now spoke, a man of outstanding but somehow useless handsomeness, seemed to be the Home Office representative. "We have as yet set no arrangements in train for the internment of British nationals. That sort of thing takes time. Your other suggestion is, as you know, frivolous and irresponsible. You're probably intelligent enough, however, to grow to a realization of the harm you've done."

"You mean because of an act of daring that did not succeed? Because I struck a quite harmless bargain with the Nazi Ministry of Propaganda?"

"No bargain with the enemy is harmless," Major de la Warr said.

"A general matter of background," said the Home Office man. "I don't quite understand why you have to have these Italian connections."

I looked at him long with an open mouth. Then I said, "My family is a Catholic family. The Catholic Church, unlike the Church of England, is an international foundation. It's not unusual for Catholic marriages to transcend national barriers. Besides, Italy is neutral."

"Won't be for much longer," Major de la Warr said. "And it's not quite neutral even now. There's another matter, isn't there, Fletcher?" He meant the policeman with the definitive dossier.

"You mean the— Yes. Oh, that can ride. He has no criminal record in respect of that. On the whole, he's been pretty discreet about it. We wouldn't have had any information at all if it hadn't been for the gratuitous laying of it. This is not uncommon in the world of art and books and so on. It's only a question of those in the know getting on to him, if they ever do. Well, he knows his duty there."

I gazed at him aghast and then at the former spectaclespinner, who said to me, "Blackmailability, you know. The setting up of situations, you know."

I said, "Oh my God. What in the name of God has my . . . How did you get . . . ? I demand to see those photographs."

"They're not of you," the policeman said.

"It's a matter, don't you see," Major de la Warr said, "of your employability.

I don't think you're employable. We should have to put in a veto with whatever department you applied to. You'd better keep on as you are, though you'll have difficulty because of the paper shortage. Entertaining the public I suppose you could call it, helping national morale. As for the matter of your security position, well, the police had just better know where you are. If you think of changing your address, report it. If you go away, even for a week or so, report at the local station. Your passport is, naturally, withdrawn for the duration of hostilities. And perhaps for a time after."

"I see. You think I'm liable to hop over to Berlin via Dublin and comfort the enemy."

"Stranger things have happened," the stiff-collared man said. He emended that: the war had only been on for a couple of months. "Will happen. Eire is supposed to be neutral but it's a very dubious neutrality." And then, amiably enough, "We're naturally terribly sorry about all this, Toomey. My wife reads your books and seems to like them. Now they seem to have been withdrawn from the local lending library. That article by that poet chap in the *Daily Express* didn't do your reputation any good."

"I replied to it. I exonerated myself."

"Yes, I know, but it's always better to be in the position of not having to provide a defense. Write a few plays is my advice. Something to take us out of ourselves. Give us a bit of a laugh."

"This needn't have happened, Toomey," Major de la Warr said, with like amiability. "You were indiscreet, no more than that. But indiscretion in wartime can be as lethal as downright treachery. The Prime Minister, I may say this now and confidentially, was deeply upset by your slander. I don't think he'll be with us much longer."

"You mean my democratically expressed lack of confidence in his administration is going to kill him?"

"Well, not quite as bad as that. But to hear that sort of thing coming from Germany in the first weeks of the war and from an author he professed to admire—"

"Chamberlain admires my work?"

"Not any longer he doesn't, old boy," said a monkeyish man with three broad strands of dyed-black hair. He had not previously spoken but he had taken lavish notes. "You've lost a lot of your admirers. But lie low, shut up, get on with your job, and you'll have them back. The main thing is to keep out of further trouble."

"Anybody anything to add?" Major de la Warr asked. Nobody. The dossiers were closed but the file, naturally, was still open. I was free to go so I went.

I went back to Albany through the blackout and under the searchlights ready to sit out the war in shame. From now till the end I would always feel that I was being followed and watched. The man in the raincoat at the end of the bar sipping discreet bitter. The man at the neighbor table in the Café Royal lunching off gravy soup and a roll, listening to me and my literary agent. Celibacy was totally enforced: if I picked up a jolly jacktar he might be an enemy agent. But the horrible security machine could not deny my private right to patriotism. I could not be prevented from writing the most popular play of 1942—*Break Break Break*, each break for a heart, the hearts respectively of three sisters, a sweetheart, a wife, and a mother bereaved, one of an airman lover, one of a sailor husband, one of an army son, but the Tennysonian totality standing for waves of time and sorrow beating vainly at a rock of British intrepidity. Shamelessly schematic, brutally sentimental, it was what the public wanted. The public also wanted a bit of a laugh, so I gave them *The Gods in the Garden*, which was about statues of Greek divinities coming to life during an air raid and interfering in the affairs of a patrician household, and the coarse army comedy *Roll On*. Cut off as I was from the realities of the soldier's life, I had to ensure the plausibility of my situations and dialogue by listening to soldiers in pubs, sometimes noting down promising tropes like "Put another pea in the pot and hang the expense" and "Roll on death and let's have a go at the angels" and "The army can fuck you but it can't give you a kid or if it can it can't make you love it."

Taking notes quietly in the Fitzroy one Saturday night I was quietly picked up by a couple of men in raincoats and trilbies. On the blacked-out street I was quietly asked what I thought I was doing. Taking notes for a play I'm writing. Might we see those notes, Mr. Toomey? I see you know my name. Yes sir, we know your name. I was told at last, the notes having been examined by the almost no light of a dimmed torch, that that seemed to be all right but watch it, sir. Watch what?

It was they, the forces of security, who were watching. Their rigor never once slackened. I was needed in Los Angeles in 1941 to write the scenario of a film about the Battle of Britain featuring Errol Flynn, but there was no question of even the temporary restoration of my passport. When I published in 1943 my annotated anthology *Breathing English Air*, which General Horrocks said should be in every literate soldier's thigh pocket, the BBC thought me suitable for delivering a little patriotic uplift after the nine o'clock news on Sundays, but I remained officially unclean and saw the assignment go to Jack Priestley. Even Val Wrigley, who had raised the flag for homosexuality before the Mother of Parliaments and been jailed for striking a policeman, who had publicly cursed Britain for its sex laws and said often that no gaybody could be a true patriot, had a job at the Ministry of Information, something to do with pamphlets on British wildlife. It was he, of course, who had published the article in the *Daily Express*. This was the article:

What would you have done if you had found yourself taking a little holiday in Nazi Germany and, being cut off from the news because of your devotion to

Nature, suddenly discovered you were in the middle of a war between Germany and your own beloved land?

Your first and obvious answer would be: I wouldn't have been such a damn fool as to find myself in that situation. But supposing you had been such a damn fool?

The obvious answer then would be: Nothing much I could do. They'd intern me, wouldn't they? I'd be stuck in a camp till the end of the war, dreaming of distant England. Just unlucky.

But, ah, dear reader, if you happened to be a famous novelist like Kenneth Toomey things would turn out very differently. As indeed they did for Mr. Toomey. The Nazis treated him like a prince. They were awfully kind. They even permitted him to go back to England.

First, of course, he had to do something nice for the Nazis. He spoke on the Nazi radio. Or rather the infamous propaganda station sickeningly called the Free British Radio. Mr. Toomey's words were picked up loud and clear in his embattled native land.

What did Mr. Toomey say? He said that the war was a great pity, that Germans and British must learn to love each other, and that Mr. Chamberlain was a bit of a fool. Patriotic language, wasn't it? And then they put Mr. Toomey on a plane to somewhere or other and then, lo and behold, Mr. Toomey turns up on his native shores bright and cheerful and not one whit the worse for his escapade. And certainly not in the least repentant.

A true patriotic British citizen would have said, "To hell with you all, killers of Jews, torturers of nuns and priests, burners of books. Do your damnedest, I will strike no filthy bargain with you. Your proffered hands reek with the blood of the innocent. I will not shake them."

But Mr. Toomey is a writer whom Nazi Germany has much admired and he had to think of his heilhitlering public, as well as his skin.

Well, if he has his German public, let him do without his British one. Let his books be swept from the shelves of our public libraries and consumed in the fires of autumn. Let the patriotic British respond to his works as to his actions —with contempt and silence.

Mr. Kenneth Toomey, best-selling novelist, you have shaken bloody hands. You have brought back with you a stink from the Nazi shambles. The very covers of your contemptible works must now seem sticky with the gore of the butchered innocent.

You and I, dear reader, can do without treasonous Toomey. To urge us in our just fight we have, thank God, better writers, more stirring singers. Let the works of Toomey be entombed. And totally without honour.

The title was THE SMELL OF TOOMEY and there was a caricature of myself shaking paws with Dr. Goebbels.

In 1940, when Plum Wodehouse was captured by the Germans in his French villa and persuaded to talk very freely and indiscreetly, though also humorously, on Berlin radio, my own case began to be forgotten by the public, though not by British Intelligence. George Orwell rehabilitated Plum as a genuine political innocent, but for a time there was a lot of unseemly sanctimony, as in *The New Statesman*, which had a competition to see who could best Nazify the Wodehouse literary tone, one entry making Bertie Wooster bleat "Cheeriheil." In the *Spectator* Val Wrigley published the following doggerel:

> *The kind of laugh that Wodehouse imparts is*
> *Extremely popular with the Nazis.*
> *On his covers let's stamp (am I being too caustic?) a*
> *Crumpet, an egg, a bean and a swastika.*

Silly. Val Wrigley kept out of my way very prudently but seemed to be looking for a new philistine public. He published much simple and tendentious verse and even had a regular poetic corner in the *Sunday Pictorial*. His poem in *The Times*—"*Wir Danken Unserem Führer*"—was considered to be the sort of thing the Poet Laureate ought to be doing:

> *Shadowing earth, our fylfot will have told*
> *History's spring and end to the eager hearer—*
> *Our earth's first blood, our titles manifold:*
> *We thank our Führer.*

I had given him that *fylfot* back in 1935. Those four final lines indicate the kind of poem it was—bitterly, though statelily, ironical. Its sarcastic praise of the Führer was, however, taken at its face value by Goebbels's Free British Radio, which did a plummy broadcast of the poem. This did Val Wrigley good rather than harm: he was showing what bloody fools the Nazis were, as well as blood-soaked devils.

I have no doubt that my own untrustworthiness was corroborated in the eyes of British Intelligence by the entry of William Joyce, known as Lord Haw Haw, into the field of Nazi radio propaganda. It was assumed that the name Joyce was a treasonous name, and it was known that I had been friendly with a Joyce with two or three kinds of bad reputation. Ezra Pound's ridiculous broadcasts from Rome also fitted nicely into the pattern. On the other hand, in intellectual quarters I began to be looked upon as a kind of failed hero: Herzog's long essay in *Horizon* on the greatness of Strehler—who it was now assumed was dead—helped me there. I was able to go to pubs like the Yorkminster and the Fitzroy Tavern and be permitted to stand half-pints to greasy men in filthy raincoats with book-bulging pockets who had evaded conscription.

I stayed in London throughout the war, firewatching, contributing junk to Red Cross sales (those thefts of Heinz came in useful), eating offal in Soho restaurants, sometimes but not too often in danger. The safe countryside was available to me, but I did not propose reporting to police stations like a delinquent on probation or an enemy alien. I preferred the bombs and the Albany shelter. Hortense sent me two food parcels, both rifled in transit. She also sent me the *catalogue raisonné* of her 1943 New York exhibition—some stones, some bronzes, a lot of cut and tortured aluminum. None of her works seemed to exalt life. In 1944 I heard that my nephew Johnny was with the Fifth Army in Italy, a cameraman in a film unit. In 1945 my niece Ann married an instructor in Comparative Literature at Columbia University. I felt myself growing old.

Strange, I derived most comfort in my loneliness from my brother Tom, whose voice survived on gramophone records, the voice of a decent man who countered the world's horrors with an easy humor. His presence was very real to me as I listened to his monologues (Columbia, plum label), and I cried every time I encountered the heroism of *Get It Off Your Chest*, which, depicting a man away from work with a bad cold, made comedy out of pain. I knew there had to be a heaven, if only to accommodate people like Tom. The same thing has, I know, been said about the overladen underfed donkeys of North Africa.

I am temporarily sick of my own voice. I will now hand over to Howard Tucker, author of one of the first books about Carlo. I have his permission to reproduce the following chapter. A fee has been agreed and will be paid.

Fifty-five

On April 26 the town of Verona, long and romantically associated with Romeo and Juliet, fell to the Americans. There was nothing romantic about it at this time: many of its historic buildings had been destroyed by allied bombing, and the Germans compounded the chaos by blowing up all of the seven bridges over the Adige before the Americans could reach it. What pictorial records we have of the sorry state of this beautiful town we owe to the intrepid camerawork of Corporal Johnny Campanati and his colleagues. Unfortunately they could not be in Genoa on April 27 to record the triumphant American occupation of the great and ancient port, an occupation prepared for by the heroic Italian partisans, who had already seized control of a large part of the city. Nor were they in time to witness and film for posterity the ignominious end of Benito Mussolini. The jeep of the cinematographic unit, driven by stolid gum-chewing Frank Schlitz of Brooklyn, manned by cranking Johnny, Lieutenant Mayer (of the film family, final segment of MGM), and Sergeant McCreery (no relation of the dour and vigorous commander of the Eighth Army), was advancing along with the armor of the Fifth Army on the Via Emilia toward the taking of Piacenza midway between Parma and Milan.

Mussolini had been arrested at Lecco, in the rugged hills above Como, while trying to make his getaway into Switzerland. The day after his arrest the form Duce, along with twelve members of his fascist cabinet, was executed summarily by Italian *partigiani*, and the bodies were speedily conveyed to Milan just before the Fifth Army entered the great industrial city, with its justly famed Duomo, on April 29. The bodies of Mussolini and his mistress were slung up from the heels like poultry, some decent minded citizen first having so secured the skirt of the hapless mistress that public modesty would not be outraged. This was in a piazza where fifteen partisans had been shot the previous year. Johnny Campanati, plying his machine among the jubilant Milanese, may have thought with a boyish grin that this was a special moment of triumph for his reverend uncle, Monsignor Carlo Campanati, Bishop of Moneta. But the supposition would have been wrong and the grin out of place, for Carlo Campanati had never taken pleasure in the unrepentant deaths of the enemies of the faith. Nothing would have pleased him better than the vision of a Benito Mussolini, forgiven by those he had harmed, sincerely sorry for his transgressions, restored to the bosom of the Church, dying in a bed in tranquil old age with the prospect of heaven before him. To Carlo there was only one enemy—the enemy of mankind and of mankind's Creator. To Carlo man was essentially good because he was essentially God's creature: evil was a property imposed by the forces of the fallen angels. I have said this before and I will say it again, but I cannot say it too often.

The allied armies continued to roll north, the cameras of the cinematographic units rolling with them. Troops of the 56th (London) Division entered Venice on April 29, while a fair sunset was gilding the historic lagoons and the pigeons of the piazza of San Marco, all unaware of the momentous events about them, flocked to their rest. The advance swept swiftly across the northern plains, and Bergamo, Brescia, Vicenza and Padua rang their bells to welcome the liberators. The Fifth and Eighth Armies thrust through the enemy's massively fortified Adige line, forcing the hard-pressed Germans back to the eastern side of the Brenta. The Brazilian expeditionary force compelled the surrender of a whole German infantry division. By the end of April the liberation of the whole of Italy was near its fulfillment. The German forces were broken and disorganized. Twenty-five divisions, the best in the whole German army, had been torn and rent and were beyond resistance. And this devastating destruction had been the work of weeks, not months. The Eighth Army had accomplished its mission in twenty days, the Fifth in only fifteen. Johnny in his jeep was fast approaching the northern limits of the peninsula: he was coming to a Moneta already liberated by tough partisans under the inspiration of his uncle. Nephew and uncle were soon to meet under the clanging of the triumphant bells of the ancient cathedral.

Who and what was this young man, just twenty in this year of victory, to outward appearances a friendly, courageous, well setup American noncom but little more? He was the son of Domenico Campanati, younger brother of Carlo and a famous musical composer. The whole world knew Domenico's music, though it did not always know who had composed it. The great film-going public pays little attention to screen credits. Many a great movie had been ennobled by a Campanati score, and Domenico was, a few years after the war, to receive the supreme accolade of an Oscar for his music to Otto Preminger's *The Brothers Karamazov*, which brought a famed Dostoevsky novel to the screen. In the fifties Domenico was to return to his first love, opera, and fulfill a youthful ambition, that of seeing and hearing a work of his performed at the great La Scala, Milan. The mother of Johnny was the noted sculptress Hortense Campanati, a woman of great beauty unhappily disfigured in an accident, unfortunately separated from Domenico in Johnny's boyhood but living a busy and productive life in New York. Mrs. Campanati was the sister of Kenneth Marchal Toomey, the distinguished British novelist. Young Johnny had swirling in his blood the corpuscles of three nations, for the Toomeys are half-French, and this blood was illustrious on both the male and the distaff sides. That he had inherited his mother's looks was generally acknowledged. In 1944 the direction of his talent was still unsure. He had had a war to fight and could not yet think clearly of the future.

Johnny had been educated at a distinguished private school on Park Avenue, Manhattan, and subsequently at the famous Choate School in Connecticut. He had volunteered for military service shortly after Pearl Harbor, had spent a year in infantry training, during which he had shown no great aptitude for the taking of orders and a certain clumsiness in the handling of weapons, and had been one of the first to transfer to a cinematographic unit when the need for recording the progress of the war on film had been recognized at the highest level of command. He had been brought up in the movie capital of the world, and his father's career in the film industry was irrelevantly taken as a qualification for the son. And so he followed the Fifth Army on its triumphant career, undergoing the normal privation and danger of a frontline soldier, fixing on film for posterity the horrors and triumphs, and the eventual victory, of the Italian campaign. In a sense the experience brought him home, back to his Northern Latin inheritance, and without doubt the highlight for him of the great days of Italian liberation was the meeting, for the first time in his adult life, with the great prelate who was destined to become the most remarkable sovereign pontiff of our time.

The uncle met the nephew in the shade of the cathedral in glorious spring weather. Johnny's own sergeant recorded the event on film, and I have watched with emotion a projection of the grainy black and white sequence—the rotund powerful bishop in muscular middle age embracing the husky blond six-footer. What film was not able to record, and what is not fully recoverable from the official archives, is the astonishing career under Nazi occupation of the man of God who feared only God, to whom last-ditch fascist and German intruder alike were poor erring souls who had permitted themselves to fall into the power of the Father of Lies.

Carlo Campanati was never willing to talk much about the ambiguous role that Pope Pius XII played during the Second World War. Here was a pontifex who, in December 1939, denounced "premeditated aggression" and "contempt for freedom and human life from which originate acts which cry to God for vengeance." Pius endeavored to use all his papal authority and personal gifts of persuasion to prevent Mussolini from dragging Italy into the European conflict. And yet the Vatican record with regard to the persecution of the Jews by the Nazi regime remains a shameful one. Pius appeared not merely not to help but actively to condone the hellish treatment meted out to the sons and daughters of Israel. Carlo's career in this connection was altogether different and quite heroic. He was responsible for organizing that lifeline which led Italian Jews to the safety of Switzerland, by which at least three hundred made their escape from the northern industrial region, and for protecting the lives of such Jews as remained through the use of the sanctuaries of the Franciscan monastery near Borimo and the Convent of the Discalced Carmelites at Sondrio. The crypt of the cathedral of Moneta was, for a time, used as a partisan armory. The Nazi authorities in the town suspected that Carlo was actively engaged in subversion. His Sunday sermons provided, in the form of easily understood biblical parallels, news of the progress of the war from the untainted allied sources which the Nazis tried to hide from the people. At the time when the partisan leader Gianfranco de Bosio was whisked out of the Gestapo cellar of the Prefettura on the Via de Guicciardi with the help of partisan grenades, it was he who was roughly summoned for interrogation. We may, with no help from Carlo Campanati himself, who was always reluctant to speak of it, reconstruct the agony of the event. And also the triumph.

A brightly lighted cellar, whitewashed, very cold, smelling of the damp earth. The day, of all the good days in the year, Christmas Day. The Bishop of Moneta, unable to sing high mass and deliver his seasonal sermon of hope and love, seated in a plain chair. Opposite him an old-fashioned dentist's chair. Dental drills and forceps lying ready on a bloodstained butcher's bench. The interrogator, dressed warmly in purloined furs. A burly operator in shirtsleeves who did not seem to feel the cold. The interrogator spoke guttural but fluent Italian.

"De Bosio is back with the Fedele group?"

"I know nothing about it."

"Where is Location B5?"

"I don't know."

"Look, Monsignore, we have our own sources of information. What we require from you is a simple confirmation that will save your people a great deal of trouble and pain."

"If I knew you might drag the information from me. There is even in me the habit of long training—not to lie, to give the truth when asked. I am keeping nothing from you. I honestly do not know."

"You've a fine set of teeth, Monsignore."

"Ah, I see. You intend to extract them without anesthetic. To make me talk. I don't like pain, especially useless pain. Extract or commence extracting and I will tell you to stop and give you what place name first comes into my head. You will waste time checking on this and then the wearisome business will have to begin again. This technique of yours is, of course, brutal. It is also very old-fashioned and slow and unproductive."

"Not *your* teeth, Monsignore." The interrogator nodded at the shirt-sleeved operator. This one went to the door and opened it and admitted a colleague who pushed before him a weeping terrified girl. Carlo knew the girl—Anna-maria Garzanti, fourteen-year-old daughter of a baker on the Via Leopardi. She screamed as she was forced to the dental chair. There were greasy leather straps attached to it and with these the two operators commenced to secure the body and arms of the wretched innocent.

Carlo said, "Very well. Location B5 is in the hills above Olivone."

"This is ridiculous, Monsignore, and you know it."

"You're right. The truth, then. The group is reforming at Cevio. Enquire there for an electrician named Belluomo."

The interrogator sighed wearily and indicated to the operators that they start their work. The girl's mouth was opened and a wooden wedge, one that, from its bloodiness, had evidently been used before for this purpose, was thrust into it. The shirt-sleeved operator grasped the dental drill. It was operated with a pedal. On this he placed his clumsy boot and began treadling. The drill whirred. "Wait," Carlo Campanati said. They waited. "Annamaria," he said. "You must understand what is happening. These people want information from me. I do not have this information. Therefore you have to suffer. The suffering will be terrible but it will not kill you. Offer the suffering to God. Remember that Christ suffered and your suffering will make you closer to him. I'm sorry I can do nothing to help except pray that the devil may depart from these poor men. Feel sorry for them if you can. You're luckier than they are."

"What," the interrogator asked, "did you call us?"

"Poor men," Carlo said. "*Arme Leute.* You're set upon by forces of evil. This must be evident to you. Consider what would make men wish to inflict torture on an innocent child. Love of Fatherland? Of an abstraction called Adolf Hitler? No. The devil has entered your entire nation. This must be so."

"Start drilling," the interrogator ordered. The operator obeyed. The drill slipped and drew blood from the girl's lip. Then it engaged the tooth and burrowed toward the nerve. It caught the nerve. The girl screamed.

Carlo prayed aloud, but not for her. "O merciful God, enlighten your three servants here, slaves to a diabolic faith. Drive out the evil from them, reinstate their lost humanity. Forgive them, they know not what they do."

"Stop," the interrogator said. The drill grumbled down the scale and ceased its ghastly melody. The girl wept and whimpered. "Now speak," he said to Carlo. "It is you who have the devil in you. It is you who are the real instrument of this girl's pain."

"Listen," Carlo said. "I say again that I have nothing to say. To say that you will be wasting your time when you resume your torture would not altogether be true. You are bound to be committed to brutality as an end in itself, though you may rationalize it as a technique of interrogation or an expression of the frustration of an occupying power that cannot fail to meet opposition from the children of light. Brutality for its own sake is the mark of the devil. This poor child's screams will be the screams of tortured nerves. Her soul, however, is intact. I say again that she is better off than you are."

"Take the forceps," the interrogator said. "Pull a tooth out. One of the incisors."

"Poor men," Carlo moaned. "Poor, poor men. O God, work on them. Drive out the evil." He saw the forceps grip the milkwhite tooth of the girl whose rich raven hair was already matted with the sweat of suffering. "You will have to bear it, Annamaria," he said. "I cannot tell them what they wish to know. Be courageous as Christ was." He could hear the scrape of the tooth in its socket as the forceps twisted it for the girl had fainted and there was now mercifully no noise of agony. The tooth was yanked out in a spurt of blood and cast to the stone paving where it tinily, dully clicked, rolled once, then lay still. To the man with forceps, Carlo said, "What's your name, my son?" The man looked at the interrogator, who minimally shrugged.

The man said, "Lenbach."

"No no, what does your mother call you?"

"Hans."

Carlo Campanati raised his eyes to the damp discolored ceiling and prayed: "O God, look down on your servant Hans with pity. He's a good man led astray by the wickedness of the enemy. He hates what he does. He sees that this innocent child might be his own daughter. He cannot see how the suffering he inflicts can help the cause of his country. Have mercy on him, O God, cleanse his soul and bring him back to the fraternity of humankind."

The interrogator said, "Get a bucket of cold water. Wake this girl up." Hans Lenbach said:

"*Es ist genug.*"

The interrogator could not believe his ears. He said, "What was that? What did you say then?"

"I've had enough of it. I don't see what this has to do with fighting a war." And he dropped the bloody forceps onto the butcher's block. His fellow-operator stared at him, his jaw dropped. "Like the priest here says, this poor girl here's done nothing wrong. I've had enough of it."

"Do you understand what you're saying, Lenbach?"

"Yes. *Enough*, I understand *enough*. Do you understand it? I don't think you do. Get somebody else to do the job." And he lumbered out. As the door opened Carlo could see a helmeted soldier in a long gray greatcoat carrying a rifle stamping on the stones of the corridor, steaming out breath like smoke. The door slammed shut. The interrogator did not call for Lenbach's arrest. Instead he looked murderously at Carlo.

He said, "You realize what we can do to you?"

"Oh yes," Carlo said. "Torture me, kill me, nail me to the cathedral door like Luther's ninety-two theses. Get on with it. The devil can't win. Luther knew that, schismatic though he was. But you *arme Leute* have forgotten Luther as you've forgotten Goethe and Schiller and Johann Sebastian Bach and the rest of the real Germans. God, man, what have you left? What in God's name are you fighting for?" This, I believe, if spoken at all, must have been spoken in good vigorous German. The girl came to from her swoon, looked about with the wide eyes of bewilderment, then fear, then spat blood and screamed. Carlo got up and went over to comfort her, unstrapping her from the chair, burlily elbowing aside the thug who had bound her.

"*Stimmt,*" the interrogator said. "We say *genug* until afternoon. We'll give you, Monsignore, time to think and remember."

"*Mittagessen* now," Carlo said. "A special meal for the *Herrenvolk*, today being the Feast of the Nativity of a notorious and subversive Jew. You have to admit that Adolf is a pretty poor substitute for Jesus. God help you, God in his infinite mercy restore you to the community of the living." He hugged the shivering whimpering girl in his arms.

"You see," the interrogator said to her, "what your holy bishop has done to you. You can blame Jesus Christ and his holy bishop for the pain you've had and the pain you're still going to have. By the time we've done with you you'll be as toothless as your grandmother."

"I know both her grandmothers," Carlo said, "and they can both gnaw bones down to the marrow." He grunted at the thug operator to open up for him, holding the girl to his warmth that the chill of the cellar had failed to impair. Then he turned to the interrogator and grinned. To Annamaria he said, "Say that you forgive him for what he's done and for what he's going to do. Go on, say it, child." And the girl, as well as she could through a torn gum and a swollen lip said, remembering some scripture lesson, *I vostri peccati vi saranno perdonati.* It would be good to conclude the incident with the thug's bursting into gross Teutonic tears and the Gestapo interrogator throwing in his job. But all we know is that the sweet voice of a child with a butchered mouth spoke forgiveness in a freezing Nazi torture chamber on Christmas Day. This must be considered a triumph.

Carlo was well aware of the location of Gianfranco de Bosio and the Fedele group.

A more complicated episode in the wartime career of the Bishop of Moneta involved the SS Gruppenführer whom Reichsführer Himmler had appointed to the task of supervising the transportation to the Reich and the disposition, in terms of slave labor and eventual liquidation, of the Jewish population of Northern Italy. This functionary was named Helmut Liebeneiner, a thin, bloodless, dyspeptic former schoolmaster from Westphalia. He had worked for a time as commandant of the camp at Oranienburg, was credited with the invention of a more vicious form of the *Stahlruten* than the SA, its first manipulators, had used, and was considered due for promotion. He was a busy man and intended his stay in Moneta to be brief but productive. All available German manpower was to be devoted not only to the rounding up of Jews but the public humiliation, before their own forced emigration to the slave camps of the Reich, of priests, nuns and monks. The stripping bare of a certain monastery load of Franciscans in a freezing piazza (it was early January) would disclose evidence of ritual circumcision. It was not yet certain what should be done with the Bishop of Moneta. He had on several occasions offered himself as victim at times of hangings in retaliation for terrorism, but his offer had not yet been accepted. Soon it might be.

Allied bombing had severely damaged the railway line between Trento and Moneta, and Gruppenführer Liebeneiner was compelled to travel from one town to the other in an Opel saloon. He did not enjoy motor travel, for his constitution was delicate and he was easily made carsick. Outside Mezzolombardo he was compelled to order his driver to stop a while, so that he might vomit at the side of the road. While he was still retching on a stomach now empty he was seized by partisans of the Fedele group. The driver was stabbed several times and then thrown into a wet ditch, though not before he had been stripped of his uniform. This, as well as the uniform of Gruppenführer Liebeneiner, fitted tolerably a couple of partisans from Bolzano, whose first language was German. An Opel saloon arrived at nightfall in front of the bishop's palace in Moneta. With harsh German cries a bloody man in gray underwear was kicked out of the car and admitted to the palace. He had been expected. The counterfeit Gruppenführer Liebeneiner went to the SS headquarters of the town, showed his papers, said there were no immediate plans for the rounding up of *Judenscheiss* in Moneta, then was heilhitlered off. Ironically, the counterfeit Gruppenführer and his driver were shattered by grenades of the Diligenza group on the road outside Campolasta. Liebeneiner's papers were found on the otherwise unidentifiable body and Liebeneiner was written off. There were bloody reprisals, but the innocent of Moneta did not suffer.

The real Liebeneiner was by now lodged in a chamber of the warren of cellars that lay, hacked out of rock, deep beneath the episcopal palazzo. He was not cold. He was dressed in six sets of the bishop's American woolen underwear, many pairs of thick Alpine stockings, fur-lined boots, and a beaver coat with hat to match. He had a mattress and eight blankets. He had a latrine bucket and a washbowl and towels. He had electric light and a select German library restricted to some of the greatest of the authors whom the Nazis had proscribed. The poems of Heine were there, and also the novels of the famous Austrian Jakob Strehler, winner of the Nobel Prize for Literature in 1935. Liebeneiner was not permitted gas or electric heating, since he might use it as a weapon against his visitors or against himself, but Carlo brought in an electric fire whenever, which was for a total of about three hours a day, he came to talk to him. Carlo himself usually brought in also Liebeneiner's meals, which were as good as those times of privation allowed—a thick vegetable soup, roast boar or stewed rabbit or hare, the heartening wine of the region, grappa, no coffee since there was no coffee. We have to guess at their conversation, though we do not need to guess at Carlo's intention: he wished to convert a convinced Nazi into a free human being.

His task was more difficult than he would ever have thought possible. It seemed to him that Nazi Germany had succeeded in producing a new type of human being, one that had abdicated the rights and duties of freedom of moral choice, that was capable of putting the abstraction of a political system before the realities of human life, that could obey without question, that was able, under orders, to perpetrate the most ghastly enormities totally without remorse, whose satisfactions were referred or collective, whose creed was mystical and insusceptible of any rational reduction. And yet this man Liebeneiner, who had after all taught the English language and analyzed poems by Shelley and speeches by Shakespeare, who loved music and had wept at the death of his dog Bruno, who had a wife and daughter whom he claimed to adore and miss sorely, had to be considered one of God's creatures and capable of Christian redemption. Carlo and he spoke English.

"You say you love your wife."

"Yes. I adore her."

"If it were to be established that she was of what is known as the Jewish race, would you still love and adore her?"

"Of course not."

"So a profound complex of human emotions, what even you might be willing to call a spiritual state of being, can be wiped out immediately at the behest of a spurious orthodoxy?"

"I do not understand all your words. You speak too fast."

"There is a line of Shakespeare you ought to know. 'Love is not love that alters when it alteration finds.' Do you think this is true?"

"I love my wife. She is not Jewish. She could never be shown to be Jewish. So I will always love her."

"What does it mean—to be Jewish?"

"To belong to a race that considers itself to be chosen by its tribal god to be above other peoples. It is a race with special physical and mental qualities. Its blood is different from Aryan blood. It has declared war on Aryan culture. And so it has to be destroyed."

"Many ethnologists, free ethnologists, scholars unbound to a particular political orthodoxy, state that racial differences are very superficial. There is no such thing, for instance, as Jewish blood. All blood looks alike under the microscope."

"This is not so."

"You have had visual evidence of this?"

"The ethnology of the Party says it is not so."

"The Party is always right?"

"Always."

And so on. And, regularly, the question from Liebeneiner: what was to be done with him, when was he going to be thrown to the partisans to be torn to pieces shouting "Heil Hitler," why was he not put out of his misery now, what trickery was this of the bishop's?

"No trickery. I believe humanity is above political ideology. I wish you to join the rest of your human brothers. You have nothing to fear. The war will end soon. Germany will be ruined, but a new Germany will arise. You will be a citizen of a free polity unanimated by false doctrine. But your career as a Nazi functionary is at an end. The Nazis are finished. God, man, is the entire world wrong except for Hitler's Reich? Is it not at least conceivable that a system built on the suppression of free thought and free speech, on racialism and genocide and the worship of power, might be an untenable system? Can you at least accept that possibility?"

"You speak too fast but I think I understand. Can you accept that your Christian Church may be wrong?"

"Every day I face that possibility. Every day I pray for faith."

"I have faith too. And I do not have to pray for it."

"The faith I represent has endured longer than yours. It is also faith in a spiritual essence, not in a mortal leader."

"Adolf Hitler is as immortal as you believe your Christus to be. When he dies in the flesh as your Christus died he will be alive in the spirit. If Germany is destroyed by your Christians it will be only as land and fields and cities and people. But Germany as the great truth of the world cannot die. The Aryan truth cannot die."

And so on and so on. *Und so weiter.* Meanwhile the replacement of Helmut Liebeneiner had arrived in the region, a certain Gruppenführer Ernst Lamprecht. Lamprecht knew very well how the war was going and was perfunctory in his rounding up of Jews and cenobites. Moneta was gaining a bad name for terrorism. The fascist mayor had been shot by partisans. A bomb had been chucked into the guardroom of a barracks taken over by the remnant of a Wehrmacht battalion, killing a sergeant, two corporals and three enlisted men. An SS firing squad, marching to its appointment with the innocent victims of reprisal in Piazza Clementi, was machine-gunned from a bombed villa. The partisans were taking control. Reinforcements were needed to stiffen the wavering Gothic Line further south. The occupying garrison heard rumors of a total German evacuation of Moneta and district. Lamprecht's polished jackboots were seen to be twinkling as he trotted to his Opel for a journey northwest. He wanted out. So did all the Germans. But one German remained, very safe, warm, well-fed, and obdurate.

"I honestly," Carlo told him honestly, "don't know what to do with you." Liebeneiner sneered faintly but triumphantly. "But," Carlo said, "there's some truth in the view that only when a man is in severe danger or excruciating pain can his brain be jerked out of the torpor of an unquestioning conviction. Have you yourself, my son, ever participated in the administration of torture?"

"I have ordered it, I have watched it."

"And also massacre, or liquidation, or mass elimination, or whatever you people call it?"

"It was a duty."

"You felt no shock of horror, no sympathy, no remorse?"

"It was a duty."

"Well, God help me, I must do my duty too." Liebeneiner did not now sneer.

He said, "I knew you would come to it. You preach mercy and kindness and tolerance and the other Jewish-Christian properties, but you find that you have to use cruelty in the end. It is in the history of your Church, with the Spanish Inquisition and the Saint Bartholomew Massacre and millions of martyrs burned in the name of your Christus." He spoke in German. So now did Carlo, who said:

"Well, you should approve. It is the Nazi way."

"It is in order when conducted against enemies of the Reich. It is not in order when used by inferior races against the master race."

"Are you saying," Carlo said, "that I belong to a race inferior to yours? I speak an older Indo-European tongue or an Aryan tongue as you would have it. I have more claim in terms of history to belong to a superior civilization than do you. I am of the people of Virgil and Horace and Lucretius. Of Dante Alighieri and Leonardo and Michelangelo and—need I go on?"

"Your civilization has been corrupted by Christianity."

"My civilization is a product of Christianity. You Nazis have nothing except barks and yelps and marching songs. What you had as members of the Holy Roman Empire you have stupidly expunged. But there's not much point in appealing to your reason. It's your soul I'm after."

To get at Liebeneiner's soul Carlo Campanati called in a couple of partisans, one of whom, Giuseppe Chinol, had worked in an abattoir, and the other, Enrico Tramontana, had made coffins. They were burly men but not naturally given to cruelty.

Carlo said to Liebeneiner, "All this should be fairly simple. Your arm will be twisted to near breaking point behind your back. When the pain becomes intolerable I ask you to revile, curse, reject your Nazi faith and the monsters who represent it. Then the pain will stop. I will know and you will know that you will not mean what you say, scream rather. It will just be a device for stopping pain. But it will be something to hear the words of repudiation. For you as well as for me. It will be the first time you will have spoken them."

"I will not speak them. You're a fool."

"Oh, you'll speak them."

And he did. Vomiting his breakfast into the latrine pail, sweating from pain and humiliation, Liebeneiner seemed to groan some ancient German prayer for forgiveness. Carlo listened kindly and with interest. "You're praying," he said. "To whom? Adolf Hitler? One of Wagner's deities? I do not know of any Teutonic tree god with the name *Scheiss*. But I should not be surprised if there is one."

The Nazis had had little experience of martyrdom. On the fourth day of his reclamation treatment, with Giuseppe Chinol ready for the harmless but agonizing twisting of his arm, Liebeneiner said surely the torture was unnecessary: he was quite ready to vilify his own faith and race and masters without torture. It was the formulae of apostasy that the bishop wanted after all, not the pain. It was not in his Christian office to want pain. Carlo shook his head sadly. He said, "If the pain is administered regularly, as it will be for as long as I think necessary, you will more and more find that you need to identify with some figure, real or mythical, who suffered even greater pain than your own. Such identification has always been necessary in the long history of religious persecution. It both exalts the suffering and eases it. Unfortunately you Nazis have no real mythology of persecution. Horst Wessel? Nothing. Thugs punched in the jaw in Nazi-Communist street fights? Hitler in jail? No. A Nazi in pain is in a situation for which his faith has not prepared him. You see your difficulty. *Bene, Giuseppe. Adesso comincia la tortura.*"

Liebeneiner screamed. "I hate Hitler, the Nazi creed is inhuman, the Germans are not the master race, for Christ's sake stop it."

Giuseppe Chinol desisted. "What did you say then?" Carlo asked.

"Bastard. Filthy barbarous swine. Filthy fucking barbarous decadent bastard."

"Words," Carlo said, "you must have heard from the beaten-up opponents of your own regime. You see how it's possible to learn even from people you despise. I note that in your transport you called out the name Christus."

"It was just a noise. It had no . . . I have to vomit."

"Vomit, my son." And while Liebeneiner retched Carlo looked sickly through a deck of large-size glossy photographs. They were part of the record of Nazi infamy in the work and death camps. The Nazis themselves had compiled this record. Their philosophy told them that there was no infamy in it. So perish all the enemies of the beneficent darkness. The bundle of photographs had been left behind in the house on the Via Giuseppe Verdi which had served as headquarters for the SS. It was a spiritual document. It had been put into the hands of the spiritual leader of the community, who now puffed one of the rank last of his stored Tuscan cigars. "I'll leave these with you to look over," Carlo said when pale sweating Liebeneiner sat again on the edge of his cot. "You'll feel something you haven't felt before—a certain kinship with some of these victims. Of course, your sufferings have been nothing in comparison with theirs. The war, by the way, is as good as over. The American Fifth Army is in Milan. The Russians draw near to Berlin. You may not wish to believe me. But if I set you free now you will certainly be torn to pieces by Italian citizens who have liberated themselves from your nauseous yoke. Shall I set you free? Ah, so you believe me. Consider yourself fortunate to be in my charge. I assure you that you shall not leave it until you are a changed man. I will come to see you again this afternoon. Bringing the good Enrico with me. A fine strong boy who would not normally wish to hurt a fly. Ah, the things you people have made us do."

Or words to that effect. It was only after a full month of beneficent torture that Liebeneiner began to see that his place was with the victims and that a philosophy of brutal overlordship availed him nothing in his sufferings. He had a vision of Adolf Hitler crucified—naked, with a creampuff paunch, quiff and little mustache intact, crying out *Eli Eli lama sabacthani?* The image was, of course, absurd. Hitler was by definition not one of the crucifiable. Yet he, Liebeneiner, faithful servant of the Führer, had been granted by the Führer no metaphysical or theological defense against agony of the body and humiliation of the soul. The Führer had let him down. By accident Giuseppe Chinol broke his arm. He swooned. The bishop was extravagantly penitent. Dr. Praz was brought in to set the arm and bind it. There was no more torture for a time. Carlo waited patiently for Liebeneiner to experience a liberating dream. He knew that a change of heart was often signaled by a sequence of nightmares culminating in a sleeping vision of hell that turned into a revelation of light. The trouble with Liebeneiner's soul was that it was not much of a soul. It was a soul made for a simplistic philosophy like that of the Nazis. And yet it was a human soul that had issued from the hand of God. God loved his own creation. He loved Liebeneiner. All he asked of Liebeneiner was such reciprocal love (and there was *love* in his name) as he was capable of giving, gratitude for the gift of moral freedom, a minimal charity to others, humility. Carlo came every morning with Liebeneiner's breakfast—goat's milk, mineral water, bread, jam—and asked him about his dreams. One morning Liebeneiner said that he had dreamed he was dead.

"Ah You are, of course, officially dead."

"I saw my dead body. It was on a great battlefield. I looked down on my own body and thousands of others. I wept."

"You wept for your own body or for all the bodies?"

"I don't know. I wept. The bodies were of my comrades dead in battle."

"You couldn't see that they were your comrades. They were just the bodies of dead men. And yet they *were* your comrades."

"There were women too. Naked. Everybody was naked. I could not stop weeping. When I woke up my eyes were wet."

Carlo looked at him kindly. Liebeneiner had not been permitted to shave since his delivery to the episcopal cellars. Nor had his hair been cut. He had been given regular warm water for washing and did not smell, except for a kind of spiritual stench that Carlo had found emanating from all the Nazis he had met, even when they were meticulously bathed and cologned. Evil and stupidity both had their distinctive odors, but it was sometimes hard to tell one from the other. Liebeneiner did not now smell too bad. With his unshorn hair and beard, which were dark brown graying, he could have passed for the Nazi idea of a Jewish intellectual. "You'll be going home soon," Carlo said. "Somehow. Münster's a long way away. And there's not much left of Münster. I pray your wife and daughter are still alive. Think what a joy it will be for them to see a husband and father resurrected from the tomb."

"Is the war over?"

"Very nearly. Your Hitler wasn't much of a prophet, was he? A thousand-year Reich, indeed. It was a stupid dream. What other dreams have you to tell me?"

"I dreamed it was Christmas and I was a boy. And there was the Christ child in the manger."

"Oh, you bloody sentimental Germans. Cruelty and sentimentality and nothing between the two. It took a hell of a long time to Christianize you, and you still don't see what it's all about.

> 'Mit blankem Eis und weissem Schnee
> Weihnachten kommt—juchhe! juchhe!'

It's time for another lesson. I shall bring my black cat down here and cut its throat with a kitchen knife. It's a wicked cat, always eating birds. You'll enjoy seeing the blood, won't you?"

"No no no no no."

"You blasted Germans. Shall I bring a Jew down then? That won't be quite as bad, will it? A Jew with a beard just like yours, and we'll shove his head into your latrine bucket and let him suffocate in good clean Nazi excreta. You'd better get yourself ready for the great outside world, Herr Liebeneiner. I've had enough of you."

Liebeneiner looked wary. His face had, during his benign incarceration, gradually learned qualities of foxy alertness and suspicion: it had become a prisoner's face, almost a human one. "I will go," he said, "when it is safe to go. Not before."

"Yes," Carlo said, "of course. You want to snuggle down here in your burrow with your blankets and your three meals a day. Rather like being in the Nazi Party, isn't it? You don't have to face the big dirty world where the winds have blown down the signposts. The world where moral decisions have to be made. Look, I have no specific desire to turn you into a Christian. I merely want to remind you what it's like to be a member of the human race, the only race there is, there's no master race and never was. The devil got into your people, and I'm not using a metaphor. A colossal force of evil thrust in and you were all too damned stupid to recognize it for what it was. Make no mistake about it, your Adolf Hitler was a big man. I say *was* because it seems certain that he's now dead. A real incarnation of evil, very rare in the world's history. If I could have had him down here as I've had you I'd have had to engage in a strenuous program of exorcism. I might not have won but I'd have had to try. I might have been blasted to hell myself in the process. As for you, there's been nothing really to work on. Not much there, Herr Liebeneiner. You always were a kind of vacuum which the Nazi Party kindly filled up for you. I'd be happier if you had real convictions, not just slogans. But, by God, I should think you've done a lot of harm in your time. Tomorrow morning I want to hear it all from your own mouth. It will be a sort of purgation. Then you can have a haircut but if I were you I'd keep that beard. It doesn't look like a property of the *Herrenvolk*. I'll get you some old clothes from somewhere and some army boots. Then you'll start walking home. You'll have a lot of interesting decisions to make on the way. Whether or not to steal, for instance, and from whom. Whether to help less lucky wanderers than yourself. What lies to tell to the various allied soldiers you'll meet. You'll have a chance to turn into a human being. Later perhaps you could write me a letter, I'll be sincerely interested to hear from you."

Liebeneiner sulked. "So we were all cheated."

"God be praised that you're beginning to understand."

"We won't be cheated next time."

"O suffering Christ on the cross, there's nothing that can be done with you people. It's not sin, it's sheer damned stupidity. O dear God in heaven."

"May your God," Liebeneiner said, "consign Adolf Hitler to a deep and eternal hell. God's curse on all of them. And you don't have to twist my arm to make me say that. It's the Jews who've won, isn't it? And the Bolsheviks. The international capitalists and the international Communists and liberals and international decadent freethinkers."

Carlo now felt that he had spoken too hastily in crying out on Nazi stupidity. "You can say," he said, "that your philosophy of power and intolerance hasn't worked. It's been defeated. Therefore it was wrong. If you Germans want to be the one great race you'll have to think of something else. You've killed off a very great part of the Jewish people. Perhaps you'll have to fill in the vacuum. The Germans will have to turn themselves into the new Jews. Strength through suffering. *Kraft durch Leid.* I'll see you tomorrow."

The next day Carlo Campanati heard it all from Liebeneiner's mouth. Confession without absolution. But it was all so statistical, so abstract. No pride in butchery and certainly no remorse. But a measure of self-pity, for pity is built into the human psyche and has to find an object somewhere: the stress of rule, the problems of organization, the screams and stenches that offended Liebeneiner's delicate sensibility. Finally, the waste. In the middle of the following night Liebeneiner, well-shod, warm-coated, wearing a cast-off suit donated by Carlo's chaplain, without money and without papers of identification, was sent on his way. He gave himself his mother's name, which was Waschneck. Two years later Carlo Campanati received a letter, in English, from Helmut Waschneck. He was teaching in a Gymnasium in Lippstadt in the British Zone. His wife and daughter and himself were well. They attended service regularly in the local Lutheran church. There was a great German for you, Martin Luther. There was another great German, Johann Sebastian Bach. The Germans had a great destiny, and that was to civilize the world. Communism remained the big enemy. It could only be countered by the example of democratic freedom. By God, the world would yet see that its only hope lay in systematic democracy and systematic free moral choice. Germany would show everybody. *Deutschland über alles.* All that Germany lacked was a leader.

The percipient reader will have observed the hand of Toomey in the above. The stress of invention is less arduous than the strain of word for word copying. I may be a bad writer, but I am better than Howard Tucker when it comes to fabricating or lying. Being uncommitted to verifiable fact, as his kind of writer is, I can indulge in the free fancy that often turns out to be the truth. The point is, in my chronicle, that Carlo fought the good fight and I didn't.

That I hadn't fought it, and that I had something to expiate, not quite treason but certainly shamefully unpatriotic, was rubbed in officially when I was ordered by the Prime Minister's office to join the parliamentary delegation that visited Buchenwald on April 21, 1945. Could the head of the executive in fact give such an order? Probably yes: we were still at war, we were all subject to direction. Why the order was given by our Great War Leader, as he was often called, was made clear by Brendan Bracken, Minister of Information, an ebullient youngish man with red hair and bad teeth who was commonly believed to be Winston Churchill's natural son. He telephoned me on April 18 to say that the Prime Minister had remarked in private conversation at a dinner party that the infamy of the Nazzy camps, as he called them, ought to be recorded in a book, and it was probably the duty of a writer like Kenneth M. Toomey, made rich through the purveying of popular fiction but not noticeably inclined to repay the British public who read him by serving his country, to write the book on the camps that His Majesty's Stationery Office ought to publish. Bracken said he was going to send me all available documentation along with photographs which would make me sick to my stomach, and that I was to fly to Weimar on RAF transport along with selected MPs to witness evidence of Nazzy infamy before the Americans cleared it all up. General Eisenhower, he might add, he added, considered, along with the Prime Minister, that it was the job of some writer to do this job and I was probably the writer to do the job.

"I can't," I said, "be ordered to write a book."

"Oh, that's taken for granted, old boy," Bracken said, "but it's generally felt that you'd want to do it, all things considered. You don't exactly smell of roses, all said and done. Anyway, that's how the PM feels about it. I'll send that stuff. Somebody will be in touch about times and rendezvous and so on. Have a good trip."

I knew none of the members who were flying with me. The U.S. Army officers' mess at Weimar gave us a lunch of grilled Spam and fruit jelly and a choice of soft drinks. While we ate a U.S. Army medical officer briefed us with such statistics as would not impair our appetites. Camp started in 1934.

Planned to contain about one hundred thousand internees. On April 1, 1945, there were 800,813. Just before the arrival of U.S. forces on April 11 the Germans removed over twenty thousand to make things look less bad than they were. Internees drawn first from German political prisoners and Jews, later as the Reich expanded all sorts, but chiefly Jews, from Czechoslovakia, Poland and so on. Camp ill-planned and ill-kept. Rough wooden huts with earth floors and no windows, no sanitation. Up to April 1, 1945, total number exterminated: 51,572. Detailed camp records with nominal rolls left behind by Nazis. Squalor and smell still sickening, despite cleaning up in vigorous American progress. For the rest, we would see for ourselves.

We saw. So did a party of German civilians from the Weimar region. It was the rule to bring such a party every day. This group was drably but warmly clad and none looked ill-fed. None looked much different from the man or woman you would meet on a Number 57 bus. They said *schrecklich* and *entsetzlich* and *grauenhaft* and so on, decent ordinary people responding to the evidence of past horrors perpetrated by others. One woman retched into her handkerchief. They were conducted by a top sergeant who chewed something medicinal and spoke the German of Milwaukee with occasional interpolations in English, such as "you goddam krauts" and "you murdering bastards" and so on. Among the members of Parliament was an overnourished Tory, very big, a former rugger blue, who said "Good God" continually as though he was being forced to sip bad port. Really, there was not much else to say.

"This," said the colonel who was our guide, "was a brothel for high-grade non-Semitic prisoners. We found fifteen women here when we arrived. Prisoners from women's camps were promised better treatment if they'd take on the job. Lucky not to be killed, all the rest were. We're using it now as a transit hospital for the really bad cases of malnutrition. Like these." The rugger Tory went *Good God*. They were all children, big-eyed, big-bellied, matchsticks for limbs. "There are over eight hundred kids still in the camp," the colonel said. "You'll see them." We saw them. We saw the sleeping huts, where six men had had, impossibly, to try and sleep together on a kind of wooden shelf six feet deep four feet wide two feet high. The eighty-foot-long hospital hut for sufferers from tuberculosis and dysentery accommodated a regular population of about thirteen hundred. Operations had been performed without anesthetics and in full view of the other patients. Corpses were flung to the end of the hut and collected by carts in the morning, some for the crematorium, some for the pathological laboratories. In a laboratory we saw shelf after shelf after shelf crammed with dusty glass jars with livers, spleens, kidneys, testicles, eyes in them. "In this place," the colonel said, "the doctors infected Jews with typhus to get serum. They experimented with new techniques of sterilization. They found castration was the best way. That was in the comparatively humane time before the extermination policy came in. See how the walls have been decorated with

death masks. They seem to have been trying to classify Jewish physiognomies."
I hardly dared to look among those noble martyred faces; I feared finding
Strehler there. Then we saw the trapdoor and the chute to the basement of the
mortuary block. They threw the rebellious and the mortally sick down there,
ready for execution. We saw the forty gibbets with their forty hooks. There was
a bloodstained Herculean club for finishing off the slow to die. Crematorium
ovens. Calcined ribs, skulls, spinal columns. "This," the colonel said in the
headquarters of Koch, the camp commandant, now reeking of glorious lysol
and full of typing clerks, "is a lampshade. It looks like an ordinary lampshade.
It was taken from the bedside lamp of Frau Koch. It's genuine human skin." It
sounded more gruesome spoken in his diphthongal southern manner—*skee-en*.
"The good Frau Koch had a number of domestic articles made out of human
skin." A socialist delegate, member for Coventry South, went out to vomit.

I was prepared to stand it all, and more. Even the pervading smell that the
disinfecting teams had not yet been able to drive out. What was the smell? All
too human, no effluvium from diabolic sources. A compound of long-standing
urine, diseased feces, rancid fat, old rags, gums ravaged by trench mouth,
cheese. Gorgonzola cheese. I could take it all. It was the smell of myself, of all
humanity. What words could I find, what words could Dr. Samuel Johnson have
found? Johnson, passing a fishmonger's shop in Fleet Street, saw an eel being
skinned alive and heard the skinner curse the eel because it would not lie still. I
saw the eel distinctly: it had the head of Oliver Goldsmith. I seemed to catch
another vision, that of mild scholarly men in doctoral robes, all Nazis, all gently
confirming that man was born, as some Church father taught (was it Tertullian,
was it Origen?), *inter urinam et faeces*. One of my shoes, rather loose-fitting,
had caught in mud like red glue; I hopped, shoe in hand, to a patch of dry
ground by a wooden wall. A fire had been lighted there and there was a half-
burnt piece of printed paper. I learned against the wall and wiped my shoe
clean. The paper seemed to have been torn from some Latin textbook. I read:
Solitam . . . Minotauro . . . pro caris corpus . . . I threw the scrap away. I could
hear behind me the southern voice of the colonel delivering some judgment that
the parliamentary delegates were competent to deliver themselves: degradation,
lowest point in human history. And, the colonel added, this camp was just one
of many and by no means the worst.

I looked at the sky, rainwashed, pure, and saw an elongated pink cloud like
a Picasso angel with trumpet. The Prince of the Power of the Air. No. This was
no Luciferian work. The intellectual rebel against God could not stoop to it.
This was pure man, pure me. A dwarf with a humped back and a shaven head
in shapeless gray clobber went by, muttering. This was Dahlke, who had already been introduced to us, a Communist who had been ten years in the camp
and had been given the soft job of firing the ovens. He now had to await his
turn for assignment to the world of the living, a world in which he could fire

ovens on behalf of some other orthodoxy. He was more man than Michelangelo's David (a disposable Jew anyway). He gave me a pattern for an image of man as very small and humped and ugly, whimpering little songs to himself as he rooted in nameless filth. Man had not been tainted from without by the Prince of the Power of the Air. The evil was all in him and he was beyond hope of redemption. Had I in my recent loneliness nourished fantasies of pure male love set free from biological urges? No, rather of manipulable bodies, often without faces set on them, to be used for careless spasms. And sometimes, when the spasm was hard to attain, the body had to be rent, the *antrum amoris* burst and disgorged its stored rubbish. We all walked or lay snug with a bloody beechwood in our brains.

There would be no need for me to pore over the photographs in the parcel from the Ministry of Information that I had not yet opened. There was no ghastliness perpetrated in the real world that a man did not already know from his dreams. Christ on the cross with a hole in his side and the hole used *penetrationis causa membrorum virilium centurionum Romanorum.* The smashed womb and the filthy slogan written in bits of entrail. No limit. Semen in the skull. The sexual apparatus torn out at the root and stuffed laughingly up the anus. The Nazis had, in a quantitative age, exploited the horror of surfeit: that was their sole new achievement. But meanwhile, and I did not know this yet though our Great War Leader knew it, the guns were being oiled to place in the hands of children to kill the shiploads of returning Russians, victims of Yalta as they were to be called. Human flesh was not precious, plenty more where that came from. Men with nosemasks on tractors would plough it all in for the nourishing of the soil. A ballet of blind beseeching as thin limbs were animated by the advancing engines, then thrust down into the slow economy of Nature. I wanted to have Carlo with me there to smell the ripe Gorgonzola of innate human evil and to dare to say that mankind was God's creation and hence good. Good, that's what I am, sir, it was the devil made me do it. Man was not God's creation, that was certain. God alone knew from what suppurating primordial dungheap man had arisen.

The passport that had been taken from me had, anyway, by now, I knew, expired. And, shortly after VE Day, I had to get to New York. I had received a letter from my niece Ann which contained terrible news. Humbly, disdaining to contact top men, I telephoned the Passport Office, Petty France, and got through to a minor civil servant, a woman with a Middlesex whine. She wanted to know where and why I wished to travel. I told her.

"My sister. She's terribly ill. She's had a terrible accident."

"Have you had a passport before?"

"Yes, but it was destroyed in an air raid. Along with other documents and personal possessions."

"Did you report this at the time?"

"Well, no, I didn't think it necessary. And there were other things to think about. What do I do? Fill in a form? Can I come round and see you?"

"You should always report the loss of a passport. A passport is the property of HMG. It's a valuable document."

"Do you understand the urgency? My sister. I have a letter here. From my niece. I'll read it out if you like."

"Even if we issue a passport you have the question of getting special permission to travel. All transport is controlled by the services. You're only supposed to travel on urgent official business."

"I'm doing official business. I'm writing a book for His Majesty's Stationery Office. On the Prime Minister's orders."

"What about?"

"The Nazi concentration camps."

"There aren't," she said justly, "any concentration camps in America. At least not to my knowledge."

"How about the passport?"

"You can't use a passport yet, for a while. There's been a war on, you know. And there's still a war on with the Japanese."

"I know, for God's sake. I read the bloody newspapers too."

"There's no call to be offensive. Please remember you're speaking to a civil servant."

"Well, damn it, wouldn't you get bloody offensive in my situation? My sister's had a terrible accident. She may be dying, for God's sake."

"You'd better write a letter requesting an official form of application. Then your application will go through the usual channels. You will hear in due course."

"Thank you for nothing."

"There's no call to be offensive."

I telephoned the Foreign Office giving my name and stating that my passport had been withdrawn for the duration of hostilities but now hostilities seemed to be over and— I was put through to a woman with a Middlesex whine. Never mind. I telephoned Brendan Bracken to urge the immediate necessity of my interviewing certain distinguished German refugees in the United States. For the book. All right then, a lecture to stay-at-home Americans on the horrors of Buchenwald. Nothing doing, old boy. Giving my name as Marchal, I went to the consular department of the French Embassy and, in my exquisite French, said that regrettably I had no passport having crossed the Channel in a small boat in 1940 to join the Free French and— I must make application in writing providing high-level testimonies to my identity. I went to the American Embassy, practicing on the way a kind of Boston accent, but the consular section was crammed with GI brides seeking visas. I wept.

In my agony I sat on the cold bed of what had been Heinz's room, the passports of Mrs. Hilda Riceyman and Miss Flora Alberta Stokes trembling in my hands. There was no means of masculinizing those first names. Besides, both passports had expired. Toward the end of July I had visitors. The entire cinematographic unit of my nephew John or Gianni. Probably with jeep parked outside. Frank Schlitz, Sergeant McCreery, Lieutenant Mayer, loaded with PX gifts. And the blond husky six-footer Corporal Campanati. Gee but it's good.

"John, oh God, John, did you get the news about your mother?"

"I got it. Kind of old news. There was a lot of mail been piled up at Genoa. What new news have you got?"

I got from my desk Ann's most recent letter.

"Had to take the eye out. Lucky it didn't pierce the brain. Oh Jesus. She's going to look like a pirate. She's alive, though. That's what matters, she's alive." And of course it was true. To come through alive was the thing. And she wasn't even a war casualty. This team must have filmed a lot of death. I liked the look of them, sloppy decent Americans smelling richly of a lavish land and easy manners: swarthy Schlitz chewing gum in a rotary motion, McCreery flame-headed and big-boned with big nervous hands that needed some occupation like whittling to keep them from mischief, thin sallow Mayer with warm moist brown eyes behind steel-rimmed army-issue glasses. I had nothing to give them, but they had brought quarts of Haig and Beefeater. I got ice and the best glasses. They lounged with their loose American limbs relaxed, thoroughly at home. Nice place you got here.

Lieutenant Mayer said, "I saw you at Metro, Mr. Toomey. You were coming out of the writers' building, sort of muttering. I was wtih my dad, he said that's the great British writer Toomey. Course I was just a kid, didn't know who you were."

"I don't feel particularly great," I said. "I feel squashed. Stuck here under the bombs doing nothing. Despised and rejected."

"I got that story from Mother," John said. "Uncle Ken," he told the others, "went into Nazi Austria to bring out this big Jewish writer before they turned him into soap to wash Hitler's ass. Then the war started and he could only get out by talking on the Nazi radio. And then Churchill or somebody got sore about him talking to the enemy so he's been kind of in disgrace." They seemed to think this was a great story.

Sergeant McCreery said, "We got some footage of the guy that was really a traitor. In a kind of cage near that place with the tower that leans cockeyed."

"He'll fry," John said. "Went on about Roosevelt was a traitor to civilization and he was glad he was dead."

"There's a lot," McCreery said, "glad of that."

"What now for you?" I asked.

"Well," Lieutenant Mayer said, "we got this short furlough. Got in on a rundown French tub from Gibraltar. Full of rats and a Chinese crew. We got rat stew every day."

"Rabbit, they said," John said.

"Too small for rabbits. They were clean rats, fat too."

"And then," John said, "we sail to New York, Manhattan, Forty-second Street, on the *Queen Mary*. Next Thursday from Southampton."

"You'll be with her," I said bitterly. "I can't get out. No passport, no travel permit. My own sister. A brother ought to have that right."

"It's governments," Schlitz chewed. "They're all shit."

"You come with us," McCreery said, strangling a velvet cushion. "The *Queen Mary*, that's a British boat, right? It's big, there's plenty of room. You just walk on in uniform and talk American. The lootenant here can give you a uniform. Maybe you'd have to be higher than a lootenant, a bird colonel would be right for a guy of your age, you being kinda old. Soon fix that. Nothing that can't be fixed." This was pure America, a gust of fresh air blowing in as if the windows were open.

"I wouldn't make it," I said in a faint New England accent. "It sounds like a fine idea but I wouldn't make it."

"Another way," McCreery said. "You could be me, right? I'd like to get over to the old country, miss the boat, what the hell, war's over, County Wicklow, I've relatives. Nothing to go back to the States for yet. War's over, they can't stop me."

"They'd bust you to buck private," Mayer said. "Send you to finish off the Japs."

"Hell, that war's as good as over," McCreery said. "Okay, we'll talk about it later. How's about checking in some place and then seeing the bright lights of Piccadilly Square?"

"You stay here," I said. "There's a big spare bed and plenty of room on the floor."

"Wouldn't want to put you to no trouble," Schlitz chewed.

"Lord Byron slept here," I said with partial accuracy. "It's supposed to be historic."

"Well, okay then. I never slept where a lord slept. Something to tell the folks in Flatbush."

"You slept where a duke slept," John said. "In that palazzo just outside of Moneta."

"Yeah, but that was only a wop dook. Here it was a real lord like your uncle says."

"Moneta?" I said.

"Yes," John said. "I saw my other uncle. He did all right. He sends his regards. He's going to be made archbishop soon, he reckons. The Archbishop of Milan had a heart attack, his third. That came through on the phone while we were there. Uncle Carlo's next in line for the job. That," he said to Schlitz, "is bigger than a lord. If he makes cardinal he'll be a prince."

London was a kind of American territory. The Americans had the money, the glamour, the nylon stockings, the cartons of Luckies, the chewing gum for the kids, the ready triple fares for the cabs. They wouldn't want me with them tonight though they were too courteous to say so. But John said, as we stood outside Albany looking for a taxi:

"Look, you guys, Uncle Ken and I, we've got family things to talk over, okay? So you go off, see you later." They were politely relieved to see that I, kinda old, would not be there. Girls, they would be after girls. I told them that Piccadilly Circus was just down there, see, a brief walk. No need for a cab. Hell, we'll grab us a taxi, no point in walking when you can ride, see, there's one, just let out that old dame with the furs and the little dog. Schlitz whistled like a bomb. Lieutenant Mayer looked like one who, already breathing the air of a society which kept the ordering and ordered apart, felt he ought to be going his own way, officers' club, high-class ladies or something. Still, they all got into the cab together. We waved them off like a wedding.

It was dinnertime. They had brought me a huge can of Spam, likewise of buckwheat flour for flapjacks, Hershey bars, Chesterfields, a pack of small tins of salted peanuts. I set the Spam to frying and reconstituted some dried egg. John ate peanuts in lavish handfuls, riding a kitchen chair. What did he know of me in his capacity as adult and soldier? I had seen him last as a boy, polite, reticent, anglicized by Choate. Had Hortense told him that his British as opposed to Italian uncle was a screaming queer? I asked most of the questions.

"What now then, John?"

"Anthropology."

"Anthro—?" Strangely I had heard the word as *anthropophagy*, wondering if he was bitterly joking, having learned in Europe of the last enormity of the abandoned and starving, seeing the pink flabby Spam as some final desperate artifact of unspeakable though piglike origin.

"Pology pology. Funny how a thing will seem to go in one ear and out the other when all the time it's sticking and growing, quiet and dark. We had this professor who came to Choate and gave us a talk about it. That's what I want to do."

"A degree in anthropology? Where?"

"I thought of Liverpool, that's where it all began. Frazer who wrote *The Golden Bough* was professor there. But there's more work been going on in the States. Chicago, perhaps."

I set down the mock food on the kitchen table. I still had a couple of bottles of Montrachet and I opened one. John, in the American manner, drank off his first glass without ceremony and with a vague glaze of disappointment: wine, celebrated in literature and liturgy, ought to be magic but never was. We both ate with fork in right hand, also in the American manner. The Spam didn't need knifing: it was beneath the dignity of true meat.

"Not Columbia? Not CCNY?"

"If you mean I ought to be living with Mother, she'll be all right. I guess. Of course, we don't know how she is. Perhaps I ought to telephone Ann."

"You'd be hours getting through. If you ever got through. Strict priorities and so forth."

"But, hell, the war's over. I mean, the Hitler war."

"Sometimes, John, I have the feeling that it'll never be over. Hitler just showed the way to the future. Showed how far governments could go with impunity. We've hardly begun to have the inkling of a realization of what this war's been about."

"Well," John said, "isn't that a good reason for wanting to do anthropology?"

"Not psychology?"

"Hell, that's just the individual mind. Individuals don't make war. We have to understand the basic principles of human society. Why societies make war. And do other things. I know nothing about it. That's why I have to learn."

"You get a degree and what then?"

"Well, I guess once I'm in Academe or Academia or whatever it's called I just have to stay there. If they'll have me. The most important study in the world and it's no good in the world. I mean, General Motors doesn't advertise for trained anthropologists. It's strictly for the scholars. But it's not library stuff. Not now."

"*The Golden Bough* is library stuff. Somebody gave facts for the books and Frazer collated the books. You collate and work out theories of magic and religion and so forth. In a library. Isn't that it?"

"Not any more. It's fieldwork now. Professors stung by mosquitoes. Speaking primitive languages."

"You've had good groundwork in learning languages."

"Not primitive ones. Anyway, that's what I want to do. It came over me going through Italy. There you had the glory of learning and faith and art"— that American curled-up *r* in *art* made its utterance seem derisive—"and what in hell did it all amount to? You end up with trying to climb mountains and cross rivers just to kill. Not that I killed. Strictly harmless shooting. But you see what I mean—I want to find the hidden patterns under the Vatican and the Uffizi and the Ponte Vecchio and the rest of the junk. What makes societies tick."

"Did you," I smiled, "tell your uncle Carlo that the Vatican was all junk?"

"No, I said that religion had to be studied as a social phenomenon. All religion. Of course, he said there was only one. And then he brought out the ink."

"Ink?"

"The local wine. He seemed to want to see how I behaved when I got drunk. *Toga virilis*, kind of. It's all anthropology."

"So," I said, "we're going to have a scholar in the family. I suppose it's time." And I toasted John's ambition with the last of the Montrachet. "Too many skills and not enough scholarship, that's us."

"And that includes Uncle Carlo," John said. "Shaman and showman. If scholars proved that Christ didn't rise from the dead, Uncle Carlo'd have the scholars shut up in his cellar, like this SS guy."

"What's this? I don't know about this."

"He'll tell you. It's a good story. Or he'd have them quietly shot. Faith and scholarship don't mix."

"Does this mean you've lost your faith, John?"

"Not in public," he said, grinning, lighting up a crackling Lucky Strike. "Let's say that I believe belief's necessary. It wouldn't exist if it wasn't. But I think it's dangerous. The Nazis believed in the great German destiny."

"Is your uncle Carlo dangerous?"

"Dangerous to the guys who don't believe what he believes. Why doesn't Mother like him?"

"Something I've never understood. Carlo thinks she's an angel."

"A one-eyed angel. Oh God. How stupid. How goddam unthinkingly stupid. I could fucking kick myself." And then, "I wonder if *he* knows. Not that it makes any difference. He wouldn't come running. New responsibilities. You pretend the past never existed or if it did it was all bad. I shouldn't have said *fucking*. Sorry. That's the army for you."

"Did you see him?" I asked. "Before you left the States?"

"I can do without him," John said. His personality confirmed that. Nothing of Domenico had emerged in it even after twenty-odd years of the possibility of gestation. Anglo-Saxon open-faced clumsiness and candor, no oiled armory of charm, no nonsense about art (how could there be nonsense with that front prolonged *a* and that retroflex burr, pioneer farmer's phonemes?). And a loose easy musculature wholly American, anephebe blondness, Hortense's ears, a chin and nose unplaceable, Hortense's eyes. "Uncle Carlo said something about God being the only father. That makes sense. What is God? God is everybody's father. That makes a lot of sense." And then, "I thought of changing my name."

"To Campion?"

He was astonished. "How did you know that? Did Mother—" What had come back was the reading aloud of newspaper necrology in a hotel room in Chicago.

"It's the nearest name. It's a good name. *Lychnis coronaria*, leaves that crowned champions. An English Jesuit martyr and an English poet and musician. I wonder if Thomas saw Edmund hanged? John Campion. It suits. You don't look like a Campanati."

"What's Campanati mean?"

"I never thought about it. Something to do with bells I'd say."

"That figures. Mother's still Mrs. Campanati and always will be she says. She says you don't play around with Christian marriage. She wears the name like a pillory."

"Did she say that?"

"She said that. I hope to Christ she's going to be all right. This Dotty or Dorothy will look after her if she's still there."

"Who is this Dotty or Dorothy?"

"A black lady. She used to be a nightclub singer. A very handsome black lady. She said hell, she needed education. She'd saved money so she went to City College. She had a fancy for French, God knows why. Now she reads Flaubert and Anatole France. A very skeptical black lady."

"Talking," I said, "about Christian marriage—"

"I've not thought about it," John said. "If that's what you mean. Not that I haven't," and he blushed. "I mean, it's expected. What do you think the other guys are doing right now except trying to get laid?"

I was very pleased with him. I said, "As for money. It's pointless your having to wait till I'm dead. If you need money . . . you three are all I have. Don't hesitate," I said.

"Oh, there's the GI Bill of Rights. But thanks." He yawned. "Sorry. I wasn't yawning at that. I'm a guy needs a lot of sleep. The other guys laugh at me. No point in you waiting up for them. They're a good lot of guys. Mayer's a prick but he knows it. Tim McCreery has cinema coming out of his ears. He wanted trick camera shots, but Mayer said what we're doing is just recording history for posterity. Kind of pompous. McCreery taught me all I know about camerawork." He yawned again. "Sorry. Some day we'll do a classic anthropological movie. Female circumcision in the Upper Wangtarara. Stranger things have happened. Nothing's wasted." I sent him to bed.

I woke next morning at eight to hear considerate whispers and padding around in socks. There was a smell that could not be muffled: fresh eggs and ham frying and coffee. I put on my endragoned gold dressing gown and went to the kitchen, where Mayer, McCreery and Schlitz, dressed but unshaven and crumpled, were dishing up. Wow, they said to the dressing gown. John slept still. Let the kid have his sleep. Chow ready, Mr. Toomey. McCreery gave me vigorous information as he ate with his right hand, crumpling a piece of toast to crumbs with his restless left. Met this guy in a pub, USAAF colonel, taking a bomber back to the States tomorrow. Okay, he said, just hop aboard, plenty room, take off oh six oh oh hours, the base is at Orford, that's in the county of Suffolk, just ask for Jake Lyman and everything will be okay. Okay, there's plenty alternatives. You want passports? McCreery dug from his hip pocket three, of colors I had not seen before.

"Where, if I may ask, did you manage to . . ."

"This one's Irish Free State, got into a fight with this big Irish guy in the alley next to this pub, where was it, Frank?"

"Wasn't there," Schlitz said, chewing. "That was when I was off with this dame said she was Free Polish."

"Polish, right, this one's Polish, you'd have to practice saying the name, look at it, for Christ's sake. It was this guy said he was diplomatic or some goddam thing. The other one I haven't seen before, some banana republic some place. You take your choice, Mr. Toomey. This dame I was with, Baron's Caught or some goddam place, heard the trains all night, she said it was the Underground, hell, I said, that's no underground, she meant subway, a GI bride called herself, waiting for a passage, she had this British passport in her drawer, U.S. visa on it, but I thought hell that'd cause more trouble than it was worth, but there you are, sir, you make your choice."

"It's awfully kind, really," I said, "but I think I'll have to do things in a more regular fashion. I lack your youth. I lack your freedom. But don't think I m not grateful. I take it you all had a reasonable night out."

"Unreasonable," Lieutenant Mayer corrected, something of an intellectual. "Feast of unreason. We went our own ways and met at dawn in a coffee shop."

"Lousy coffee," Schlitz said. "Not like this joe here."

"London's okay," McCreery said sagely, "if you know your way around. Bulging with stuff. These eggs, that ham there. Went with this little dark guy, Lithuanian he said he was, to a garage some place. Crammed with it. Very hungry for dollars, this guy. I tell you, you can fix anything."

"A Lady Bloomfield," Mayer said. "You ever hear of a certain Lady Bloomfield, Mr. Toomey? Quite a girl."

And then John came in, tousled and near cracking his jaw with a yawn. He wore only an army shirt. He took coffee like the kiss of life, wordlessly. John Campion, predestined martyr.

fifty-eight

It was not until after VJ Day that I was able to leave for New York. Warner Brothers in Burbank, in the talking person of a man called Buzz Dragon, came up with the notion of three or four little films based on short stories I had written, bound together into a whole called *Troika* or *Foursquare* or something, depending on number, with myself not only scripting but also linking the elements with a few well-chosen words. There had been a change of government in Great Britain. The old gang, led by Churchill, was out. The new world was for the workers, and I, as I loudly proclaimed in the corridors of bureaucracy, was one of them. I had the right to get out there to the States and start earning dollars, part of the export drive. The new world was also the world of the atomic bomb, and the prospect of everything blowing up fairly soon seemed to have a quietening effect on those official forces that might otherwise on principle have opposed my getting a new passport and an American visa and a passage on the *Aquitania*, New York outward bound from Liverpool.

There were a lot of GI brides. There was also the Archbishop of York, quondam Bishop of Gibraltar and later Bombay. He had not changed much. Thin and boyish, his unthinning silver hair looking like an allochrome of blondness rather than gray, he greeted me cheerfully in the bar and said, "I take it you were first to get the news?"

"What news?"

"Milan has a new archbishop."

"Ah."

"It was on the radio this morning. They had it on in the breakfast room at that damnably grimy hotel. Why is everything so damnably grimy here? Look at that monstrosity of a Liver Building. The news, yes, not as important as computing the casualties at Hiroshima and Nagasaki, and naturally jazzed up a bit. Bishop Campanati, burly cigar-puffing freedom fighter who spat on the fascists and snapped his fingers at the Nazis. Very popular choice, one gathers. I suppose the red hat will come through at the next consistory."

"I'd better go to the radio room. Send off a congratulatory cable. How are you, by the way?"

"How am I?"

"Do you still have trouble remembering the Athanasian Creed?"

"What a memory you have, Toomey. That must be all of twenty years ago. A lot's happened since then, ah yes. Pretty little things, aren't they?" He meant the sororities of GI brides with their gum and nylons. "One of the functions of war, the promotion of exogamy. Biology moves in a mysterious way. You going stateside to lecture, film?"

"Film."

"I'm attending an international conference at Washington. On birth control. And these deliciously vulgar little creatures here are traveling in the service of natural increase. Their wombs are already at work manufacturing the postwar generation. Look at that one there, six months gone if she's a day. Ill-timed, this conference, when you consider how hard the major Malthusian check has been operating these last years. Millions dead, Toomey, scores of millions." He beamed.

I had in my tweed jacket pocket a paperback edition of Thoreau's *Walden*. I took it out and flicked through it. "Listen," I said and read:

"There was a dead horse in the hollow by the path to my house, which compelled me sometimes to go out of my way, especially in the night when the air was heavy, but the assurance it gave me of the strong appetite and inviolable health of Nature was my compensation for this. I love to see that Nature is so rife with life that myriads can be afforded to be sacrificed and suffered to prey on one another; that tender organizations can be so serenely squashed out of existence like pulp, tadpoles which herons gobble up, and tortoises and toads run over in the road; and that sometimes it has rained flesh and blood."

The archbishop did not now beam. "Rained flesh and blood, eh? Strong appetite and something or other health. Hm. A bit too eupeptic for my taste, Thoreau. Talking about the raining of flesh and blood, I heard some talk at high levels of your writing the big definitive book on the concentration camps."

"That was Churchill's idea. But I don't have to bother now. The old bastard's out of office."

"Weeping all the time at the ingratitude of the British people, they tell me. Emotional lability, Toomey, very embarrassing."

"From now on," I said, with a sudden anger that surprised me, "I write books for myself only. You remember a particular book I was bludgeoned into putting together about the New Christianity? You were there, *vox* and nothing else like the nightingale, and Carlo bullfrogging back at you."

"The great synthesis," he said with great sincerity. "We're on our way toward it, Toomey." He looked kindly again at the pretty lower-class girls who, as the ship boomed its first warning of leaving, prepared to enter the classless comity of the New World. Their accents were eclectic film American: one girl seemed to believe that the Bogart lisp was part of the general phonemic inventory, another had made herself Bette Davis southern jezebel. They would do all right over there. "We have to think," the archbishop said, "of the generation they and their coevals everywhere in the West are going to bear. The adolescents of the early nineteen-sixties. The new faith will be for them." I did not know at the time that my niece Ann, in an apartment on West End Avenue, was now quick with one of those adolescents.

When we arrived at New York I went, straight after clearing customs, to the Algonquin Hotel. I would not claim as of right a room in my own flat, since Hortense must now regard it as hers. After a couple of whisky sours in the Blue Bar I walked up Fifth Avenue. The September heat was intense and the air was all woolen shirts aboil. The town was full of jumbo steaks and ice cream, the shops pleaded that we buy useless gadgets. This was not Europe. This was very far from being Europe. Victory in Europe and Asia confirmed the excellence of the American way of life. Strong appetite and inviolable health. The afternoon sun was higher here than in any town of Europe, forced upwards by the sky-scrapers. The place was rife with life. The question punched me as I waited at a crossing, watching large cars rife with cheap gasoline hurl toward the East River or the Hudson: where was I now to live? Not England, no, not ever again. Look, we have come through. The world offered itself to me and I drew back from its giant tray of rich pastries. I was fifty-five, not too old, and a reasonable working life stretched before me, but I felt timid, dusty, a failure, unloved and unloving. And now, as I entered the apartment block and told the uniformed concierge I had come to see Mrs. Campanati, I began to tremble.

"Mrs. Camper Neighty. Yes *sir*. Tenth floor. Number one oh fahve."

I rang the bell, trembling worse, and the door was opened by a black woman who radiated warmth like a stove. "Dorothy?" I said with caution. "Dotty? I'm her brother."

"You don't have to tell me, Ken. Just great to see you, great. Come right in." She was a very lovely woman in her late thirties, in a silk dress of screaming scarlet that would have etiolated a white woman to bled veal. Her hair had been straightened but lacquered to a becoming complication of billows and puffs and curlicues. Black is no color, merely a brutal politico-racist abstraction, and it was the texture of her skin that struck before its indefinable hue, or rather was inseparable from it, the pleasure of the sight of it only, one knew, to be com-pleted by the most delicate palpation: as if honey and satin were one substance and both alive and yet sculpted of richest gold. Hortense, I felt, should take to painting and devote her life to the exact rendering of this glorious creature's beauty. And now, in the salon that was not the salon I had known before the war, here was Hortense.

She was dressed simply in a beige suit of kneelength flared skirt, low hip-length jacket with elbowlength sleeves, tailored belt with long gold buckle, welt pockets, tailored collar and revers. Her elegant legs were skinned in bronze nylon. I dared to look at her face. It was the left eye that had gone. She wore over the hollow a pad that matched her suit and wore a melleous wig with a tress flowing down to her cheek. I held out my arms, my eyes flooded. I grasped her, hugged, kissed her cold lips, sobbed my darling my darling. "Leave you two a while," Dorothy said. "Bring you some tea, real British style hot and strong in say ten minutes, okay?" Okay okay. Hortense held me loosely. She gave off a whiff of patchouli but also of raw gin.

"I tried the moment I got Ann's letter. I went on trying. They made the war being over an excuse for not letting me go. My dearest sweetest darling girl, what have they done to you?"

"What do you mean, *they*? I did it myself, didn't I? You always did talk wet, Ken Toomey." And she not only suffered my embrace but returned it keenly. I knew the first solid sexual response for years to a stimulus not merely imagined. She led me to a long russet couch with tossed humbugpatterned cushions. We sat close, my arm loosely about her waist. I took in distractedly deep grassgreen carpeting, Calder mobiles turning sluggishly in the conditioned current, her own metal sculptures of attenuated epicene bodies. The hard Manhattan afternoon light was on her, no longer a young woman, in her mid-forties, the chin thickening charmingly, the skin above and below the eyepatch puckered. She was hurt, aging, in need of protection, so my glands told me. She said, "What have they done to *you*? You're so gray."

"Worrying about you." Distractedly, photographs of John in uniform on a white baby grand piano, probably Dorothy's. The noise of cups in the kitchen. Beefeater gin on the bar. "God, you're all I have." I had a base desire to see the inert horror under the beige shade, the shriveled lids closed on nothing. My glands spoke of this desire. Jews in the ovens in Europe, corpses with stick limbs ploughed under, now this. It was of the same order, it provoked the same hopeless anger. "My dear angel. And I still don't know how it happened. Ann's letters just talked of an accident, very vague." I felt a shudder under my hand.

"There's no point in going over it. It happened. Worse things have happened to others. Call it my contribution to the war." The voice was harder than I had known, and not only in stony reaction to long floods of wholly just self-pity, also roughened with gin and smoke, perhaps also assimilated to New York induration, the hardness of culture as well as of pain. She had no softness in her now; my embracing arm was discouraged. She leaned to the onyx cigarette box on the coffee table, a slab of marble set on piled thick slabs of black glass. I lighted up her Chesterfield with my gold Rocher.

"I have to know. You know I have to know."

"In the studio," she said, and coughed. She detached a tobacco fiber from her lower lip. "In the Village. I was shearing aluminium, what they call aluminum here. A heraldic lion, commissioned. Then the girl who used to work with me rushed in. She had the cold water flat at the top. She'd been out for lunch and she met the telegraph boy in the street. She ran in yelling *He's dead, John's dead*. Then my hand slipped. There wasn't any pain, just blood. And before I passed out I realized it was her husband, not my son. John's a common name."

"Christ," I said.

"She's dead," Hortense went on. "I don't think she meant it, but she's dead. Drink and barbiturates. I'm still alive. And my John's still alive. Or was when he telephoned from Chicago an hour ago. And if he dies now I'll never again have any way of reacting. I've done my reacting. But if he got through wartime Europe he'll survive peacetime Chicago."

Chicago, town of the lengthy necrologies. I was blushing with helpless fury. Somebody had to be blamed. "The stupid silly little bitch," I said.

"Oh, you and your bloody wetness. I should have taken a deep breath and remembered that there's more than one John in the world. Her John shouldn't have been killed. She shouldn't have been stricken to death. There shouldn't have been any war. People shouldn't be killed in air crashes and road accidents and by choking on peach stones. Hands shouldn't slip. Everything should be different. The world's been made wrong." And then, fiercely, "Bloody stupid Carlo."

"What's Carlo done to you?"

"He doesn't believe the world was made wrong. He wrote me a smarmy religious letter about sacrificing my beauty to God. Who told him, anyway?"

"John may have written. I didn't. You know he's an archbishop now?"

"Oh yes, he was bound to be. Some day he'll be a bloody saint. It's his job to smarm about God's will and leave the suffering to others."

"If only it could have been me." I tried to embrace her again but she held me off with her cigarette.

"There's nothing to stop you stabbing your eye with a fountain pen. You'll be all right, you'll always be all right. I'm all right too. I can work well enough the way I am. Not metal any more, though. I could work totally blind with clay or stone. Sculpture's a matter of touch. Like love."

She'd never mentioned physical love to me before. I said, "Money."

"I'm all right for money. I get commissions. I get alimony. I'm all right for everything. I even have faith still. I accept Christian logic. But I don't want to be smarmed over by an Italian bishop. Archbishop," she emended.

Dorothy or Dotty came in rattling and radiant with a tea tray which she set down with great grace on the marble slab. "Dorothy," I said, "accept a brother's grateful thanks."

Hortense wailed. "Listen to him, Dot. He talks like Shakespeare. Pity he doesn't write like him. Brother's grateful thanks quotha or forsooth or whatever it is."

"It's nice to be called Dorothy again," Dorothy said. "I get tired of being Dotty or Dot. Too big for a dot and too sane to be dotty. I hope this is how you like it, Ken." And she poured black tea into big cups, no delicate china nonsense. She had made tiny sandwiches in the British manner. There was a dish of the cake called devil's food.

"Fine, perfect," having sipped. "However ineptly I put it I mean what I say."

Dorothy was seated on the carpet beyond the marble disclosing long bare legs of a strong but exquisite molding. "Hortense," she said, "looked after me in a bad time and still does in a good." And she fired love at my sister with a directness that would have been impossible in a white woman schooled to the deviousness of the long European tradition. Her purple lips that gleamed with tea glowed with love as much as her great eyes, the fine wide nostrils dilated with it. I felt a prick of complicated emotions. It was evident they went to bed together. I saw them an instant writhing on crimson sheets and felt a sharp aesthetic joy, like the joy of imagining incest. All beauty hath a strangeness in it, or an element of the forbidden. In a sense my own more than brotherly love for Hortense was sanctified by the vision. And of course one of the emotions was jealousy. There were also rage and frustration though damped or much muted.

Dorothy said, "There's a room all ready for you, Ken. I hope you'll be staying a good long time."

"Alas, I have to fly to Los Angeles the day after tomorrow. And I, well, I didn't want to presume. I booked in at the Algonquin."

"But why?" Dorothy looked operatically hurt, prolonging the vowel operatically. "This is your place."

"Yours, yours. Where shall I take you for dinner?"

"We don't go out for dinner," Hortense said quickly. Yes. Stupid drunks going yo-ho-ho at the pirate eyemask. "Besides, you've got to see Ann. Mrs. Breslow. And Professor. Dot bought a big turkey. With all the fixings. Like Thanksgiving." She gulped at that and Dorothy got in quickly with:

"Well, there's a lot to give thanks for, isn't that the truth? The war's over and we're all alive and families aren't separated any more. Thanksgiving, right, why not?"

"I think I'd like a drink now," Hortense said.

"Oh, honey, no." I could tell this was a regular, almost ritual, cry of distress. "Isn't tea a drink, good, strong, hot, crammed with stimulating tannin?" It was a desperate mockery of some unctuous radio commercial voice. "Give it another hour, okay? Soon as I put the turkey in the oven we'll all sit at the bar and have a nice long cool highball, okay?"

"Not too long not too cool," Hortense said. "Sing us something, Dot. Ken's never heard you sing."

"Well, sure I'll sing," and Dorothy looked at me in a way that seemed to signify: don't let her nip over to the bar while my back's to her at the piano she's clever at grabbing a quick one. So she got up with wonderful grace and went over and sat and struck some blue chords and began to sing:

> *"Ich nehm' ein' Zigarett'*
> *Und ich fühl' du liebst mich nicht mehr*
> *Und ich weiss es ist aus*
> *Und da macht mein Herz so schwer."*

She paused to smile at me, expecting some comment. I knew the song: I'd heard it in Berlin in 1935.

I said, "Where on earth did you—I mean, such a perfect German accent." Such a rich terra-cotta voice too, like a meat extract that was also an aphrodisiac.

"I've been around," Dorothy said. "That's my Dietrich style. Now I'll do it in English." And she did, right to the end:

> *"Yet*
> *With my cigarette*
> *Though I give no more than I get*
> *There's no sigh of regret*
> *At the end of my cigarette."*

During the song Hortense made a move to get up, but I held her hand tight.

I said to Dorothy, "You fire me with a desire to get back to the musical stage again. It's a long time since I did book and lyrics. God." And I saw it: Cleopatra. "Cleopatra, with you in the lead."

"Cleopatra was white, wasn't she? Greek. I'm black, brother, all black."

"Cleopatra was what you are. To hell with the facts of history."

"I'll get that turkey started," Dorothy said. "Good little *Hausfrau*, that's me, right, Hortense honey? With a little French literature on the side."

"You're wonderful," I said. "What stage work have you done?"

She did a mock or genuine curtsy to my compliment, saying: "I was in *Porgy and Bess* in Atlanta, but it's not really my style. I'm a gal strictly on her own, me and my lil' piano. I did nightclubs. Now I stay in nights. I'll see about dinner." And with great humor she danced her way to the kitchen, doing another curtsy at the door. I clapped.

"I'll have that drink now," Hortense said.

"No, you heard. We all have a nice long cool highball together."

"I want a quick sharp neat gin. And I want it now." She was quick in getting up. I was quick enough to grab her and hold her halfway to the bar. "Let me go, bloody Ken Toomey."

"How much are you drinking?"

"None of your bloody business." We stood there in the conventional posture of struggling woman and importunate man.

"No, but apparently it's Dorothy's business. Take it that I'm just standing in for her." She relaxed in my hold. I let go. There was probably another reason for their not going out in the evenings: Hortense's intake not easy to control in public, people seeing at once why she drank and saying poor bitch no wonder. "Perhaps we ought to go and help her get that turkey in the oven," I said.

fifty-nine

My niece Ann, whom her husband called Annie or Annikins or Roo for Little Annie Rooney, had grown into a rather stupid though undoubtedly voluptuous young woman. She had been led to the marriage bed, no question of it, too early. The warm wet brown eyes of Professor Michael Breslow could not leave her alone, even at the dinner table. He was over ten years her senior. They had met in no context of higher education, unless the term could be applied to the readings by distinguished writers held at the Poetry Center on Lexington Avenue. Ann had been taken by a girl friend to hear a very drunk American poet of the Black Mountain school slobber unintelligible verses, and, taking coffee after, she had met Professor Breslow. Breslow had taken her to the cinemas near Columbia University which specialized in foreign or American classic films. Like Samuel Taylor Coleridge, he had sought the lineaments of gratified desire in a prospective bride rather than the prospects of intellectual companionship. On the other hand, little Ann Campanati was very well connected in terms of the arts. Breslow knew my name and even some of my works, but he taught none of them in his Comparative Literature courses. He knew the artifacts of Ann's mother and had heard subliminally the croons and crashes invented by her father for films sometimes seen at the Thalia cinema. He understood there was a distinguished Roman Catholic ecclesiastical connection, but that was a long way off and not in his line of interests. He was a freethinker and disclaimed as far as he could his Ashkenazi ancestry, but he had suffered vicariously with the victims of Hitler. He had not himself served in the armed forces against the Jewkillers: he had a number of small disqualificatory physical disabilities of kinds not well known or, if known, taken with the right clinical seriousness in Europe. He had graduated at City College but taken his doctorate at Columbia. His thesis had been on Symbols of Decay in *Bleak House*.

Ann's twinhood with John was proclaimed in coloring, admirable physique (though now distorted by pregnancy), and shape of nose and chin, both masterful. Her face, though, lacked the seriousness of John's: its features were not well employed in discourse. She twisted her lovely mouth in comic gestures learned from Abbott and Costello films, she crossed her eyes and rolled them. She wolf-whistled at Dorothy's evening frock of deep purple. She performed a double Zulu click of pleasure at the sight of the strawberry flan dessert. She had inherited the slight venerean strabismus which her poor mother had now lost, but on her it looked not good but a disability. She used expressions of enthusiasm like *wow* and *this I like.* Her greeting to me after long years had been "Hi." She wanted a boy. Her husband wanted a girl. They performed to weariness a crosstalk naming act. Ann's blondness was streaked, as though she had tried to dye it mouse and then lost heart. She had been educated at the Bodmer School in Connecticut where the male instructors had not taken their charges seriously, except when they reached the seducible phase. There had been courses in witchcraft and astrology. A few plays of Shakespeare had been taught in a modernized version devised by one Con Roebuck, a young heavily bearded instructor now understood to be in jail, though not for turning Hamlet's chief soliloquy into "To live or to die—that's the choice, I guess," and the rest in the same style. A girl's cleverness had been privately judged on her capacity to avoid seduction by the faculty or, if not to avoid it, use it for purposes of blackmail or marriage. By the first alternative of this standard Ann had to be adjudged clever; it was her only cleverness. Over the dinner table there were jokes about Ann's raw turkeys and charred chops: Dorothy's feast was, as was to be expected, delicious. Ann had, before her early marriage, done such war work as a girl of her age and educational attainments might be expected to do: blowing up the coffee urn in a services canteen, being dismissed from an aircraft factory as a liability, packaging parachutes with a potential lethality soon fortunately detected by her overseer. She was a happy girl. Her husband was happy too. He said to me over the turkey and sausages and chestnut stuffing and cranberries:

"I heard about what you did, sir, for Jakob Strehler. We brought in Strehler for the first time this semester. Just started. The Mann Strehler Hesse course. What you did was heroic."

"My gesture was not well appreciated in wartime Britain," I said. "For your appreciation, my heartiest thanks."

"Quotha," said Hortense.

"You might like to know, sir, that your name came up for possible inclusion in a Contemporary British Fiction course. Along with Somerset Maugham and Compton Mackenzie."

"All three of us were thrown out, I suppose?"

"Well, yes, sir. It's not a question of readability or enjoyment, Professor

Eckhart said, chairman of the department, it's a question of what you can get your critical teeth into."

"Flawed greatness, you mean."

"Well, yes, sir, it's only the great that have the interesting flaws, practically Eckhart's own words."

"Oh, I've never had pretensions to greatness."

"I read one of your books, Uncle Ken," Ann said. There was a single cranberry like a blister on her lip. "And I thought it was just great. The one where this girl falls in love with this older man."

"A lot of them are about that," I said. "The Daddy Longlegs syndrome."

"More turkey, Ken?" Dorothy said.

I passed my plate; I said, "This is not flattery, my dear. I've not had a meal like this in six years. God bless America. God bless you."

"God bless us every one," went Hortense. She was in midnight blue with a midnight blue eyeshade. She had got through a bottle and a half of Chambertin on her own. She had eaten little.

"Tiny Tom," Ann said.

"Tim," corrected Breslow, to whom, the Dickens specialist, we left the correction. "Tom would be too rotund a name. Tim's kind of thin."

"Timothy Breslow," and Ann tasted the name.

"Felicia Breslow."

"Nathaniel Breslow."

"Penelope Antigone Persephone Breslow."

"Oh shut up," Hortense said. "Counting your chickens. Pray to God that you'll get a kid you won't want the doctor to smother at birth. The next generation at Hiroshima's going to have three legs and four arms or none at all. So *Time* magazine says. Kids with one eye in the middle of the forehead. Proper little cyclones or whatever the hell they're called."

"Cyclops," said the professor. "I think a lot of this speculation is exaggerated."

"Quotha." And then, "For Christ's sake Ann lick that thing off your lip. No, the other side. Better."

"Kind of grouchy, Mom."

"I'll get the dessert," Dorothy said, getting up. "Annie's favorite." She went out.

"Oh yum yum yum. I know what it's going to be."

"Greedy child," Hortense said. "You're supposed to eat enough for two not three. I've been watching you, you gutsy horror."

"A very British locution," Breslow said.

"Well, what's wrong with a British whateveritis? I *am* British. I'll show you my passport if you like."

Dorothy brought in the strawberry flan. Ann did her double Zulu click. "My my," her husband said deferentially. Hortense blew cigarette smoke over the dessert.

"That's a dirty thing to do, Mom," Ann said. I smelt more than Hortense's cigarette smoke.

Hortense said, "I'll have my brandy now. My gutsy daughter still has a lot of eating to do."

"Oh honey," Dorothy wailed. But she made no additional protest when Hortense glided over to the bar to pour a large measure of Martell's Cordon Bleu into her wineglass. Ann and her husband both began to say something simultaneously. I heard the word *Hollywood* from Breslow and said over quickly:

"They're going to take a few of my stories and make a kind of anthology film. With me saying a few words to link them. Should be rather fun."

"Rather fun," Hortense mocked, coming back to the table with her spilling cognac. She blew more smoke over the dessert and said, "Dirty, Mom. Go on, shovel it down, you little gormandizer. You'll probably give birth to a Boston cream pie."

"That's not nice. That's unkind. You're behaving like a real grouch, Mother. It's not fair to Uncle Ken." And with evident reluctance she pushed her still half-filled plate away.

"Oh honey, eat it," Dorothy cried. "Don't listen to your mother. You know she's only having her little joke."

"I get tired of her little jokes, Dotty. It's not my fault if—" She stopped and gulped and then pulled back her plate speedily.

"If what, Ann?" Hortense said quietly.

"Oh, you know." She ate sulkily.

"Meaning that if that telegram had had a different name in it a certain event would not have transpired." She turned to me and said, "Quotha. Or should it be forsooth?"

"*Quotha*," Breslow explained, "is really *quoth he*. Meaning *said he*. *Forsooth* means literally *for truth*."

"Hortense," I said. "Please." And then the thing happened to me that had not happened for so long. I was aware of my heart as a sudden vacuum. Sensation evacuated my feet and my left arm. I bowed involuntarily as in prayer and then was aware of the comedy of my face approaching the almost untouched portion of strawberry flan before me. Before the squelch I passed out. I came to to hear voices of concern but to see Hortense draining her glass of cognac. Dorothy was wiping jammy mess off me with a napkin. "I'm okay," I said, "really and truly okay." But Dorothy and Ann, with Breslow hovering with professorial ineptness, were taking me to bed. "It sometimes happens," I protested. "A kind of fuseblow. I always feel just fine after." But they were taking me to bed. I smelt goo from Ann and from Dorothy something refined and Parisian. Hortense was at the bar getting herself more Cordon Bleu.

The bedroom was, I presumed, John's. It had a no-nonsense young man's austerity about it. Out of the sack and up for chow. "Into that bed," Dorothy ordered and began to undress me as far as my shirt and shorts. "It's the aftermath, I know. The war. A lot of things." I said, "I love you, dear Dorothy. But really I'm fine. And I have this suite at the Algonquin." She fussed. "Get in there. Nice clean sheets." They were primrose and breathed lavender. "I'll go round myself and get your things. You're staying here, Ken. Home. I guess you know the word." I said, "I love you, Dorothy." And then I passed out again. I came to healthily tired. "I'll sleep a little," I said. I might as well be in bed as elsewhere. Sleep as well as anything else. Dorothy kissed my forehead with cool dry but generous lips. Ann, after hesitating, pressed thin wet ones on my cheek. The air conditioning was slow to dry the mark. I dropped off.

I woke to find a dim lamp on on the table which had John's books on it supported by mahogany butting bison. The lamp was austerely shaded with a parchment cylinder on which the letters j o h n were disposed in arbitrary order and in various sizes. Hortense sat by the bedside in a cerise dressing gown, smoking a cigarette and looking at me. "Oh Christ," I said, "you've taken it off."

"You said you wanted to see it." Smoke curled about the flat shut emptiness and the scars and then was sucked into the conditioning unit. She wore no wig: her graying honey-colored hair was still short after the premedical shearing. The deformity was clear but in shadow. She put her head nearer the lamp. "Horrible, isn't it?" She sat on the edge of the bed. "Go on, take a good look." Overcome with pity and love I raised myself and kissed it. I put my arms about her and she suffered the embrace stiffly. I kept my lips pressed to the untenanted hollow; there was no flutter of eyelashes.

"Lie down with me," I said, "just for a little while." I spoke to the butchered and mended cheek. "Lie down. With my arms round you."

"What is this?" She was amused but spoke acutely. "Are you trying to make yourself normal? Through a different kind of abnormality? Dot would be very shocked."

"Quotha," I said, "since the context could be taken as Jacobean. Give me one of your cigarettes." The mood of tenderness was not really broken. She gave me an English Player from the crushed pack in her dressing-gown pocket; she even lighted it for me with a plain worn Zippo.

"What are you talking about?"

"Oh, my mind went back to Monte Carlo and the twenties and the great impotent sex man Havelock Ellis. He said something about the origins of homosexuality. And then talked at the next table in the Hôtel de Paris about that incest play by John Ford. Jacobean. Do you remember the occasion? It was when your marriage was arranged."

"I don't remember."

"Not a thing you might want to. I was worried about my homosexuality then. We all want to be like the rest of the world. And then there was the Church and poor Mother. And then I discovered what I thought was a mode of transcendence. In Malaya. Carlo said I was being drawn to the love of Christ. A family of saints. I've no doubt that Tom's a saint. Carlo believes you're an angel."

"How is it we can never talk about anything without bringing bloody Carlo into it?"

"Why do you hate him?"

"He means harm."

"As a prince of the Church and loud-voiced bearer of its multifarious messages? Lie down here beside me. When I was fifteen and you were six you used to."

"I was innocent then."

"And now both your eyes are open. Oh Christ, what a stupid, what an unutterably inept and brutal—"

"All right all right all right. Dot said something yesterday about me keeping my eyes skinned for something. She didn't even notice. Carlo means harm, I tell you. Carlo stands for innocence. He'd put a six-year-old kid in bed with a sex maniac and swear that sex mania didn't exist. Nobody can afford to be innocent any more. His Church isn't mine."

"What is your Church?"

"A thing that explains why we have to suffer. There's no such thing as a Jesus Christ triumphant. Christ didn't rise from the dead."

"That means you're not a Christian. Rising from the dead is the whole bedrock. It strikes me you've been reading something. Or talking to somebody."

"Dot. Dot's father was a preacher. In Georgia somewhere. One of the old Bible thumpers. He thumped the Bible into Dot. And into her kid brother Ralph so that it nearly drove him crazy. Dot's come through pretty sensible about religion. Very skeptical about pie in the sky. She agrees with me. Or I agree with her I guess, suppose. It's all about suffering."

"Dorothy doesn't seem to me to be a great sufferer." And then I saw that I was wrong. "No, she suffers about you."

"I'll give up the drink, I will, really. It's just the aftermath." Dorothy's word to me. "She suffers about other things. Who the hell can help suffering these days? And it's hardly begun, the suffering. The Germans tried to wipe out a whole race. And now we've found a quicker way of doing it than gas ovens. Who's the enemy? There's no enemy except the big bad father you can't get back at. Christ was his son all right. You can tell that by the way he treated him. The Promised Land across the Jordan. Dot's father, who faced up to the nightriders, believed in that even more when they'd got the whip to him. If we suffer enough here we'll kindly be allowed to sleep. Christ at least wrung that out of the father."

"You're not making much sense, dearest."

"More sense than Carlo. It's a horrible thing to be flung into the hands of the living God. Or words to that effect. Carlo shakes God by the hand. The innocence of a child trying to stroke a tiger. I bet I believe more than Carlo does in what happens at the altar. I get Christ all right, moaning in my mouth but saying it's all right I'm with you. The inventor of love."

"Does Dorothy go to mass with you?"

"Oh no, the Church of Rome is still the Whore of Babylon to her. She's Baptist way deep down. Suffering and love. The big solace you've always got to be scared of losing. We have that, I think. I'd better get back to her. She puts her hand out in her sleep and if I'm not there she wakes up and cries. She thinks this time I've gone for good. But then I'm back and everything's all right again. Believe it or not, I got up to take some Alka-Seltzer. Drink gives me heartburn. And then I felt remorse and came in to see my brother. After all, he had what looked like a heart attack during dinner and I just sat there swigging."

"Do you sleep without that thing on?"

"Yes. Dot kisses it better too. It doesn't put *her* off either. Wasn't there some saint who went round licking sores?" And then, "You love who you want and how you want. God's the big biology professor. Christ just taught love." And then, "Are you tied up with anyone at the moment?"

"Alone on a wide wide sea."

"I wish you'd do something about Ralph. You know, Dot's brother. He's only a kid, product of aging loins, quotha forsooth. Like John the Baptist. Brought up Baptist like Dot, Bible for every meal, not that they had many meals. About twenty-five. He reads. He tries to write. He wants to be the big black T. S. Eliot but he has no talent. He's not so stupid as to say that that's all the fault of the white oppressor. He'd make an acceptable companion-type secretary. He'd love to travel."

"Does he talk much about white oppressors?"

"A question of which is the real oppressed minority. His friends in adversity have been black, brown, white, yellow, heliotrope for all I know. The cops say you fucking fag before they say you fucking nigger. You see what I mean."

"Where is he now?"

"He's just stopped trying to run what he calls a minority theater in Brownsville. That's in Brooklyn, the filthy pestridden asshole of the borough as they call it. There's a derelict store he tried to fit up as a playhouse. Not much of an audience to see plays about black and brown and heliotrope and fag suffering. It's gin they want. Some of them even want jobs. Now Ralph's holed up with a friend somewhere in a tenement trying to write a kind of fag *Waste Land*. He's all right. We give him a big dinner on Sundays."

"I'll think about it. If he has any of Dorothy's qualities he has to be all right."

"Dot got a cab and brought your bags over. She unpacked them quiet as a little mouse. The things are in that wardrobe there. Your shaving stuff's all laid out in the bathroom. Dot is like that."

"I'd love to stay."

"Come back to us when you've finished this stupid job in Hollywood."

"You mean that?"

"And find out how Domenico's getting on with his fourth or fifth wife. Woman's curiosity. Oh, I know I bitch at people but it's only a façade. I don't really blame anybody for anything. All the blame of the world lies in one place."

"So none of us are free?"

"Sister Gertrude at school used to quote *Die Meistersinger* at us. You know, Hans Sachs: *Wir sind ein wenig frei.* A little bit free. I'm free now to go back to bed and find Dot there. But I wouldn't put it past the great eternal swine to whisk her out of it and make her dissolve into thin air." She bent and gave me a full kiss on the lips. Then she left. I couldn't sleep. It was getting on for dawn. I found a volume by Anatole France among John's few books. It had on the flyleaf the name Dorothy Alethea Pembroke—aristocratic, as all slave names had to be. The story was the one about Saint Nicholas and his resurrection of the three young clerks from the innkeeper's pickling tub. He adopted them and brought them up holily but they all behaved in a most villainous manner. One of them even denounced him to the Vatican for all kinds of fictitious sins. Saint Nicholas acknowledged God's greatness but found it hard to believe in his goodness. Jesus Christ, of course, was a very different proposition.

It was a year or so before Ralph Pembroke came into my service, or I into his or we into ours. When I say now that I remember well lying in bed with him one Sunday morning in our suite in the Beverly Wilshire Hotel, I am pricked with an immediate doubt as to whether this was near the beginning or the end of our relationship. Like all, or the few, relationships I had in middle and old age with younger men who were nominally, or not so, engaged as secretaries, there was the whiff of breakup even in the early and ardent enthusiasms. I see myself as a bronzed man in his sixties, pared, fit, but not unravaged. The sexual impulse, as my coevals will know, does not die with age: it becomes merely intermittent, abating little of its pristine ferocity on the occasions of its resurgence. It needs, however, to be stimulated by youth and beauty, and this implies a certain one-sidedness of passion, for what youth and beauty, except in instances of geronto-phile perversion, is reciprocally stimulated by wrinkles and gray hairs? True, as I moved toward my final infirmities it was companionship I needed more than sex, but it was not, as in marriage, the companionship of one of my own generation. I wanted companionship with the connotations of amorous excite-ment, meaning the electricity of touch, of entwining, of verbal endearment, the reassurance in the night of a body, so long as it was youthful and comely, breathing next to mine. I was grateful for the added gift of intelligence made piquant by a comparative lack of worldly experience. Let me say that, this May California morning, the end of the relationship was closer than its beginning, but let me record words more appropriate to the beginning than the end. I wore my heliotrope pajamas while Ralph lay naked. He was beautiful as only one of his race can be, especially when nurtured on the benefits of American civiliza-tion, but the serenity of those relaxed muscles and the sumptuous sheen of his exquisite skin found no correspondence in a visage that had acquired a white man's discontentedness, the brow often corrugated, the mouth peevish, the eyes shifty, unstill, unhappy. As now.

I said, "I refuse, dearest Ralph, to say the thing that is not." This was a Swiftian trope we shared. Ralph loved horses, seeing in them a nobility which he believed to attach to his own people in their native habitat. I had, some years before at a riding school near Sitges, enjoyed watching him acquire equestrian proficiency. He and the horse became one, were centaurized to a degree I had never previously seen even in crack show jumpers. He called horses Hou-yhnhnms and spoke to them in snorts and whinnies. He had, in this time we had been spending in Hollywood, with myself working on the scenario of an ani-mated cartoon version of H. G. Wells's *The Food of the Gods* for Max Fleischer, been able to employ his riding talents in a Western. He stood in for the leader of an avenging posse, though, because of his implausible blackness, only in very long shots. The Houyhnhnms, you will recall, have no word for *lie*.

"It's what it's about that's important," Ralph said. "Okay, so what if it does limp and the rhythms are cockeyed and it's what you say, derivative?" The vibrancy of his speech was transmitted as a bodily sensation across the bed, probably by virtue of the mattress springs. His speech was as thrilling as his sister's singing. Educated black speech is probably the finest sound of all North America.

"No, dearest Ralph, no and again no. If you want to write a pamphlet, of a severely polemical nature, do so. Tell the world of the sufferings of the American Negro, but don't try to turn it into art. Because you can't do it, you know."

"We don't like this word Negro. We prefer the word black."

"Who's we?"

"Blacks."

"Meaning the descendants of West Coast African slaves now full citizens of these United States but powerfully aware of continuing wrongs. There are, you know, other black people." I saw an instant the smile of the purpleskinned magician and shuddered. "The bloody Tamils, for instance. All I'm saying, dear Ralph, about your poem I mean, is that, attempting to be both art and propaganda, it fails to be either. And I doubt whether it's possible to express sectional sentiments through the poetic art. I mean, Othello's color doesn't really matter. It's the jealousy that counts. In a high school in Malaya I saw a very interesting adaptation of *Othello*. There was only one white boy in the school, so they turned him into a jealous Irish police officer called O'Tallow. Ee Ah Goh was Chinese, Desdemona was Tamil, black as the ace of spades, and Michael Cassio was Eurasian. It worked."

"Ah shit," Ralph said. "I think it's pretty good. I'll send it to *Wakati*." (*Wakati*—its name the Swahili for *Time*—was a literally black magazine, the type white on it as in a photographic negative, part-financed by the Time-Life organization.)

"I don't doubt they'll publish it," I said, "but that won't make it good. Another thing. Your newfound black militancy—is it replacing your former militancy on behalf of the sexual tropism you and I both represent, or are you looking for a way of combining two very distinct social grievances? I mean, supposing the blacks ran the United States of America instead of the pinkos, would the situation of a white homosexual automatically improve?"

"Minorities," Ralph said frowning, "speak to each other."

"Well, you ought to be looking for poetic symbols to express that constatation, oughtn't you? Not that you could. You know that. I'm going to get up and ring for breakfast and then bathe. What will you take for breakfast? Something *black*, like hominy grits and chitterlings and watermelon?"

"It's pronounced chitlins. I've been corrupted by white culture. I want a steak, medium rare, and two eggs fried sunny side up. Listen, this *has* to be good:

> '*I sat in the bleachers, among the bleached*
> *And watched them bitterly at their game,*
> *And in warning the black cloud reached*
> *Its hand out to cover the sun. But all eyes*
> *were on the*

Smitten balls, black balls, black heads,
Not seeing that the game would stop in black rain
And there'd be no raincheck, no, not ever again.'"

"No, Ralph my love," I said, "no, no."

"And who the Christ Jesus are you to say no?" He was out of bed now, naked except for his Longines wristwatch and the typescript he waved at me. The beauty was all in himself, he would never create beauty: God, or something, never gave it you both ways. "You've never written one thing in your whole damned life that had any pretension to being art."

"Pretension is right. I've never had pretensions. But I know art when I see it. I cry with self-pity when I see real art. I'm not crying now."

"You bastard. You *white* bastard."

"Ah, white now, am I? Watch that, Ralph. You'll end up saying that only blacks have any real moral and political and spiritual and aesthetic values. That's only the Nazi philosophy in blackface."

"Look at yourself," he sneered, as I took my pajamas off. This, of course, may have been somewhere else and on another occasion. "Little pink prick and shrunk shanks and potbelly. And you talk about aesthetic values."

"Blueish prick," I corrected. "Purplish. Little, I grant you. And the rest of the attributes, dry fruits of senescence. Well, the potbelly—shall we say not so ripe as many? Not by any means a record of Falstaffian self-indulgence. It comes to all of us. Albert Einstein had one, you know. I saw it when I visited him at Princeton." I find it hard to believe that I just stood there naked chattering, suffering the sneer of this polished beautiful boy. A lot of the past is incredible. "I leave it to you," I said, "to order breakfast. Dry toast for me and Oxford marmalade. Orange juice and coffee." And I went to take my bath.

Ralph and I were at this time more or less domiciled in Barcelona, in a sizable apartment not far from the Barrio Gótico. Why Spain, or rather Catalonia, which is not quite Spain? Because mild fascism semed to be at the time to be better than confiscatory socialism. Because of the architecture of Gaudí and the cuisine of Los Caracoles. Ralph, at first muttered and even spat at because he was taken for a Moor, liked it well enough when he was recognized as primarily an American. He learned Catalan with the relish he was later to give to the East African dialect called Oma. The truth is though that we were out of Catalonia more than we were in it. I was called to towns like Helsinki and Stockholm and Rio de Janeiro for literary conferences that had more of politics in them than literature.

I was yielding to the temptation of being the Writer as International Figure, meaning one who talked more than he wrote. I was feeding off my prewar literary fat; there was no great urgency about producing new books and plays. There was the medium of television available for the easy projection of inchoate ideas and a pretty well fully formed persona. My persona was mildly liked by television audiences. Its features were recognizable and caricaturable—the cigarette in its Dunhill holder wielded as gracefully as a Queen Anne fan, the Savile Row suitings whose conservative elegance was contradicted by open-necked silk shirts from Kuala Lumpur or by cream polo sweaters, the sharp ravaged profile which the cameras loved, the slight lisp, the dogmatic pronouncements on the mores of the postwar world, the occasional assumed ferocity. French television knew me as well as anglophone. I could modify the deliberately prissy British image with handweaving and patois. Soon the Germans would see me on their screens and hear me barking.

There was also plenty of work for me in Hollywood. *The Food of the Gods* was never to achieve filmhood, nor was the projected musical on Shakespeare's life called *Will!*, nor the colossal *Middlemarch*, nor several other conceptions in which I was involved, but I was paid, overpaid, and accommodated with my secretary companion in Regency suites with uncountable telephones. I had, this Sunday morning in the Beverly Wilshire, the satisfaction of knowing that my work on *The Food of the Gods* was virtually finished. It had been amusing to think in cartoon images, very Victorian British, and reduce Wells's dialogue to a few whatwhats. The following day, Monday, I was to fly away from Los Angeles to deliver a lecture at a college in Indiana while the rewrite men gnawed and worried my final script. At this college, named for its founder Oswald Wisbech, my nephew John Campion was a professor in the growing department of anthropology.

"I'm off," Ralph said when he had finished his steak and fried eggs and quart of coffee. I sat in my lime and gold dressing gown, smoking and looking amiably at him. He was dressed in a gray suit of a vaguely military cut, tan Gucci loafers, an indigo silk shirt buttoned to the neck and embellished with a silver hand of Fatma dangling on a silver chain. I paid him a salary which he hardly earned, I dressed him, protected him, gave him my affection.

I said, "There are a great number of letters to look at. When you come back late tonight from your session with Nat Fergana Junior and his friends you will be too tired to look at them. Tomorrow and the next day I shall not be here to urge you to work. I make no complaint. I merely point out that there is a lot of work to do."

"Yeth, there thyure ith," Ralph mocked. "But even slaveth were entitled to Thunday off."

"Another thing, and please don't think that this is in any way an accusation. What I mean is, I'm not accusing you. Perhaps I'm merely accusing my own absentmindedness or perhaps initial stupidity in being so careless. You're always telling me not to carry so much cash, but I can't help it. I was born in an era in which cash was carried and used for payment on the nail."

"Oh come on, Ken, what is it?" And he looked frowning at his Longines.

"I had a thousand dollars in what are known as C notes. They were in the inside pocket of the jacket of my fawn suit. I checked after my bath and they're no longer there. It's no good complaining to the management, they have a written notice about the danger of keeping valuables in one's room. And if I accuse the Mexican hotel staff I'll wake up with a knife in my guts. I'm just hoping that you took the money for my own protection or to teach me a lesson or something benevolent of that sort. I can afford to lose the money, I suppose. But I do hate being robbed. Tell me I haven't been robbed."

"You've been robbed all right old boy old boy. I don't have your thousand bucks. You know that. You are generous to what they call a fault and I don't have to go picking in the dark. But I'm sorry you said that. It sets up something between us not very nice."

"I just wanted to know, Ralph, that's all. Let's take it that I've now learned a valuable lesson about being careless with cash and in future I'll use checks or credit cards or something. There will be Mexican faces grinning out at me from rooms being serviced each time I pass along the corridor, but no matter. We shan't be here much longer anyway."

"Oh no, not so simple." He did not lisp it. "There'll be some corner of your little mind in which little scenes will be enacted. You know, nasty black Ralph needing a lump bigger than usual for the paying of blackmail or gambling debts or helping some little boy in dire need he meets at Nat Fergana's establishment. And a little corner of my little mind in which you are seated as before a little stage watching some such little enactment. I guess this sort of thing had to happen."

"Ralph, dear, this is not so. I've forgotten the matter already. I'm being absurdly overpaid by the studio and can well afford to lose a thousand dollars to some indigent Mexican family or other. Please forget that I spoke."

"Aw, you had to speak. It'd come out sooner or later. Have you had a good look, you know, in other pockets, under the carpet, under the mattress? You're welcome to search in my bedroom. You're welcome to search me here and now. I don't have your thousand bucks. And now I can see you wishing that my big black face would crack into a big toothy smile and me pull the cash out and say, Let this be a lesson old buddy and don't put temptation in the way of the poor and unscrupulous. But that ain't gonna happen nohow, no sir, massah. Can I go now?"

"What precisely," I said, "do you do at the house of Nat Fergana Junior? Does he dance for you or show you his old movies? Or is it good solid black *agape?*"

"Not *agape*," Ralph said. "You look *agupe* up in your dictionary sometime. Fun and games, old chap, nothing spiritual. But black, yes, aaaaall black. Spend a little time looking for that lost grand while I'm gone. And a fine black fart in the face of Nick Campanati." Who was coming to lunch with me. The telephone rang, meaning all the telephones. I was nearer to the nearest and answered. It was a young woman with some such name as Randy Reinhart, one of the staff of the book section of the *Los Angeles Times*, surprisingly at work, or at least thinking of work, on a Californian Sunday. She wanted an interview. Not today, natch, but sometime in the week. I was vague, watching Ralph leave with big gestures of servitude, putting out wrists joined as though manacled. Thursday, cocktail time, here? That would be just fine. Ralph went from our huge drawing room into the vestibule that abutted on my bedroom and then seemed all of twenty seconds getting from the vestibule into the corridor, door shutting over-audibly, then off.

It was as I had thought it might possibly be. I found the bundle of hundred dollar bills bound with elastic on the dark floor of the clothes closet of my bedroom. I also heard my toilet cistern filling up. I could pin nothing on Ralph. Ralph was not like Heinz. I had met Heinz again a few years back working in a bar on the seafront of the little resort of Sitges. It was a bar run by an English-man named Bill Gay, and it was called the SS, initials standing if need be for Sweet Sixteen or Stars and Stripes or whatever Gay's casual fancy suggested on enquiry. Gay had been an intelligence agent tortured, like the White Rabbit, by the Paris Gestapo. The swastika brassards and steel truncheons which dec-orated his bar had to be seen as trophies rather than symbols of perversion. One day while I and Ralph were there a drunken British customer shouted "Come here, Gay," and Gay replied campily, "*Ich habe ein Handel zu mein Name*, have I got it right, Heinz ducky?" And then a blond young man, excessively bronzed, turned from the dart board where he had just said to a player "That were a bloody good un, Alf," and revealed himself as Heinz. He had been put to farm work in the North of England and now spoke fluent dialectal English. He and Ralph, I saw with a pang later, made a lovely pair. Kidlings bright and merry. Heinz seemed to have got over his racism. Ralph's was yet to begin.

Nick, or Domenico, was sixty or so now and looked it. He was jowly and paunched and was still Italian enough not to give a damn. No cottage cheese and lettuce for him. From room service I ordered spaghetti and meatballs with a large steak to follow, pêche Melba to follow that, a bottle of Valpolicella to wash all down. That was for Domenico. I had cottage cheese and lettuce. We sipped very dry martinis while waiting for our food. Domenico unrolled a magazine which he had been tapping on the glass-topped table like an irritable baton. "You see this?" he said. I took it. It was a copy of *Life* with a portrait of Carlo Campanati on the cover. He was got up as a cardinal and, his big back to the Duomo of Milan, he sardonically blessed the prospective reader. The legend was MIRACLES IN MILAN. This, I knew, did not refer to real miracles of that Chicago hospital order: it signified that Carlo was demonstrating the relevance of Christianity to truculent Milanese factory operatives. He had had much to do with the settling of strikes. The Church, he said, despite the evidence of past history, had been founded for the workers not the bosses. He had filled the Duomo with workers and taught them the Catholic message of Marxism.

I said, "I'll get a copy in the shop downstairs."

"Keep that, keep that, keep that. I don't want the goddam thing."

"You're still bitter, Domenico. You still remember that arrested orgasm. You must have had many unarrested since to make up for it."

"I've done with women. You know Sindy's gone off with that Mexican bastard?"

Sindy was Cynthia, née Forkner, a starlet from North Carolina and Domenico's third wife. Perhaps she wanted children. "No, I didn't know. Should I say I'm sorry?"

"The time's come," Domenico said, "for the parting of lots of ways. I've finished with Hollywood. I've finished with shoveling auditory shit on sound tracks. I want to write real music again." That *again* was not perhaps appropriate.

I said, "You got an Oscar for that Dostoevsky film. You produce some of the best film music in the business. What do you want to do? A symphony?"

"No. An opera, what else? Milan's got fucking Carlo. It's time Milan got me. And you do the libretto."

I said nothing for the moment. I opened the door to the Latvian waiter, who wheeled in a table and a load of covered dishes. I said nothing while he laid it all out and brought chairs up to the board. I signed the bill and gave the waiter two dollars. "Enzhoy your launch, genlmen," he said and shambled out. Domenico at once began fiercely to tuck in. A dew of concentration appeared on his brown bald dome. "I did a libretto before," I said, picking with my fork, "and it turned out to be a great waste of my time. I take it you have in mind some big *opera seria*, three acts, the works. Something of archiepiscopal magisteriality."

"That was a gamble, we were both young then, now it'll be a sure thing. I saw Giulio Orecchia in New York at the Met six, seven weeks ago. He said yes and again yes, start yesterday. So what ideas do you have, I want a libretto by early fall at the latest."

"In New York did you pay any family visits? See your growing grandchild, for instance?" A granddaughter called Eve, a pretty blond romp who called me tunkie for great-uncle.

"Look, Ken, I married into three families and I kept away from them all. That's the only way to be."

"This family's somewhat different, Domenico. It's your first. The Church would say it's your only. So you didn't visit Hortense?"

"I didn't visit Hortense. I'm sorry about what happened to Hortense, but I didn't visit her. It's all over."

"She still calls herself Mrs. Campanati. It's under that name that she's finishing her own magisterial work of art for Milan. It was good of Carlo to fix the commission. She needed it, it stopped her moping."

"What is this?" Domenico glared in fear and suspicion. His lips, indifferent, sucked in spaghetti ends. "What's been going on?"

"It's a basso-relievo representing the career of Saint Ambrose, patron saint of Milan and Carlo's distinguished ancestor in office. She's working on it in a new big studio in the Village and it promises to be very impressive. You see the infant Ambrose with bees swarming round his lips, you see him as bishop excommunicating the emperor Theodosius, you see him trouncing the Arians. Ambrose, a great naked muscular figure—"

"Naked?"

"More or less naked. I seem to remember a miter and a crosier as well as muscular nudity. It looks like being the best thing she's ever done. The name Campanati is going to be a great name in Milan. A great archbishop, a great sculptress, and then you. If you can do it."

"It's my name before it's theirs. Christ, what are they all trying to do to me? When's this thing going to be ready? This damned blasphemous thing of that *puttana* who called herself my wife?"

"How do you know it's blasphemous? And why should you, expert in serial polygamy, take up any moral attitude?"

"She's living with this black bitch, isn't she? When's it supposed to be ready?"

"The dedication's fixed for Saint Ambrose's feast day the year after next. December seven, I seem to remember, the day after the feast of Saint Nicholas. The thing has to be shipped and installed. Good God," I added, for I had just thought of the subject for a libretto. "What absurd idea do you have in mind, Domenico? Do you propose trying to get in before your former wife, still your wife incidentally but let that pass, bursting in a blaze of music at the Scala while Saint Ambrose is still on the high seas pointing toward Genoa? You know how long it takes to set up an opera."

"There are shortcuts. I'm taking back this boy Vern Clapp with me—"

"Who?"

"Vern Clapp."

"Is that a real name?"

"Vern stands for Vernon. He can help with the orchestration." Domenico was now on the pêche Melba, spooning it in rapidly, time being awasting.

"Taking back, you say. You're leaving America?"

"Sure I'm leaving America. I've had out of America everything that America could give me, mainly money. I'm going to Menton or Nice or some place, work in peace. Now how's about that libretto?"

"Saint Nicholas," I said.

He stared at me for several seconds, chewing. "You mean an opera about a saint? You don't have operas about saints. Saints are for oratorios. Like Mendelssohn and Handel and all that shit." He swallowed a lump of ice cream as though it were something warm and sour. I explained. He listened.

"You see," I said, "you could have the legend of the resurrection of the three young men in a pickle barrel done as a kind of highly stylized prologue. And then realism for the real story. The first of the adopted sons tries to turn Nicholas's house into a brothel, and Nicholas yields to the temptations of the flesh. After that, of course, he flagellates himself and gets himself holy and ready for the Council of Nicaea in order to denounce the Arian heresy."

"Oh Jesus."

"Jesus, Father and Holy Ghost to be exact. The denial of the doctrine of the Trinity. Arius said the Son wasn't coeternal with the Father."

"You can't put that in an opera. Where did you get all this crap anyway?"

"The basic idea's in a story by Anatole France. The second adopted son forges documents to prove that Nicholas is a bigger heretic than Arius, and the act ends with a big choral denunciation. Nicholas begins the third act in sackcloth and ashes, you know, in enforced repentance. He gets his bishopric back, but the third adopted son has become a military leader and is going to slaughter women and children in the name of God. The enemy are the Arians and Nicholas is supposed to be all for exterminating them, but at the end the ravaged corpse of a child is brought in. With the child in his arms he raises his eyes to the invisible God and says: What is all this about? What's going on? Why did you let me bring these bastards back to life if you knew what they were going to do? And then curtain. Or, to be on the safe side, an epilogue, stylized like the prologue, in which God says, one could do this in the manner of Blake's Book of Job illustrations, all this was the temptation appropriate to a man destined to be a saint, and Nicholas came through without cursing God and he's passed the test. Apotheosis."

"What's that word?"

"He goes up to heaven. This is only a rough outline, naturally. What do you think?"

Domenico poured both of us coffee from the big pewter pot and leaned back in his chair the better to caress his belly. I could tell he was thinking musically, in terms of sonic lumps rather than plot and psychology and the boring realities you left to the mere wordman. "No big soprano part," he pronounced.

"But a bloody big tenor one."

"Too many men all round."

"You've got whores and wailing mothers. Angels too if you like."

"Why can't one of those three be a woman? She's been disguised as a man and the other two could be monks running away from a monastery and taking her with them running away from a convent. Nicholas only discovers this in the first act after the prologue thing. She could be a real bitch. She could even be a black bitch."

"You have the heart of the matter in you, Domenico. What do you say, then?"

"Try it. Get me a draft done."

"Who pays?"

"Ah Jesus. You know all about show business. It's the public pays. Not too many words, remember. Numbers. Solos, quartets, choruses. Get down to it now."

"*You* can get down to the prologue now. No words. Like a little ballet suite. You could have that played in the Hollywood Bowl in a week or so. Cool and pre-Raphaelite like early Debussy. I can hear it." Domenico wiped his mouth and then face and finally head with his napkin. He got up as though really ready to start.

He said, "What do we call it?"

"*The Miracle of the Holy Saint Nicholas.*"

"That sounds like what they're not going to get."

"It's meant to be ironic."

"Get started, Ken. Thanks for the lunch."

"Thank my employers."

That afternoon I read the long article on Carlo in *Life*. It was written by somebody who sounded like a *mafioso*, Turiddu Genovese, and it was full of the quoted Wit and Wisdom of the Archbishop of Milan. I had a feeling that Carlo would not now, to use his own expression, make Pope. *Life* was making him into a world personality before his status warranted it; after all, he was only a provincial prelate. He would be dead as news when the next papal election arrived; his newsworthiness was being spent, in terms of that, most prematurely. Nor would his fellow cardinals much care for this stellar elevation. If he was being celebrated in *Life*, *Stern* and *Paris-Match* and *Hoshi* and *Kochav* must also be ready to put that fat ugly blessing mug on their covers, if they had not done so already. Although the early part of the article made much of the part Carlo had played in 1929 when the Vatican had been turned into a great instrument of capitalism, the living capitalists of Turin and Milan would not be taking kindly to his siding with the workers in industrial disputes. Here was Carlo on Carlo Marx:

"Most people who call themselves Marxists have never read the works of that remarkable reformer. I have devoted much time to his books in the original German and find none of that atheistical materialism which has so stupidly been lauded. Marx has been misrepresented by the political leaders of the Soviet Union, especially Josef Stalin. Here was a man who, taking his wife and children home to Soho after a picnic on Hampstead Heath, would recite canto after canto of the divine Dante, finding in him the ultimate truth which feeds men's souls, while economic reforms and social revolutions merely benefit their bodies. Marx knew that man does not live by bread alone.

"Marx wished the generality of mankind, the workers not the capitalists, to find moral power and be given social justice. This has always been the aspiration of the Church of Christ, which teaches that a camel can get through, et cetera, et cetera. Marx taught the dynamic principle of social change, the long and necessary struggle to improve the physical lot of the people and grant them the leisure to contemplate things higher than mere subsistence. The Church teaches the slow working of God's grace like yeast in the heavy dough of a human history that has been mostly hard to swallow. More than anything, Marx emphasized the essential decency of man, a decency too often obscured by the wretched condition of the need to survive imposed by capitalism. The Church tell us that man is God's creation, and hence perfect, and his imperfections are the work of God's enemy. As for the classless society, I see it as an analogue of the communion of saints. Russia blasphemes by assuming that she is the Church Triumphant. We move slowly toward triumph, but it is not given to mortal man to attain it."

The apothegms attributed to Carlo were specious. *Reader's Digest* stuff. He said: "Christ considered alcohol as necessary as bread. He turned himself into both, and still does" and "Whisky and God have much in common—both are spirits" and "The sexual act is fulfilled in a nine months' miracle, not in a two-second shudder and sneeze" and (of Italian film goddesses) "God made the female bosom. He also made the sun in the sky. We must look at both with our eyes closed" and "Hollywood and Belsen alike proclaim the cheapness of human flesh" (surely I had said that?) and "A man needs a good meal before he listens to a bad sermon" and "The simple life is all too simple. There is no loss of breath in going downstairs" and "A good meal is God the Father. A good wine is God the Son. A good cigar is the Holy Ghost. At mealtimes, as at all times, I believe in the Holy Trinity" and "There are people who see red when they look at me. I was destined to be a cardinal" and "Good and evil have their own smells. Good smells of a child's body. Evil smells of his napkins" and "Evil comes of inattention more than intention. The Germans shut their eyes for an instant and Hitler streaked in" and "Man's Fall was followed by Man's Winter. It has been a long one. But I think it must now be about the beginning of March" and "The first duty of a government is not to govern but to exist. The same may be said of the amoeba" and "We need priests, alas. We need garbage men, alas. Both are consequences of the Fall" and "People ask why the Redeemer was born in Palestine in the reign of Augustus Caesar. If he were born in Wisconsin in the reign of President Truman they would still ask why. I ask, why not?" and "A Jew is only a Christian without Christ" and so on, these poor little epigrams being set in boxes at intervals throughout the article.

There was a paragraph about Carlo's family—the mother who had died trying to shoot Himmler (no reference to my shameful part in that event), the brother killed by Chicago gangsters, the brother who was an Oscar-winning Hollywood composer and, as a limp afterthought, the mother superior sister. Too much glamour altogether. Then Carlo's practical charity: three-quarters of the archiepiscopal palace housing the homeless. None of this would do; this was jumping the gun. It was as though, impossible of course, Carlo were employing a press agent. The fact was that something new was happening in the Church, and the new is the essence of news. I did not know the word at the time, but the word was *aggiornamento*.

I went to bed early after a steak and a bad bottle of Cold Duck. Ralph came back very late and shook me awake with black anger. He seemed to me to smell of a variety of other men's semina as well as of the smoke of some sweet herb. "You bastard," he cried, and then, by an easy transition, "you bastards. You deprived us of a history. You realize that, man? We got no goddam history." His speech had been much coarsened by contact with his Sunday friends, including the great black singer and dancer Nat Fergana, Jr. "You fuckers took every goddam thing away, including our goddam fucking history. Slaves don't have a history, did you think of that, you bastard?"

"Ralph," I said tiredly, "I refuse to take the blame for the wrongs perpetrated by a few Anglo-Saxon slave owners. The men you should blame are resting at peace in expensive graves. Now let me too rest in peace. Get into bed and sleep."

"I sleep in my own bed tonight, you bastard white fucker. The sight of your white skin makes me want to fucking throw up."

"Do as you please, dearest Ralph, but please remember I have a very early plane to catch tomorrow. And," I added, "do something about that unanswered mail, will you? I've scribbled rough replies. All you have to do is expand them, using cold correct English."

"Fucking English. You even robbed us of our own fucking language. I'll answer the letters when I feel like doing it, you ofay pig, and I'll tell them all to fuck off."

"Thank you, by the way, for returning the thousand, ah, bucks. It was a decent if surreptitious gesture."

He danced, but not with the toothy goodwill of Nat Fergana, Jr. "Bastard bastard bastard. I never touched your fucking money, you stinking white fucker. You listen to me, pinko, I'm getting out of here, I've had a bellyful, you answer your own fucking mail."

"You mean you wish to terminate your employment?"

"Haw haw haw old top and all that sort of rot, that's just what I fucking want to do and will do, you effete decadent etiolated moribund sonofabitching white bastard."

I had had this sort of sincere abuse and insincere rebellion from Ralph before and would have it again. Wearily I told him to get into bed and not be a fool, but, after hurling my hairbrushes at the air-conditioning unit, asperging the carpet with my hair lotion, and pulling the sheets off me recumbent, he stamped out yelling. I could hear a lamp in the sitting room go over. Then whatever he had to cry from his own room was too far away to be audible.

The petulant boy who had objected to making love in the faint redolence of bully and onions in Baron's Court had turned into a kind of Walt Whitman, all uncontrolled gray hair and beard. He sat in the front row of the Agnes Watson Auditorium and said, as I came in at the side door with Professor Korzeniowski, "Hello, old thing" quite in the manner of the First World War. I stared and frowned, pausing in my walk. "Val," he said. "Wrigley. Poet in residence. Get up there and give it us and for God's sake don't be a bore."

As Jesus Christ had to be born somewhere, so Val Wrigley had to live somewhere, and why not then on the campus of Wisbech College, Indiana? Still, it was a surprise. "I haven't forgotten," I said. "Bloody treachery."

"Oh, go on, get up there."

So I got up there and waited with Professor Korzeniowski until the college carillon, mounted high above the Agnes Watson Auditorium, celebrated the hour of four with the bone of "My Country 'Tis of Thee" bobbing in a thick ragout of harmonics. I looked at the five hundred students and faculty. I tend to see the students in memory as jeaned and afroed, but this was the fifties and they were dressed as young ladies and gentlemen. Professor Korzeniowski, a specialist in Spenser, the only man I had ever met who had read *The Faerie Queene* right through, had no apparent qualification for chairing my lecture. He did not, I was to learn, read novels. Of course, like Spenser, I was a British writer. Perhaps Val Wrigley had suggested a fanciful relationship between Spenser's title and my own state. Anyway, bald Korzeniowski with the Middle West accent introduced me as a distinguished British novelist who would talk about what it was like to be a novelist, here he is then, Kenneth Marchal Toomey.

I talked informally about fiction as a trade more than an art. Political engagement? Social engagement? "I remember those expressions coming up in the presence of Ernest Hemingway when I was staying in that run-down house of his set in its own private steamy jungle in Key West. The only engagement an author should think of, he said in his forthright manner, was the engagement of the seat of his pants to the seat of his chair. Thomas Mann, this was in Hollywood, said that a writer was essentially a creature that put down words without being too sure of their meaning. Everything a writer writes is an allegory of something else, and it's the task of critics to argue about what that something else is. Those of you here who aspire to be novelists, do please remember that the mechanics of the craft are more important than angling for ultimate truths or changing the world. If your work changes the world, well, it will not be because of your purposing. As for truth, Pontius Pilate asked a very good question about it, though his choice of time and place were infelicitous. I remember the present Archbishop of Milan saying something to that effect in Chicago, I think it was." I dropped names freely and added bonuses of personal quirks which were intended to remind my auditors that authors were, above all, fallible and imperfect human beings. T. S. Eliot kept pieces of cheese in the drawers of his desk at Faber & Faber's, Russell Square. H. G. Wells was a satyromaniac. James Joyce called a particular white wine archduchess's urine. I talked until the carillon hammered a "Yankee Doodle" sad but encrusted with the brilliants of upper partials jump on five o'clock. Any questions?

"What was it that guy, Poncho somebody, said about truth?" This was a tall girl with frizzed ginger hair somewhere near the front.

"Heavens," I said, "don't you know your New Testament?"

"New what?"

"Never mind. Somebody please tell her." After a pause somebody told her. A youth who looked Melanesian got up to say:

"I disagree with what you said, sir. I mean when you said a writer doesn't know what he's writing. I mean the important writers say important things and they know they're important, if not they wouldn't write them. Like God Manning."

"Like *who?*"

There was amusement and some anger at my ignorance in the middle right segment of the audience. Several young voices repeated the name.

A fat sallow girl in unbecoming violet rose to inform me: "He wrote *Call Me and I'll Answer*. Godfrey Manning. But he's called God for short."

"I see," I said, baffled. "A theologian, I take him to be. He proclaims his subject in his pet name. I'm afraid theology isn't my province."

"The way and the truth are everybody's providence," the girl said. "I haven't read your books, but you seem to me to be what I'd call kind of frivolous."

"Perhaps," I said, smiling with irritation, "that's because I'm *kind of old*. I leave earnestness to the young."

"That," she said, "is a kind of a frivolous thing to say."

"Let us keep to the novel," my chairman justly called. A member of the faculty stood, his glasses flashing in the electric light, and said:

"Have you any information on the ultimate fate of Jakob Strehler?"

"Strehler," I said, "joins the millions of Jewish dead. I saw him led off to imprisonment and, I cannot doubt, eventually the gas chamber. He went off lightheartedly enough. He knew his work was finished. He knew it would outlive the Nazi butchers." A dour glee rose in me. "I attempted to smuggle Strehler out of the Reich. He was reluctant to be so smuggled. Both of us were cut off from the big world of news and terrible enactments and didn't realize the war had started when the forces of the state came to arrest him as a Jew and myself as one of the British enemy. I spoke on the Nazi radio to buy my way out of the Reich. I said nothing unpatriotic. Your poet in residence here, my old friend Valentine Wrigley, publicized in the British press my reasonable act as a treasonable one. I'm glad to have this opportunity of inviting him to take back his harmful and unfriendly abuse." There was a stir in the audience; unexpected, a bonus, the intrusion of scandal. Val just sat grinning through his great gray poet beard, arms crossed on his belly. Without rising he said very clearly:

"I never take things back. Mr. Toomey should have defied the enemy and gladly suffered internment. Mr. Toomey, an old friend or should I say former friend, displayed on that occasion the qualities that have marred equally his life and his craft—I will not say art, nor, to give him due credit, would he. I mean the easy way out, the path of compromise."

"Has," I sneered, realizing too late that I should not have provoked this situation, not here, not in the presence of five hundred strangers, "your career been very different?"

"I," Val said, "have practiced a rigorous art with the minimum of financial gain. I have written what I wanted to write, not what the public wanted. I have stood up against state oppression of minority views and minority practices. I spent an admittedly brief time in prison for being what I am and not what the gods of the norm would have me be. Mr. Toomey has grown prosperous through selling out. One of our students here found the right word—*frivolous*. I would not have said any of these things unless I had been invited expressly by Mr. Toomey to speak. He wanted a retraction. I think I am justified in stating why I find myself unable to retract."

Some of the students applauded. I felt the terrible chill that all speakers know when they find their audience turning against them. I had to hoist the sails of rhetoric. "I have devoted my life," I cried, "to the production of objects designed to please, to enhance life, to allay sorrow. Is it so terrible a thing to wish to entertain? Is it so ghastly a return to see one's works read, loved, deeply loved, as mine have been? I have been the loyal servant of the public. I have given the public for over forty years a measure of diversion, solace, and, may I say, joy. If I recognized that it had not been given to me to reach the more exalted reaches of art, at least I knew where the true excellence lay and I risked much to save the life of one of the most shining exemplars of literary attainment. For this I was reviled, reviled by a comrade and fellow worker in those laborious mines where truth is quarried from language—"

"What is truth?" somebody called, one who from his vocal resonance must have been a member of the faculty. Val stood and cried, and it was strange to me, who had never seen him show evidence of knowledge of the works of Shakespeare, to hear words of Shakespeare from his lips, bearded or otherwise:

"This above all: to thine own self be true." And he rolled out, terrible as a prophet, by way of the aisle, applauded and even cheered.

"We'll go out the back way," Professor Korzeniowski said. And we did, by way of the stage wings. "That finished," he said, "not quite, well, the way we would have wished." I noted the Spenserian music of the semivowels. "Wrigley," he said, as we tripped over electric cables in the neardark of the wings, "is near the end of his year with us. Having no interest in tenure he feels free to shock. He has shocked and will shock more before he goes. The sequence of poems he is writing and reads aloud to his creative writing class. Shocking. Just now he was shocking. Of course, he is popular with the students. Popularity is a siren singing on a rock. It is never a thing to be aimed for, not in my opinion." And then, as we came into sunlight by way of a door, he looked many things at me: confused, apologetic, embarrassed, reproachful. I had claimed to be popular and now that was my sin. It was Val, the unpopular, who was popular. Professor Korzeniowski had been dragged from the Bower of Bliss to preside over my unpopularity. He had better get rid of me. "You will find your nephew," he said, and pointed, "in the Wilmore Wertmueller Building. He is not unpopular." Beyond the little congeries of low blocks that made up the college the endless flat Indiana landskip basked. There was a faint smell of tomato ketchup on the mild May wind. A tomato processing factory stood a mile off.

A misshapen lad with glasses and an eager open mouth limped up to us.

Under his arm he had Sapir and Bloomfield, others. "Pardon me, sir," he said, "I was interested in the common possession of a species of sigmatismus demonstrated by yourself and by Professor Wrigley. You said *thorrow* and he said *thine own thelf*. Is this typical of British educated speech?"

"Sod off," I said with a clear sibilance. He did not understand the expression. I relented. "Read Professor Sodoff on the phenomenon." He thanked me.

John, Professor John Campion, was lecturing to a small group on what I took to be some aspects of linguistic anthropology or anthropological linguistics. "The linguistic specialist," he said, "is scared of the semantic element in his subject. Phonemes and morphemes cause him no difficulty, but once you start studying meaning you're into culture. And what is culture? A. L. Kroeber said it was 'that larger whole which is the common property of all groups of men and which distinctively sets off mankind from all other animals.' This is what anthropology studies. Linguists, says Kroeber, equate culture with the lexical element of their subject, but, as Professor Borghese put it, they prefer the study of forms because, once they let meaning in, the laboratory door is torn from its hinges and life comes rampaging like a gang of louts.

"We can see the problem of meaning only when we look at it in an anthropological context. Let's take what Professor Eugene A. Nida recently said in his work on linguistics and ethnology, where he examines the translation tasks of the Bible-bearing missionary, traditionally the pioneer in anthropological inquiry. There was a particular problem facing a missionary who wanted to translate the phrase *bill of divorcement*, as it appears in the Gospel of Saint Mark, ten, four, into the language of the Totonacs of Mexico. Now when the Totonacs want a divorce they pay the town secretary to strike their names from the civil register. If divorce is by mutual consent, the fee is small; if only one party wants a divorce, the fee's a good deal higher. But the whole thing is regarded as legal, and the Totonac word for *divorce* has, as its root meaning, *erasure of name*. If you translated *bill of divorcement* literally as something like *a letter stating that a man is leaving his wife*—well, the Totonacs would be disgusted by the whole concept of a religion that permitted such an abomination. When the Totonacs had read out to them another passage in Mark—fourteen, thirteen—the one about a man carrying a pitcher of water, well, they were both amused and disgusted. Water-carrying to them is woman's work, and, to quote Nida, 'they were astonished at the man's ignorance of propriety.' With some African languages the problems are hair-raising. One man rendered into one East African dialect the term *Holy Spirit* into a word meaning something like (I quote) 'a spirit, probably an evil one, which has acquired a tabu by contact with some other spirit undoubtedly evil.'

"It's not only a matter of lexis. Linguistic structures tell us a great deal about what is laughingly called the primitive mind, which usually turns out to be less primitive than that of many a full-blooded meat-and-potatoes American. I'm delighted to welcome here today my uncle, the distinguished novelist Kenneth Toomey—" All turned to look in amiability and wonder: none had been present, thank God, at my lecture. "—He, who spent some time in Malaya, will confirm the existence in the Malay language, as also in the Chinese, of a feature called the numerical coefficient. The Malay word for one is *satu*, the Malay word for a house is *rumah*, but you don't translate *one house* as *satu rumah*. It has to be *sa-buah rumah*, where the *buah* literally means a fruit but is used here to signify something bulky. *Biji* literally means a seed, but *one egg* is translated as *sa-biji telor*, *biji* being the right numerical coefficient for a small smooth object. According to Benjamin Lee Whorf, the Navaho Indians have an even subtler system of classification. The Navaho world of inanimate objects is split into long things and round things, and these affect the verb stems of the language. You need one verb stem for a round thing and another for a long.

"Then there's the question of tricks played with linguistic structure in accordance with ritual and other cultural traditions. As I have one uncle here in this room already, it seems appropriate that I should invoke the spirit of another, now alas dead, to demonstrate how even in British English the ludic element, as we may call it, can be used for a quite serious purpose." I had not noticed the black box which, I now observed, contained a record player that John began to operate. He put on a disc and, from the loudspeaker set above the blackboard, there came out scratchily the voice of my brother Tom speaking cockney back slang. I remembered the act well: Tom was being a pert cunning spadger in a dry goods shop, calling his assistant for some delo nocab for the delo woc and telling him to trosh taiwy her on the araremed ragus. It was a strange moment, it brought tears. John explained. "Here you have a reversal of letters rather than phonemes, deliberately mystifying, but only to the customer in a shop whom the assistants wish to cheat. The *delo nocab* is old bacon, and the *delo woc* is the old cow. She is to be shortweighted on the Demerara sugar. And so on. Now consider what happens in southern Mindoro in the Philippines. There the jungle people known as the Hanunoo have to learn phonemic substitution as a prescribed skill of courtship. If the courter belongs to a particular social level, there is a certain relaxation of the taboo on endogamy. The courted is closely related to the courter but he has to pretend that she does not know this. Hence there is a pattern of disguise—blanket over the head, unusual mode of speaking. *Barang* becomes *rabang* and *katagbuq* is deformed to *kabugtaq*."

And so on. It was well done. Here was a bright young man, blond and big, his manner informal but his subject matter under rigorous control, the handsomeness in which I saw so much of Hortense qualified only slightly by the wide-eyed dementia of the academic. After his lesson we went together to the office he shared with a certain Professor Bucolo, an African specialist who had a day off. We drank coffee among the crammed bookshelves and the small trophies of anthropological exploration. John had not as yet been far: he had stayed on a

Nipissing reservation and examined some folk customs on the Isthmus of Tehuantepec. His professorship was provisional, he would be some time attaining tenure, he was still at work on his doctoral thesis. "It was strange and moving," I said, "to hear the voice of poor Tom, not only here in Indiana but in the course of an academic lecture."

"Oh, you know what they're like at Choate. Very anglophile. One of the staff had a complete set of the Tommy Toomey records. He's supposed to represent a great dead culture."

"Yes," I said. "Comedy without cruelty. The tones of a kind of helpless amiability. A lost empire. That bastard Val Wrigley once said that Tom was a saint. Why didn't you warn me Wrigley was here?"

"I'd no idea you knew each other. In what way is he a bastard?"

"He reviled me for lack of loyalty to various things. After my talk, that is. The students applauded. I think," I said, "I'll skip tonight's party in my honour."

"Don't, please. They'll find a way of blaming me. It was I who suggested you for this year's Berger Memorial Lecture."

"Nepotism the other way round. Is there a word for it?"

So I went. There were drinks and a buffet supper at the house of the college president, Dr. Ovid F. Pargeter. It was a terribly new house and terribly clean. Engravings of Greek antiquities were set on the salmonpink walls at exactly ruled distances from each other. The furniture was Scandinavian. Outside the windows open to the warm evening air there stretched on all sides terribly flat Indiana. I have a memory of flashing glass, in hands and on noses. The faculty wives mostly knew my work: their glasses flashed flirtatious admiration. I was old enough to be a kind of classic, though not of Dr. Ovid F. Pargeter's kind. There was a word for the sort of devotion that led more or less straight from the baptismal font to an adult life of close specialization. Dr. Pargeter had been named for the obstetrician who had presided over his difficult birth in Dayton, Ohio. Pargeter père had never even head of Publius Ovidius Naso (43 B.C.–? A.D. 17), and now here was his son, risen to academic heights through his famed editorship of the *Amores*.

"What would the word be?" I asked him. "Eponymy?"

"That properly refers to the derivation of place-names from personal ones I would say, Mr. Toomey."

My nephew John brought Professor Bucolo to be introduced, a small swarthy man who had also risen: in his instance from Mulberry Street, Manhattan, to a study of primitive African taboos. He held two books. One was my own: *New Roads to God*. He wished me to autograph it.

"Heavens," I said. "I thought this was long dead and buried."

"There are copies around," Professor Bucolo said. "Thank you," as I signed it. "I have nothing of comparable weight to offer in exchange, but I hope you'll accept this in token of my esteem." And he handed me, already floridly empurpled with his signature, a little pamphlet entitled *Language and Culture Among the Oma People: Notes for a Survey.*

"Who," I asked, "are the Oma people?"

"One of these days," the professor said, "I hope to make a more direct and prolonged contact than has so far been possible. There is the question of obtaining an adequate endowment. This is based mainly on what I learned on a brief visit to Kilwa Kivinje. There were five members of the Oma tribe recovering from a disease somewhat like yaws in the missionary hospital run by a certain Father Alessandri, a Frenchman despite his name. You may," he said with cunning insight, "find things here useful for seasoning your fiction. Like the fact that the Oma people cannot count beyond two. *Ok, fa, rup.* One, two, many."

"We're the same," John said, "when we count in Latin. Unilateral, bilateral, multilateral."

"This book of yours," Professor Bucolo said, weighing it in his right hand, "has an interesting chapter on the adaptation of Christianity to the needs of so-called primitive peoples. For my part, I consider such notions as it contains somewhat implausible. Christianity cannot be adapted without danger of loss of its essential principles."

"As I say in the introduction," I said, "these ideas aren't mine. I present myself as a kind of popularizing editor." A drinking faculty member lowered his glass and flashed his glasses in my direction on that word *popularizing.* I was glad to see that Val Wrigley was not around. I gathered he was running an informal beery poetry reading session in his own quarters. "But the ideas propounded were formulated by genuine Christian churchmen."

"Including mainly," John said, "Uncle Carlo. I can hear his voice. Did you see *Life* magazine?"

"I saw it."

"When," John said, "I saw Uncle Carlo all those years back, he put an idea for a book in my head. He seems good at that sort of thing."

"His mother, your grandmother, was good at it too, rest her soul. What book?"

"When I told him I wanted to study anthropology he said I ought to make my life's work a big book on the religious impulse. A kind of *Golden Bough?* I said. As well written, he said. I was stupidly surprised, I didn't think a bishop would have read it, but of course he had. He knew all about the Hanged God and Attis and Osiris. The idea was that I should show man's universal helplessness without a redeemer. Anthropology as Christian propaganda? I said. Then he started shouting, you know his way. Just look for the truth, he yelled. And then he dragged out a three-gallon carboy of the local wine. The search for a man who was really God, he yelled."

"Who," I said, "is God Manning?"

"A poor wandering demented preacher creature," Professor Bucolo said. "He gets in among students in coffee shops and sells them a demented pamphlet of his about the way and the other thing. Some of the kids swear by him for a time. Then they forget when a wandering yogiman or bald bogus Buddhist comes along. The religious impulse can be very dangerous. It damages, sometimes permanently. But most of these kids are healthy and young and pagan."

John looked at his wristwatch. Bucolo grinned. "She's late," John said.

"Who?" I said.

"The lovely Laura." Bucolo grinned. "She has a short story writing group." John flushed charmingly. I liked that. He had inherited normality from somewhere. A Philippine houseboy in a white jacket, not, I presumed, from the Hanunoo tribe, smiled at Mrs. Gloria Pargeter from the arch of the dining alcove. We were all begged to join the chow line. The girl Laura came rushing in as I was taking *asperges en vinaigrette*. She kissed John, who flushed again. Lovely, yes, I saw as she was introduced to me. Her long lovely American body wore an orange wool crêpe dress with short sleeves, fitted bodice, full skirt. The hair was blueblack and untortured to a style: it was parted in the middle, madonnalike, and swung heavily to her shoulders. Her eyes were iceblue but warm. There must be Irish blood there. She was delighted to meet me.

She said, "Did you know you were the only living master of the short story? We were dissecting one of them tonight in your honor."

So. That was possibly where mastership lay: in the things one threw off carelessly for quick dollars. "I'm honored. Which one?"

"The one about the nun in the convent who's trying to go to sleep and sex keeps getting in the way. Then she concentrates on the crucifixion and finds the hard muscular body of a centurion getting in the way. 'Children of Eve.' "

I had forgotten it totally. "I'm honored," I said again.

"Could you come and talk to my group tomorrow?"

"I should be honored. So long as it's in the morning. I have a plane to catch after lunch."

"It's in the morning. Johnny could pick you up. That's fine," she said. "Gosh, the kids will be delighted. Thanks a million, Mr. Toomey."

I felt very warmly toward them both. They seemed genuinely in love with each other. As they joined the line together, scooping food with young hunger, the wrists of their scooping hands kept touching, her fine full hip swung to collide with his bony one. The buffet was ennobled to the amorous and sacramental: the spiced beef stew smoked to heaven, the lamb was for the supper of the lamb, the summer syllabub ("Gloria's specialty," said Professor Bucolo) was richly fruitful. There was no reek of tomato ketchup on the night air. They would marry, I knew; they must be helped. Why should my money sit grossly accumulating to a sterile end? Laura kissed me wetly on the cheek when I left.

Back in the president's guesthouse I found that the graduate student who lodged upstairs and had the job of attending to the minor needs of visiting lecturers had set out on the kitchen table a crock of milk, sugar, a Mickey Mouse mug, and a large jar of something called Malto: it had on its label a sleeping smiling crescent moon. There was also a typed note saying: "This will help you to sleep. You mix it with milk. You can drink it cold but it is better warm. There are matches next to the gas cooker. Prof. Wrigley came and left this envelope. I hope you sleep well. Yours cordially, Jed Bezwada." The envelope contained some photocopied sheets of what looked like verse. There was a title page saying *The Love Songs of J. Christ*. Oh my God, deranged, sometimes permanently. I saw: "Your lance was in me, not in my side." Oh my God. A scrawled note said: "We always have another chance. Let's see what you do this time. Val."

"You are now," I said to Ralph, "in Africa." I nasalized the A campily, overstressing the syllable and introducing it with a comic Jamesian gasp. It was meant to reduce Africa to the tiny and absurd. "That big burning bright light bulb on the high blue ceiling is the Afric sun." We walked in sweat from the Air Maroc plane to the terminal of the Marrakesh airport.

"It's not Africa. Not real Africa."

"Meaning that you see none of your own color. Nevertheless this is the continent you're always fantasizing about. The great mother from whose breast the white man wrenched you yelling. With the assistance of greedy black entrepreneurs. It's a bloody big place, Ralph dear. Look, there, see, the Great Atlas range. Beyond it the heart of darkness starts its first tentative beats. But here we have Islam and an old empire which was built on slavery. Like every other damned empire. White men were slaves too. My fellow novelist Cervantes for instance." In the terminus there was a map of Africa which covered an entire wall. "Look at the size of the damned place." He saw.

He said, "How do you get to Nairobi from here?"

"Why Nairobi? The West Coast is your ancestral home."

"I want to go to Nairobi."

"The best way, Ralph, is to start from somewhere else. Rome, for instance. Of course, you could walk. No nasty big sea getting in the way. Desert, though, jungle, nasty little men with spears."

Ralph, like a European, shuddered.

Outside the terminal, its lower walls striated with Berber piss marks, the powerful reek of wild mint struck. Tizra and palmetto leaves acknowledged the tired gesture of a breeze from the west. A Moorish taxidriver in a filthy shirt said, "Where you go, Charlie?"

"To the Hotel Moghrab."

"You Merican, Charlie?"

"*Ce monsieur*," I said. "*Cent per cent. Moi, je suis ce que je suis. On y va.*" Our bags were put in the trunk. In the taxi Ralph sniffed with apprehension the effluvia of its driver: stewy sweat, sweetish kif (from the Arabic *kayf* meaning pleasure), rank goatish urine. A laden donkey got into our path. The driver turned; the hard light beamed from his eyeballs:

"You want boy, Charlie? I find you plenty boy."

"One thing at a time." Ralph got out at the French-run hotel with our bags. "Now," I said, "take me to the Villa el Filfil. Near the Djemaa el Fna." Soon we were coasting about the periphery of the great market. Snakecharmers and storytellers were at their trades. A small boy went bouncing heavenwards from a trampoline. A sort of shawm skirled and drums were languidly spanked. Aimless pocked brown dirtyrobed Moors spat dryly and sauntered. My driver could not find the Villa el Filfil, so named from the pepperbushes in its garden. I thought I heard the crash of a piano chord muffled by leaves of cedar, fig and apricot. "There," I said. "Here." I gave him too many dirhams and then walked through the open gateway through overgrown greenery live with lizards and entered the full noise of Domenico's piano.

Domenico had come here from Menton, fancying dry heat. His assistant, Vern Clapp, a kif cigarette in his mouthcorner, stood at a high desk ruling bar lines on scoring paper. "Hi," he said. At his hired grand piano Domenico sat, singing my words:

> "*You whom the fisherfolk of Myra believe*
> *To have power over the sea*
> *Acknowledge a power as old as Eve—*
> *The sea's goddess, Venus, me!*"

And then, necessarily adding notes, Bevilacqua's translation:

> "*O tu che a Mira ogni pescatore*
> *Venera pel potere che hai sul mare*
> *Conoscer devi la potenza arcana*
> *Di Vener, dea del mar, me, soprumana.*"

"The English is better," I said. It was a big empty room, shuttered against the sun but open to the luminous gloom of the rear of the garden. It was pared to function—tables, piano, desk, music paper. There was no pederasty here: rather there was a faint odor of fairly recently departed Moorish woman.

"Finished?" Domenico said. He looked very slummy Italian, unshaven, hairy belly pulsing, shirt unbuttoned, feet sandaled. "You want a drink?"

"Whisky and Vittel. Ice."

Domenico went himself toward a dark space beyond an arch. "No boy," he said. "Goddam thieves, all of them."

"Is Bevilacqua here?" I asked Vern Clapp.

"In bed with the squitters. Eating unwashed fruit." He was penciling notes in now, frowning down at Domenico's short score.

"Yes," I said, as Domenico handed me a dirty brimming clinking tumbler, "all finished. Including the epilogue. Apotheosis of holy much-tried Nick."

"We're not having that," this other Nick said. "We're going to finish with him holding the dead kid in his arms, cursing God for an unfeeling bastard."

"You can't."

"It's the only way. War going on outside and he yells at God over the noise and the curtain comes down while he's still yelling. A riot."

"There'll be a riot all right. You'll be proclaiming in your own brother's archdiocese that God is an unfeeling bastard."

"Just what I said. Anyway, he *is* an unfeeling bastard."

I sighed profoundly. "Remember, Nicholas is a saint. This is an opera about a holy man, not one who ends up screaming that God is an unfeeling bastard."

"Which he is, like I said. All those dead Jews and the atom bomb. This last act says it all if you've written it right."

"The epilogue," I said, "should last about ten minutes. It needn't be a separate scene. The noises of war recede and there's unearthly music and an angelic chorus. A subtle lighting change, the amplified voice of God is heard, basso profundo, Nicholas is haloed in light, he kneels. Angelic voices in crescendo. Chord of C major. Curtain."

"And how's about this dead kid he's holding?"

"He puts it down somewhere. Angelic hands take it away. No, he still holds it. But the child's no longer dead. Nicholas, patron saint of children. Light floods them both."

"And," Vern Clapp said, "the orchestra plays 'Jingle Bells.' "

"It won't do," Domenico said.

"Oh, it will," Vern Clapp said through kif smoke. "Ken here's right. Of course, you could have alternative endings. One for Moscow, the other for Milan."

"We'll think about it." Domenico scowled. "You want to hear the whole of the first scene?"

"With you singing all the parts?"

"You'll get the general idea."

"No," I said, "thanks all the same. I'm just delivering the goods. Such as they are." I took from their slim Gucci case the few sheets that would feed an hour of Domenico's music and placed them in the dust of the upturned piano lid. "I must go to the hotel and make sure that Ralph is not abducted by Moghrabi traders. Perhaps we could have dinner together somewhere."

"That black bastard's still with you?" Domenico scowled deeper. "Too much of a fucking pattern, isn't it? Hortense was in some magazine some place. Hacking away at the bishop with his balls on show. That black bitch cut what they call an album."

"What talents we all have," I said. "Except for Ralph. No talent at all, poor boy, and he resents it. Shall we say the bar of the Maimunia, sevenish?"

"That the place with Winston Churchill's pictures all over the walls?" Vern Clapp asked.

"The place where he and your late president," I said, "decided to send the Cossacks to their death. Or was that Yalta?"

"Okay," Domenico said. "Bevilacqua needs to get out of his bed and have some semola or rice or something stuffed into his guts. Eating apricots straight from the garden, fucking idiot. We'll drag him along."

"Solo oboe here?" Vern Clapp asked. "Or is it with flute an octave higher?" Domenico padded over to see. I left. I picked up a *petit taxi* near a stall that sold warm-looking yellowish drinks and went to the hotel. In the bar of the hotel I found Ralph at a little table nursing a Pernod. At another table sat an old man who looked like Frederick Delius, blindness and all. He was in an open-necked silk shirt and a white suit. This was the quondam Archbishop of York, now retired, or abdicated, or whatever episcopal dignitaries did when their health failed.

"Toomey," I said, taking the long thin cold now ringless hand.

"Ah, Toomey, you here? I was just telling this young American how badly his race treats the Negroes."

Blind, batblind. "He prefers to be called black."

"Whatever he prefers to be called, he and his kind treat the Negro population shamefully. So, you here too, Toomey. Can't see you, I'm afraid. Have to rely on the inner light now. Glaucoma, you know. Everything all right, then? I had a visit from dear Carlo. Such a comfort. His robust health continues. I could feel its radiations."

"Here?"

"In Rome, in Rome, cradle of the faith. No, not that really when you come to think of it. Jerusalem? Mecca? There is only one God, Toomey."

"I never doubted it."

"Have you ever considered that our Muslim friends have come closer to a reasonable nomination of the deity than either the Christians or the Jews? God is Allah, but the root is the single consonant L. A mysterious sound, Toomey, a kind of song. It floods through the African morning from the minarets, very thrilling. Gibbon said, you know, that if the Muslims had pushed just a little further, from the Loire to the Thames, the ah, let me see if I can remember the exact, let me see. Yes, 'perhaps the interpretation of the Koran would now be taught in the schools of Oxford, and her pulpits might demonstrate to a circumcised people the sanctity and truth of the revelation of Mahomet.' Very elegantly put, Toomey. This gentleman," he said to Ralph, "is Mr. Toomey, the noted British author. We are old friends. Toomey, at my age, and with all this enforced leisure, I find myself in an interesting situation. I have given my life to the Church of England, and I have given much thought necessarily clandestine, as you must know, to dear Carlo's dream of a reunited Christendom. And now, having spent six months within hailing or Allahing distance of the mosque of Sidi Bel Abbas, I find myself drawn to the scimitarlike simplicity of Christendom's ancient enemy. I think there must be in every Englishman a touch of the Islamic tarbrush. Doughty, Burton, Lawrence are but a few of the names we think of in this connection. Think of it, Toomey—the one God and the faceless prophet, the cleanly diet, the five prayers daily, the genuine Lent of Ramadan."

Ralph took from his fawn moygashel jacket pocket the little book on the Oma people and their language which I had passed on to him. He dissociated himself from the two old white fags and recited primitive words under his breath. "So," I said to the retired prelate, "the final road is to Mecca."

"Ah, it doesn't work out that way at all, Toomey. The final road is back to the unformed mentality of childhood. Faith and loyalty and duty. The church on the hill and the known names in the graveyard. Dear Carlo is wrong. Faith cannot move forward to new loyalties and duties. If Carlo can do it, he is exceptional in his loneliness." Very acute, very. "We are loyal only to our mothers. We strive for the new but cannot attain it. We travel a circle. We want to get back."

"Back to what?" Ralph asked suddenly.

"Ah, my American friend, are you still there? In your case, back to Boston or Milwaukee or wherever you come from, I was never much good at American accents, all sound alike to me, back to your childhood there and all that that childhood inherited."

"My people were slaves."

"Slaves? Really? Your people? Then you must be an American Negro. I would not have thought it."

"My people prefer *black*. I inherited a white culture and I don't want it any more. How far back do I go searching for faith and loyalty and the rest of the—" He was about to say *shit*, but this was after all a clergyman, just like his father, who would never permit foul language in the family cabin. "That nonsense?"

"It depends on how Negro, excuse me, black, you feel." That too was acute.

"Black enough to want to get away from the whites."

"You can't do it, you know. You've absorbed too much from them. You might become Muslim, of course, but that would, in your view, only be exchanging one exotic abomination for another. Whatever you do, my boy, don't yearn after some long-buried juju. And never feel bitter about slavery. All races have at one time or another been enslaved by another race. Slavery is a mode of cultural transmission."

"Don't call me *boy*. And don't give me that high-sounding crap." He had let the word come out without thinking but the quondam was delighted.

"Craps," he said. "You remember, Toomey? Baby wants a new pair of shoes. Come on seven eleven. Ah well. Still, I hear there are Braille playing cards. You, sir," he said sternly to Ralph, "may cherish some romantic Rousseau dream of rational savagery, but let me warn you of its dangers. You will have to shed hardly won skills, especially in language. As a young clergyman in Africa, not this part of course, I saw what savagery was like. That would be going back *too far*. You, like our clerical friend Carlo, not yours of course, Toomey's and mine, are forced to go forward. No nostalgia for either of you." And then, petulantly, "Where is my companion, as I must call him? He is plucking sleep, as Virgil puts it, the flower of the siesta. I wish to go to my room. If you could telephone him, Toomey. His room number is eighty-one. His name is Gordon. He is a young Scotchman. He prefers to be called a Scot. All these taboos."

"I'll take you," I said.

"Would you, will you, Toomey? A very Christian act. Oh, how stupid, how narrow. My blind man's stick is somewhere."

Ralph, who could very occasionally find pity for others than himself, took the quondam's right arm while I took his left. We got him to his room through various Moorish arches and along wide cool corridors with bronze shields on the walls and found ourselves near to our own two adjoining. I wanted Ralph naked in my arms for a space: the warmth and known lax ambience invited it. But Ralph was petulant and unwilling. Very well, then. There were things to tell Ralph, and these were not directly about love. I said, as I lay on the coarse Moorish coverlet on my bed under the ceiling fan and he sat flopped frowning in a wickerwork armchair:

"Ralph, I fear we shall have to leave Barcelona. For good."

"And come here?" He was quick enough when he wished to be.

"Here, this town, I think not, but I was anxious to see it. Perhaps Tangier, which I know well enough and find sympathetic. The fact is that I received a visit from the Deputy Chief of Police while you were, according to you, spending the day at the Museum of Catalan Art."

"You kept this quiet. Why?"

"Because you might have responded to what I reported with unseemly and perhaps criminal behavior. You are what is known as a persona non grata, Ralph dear. Nothing to do with your race, I assure you, though that makes you conspicuous. It's just the way you carry on when not under my restraining influence. The police, in fact, have been very tolerant. But in several bars you have been heard saying derogatory things about General Franco and once it was alleged you attempted to urinate on his picture—difficult, as it was high on the wall. There are other things. You held a very noisy party in our apartment while I was seeing Gomez in Madrid. You played jazz on the harpsichord I bought you and then tried to throw the instrument into the stairwell. Black American sailors were present. Two of them did a mime of sodomy on the landing in the presence of Dr. Borges. When the neighbors sent the police round you were all abusive but you most notably so because you were abusive in fluent Catalan. These things add up. The Chief of Police and his deputy know my work and my reputation. They do not want scandal. The view is that we might be happier somewhere else."

Ralph brooded on that. "Just me, isn't it?" he said at last. "You're the discreet English gentleman, the quiet bugger, what what. Okay, you stay and I'll go."

"We're supposed to be together, dear Ralph. I believe in the ancient virtue of loyalty. I wanted to come back to Morocco to see how things were. Marrakesh seems a little dull and run-down. In Tangier there are expatriate writers like myself. There's a great deal of tolerance for, well, aberrations. Poverty, though, slavery even of a kind, thievery. My more precious possessions could be put in store somewhere, I have looked on them long enough. We could rent a little house and have smiling Moorish servants. A little garden, too. There are the charms of the *souk*. We could at least try it."

"No," Ralph said. "You brought me to this mock Africa. Now I want to see the real thing. I might even find something to do in black Africa."

"You mean *revert*? You heard what the former Archbishop of York said. The romantic Rousseau dream. Douanier and Jean-Jacques together. You're not talking sensibly."

"Okay. It was you who said that failure in art can only be compensated by a life in action."

"Did I say that? I think not. I probably said that people like Hitler and Goebbels and Mussolini got angry when their artistic drive was frustrated and could only find an outlet in revolutionary politics. You, dear Ralph, can't write but you can do other things. You played Mozart very nicely until you decided he was a white reactionary slave-owning fag. You can direct plays. For God's sake don't start believing that you have a place in any of these damned revolutionary movements that are fomenting in postcolonial Africa. Stay with me. Don't desire to move too far from the Atlantic or the Mediterranean. We'll start househunting in Tangier. The day after tomorrow, if you like."

Ralph sulked, and I could have torn his clothes off with anger. "Don't you start thinking of the two of us settling in Tangier. The time's come for you to settle, I can see that. With me its different."

"Ralph," I said, feeling my glottis constrict, "have you no love or loyalty? Does it all have to be on my side?"

"You pay me a salary. I'm kind of an employee. Those two things don't have to come into it."

"Yes," tears were starting, "and if it weren't for my own love and loyalty I'd say that you were a bloody bad employee."

"You mean I don't hold my ass at the right angle?"

"That's a cruel thing to say. I mean that you sent a letter to my British publisher saying *Fuck off* and signing it with a facsimile signature that was taken to be my own. I mean other things. I mean that my love for you, which cries out for a physical expression you tolerate brutishly, induces a cecity to your inefficiency and your bad behavior. I don't want to think of you as an employee. You are given all the money you require, and it is far more than I would give to an employee. I want to think of you as my loving friend."

"Oh Jesus." Ralph grinned. "Loving friends. Like that story of your about the other fucking Ralph. *Let me take your pants off, darling.*"

"That too is cruel. If you were a *real* writer instead of a bungling amateur, you would know that the names of one's own fiction can take on a kind of magic, can achieve something like prophetic stain, I mean strain. I have to confess that, when my sister suggested you as a secretary and companion, your name was much in your favor. Now please let us try not to be unpleasant to each other. Perhaps you and I could arrange a little trip to East Africa. The British Council has frequently proposed that I exhibit myself on their African ah circuit."

"Ah shit," went Ralph, beautiful wretched boy. "You keep missing it, don't you? Uncle Tom colleges. I want to see where I come from."

"As I have said many times, your provenance is the West Coast, where a gentle artistic people allowed itself to be exploited by predators of many colors. You will see genuinely black Africans on the East Coast, as well as Arabs and Asians, but they will have nothing to say to you, nor will you have to them. This is the worst kind of uninformed romanticism."

"Listen," Ralph hissed. "Blacks don't stand an ice cube in hell's chance in the States. What history meant by black slavery was equipping a whole continent in retaliation with the ideological and technical resources of the West to rise in power and authority and dignity to make the whole fucking West tremble. And you talk of the British fucking Council."

"You have been reading something," I said. "And I don't mean just that little book on the Oma people who can't count beyond two. You have been reading the windy rhetoric of some of the new African politicians. I don't like it, Ralph."

"Okay, you don't like it. But don't talk to me any more about seeing the tourist sights. Life's short. And I'm hungry."

"Hungry for what?"

"Hungry for food. Jesus, come down off it. What they gave us for lunch on that Sopwith Camel was like a snack for a canary. Let's go out and eat someplace."

"We're meeting the ah operatic contingent in an hour or so. We eat then."

"Listen, I'm not eating with Nick Campanati. You call him and cancel it."

"We have work to discuss, dear Ralph. I came here primarily in connection with work."

"Give me money then. You brought me to what you call Africa, okay, I'll go and see what it has to offer. Money money."

"I gave you money."

"I spent it on those shirts at the airport. Money, give."

I sighed and sighed. "In my inside pocket there you will find a supply of what they call dirhams. Take what you wish but leave me enough to pay for dinner."

A very ungracious boy. I dined with Domenico and his in situ colleagues not at the Maimunia, where we only drank, but at a dark and oily garlicky restaurant more Neapolitan than Moroccan, though its name was the Shiwa, a sardonic name since there was no roast beef on the menu. Bevilacqua, who was pale and shivery, dug away at a mound of plain rice with lemon juice squeezed onto it. The rest of us had a bland couscous which we enfired with *harissa*. Domenico had now reached the stage of hearing voices in his skull. "Mazzotta," he said, "for Nick. Gregoretti for Venere." We had decided that one of the three unpickled and revivified by the saint should be not only a woman but a personification of the goddess of love and that Act One, Scene One should be a kind of Venusberg.

"Gregoretti looks it," Vern Clapp said, "but she's weak in the high register. Is that rice holding?" he asked Bevilacqua.

"Better. I think it will stay."

"*Controllo muscolare*," Domenico said, "*è quello il segreto*." And to me, "I think we're going to finish like I said. The kid dead in his arms. Hiroshima. The death camps."

"Morocco," Vern Clapp said. "The Bronx. Any darned place you like."

"While we're talking of muscular control," I said, "don't ever think of letting art relax itself into propaganda."

"It's not propaganda," Domenico said. "It's the way things are. God doesn't give a fuck about men and women and kids."

"You can't write this opera that way."

"Ken's right, like I said," Vern Clapp said. "Let's finish with that heavenly choir."

"The point is," I said, "that the responsibility for the music is yours. The words are mine. And his," I added, nodding toward grimly rice-stuffing Bevilacqua. "Let's have some more of this local wine."

"It tastes like catarrh," Vern Clapp said.

"Don't put Renato off his rice," Domenico said. And to me, "It's the music that speaks and always did in opera. The words are only a kind of, what's the word—"

"Excuse? Pretext? Subterfuge? I'm not having that."

"You hand the words over to me," Domenico said. "And then I do with them what I have to do."

"That," Vern Clapp said justly, "is because you've been taking orders too long. Give us a sound meaning that Cary Grant has indigestion. Give us a tune that sounds like what Lauren Bacall looks like. You're overreacting, Nick boy. Ken's right. It's his story not yours."

"Maybe you don't want any music at all," Domenico said, hot as *harissa*. "Maybe you want a nice little play about God shits on you but he's still the big good God. That would please the big good cardinal."

"You're bringing family matters into it," I said. "Don't, Domenico. Art, art, art. Composite art. Wagner didn't put the music first."

"That's because he wrote the words too," Domenico said.

"Well, you try it," I said. "You write the words. Then you'll get what you want. Do you want me to withdraw my libretto?"

"When I've done the first scene and am halfway through the second? You must be crazy. And that's a nasty thing to say, Ken. That's prima donna stuff."

Bevilacqua said, "*Devo per forza tornare a casa, non mi fido dei gabinetti di qua.*"

"What's he say?"

"He says," Domenico said, "that he's got to get back. He doesn't fancy using the bathroom here. Okay, who pays? You pay, Ken, right. It was lousy food anyway. Right, we do it your way and then see what the critics say. Always chop that bit off."

"So long as you chop my name off the credits."

"We'll see. Get the second act done first. Then think about it."

"Ken's right," Vern Clapp said.

"*Devo andare. Subito.*"

They went off in a *petit taxi* and left me to wander a while in the warm March air. An odorous old Moor tried first to sell me kif and then a boy. He had a goat too, he said, female if my tastes ran to American-style normality. I went back to the hotel and to Ralph. Ralph was in his room sobbing.

"Ralph dear, angel, what in the name of . . ."

He stopped sobbing and got up from his bed showing a wet face. He wiped the tears off with his shirtsleeve. "Okay," he said. "Okay okay okay. I want to go home." The vowel of *home* threatened to prolong into a howl, but he bit it off, the more easily because tears had denasalized his speech.

"Something bad happened? Where? What did they do?"

"Home, where the white liberals are real nice to niggers so long as they don't claim their rights. Cokes and burgers and Jell-O. Home."

"I want to know what happened."

"Oh, what I might have expected. I went round some dark alleys and there was the sound of this woman wailing one of these Arab songs, and I went to the door which was open, I thought it was some kind of a Moorish nightspot, and then these four black guys jump me and I get rolled. Black, man, black guys. My watch, money, the lot."

"A rich American, Ralph, that's all you are to them. Black? They must have been Berbers."

"And then they try to get my pants down and stuff it up."

"Oh no."

"I want out of here. I want to go home."

"Home is with me, Ralph. My only desire in life is to look after you. Oh my God, they did that."

"They tried it. They didn't get far. A police car comes by and they run. And the police tell me in French and I say make it Spanish, they tell me in Spanish to keep out of these places, not for tourists, you go back to your rich hotel, sucker Americano. They don't even give me a ride there. Okay, that's Marrakesh. That's Morocco."

"Tangier is very different, you'll see. Gang rape, oh my God."

"Fuck Tangier. I want New York."

"Come into my bed, Ralph. Cry yourself to sleep. I'll be watching over you every minute from now on. This sort of things happens to all of us."

"A mockery, that's all. Humiliation, you know that big word?"

"I practically invented it."

"A fucking mockery."

sixty-four

"Naughty," said the fat man in white, Lord Somebody, "not to put too fine a point on it."

"He'll be for the chop all right."

"How did they *dare?*"

So goodbye to Barcelona with Gaudí's Church of the Sagrada Familia, almost esculent, crisp burnt baguettes aspiring to heaven, and his Park Güell, fairy decadence, the stalls in Las Ramblas and the winds of Tibidabo, the ten o'clock dinners of octopus in their own ink. To say that I spent the next decade and half of my life in Tangier would not be strictly true, since my sixties and seventies were as restless as the fifties and sixties of the century, and I jetted about the globe being a personality, spent six months in Australasia, a year in New York, two years traversing Latin America for a possible book, odd rags of time in European capitals. Nevertheless, Calle Mozart 21, not far from the Teatro Lope de Vega, became my official home until my flight to Malta. The house, built in the thirties, was of two stories, a box with little elegance though ample amenity, surrounded by a garden with a pair of cedars and walnut and orange and lemon trees, the garden surrounded by a thick high wall surmounted by broken-bottle chevaux-de-frise. While Ralph, moody but for a time chastened, was still with me, I managed to work well on a new long novel entitled *Walter Dunnett*, somewhat autobiographical save for the hero's heterosexuality. It would, from the technical angle, have seemed unremarkable when Arnold Bennett was a boy, what with its firm plot and stodgy dialogue, as also its inexplicit love scenes. I still had my audience, large if aging, but American scholastics were beginning to find in my work elements of irony and patterns of symbolism that were not, so far as I knew, really present. Meanwhile in France a new breed of writers was producing the *nouveau roman*, based on the rejection of plot and character and, indeed, everything I had always stood for. It was perhaps with unspoken relief that, admiring these, professors of fiction took my own works to bed and, enjoying them, had to rationalize their enjoyment in terms of my consciously, in a kind of revolt against postmodernism, ridiculous term, reverting to an earlier tradition. I was not, of course, reverting at all.

"I know why they *dare*. They want to make a case of it. About time too."

I was drinking sherry with Ralph in Al-Djenina, a bar not far from the Hotel Rif, and a number of expatriate writers, each with his Tangerine young man in smart suit with briefcase, were discussing *The Love Songs of J. Christ* by Valentine Wrigley. This had recently been published in London by Macduff and Tannenbaum.

"The case is already about to begin," I said.

"You've read it, Toomey?" This was a man in middle age best known for his loving biography of Lord Alfred Douglas.

"I read it in typescript," I said, "in the States. And I have just received a request from the publishers' solicitors to present myself as an expert witness when the time comes. The time is coming. The Director of Public Prosecutions has been compelled to take action."

"Will you go?" asked the lord, a viscount to be exact, a young and muscular man dabbling on a family remittance in the worst kind of Moorish pederastic dirt.

"I think I shall have to. Thank God the law forbids my delivering an aesthetic judgment on this book." The courtyard of the bar was full of tame birds, gaudy but songless, that were beginning, with chirruping and irritable preening, to settle on their perches for the night.

"It'll be magistrate's court," said the Alfred Douglas man, who looked ascetic, even High Anglican clerical. "Marlborough Street. I remember the *Well of Loneliness* case. I was there. Terribly ill-written book. But one had to speak out, you know, as much as one could. Never cared much for lesbians, perhaps unreasonable of me. Never cared for Tiggy Hall."

"Is that what she was called? I thought it was Boopsy or something." This was a twitching man who managed to live out here on two novels a year, a sale of three thousand for each. No tax, cheapish cigars. He was chewing one.

"I was made to feel guilty," I said, "for not putting in a word there." It seemed that my brother Tom, silly eventually faithless Estella peeping over his shoulder, was looking at me in sad retrospective reproach. This is the way the brain works. "I suppose I'm really making amends."

"Not really a trial at that stage," the Bosie man said. "The magistrate regards Marie Corelli as a daring authoress and Hall Caine as a pornographer and they have a counsel who just asks polite questions. They're trying to find out if there's a possible defense, really. That sort of thing. Court of enquiry."

"The point is, I think," I said, "that Macduff and Tannenbaum want to make a sort of bargain with the law. They paid big money for this big novel by Ralph's compatriot—"

"*Dear* Ralph," said a small man called Pissy who seemed to have no other name, twinkling and drawing his upper body together in a gesture meant to be seductive.

"That would be Foulds," the two-novel-a-year man said with bitter envy. "*The Cry of the Clouds*. A very dirty book. Long as well. Like *War and Peace*. There was an American woman in the Miramar with a copy. Anything gets through in the States."

"You see the situation," I said. "This volume of Val Wrigley's gets banned, they're not going to follow right away with another prosecution. If they say, as they may do, this is only a book of pseudopoems with a limited audience, let it go, then there's a great victory for free speech and so on. They practically threw it at the DPP."

"Black, isn't he?" the viscount said. "Saw a photograph of him somewhere."

"Yeah, he's black," Ralph drawled, "all black, man. You any objection to him being black?"

"How touchy you chaps are," said the Bosie man. "We love your rippling black velvet bodies and you know it."

"But not our rippling black velvet minds."

"All right, Ralph," I said and drained my Amontillado. "Don't start anything."

"Foulds shows up you bastard little *littérateurs*," Ralph said. "A big book, right. And big money. But he took the money home, right?"

"East Africa is *not* his home," I said, "any more than it's yours, dear Ralph. You and I will now go to *real* home. Ali gets upset if we're late for dinner." The marine sky was all plum and apple and honey touched with a little greengage. There were old-fashioned farewells from the others, who did not seem to propose going home, not till their Moorish boys carried them thither. "Tutti frutti," and "Be good, you old whore" and so on. Ralph and I walked home, myself panting little more than he as we engaged the brief hill. Ali, whom you have already met, smiled that we were not late. He served us avocado followed by coq au vin, cheese and a shop-bought apricot flan to finish. We ate in a room bare except for its monastic dining furniture and Moorish rugs on parquet floor and walls. After dinner Ralph got down to some serious practice on his harpsichord: there was talk of his playing Mozart at a little concert that Gus Jameson, an expatriate Scottish composer, was arranging for late December. I went to my study and, sighing, numbered a new sheet of foolscap (140), recalled some of my characters from their brief sleep and set them talking. They started talking, to my surprise, about the novel which contained them, rather like one of those cartoon films in which anthropomorphic animals get out of the frame and start abusing their creator.

"A novelist friend of mine," Diana Cartwright said, "affirmed that a satisfactory novel should be a self-evident sham to which the reader could regulate at will the degree of his credulity."

"A sham, eh?" Walter Dunnett said. "Even when there are verifiable historical personages in it? Like Havelock Ellis and Percy Wyndham Lewis and Jimmy Joyce?"

"They're not the same as what they would be in real life. The whole thing's a fake. We're fakes too. We're saying what he wants us to say. You see that Degas over there—he could turn it into a Monet at a stroke of the pen. He could reduce the number of oranges in that bowl from eight to three. He could make me die now with a heart attack,"

I nearly wrote: *She died at once of cardiac arrest.*

This would not do at all. I got up and walked round my study. For the first time I was being made to realize how tenuous my art, such as it was, was. This was the impact of the age, in which the suspension of disbelief was slowly being abandoned. The young, certainly, were done with art. I sat shakily down at the little table where Ralph, when he felt like working, typed my letters and sometimes my manuscripts. To the left of his typewriter was a low pile of magazines, including five or six successive weekly issues of the new *Nywele*, an international periodical dedicated to what was called the International Black Movement and published in Kampala. As was appropriate to life, though not to fiction, the copy I picked up opened at an article, in English, on the black novelist Randolph Foulds, complete with brooding thick-necked photograph. He had made several million dollars out of *The Cry of the Clouds* and he had invested it in the strengthening of the military regime of Abubakar Mansanga, who was building a modern state in Rukwa and converting a tribal congeries into a totalitarian unity. It was to be a model African state in which neither the imported white technological experts nor the Asian men of commerce would much longer be allowed to dilute the *echt* negritude of a territory whose boundaries were, as yet, unfixed. Here the African Future was already being proclaimed. I heard Ralph repeating and repeating an elegant rococo right-hand run on his harpsichord, and I shuddered. I went back to my novel, crumpled the sheet I had started, and forced the characters back into total servitude to my will. Slaves, sort of, with only the illusion of freedom. Like all of us. The novel form was no sham.

The letter I received from Lightbody and Creek of Essex Court, Strand, informed me that the hearing would begin at Marlborough Street on December 5, and I was requested to render myself available at 9:00 A.M. on that date. This was a nuisance. The opera *Una Leggenda su San Nicola* was to have its premiere at La Scala on the feast day of its protagonist, December 6, and I wished to be present at the dress rehearsal. Those readers knowledgeable in the operatic calendar of Milan will be aware that the season does not normally begin until the following day, the feast of Saint Ambrose (this is a solidly holy segment of the Milan winter, with the feast of the Immaculate Conception coming on December 8), but an adjustment had, after several committee meetings, been made out of a reluctant sense of celebratory fitness. Well then, everything was coming together, as in a well or mechanically plotted novel, since I had heard from Hortense in New York (who would not be in Milan) that the basso-relievo had arrived at Genoa on the *Michelangelo* as early as November 11.

I said to Ralph, "Ralph, I must fly to London on the fourth. For the trial of *J. Christ.* Do you propose coming with me?"

"I'll be okay here."

"Are you sure you'll be ah okay here? Are you quite sure you won't get into mischief in the Casbah or somewhere?"

"I want to go to Rabat to look at the horses. Arabs, man. And I could see the tombs of the Marinide sultans and all that crap. I'll be okay."

"Do you propose to be with me in Milan for the opening?"

"Opening of what?"

"Ralph, you're terribly distracted these days. You know what."

"Aw, that. I'll get the records later."

"Very well, then. I shall fly from London to Milan and be back here, God willing, on the eighth or ninth. I'm delighted, of course, that you should wish to go to Rabat. I can give you a letter of introduction to the royal equerry if you desire it."

"Give me some money is all I desire."

"You're very sullen these days, Ralph. I much prefer you in your loud and vicious moods. No, no, I was only jesting. You shall have your money."

I flew by Air Maroc to Gibraltar and waited two hours in the airport bar under the looming north face of the great rock for the BEA flight to London. I was the only first-class passenger, and the stewardess kept bringing me small gifts of the line: miniature liqueurs, aftershave lotion, a pack of samples of British cheeses, finally a tiny flask of Givenchy perfume "for my wife." At Heathrow I found a message in the rack by the luggage carousel. Nay, I found two, but the first was not for me: WAITING AT HOME FOR YOU LOVE TOM. It was for a Mrs. Timpson. For Toomey there was a curt warning signed "Wrigley": DON'T YOU EVER LET THE SIDE DOWN AGAIN. I took a taxi to Claridge's.

The Marlborough Street court was, the following drizzly London morning, frowsty, dark, Dickensian but, or and, somehow festive. Aberrants in bright colors as well as a number of vulgar pressmen were awaiting the fun. The corridor at the side of the little pitch-pine courtroom was filmed with mud and planted with shoe-crushed cigarette butts that had opened like flowers. I kept myself to myself near an unwashed open window that opened onto a space too small to be a yard, inaccessible also except by that window. It was scattered with the detritus of sordid decades: a broken bottle that had contained beer brewed by the successors to Johnson's friend Thrale, a browned fragment of a *Police Gazette* that possibly announced the arrest of Charles Peace, fag-ends of Crumbs of Comfort and Mermaid Whiffs, even condoms. I stood there looking, smoking, not wishing to be associated with the smutseekers, dotty literary, reporters. They all knew who I was. Lights suddenly went on and there was a cheer. I saw, to a kind of quiet, Sir Arnold Wetherby the magistrate go in. He was accompanied by a curly bronzed man of forensic handsomeness, the well-known barrister George Pyle. Sir Arnold had a curved Dunhill pipe which he extinguished at his leisure but kept gripped as a kind of gavel. Both men were laughing.

When I was called I had to take the oath and I was given a selection of
Bibles. I chose the Douay Version. Then there was a session of great affability
and informality, with breaks for a smoke every fifteen minutes or so.

"I don't think you have to be introduced, do you? You're Mr. Kenneth M.
Toomey, novelist, playwright, at present living abroad. The court, I think I may
say this, is cognizant of the inconvenience to which you have voluntarily sub-
mitted in order to be here and conveys its thanks."

Sir Arnold accepted Pyle's speaking on his behalf and said, "Glad to see
you here, Toomey. Damned bad weather for you to come over to, but there it
is. Read quite a number of your things. Enjoyed most of them. Not like this
thing, eh?" And he waved a copy of Val's book at me. It was a thin book with
the title, on a pure white ground, engrossed in a kind of Celtic lettering.

"No, your honor."

"What," Pyle asked, "is the meaning of the initial M? In your name, I
mean?"

"Marchal. It's French. My mother's name. My mother was French."

"A lot of the influence of Guy de Maupassant in your stuff," Sir Arnold said.
"A sort of cleaned-up Maupassant. Not that I've read much Maupassant. Do
you agree?"

"That you haven't read much Maupassant, your honor?" This got a laugh.
What masochism, what fundamentally cynical irreverence for institutions and
principles makes us British make comic butts out of each other on occasions
when comedy is totally out of order? There have been murder trials that were
positive orgies of hilarity. "I'm sorry, your honor. Your other statement, yes,
that seems to me to be a very astute literary judgment."

"Jolly good," Sir Arnold said.

"As you know, Mr. Toomey," Pyle said, "this volume of alleged verse—is
the author present? No, I see he is not—I say *alleged* without disparagement, it
is published as verse, but much of it seems to be chopped-up prose—"

"*Vers libre,*" Sir Arnold said, and looked at me as for approval. I nodded.

"This volume is arraigned on the grounds of its capacity for moral corruption. You have read it?"

"Naturally."

"You have read it, naturally. What do you find in it?"

"You mean its content?"

"Yes, let's say its content. Please tell the court."

"It is a series of twelve longish poems, each in the style of Mr. T. S. Eliot's
Love Song of J. Alfred Prufrock, which the title is probably meant to evoke.
That would explain the *J. Christ*, not in itself, when seen in the Eliot context, at
all really blasphemous."

"*Vers libre.*"

"Quite, your honor. Jesus Christ seems to be writing a letter to each of his twelve disciples after his death, resurrection and ultimate disappearance. He affirms his continuing love for them, even for the traitor Judas. As the medium is poetry, an intensely physical medium, he expresses the love in physical terms."

"To be exact," Pyle said, "homosexual terms."

"Necessarily, since the disciples are men. He stresses physical love as primarily a means of expressing affection, as a figure of the intense love God feels for humanity, and not as a means of procreation. The end of the world is coming, and the biological purpose of sex has no further pertinence to human life. Historically, if I may say so, there were Jews in Palestine during the reigns of Augustus and Tiberius who believed that the world was coming to an end and people had to learn the importance of loving their neighbors before the final judgment. Hence the urgency of John the Baptist's message and then Christ's."

"I don't see," Pyle said, "the, to use your own term, pertinence of all that to the issue at hand. Christ is presented as a homosexual. The average Christian must regard that as blasphemous. Don't you agree?"

"I agree," I said, "but the average Christian may well be wrong. Just as the average Palestinian Pharisee seems to have been wrong in regarding Christ's teaching as blasphemous. It may well be the job of a certain kind of writer to make the average Christian look at Christ with new eyes. Christ was part divine, part human, so we are taught. The human aspect ought to encompass sexuality. It seems to me very probable that Christ was not altogether celibate. What I mean is, celibacy was no more esssential to his mission than it is in the pastorate of the Church of England. If Christ were presented as writing a love letter to, say, Mary Magdalene, would that be regarded as blasphemous?"

"We have to ask the questions, Toomey," Sir Arnold said. "Sorry about that, old man."

"I understand, your honor, but I suppose I'm really asking for guidance. D. H. Lawrence wrote a story about the resurrected Christ called *The Man Who Died*. In it he has Christ recognize the importance of sexuality. The book was regarded by many as extremely reverent. It was not, I think, banned."

"It would have been a big job," Sir Arnold said, "banning all of that chap's books. There's one banned, though, and likely to remain banned. That *Lady Chatterley* thing. Whether it's ordinary sex or the other kind, the law lets you go so far and no farther. This poet here has enough descriptions of ah ah sexuality to merit suppression. I mean, would Thackeray want to write this sort of thing? Would Dickens? Would you yourself, Toomey?"

"I appreciate your grouping my name with those distinguished ones, your honor. If I myself would not it may confess an unworthy limitation of temperament. I am naturally shy of explicit sexual description. But I tend to applaud explicitness when I find it in others. Joyce and Henry Miller, for example. It seems to me a mark of literary courage."

4 9 0

"These poems," Pyle said, "if I may call them that, seek to establish a homosexual relationship between Jesus Christ and each of the twelve disciples. Sometimes the relationship is expressed in terms which I suppose the author would regard as ingeniously appropriate to the person addressed. The sound of Judas's ah ecstasy is likened to the tinkle of thirty pieces of silver. Saint Peter is complimented on his lusty fisherman's rod."

There was a buzz of amusement and, from a reporter, a vulgar laugh at once muffled. Sir Arnold himself smiled and then put his dead pipe in his mouth to convert the show of yellow teeth to a stem-gripping rictus.

"Evidently," I said, "these symbols are not without wit. Wit was once regarded as a legitimate element in even the most devout literature of religion. I mean, Donne, Crashaw, Jeremy Taylor. Crashaw, referring to the infant Jesus being suckled by the Virgin Mary, mentions another teat that will be given to him. A bloody one, he says, and adds 'The mother then must suck the son.' That is wit in the sense of irony. It is not meant for laughter. It may be regarded as sexually perverse. But it is deadly serious and meant devoutly. I submit that these poems of Wrigley have something of that quality. Mr. Eliot, a noted churchman and even vicar's warden, helped English poetry to recover that quality. Another thing. Sexual imagery, perverse or otherwise, has constituted an aspect of a great deal of religious poetry and has never, to my knowledge, previously run into conflict with the secular law. The poems of Saint John of the Cross, depicting the marriage of the soul to the bridegroom Christ, are fiercely erotic. Bernini's sculpture of Saint Teresa, if I may change to another art, shows the saint undergoing what is clearly a kind of orgasm. The Bible itself, in the Song of Solomon, gives us the most sensual poetry in the world, but Christians take it as an allegory of Christ's love for his Church. These poems of Wrigley must be seen in the context of a long and distinguished artistic tradition."

"The point is," Pyle said, "that these poems are homosexual and, to use your own word again, explicitly so. The depiction of Christ as an active homosexual constitutes, does it not, a very offensive and scandalous flouting of another tradition—that to which all decent Christians subscribe."

"But," I said, "it is nothing new to present Christ as a homosexual. Christopher Marlowe, our greatest playwright after Shakespeare, said that Jesus Christ was nought with the beloved disciple John—"

"Was what?" Sir Arnold asked. "What was he?"

"Nought," I said, "your honor. An Elizabethan term meaning mistress or lover. Actually, nought being represented as a circle, it signifies the organ of ingress. It was in very common use. May I add that in Renan's *Life of Christ*—"

"All right, Toomey," Sir Arnold said. "We're coming to the point, I think. This is homosexual poetry for homosexuals. A homosexual point of view deeply offensive to ordinary people, isn't that it?"

"Homosexuals may be in a minority, your honor, though I submit that there is less thoroughgoing heterosexuality in the community than orthodoxy would have us believe. Nevertheless, homosexuals have a right to an expression of their own view of life and love. Our literature has been grievously harmed by the suppression of that right. So, God help us, has society in general. No man or woman can help being homosexual. I cannot help it myself."

It had been said, or very nearly. The declaration had been made, as good as.

Sir Arnold said, "You needn't have said that, Toomey, you know."

"Having said it, your honor, I'd better say it clear and loud. My own work as a creator of fiction has been severely harmed by the taboo on the depiction of the homosexual act of love. My own life has been spent in exile chiefly because of the draconian British rejection of the homosexual sensibility as a legitimate endowment. As a homosexual I speak up now for other homosexuals. And for homosexual art. This book of poems is a sincere expression of an image of Christ very comforting to homosexuals but totally forbidden by a Christian Church hostile, sometimes hypocritically so, to what it regards as a willful aberration. It is not a willful aberration. It is as natural a tropism as the other."

Murmurs of approval and even some tentative claps were quelled swiftly by Sir Arnold's pipe gavel.

"Well," he said, "you've spoken up, Toomey. Thanks for your ah contribution. Anything else, Mr. Pyle?"

"Nothing else, your honor."

"Right, we'll take a break, shall we?"

sixty-five

I could not get a flight to Milan that day, at least not the first-class passage to which old age and comparative affluence, and I might now add moral courage, seemed to entitle me. I presumed that a number of distinct and separate British trade commissions had preempted all first-class seats on all flights to Milan. Well, it would be enough for me to be present at the performance and to hell with last-minute changes in the text. Alitalia offered me a near empty cabin the following morning at 9:50. So, dining alone in my suite on braised endives and an *assiette anglaise*, I was able to read at leisure the reports on the first day of the *J. Christ* preliminary trial. I and my confession received the bulk of the journalists' attention: a famous writer's homosexuality had become headline news. The witnesses who had come after me, some of whom I had stayed to hear, seemed to take their arguments from my own, but none had made a similar declaration. What would the law have done if the entire British literary establishment had, not at all impossible, confessed itself homosexual? My heart prepared to lift when Jack Priestley got into the box, but he merely spoke dourly of the sacred tradition of freedom of expression and quoted *Areopagitica*. There were some simpering poetasters, school of Wrigley, who did the cause no good. The cause, I thought, was a lost one.

So there I was, an avowed lifelong lover of male flesh, receiving telephone requests for interviews but saying no; I had already said all there was to say. I slept peacefully enough except for two brief dreams. One was of my brother Tom being wound up dripping from a deep well. The other was about Carlo thundering an unintelligible Latin or Tamil: it seemed, from his gestures, that he was deploring the lack of bristles on a sweeping brush.

There I was again next morning, a bitter and foggy one and all flights delayed. I sat in the departure lounge at Heathrow and read about myself in *The Times* and *Daily Telegraph*. The *Daily Mirror* had dug up a photograph: I was in a flower-patterned shirt and gesticulated with a flash of rings. I was sure that many in the lounge knew who I was. Look, Mildred, there he is, he's not ashamed of being called a poofter. It suddenly struck me that I was on my way to Carlo's city and Carlo would soon be learning of this declaration and not with pleasure. More, I had publicly defended evident blasphemy. Not that it really mattered to me. I had been out of touch with Carlo, except for a brief meeting in Rome on one of my dental visits and a couple of letters about poor Hortense and the sculptural commission which had not gone unopposed by Italian patriots (what can America do that the country of Michelangelo cannot?). Of course, I had not felt out of touch. If Carlo's elevation had placed him out of the reach of social and even familial intercourse, he was still of a high visibility and audibility. There was no question of my wondering what old Carlo was up to these days. He was up to defending strikes and making enemies of the Turin and Milan capitalists. He was up to sermonizing on texts of Karl Marx. Pius XII was intermittently ill, and the non-Italian secular journals had no doubt who was to be his successor. The trouble was, and Carlo must surely know it, the voice of the popular press was not the voice of the Holy Ghost.

I took a taxi from Linate airport to the Hotel Excelsior and, settled in with a glass of gin before me, telephoned La Scala to ensure that a ticket for the gallery was available for me and would be waiting at the box office. I preferred to take in modern opera from high up: often the real drama was proceeding in the orchestra pit, which was not visible from the stalls. Then I hesitated. Should I at least perform the courtesy of informing the cardinal archbishop that I was here? But I knew that I would be screened from him by auxiliary bishops and chaplains. Finally I decided to call Luigia Campanati, mother superior of the convent in Melzo. I got through to her with little difficulty. She did not at first remember who I was. It was an old sharp voice.

"Kenneth. Kenneth Toomey. Sister of Hortense who married your brother Domenico." I spoke English.

"Kenneth, yes. Ah yes, Kenneth. What are you doing here?"

"Question of an opera. Opening tonight. A very happy and holy feast of Saint Nicholas to you and yours."

"I pray every day for Domenico. He has broken all our hearts. I heard of this opera of Saint Nicholas. I trust it means that God's light is showing to him again. I shall not be there. We do not go to theaters."

"How is . . . how is ah the cardinal?"

"He does not go to theaters either. Will you see him?"

"Is he difficult to see?"

"Very difficult. Tomorrow is our great day."

"Saint Ambrose, yes."

"You will be at mass at the Basilica? You will see the dedication of the new statue?"

"It's not a statue. It's a basso-relievo. It's the work of my sister Hortense. At last the Church acknowledges the artistic gifts of its daughters. God, if I may say so, be thanked."

"No good will come of it. All change is change for the worse. There is always trouble. I come to bring not peace but a sword. We must prepare for great manifestations of evil. Tell Domenico I have no wish to see him."

"Has he already made contact with you?"

"He has not. Perhaps he is ashamed. Let us hope that that is so. Carlo said your sister is a saint. I have tried to see her in visions. Hard times, I say, are coming to us all. I am not well. I have pain. I must keep to my bed. God's will be done."

"What's the trouble? With what are you not well? May I come to see you?"

"It would do little good. Pray for me. Pray for Carlo. Pray for my dead mother and brother in purgatory. My father, I think, is past the help of prayer. Pray for the whole world." And then she put the receiver down.

Cloistered virtue, which neither John Milton nor Jack Priestley loved. Its rewards old age and infirmity. Carlo had never approved of nunneries. He wanted women dedicated to God to face the world for which she asked me to pray, short-skirted, armed with skills, unafraid of rape. She had talked once of going to Africa but, after all, stayed where she was, erotic energy perverted to the hysteria of visions, sadistic authority, an impossible austerity, a wasted life. But who was I to talk?

A certain gloom on me, I dined lightly and went to the great historic theater in good time. *In Prima Mondiale*, the posters and programs said. The names: Campanati, Bevilacqua, Lanuzza, Cechetti, Focchi, Perlini, Nascimbeni, Sudasassi, Sancristoforo, Castelli, Castaldi, Giuffrida, Mangano, Pautasso, Ronfana, Kristeva, Verdiglione and the rest, with Toomey a lone exotic. Lone too standing about in the lower *ridotto*, while smart Milan showed off its jewels and paunches. I was not known here. I drank a champagne cocktail in the bar. Alone, grim, praying for the whole world. The bell rang and I climbed to my *galleria* seat. My companion was a slim structural pillar. Behind me a woman with streaky hair was already humming generic arias. We were thirty-five minutes late starting, but that was, by Italian standards, early. The house was near full and still filling as the lights dimmed. Domenico, a lime spot on his baldness, in tails with a loose collar for comfort, entered and toddled to the rostrum, baton gripped tight like a weapon of offense. He was clapped but not cheered. He surveyed his orchestra, which had a swollen percussion section, including vibraphone and bongo drums; the *sonorità di Hollywood* a man near me quipped unkindly. The floats glowed. The desklamps glowed. Domenico raised his baton. Pianissimo chords on muted horns and trombones and a slack roll on the deepest kettledrum. Debussyish consecutive fourths on oboes and clarinets. The curtain rose.

Verdiglione, producer and stage designer, had done his work well. The set, depicting the interior of an ancient tavern, was remote from realism: we were into fable. With steps near balletic three robed and cowled figures entered. They were greeted in gesture by a rotund innkeeper whom the orchestral brass designated as evil. They sat at table, a flat with trenchers painted on it, unforeshortened as in a primitive canvas that had not yet discovered perspective. In stylized motion the three were smitten down, bags of presumed silver abstracted by the innkeeper's wife. Not a word sung. A pickletub flat was wheeled on. The three corpses, which palpably assisted the dragger, were dragged and placed behind the flats. Domenico's music tried to depict the acid action of the pickling liquor. There was some amusement in the audience: this was not opera; this was Mickey Mouse. The lights went briefly down on the three pickled, cowled, heads bent, hands crossed on breast. A knock, threefold, on Chinese block was turned by the woodwind into a leitmotif. Lights came up on the entrance of Nicholas, dressed in traveling clothes but carrying a crosier. It was Mario Cechetti: he was applauded while the orchestra held a *fermata*. Singing began. Nicholas would have meat. Chicken? No. Beef? No. Veal? No. He would have the meat in a pickletub which he was sure lay behind that curtain. He drew the curtain back. He made the motions of blessing as the three cowled corpses were revealed. The innkeeper and his wife sank to their fearful knees. Hidden choirs in antiphony sang alleluia as the miracle of resuscitation was performed. Male voice trio: Nicholas and the two outer resuscitated. The middle one, of course, was the coloratura Julia Kristeva, known as the most voluptuous Salome in the business. The time for the revelation of her sex and mission was not yet.

Not till the first act proper, which followed without break on the prologue. The set was changed in the view of the audience: it became, with the frank raising and lowering of flats, the interior of Nicholas's palace. The music became grayish and devout. Nicholas and the three resurrected had not moved from their former positions. Now there was an aria from Nicholas as he spoke his intentions, and the three inspected, like sniffing cats, their new home. They were bidden stand at three lecterns to start studying Scripture. Nicholas came downstage to a prie-dieu. His back to the trio, he knelt and gave thanks to God for the miracle and prayed that the adopted sons—Fra Marco, Fra Matteo, Fra Giovanni—would prove worthy of it. Meanwhile the three indicated their diabolic provenance by making fire flash from a Septuagint. Marco and Giovanni grinned devilishly at Matteo and then quietly left. Turning, Nicholas saw that Matteo was ripping off his habit, to be revealed as a woman of terrible allure, scantily clad: Venere herself. The music began to swell as if accompanying cinematic sunrise over the desert. No no no, Domenico did not have it in him. The woman behind me began to hum the theme as if she, which in a sense she did, knew it already. Julia Kristeva from the Dalmatian coast loosed aphrodisiacal syrup that stirred even my scrotum. The temptation of the senses of Nicholas began: it owed something to Flaubert's *Tentation de Saint Antoine* and involved phantasmagoric images of wine, food and copulation. Nicholas desperately invoked the figure of the suffering Christ. Christ appeared, only to reveal himself as the naked god Pan. Ballet of hetaerae and houris, choreography by Italo Castaldi. Nicholas fell. Great love or sex duet between himself and Venere. The music mimed coitus. Some woman to my right tutted loudly. The coitus was interrupted in mid-chord. Was this Domenico recalling that terrible event of the Hollywood party all those years back? In an updated *Tannhäuser* downward glissade of strings the scene of riot vanished, leaving a half-naked Nicholas to repent, lash himself with sauna birchtwigs. The three, demure in monk's robes, resumed their former stances at their lecterns, singing a holy trio, Venere or Fra Matteo's part well below the stave. Nicholas bewildered. Had it happened in truth, or had it been but an unholy dream? God God, what is happening to me?

End of scene but not of act. Audience murmurs during interlude of ecclesiastical counterpoint on brass. It came to me for the first time that I had not consulted the executors of the estate of Anatole François Thibault, or Anatole France, as to the availability of permission to adapt his story to the stage. I felt the shiver of impending danger from that quarter. Not that there was really anything of the story left. When the curtain rose the décor had changed to classical pillars, a vista of palms, and chairs and thrones for the assembling bishops of the first ecumenical council of Nicaea. Gianni Pellicani, a deep Roman bass, was Athanasius; Arius the heretic, historically an old man, was played by the young sexy tenor Tito Sudasassi. Nicholas in full episcopal robes. In the background, a humble carrier of documents, Fra Marco. Sudasassi sexily proclaimed his heresy. The Son was not coeternal with the Father. The Son was a created being, though far surpassing all others. Tell the world that Father and Son possessed the same substance and you would be encouraging it to believe in two Gods. *Homoousis homoousis*, chanted the bishops, onesubstance onesubstance. Too many male ensembles, I thought, everybody would think. One needed the clear yellow light of female voices. Domenico must have thought so too, for now a chorus of sailors' wives and sweethearts broke into the assembly, imploring Nicholas, as a kind of Christian Poseidon, to still the turbulent waves of the Mediterranean: they had seen the homeward-bound ship manned by their men tossing and bucking in the distance, impelled toward the dreaded Macheri rock. Out out, women, cried the bishops: we are at holy and important work; we are quelling a heresy that will destroy more than a mere rock will. Nicholas agreed but, to bring the proceedings to an end and enable him to perform his salvatory mission, he swung into a cabaletta which summed up the argument against Arius and then, fired, struck the heresiarch a knockdown blow. Consternation, condemnation of unbishoply conduct. Fra Marco now, with his shrill tenor, dominated the conclave. Nicholas was the true heresiarch: here were documents to prove it. He had proclaimed that the one true divinity was Venus, in a sexual transport he had proclaimed it. Nicholas could not utter a word of denial. He choked, gurgled, sank to his knees. Episcopal fingers shaking in horror pointed. Athanasius's voice led all the rest. Arius, recovering from the blow, rose to add his sexy tenor to the ensemble. The sailors' women appeared again, this time as a mourning chorus: too late, too late, the ship was wrecked, Nicholas had let everybody down. Curtain. End of first act. Lengthy intermission.

Well, there was something of myself in that turbulent scene, but far more of Bevilacqua. Let Bevilacqua take the knocks, if any, from the Anatole France executors. Dramatically none of it was bad, but the music was of the kind that gets a man an Oscar. I met Vern Clapp in the upper bar. "Well," he said, and knocked back pure Bosford's gin. "It ain't," he said, "Wagner. Or Puccini. Or Alban Berg."

"I note that my libretto has been rewritten in many places. It's just like Hollywood."

"You'll find," he said, "even more rewriting in the second act. That Bevilacqua's quite a boy. You should have been around. To protect your property."

"I've had various things to do."

"Yeah, I read about one of them. In today's *Daily American*. You got quite a write-up. The day of justice for deviants is dawning. Say, that would set well to music." I heard what I took to be a music critic behind me uttering terms like *banalità*. I heard a female voice crying *bestemmia*.

"I don't," I said, "find the Voice of God in the program."

"Done by a male chorus," Vern Clapp said vaguely. The bell rang.

The second and final act began with Nicholas in sackcloth doing penance. Word came from Rome to say that all episcopal duties and privileges were now restored. The Pope was well pleased with Nicholas's treatise on the Holy Trinity and his eloquent denunciation of Arius. Unfortunately, a great number of Germanic tribes had been converted to Christianity by Arians and the heresy was deeply rooted among them. Fra Giovanni appeared to announce that he had been given a special imperial appointment to extirpate with fire and sword the damnable aberration. You? Yes, I. And the friar removed his habit to reveal himself clad in armor. Kill them all. Torture them before killing. Cleanse them with fire before plunging the knife in. No no no, our faith is a faith of love, cried Nicholas. So we love the foul heretics who believe Christ to be non-coeternal with the Father? Nonsense. War. The vaguely ecclesiastical décor, with its pillars and mullions, ascended to the flies, and the scene thereafter was a kind of blasted heath, with Nicholas crying like Lear against the roar of the tempest, the tempest being battle conducted in the orchestra on good Hollywood principles, mainly plagiarism of Holst's *Mars*. The producer, helped I presumed by Bevilacqua and abetted by Domenico, had episodes of Nazi-style interrogation slotted into scenes of massacre, and all the time Nicholas protested or looked on helpless. *"Dove sono i carri armati?"* a man asked behind me, and he was answered by bits of film of modern war projected onto the cyclorama. At one point Nicholas besought heaven to send down Love, and Venere herself appeared as a goddess of brothels for soldiers. Bereft mothers pleaded with Nicholas for a miracle. One of them placed the bloody corpse of a child in his arms. And then Nicholas was alone with the child, his eyes again up to heaven. The noise of war receded to allow him to ask God why why why. There was no answer. "You are a God of hate," Nicholas cried, "a God who murders the innocent. Why did you permit that miracle? See what that miracle is doing to the world? Tell me why you put that power into my hands." I waited for the racket to modulate into soothing chords for high strings, roseate clouds to gather and hover, the blasted heath become an Edenic landscape, angelic voices intone a hymn, the voice of God say this was all a temptation to Nicholas to curse his Creator and, see, he had come through uncursing: get ready for sainthood. But all that happened was that Nicholas gave out *Maledico maledico* on a high B flat and, as the curtain slowly descended, was drowned by the renewed din of war, the child still limp in his arms.

There was applause enough, but there were also catcalls. Spectators in our gallery began to get down to the rails to look at what was proceeding in the stalls, for the shouts of battle seemed to have been transferred thither from the wings. Conservative musicians were standing to denounce the work as a disgrace to La Scala and one another as insufficiently conservative or something. The young were cheering: the God addressed by Nicholas was really the Italian establishment. Punches were launched at the young by the less young. The less young were punched back by the young. The singers took their bows and were mostly bravoed. Small contained fights went on in the auditorium. A fracas with unhandy blows began not far from myself. Domenico appeared on the stage with the singers and was booed and acclaimed. I got out.

sixty-six

The bas-relief representing the birth, life and death of Saint Ambrose, patron of Milan, was, until Carlo's successor removed it, to be seen in the Duomo di Maria Nascente, affixed to a patch of wall near the marble altar created by Martino Bassi, with Giulio Cesare Procaccini's statue of Saint Ambrose not far away. It should, if a modern monument to the saint were required at all by the Milanese, properly have been set up in the Basilica di San Ambrogio, but this has always been a near autonomous temple, with its own (Ambrosian) rite and confidence in its own principles of sacred art, which do not encompass the modern and exotic. The marble which Hortense had incised was good New York State stone, as firm and lovely as Carrara and far better than San Pietro. On it she had sculpted the infant Ambrose's head, with bees swarming about his lips in token of heaven's favor; the young Ambrose togaed as prefect of Milan; Ambrose naked, casting off his garments along with his wealth; Ambrose in full bishop's fig from the waist up, all balls and leg muscles beneath, cursing Arius; Ambrose raising a stone head of Zeus to smash it, cursing Aurelius Symmachus; Ambrose naked on his deathbed, singing one of his own hymns. The style, which mixed Eric Gill and Epstein, was not appreciated by the Italians, and there were powerful complaints about Ambrose's explicit masculinity. It was likened to a strip cartoon in the *Daily American*: it needed only *fumetti* with ZOWIE and EEEEK; one critic called it SUPERSANTO. Carlo stoutly defended it as a tribute from the New Catholic World to the Old; the Milanese must start learning the meaning of the term Catholic.

I did not attend the dedication of this work (for which Hortense was paid five thousand dollars) on December 7. Instead, after writing a letter to Domen-

ico deploring the alterations to my libretto, especially the blasphemous trunca-
tion, and demanding that my name be withdrawn from the programs and
posters, I flew back, via Rome and Madrid, to Tangier. I was angry, but my
anger was a little appeased by the notices in the Italian newspapers. The critic
in the *Corriere della Sera* said that the opera was an affront to the cardinal, the
saint, and all true believers, but its perversion of the hagiographic truth could
have been swallowed had there been copious drafts of music with, if not originality, at least character to wash it down. *La Stampa* of Turin called it a
Broadway musical without tunes and hinted at a vendetta within the Campanati
family. *Il Messaggero* said that the true blasphemy was not the cynical twisting
of a sacred legend but the pollution of a noble temple of art by a confection
which was pure Hollywood. The communist papers on the other hand praised
the work as a slap in the face for the forces of reaction, though they ignored the
music.

When I got back to the house on Calle Mozart I found that Ralph was still
away in Rabat. Ali said, with all the deference in the world, that I had neglected
to pay the wages due at the end of November: much on the señor's mind, no
doubt, a trivial matter like wages easily forgotten, but if the señor would be so
good— I apologized and went round to my branch of the Banque du Maroc on
the rue Spinoza: I was quite cashless after my trip. I made out a check and the
clerk took it away. He returned puzzled and apologetic. He said that, except for
a few dirhams, I had drawn out the entire balance of my current account on
December 5. Impossible, I was away in London on that date. He brought the
check. The sum drawn was one million four thousand two hundred and fifty
dirhams; the date was as he said; the signature was mine. The signature was not
mine; it was Ralph's facsimile of mine; he had shown that minor talent before,
in abusive letters to publishers and others purporting to come from me. *"Mon
secrétaire?"* I said. *"Le monsieur américain?"*

"Oui, le monsieur nègre."

He'd brought checks signed by me before for encashment, though never
before for a sum so large. I kept calm before these bank menials with their large
wondering brown eyes. I even smiled. I gently cursed to them my absentmindedness. I would cable Geneva and arrange for a transfer of funds. Meanwhile I
needed cash. *"Bien sûr, monsieur."*

I went home, paid Ali his wage and gave him money for marketing. Then I
looked at Ralph's room. Everything was gone, but there was no farewell message. There is no need to transcribe my feelings. Indeed, feelings are always a
most difficult thing to convey. I rage I melt I burn and so on, like Polifemo in
Acis and Galatea. And yet it had always been to be expected, it had always
been in the nature of the relationship and every relationship of that order. The
foreknowledge had been part of the furniture. Still, I felt excoriated, flayed,
dreadfully abused. All over, good riddance, forget him, yet I could not forget

him. The musky exhalations of his skin were printed on my epithelium; I saw his fingers walking on the harpsichord keyboard, his teeth stained with fig juice; I heard the resonances of a voice hued like his body.

I watched the mail, I watched it for a month, hoping for a letter whining that he was stranded in Mombasa or on Aldabra Island, disabused, desperate, begging to be taken back. I had no doubt that it was to East Africa he had gone, thinking he was homing. I am here in Mogadishu, and it's hell, man. Dearest Ken, please fly to Arusha and bring me back, I've learned my lesson. And then, in February, when I had experienced the first sweet pangs of awareness that I could adjust myself to his absence, I received a letter, the address typed, the stamp the gaudy assertive one of a new African state, with the name RUKWA crowning a black Mussolinian profile, gaudy jungle flora behind. "Dear Ken," I read, "I know you regarded the taking of the money as the least of my crimes. One of the good things about you was not caring too much about money. If you want the money you can have it, though there will have to be some fiddling because there's a severe limitation just been put through on the amount you can legally export from Rukwa. As you see from the letterhead I'm working in the Information Department. The official language is English at present and English will be the second language when Rukwayi has been properly modernized and established, which will be a long job. I knew I was right to come to Africa. Randy Foulds is here with the official title of Minister of Education but he spends most of his time on a new book which he says will be the first real African novel. The big job is total Africanization. You don't want to hear about making omelettes and having to break eggs, but some Asian hearts have to be broken. All the commerce in Tukinga, which is being built up into a modern capital city, has been in the hands of the Asians for as far back as you can go, but now there has to be expropriation and enforced repatriation and the rest of it. That goes too for the whites including the missionaries who run the hospitals and the technicians who were brought in under the late unlamented Hossan Zambolu. Peaceful unification is another of our slogans, which means working on the tribal mind, as the boss calls it, and instilling the idea of a bigger patriotism. No violence, no police state methods. My knowledge of a little Oma surprised the boss and showed him I was serious. I've a hell of a lot to do. But I'm happy, very happy. For the first time. You might not recognize me now in my red handwoven robe. I sign myself as always but I have to think of myself as Kasam Ekuri. Believe it or not, but the name Kentumi exists here. I tell them there's only one Ken Toomey."

There was more, but not much more. My heart sank further with every line I read. The innocence of the boy, the political ignorance, the damnable optimism. He made it easy for me to put him out of my mind. Ralph didn't exist any more. There was a black functionary in a new state that would soon learn to be repressive. He wore a red robe and was named Kasam Ekuri. I did not know the man.

On the very day I received this letter that terrible issue of *La Domenica Ambrosiana* appeared which, under the title *Peccati Cardinali* and the by-line Massimo Fioroni, devoted many pages to the denunciation of that other innocent, Carlo Campanati. I did not see a copy until a fortnight after its publication. I was taking a gloomy cocktail in the bar of the Rif and saw an Italian tourist yawning over the magazine. There was Carlo on the cover, caught by a camera in an unfortunate posture—raising a glass of what could have been blood, Tuscan cigar in mouth, cigar smoke billowing as amply as steam at night from a Manhattan street grating. I asked if I could borrow. The man said I could keep, he had done with it. But, with reference to the picture on the cover, he showed fine vicious teeth and made a thumb-down gesture. That was a fair précis of the article. I read:

"*I membri del regno si possono riconoscere sempre: dai loro frutti . . .*

"Those who belong to the kingdom are easy to recognize: by their fruits shall ye know them. We may ask: which kingdom? We may also add to fruits circumcrescent greenery. With the failing health of the Holy Father the question of his successor inevitably arises, and among the number of the *papabili* the name of Carlo Campanati, Cardinal Archbishop of Milan, has been glowing, especially in the gutter press, with a proleptic nimbus of election. It is time to consider not merely the fruits of his reign in the archdiocese of Milan but also the odors of his associations." I regret that this does not always sound like English. Pompous Italian journalism translates ill. "The Campanati stock offers much of bizarre fascination to the student of family backgrounds in the Italian prelacy. Its commercial side began humbly enough with the production and national retailing of one of the more famous, and certainly most redolent, of our cheeses. Later it branched out and grew an American affiliation. The father of the present Cardinal Archbishop of Milan married an American lady of mixed Northern Italian origins and begot three Italo-American sons and one Italo-American daughter before fading out of both commerce and society to await the lethal outcome of a disease whose dire nature may be surmised if not, in the considerations of decency, named. The daughter became a sister of the contemplative order of Saint John the Divine and reached the venerable eminence of mother superior. The youngest son became a musician of mediocre talent who found his vocation in the composition of mediocre music for mediocre Hollywood films. The eldest son emigrated to Chicago as the director of an organization dedicated to the importation into the United States of Italian foodstuffs. We know what the third son became.

"Before we examine this son's career let us consider what happened to those members of the family which remained in the secular world. The mother courageously allied herself to the cause of persecuted Jewry during the time of the Nazi regime, contracted a deadly disease, and sought a way out of her own suffering by an action which might technically be considered suicidal but which the more charitable could construe as a self-elected matyrdom. Attempting to assassinate Heinrich Himmler outside a Berlin cinema, she was deflected from success by the prompt action of a companion of the Reichsführer and herself met a prompt end at the hands of gunmen of the SS. The eldest son had, some time earlier, been drawn into conflict with Chicago gangsters. Apparently ill-equipped to fight Al Capone and his myrmidons with the right moral and legal weapons, and certainly quite unequipped to oppose him with a more telling armament, he met mutilation and death in the sordid circumstances inseparable from a Chicago gang warfare which most of my readers will be acquainted with only from its glamorous exploitation on the cinema screen.

"This brings us to the youngest son, whose association with that same cinema screen began in the first days of the talking films and only recently came to an end with an ill-advised incursion into a field of art somewhat beyond even the most ambitious exertion of his talents. A composer of film music and a denizen of the film capital of the world, he succumbed to the immoral ambience of a culture dedicated to money and pleasure, blatantly forsook the faith of his fathers, and immersed himself in the Mussulman joys of the serial polygamy which the American divorce laws countenance. He had, be it noted, contracted a Catholic marriage to a member of a British family but, suspecting, with justice as it later transpired, that the two children of the marriage were not his own, he effected a separation to be shortly transmuted into a civil divorce.

"He had married into the Toomey family, and the most distinguished member of this family is Kennet [sic] Toomey, the novelist and playwright, whose works are well known in Italy as the kind of superficial diversion which, acceptable in its own terms, is not to be confused with genuine literature. Kennet [sic] Toomey recently announced in the British press, with temerity rather than courage, that he is of the homosexual persuasion. His sister, in an interview which appeared in the American press somewhat before Kennet [sic] Toomey's declaration, admitted on questioning that she was living in an undisguised relationship of lesbic pseudomatrimony with a Negress. Both Kennet [sic] Toomey and his sister, who still fulfills the nominative regulations of Catholic marriage by terming herself Mrs. Campanati, swam into the Milanese orbit recently with what they both no doubt considered as contributions to Italian culture. Mrs. Campanati's sculptural comic strip of the career of Milan's own patron saint was solemnly installed in the Duomo. One may legitimately enquire into the motivations which prompted His Eminence the Cardinal to commission this work, paying, against lay and clerical opposition which his authority easily overrode, several million lire out of the archdiocesan funds. The work is certainly incompetent, if not blasphemous, and it insults the genuine, and genuinely devout, Italian art which glorifies the Duomo. His Eminence has defended the work of his sister-in-law as high and holy, and even spoke of the sanctity of life of this alleged artist. This is a somewhat unorthodox interpretation of a lesbic ménage. The incompetence of the piece of sculpture could be perhaps excused in terms of the disadvantages of monocular vision, since the lady was transformed, in circumstances somewhat unclear but perhaps sufficiently romantic, into a female Cyclops.

"Kennet [sic] Toomey's contribution to the art of Milan was the libretto of the opera *Una Leggenda su San Nicola*, which had its premiere at La Scala on December 6 last but was withdrawn after fewer than the number of its scheduled performances. This, loosely based (without, it has transpired, the permission of the copyright holders) on a story by Anatole France, employs a travestied version of a legend of the great saint to hammer home, in gross words and grosser music, the interesting thesis that God is evil, and that even divine miracles may be employed as devices for propagating evil in the world. It is true that there was no consultation, on the part of either the homosexual librettist or the renegade much divorced composer, of the highest religious authority in the city as to the legitimacy of the project, and the great prelate himself has washed his hands, in good Pilatian fashion, of responsibility for the secular activities of his archdiocese, but it might be supposed that the long announced title of the work would excite interest in His Eminence, especially as its composer was his own brother and its librettist his friend.

"The friendship between Kennet [sic] Toomey and the cleric who began as Don Carlo, became monsignore, and, if his admirers can overcome the workings of the Holy Spirit, may yet be a genuine candidate for Saint Peter's throne, is of long standing. It reached a practical fulfillment in a strange collaborative act which, at the time of its perpetration, caused little stir. Kennet [sic] Toomey mysteriously presents himself in a book entitled in Italian *Cerchiamo Iddio* and published by Einaudi as the secular voice of many religious voices, meaning that he has taken it upon himself to present in a popular even diverting style the deliberations of a number of progressive theologians and pastors on the future which evangelical Christianity ought, in their collective view, to take. Some of the proposals are startling. The great term is *ecumenical*. The final vision seems to be of a unified Deism, in which traditionally firm Christian dogmas are modified to a convenient vagueness when not liquidated entirely. The vagueness is peculiarly helpful to the kind of disordered intelligence which can reconcile Christianity with Marxist materialism. Attentive listeners to His Eminence's sermons in the Duomo, as well as to his frequent weekend homilies on Radiotelevisione Italiana, attentive readers of His Eminence's pastoral epistles will already have found promulgated, in admittedly a form more rhetorical than rational, some of the bizarre new doctrines of which Kennet [sic] Toomey consented to be the nominal promoter. It will be noted, strangely enough, that the book makes no provision for the reconciliation of homosexual practices with the teaching of even the laxist oneiric Church envisioned in a work which, whoever the other anonymous collaborators may be, bears the strong personal stamp of His not yet achieved Eminence.

"But the great prelate is not yet demented enough to sponsor sexual perversion. It was left to Kennet [sic] Toomey to combine on an all too public occasion, namely in the course of a criminal prosecution against one of his own friends, a notorious British homosexual poet, a declaration of his own sexual position with a spirited defense of a book, published by that same poet, in which Our Blessed Lord and Redeemer is presented as a pervert of his own stamp. Words are inadequate to express the shock, horror and literally physical nausea which even the most general articulation of such a blasphemous concept inevitably occasions even in the soul of a nonbeliever. The true believer will hardly find it credible that such a filthy farrago as the volume represents should reach the public, however low a view he may have of the capabilities of a Protestant culture. That the book was suppressed only after long debate, and that the decision of one court of justice may well be set aside by another, sufficiently indicates the perilous condition of that culture.

"The cardinal archbishop has strange friends. He has also a strange family. He has strange notions of Christian doctrine. He proclaimed many years ago his abhorrence of the most fundamental dogma of the faith—that doctrine of original sin which, long before the Word was made flesh and dwelt among us, presupposed the necessity of divine redemption. Man is God's creation, His Eminence preaches, and hence is good. Evil is wholly external, entirely a diabolic monopoly. Evil is exorcizable. In spite of the evidence of human depravity, the wretched years of a shameful history through which we have all recently lived, the hardly credible enormities which men have suffered but, in the terrible human paradox, also willed, he holds fast to a misguided belief in a spiritual immaculacy which, as Holy Church teaches, was vouchsafed by God to one human creature only, God's own mother.

"In the secular sphere His Eminence exhibits a cognate eccentricity. The spirit of man in our age, according to him, is most nobly manifested in the proletariat. The aspirations of this proletariat, as voiced by the syndicates, are, in his view, totally reconcilable with the Augustinian vision of the City of God. What Marx wanted, God wants also. In his obscure logic, His Eminence locates the secular equivalent of theological evil only in capitalism and cannot find a trace of the morally reprehensible in even the most irresponsible acts of syndicalism. If we place the template of his perverted theology on the scheme of his anarchical philosophy, we shall find the Father of Lies snugly located in the citadels of capitalist endeavor.

"I have said enough for the moment, but I speak with only the authority of decency, reason and orthodoxy. Can there be any doubt of the necessity of the raising of voices in which a stronger, I might say a Petrine, authority vibrates? The Vatican remains silent on the subject of the vagaries of one of its princes. It is a silence, one presumes, of prolonged and pathological shock rather than of complicity. Let us now hope to hear the thunderings of the Pilot of the Galilean Lake and the rattle of the omnipotent keys."

So. "*Il tintinnio delle chiavi onnipotenti.*" That *tintinnio* was a bit inept, sounding like the tinkle of car keys. The rest was resonant enough. Actionable? I doubted it. I had, in my career as a novelist, learned something of the law of libel. Nastiness in itself was no tort. This journalist, whose name was unfamiliar to me, had taken care to get his facts right. Behind him were foreign press bureaus. Behind him, more particularly, was money. It was capital, far more than faith, that Carlo had outraged. I dreamed for a while of commissioning one of the mercenaries of the Casbah to get over to Milan and assassinate this Massimo Fioroni on behalf of Hortense and her children. But surely it was up to Carlo to shrivel up the pusillanimous wretch with roars more terrible than tenpenny daggers.

Whatever response Carlo intended was never delivered. Getting up into the pulpit of his own cathedral on the second Sunday in Lent, he emitted a sudden bellow like that of a bull that feels the shears of the gelder and then collapsed. The hand of God had struck him, some said; others, the hoof of the devil. A cardiac arrest, the more rational presumed. As he lay still on his back he let out a row of Falstaffian snores. They would have made shudder, like a thirty-two-foot organ pipe, a sacred edifice less massive. It took six servitors to carry him off.

sixty-seven

I had my own affairs to attend to. Nevertheless, I wrote a long commiseratory letter to Carlo, who was sent for a rest to a nursing home run by nuns at Bellagio on the Lake of Como. I received no reply. I traveled, an aging man who, though the whole world knew him to be homosexual, had been restored to his habitual loneliness. Early in October 1958 Carlo, back on much reduced duty, sent me a cable. I was ordered to spend a weekday with him at the Hôtel de Paris, Monte Himself. His secretary had made all arrangements. I was prepared to disobey the order, having already been invited by His Majesty of

Morocco to attend a banquet and reception for the U.S. Secretary of State in Rabat. But curiosity, shame and even affection prevailed. I flew to Barcelona and thence to Nice. I rode in a taxi along the Corniche. The sea was calm, the sky was clear, the air was mild. At the hotel I was informed that His Eminence had already arrived. I was shown to my room and then to his suite.

Carlo was seventy-odd, nobly fat, wonderfully ugly, apparently recovered. He was dressed in the total red of his rank. He had come, I gathered, alone. He offered me whisky, the rare brand Old Mortality. He said, "They told me the Casino was reserved for some visiting oil sheikhs. I was not having that. Would you put the infidel before a prince of your own Church? They then telephoned through to say that His Highness Hussain ibn Al-Haji Yusof or somebody would be honored if I joined the party. So. We play first. Dine after. Does that suit you?"

"How many years is it now since we did that? Forty?"

"Forty. There were three of us then."

"Yes, three of us." I sensed that there was a taboo on mentioning the third by name. "How are you, Carlo?"

"Well enough. You realize that the moment of truth is coming?"

"You mean a certain death is imminent in Rome?"

"Yes yes yes. You remember before the war, in Moneta, we discussed Greek tragedy. I cannot remember whether the term *hubris* came up."

"I don't think it did."

"Have some more whisky." He appraised me from his plush armchair. "Help yourself. You're thin. You look old. How old are you now?"

"Sixty-eight."

"Old, and you haven't yet come through to what I said." All this talk was very cryptic. "The revelation has not occurred."

"Revelations of human turpitude. Plenty of those."

"Human turpentine," he said in sudden jocularity. "Serpentine turpitude. You know why I was sick?"

"I assumed—"

"So did many. In fact it was the exhaustion of the hardest struggle of my entire career." His English accent was more British than I remembered: it came fairly close, in vocalic length and intonation, to that of the quondam Archbishop of York, but there was no fluting, the resonance rose from the belly still. "There was a child in a poor family in Novara, bored through like a cheese with infernal presences. Quell or quench one, whatever the word is, and another would take its place. The usual silly little names—Popo and Cazzo and Stronzetto. The usual silly little blasphemies. Then one day there was silence from all these, as though they were waiting for a tyrannical schoolmaster and could hear his footsteps in the corridor. I waited too, and then came the authentic tonalities of the master. Well-read in many languages, courteous. He quoted that damnable article with great accuracy. He performed little conjuring tricks in a bored manner. He made the electricity go off and come on again, projected a kind of film of my early life onto the ceiling, produced vile odors for which he apologized and which he replaced with the scents of our garden at Gorgonzola. He recited the ordinary of the mass very devoutly, but at the same time he devoured the body of the child, on whose face was set a kind of comic grin."

"Devoured?"

"The limbs visibly wasted but the belly grew like a balloon and I knew it was going to burst like that of a poisoned dog. I felt I was powerless. He knew the Rituale Romanum far better than I. The stress wore me down very badly, especially as I was fasting. Many days of it, and only a few hours of rest. I did not use the prescribed order of exorcism. I prayed and prayed and I failed. He said *vale sancte pater* and broke the child's neck. Broke it as you would break the neck of a rabbit. It was all over and I had failed. It is no wonder I became sick."

"He spoke Latin?"

"Latin. And then the poor child's neck snapped, and then there was silence."

"There's only one man who can be addressed as Holy Father. Can the devil speak true?"

"The Father of Lies?" He gave a huge shrug. "If he lies all the time then he must be telling the truth. But he does not lie all the time, and that is why he is a great liar." And then, *"Hubris, hubris.* Shall we go now and play?"

In the lobby of the hotel Carlo received obeisances and dispensed blessings. One or two open-necked Americans merely gawked and one said, "Whadyaknow, a commie reverend." But Carlo did not hear. He had gone to the statue of Louis XIV and was stroking the raised foreleg of his horse. It gleamed a richer gold after all those forty years. "It is not," he said, "the kind of luck which you think it is that I seem to be asking for, not that I ask for anything," still cryptic. We went out into the mild evening and crossed to the Casino, Carlo blessing blessing all the way.

The little gambling principality was, after a time of slump in which it had watched Nice, Antibes and Cannes eclipse it in popularity, now recovering, thanks chiefly to its ruler. His recent marriage to a lady of good family of Philadelphia, who had achieved world fame as a screen actress; the association, later to be broken, with a vulgar but lucky Greek shipping tycoon who had sought to add Monaco to his fleet; the promotion of thalassography and the encouragement of art—these were bringing fresh fame and glamour to the tiny state, whose prosperity and independence its great neighbor France begrudged and snarled at. The Casino, usually thronged, tonight had the tranquillity of a church or mosque. The visiting Arabs had, it seemed, insisted for some security reason or other, or out of a sheer show of insolent wealth, on the closure of all rooms except the single *salle privée* reserved to them. To this rococo chapel of play we were bowed. The prince had, in his kindly wisdom, reinstated the old custom of providing free refreshments for serious gamblers, and Carlo eagerly accepted the misted flute of Mumm he was reverently offered. There, sipping orange squash, stood the white-robed magnates of the desert, ten or so in number. Three of them wore dark glasses against the mellow enough light of the chandeliers, and these were introduced to Carlo and myself by a well-spoken functionary in a Savile Row suit and Old Etonian tie. Their Highnesses the Sheikhs Fazal ibn Sayed, Mohamed ibn Al-Marhum Yusof, Abdul Khadir ibn al-Haji Yunus Redzwan. This last name, I remembered from Malaya, meant the same as that of Monaco's princess. And there she was in a painting on the wall, softly illumined. A banal romantic theme of poor Domenico's swam into my head: he had composed the score for *No Way Out*, in which, in her previous incarnation, she had appeared with Cary Grant. Carlo made out, with a gold pen, a check on the Bank of the Holy Spirit and received, with bows, plaques of large denomination.

"Roulette?" The suggestion was that of His Highness the Sheikh Abdul Khadir.

The prince of the Holy Roman Catholic and Apostolic Church replied, "*D'accord, pour commencer.*"

We had the requisite number of croupiers in attendance, despite the exiguity of the party—one at each end of the table, two close together in each of its curved waists, the *chef de partie* on his raised throne.

"*Messieurs, faites vos jeux,*" and the wheel spun, the ivory ball trundled in the wooden basin and rolled against the direction of rotation of the wheel. Carlo handed over three chips and asked for *finales sept par dix*. The croupier obediently placed the chips on 7, 17 and 27. The princes bet the maximum, sixty thousand old francs each, *en plein, à cheval, carré*. I took a humble *chance simple* and made a gesture of self-depreciation: I was not really here myself to play. "*Les jeux sont faits, rien ne va plus.*" The ball lost velocity, struck the diamond-shaped metal studs of the basin, grew drunk and arbitrary of motion, reached the wheel, fought the raised metal edges of the numbered compartments, came at last to rest. The croupier announced: "*Dix-sept, noir, impair et manque.*" Chips were raked toward Carlo: he did not seem overjoyed.

He did not seem overjoyed when, trying all the *chances multiples—transversale, carré, à cheval, quatre premiers, sixain, colonne, douzaine*—he won a great deal more than he lost. One of the minor princes, whose name we did not know, said in fine English, "The money will go to the poor, your eminence?"

Carlo replied, cryptic as ever this evening, "The poor you have always with you."

"Trente-et-quarante?" Sheikh Fazal ibn Sayed suggested. So trente-et-quarante, the rich man's game, it was. We moved to the shieldlike table, simply emblazoned with its diamond *noir* and *rouge*, its *couleur* arrow and its chevron

for *inverse*. Two of the croupiers retired for refreshments: they were not needed
here. The *tailleur* produced his six packs of playing cards and broke the seals.
He shuffled each pack separately then all six together. With a kind of genuflec-
tion he invited Carlo to cut. Carlo cut. The cards were shoved into the shoe.
"*Messieurs, faites vos jeux.*" Large sums were bet on *rouge* and *noir, couleur*
and *inverse* being for the present ignored. The *tailleur* laid out his two rows, the
upper signifying *noir,* the lower *rouge.* We watched with bored impassivity.
Carlo smoked a Romeo and Juliet. The top row came to 37, the lower to 32.
"*Rouge gagne.*" Carlo had won. Carlo went on winning. *Noir-couleur, noir-
inverse, rouge-couleur, rouge-inverse.* He lost a little, but the plaques piled up.

Sheikh Fazal said, "The devil's own luck, as we say in our language."

"Only the devil has luck," Carlo said, adding to the Wit and Wisdom of.
"God does not need it. Shall we break briefly for refreshments?" We broke.

We drank champagne and ate exquisitely fashioned but innutritious canapés. Sheikh Abdul Khadir told, in French, the joke about Moses taking the
wrong turn in the desert and so missing the oil. "Is there," Carlo asked, "some
mystical connection between oil and Allah?" This gave offense expressed in
greater cordiality. The *chef de partie,* who had been computing Carlo's plaques,
came up to him and told to his ear the amount of his winnings. Carlo nodded
and said, "The ill-gotten gains of the Church confront those of the Sons of the
Prophet. I am prepared to stake all on the turn of a single card. Would any of
you gentlemen care to play?"

Sheikh Fazal said, "The sum in question?" Carlo told him. The sheikh said,
"It is large, very large. But not overlarge. The wealth of the soil that Allah
blesses is limitless. Your Church was founded on a rock not rich in mineral
deposits."

"*Tu es Petrus,*" Carlo quoted, "*non Petroleum.* You may confront my small
sum with ten or twenty times the amount. If I win, the money will go to the
poor."

"The Christian poor," Sheikh Fazal said.

"Or the Muslim poor if you wish. Poverty is its own religion."

"Very well. Now?"

Carlo drained his flute and belched tinily. "Mr. Toomey here can preside
over the ceremony."

"He is a Christian."

"Not overwhelmingly so." And Carlo shot me a look of what seemed brief
malice.

"Let us have instead *monsieur le chef de partie.* He has his own religion. We
must also respect a man's métier."

"Good." We went over to a plain baize table with a shaded lamp above it.
Carlo sat. Sheikh Fazal sat. The *chef* bowed and sat with them. A croupier
brought, bowing, a new pack. The *chef* ceremoniously ripped the seal.

"I stake," Carlo said, "the sum of one million six hundred and seventy-five thousand francs."

"To make a round figure, I respond with twenty-six million. Ace is high?"

"Indeed."

The cards were shuffled and cut. We held our breaths, all except Carlo, who puffed smoke. Sheikh Fazal drew first: the ten of clubs. Carlo replied with the queen of hearts.

"Congratulations, your eminence. Let us drink to the poor."

"Wait," Carlo said. "The best out of three. You accept?"

"If you say so."

Carlo drew the three of spades, the sheikh the seven of clubs. The cards were reshuffled. The sheikh drew the king of hearts. Carlo drew the eight of the same suit. He whispered: *"Deo gratias."* And then, aloud, "May we still drink to the poor?"

"As you said before, your eminence, the poor we have always with us."

Bows and bows and bows. As we crossed back to the Hôtel de Paris I said, "I descry superstition. A possible belief in *Schicksal,* or *qismat* as the Arabs call it. What did that mean?"

"It means I've played for the last time. As for the other thing, no. We're free."

"I've ceased to believe it. We're not free. We're damned."

"Not overwhelmingly so, as I said. A Christian, that is. Let's dine."

Bows and bows and bows. Crystal and light. Not so many elegant ladies as there had been forty years before. A plain woman with ginger hair chewed with her mouth open. A table was served with Coca-Cola in a beautiful misted silver bucket. All eyes were, for a time, on Carlo. He was hungry, and he did not hide his greed. It was as if he were enacting the stock rôle of the sybaritic prelate. His great ring lightninged in the *belle époque* chandeliers as he drank his wines with a kind of valedictory relish. Dom Perignon with the seafood, a Corton Bressandes with the meat, Blanquette de Limoux with the dessert. "A kind of valedictory relish," I said. "You have a funeral ahead and then a conclave. What is the news?"

"He'll be dead tomorrow. I come from one funeral to another." A dozen *praires farcies,* then *rougets barbets,* then, the marine lust continuing, *barbues à l'oseille.*

I swallowed my sixth and last oyster. "Whose?"

"My sister. You didn't hear. Of course, you've been out of touch. My sister, I say. She died believing we were blood of each other's blood. Now, no further deception."

"I spoke to her on the telephone. The day of that infernal premiere. Her last words to me were about Domenico at last seeing the light. Believe me, that was none of my fault."

"No further deception. She rambled a good deal before she died. The mother superior talked to the ceiling about the sins of the flesh. She wept."

"She committed no sins of the flesh."

"That, presumably, is why she wept. You're eating nothing."

"I've lost most of my appetites. I understand that the most horrible food is served at these conclaves. That the length or brevity of the conclave is a gauge of the badness of the cuisine."

Rognons de veau entiers flambés. Carlo watched kindly the cognac flames flare. "In hell," he said, "we eat. In heaven we are eaten. Who said that?"

"I don't know. It sounds an extremely stupid aphorism." He nodded, as though expunging it from the Wit and Wisdom of. "Do you think," I said, "that it will be you?"

"The elected one," he said, chewing kidney, "is supposed to show a great humility and declare himself unworthy of the holy burden. The Holy Spirit chooses. But he chooses through fallible men. I may be unworthy of the office, but I have things to do. Is that *hubris*?"

"You mean you want to send a great wind blowing through the Church. The Holy Ghost appears as a wind, doesn't he? Fallible men. You have enemies."

"Oh, one always has enemies. Fortunately, enemies are inimical for a diversity of reasons. They are not a united foe clashing armor in the same rhythm. I have capitalistic enemies, but I have Marxist enemies too. The spiritualization of the *Communist Manifesto*—unthinkable. The unification of the churches. The vernacularization of the liturgy. Those who disapprove of innovation in some areas accept it in others. Enemies cancel each other out. The great thing, perhaps, is not to have friends."

"What do you mean?"

He said nothing till the *prunes à l'eau-de-vie* appeared, with a *glace meringue Chantilly* on the side. He did not answer my question. "The time," he said instead, "is fairly short. The medical men don't like the state of my arteries. I have to watch my diet. If I can have five years, even four—"

"What was that about not having friends?"

"No friends. No brothers, no sisters, no father, no mother. Like *Oedipus*, you remember." He spat a stone onto his spoon. "If God can accept loneliness, so can his servant. I don't want any of you."

"Say that again."

"I don't want you. You're a hindrance. Can you understand that? I elect loneliness. Whatever happens, I shan't go back to Milan. If the Holy Spirit rejects me, I shall enter a house of contemplation. If not the highest, then the lowest. But whatever it is, loneliness."

"This, then, is a meal of valediction. A ceremony of rejection. There was a time when you called me *fratello*."

"God preserve me from brothers."

"And from sisters?"

"I don't want you. Any of you."

I looked at him hopelessly as he spooned in his Chantilly. It left a thin white foam round his mouth. "Well, then," I said stupidly. "*Nunc dimittis.* May I wish you—no, luck doesn't apply, does it? That's just something for the Casino." I folded my napkin with prim neatness. I got up and said, "*Vale, sancte pater.*" He seemed to snarl, or it may have been merely a chewing motion. Then I went to the bar, leaving the bill to him.

sixty-eight

Knowing, as on that previous occasion, my connection with the Italian prelacy but now a more particular connection with one of its *papabili*, the London press urged me to go to Rome to cover the funeral, the conclave, the election. There was even a call from *The Times* the following morning while I was just leaving the hotel. No. Nothing doing. I was old, I was tired, I was not interested.

And yet, back in Tangier, I followed in the newspapers of four languages the empty reports, all color, no news, which emerged from days of waiting for a gush of white smoke. Later, in books like Peter Hebblethwaite's *Rebirth of a Church* and Conor Cruise O'Brien's *Morning in Their Eyes*, we got the whole story of the conclave of 1958. It began with the gathering of one hundred and twenty cardinals in the Pauline Chapel, with its frescoes by the great homosexual of Saint Peter's seeing the world end upside down and Saint Paul stupefied on the road to Damascus. Red in cassock, biretta and mozzetta, snowy in surplice, they were led by Monsignor Pierluigi Bocca, the papal master of ceremonies, through the Sala Ducale into the Sistine Chapel, whose choir went before chanting *Veni Creator Spiritus.* Two long narrow tables faced each other, with straightbacked chairs of great discomfort cynically masked by red velvet. The cardinals grunted, whinnied and squinted, looking for their place cards. There were prayers, and then Monsignor Bocca cried "*Extra omnes.*" Choir, servitors, workmen got out. The entrances were blocked with double slabs of tough wood. Then the assembly swore to follow the apostolic constitution, nodded over a long dull discourse from the chamberlain, Cardinal Percini, and went to eat a bad though atoxic meal in the Sala Borgia. After that they retired to their cells, which were frequently renaissance drawing rooms forty feet high, crammed with sofas and chiffonniers, with the lightswitch a long obstacle race away from the bed. There, presumably, Carlo prayed that he be made Pope.

The next morning at breakfast Cardinal Casorati, the aging (they were all aging but he more than the others) Patriarch of Venice, looked ill. He recovered after a swig of Brandy Stock (*con il gusto morbido*) and all proceeded to the Sistine Chapel for the first ballot. On the tables were papers with the printed formula *Eligo in Summum Pontificem*. The cardinals wrote down the names of their choice, disguising their handwriting as best they could so that nobody would officially know who was voting for whom, and, with the paper folded in two, went one after the other to the altar, knelt in prayer, and said "I call to witness Christ the Lord who will be my judge that my vote is given to the one whom before God I consider should be elected." The terrible musclebound Christ of *The Last Judgment* looked down as the papers were tipped into the chalice. The papers were shuffled and then scrutinized by the three scrutineers. The names were read out and the cardinals made their own scores. Manfredini 25. Casorati 23. Campanati 21. Giustolisi 10. Schneider 8. Parenti 6. De Neuter-Strickmann 4. Trione 2. Geblesco 2. All the rest were single votes for names like Chin, Ngoloma, Sacharov, Lang, Prado, Willoughby, Rasy, and (unjust but impossible) Papa. That the Pope had to be an Italian was, in those days, taken for granted. Manfredini, a Florentine set over Florence, a favorite of the defunct pontiff, anemically saintly, desperately conservative, was heading the list in a mere gesture of respect and affection. He did not stand a cat in hell's chance of commanding the two-thirds votes needful. This was why, in the second ballot, he went down to 10. But Guistolisi, who had been shoved forward by a cabal in the Curia, shot up to 30, with Casorati just behind with 28. Campanati had sunk to 19. The third ballot, taken after lunch and presumably a measure of hot discussion in corners, drove Casorati well ahead with 56, while Giustolisi dropped to 27. Campanati went up to 31. At the end of the day a searchlight from the Gianiculum fingered black fumes from the stovepipe. Try again. And again.

The next morning the Frenchman Chassagny received, after God alone knew what nocturnal pressures, 5. The Cardinal Archbishop of Chicago, F. X. Murphy, got a surprising 2. Casorati had, perhaps because he had looked ill again at breakfast, only 50. Campanati had risen to 33. Campanati and Casorati rose and fell, fell and rose as the hot October day crawled to exhaustion and dinnertime. 55, 27. 51, 33. 57, 34. Neither could climb to the necessary 80. Black smoke again.

It was on the third day that the event occurred which bred much fanciful speculation of a horrific kind and even inspired a detective story called *Murder in the Conclave*. In the early afternoon the ballot recorded 91 votes for Casorati. There were murmurs of *Deo gratias*. And then the venerable Patriarch rose from his seat, thrust out an arm, cried "No no," then collapsed onto the fawn wool felt carpet. He had had a terminal heart attack. Secrecy forbade the conveying of the news to the outside and even the importation of a doctor. The younger and fitter cardinals carried with some difficulty the corpse to the nearest cell, which was not far from the Sala Borgia. Prayers were said and the ballot was resumed. Its result was definitive. Carlo Campanati gained his own votes as well as most of those of the dead Patriarch. It was a walkover.

It was the right time of day for the gushing of the white smoke. People were coming home from work. There had been a light rain on the city at about the hour of the Patriarch's collapse, but now the sun was radiant before bedding down in clouds shot with all the colors that Italian painters had ever, sighing or frowning or triumphant, ground. The piazza was packed, cameras dollied or were held ready to click, the one hundred and forty saints stood high (journalistic cliché) and waiting. Cardinal Focchi appeared on the central balcony of St. Peter's and said to the microphone: *"Annuncio vobis gaudium magnum. Habemus papam, eminentissimum et reverendissimum Dominum Carolum, sanctae Romanae ecclesiae cardinalem Campanati, qui sibi nomen imposuit Gregorium Septimum Decimum."* The crowd gaudiated magnally: old ladies in black wept, teeth gleamed in stubbled faces, strangers shook hands with each other, children jumped as though Mickey Mouse were soon to come on, the horns of Roman cars rejoiced plaintively. And then, to roars, Carlo appeared in a skewwhiffed skullcap, all in white, fat and loving, everybody's daddy. He stilled the roars with fat arms and said:

"Ho scerto er nome Gregorio—" The laughter was immense and affectionate. He was speaking the Roman dialect in a deep Roman bass. Then, as if to remind himself that this was only appropriate in a parochial context—relevant for a Bishop of Rome but not for the Father of All the Faithful—he switched into plain television announcer's Italian and told the crowd briefly why he had chosen the name Gregory. It was primarily because of Gregory the Great, who had reformed the Church and spread the Gospel. There were other Gregorys too, not all great: Gregory VI bought the pontificate from Benedict IX; Gregory XII got into trouble and was banished to Naples. The annals of the Gregorys comprised all the shames and triumphs of which man was capable, and he, Gregory XVII, was no more than a man with no claim to greatness. But he would keep the shining image of Him who was Great constantly before his eyes. Then he said:

"Praised be Jesus Christ."

"Now and forever," the crowd went.

"Dear brothers, dear sisters, my brother cardinals have called a new bishop to Rome. We are sad with the knowledge of the death of our beloved father Pope Pius the Twelfth. We are sad with a more recent knowledge. This very day, when God called him, and not myself, to the throne of Peter, our dearly loved brother Giampaolo, Patriarch of Venice, collapsed and died." The crowd hushed;

some crossed themselves; a number of men covertly warded their balls against evil with horning fingers. "God's ways are mysterious. God's time is not ours. In the moment of choice our brother was snatched to beatitude by the operation of another choice. *Requiescat in pace*."

"Amen."

"I come to you, then, as a second best. I come in humility. I come with neither the holiness, nor the fortitude, nor the learning, nor the pastoral skills of our deeply mourned brother. Nevertheless, accept me for what I am. Let me now divulge a truth which has been long a secret. I come to you as an orphan. I come as one who has known neither father nor mother, neither sister nor brother. The very name I carried was not my own. Today I am reborn, with a new name. Through the mystery of God's will and the benison of his even more mysterious love I am become a father and a brother. You are my family now. Accept my love. Give me your own. God's blessing be upon you." And then the fat arms blessed *urbem et orbem* and the crowd wept and howled with joy and pity and affection. I could imagine him going inside and saying to his brother cardinals: "That seemed to go down all right."

The vaticanologists have deliberated hard on the circumstances of Pope Gregory XVII's election. It is certain that the Italians did not want him, nor did the French. The anglophone cardinals, on the other hand, saw him as one of themselves. The cardinals of what is now known as the Third World appreciated the dynamism of his social philosophy. The piquancy of referred scandal was something of a recommendation in America, the home of the cult of personality. But he would never have become Pope if the conclave had not been thrown into fearful confusion by a death which seemed to many a sign from heaven that, despite the qualifications of the stricken candidate, the wrong choice had been made. The Holy Spirit seemed to have bullied the enemies of Carlo Campanati into a flash of revelation that they had better not be his enemies. As for the theory that Carlo had willed the death of the Patriarch of Venice, or even poisoned his coffee, such a supposition was unworthy. Of the holiness of Pope Gregory XVII there has never been much doubt. Was I not one of the agents of his canonization?

On that early October evening in 1958 Carlo Campanati left my life and his ample flesh spilled over from the confines of memoirs into the arena of history. You know as much about Pope Gregory XVII as I. Henceforth I was to see him only blessing fatly in the media, kissing the feet of the poor, weeping with earthquake widows, treading the Via Crucis, embracing criminals and communist leaders, inaugurating the Vatican Council which, under his leadership, his goading and coaxing and bullying rather, was to modernize the Church and bring it closer to the needs of the people. He was, as you know, everywhere: in Montevideo and Santiago and Caracas, pleading inviolate the rights of man against corrupt and tyrannical regimes; in Kampala, encouraging the formation of an African Church; in Canterbury, fraternally embracing an archbishop who presided over the morganatic legacy of an uxoricide; in Sydney, responding to cries of *Good on ya*. There were strip cartoons in which he was the hero. Kids in jeans and T-shirts sang songs about him.

> *Pope Gregory, Pope Gregory*
> *Free our souls from sin.*
> *Rescue the world from beggary,*
> *Let the light shine in.*

One of the new Gregorian chants. The Holy Spirit had spoken.

sixty-nine

He was in the United States at the same time as myself. I was trying to assuage my loneliness, not, like his, deliberately elected, with a fairly lengthy lecture tour of the universities. My agents were ACM (American Circuit Management), 666 Avenue of the Americas, New York City: they took a commission of thirty percent and arranged meetings, travel and hotels. The hotels were mostly Holiday Inns—the same double-bedded room from Florida to Maine, with its ghost of a reek of old tobacco and air-conditioning machinery, its sanitized toilet and television set. The Pope was here to bless the American people, whose tongue he spoke so well, to address the United Nations, to officiate at masses with huge congregations in football stadia and baseball parks. I watched one of these latter ceremonies on television in, I think, Prescott, Arizona, lying on my bed the afternoon before a lecture, Coke can in hand. There were several thousand worshipers in this stadium in Newark, and the holy words boomed and rebounded rah rah rah from a multitude of loudspeakers. The mass was in English, an English direct and businesslike rather than arcane and mysterious. There was no nobility, which was in order, but there was a certain ineptitude of phrasing. "The Lord be with you" had to be answered by "And with you," but the need to stress that second *you* produced a kind of petulant squeaking. There were gimmicks of audience participation like the kiss of peace. The altar had taken on the look of a lacy conjurer's table or even butcher's block. But you got the full round face of Carlo, with his huge complicated nose and his shrewd eyes glazed in devoutness, swigging the chalice in unabashed view, instead of his broad back engrossed with the cross. The host was administered by a host of delegates: I thought of the bushels of wheat entailed. I was sourly moved.

In Boise, Idaho, the evening before my lecture, I saw and heard Carlo on a prime-time talk show. Beaming sweatily in the studio lights, in slightly soiled papal white and rakish cap, he fielded questions from unbelievers. A spotty girl in jeans wanted to know what proof there was that there was a God.

Carlo said, "I could give you the famous traditional five proofs, but first I'd better ask you what you mean by a God. What do you mean?"

"Like somebody up there who like made it all, you know, and knows what we do and is hot against, you know, sin and sends people to heaven or the other place."

"The universe exists," Carlo said, "and somebody had to make it. You accept that?"

"It could have like made itself."

"Can a clock make itself, or a television set, or a book or a piece of music?"

"That's like different."

"The same rules apply. The constellations and the planetary systems are far more complex than a clock or a radio. There has to be a Creator. This Creator created everything, including us. You want to know what creating a universe has to do with virtue and sin and heaven and hell—"

"Right."

"The whole complex movement of the universe represents order. The Creator loves order and hates chaos. Virtue is order. Sin is chaos. Virtue is creation and the maintenance of creation. Sin is destruction. The sinner often doesn't understand the extent to which he destroys order. He has to find out. That's why we have the doctrine of hell. The soul dedicated to order joins the ultimate divine order."

"What do you mean by a soul?" a sporty-looking man with a postiche asked.

"What's left of the whole human complex when the body is taken away. The part of the human totality concerned not with the business of living in the world but with values—those essences which we call truth, beauty and goodness."

"How do you know that goes on existing after death? Nobody comes back from the dead. Except in ghost stories."

"I won't mention the resurrection of Christ, which is the cornerstone of the Christian faith," Carlo said. "Nor the resurrection of Lazarus. Let me say instead that there are things we *know* go on existing after the death of the body. Certain truths, for instance, like a plus a equals 2a. If Beethoven's Fifth Symphony was not played by an orchestra and all the printed and manuscript copies of the music were destroyed by fire, we wouldn't be right in saying that the work doesn't exist any more. If ideas, if works of beauty and truths exist outside the mortal flesh, they have to exist in a sort of mind belonging to a sort of observer. You see now what I mean by a soul?"

"Okay," a woman with a castellated hairdo said, "but what do you mean by a soul in hell?"

"A soul at last aware that truth and beauty and goodness, as expressed in what we may call the personality of God, go on existing but quite beyond the hope of that soul's being able to get at them. The condemned soul knows what it wants, but it can't have what it wants. That's hell."

"But," the same woman said, "can you really accept that a merciful and loving God would send souls to it?"

"Hell is an emanation of God's justice. But we believe that his love is greater than his justice. Hell has to exist—it's a logical proposition—but there may be nobody in it. Remember, man and woman were made perfect because they were made by God. But they're made evil, which means blind to virtue, by a force which God also made and which he can't unmake."

"Can't?" croaked a man with a piebald beard and a turquoise pullover (turquoise? Am I inventing that, or was I watching, in 1959, a color set?). "Can't? When God according to Christian teaching is omnipotent?"

"Oh yes," Carlo said. "There are certain things that God can't do. He can't not be God, for instance. As a Creator he has no power of destruction. He can't even destroy a human soul. He can only make it suffer eternally. He created the angel who created evil, and he can't uncreate him."

"But," the turquoise man (I distinctly see turquoise) said, "he must have known that there'd be evil. He knows everything, right? If he knew, why did he let it happen?"

"Here's a great and awful mystery," Carlo beamed. "God gave his creatures the most tremendous endowment, the thing most like his own essence—I mean freedom of choice. If he knows in advance what his creatures are going to do, then he's denying them freedom. So he deliberately blacks out foreknowledge. God could know if he wished, but out of respect and love for his creatures he refuses to know. Can you imagine any more awesome gift than this—God denying himself out of sheer love?"

This was on the NBC network. More awesome than Carlo's avowal of God's love is my memory of commercial interruptions. Not so many as normally: one every thirty minutes. I am fairly certain I now saw ungreasy fried chicken proclaimed by a radiant black family, Italian tomato paste, a cough mixture called Nyquil. Carlo would not be outraged by the intrusion of consumerism into elementary apologetics: time for a swig of cognac from the flask carried by his batman or familiar. When he came back on again somebody was asking okay God, but why Jesus Christ? Are the Jews wrong and the Indians and the yeah Chinese and the Japs?

"Let all who believe in God," Carlo said urgently, "unite in the brotherhood of that belief. But within that brotherhood is another fraternity—those who accept that God became man at a certain place and at a certain time, in a word, entered human history. I mean the Christian fraternity. Inside that, until recently, it was assumed that the fraternity of which the Bishop of Rome is the head was sealed off, arrogant in its claim to sole legitimacy, the only begetter of Christian authority. I think that view is dying now. I think that I and my brothers are helping to kill it. So I say that Christianity is the tin Baptist chapel in Arkansas as well as Saint Peter's in Rome. But to return to your question: why Jesus Christ? The answer lies in many places. It lies, before history brought about the Incarnation, in logic. We have talked of an omnipotent God. An omnipotent God who loves man. What more logical than that he should show himself among men? We have talked of sin. That man does not properly understand the nature of sin, thanks to the blinding power of the devil, in no way mitigates the horror of the impact of sin on the pure radiance of God. The sin that man commits must be paid for. Not by damnation but by sacrifice. No purely human sacrifice could wipe out the horror of sin. Hence the divine sacrifice."

"Okay," a housewife in beads said, "but why did Rome ever think it had the right to set itself up as the only ah ah religious authority? I mean, you're the Pope, right?"

"Right," the Pope said, rightly.

"I mean, why should Luther be wrong and ah ah Calvin and Henry the Seventh no Eighth and ah ah Billy Graham and the Holy Rollers and William Penn and ah ah right?"

"The Church of Rome represents the primal historical authority," Carlo said. "There's an unbroken line of succession from Saint Peter, crucified in Rome in the place where the Vatican now stands, to myself who am, as you accurately remark, Pope. No sensible Catholic now denies that, in the sixteenth century and after, reform was needed in his Church. He regrets that such reform took the shape of new foundations of protest. But the important thing today is the whole Christian fraternity. Of that I may claim to be not the head but the coordinating minister. Such a claim is reasonable, being based on a historical tradition. Rome is the symbol of Christian unity, no more. We must talk no more of Catholics and Protestants—only of Christians."

I switched off. I had had enough. I knew all the arguments, which could have been as confidently entrusted to a wet-eared seminarian. But if the President of the United States could be expected to submit to the democracy of the small screen, why not the Father of All the Faithful? If you want the dope, go to the bossman. The bossman had been seated in the parlors of millions of Americans, dealing out the Christian truth, straight from the horse's. Dope was, perhaps, the word. Tidings of comfort.

I went to bed with a paperback copy of the novel called *Africa!* by Ran dolph Foulds, alias Ngolo Basatu. Seven hundred and fifty pages. Six million copies sold in the hardcover edition. Soon to be a major motion picture. I had bought it down below in the little gift shop of the Holiday Inn. I had not read *The Cry of the Clouds*, but I gathered it was rather like this: black sex and violence. It had sold well in Britain, where, despite cries for its suppression, the law had not pounced. The law had chewed up *The Love Songs of J. Christ* and was temporarily satisfied. I read a few pages of the later opus but found it tough going. The whole of Africa seemed to be turned into a bed on which a massive muscle-bound character named Bmuti thrust his fiery rod into everybody. Bmuti stood for the new prevalent black. He could have been the ebony Pantagruel or the Los of the Niger, but he lacked humor and poetry. He was a media robot with three or four computerized facial expressions. On page 23 he seemed to be polishing his weapon for insertion into a character named Bowana, whose model might well have been Ralph—a cultivated American black who didn't know the best way to become Africanized. I fuck you man but good. Dat de best way.

seventy

"Next year," my nephew John said, "*Africa!*"

I seemed to hear it in italic with an exclamation point after. "You and Professor Bucolo?" I was back at Wisbech College in Indiana. Val Wrigley was no longer there to taunt me with frivolity and irresponsibility: nor would he now have had cause to. Val Wrigley, I gathered, was now in Christopher Isherwood country, Santa Monica or somewhere. I had given a lecture entitled "What Now in the Novel?" I had been fed and drenched by a students' committee. I was in John and Laura's campus house, taking a forebed whisky. They had been married about eighteen months, their wedding a solid old-fashioned Catholic one in Laura's hometown of St. Louis. John had gained a doctorate for a thesis on the matriarchal culture of a Mexican Indian settlement near Zacatecas. He had a full professorship with tenure. Wisbech College was notable for the close working relationship that existed between its Department of Anthropology and its Department of Linguistics. John was now working on analogues of familial structure in the structure of language.

"Yes, Jimmy Bucolo. He got us the grant. A pretty stingy one but it will have to do. One of these charter flights to Marseilles. Then a run-down steamer to Port Said. Then a Hawaa Masir trip to Jibuti. Then the Erinmore Line takes us through the Gulf of Aden. And then— As you can see, too much time spent on travel. Of course, if we could both have a sabbatical . . . four months' vacation doesn't give us much chance to see—"

"What do you expect to see?"

"Well—" A big handsome dedicated scholar with so much of his mother in his looks, he sat on the edge of the chunky russet sofa and clasped his hands as in prayer. "I've been gathering a lot of material from this side of the Atlantic on a particular marital custom. Among the Akanyi, the Ptotuni, the Zoloar tribe near Tegucigalpa—the names won't mean much to you—"

"Not a thing."

"Well, what happens when a girl marries is a kind of ritual incest without impregnation. It's the girl's uncle or even great-uncle that spends a week with her—sexual initiation partly, partly a sort of reminiscence of endogamy. Sometimes it's a week, sometimes more, less—more than two days, anyway. What happens to the language as spoken by the whole group during that period is of huge interest. Sentences get inverted, and if anybody forgets to invert there are punishments—not severe ones, more like comic humiliation. About a dozen words in the lexis—sometimes more, sometimes fewer: 9.05 on average so far—come under taboo. All the words belong to the same semantic area—I mean, they all have something to do with covering things up—loincloth, lid, including eyelid, palm of the hand, darkness, the skin of an animal—you get the general idea. The words can't be used except under penalty. The substitute words are sort of complementary to the taboo ones—you can talk about the covered but not the covering—you can even use the word for genitals, which is normally taboo in a lot of the groups I studied. But only during this period."

"Fascinating."

"You think so? You really think so? Now in the Americas the possibility of cultural transmission can't be left out of account, but Jimmy feels sure the same sort of thing goes on in Africa. You remember the Oma people? He gave you that offprint, didn't he? He couldn't understand why the word for eye was *oro* and the word for eyelid the same. He must, he thinks, have been in touch with somebody who'd gone into the mission hospital while a taboo of that kind was operating. And this guy was stroking the hospital cat and he called its fur its kidneys, which is the generic word for the insides of an animal—"

"Fascinating."

"So it may be there's something built into what we laughingly call the primitive mind—you see what I mean?"

"Is Laura going with you?"

"You kidding? On a grant that size?"

"John," I said, "I've told you before that you must not be afraid to ask me for money. The money I have has been earned through the purveying of a kind of trash—"

"Don't call it that. A lot of it's very good."

"On the strength of my reputation as a purveyor of this trash I've been paid two thousand dollars for a single lecture at your own college. How much will you need to get the three of you to East Africa in moderate comfort and at reasonable speed? And back, of course. Ten thousand? Would that help?"

"Uncle Ken, you're too good."

"No, I'm making amends for a wasted life. I'm proud to be contributing to scholarship."

"Well, you know, I don't know what to say. Except thanks."

"I'll make out a check in the morning. My checkbook's in my luggage in the president's guesthouse."

"Thanks and thanks again. When do you leave and where for?"

"I lecture at the University of Oklahoma on Monday. I'm spending tomorrow night in New York. There's a flight after lunch."

"Fine. Tomorrow morning you can see the film that Dotty's brother sent. Of course, you know him, I'd forgotten. The glories of Rukwa, rather a nice bit of propaganda. They want black American skills. The building of a modern African state. At least I know what the place looks like."

"It's there that you're going? I hadn't thought."

"There seem to be a fair number of unassimilated tribes on the borders. Including the Oma people." And then, "Dotty's far from well."

"I heard that. The great twentieth-century slayer. Evil made flesh. Not flesh, rather antiflesh. Ah." for Laura had just come in from a visit to a neighbor, Professor Szasz's wife, immobilized with a slipped disk. So lovely a girl, spilling over with health, those startling warm iceblue eyes framed in well-brushed lustrous blueblack, the neat pliant body in a shift dress of cinnamon wool.

She said, "How's my favorite writer?"

"Laura dear, your job is to improve literary taste not debase it. You must really stop feeling such enthusiasm for my work."

"Okay, the short stories are great, the novels are lousy, will that do?" And she dimpled with a flash of serried snowgems.

"Laura, you're going to Africa. Uncle Ken's putting up the money."

"Say that again."

"Africa. Not just Jimmy and me. You too. And not on banana boats either."

"Oh gosh," she said, sitting with grace in the second of the chunky russet armchairs, myself being in the other. "You mean that? Hemingway country. Oh gosh."

"*Not* Hemingway country," John said. "*Not* safariland. A bit rough, some of it, but I'll keep you away from the more harmful fauna. You'd better get that cinecamera mended."

"Dear Uncle Ken," she said, and she came over and sat in my lap and kissed me. Then she sprang up very lithe and switched on the television set. "There's your other uncle on, Johnboy. I want to hear what he has to say about birth control. Sorry, Uncle Ken, I have to know, we both do. But thanks and thanks and thanks. I can hardly believe it."

John said, eyes narrowed, as she turned the dial and got the NBC channel and a fat splotch of blessing papal white, "He's not my uncle. Everybody's father and brother but nobody's uncle. We all let him down. He's disowned all of us."

"Oh, come off it, Johnboy. Listen."

We listened. Carlo was quite at his ease among a mob of militant women. The venue seemed to be a press conference room, the women, from their hard smartness, journalists. "Ordained priests," one of them was saying.

Carlo replied, "Once you grant men the power to bear children your sex will have a powerful claim to the right to ordination. Not before. Remember, all women are, in fact or potency, vessels of the mystery of birth. Kindly, ladies, permit a few men to enact the mysteries of the priestly craft. Another thing, the priest is the inheritor of the mission of Jesus Christ. God in his mysterious wisdom incarnated himself as a human creature of the male sex. He granted, as God the Son, the right to spread the Gospel to male missionaries, not to their wives. Things may change, things *will* change. But not while I sit in Saint Peter's chair."

"Why can't priests marry?"

"There's no doctrinal reason why they shouldn't. But there's every possible commonsensical reason why they should remain celibate. The story is told of an Anglican minister and a Catholic priest sharing a friendly glass of beer in London at the time of the Battle of Britain. An air raid began. The Anglican said, 'I must get home to my wife and children.' The Catholic said, 'I must go and look after my flock.' The family of a minister of the faith is his congregation, and a special, more personal relationship would be an obstacle to his impartial love and devotion. As for sex, don't think that some of us have not known, and still don't know, the agonies of sexual frustration. Deprived of a wife, must a priest then go to a brothel? Sexual deprivation is a cross the priest must bear. And the Pope too. It is a fleshly sacrifice he offers daily, hourly, to God."

"Why won't the Church permit birth control?" asked a woman with big blue granny glasses and an evident pregnancy.

"Ah, that question," Carlo smiled. "It will plague me to the end of my ministry. Human seed, containing as it does the mysterious potency of new life, must not be regarded as a mere by-product of the sexual spasm—sometimes kindly permitted to do its biological work, sometimes regarded as a deadly nuisance. If Mr. and Mrs. Shakespeare had indulged in birth control there might have been no William Shakespeare. And so for the parents of Saint Paul, Abraham Lincoln, President Eisenhower. And so, if I may say so, for my own parents, whoever they were—"

"The ultimate celibacy," John said. "You wipe out the past as well as the future."

"Quiet, Johnboy."

"—What we have to think of is the immense potentiality of the human seed, the desperate turpitude of wasting it. Very well, very well, I can anticipate your objections to these words, which are not, remember, words I utter in uncaring callousness. They are the words of the Church I inherit, not of the Church that is still to be made. Tradition says that a woman's chief function is to produce new human souls to the glory of God. Our own age says that a woman has duties to her own soul, and that she must not be condemned to a life of labor pains. Well, the control of birth lies in the will of the man and woman alike— the will to abstain from total sexual congress. This may be difficult, but it is also good, even holy. But remember"—he grew fierce, his chin jutted in a Duce manner, his nose trained itself on his audience like a dangerous weapon—"we must beware of accepting the deadly heresy that life is sacred only when it crosses the threshold of the womb—that, as yet unshaped, as yet unnamed, it is expendable. It is a short step then to condoning abortion, which is no more than a form of infanticide."

There were angry shouts from these hard and emancipated women. Carlo's great voice rose like a lion's above them. "Love," he cried, "love is greater than animal coupling. The love of man and woman which is a figure of God's love for humanity. Are we to be no more than brute beasts howling in perpetual heat? Can we not learn that love of the spirit that transcends the lust of the flesh? Love, love, let us have love."

The anger had to subside, because it seemed now to be directed against love. Carlo spoke more softly. He even smiled as he said, "Your Heavenly Father is not a personification of biology. He knows your problems. He weeps over the spectacle of a hungry world. Do not blame him for his own hunger, which is a hunger for human souls."

"Baal," John said, "Moloch."

"Johnboy."

"Heaven is limitless. It is not confined as our earth is confined. Its crops do not fail, no famine oppresses it. And yet, says the Lord, this house must be filled. Filled with countless human souls, and each one reveling in its divine uniqueness."

"Mongoloids?" someone shouted. "Thalidomide cases?"

"Souls, souls, I speak of souls. And I speak, and will always speak, of love. Let me end on that note. God's love is great enough to condone our weaknesses. He asks us only to do what we can to fulfill his kingdom. He does not ask the impossible."

"Switch him off," John said.

"Yeah, switch him off," obeying. She sat down again and we looked at each other. She was a good housewife as well as, I gathered, a fine teacher and, I could see, a lovely girl. This little drawing room was conventionally enough furnished with its wedding-gift suite and rocking chair and coffee table with coffee-table Tiepolo album, but there were her own touches of greenery—fern and wandering jew—as well as a well-dusted disposition of knickknacks (John's jujus and totems, her own pieces of colonial glass and china) and flower paintings on the strawberry and cream walls—love in idleness, love in a mist, love lies bleeding. She was, I knew, a good American cook, expert at spareribs, pineapple-orange glazed ham, southern luncheon bake, frosty ribbon loaf, dad's denvers. Tears came to my eyes as I looked at her: what I had missed, what I had been predestined to miss. The tears welled and had to be sucked back as I looked fondly at them both. I saw them in bed naked together, intent on each other's joy, not engaged in the making of a new William Shakespeare, while Carlo frowned down from the ceiling.

"Another whisky?" John said.

"One for the road. A lionfrightener."

"Condone our weaknesses," Laura said. "What did he mean?"

"He meant, I think," I said, "that the seed containing a new Abraham Lincoln may flow but not be too upset if it meets obstacles. So long as it doesn't know in advance that it's going to meet obstacles. If it knows this, it had better not flow."

"It didn't sound to me as if he meant that."

"You wait. As his tour of the Americas continues he'll talk more of love and less of dogma. He'll shelve more and more of the hard questions. He'll talk of love because he wants to be loved himself. Gregory the Beloved."

John gave me my nightcap. "Did you hope," he began, "I suppose I shouldn't ask. What I mean is—"

"Did I hope that the new Church would condone my particular weakness? No, I didn't. Not that it applies any more, at least not to me. The fire has been doused. I'm an old man. I could go back to the Church tomorrow if I wished."

"Do you wish?" Laura asked.

"I've got on well enough as a cynical rationalist."

"Come on," she said. "What you write isn't like that at all."

"Sentimentality," I said. "That's the other side of the coin." I drained my drink and got up stiffly, an old man as I'd said. "Can you pick me up?" I said to John.

"Is ten too early?"

"Fine."

"Thank you again," Laura said, "a million times thanks." She got up to kiss me goodnight. And then, her lovely eyes full of it: *"Africa!"*

The film was called *Rukwa Reborn*. John ran it for me himself on the sixteen-millimeter projector which belonged to his department. I recognized the voice of the commentary: Ralph's. Its vibrations struck my glands and gave the lie to my talk of the dousing of the fire. And there was Ralph himself onscreen, in hot-colored robes, tigerskin shako, leather riding boots, mounted on a white Arab, leading a kind of detachment of native cavalry over a grassy plain. We saw oil rigs and earnest black technicians in hard silver hats poring over charts, a black finger pointing, a black head nodding. There was a black technical college with black students in snowy shirts and well-cut pants examining the gleaming maquette of a power station. Backward tribes were being gently taught, seated on grass on loinclothed haunches before a whiteboard and bespectacled black teacher, about the need for their assimilation into the new progressive state. A black audience laughed its head off at a black comedy film in color. Here was the capital with its white-box commercial buildings, football stadium, the ten-story Mansanga Hotel. "They seem to be doing all right," John said. Ralph's commentary, more grandiloquent, said the same thing. It also said something about freedom of worship while a black muezzin called to the blue heavens and black schoolchildren, led by a black nun in white, trooped to a little church with one clanging bell. Ralph admitted that the state had problems: jealousy on its borders, no direct access to the Indian Ocean, heavy duties imposed at the port of Kilwa. But all problems could be solved with good will, the right Pan-African spirit. The author of *Africa!* appeared, smiling, muscular, a possible candidate for the Nobel Prize. And, finally, there was the great Mansanga himself, greeted by a loving people with excellent teeth, or getting a laugh in the council chamber, or inspecting troops from the saddle of a black Arab, while Ralph rode behind him on his white. Jaunty music, weak on melody but rich in polyrhythms, swelled on pipes and a multitude of drums. The film was over.

"Yes," I said without conviction, "they seem to be doing all right. So long as the oil lasts."

"Meanwhile," John said, "the tribes get corrupted and lose their gods to the god of uniformity." And then, "Dotty's brother seems to be doing all right too. The poet as man of action."

"He was never much of a poet."

"Give my love to Dotty. And, of course, to Mother."

Dorothy was, I saw, far from well. She lay in bed limp, her once glorious hair graying and without life, the once sumptuous lushness of her skin now taking on the hue and texture of an elephant's hide, her fine eyes at the mercy of tearducts which never dried. I kissed her with affection and compassion; she put her bare thin arms lovingly about my neck. "How is it?" I asked.

"It comes, it goes. We just had Hortense's brother-in-law on about offering pain up to God." At the bottom of the bed was a small television set, now off. Hortense was seated on the bed, her arm about her friend, her one tired eye on me.

She said, "You're old, Ken."

"I don't deny it. Old and lonely." She herself did not look old, save for a crepiness about her neck. She was in blue linen, bell-shaped skirt, boat-shaped neckline, bow tie, short jacket with welt pockets, bronze stockings. She had kicked off her high fine stiletto heels. Her eye patch was a frank accessory, attractive in itself: a cluster of miniature blue roses on a green ground. Her hair kept, though cunning cosmesis, its schoolgirl color: the blue roses peeped through a flow of its honey.

"Stay with us," Dorothy said. "For good, I mean." And then her eyes brimmed. "No, not fair to you. You don't want to see—oh hell." Hortense hugged her.

Hortense said to me, "Before I forget, your agent called. Something about somebody filming one of your books. He thought you'd be here earlier. He's gone to Martha's Vineyard, you won't get him now till Monday."

"Which book?"

"The one you wrote while I was still at school. About Socrates. I'd forgotten it. Then his mentioning it brought it all back."

"Socrates on the screen. Well, things are looking up."

"I had another call too. From one of the Campanati brothers."

"What, His Holiness actually deigned?"

"No, it was the other one."

"For God's sake, bloody Domenico."

"I just love that *bloody*," Dorothy tried to smile. There were teeth missing. "Real breath of Oldy England."

"Where was he, is he?"

"Menton or somewhere. He must have remembered a happy day we spent there together. All those years ago. He wants to come back to me. He says he's failed in everything. Couldn't we, what's Mr. Eliot's phrase, make *a fresh start*? He sounded drunk. Maudlin tears over the transatlantic cable. Too late, I told him, saddest words in the language." She hugged Dorothy more tightly.

"Poor Domenico," I said. "Last I heard he'd taken the way out of all hopeless musicians. Noises. A Moog synthesizer. Birdsong played backwards."

"Oh Christ," Dorothy suddenly went. "Sorry sorry sorry. It's the not expecting it that— Oh Jesus." The sweat of pain was frightful in its copiousness. Hortense tenderly wiped her with one of a number of towels that lay in crumpled disarray on the table by the bed. A double bed, the one I took it they still shared. "You go, Ken," Dorothy gasped, "you don't want to—Christ, it's not—" Dignified, she meant; she was right. Then the spasm passed. She lay very spent and said, "Hemlock," smiling weakly. "*Ciguë.* You remember that *Socrate* of Satie? They say there's going to be a recording of it."

"I'll watch out for it," I said, "and send it."

"I didn't mean that, honey," smiling twistedly at Hortense. "It's just the sharp jabs when I don't expect . . . it's the surprise." I caught, with a sharp jab, that day in the Chicago hospital thirty years before. Carlo was now, I knew, being pelted with paper as he drove blessing along cheering Fifth Avenue; paper like palm fronds was under his holy wheels. I had had taxi difficulty getting here, streets closed to traffic, honking jams. *De Pope*, the driver had explained through his wet chomped stogie. Please come and perform another miracle. The friend and lover of the woman you said was a saint. No, one didn't beg favors any more. The power, I had been shown, fell where it would, indifferent as grace, wild like goodness. No favors to friends, no friends.

"I'll be back before bedtime," I said. "I promised to spend the evening with my niece. And—should it be grandniece or great-niece? I've never really known. Both seem to be preposterous titles."

"A preposterous girl," Hortense said.

"Oh honey, she's okay. She's just like the rest of them."

"Yeah," Hortense said *echt* Americanly, or really (*gea*) *echt* Alfred the Great. "One of the inheritors."

"It should really, I think, be inheritrices," I said.

"Dear Ken. Dear bloody Ken. You write as badly as hell and yet you're pedantic as hell. I must do a bust of you." I did not see the connection.

seventy-one

My niece Ann cooked a dish called New England Boiled Dinner, which tasted of little except sponges and salty water. It was followed by a Sara Lee banana cake, insufficiently defrosted, and caffeineless coffee: none in that household could tolerate caffeine. When I started to light up a Romeo and Juliet Ann said:

"Please don't smoke, Uncle Ken. Eve's allergic to it."

Eve said, "Gimme one more slice of that, Mom, and then Tunc can smoke all he wants. Bob's taking me to the movies."

"What are you going to see, dear?"

"*On the Beach.* At the Symphony. It's Gregory Peck and Ava Gardner. About the end of the world in nineteen sixty-two."

The father and husband was away in Denver, Colorado. There was a weekend Comparative Literature conference, and he was reading a paper on Strehler's Debt to Kafka. I remember distinctly Strehler's telling me, the day before the Gestapo arrived, that he had not read Kafka, or rather that he had started to read *Der Schloss* but had been so appalled by the quality of the German that he had been unable to go on. Still, I had no doubt that Professor Michael Breslow would make, or had already made, a very plausible case for the alleged debt. You could prove anything in literary scholarship. Why, somebody had somewhere read a paper on my indebtedness to Sir Hugh Walpole.

So I drank my caffeineless coffee unmitigated by smoke while Eve, my fourteen-year-old great- or grandniece, ground at her second portion of banana cake. I could hear her little teeth engaging the thin ice of its surfaces. What can I say about her except that she was doomed? She was emptily pretty like her mother, with a firm little bosom upheld by a Maidenform brassiere. She wore an off the peg dirndl dress, not every young person at that time wearing jeans, and on her long American legs were lime woolen stockings. Her pretty little feet were in scuffed black ballet slippers. Her squeaky clean yellow hair was caught just beyond the crown in an elastic band and it wagged behind in a ponytail. She had delicate little pink ears and a charming piggy nose. Her brain was furnished with all the rubbish that the earnest promoters of American values, comforts and stimulants could provide. She was indeed one of the inheritors or inheritrices. While Nevil Shute's vision of the end coming to South Australia was being rerun at the Symphony Cinema on Broadway, Eve's other great-uncle was telling, in Madison Square Garden, of a new beginning coming to everybody. Eve was the inheritrix of a joy and a despair which were somehow cognate.

While she was scraping up the last of her Sara Lee the doorbell did a jaunty eyetiddlyeyetie and, a second later, pom pom. "It's Bob," she said. Chewing she ran to the door and let Bob in. Bob was another of the inheritors. He was six and a half feet tall but had not yet put on the mature flesh that his skeleton demanded. He gangled. He wore glasses. My idle brain wondered a moment why the cartoon American male had always worn glasses. A stronger sighted race had never before existed. It was something to do with the consumer philosophy, perhaps. If there was a space, you filled it. Pangloss had praised God for providing nose and ears for the fitting of spectacles. Carlo, man of many voices, probably approved of Pangloss. I had never asked him if he read Voltaire, and it was too late now. On the other hand, I did not deem it too late to make a more urgent communication. I had that afternoon sent off a note to him care of the Archbishop of New York: the reader will know what was in that note. I had no hope of a response.

"This is Tunc," Eve said. "Mr. Toomey the great writer. This is Bob."

A long thin cordial arm shot out. "Hi, Mr. Toomey. What kinda things do you write?" He was in endlessly long fawn trousers and an acidgreen windjammer. In the young face there was a whole continent of innocent benevolence.

"Novels. Like Nevil Shute. Well, not quite like Nevil Shute. He's an engineer, you know. He helped build the R-101."

"Is that so?" He had never heard of Nevil Shute. "I don't read much, Mr. Toomey. Eve and I go to the movies a lot. Sooner or later you get all the books in the movies. Just a matter of waiting."

"*On the Beach* is by Nevil Shute."

"Is that so? Well, like I say, all you got to do is wait," with a most charming intonation. "You ready, Evie?"

And off they went, inheritors of movies with popcorn and Coke machines in the vestibule. And also, though some place else, mushroom clouds and starvation. I was permitted to smoke now. Ann left the dishes till later. We sat in a pair of rocking chairs in the long drawing room that was really Professor Breslow's Comparative Literature library. It was a fine spring evening. The window looked onto West Ninety-first Street and, if you opened it and craned left, Riverside Drive and a fine chemical sunset over the Hudson. Well-fixed, this family, a decent future to anticipate. My niece Ann, in her middle thirties, was as sweet and innutritious as a Hershey bar. Teeth good, complexion radiant, plumping figure well contained.

"I was just thinking," I said, "that those two kids prefer to go and see the end of the world through the southward drift of toxic atomic dust than to hear the new word of the Lord in Madison Square Garden."

"Bob's a Baptist," she said. "Eve just doesn't care much for religion. Don't tell Mother that, though." Mother? Of course, Mother was Hortense. "Mike had this idea that kids ought to choose what to believe in when they get old enough to understand what it's all about. He didn't want a repetition of his own childhood."

"Ironic. There's Eve's other great- or granduncle as head of the faith, and she prefers atomic fallout."

"I told Mike that you've got to start them off early. He insisted she went to schools where they didn't teach religion. What she's never had she doesn't miss. I told her about Our Lord dying on the cross and she said 'Poor guy. Did it hurt much?' She'll come to it when she needs it." And then, "He's not really any relation, is he? I can hardly remember Father, and then he ran off and said we weren't his children. And Mother said nothing."

"Legally," I said. "Legally." I said, "Your mother got a telephone call from your legal father. Did she tell you?"

"She tells me nothing. I don't see much of her. She doesn't like me. Never did. It was always John John John. What did he say?"

"He wants to come back to her. Catholic law and Catholic guilt are nagging him in his old age. Indissoluble bonds. She won't have him, of course. He'll probably drink himself to death."

"Would you like some homemade lemonade?"

"I'd prefer brandy." She went to a cupboard underneath shelves full of Comparative Literature and a photograph of Thomas Mann as a disdainful Hamburg industrialist. She had her mother's elegant legs. She brought out a bottle of Christian Brothers. She said, pouring, myself saying *enough* very soon:

"You had time for a talk with Eve. What do you think of her?"

"Too soon to say. A nice child, but for God's sake what do they teach them these days? Her mythology's the Saturday morning TV show of kids' cartoons. She started to read *The Catcher in the Rye* but couldn't get on with it, found it kind of hard going. It's difficult for someone of my generation to converse about Superman and Donald Duck and Debbie Reynolds. God, you were brought up on French and Italian, but she knows no languages. They read twenty lines of Virgil at school in bad English prose. She saw a movie about Helen of Troy. The past is dead and the world outside the United States doesn't exist. Haven't you even taken her to Europe?"

"We went to France but the food made her sick."

"I fear," I said prophetically, "the great vacuum. You can fill it for a time with Walt Disney but some big wind is going to blow that fluff away. Stronger anodynes. She tells me that one of her instructors was onto drugs. He'd read a book by some guy, she said, I might know him, it turned out to be my old friend Aldous Huxley. All about visions and reality and you got the truth the easy way, like switching on the TV."

"Yeah, that was a teacher called Perrin. They had to fire him."

"Well," I said, "she's your child. And America's. But, speaking as a decadent European, I'd say she needs stuffing with something solid. Not candyfloss and wow and zowie."

"She's just a good normal healthy teenage girl," she said defensively.

"With an allergy to cigar smoke. And, she tells me, to tomato skins. And goldenrod in the season of goldenrod. And she gets all itchy when she touches the cat. These are substitutes for European guilt."

"She's normal sexually, anyway," Ann said. That seemed to be a crack at me. And of course her mother. "Thank the Lord for that."

"You mean she's already slept with that long youth who takes her to the movies? And had the right physical responses?"

"That's just dirty, Uncle Ken, and you know it. I mean she likes boys and scored eighty-five in that sex quiz in *Mademoiselle*. She's normal. And she's good." Ann then blushed. "She started to read an article in one of those literary magazines that Mike had. It was about what it called the homosexual strain in the British novel. She saw your name there and said there's a bit here about Tunc, I didn't know they wrote about him in magazines. And she said, 'What's it mean, homosexual?' That's how innocent she is."

"And you, or Mike, enlightened her?"

"Mike was very good. He said homosexuals liked men, that's what *homo* meant, man, and she said, 'Well, that makes me homosexual.'"

"His etymology's at fault. Well, so her Tunc or Tunkie is a kind of corruptive influence. And Superman and Gregory Peck and Senator McCarthy are just fine. I'd better go. A little chat with your mother before bed."

"You won't say what I told you about Eve not going to church or anything?"

"She's not particularly interested in Eve. She's got enough on her plate at present."

"Look, Uncle Ken, I didn't want you, you know, to be offended. I mean, I know you can't help being the way you are—"

"The way I was, Ann. I'm now what your daughter thinks I am—past all that, you know, a hundred years old and all the rest of it. Thanks for the dinner." And I gave a dry kiss to her narrow forehead.

Hortense was at the bar in a tigerstriped housecoat. She was weary, I could tell, and she was sipping pure scotch with a lot of ice. "Is she asleep?" I asked.

"She got off about half an hour ago. I gave her a shot of PT6. The shots have to get bigger all the time. She was on again about hemlock, and then she said sorry sorry. I think she's right about the hemlock."

I took a shot of brandy unblessed by Christian brothers. I felt, while pouring, a faint simulacrum of the pain that Dorothy was suffering. The growth was located in the lower bowel. Inoperable. "What's the modern version of hemlock?"

"I'd say a bottle of scotch and about a hundred aspirins."

"Cumbersome. And Carlo wouldn't approve. Did you by any chance hear anything from Carlo?"

"You mean on television? We had him on for about fifteen minutes telling the world about love. Then Dot said let's have an old movie. So we had Bette Davis in *Dark Victory*. Not the best of choices."

"I meant something personal. A personal message or something. He always thought highly of you."

"That changed when the Milanese discovered that Saint Ambrose had balls. No, nothing from him and I expect nothing. Let him keep out of my life. I was grateful that time for the commission, but I would have been grateful to any-body. And it won't be long before I'm grateful to these people in Bronxville."

"What people?"

"Wheeler College. They'd like me to teach the History of Art. I gave them a talk once on the technique of sculpture. It went down well enough. I'm going to need a job. Not for the money, of course."

"Poor poor Dorothy. How much longer can she stand it?"

"How much longer can I? Christ helps a bit. But I don't think crucifixion could be as bad as cancer."

"Do you think Dorothy will—well, seriously ask?"

"She'll seriously scream. And I'll take that to be seriously asking."

"I've had trouble sleeping. Doctors in Morocco don't have any qualms about overprescribing. In my bag I have one hundred brown pills. I know that will do it. Poor Jack Tallis in Tangier sailed off on thirty-five. That wasn't cancer, it was thwarted love. I'll leave them with you. Having them there makes it easier to put off and off and off till you can't put off any longer. Why don't you get some sleep? You won't need any tablets."

"She'll wake in an hour. Or less. I have to be ready. I slept this morning when the nurse came for her two-hour stint. I'll sleep again tomorrow. I don't need much sleep. I'll sleep while the bells are clanging and Carlo's proclaiming love and peace to the TV cameras." And then, "I'm sorry about Ralph."

"Ralph's doing all right."

"No, I mean you and Ralph. It was my idea, after all."

"Oh, it worked for a time. But I'm old and scrawny and also of the color of the damned. It couldn't last. None of my sort of thing ever can."

"A good title," she said, *"The Color of the Damned.* For James Baldwin or Ralph Ellison or the other Ralph's pal out there. There was a nasty thing happened in Central Park. A white kid was dragged into some bushes by the Hans Andersen statue and his balls were cut off. He'd gone for a pee and his mother wondered why he was so long. And bloody Carlo preaches about a new age of love and tolerance. You get off to bed, Ken. Dream about love and tolerance."

The following morning I embraced poor Dorothy for, I knew, the last time. She knew it too, for she wept and clung to me. One more last thing to be filed: last trip to the movies, last meal in that Belgian restaurant on West Forty-fourth Street, last sight of crocuses in Central Park, last meal cooked in her own kitchen, last sight of Ken Toomey, old, dry, but horribly healthy. I embraced Hortense with love and pain, left, with no word, my bottle of barbiturates on the dining table, then went down to get a cab to take me to La Guardia. There I caught the noon flight to Oklahoma City.

I have confused recollections about the loose forking together of my university visits, which in memory congeal to a single and generic one, and Carlo's American mission as read of in the papers and seen distractedly on the motel screen. I don't know whether I'm being just either to time or the potentialities of his *aggiornamento* when I say that I associate this continental tour (not, after all, my last) with the more bizarre of the innovations, ritual or doctrinal, which his strong podgy arms blessed. Was it at Rockhurst College in Kansas City that I witnessed a mass whose liturgy derived from Coventry Patmore's *An Angel in the House*? Was it in the town in Pennsylvania confusingly named California (from a long-exhausted mineral strike) that I saw a little of a rock mass, with guitars and trapdrums and a Kyrie that went

> *Lord, Lord, have mercy on us, yeah*
> *Christ do the same, yeah*
> *And if you have mercy on us, yeah*
> *We will bless your name, yeah*
> *We'll sure bless your name?*

I did not see the ballet mass put on in Chicago, with its priest in tights (Hortense's orchidelic bas-relief was, then, prophetic), but I was invited, in Iowa City, to a folk mass with loaves rushed hot from the oven and applejack served to the congregation as Christ's blood (was this really in defiance of the Council of Trent? Did the Council of Trent matter any more?). In Bowling Green, Ohio, or else Kalamazoo, Michigan, there was an open-air confession session with a priest in gaudy mufti and a tie that looked like two fried eggs sunny side up lolling on his crimsonshirted chest. These things can be believed as having taken place in America, where there is a tradition of religious razzmatazz. Were similar things happening in Mexico, Peru, Guatemala? A middle-aged priest in unfashionably rusty black told me, in a bar in Minneapolis, that he did not know where the hell he was.

"Like God," he said. "I used to have a pretty clear idea of God. Now we have these new theologians who say God's inside here not up there or he's an impersonal noosphere and the anthropomorphic image is out. Three unpersons in one ananthropomorphic noosphere. Our nada which art in nada, nada be thy nada."

"A clean well-lighted place," I said. "That's all he wants. What you're objecting to is the great opening up."

"To open up is to loosen. Holy Father, says the Archbishop of Boston, I've forgotten everything except my penny catechism. I've forgotten even that, says His Holiness. Let's forget everything except love, come to my arms little brother. That's not really inconsistent with this noosphere junk." He irritably indicated to the shortskirted bosomshowing waitress that he wanted another whisky sour straight up. A whisky priest. "We got nuns dressed like that now," he said. "We got sexy priests, God help us. Thank Jesus I'm not sexy."

"The Church," I said, "is coming to the people."

"The brothel," he said, "is coming to the clients."

This was going, I thought, too far. Christ spoke in the language of his hearers. Like the chaplain of Erie County Jail, New York, who gave out the Twenty-third Psalm as "The Boss is like my Probation Officer He makes me play it cool and feel good inside of me He shows me the right path so I'll have a good record and He'll have one too." I heard that. It went down well. God is like for real, man. Those kids didn't know what the hell a shepherd was. A Lord was something in old movies.

Carlo spoke to the blacks in Harlem. He didn't use their language but they understood him all right. He spoke in the thin spring sunlight on a street of ratgnawed tenements not far from 125th Street. "First," he said, "let me tell you what I am. I'm an Italian from Italy, not from Mulberry Street. Big Italy, not Little. I've nothing to do with the Mafia. I'm white, okay, and that goes against me. I can't help being white. That's a matter of luck, good or bad. Blame my parents, if you can find out who they were. I never knew them. I was an orphan very early in life and I got adopted. Now I'm the Pope, which means I'm head of the Christian Church. Now I don't want you to think that the Pope's always got to be a white man. He hasn't. Saint Peter was the first Pope, and he was a swarthy Jew, a fisherman without a dime for a cup of coffee when Jesus took him up. Jesus was pretty dark too, not black but sunburnt. It's not a white man's Church, and if a white man's at the head of it now, well, that's just an accident. Next time, who knows, we may have a black Pope. Or a yellow one. Color doesn't matter much, after all, except the color of your soul. And let's not talk about black souls and white souls. Let's talk instead of dirty slimy stinking souls and clean shining polished ones. Of dustcarts and Cadillacs, if you wish. If our souls get dirty, who do we blame? You know who. Now listen to me. The devil has his best chance among the ignorant, the deprived, the homeless, the jobless. That's why we can't have true religion till we've wiped out squalor and hunger and unemployment. I'm here in America for many things. But the big thing is to call for a change of heart. Your people have suffered from slavery. You, the children of slaves, suffer from the lack of justice. You have suffered too long. All this has to change. You're still in Egypt's land, whipped by Pharaoh. I stand here now and speak with the voice of Moses. I cry not *Let my people go* but *Let my people live*."

He left Dulles Airport after animating Washington with sermons both radical and reactionary, according to milieu. The words, indeed, grew less and less important. He communed with his smile, fatherly arms, bulky earthy solidity. Of his goodness no one was ever in doubt. He moved to the oppressed states of Latin America to diffuse this goodness further. It was not a goodness that noticeably, at least not yet, seemed likely to change the world. The technological progress of that year of papal travel was unrelated to the motions of the heart. *Pioneer IV* went in orbit round the sun; the basic molecule of penicillin was isolated; the Rajendra bridge spanned the Ganges; Jodrell Bank bounced a message to the United States off the moon; Auckland Harbour bridge was opened; the Vickers *Vanguard* turboprop airliner flew two and a half thousand miles in five and a half hours; Russia fired *Lunik III* and photographed the moon's glorious behind; the atomic icebreaker *Lenin* cracked its way into the Baltic; the first nuclear merchant ship *Savannah* was launched by Mrs. Eisenhower; CERN's proton synchotron went into operation in Geneva; the French Premier opened the four-hundred-mile Sahara pipeline; a U.S. Air Force pilot set a new world speed record of 1,520 m.p.h.

Nature was equally unresponsive to the message that love could conquer all human problems. The world's population, already 2,800 million, increased by another 45 million—the result of love or something like it; the South America to which Carlo flew suffered the greatest flood disaster of the century; a typhoon in West Japan killed five thousand and left a million homeless. Humanity in the mass, or through the abstract actions of politics, remained unregenerate. States of emergency were declared in Southern Rhodesia and Nyasaland; the communist guerrillas in South Vietnam, soon to be known as the Vietcong, set up their National Liberation Front; there was an uprising in Lhasa against Chinese rule and the Dalai Lama fled to India; desperate riots tore townships in Durban; the Prime Minister of Ceylon was assassinated; Russia glowered at the West and the West glowered back; the East glowered at everybody. Technology and power politics conjoined in the setting up everywhere of nuclear installations which potentially outdid in terror mere floods and earthquakes. City streets began to be unsafe at night. A change of heart was, however, the answer to the growing world mess, a cultivation of the technique of love. Could anyone honestly say that this was really wrong? The Pope of Rome may not have been all that realistic, but he was more realistic than the secular statesmen.

Of course, it was a comfort to know that man was not really bad and that everything could be blamed on a kind of moral virus that had landed in Eden in a spaceship. If the sophisticated could not hear of the diabolic power without a smile, the young were very ready to believe in him. There were many cases of juvenile crime, including *actes gratuits* of rape, torture and murder, which were laid by the defendants at the devil's door. The devil became as tangible a reality as Christ for Kids or the Big Black Jesus: his horns and eyes decorated many a bass drum of rock groups; he was invoked in drug sessions and was a blazon on T-shirts. If Carlo had convinced a section of the Christian population that there was a palpable malevolence at large which had nothing to do with original sin, then he had partly succeeded in his mission.

Anyway, he was there. It is still hard for me to accept that the little greedy cleric I had given lunch to in Sardinia at the end of the war to end war had become father of the faithful and a potent myth. It would have been proper for the man who had once been his brother to celebrate this elevation in some Berliozian *Te Deum* scored for quadruple woodwind, ten horns, six trumpets, the same of trombones, three tubas, massive kitchen department, a hundred strings, organ, and voices voices voices. *Te Deum* would, of course, have had to be vernacularized. But Domenico, having made his drunken plea for marital reinstatement and, so far, been rejected, settled with his whisky and Moog synthesizer in Menton, one who had fathered neither children nor great music, and brooded on his loneliness. I was lonely too, and so was Hortense after she had fed poor Dorothy her hemlock. This record, I see, has now to become not merely a chronicle of loneliness but of death, but that is in order for a chronicler who is dying himself. Yet the message of lonely Carlo, due for death five years after his crowning, was really life.

seventy-two

Laura Campion sent me, as a gesture of thanks for my gift of her trip to East Africa, almost daily letters and postcards. The pictures on the postcards showed sunny main streets not much different from those of the American South, except for public statues of great anonymous blacks. "I'd thought," she wrote in a letter, "that it would be plunging into the Heart of Darkness, but of course we're only nibbling at a coastline where Arabs and Syrians seem to be running things, hardly black Africa at all. As for Johnboy's anthropological researches, that's a business of consulting other anthropologists—I'm amazed how many there are, it's as though everybody's trying to grab what they can of primitive or tribal Africa before big modern Africa takes over. Not that it's possible to get any idea of Africa Africa, I mean the lot, the totality, the whole continent— that doesn't exist, it's much too big, the mind can't take it. Anyway, tomorrow we start journeying inland, that's by train from Dar-es-Salaam to Dodoma, then by road to Rungwe—from then on I don't yet know. Johnboy's found out, at second hand, but that seems to be the only way, that there *is* a relation between linguistic structures and familial constellations, and that when anything like incest creeps in language does go haywire—so it seems that his theory that the thing's universal will hold water. I think it's gorgeous so far, what I've seen, and what I've eaten too—roast birds I can't give a name to, and big hairy fruits that are smoothly delicious inside, and fermented coconut milk that smells like burning paper but gets you nicely not nastily high."

Of the State of Rukwa she wrote: "This is a very small republic which all began with a settlement round Lake Rukwa and expanded as far south as Lake Nyasa. It's very progressive but a bit dictatorial. There are elements of dissent which make for terrorism, which explains the strong police force and what are termed Emergency Regulations, and border incidents which may or may not be provoked by the Big Boys to the north. Oil is the wealth here, oil, oil, but the white prospectors are strictly out and the technical knowhow is all black. There are a number of black American technicians who are not well liked by the natives—they call them *uruwe yanki* or Yankee pigs, or sometimes *tumbo cocacola*. Your old friend and the brother of poor Dorothy is aide to the boss, who as you might expect is big and forceful and charismatic and very far from being unintelligent. I do honestly believe he means well for his people, unusual in African leaders, American for that matter. Kasam Ekuri who used to be Ralph worked up the Department of Information and then handed over to a North Carolina black who was Jack Anderson and is now Garapa Mubu, now Ralph's big title is colonel of the *gaysh hisan*. These horse soldiers we saw on that film, they're more ornamental than anything, but they look very nice riding along the plain in the sun, flash flash. The Oma people, whom Jimmy Bucolo knows a bit about, are all now in what's called a *kijijipya* or new village near the northern border. They're peaceful and kind of feeble—too much inbreeding?—and used to be preyed on by the Kwanga till a protective garrison was brought in. The Kwanga are over the state border, but they don't know what national frontiers are, any more than American Indians knew what the 49th Parallel was. The Oma people were Christianized by Jesuits, but there are no white missionaries any more. I'm loving it all and can't say thankyou thankyou often enough . . ."

I had to go to Cannes as a member of the jury for the annual film festival, so Laura's cards and letters dropped for some weeks into the slot of a deaf house. The festival organization paid for my room and *table d'hôte* at the Carlton, but I paid my own supplement for a suite and chose from the *à la carte*. My fellow jurors were Rayne Waters, the embodiment and I mean no cliché of stupid glamour; the Italian director Gabriele Bottiglieri; the Israeli singing actor Alon Schemen; Kiyoshi Araii, the Tokyo epigone of Federico Fellini; the Spanish hidalgo actor Carlos Corces, devil for young girls; fat old Sonya Lazurkina, there only to vote for the Soviet entry; a number of dim French cinematic journalists who pronounced *génial* on nearly every bad experimental film we were shown. It was an arduous viewing schedule—two main movies a day and a number of shorts, with a tall sunburnt blonde of great elegance and ugliness taking our names at every session. Rayne Waters breathed patchouli on me one evening and said, "Love, I've got to spend the day on Ari's yacht tomorrow, you sign me in honeybunch, okay?"

The tall blonde said, "*Mais non*. No dice, *bébé*."

If you missed a morning projection, you had to put on *tenue de soirée* and fight gendarmes, photographers and general public in order to see it in the evening. The preliminary voting sessions were irritable and chauvinistic. The Soviet film was a three-hour war epic with stereophonic effects, landmines going off under one's seat, bombing planes crescendoing from projection room to screen, and its aim was apparently to demonstrate that the Russians beat the Germans singlehanded. "Propaganda," I said, "not art. I vote that it be eliminated as ineligible for serious consideration."

"*Mais*," Comrade Lazurkina said, "*c'est évidemment le meilleur film, on ne peut pas douter sa supériorité aux autres*," meaning that she would be sent to the saltmines unless she reported victory.

"Art tells the truth," I said, "and this does not. The Americans were in that war too, and also the British. We suffered, you know, London was nearly destroyed not just Leningrad, we faced Hitler alone—"

"You," M. Brochier the journalist said, "spoke on the Nazi radio. I do not consider it convenable for you to speak on this subject in connection with this film." He was a Marxist; Comrade Lazurkina was assured of his vote; he had evidently done his homework on his fellow jurors.

"I am making an aesthetic judgment. My personal biography is totally irrelevant."

All this had to be translated for Rayne Waters. She nodded in incomprehension and said, "Surely, surely."

A screaming rock opera about Christ and Judas, with Judas a hero of progressive if simplistic politics, was adjudged *génial*. I condemned it for blasphemy and vulgarity, for the implication that Jesus and his betrayer were locked in homosexual lovehate—M. Brochier was ready again with his dossier: "You did not feel it was blasphematory when you defended the poems of your friend in London. Your own proclaimed homosexuality is mondially known. You have what is called the double standard." Rayne Waters could be heard loudly whispering to her translatrix:

"A fag? Who's a fag? He's a fag? My my."

I did not, then, enjoy these sessions. Nor did I enjoy entering the vestibule of the Carlton after them, hot and weary, to be assaulted by posters and stands taking orders for commercial pornography. Alon Schemen and I would escape to small dark bars and share a bottle of chilled wine of the province. He was a plumply handsome man of forty, no wencher, devoted to unglamorous wife and children in the suburbs of Tel Aviv. He had made his world name in a singing film about dybbuks, based on a story by Isaac Bashevis Singer, a very irritable Yiddish writer I had met in New York. He looked not unlike my idea of—

"Leopold Bloom," he said to me one early afternoon in a bar off the Croisette. "It's just been offered to me."

"God," I said, "how astonishing. I was just thinking how absolutely— A film based on *Ulysses*? Sam Goldwyn wanted to do it, you know. Joyce wanted George Arliss for the part. But yes, you— It will make no money," I added.

"I do not know the book, though I've heard of it. No, this is a Broadway musical called *The Blooms of Dublin*. Lublin I thought I heard, but, no, Dublin. I must learn an Irish accent."

"*A musical?*"

"They say *The Cohens and the Kellys* and *Abie's Irish Rose* were great successes. This they think could be the same. It will be good to be back on the stage. I think you know the man who is to write the music. I went to Menton to see him last Sunday evening. He played me one or two of the songs. How does this sound to you, if I can remember the words?" And he sang, drumming a Bom da rara rhythm on the table:

> *"Today*
> *It's the sixteenth of June today*
> *And from morning till moon the*
> *Hours to come*
> *Will add up to a humdrum*
> *Sum*
> *Mer's day—"*

"You mean Campanati?"

"Yes. Does that accent sound all right to you?"

"So he's left off his Moog and backwards birdsong. Good. It will save his life. Not that it's worth saving."

"The bridge goes

> '*Plenty of fleshly exposure*
> *Napes and strawberries are red*
> *Buttocky peaches in a basket*
> *Racing on at Ascot*
> *In the royal enclosure*
> *Ted*'

The words are not always easy to sing. A young New York man is writing them, Sid Tarnhelm. The accent is right?"

"The accent's fine. Now we have to go and see this Peruvian horror."

In the vestibule of the Palais I saw my West Coast agent, just arrived, in a magenta shirt with a montage of Greek heroes in profile. His keen agential eyes were hidden from the Côte d'Azur by dark glasses that were also the new insolent golden mirrors to be favored by him who was soon to enter my life. The parrot beak sat ill between the jowls. His name was, even now hard to accept, Lev Trapeze. He said, arms out, "Ken, baby. You look beautiful."

"Old," I said.

"Yeah, but only the old are beautiful. You think about that, kid," he said to the exquisite leggy brunette nonentity in linen shorts beside him. And to me, "They took up the final option on that Heracles thing."

"Socrates?"

"That's the one. Principal photography starts in the fall. A guy called Wrigley did the script."

"Oh my dear God."

"This Greek guy called Lilliputtopiss or some shit like that, they have the weirdest names, he's playing the lead. Very mysterious money in it, Ken baby, but their check ain't no condom, like they say. You going in there?"

"I have to. C'est le boulot."

"Pedophilia Productions they're called now. Philadelphia? I ask them. Then they spell it out. Where's that? I ask them."

"Oh my dear God."

"What is this movie now? Is it the one with Bardot naked and the performing seals?"

"This is Peruvian. Peruvian and seals have something in common. Think about it, Lev. So long."

Next morning we watched the Quebec entry, *Et Patati et Patata*. The French jurors protested that they could understand neither the Canadian French dialogue nor the English subtitles. I raged at them and said: Christ, it's only eighteenth-century Norman. The projection was intermitted while a simultaneous translator was sought. Finally I did the job myself. With a parched mouth and thuds in my skull I tottered into the Carlton vestibule at lunchtime: the posters (REAL! NOW! FOR THE FIRST AND LAST TIME!) hurt my eyes. A limp hand touched my sleeve. The face looked familiar. I frowned at it.

"Bucolo," he said. "Jimmy Bucolo. Professor Bucolo. You know me."

"You," I said, "are supposed to be in Africa."

"Could we talk? Alone?" He was in a dirty beige tropical suit and his face and head were so wet with sweat that it was as though he had been dunking them for a hangover. "Alone," he said, "like me, alone. I came back alone, you can see that. Nairobi to Casablanca via El Obeid, Murzuq and Tuggurt. I telephoned from Casablanca and they said where you were. It's been a long trip but I had the money, you gave it. I booked one way for all of us, I might have known." All this was spoken manically. Passersby in the vestibule frowned or grinned at the ham actor demonstrating a role: this was not the place, this was strictly for commerce not art. I felt cold and my head cleared of its ache. I led Bucolo to the elevator, "I've these bags," he said. "A lot of luggage." I signaled to the porter's desk.

Up in my sitting room I poured whisky into him. He sat hunched and thin and ill and haunted. He could not take the whisky. His face bulged, he got up and staggered, looking for a place to throw up. I pointed, he ran tottering. I sat trying to take in the news. The evidence he had placed on the round glass-topped table seemed irrelevant to anything I was able to, meaning wished to be able to or perhaps unable to, believe. Two certificates headed REPUBLIK RUKWANI with a crouching leopard, the subheading *Sertifikit Kifo*, the two names and the numbers of two passports, as though for the immigration control of the next world; a Bank of America credit card; John's notebook. Bucolo came back and flopped on the couch facing me. He was not far from total breakdown.

He said, "There's no need to look at me like that."

"How am I looking at you?"

"As if I should have gone with them. But I gave up the faith, you see. Reaction to my brother, my father and mother liked him better than me, he became a priest. It's not uncommon in families, you know that. I don't go to mass any more. Besides, I'd had to go to Morogo, you see, to see the snake ceremony. It was safe enough for them, you see, everybody said that. It was just a matter of a few miles in the Land Rover. A real paved road, you know, and open country, a couple of abandoned shantytowns and some scrub before they got to the new village. And everybody said that the terrorists had been contained, you see that. Shinya had been executed publicly. By firing squad. Near total pacification." He started to laugh.

"Stop that stop that now for Christ's sake. What terrorists, what are you talking about?" He went on laughing, showing brown teeth. I slapped him. He stopped.

"Thanks. Thanks very much. Thank you very much, that was the right thing to do, thank you. It's Mbolo's party really, but they put Mbolo in jail and they want Mbolo out of jail. They'll kill anybody, but whites are best, Africa for the Africans, you see that. They're still killing but it was put out about total pacification, you know. Containment, you see that."

"You saw, you saw—"

"I saw them, I had to identify, you see that. I saw the faces, the bodies were covered, they didn't want me to see the bodies. *Damu damu* this man kept saying in Swahili, that means blood. Robbed of everything, clothes, watches, money, everything. Except passports, they didn't want the passports. There's a man representing the United States who came in from Kipila, an honorary consul, you see, black of course. He took the passports. They were given a proper burial, taken to the Christian graveyard in Kilwa Kivinje, that's outside the territory, you know. There was a black Catholic priest did the ceremony, you see that."

"Let me get this clear," I said. "They were going to mass and they met a roadblock near a shantytown and then the terrorists got them. This was in broad daylight?"

"No, night, night, you see, they were going to a night mass, they always have mass at night. If they hadn't been going to mass, if they'd lost the faith like me— You see that."

"John had as good as lost it. He got it back through Laura. Oh Christ, I got Laura there."

"You got us all there. But you mustn't blame yourself, blame the badness in these bastards, that's all, it could have happened any time any place. There's only Laura, yes, she wouldn't have gone if it hadn't been for . . . but it could have happened some place else some time else."

"Black bastards," I said, "black filthy bastards. What did fucking bad filthy Ralph do about it, eh, Africa for the filthy fucking Africans, cut the white man's balls off. You didn't see the bodies, no, you said that, no, you didn't."

"They wouldn't let me see them, only the faces, you see that. I think the bodies must have been cut up. They don't have guns, they have the *kisu* and the *sikkin*. Can I have some hot tea with mint? It's the only thing that stops my stomach churning. I'd appreciate it if you . . . if you . . ."

"You can have tea but no mint. This isn't North Africa. The French don't go in for mint. I'll order some for you. Then I have to go. I have to watch a film."

"You have to what? You have to *what*? You mean you could after what I, you mean you could . . ." Old Mulberry Street proprieties were being outraged. "Christ, to go to a *movie*."

I telephoned for tea for him. "The job goes on," I said. "I said I'd do the job and I'm doing it. What do *you* propose to do?"

"I'll rest here if you'll let me. Stay the night if it's no bother. Then I can see about getting back home from Nice. I'll leave their things with you. These." He made hand movements at two of the bags. "When I get back I'll get down to telephoning to St. Louis. You can give the news to John's mother."

"Why me? And what do I want with this dead luggage?"

He opened his mouth at my hardness of tone. "You're his uncle. His nearest relative. I mean nearest in space. I mean, the same continent, though you're in Europe now, I see that. I mean, what the hell can I do, send a cable saying: John dead?"

"You'll be flying to New York. Give her the news in person."

"I can't I can't I can't."

"All right," I said sighing. "I've missed lunch. I have to grab a sandwich or something. At the bar downstairs. You stay here. Rest. Would you like a sleeping tablet?"

"I have some of my own. They only bring bad dreams. I can't sleep. I'll just lie down here if it's all right with you. Oh Christ, my stomach." But it was his belly he grasped.

The film I had to see that afternoon was an ill-made Brazilian feature entitled *Os Cidadãos*, all about low life in Rio, with a norm of gratuitous violence in gaudy psittacine colors. I heard the French journalists saying *"génial"* whenever a particularly gross cinematic cliché presented itself. I saw the violent killing of John and Laura very clearly in my own inner projection room. It became part of some other film full of outrage in exotic settings, it was half-cleansed to bad art, it was a help, it would in time become an abomination I had been forced to look at as juror at Cannes, title and plot forgotten, that one scene enacted with terrifying conviction but still a cliché, *génial*. When we staggered out into the huge marine light after the cozy dark shot with screams and stripped bodies, I knew what I had to do.

I went back to my suite at the Carlton to find Bucolo at the escritoire scribbling madly. He looked at me with demented brightness to say, "I'm doing it. I'm writing letters. I'm telling them all about it."

"To John's mother too?"

"I got to. It's my duty. I was head of the team."

"Don't. I'm seeing about that now." I looked up Domenico in the Alpes Maritimes telephone directory—boulevard Garavan 22—and then ordered a car to take me to Menton. "I'm going," I said, "to see John's father."

"You mean his real father? You've found his real father?"

"What the hell do you mean, real father? There are no real fathers, only legal ones. Mothers are different, mothers are all too real."

"So I don't have to write?"

"Later, very much later."

It was a gorgeous early evening, ideal for a coastal spin. The uniformed chauffeur was inclined to talk, making much play with his heavy shoulders and short thick neck. He was a devotee of the cinema, the Cannes festival cared not a turd for art, only for the commerce of the flesh, look at these would-be vedettes thrusting their naked bellies out at the world, being laid by fat Arabian Jews. We sped through Monaco, which he castigated as a principality made rich on human weakness, did I know the book by Dostoevsky about the agonies of a gambler, that would make a great film. At length he dropped me on boulevard Garavan in Menton, which town, he told me, the Italians called Mentone and claimed as their own. Was he to wait? Yes, he was to wait.

I could have found Domenico's third-floor apartment blindfolded. It was a matter of climbing as far as a loud composition made up of birds, glissandos and electronic ostinati and then knocking at it. At my knock the noise left off. Domenico opened up. He looked terrible. He was old, though some years younger than myself, but he was far gone in decrepitude. He was in dirty white like a Conrad character going to pieces in the tropics, his belly was huge, he was totally bald, he was leaning heavily on two thick sticks. I had not seen him since that bad time at La Scala. He seemed prepared to fend me off with his right hand stick. "All right, all right, Domenico," I said, "I come in peace."

He growled, "I heard you were in Tangier. What are you doing in these parts?"

"Cannes, Cannes, Cannes. Where I heard about this musical *Ulysses*. Congratulations. I'm sure it'll be a riot."

He was living near monastically in three rooms, though the biggest room appeared, apart from its upright piano, to be equipped with machinery apt for propelling a nuclear submarine. That would be the synthesizing apparatus. In another room there was only a camp bed and music paper. The living room had one armchair and two canvas chairs of the kind used by film directors on location, no carpet, a kitchen table with metal legs and a jazzy plastic top with three stained coffee mugs. I caught a glimpse of what looked like a submarine galley, too small to hold that table, a cooker filthy with spilt coffee and tomato sauce. The splendid evening light fought to pierce dirty windows. Domenico settled heavily and wincing into the armchair. It was old and it creaked. "What's the matter with the legs?" I asked.

"The arteries are getting clogged. It's agony most of the time. Sometimes it lets up. But not for long."

"I know. Intermittent claudication. Why are you living like this? Surely you've plenty of royalties coming in?"

"Alimony. Money's no good if you can't buy services. You can't buy services these days."

"I'm glad you've gone back to composing real music," I said. I did not trust the canvas chair I was sitting on. I got up and sat on the edge of the kitchen table. "I mean tunes and so on."

"I got a prize at the Venice festival of electronic music," he said gloomily.

"But you hanker after the big world of the tone deaf?"

"This *Ulysses* is supposed to be a great book. I remember in Paris everybody saying it was the book of the century. I remember Joyce, that thin drunk blind man. I worked with Irving Hamelin once. It was his idea I should do the music. You've caught me just before I go to New York."

"Traveling must be pretty painful."

"They have wheelchairs at all the airports."

"You need somebody to look after you. A wife, for instance."

"You know all about that. You know I tried. Telephoning on my knees, damn it."

"Less painful than standing?" A telephone wallstand was the only item in the vestibule. "Listen to me, Domenico. Listen to me with care. I want to talk about your son John or Gianni."

"He's not my son."

"Look, we're not getting into all that again. Paternity is a fiction. The law says you're his father."

"How can it say that when it says his mother is not my wife?" That was a complicated statement for Domenico, a twelve-tone ground with a couple of *appoggiature.*

"You know perfectly well what the Church says, and to hell with the secular laws of America. You were married once and once only. You're still married. And you're the legal father of two children. You have a certain duty to perform."

"Try and tell Orténsia about the duty. I'm ready to go back. But not as the father of those two kids."

"You thickheaded bastard, can't you take in what I'm telling you? The Church says you are the father and the Church is right. And the duty you have to perform is to tell your wife that one of your and her children is dead."

He grunted at me with his eyes wide: the whites looked as though they ought to be washed. "Dead? Who's dead?"

"Your son John is dead. And his wife Laura, your daughter-in-law. I got the news today. Along with their wretched orphaned luggage. They were in Africa. They were killed by terrorists in the tiny republic of Rukwa. Somebody has to tell John's mother. You know what happened fifteen years ago when that stupid girl went in with a telegram screaming. Somebody has to tell her quietly, gently, before any fool sends her a devastating letter. I just stopped one fool from doing it."

"Johnny's dead?"

"John is dead. I think the responsibility of telling her is all yours. Carlo, if he were interested in anything but humanity in the round, would think the same thing. I'm only Hortense's brother. I've already suffered enough with her. I'm suffering now, prospectively. But I'm not going to bear the news and see her collapse. That's your job."

"I hardly saw Johnny. I don't know what he looked like even. He changed his name. He abandoned me."

"You did the abandoning, you bloody fool. When are you going to New York?"

"Day after tomorrow. I'm sorry he's dead, I'm sorry when anybody's dead. Anna will know already. She always did know when he was sick at school or something. I knew that. She wrote letters to me for a time. I didn't answer. It comes of being *gemelli*."

"Twins, I know. Twillies, the doctors call it. Twins' ESP. Domenico, you and Hortense are going to be together again. She's alone now. She won't say no this time. You have to give her the news."

"I don't want to, I can't. Jesus, the trouble we all have."

"I know. But it's better to have the trouble and not be lonely. It's hell being lonely. I've been lonely all my life. When Carlo opted for loneliness I knew what I'd always suspected. That he wasn't, isn't human. It's like opting for hell."

"It's hell all right. Carlo thought we'd all let him down. By being human." And then, "How did Johnny die?"

"Simple. He died by being in big dirty black Africa. A place where white men are supposed to die. White women too. I paid her fare. But I take no blame, none at all. You must never blame yourself for good intentions."

"My intentions were good," Domenico said, "with our Saint Nicholas thing. I mean, I mean that God's a bastard. He is too." His eyes began to wash themselves. I could see that he was seeing himself as Nicholas, after all Hollywood had called him Nick, with a dead kid in his arms. He dried his eyes on his sleeve and said, "I see what you mean about it's my job. It's a hell of a job."

"Nobody else can do it, Domenico."

"You're right at that." And then, "That apartment in New York. It's yours, isn't it? There are some things a man can't do. I'll have to look around."

"Don't talk wet," I said in Hortense's manner. "If I gave it to her I gave it to both of you. One flesh as they say."

"That's out," he said. "That's all over. That's what makes it possible to think of starting all over. Sex," he said, "is a fucking nuisance. Thank Christ I'm over it."

I went back to Cannes. Bucolo had gone, taking all that luggage with him. He had left a note: "I tore up the letters I wrote but writing them got a lot out of my system. I'm catching the evening flight to Paris. Professor Lévi-Strauss is giving a lecture on incest and riddles at the Sorbonne. I intend to hear the lecture and get very drunk and then be poured on the plane to New York. I'll leave telling poor John's mother to you. Thanks for having me. The hot tea did a lot of good."

The final meetings of the jury were vituperative. The Russian war epic kept getting two votes only— Comrade Lazurkina's and M. Brochier's. A message came through telling us that if the Algerian entry, *Feu et Fer*, did not receive the award for best film a bomb would go off in the Palais. There was much hot talk about honor and impartiality. M. Brochier worked my dossier to the limit and combined with his journalistic *confrères* to denounce the perfidious and pederastic Albion I personified. The prize for best film went to a Yugoslav entry which nobody liked. The best director was the director of *Feu et Fer*, which was disgustingly directed. The best *court métrage* was the technically incompetent Soviet cartoon film *Shtopor*. Thus Comrade Lazurkina's sentence might be mitigated to public castigation and expulsion from the appropriate union. I feebly hit out at M. Brochier during the final buffet party and was much photographed. M. Brochier grabbed my weak wrist and sneered. "*Sportsman*," he said. "*Gentleman. Fair play. Vous êtes tous foutus. Tous.*"

seventy-three

The Broadway first night of *The Blooms of Dublin* came after tepidly received tryouts in Toronto, Boston and Philadelphia. The book and songs were frantically worked upon during this provincial run, like repairing an aircraft in flight. Action was what was missing from the original novel, and this had to be coldly injected, like adrenalin. Haines, the Englishman, went round with a gun and the intention of killing Stephen Dedalus, whom he identified with the black panther of his dreams. A strangulatory rope was made ready for Leopold Bloom in Barney Kiernan's. There was a copulatory chorus of drunks and whores in the brothel scene. The songs, I thought, were good: Domenico's Italianate lilt was not inappropriate in an ambience where bad Italianate opera was adored. In the first scene Buck Mulligan (played by Roy Hahn) did a Greek dance and sang "Hellenize the Island":

> *Let's turn this dim necropolis*
> *Into a real metropolis*
> *Put a ton of high explosive*
> *Under Mary and St. Joseph*
> *Groves where no lime or lemon is*
> *May still see agapemones*
> *Ouzo drinking will spell finis*
> *To the wealth of Arthur Guinness*
> *Exorcise all gloom and sin*
> *Let the pagan sun shine in!*

Stephen, played by the fine young tenor Tony Haas, sang an acrid mother song:

Mother Ireland
How many lice in your comb?
Bitter and bitchy though sweet of tongue
The original sow that devoured her young
I gave you my heart—what more can I give?
For God's sake let me alone and let me live.

Mr. Deasy during this first scene in the Martello Tower came in to announce that there was no school today and to foretell the death of the British Empire:

England's in the claws of the Jews
The paws and maws of the Jews
Swarming in monied hordes
Into the House of Lords
Corrupting youth and the truth
With their organs of news
The children of Israel own
The imperial throne

And then, with his line about Ireland's never having persecuted the Jews because she had never let them in, the lights dimmed and came up on the great Alon Schemen as Bloom singing that today was the sixteenth of June:

Let's see
If there's anything else in store
Let's be having it soon
This sixteenth of June
Nineteen hundred and four
A.D.

Molly, the professional soprano, played by the voluptuous Gloria Fischbein, herself a professional soprano, sang in bed a duet with her own recorded voice, a counterpoint of "Love's Old Sweet Song" and

At four o'clock this afternoon he's coming
Twirling his mustachios and gaily humming

with, later, Bloom adding his own baritone counterpoint about Boylan Boylan Blazes Boylan. In the newspaper office scene Schemen had a superb long sung monologue about the tribulations of the Jews—"Wandering, Wandering"— and, in the middle of a reverie near Nelson's pillar, the hit song of the show:

> *Flower of the mountain*
> *Crown of the Head of Howth*
> *That's what I called you then*
> *Day of full summer*
> *Day of the spring of love*
> *Will you come back again?*

The décor, mostly backcloths based on Edwardian photographs of Dublin, was the work of Hortense Campanati. She, with her husband, was present at this Palace Theatre premiere, slim and elegant in her early sixties, the eyeshade now wholly accepted as a property of *couture*—tonight a flash of brilliants flung onto a black velvet ground, the hair, frankly a blued gray, falling in a coil over it. She sat in the back row of the stalls, near the aisle. Next to her, in that aisle, in the wheelchair which she had herself propelled into the theater, sat Domenico Campanati. Was, I wondered, this musical remake of a, to be totally honest, totally unadaptable masterpiece of literature recalling for them the good Paris days of the avant-garde, youth and hope?

When, in the first act, Æ, George Russell, walked on briefly with a copy of *The Pig's Paper*, I recalled vividly the event that Dublin day which demonstrated to a young boy the nature of his sexuality. *Ulysses* had given Russell an alibi which no appeal to history could break. At the going down of the first-act curtain, with applause and the deafening cuckoo song which bellowed to the world Bloom's shame, I thought, grinning to myself, of how times had changed and I had had something to do with changing them. It was now possible to publish, in the *Joyce Newsletter* or something, an article on the maimed historicity of that novel, revealing why Russell had not been able to be in the National Library when Joyce said he was. Going into the vestibule I saw Professor Breslow, husband of my niece, and said:

"I was in Dublin on that memorialized day. I lost my innocence in the Dolphin Hotel. I must tell you the story sometime."

"Do." But he was not really interested. "I never thought," he said with scholarly resentment, "that they'd be able to make a public entertainment of it."

"I agree. First they've had to turn it into a genuine novel, with action and motivation. Great though *Ulysses* may be, novel it is not."

"They'll be doing *The Magic Mountain* next. Or Strehler's masterwork."

"Strehler wouldn't have minded."

"Or *Der Schloss*."

"That's been done," I lied. "A very perky Broadway style version. I saw it in West Berlin."

"I don't believe it. Shall we go for a drink?" There was a little bar almost next door to the Palace drama. We fought our way in and I automatically ordered Guinness.

"So Ann didn't come," I said. "I thought she liked the lighter kinds of theater."

"Ann," he said, with froth on his lips, "is far from well. She's had fits of suicidal depression after the hysterectomy. Not well at all. They're giving her a course of electric shocks at the Hedley."

"I didn't know. I've been out of touch."

"First the death of her brother. That hit her harder than I thought it would. They were never close. Except in the sense that they were twins."

"I know. Twillies."

"And then the business with Eve. That made her very hard, very shrill." A strange choice of word, a literary academic's choice. "Very Victorian father."

"What business?"

"Didn't anybody write to you?"

"I've been on my travels," I apologized. "Mail wasn't forwarded. I flew to New York this morning from Copenhagen. I went straight from Idlewild to the Algonquin. I came straight from the Algonquin to the theater. Tomorrow I have to fly to Los Angeles. You see the situation."

"Los Angeles?" he said fiercely. "Go and see her. Tell her I want her back. Her mother may not, but I do. Tell her to come home, baby as well."

"Do you mind starting at the beginning?"

"Eve," he said, "had a baby. Illegitimate, naturally. This is the great new age in which everybody is good and everything's moral and natural and nobody has to be blamed. I was tolerant. Annie was not and is not. As I say, like an old-time father, not like a mother at all. No compassion. Okay, the kid was foolish, but all kids are foolish these days. Eve had her baby in a public ward some place in the Bronx. The father came from the Bronx. That's all we know about the father. There was some big rock music rally in Cliffside Park, New Jersey. Teenage copulation. That's where it happened. Then they followed that up with a couple of carefree nights in an old tenement building in the Bronx. A kid of sixteen, God help us, claiming her right to illegitimate motherhood. Now she's taken Belial, as she calls her kid, to California. Redfern Valley. To join the Children of God."

"Don't say all that again. Just say what name she's given her baby."

"Belial. And she didn't get the name out of *Paradise Lost*, either. They call kids names like Beelzebub and Mephisto. It's the new freedom."

"What are these Children of God?"

"It's this evangelist God Manning as he's called. He runs a big closed religious community. The Children of God. It's an old army camp. Now they're tending the soil and keeping pigs and cows and cutting themselves off from the dangerous modern world."

"God for Godfrey. The name rings a bell."

"We got a letter saying she'd found religion at last. I never thought she'd find it that way. I never thought it would be that kind of religion."

"They're going back. I don't suppose you feel like going back. A travesty of *Ulysses* to add to your other worries."

"I've got to see it through to the end. We're doing *Ulysses* this semester. The Joyce Proust Mann course. I have to explain why it can't be turned into a musical."

"But, Christ, they've turned it into a musical."

"It can't be done."

Breslow was up in the balcony, I was in the orchestra seats. On my way in I stopped to address words of greeting and congratulation to Hortense and Domenico Campanati. They seemed not to have moved from their places during the intermission. They had near-finished drinks in their hands. Somebody had presumably brought those drinks to them. I greeted and congratulated. They were polite, even friendly, but they did not behave like my sister and brother-in-law. It was probably necessary for them, holding like an expensive artifact of crystal on a windy and violent Fifth Avenue their newly reestablished relationship, to exclude the associations of their sundered state. "I'm sorry," I said, "to hear about poor young Eve."

"An abominable child," Hortense said.

"Congratulations again." We sort of all bowed at each other.

The second act began in the Holles Street lying-in hospital, with Bloom and Stephen meeting for the first time among students who blasphemed against fecundity. Stephen, dubbed bullockbefriending bard because he had placed Mr. Deasy's letter on a cure for cattle disease in the evening paper, and Bloom, a father, alike proclaimed their veneration for the fertile Oxen of the Sun. But a couple of students, with sticks and straw cadeys, sang:

Copulation without population
That is the thing the world requires
Why fill our flats and houses
With dirty squalling brats?
We need every square inch we can spare
For parrots dogs and cats
Pedication as a variation
Sets trilling all the hot erotic wires
But love's true end is uteral so all the poets
state
A prelapsarian paradise for Adam and his mate

With RAISING CAIN FORBIDDEN written on the outer
gate
And COP U LATE

Then Buck Mulligan came in, rainwet, followed by Haines with a gun. Bloom disarmed him. Stephen fled to nighttown. Bloom followed. Now came the big phantasmagoric scene, with the unconscious rawly exposed, the chorus with much to do, Stephen's mother whizzing up from the grave, Stephen smashing the chandelier with his ashplant, getting the hell out, beaten up by tommies, Bloom leaning tenderly over him and then catching a vision of dead Rudy. There were tears in the audience as at an adaptation of *Little Women*.

Bloom and Stephen at the cabman's shelter, the chantey-singing Murphy, a tenor and baritone duet before parting but promising to re-meet, based solely on the words "The heaventree of stars hung with humid nightblue fruit." Then the final scena for Molly, a virtuoso twenty-five minutes. The viewpoint of the audience was a point in the wall of the bedroom in Eccles Street, so that the floor tilted up and the bed was raised. We were looking down at Gea Tellus from the moon. Molly sang, monologuized, ended with a flamenco reminiscence of Gibraltar and young love, the kiss under the Moorish Wall mingling with another on the heights above Dublin, a reprise:

> *Flower of the mountain*
> *Crown of the Hill of the Howth*
> *That's what you called me then*
> *Day of full summer*
> *Day of the spring of love*
> *Will you come back again?*
> *Will you come back again?*

And then came the coda with a crescendoing and diminuendoing chord of C major, the last whispered *yes*. Curtain. Applause. Much applause. By God, I thought, if the New York critics don't pan it it may run.

I met Breslow coming out. "It doesn't work," he said, "because it can't work." He was very dejected, a Bloom whose wife's womb had been cut out and whose daughter had been put in the family way at Mullingar.

"Come back to the Algonquin with me," I said in pity. "A little drink in the Blue Bar."

We walked to West Forty-fourth Street, only a couple of blocks. There were a lot of obstreperous Afro-Americans about. I caught a stupid vision of Carlo blessing with fat arms man's innocent violence from a lighted window forty stories up. Hellsmoke curled from the gratings. Red and yellow light flashed on and off faces gleeful with gratuitous malevolence. In the bar we ordered scotch on the rocks.

"The hysterectomy," I said.

"Something there, something growing, malevolent, you know."

"Malignant?"

"Is there a difference?"

"Look," I said. "I'm going to California to see a film based on an early novel of mine. About Socrates. I'll also see Eve. Where is this place?"

"Redfern Valley. About thirty miles out of Los Angeles. They won't let you in. I know, I've tried."

"But, Christ, a man has a right to see his own daughter."

"The message they give you is that nobody wants to see anybody. Wrapped warm in the love of God Manning or Jesus or somebody. No contamination from outside. I got a little note saying Go Away Dad, I'm Fine. It was Eve's writing all right. What the hell could I do?"

"Get the police. The FBI. The state governor."

"That's crazy. It's private property. You can't just break in. They'd love the police to try. Then they could propagandize about the state being against God. They have their own radio station."

"Does the press ever get in?"

"Manning isn't averse to publicity if he can check everything first. You mean you'd try and get in as the press?"

"As a representative of the London *Times*," I decided. "I know Kilduff at the Washington bureau. He could fix it for me. I take it these people are on the telephone?"

"I got on the telephone to them. They put a girl's voice on. It didn't sound like Eve. It was the same message. Go Away I'm Happy in the Love of the Lord. The London *Times*," he said, "has a big reputation. It might work."

"I'm desperately sorry about all this, you know."

"Look," Breslow said fiercely, "I've always been right about religion. Religion's dangerous. You just don't know what you're tuning into when you listen for the station GOD. Now your Pope comes along telling everybody that everything's beautifully clear-cut and God's here and the devil's there and the devil doesn't smell of roses and runs off yelping when you make the sign of the cross. I'm a Jew and I know it isn't that simple. If Jehovah exists he's schizophrenic. Loving father and dirty bastard. But I don't think he does exist."

I looked at him and very nearly said: Here are you teaching Comparative Literature, the big subtle stuff crammed with ambiguities, and you've been put in a situation of melodrama, very simple and crude, a teenage daughter turned into an unmarried mother and a wife distraught with the shame of it, yourself a sorrowing father. Get off Comparative Literature: it doesn't help you to cope with life; read the disregarded works of Kenneth M. Toomey, they're pure melodrama, full of erring sons and daughters and heartbroken parents. But I said, "I'll get on to Kilduff now." Breslow nodded dumbly, finished his drink, then went out to engage the hell of the streets and the IRT. I went to my little suite and telephoned Kilduff. He was home and not yet in bed. He went along with my proposal.

The place I went to the following day was the little seaside town of San Jaime, almost midway between Piedras Blancas and Santa Cruz. To reach it I had to fly from Los Angeles in a twelve-seater aircraft operated by Coast Range Airways. The name of the town carried two pronunciations, like Los Angeles itself. The pilot called it San Jamy, and I could not help saying to myself, as we landed, "By the mess, ere theise eyes of mine take themselves to slomber, ay'll de gud service, or I'll lig i' th' grund for it." Meaning the next day, not today. Today was the film, entitled somewhat Ibsenishly *A Corrupter of Youth*, and here, on the little airfield, was Sidney Labrick, the producer-director, a saturnine man with a pepper and salt beard, and with him, now entering my life, Geoffrey Enright.

Geoffrey Enright said, "Well, the man isself, Gawd bless and sive us, not looking a day over seventy and fit, by God sir, yes, fit, fit, and sexy wiv it."

"Geoffrey," Labrick said, in American, "has been helping me." And he looked at Geoffrey with cold eyes half-shut against the sea wind. "At least, he *called* it helping."

The town we now entered in Labrick's Studebaker was, and still is, a male homosexual colony. The ingenuous reader will regard this as too improbable even for fiction, but it is the truth I am writing. California has always been notable for excess, or originality, or the pushing of logic to the Cartesian limit. No decree of Californian law had made this town into a male homosexual enclave: it had gradually become that, with heterosexuals quietly leaving as white folk left the prosperous black districts of Queens in New York, except that here black heterosexuals moved out along with the white, and lesbians both black and white moved out also. The police were homosexual too, and of course the mayor. There were absolutely no women. When I was shown to my room in the Holiday Inn, the Push It Well In, as Geoffrey termed it, a fair-haired youth with a frilly orange apron on was still hoovering it. "Oh my dears," he sibilated, "we're so late today. Not a pisspot emptied and the house full of spaniels." Such ephebes as he were rarer than they had been. Most of the citizens I had seen walking the streets were butchly muscular, dressed as cowboys. I dumped my bags and we went to the bar for a few Ramos fizzes. The barman was black, tough and charming. "The *size* of it, my dear," Geoffrey whispered to me. "He can lay ten dollars' worth of quarters along it and flicked them all off with one seismic lash."

"You know," Labrick said, "the situation. This movie will never get a public performance in the present condition of the law. The law will change, it's changing already, following that change in morality which has to precede legal change. I reckon about seven years will go by before we see the permissive society." I had not heard the phrase before.

"Speaks lovely," Geoffrey said, very close to me. "Like a real shonnary."

"A what?"

"A shonnary. I always leave the dick out." Then he made a comic gesture of horror at an imagined open fly. A very amusing young man, dressed in a parody of British smartness—dark woolen suit with stiffish shirt collar and a blue tie with phalloid shapes in gold. He was not yet running to fat, though he was on the way to losing his hair, which had the color and patina of tan boot polish.

"I don't quite understand," I told Labrick. "About the film not getting a public performance, I mean. There's nothing bannable about the life and death of Socrates."

"Ah," Geoffrey said, "but there is the way Sidney's done it. He's played up the *love*, haven't you, Sidney?"

"History," Labrick said, "has been unfair to Socrates. Just as it's probably been unfair to Christ. History is too often written by heterosexuals."

"I gather," I said, "that Val Wrigley wrote the script. I see the tie-up. Between Socrates and Christ, I mean. I wonder if I should have sold you the rights to the book."

"There's not much of the book left. We had to buy a book to please the backers. I said the whole thing's in the public domain. But no, they said I had to buy a book."

Geoffrey was looking at me in the manner of a preparatory school master shocked by a pupillary solecism. "My dear," he said. "It's you whom we consider to be the great opener of flies. None of us will ever forget that *fearless* declaration."

"All I mean is that Socrates is a philosopher in my book. The pederasty hardly gets a mention."

"You wrote that book a long time ago," Labrick said. "Anyway, don't judge till you see. And remember you get points. This movie is going to get a very wide private showing. And by private I mean full-size moviehouses hired by clubs. When the permissive age begins it will be universally recognized as a landmark."

"Val Wrigley," Geoffrey said. "I gather you and he were ah ah ah"—he gasped quite in the Henry James manner before uttering the word—"*buddies*."

"First World War," I said. "Nearly as long ago as the book. Is he here?"

"Just about here," Geoffrey said. "He is very very," in a Noel Coward tone, "old."

"Younger than I."

"Ah, but time hasn't been good to him, dear. You, on the other hand, the enemy has positively *coddled*. Still, he looks very distinguished and venerable in his robes."

"Oh Christ, is he an autocephalic archbishop?"

"You'll see him this afternoon if you come." Naturally he made the word sound like an ejaculation. "You are cordially invited to a bout of holy matrimony, or perhaps it ought to be patrimony. Loads of champers at their stitely aum awfterwards. Both William and Evelyn are well oiled or is it heeled? Oiled as well."

"Let's eat," Labrick said.

seventy-four

So I was taken that afternoon to the wedding of two young men in the Church of John the Beloved Disciple. There seemed to be two or three autocephalic archbishops officiating, but Val Wrigley was very senior, crotchety and authoritative. I was interested in the form of the service, which asked William if he would take Evelyn to be his wedded husband in the sight of God, and asked Evelyn if he would take William to be the same thing in the same perspective. Both said *I do* in powerful cowboy tones. Everybody in the church, which was positively loaded with lilies, was very well dressed, and there were tears from the sentimental and labile. The organ played "Promise Me" and, for some reason, Debussy's *Clair de Lune*. I was tremulous with mixed emotions when Archbishop Wrigley declaimed a good deal of my perverted Genesis, once put out by the Black Sun Press in Paris in a limited edition and now, it seemed, an aspect of anglophone homosexual folklore. Geoffrey, who sat next to me, said, "You all right, dear? You seem *affected*."

"I wrote that," I said.

Geoffrey said, "You clearly need to be very well looked after. Do you think I will like it in Tangier?"

"I wrote that, I tell you. A long time ago, but I wrote it."

"It would have to be a *very* long time ago, wouldn't it, dear?" Shakespeare had merely gotten his name into the Bible (Psalm 46); I had actually written a book of it. I said nothing. The congregation began to sing a kind of recessional hymn, tune the "Old Hundredth," words by, I presumed, the senior autocephalic archbishop:

> *"O God who made us what we are*
> *Shine down thy love upon our love*
> *Illumine it with sun and star*
> *And dub it with the choirs above*
>
> *Released from biologic ends*
> *It soars to seek the heavenly sphere*
> *The golden ecstasy of friends*
> *A song attunéd to thine ear*
>
> *In thee at last our loves shall meet*
> *All loving faces in thy face*
> *Eternal spendings shall be sweet*
> *Yet never spent in thine embrace"*

Geoffrey made a soaring descant out of the Amen. Then we left the church, his arm on my elbow, and went to the reception at the fine house on Alfred Douglas Avenue. There was too much campy play under the influence of the champagne and I looked sourly upon it.

Geoffrey saw this and said:

"I quite understand, my dear. A very artificial atmosphere, isn't it? I mean, too much *set up*. A certain lack not only of dignity but of danger. Do what thou wilt and so on. No disapproval to provoke, except perhaps from Archbish Wrigley over there, but with him it's only sacerdotal camp. Do tell me all about those dirty brown boys in Tangier."

"What's your job? What have you been doing with Labrick?"

"Lubricious Labrick, yes. Oh, helping, you know. I'm rather a good secretary. I type terribly fast for one thing. Very fast all round they tell me I am. I'm used to the literary as well as the illiterate, which is what Lubrick really is, all visual and motor sensations, my dear—look at him now with that horrible little slut who plays Alcibiades, as you shall see later. I worked for Irving Pollard, you know, till he got ratty. Daylong sipping I can tolerate, but, my dear, with him it was gulp gulp gulp all the time."

"What did he get ratty about?"

"Oh, everything. Nothing was right. I wet my pillow frequently, frustration, you know. Then I was companion to dear Boyd Chilling. Well named, I can tell you. Fair crackled with ice he did. I want *home*, my dear. I'm a European, I fancy our great blue mother the Med and our indulgent dad the sun, sweat trickling down into my tummybutton. Of course, there's plenty of sun here, but it's all enrobed in dirty smog. A day on the beach and I feel my little body positively *inquinated*. I'm an African too, of course, if that is required."

"Don't mention Africa to me."

"Suffered, have you? Hm, I can tell. Say no more. I can be whatever is wanted. I leave dirty Labrick tomorrow. I'm all yours. Just say the dickybird."

Val Wrigley came up to me. He had changed out of his robes into shimmering black barathea with a dog collar. He held a chalice of gin and tonic. He did not bless me.

I said, "Quite the little Cardinal Newman. Lead kindly light and all that sort of thing. When do you write your *Dream of Gerontius*?"

"You were always," he said, "a mocker."

"I stood up for you," I said. "I got no thanks."

He had effected the change well from Walt Whitman to a kind of Gerard Manley Hopkins grown, which Hopkins never had, old.

"You never could understand," he said, "things like faith and trust and unity. We are all members of one another. For me you did nothing." A fair-haired youth came round with canapés of pâté and caviar, all exqusitely tailored. "Do you have such a thing," Val asked him, "as some stewed corned beef with onions?" The youth, whose mouth was full, negated prettily.

"That's cruel, Val, that's desperately cruel."

"We all carry the cross," he said. "Those who belong to the Church Militant at length become members of the Church Triumphant. You never had the stuff of the martyr in you."

I could not clearly understand my angry tears. "Blasphemer," I said. "Bloody fucking blasphemer." He turned his back on me and began to give spiritual advice of great gravity to a bulky young man with very sweet lips. "I'm going," I said to Geoffrey. "I have to lie down for a while. What time is the film?"

"Oh, I'll come and pick you up about seven-thirty. Are you sure you're all right alone? You seem terribly shaken."

"I'm all right alone. For now at least. I'll tell you about Tangier tomorrow."

The film was shown in the Erato Cinema, a private showing, of course, since the public morality of the State of California applied even in this pornotopia. Geoffrey sat next to me and held my hand, or tried to. My hands were in fact much concerned with gestures of distaste and even horror. Socrates, played by the ugly snub-nosed Athenian Pericles Anthropophagoi or something like it, began the film as a brave soldier, saving the life of Alcibiades at Potidaea and then very explicitly pedicating him. Dubious about the morality of homosexual love, Socrates married Xanthippe, a comic shrew played by Timothy Rhinestone (present, like most of the cast, in the audience), who fed him on cold stewed lentils and threw the contents of the pisspot at him. Disenchanted with marriage, the philosopher now sought the company of handsome young men and taught them wisdom by the Socratic method, which consisted in conducting simple catechisms during the sexual act. Everybody was buggered by or buggered Socrates, including Plato, and at the Symposium all possible positions and combinations were tried out to the Laocoontic limit. As for the wisdom Socrates purveyed, it was to do with seeking virtue and truth and justice. Hated by the archons of Athens for his fearless condemnation of municipal graft, he was hypocritically arraigned on a charge of corrupting Athenian youth. His wife Xanthippe, as well as the evil leather-seller Meletus, were to the fore as witnesses for the prosecution. He sinned, they said, against Nature as well as the polity. Socrates defended himself with spirit, spoke up for love between man and man, asserting that the cold abstractions of the enquiring mind had to be balanced by the warmth of fleshly embraces, man being a mixed creature in which opposed elements must be reconciled, but he was nevertheless condemned to death. Xanthippe relented of her harshness and Meletus hanged himself. The hemlock drinking scene was sentimentally rather than fiercely carnal. When Socrates whispered that he owed a cock to Aesculapius, Alcibiades said that he owed a cock to nobody. Death and transfiguration. The end.

Geoffrey tried to still my shaking with both hands as the lights came up to cheers and congratulatory embraces, Labrick, with smiling lips and cold eyes, bowing and bowing. "Let me get out of here," I whimpered. "Sex, sex, sex, Christ, is there to be nothing in this world but bloody sex?"

"You have to admit, dear, that parts of it were very very moving."

"Yes yes, flesh moving, bloody hoi phalloi never bloody still, is that what the world's coming to?"

"I think," Geoffrey said, as we stood outside on the street, the exiting audience milling their way off to a party somewhere, "you consider yourself to be past all that kind of thing. You consider yourself to *have come through* to a plateau of fleshly renunciation. I think you may well have to be taught that such a location exists in no known gazetteer. Am I or am I not to be with you?"

"I don't want anybody. I want to be left alone."

"Yes, that's your feeling now. A feeling that will change. See, I have written down my telephone number. I'm staying temporarily with Robin Cathcart, who played Plato. Call me tomorrow. Without fail. I have to know, you see, dear."

I went back to the Holiday Inn, which was only a couple of blocks away, and raged for a time quietly in my room over the bottle of scotch which was part of my luggage. A message, I noticed, had come through from Kilduff in Washington. I had given him this number in New York, having found waiting for me at the Algonquin a confirmation of my booking here. The message said: OKAY ANYTIME TOMORROW.

I slept fitfully having asked for an early call, then caught the dawn flight to Los Angeles. The Quartz agency at the airport provided me with a car and driver to take me to Redfern Valley. We traveled east through smog and architectural vulgarity toward Mojave. Scrub and sand and commercial hoardings and filling stations. "This," the driver said, an expatriate from Sydney NSW, "seems to be the plice." He meant a decayed village where the vestiges of failed enterprise were beaten by brassy sun and a dry wind—Ye Jollie Olde En-gglisshe Pubbe, a chicken farm, a reptile store, a flapjack parlor. The army had been near here but now the army had gone. The Children of God supported no commercial substructure. The driver found the camp with no difficulty, about two miles southeast. The physical atmosphere was still military—a periphery of high tough woven wire, huts, even a guardroom. Above the closed metal gate was a huge arc of metal, on which the name of the community had been painted in cartoon lettering. In the vast enclosure, where grass was losing a war with sand drifts, I could see what looked like a dispirited platoon, men, women, whites, blacks, browns, marching off with hoes and spades to hopeless agricultural work. I heard the massed grunting of hogs some way off. "Rather you than me," the driver said. "You want me to wite?"

"Come back in two hours or thereabouts. Get yourself some lunch."

"Lunch, for Christ's sake where?"

"There's bound to be a McDonald's somewhere. Even in this bloody desert."

He went off, his exhaust snorting, and I went to the guardroom. There were three blacks in a kind of uniform with COG brassards. All were armed with pistols, and there was a small armory of rifles against a wall. "Guns," I said with fearful jocularity, "in a holy place?"

"God," the senior black said kindly, "he got lotta threats from nuts and commies and suchlike." He telephoned somebody from a wall telephone. A portrait of Godfrey Manning looked at me with calculation: a handsome forty-odd, lustrous sideburns, sensuous mouth, eyes wideset like a dog's and narrowed to the divine light. "He say *The Times*. He say he got an appointment. Yeah. Yeah." Then to me, "Jed here take you to the big house. They waiting for you." Jed was exophthalmic and limped. "I do that," he said. "You come longa me." The big house referred to had not been visible from the entrance. The way to it was by a path on which Johnny-jump-up grew through the sand, past plain wooden huts which doubly encircled it. Nobody seemed to be in the huts at this hour of the late morning. The house was of white clapboard, two-storied with a mansard roof, a verandah all about, a surrounding garden, the soil evidently imported, forsythia and bougainvillea flourishing. A young lithe man with dark glasses, dressed in white as for overseeing toiling coolies, got up from a swingseat as I approached. He came down the steps with vigor, welcoming hand out.

"Hi," he said, "I'm Jim Swinney. You go back now, Jed."

"Toomey of *The Times*," I said. "Great interest in your ah community in my country. Thank you, ah Jed." I then saw Professor Bucolo in my head and wondered why. Of course, God Manning, a sort of preacher creature. "Some years ago, when I was lecturing in Indiana, I was introduced to his ah book.

Hence my personal interest. I am myself a writer of books. I am not actually an employee of *The Times*. Toomey," I said. "Kenneth M. Toomey. Author myself of a ah theological work."

"Fine fine, just fine." He had clearly never heard of me. "Of course, we've come a long way since those days of the wandering. This is the Promised Land of the Children of God. Come unto me all ye et cetera. God is due back about noon from Los Angeles, business in the mission there, you've seen it of course, the Temple, eighteen fifty-nine Sunset Boulevard. This is our Mecca. This is where we are."

"Yes," I said, "so I can see."

"Fifteen hundred disciples," he said. "The number's growing. The sick and the lonely. He cures the sick and he comforts the lonely." He was leading the way toward what looked like a small aircraft hangar.

"He cures the sick? Literally?"

"Fifty-five cures where all doctors failed. Killing cancers. Leukemia. Jesus said go ye and do likewise. This afternoon after lunch you'll see. This is our Place of Prayer." He meant the hangar. We went in, meeting in the vestibule a high gesso statue of the Lord holding out wounded hands: the face, unbearded, was not unlike the one I had seen in the guardroom. The hall itself was like a theater, with fixed bucket seats and a curtained stage. Spots and floods, blind at present, were everywhere. The house lights were dim and religious but, I had no doubt, could be cunningly modified on an electronic board to stimulate, with the aid of the electronic organ near the front at the left, whatever emotional atmosphere was required. "Holds two thousand," Jim Swinney said. "Sometimes we show devotional movies. We have our own choir. You'll know the album *God Is with You*. Sold two million."

"Yes indeed. Is that the sort of thing you live on? Record royalties, I mean, that sort of thing."

"We're self-sufficient, that's a fact. We make our own bread, donations, book sales, record albums, they're the butter."

"State taxes, federal taxes?"

"We're a religious organization. We pay no taxes."

"Do you mind if I smoke a cigarette?"

"Give up that killing weed, brother. It rots the soul as well as the lungs. No smoking here, no liquor either. No toxic abominations may pollute God's good air, that's our rule. Now I'll show you what work we do."

It was a long trudge to the farming area. There had been a serious effort to feed bad ground. Potato fields, acres of cabbages. Workers, black, white, of poor deprived stock all of them, except for the occasional crazed thin clerkly-looking man, librarian-looking woman, unbent their backs from their tasks to greet and be greeted. Hi Jack Enoch Jethro Mabel. Hi Jim. At me they looked with suspicion. I could not see young Eve anywhere.

I asked, "What do the children do?"

"Schoolhouse is down there in the Matthew area. We have four areas, named for the evangelists. School will be out in half an hour."

"And the very young children? The infants?"

"We have this, what do you call it—"

"We British call it crèche."

"That's a French word, we don't like anything foreign. We call it a kiddy center."

"Is there a hospital?"

That's not a foreign word, right, but it's kind of a dirty word with us. Healing is in the hands of God."

"The deity or er Mr. Mannning?"

"One through the other. This here is the piggery. See that fine Jersey herd. Self-sufficient, like I said." Nowhere could I see little Eve. "With corn we're not self-sufficient. We buy that. Bakery's over there. Own generators. Sewerage system. That was put in for the chemical warfare unit that was here."

"What's that building there without windows?"

"That's the special meditation center. The children are sent there for special meditation on their sins. Thank the Lord that's not too often. The devil bites them when they're not keeping a sharp lookout. The children of the Lord are good children."

"Precisely what my sister's brother-in-law says."

"Well, he's right." A jangle of jubilant bells rang through the camp. I looked for the source. Loudspeaker grilles flush with hut walls just under the eaves. "God's back. We'll meet him at the big house." This young man's background was hard to place, both socially and regionally. The voice should have been southern Baptist but was in fact half-educated, say, Nebraska.

I asked, "How long have you been with ah Mr. Manning?"

"Just call him God, to his face too. No ceremony with us. How long? Seven years, since he came out of the wilderness. I'll give you all the facts you want, we're not ashamed of the facts. Before that I managed a pool hall in Concordia, if you know where that is."

Northern Kansas, not too far from the Nebraska border.

"You'll not believe me, since you're one of the unbelievers, but I heard the voice call one day in the click of the balls. The balls clicked and kept saying Come come come. So I came. God was in Concordia that night, preaching, selling his book. I bought the book, I knew about books, always a big reader of filth and frivolity before that. I was educated at Kansas State in Manhattan, if you know it."

"I know it."

"I fell on evil ways. I was rescued. Praise the Lord."

"Amen."

By this time we had arrived back at the big house, and Godfrey Manning was awaiting us on the verandah, arms outstretched. His voice was of the superfatted melodiousness you find only in America.

He greeted: "Kenneth. Kenneth. Brother. In the name of the Lord many many welcomes."

I did not wish to be embraced. I climbed the steps to the verandah but kept my distance. "It is good to be here," I said hypocritically. He was big and broad, a steak-fed man. The hair was too black to be other than dyed; I thought I detected a toupee. He was dressed in a very good clerical gray woolmixture suit. He wore a cream silk shirt with conservative collarpoints and a plain thin gray tie. No razzamatazz. The eyes were blue and remarkable. I had read of Napoleon's eyes, which were like cannon, cantharides, heaven's deeps or whirlpools. The eyes that had held together an empire. Manning's eyes were less, or more, ambitious. Such eyes were as much a free gift as any other physical beauty, and there was as little necessity for them to be an expression of a great intellectual or spiritual endowment. This man was neither holy nor intelligent, but he was very shrewd. He had not, being given my name by Kilduff in Washington, known who the hell I was, but he had found out. Do a rundown on this Toomey. *Who's Who* would tell him my achievements but not my weaknesses. See what Jack Javers at the *San Francisco Chronicle* can dig up about this guy.

He said, "This is a double honor, Kenneth my brother. You come from the greatest newspaper in the world. You are one of the world's greatest writers."

"That goes a little too far perhaps, Mr. Manning. I'm merely—"

"You must call me God. Away with the constricting clothes of surnames." Where the hell had he got that from? "I'm conscious of the pretentiousness of the nomenclature. But it's merely short for Godfrey. I was named for Godefroy de Bouillon, leader of the First Crusade and first ruler of the Latin kingdom of Jerusalem." He pronounced Bouillon as bullion. "Bouillon," he said, "survives as the name of a soup. Let's go and eat, I'm hungry. I trust Jim here has been looking after you adequately."

"I could not have had," I said, "a more conscientious or amiable guide."

"Take all the compliments you can get, Jim. In we go, Kenneth my brother." We entered the house by way of french windows leading into a chintzy drawing room with well-polished parquet. Then on to a corridor smelling deliciously of lavender and beeswax. Then into a dining room with an oak refectory table and what looked like a genuine Florentine credenza. The pictures on the walls seemed to be family portraits. There was a painting, not badly done, of a blond woman seemingly asking the painter a question. Manning saw me looking at it. "My dear wife," he said. "Passed on. Still my morning and evening star, the light of my inspiration." Another man came into the dining room, big-nosed, bespectacled, hair a mess, in a kind of tracksuit. Also a woman like a wardress. "Tom Bottomley," Manning introduced. "Irma Mesolongion. Kenneth, our brother, great writer from a great paper. Let's say grace." He cried to the ceiling: "Your gifts, Lord, your gifts. May we consume them with gratitude. May they nourish body and soul to your greater glory." We sat. I half expected Eve to come in with the bouillon or whatever it was to be, her to drop the bowl in shock at seeing me, Manning to say *deceit deceit my homosexual enemy and friend of blasphemers drag him to the dark shed of penitence*, but a boy from the Philippines entered with a shrimp salad and Manning said, "What delicious treat has Jessica prepared for us?"

The boy said, "Yes."

Manning said to me, "Toomey is an Irish name. Your father is Irish?"

"My father is dead, of course. Yes, my grandfather came from Ireland. He was what was known as a potato Protestant. My mother, a Frenchwoman, brought back the faith to our family."

"The Romish faith, of course." I had never heard the expression though I had read it in John Milton. "But we are past the days of division and hate. Your Pope has done," he said ungrudgingly, "good work." Water was poured for us all. "You will have expected," Manning said, "some rare vintage wine with your European tastes. But all stimulants are an abomination. Including tea and coffee. Our drink is water bright from the crystal stream." From the mains, chlorinated, tasting a little of my father's surgery.

Unwisely I said, "Prohibition brought much harm to America. It killed—" But soon, under that steady blue luminosity, I would be blurting out the whole joint chronicle of the Toomeys and Campanati. "I mean, Christ turned water into wine and wine into his own blood."

"Pure grape juice," Tom Bottomley said tonelessly. The shrimp salad was removed and a dish of hamburger steaks in deep brown gravy replaced it. Manning served them out, the Filipino helping.

Manning said, "To think of a savior of mankind high-flown with wine is a blasphemy. Irma here knows all about the horrors of the fermented grape."

"I," Irma said, as tonelessly as Bottomley, "was an alcoholic till God rescued me." She was dim, blotchy and shapeless and looked as though a drink might do her good.

"We have all sinned," Manning said cheerfully. "If we do not sin how can we be redeemed? You, my brother Kenneth, have sinned." Ah, he knew. "But the divine mercy is without end."

"Amen," I said. "Here, though," I then said, "is an end of sin. There are, I should imagine, few opportunities for sin in this ah holy community."

"Don't you believe it," Jim Swinney said. "The devil's a real tough customer."

5 6 6

"Sex," I said, "is probably the perennial problem."

"Sex," Manning cried, "abases itself in the presence of the Lord. We make sure it abases itself."

"How?"

"Work, prayer, meditation, medicaments."

"Ah. Something in the water?"

"Something," Tom Bottomley said, "in the body of the Lord." A canned fruit salad was brought in, embedded in a kind of frogspawn. "The devil has to be fought." I wanted to get out of here. I had no further desire to contact Eve and persuade her to go home to her sorrowing father. I could always say I had done my best. While we were finishing off our medicated water that great peal of joyous bells clanged through the house and, I presumed, the camp.

Manning said, "Jim, be sure our brother Kenneth is well seated." And then he cried a grace after meat over the bells. "Your gifts, Lord, your gifts. We have consumed them with gratitude. Nourished, we resume with vigor your holy work."

Outside, I saw platoons being marched to the Place of Prayer. The recorded bells slammed away spilling overtones. The Californian blue swallowed them like a pig swallowing peanuts. We went. We kept our distance from the worshipers filing in. Each one, I noticed, was given by a black or white or brown sexton or servitor or sidesman in a gray gown what looked like a communion host in a square plastic wrapping. "The body of the Lord?" I said.

"Yeah, quicker this way. They take them in, then at the signal they consume. No waiting at altar rails. All in together, one body."

"After the act of consecration, I presume."

"Oh yes, they get consecrated."

I still had not seen Eve. But now I saw her. She was going in with a group of females of all ages. All were clothed in what seemed to be drab floursacks corded at the waist. Eve's hair was lifeless, her face set, like the others, in puddingy holiness or resignation to the hard word of the Lord. She was not the girl I had previously seen, scoffing her Sara Lee, eager for the atomic end of the world at the Symphony Cinema. I doubted if I should be permitted to have a word with her.

I was given a seat right at the back of the Place of Prayer. The light was, as before, dimly religious. The organ, played by a kind of reformed schoolmistress, gave out quiet generic Moody and Sankey. The congregation, fifteen hundred strong, sat quiet. Some faces turned suspiciously or curiously to look at me, the stranger and infidel. One of these faces was Eve's. She recognized me all right. Her eyebrows rose nearly to her hairline. Her mouth became an O. She shook and shook and shook her head. I frowned at her and made a shushing gesture. The organplayer footed the swell, the music rose, the curtain opened, the spots crescendoed from dim rose to the bright rose of revelation. God Manning was on the stage, a doctor's gown about his natty clerical gray. He raised his arms. The music stopped. Without preamble he shouted: "Do this in remembrance of me and my long and bitter suffering. For herein am I present and shall be with you so till the end of the world. Take and eat." The congregation broke open, some with difficulty, the plastic case on the communion wafer. "This is the body and blood of the living Lord." So the Council of Trent operated here: it was a kind of ecumenicalism. The congregation reverently took the body on its collective tongue. "Purge us, bless us, glorify us," Manning cried, taking no wafer himself.

After this act, in the Catholic Church the climax of the sacrificial drama, here a therapeutic preliminary, God Manning relaxed and smiled. "We welcome today to our midst fifteen new brothers and sisters." A side door in the auditorium opened, down near the stage, opposite to the organ, a flood shone, a group of the clearly dispossessed, mostly old black women, shambled in, blinking bewildered in the lime glow that warmed them. "You will learn their names in God's good time," Manning cried. "Now they come to us merely as God's abandoned children in sore need. But one name I utter—Rebecca or Becky Fawldon." An old black woman tried to hide her face in her hands. "Be not afraid, Becky. The Lord will work on you. Sorely diseased of a cancer of the bowel, she comes to us in the direst agony." How she could stand there nursing a cancer of the bowel only God knew. "Take her," Manning said to a couple of youngish women who now got up from the front row, "to the Room of Healing." The women grabbed the poor black sufferer somewhat roughly. They led her sobbing, probably more with embarrassment than pain, up the center aisle. She passed me, her elephant skin wet with sweat and tears, giving off an odor of sickness and poverty. Then a door opened and closed behind me. Manning said, "Stand. Sing to the Lord our God." The organ started up again. They stood. They sang "Let Us Gather at the River." The tempo quickened for each fresh verse. There was concerted handclapping led by Manning. This was the true southern revivalist condiment. The hymn ended. Manning caught his congregation on the cusp of exaltation. He shouted:

"Lord Lord Lord deliver us from iniquity."

"Deliver us O Lord."

"Lord Lord Lord save us from the fiend of hell."

"Save us O Lord."

"Lord Lord Lord cleanse our bodies from disease, cleanse our souls of every abomination, cleanse the filthy world about us that it may be fit to be the golden throne of your coming."

"Cleanse us O Lord."

Much more of this. I longed for a stiff whisky and a cigarette drawn deep. The door at the back of me opened and one of the youngish women began to run down the aisle, clutching something black, dripping, shapeless, nameless in a napkin held high. I caught the smell of profound putrefaction as it flew past me. I wanted to pray, but to no God known here. The youngish woman cried: "Hallelujah, praise the Lord."

"Your servant," countercried Manning, arms held aloft, "is by your grace healed of her affliction. Praise him praise him praise him." The congregation did its own arm-raising and praising. I had had enough. I got up and got out. Nobody hindered my going. Not even Manning, I think, saw. I met the poor old black woman at the back, weeping copiously in what might have been joy, clutched in the arms of the other youngish woman. Outside in the air I committed a foul sin. I lighted a cigarette and drank in its smoke like salvation. A black sexton or servitor came from round the corner of the Place of Prayer and, wordless, gentle, reproachful, took the cigarette from my mouth. He held it as though it were that black dripping horror within. I shrugged and smiled and waited. I was going to get Eve out of here. It was, after all, supposed to be a free country.

Jim Swinney was out first. "You didn't stay till the end," he said. "You missed the healing of the halt and the lame."

"I saw the healing of a cancer. Indeed, I saw the bloody cancer. That's enough for one day. Now I want to see my great-niece."

"Your what?"

"Great-niece or grandniece. I'm never sure of the right term. I saw her in there. A little girl called Eve Breslow. A girl who came here with an illegitimate baby. I have a message for her from her father. I want to see her alone."

"Only God sees people alone." He took up a stance and put on a smirk signifying that he had seen through me. "That's why you came, is it? Not to do an article for this British paper."

"Oh, that as well. But I see nothing wrong with delivering a message. A paternal one. Is there some rule against it?"

"Christ said we must leave our fathers and mothers and follow him. What you're asking is irregular."

The congregation, tranquilized by the Lord's body but elated by the works and words of God, started to come out. "There she is," I said. "Eve," I called. Jim Swinney also called. To him, not me, she came.

She said, "I did nothing wrong, Jim. I swear."

"I know you didn't, Eve. Do you know this gentleman?"

She didn't know whether she ought to say she did or not. She squirmed. She tried to tighten her rope cord. "Yeah," she said at length. "He's my mother's uncle." And then, with a pathetic teenage salute of greeting, hand circling away from right temple, "Hi, Tunc."

"Ah hi, Eve."

"You got anything to say to him, Eve, anything to take back to your father and mother?"

"Yeah, that I'm okay. That I'm happy. That I found salvation. That I love God."

"How's the baby, Eve?" I asked.

"He's okay, I guess."

"That's about it," Jim Swinney said. "You have your message."

"Could I talk to her alone?"

He thought about that, chewing the inside of his lower lip. "It's irregular," he said. "But we might arrange something." He called a black sacristan or beadle. "Dick," he said, "take these two to the interview hut." Then he said something quietly to Eve.

And so it was that we found ourselves, Eve and I, suspiciously alone, in a kind of wooden prison with a made up bed in it and two plain chairs. It had the smell of something long baked in radiant heat. The single high window would not open. "Kind of hot," I said. "Eve, your father wants you back."

"My mother doesn't. Besides, I'm okay here. I found the way and the truth."

"If you wanted the way and the truth your other grand- or great-uncle was better qualified to give it. The Catholic Church is at least civilized. This seems to me to be very suspect. I don't care much for this God Manning of yours."

"He's wonderful. He's the living witness to the truth."

"Love him, do you?" I said brutally.

"With all my soul. He's the living witness. My days and nights are given up to the worship and praise of the Lord. Through him I found the way and the truth."

"You're only a child," I said. "Christ, you've read nothing, learned nothing. You've been taken in by a ah phony."

"Now you're blaspheming. I don't want to hear any more."

"You're coming with me, Eve. I'm taking you back to New York."

"I'm not I'm not." And then she did a thing to me at that moment totally inexplicable. Standing as she was now, and just by the door, she tried to rip her sack garment. It was too tough for her small fingers. She untied the knot of the waistcord and threw the waistcord down. Then she lifted the garment over her head and stood there naked except for a pair of pants, her own I assumed from their flimsiness, not Godgiven. Then she screamed and screamed and banged at the door. I should have known it would be locked. It was very speedily un-locked. God Manning himself was there, along with Jim Swinney and the blotched former alcoholic. They were none of them shocked by the sight of the naked girl. Irma Mesolongion even had a bathrobe ready. Manning himself picked up the discarded sack from the floor. Then he started on me. Eve meanwhile sobbed in the arms of Irma the reformed. Manning told me of my filthy libidousness, my incestuous lust, my disgusting senile pervertedness. Vari-ous Children of God, perhaps kept hanging about for this purpose, closed in the better to hear. Manning made it clear that it was only by the holy strength of his presence that they did not tear me to pieces as dogs tore the defiled flesh of Jael.

"This," I said, "is ridiculous. I have never touched the body of a woman in my life. To suggest that I would do it to a girl, to my own grand- or great-niece. My tastes," I said mildly, good old former comedywriter Toomey, "are quite otherwise."

"Son of Sodom," Manning cried promptly, "spawn of Gomorrah. Out of the abode of the blessed with the curse of the living God upon you. Liar and cheat, without doubt the author of filth, though thank the Lord I have never read you. Out."

It was a fair trudge back toward the gates and the guardroom. I saw, thank the Lord, the hired car waiting outside. Behind me marched the troop of the saved, murmuring, even barking (Filth fornicator dirty sinner perhaps even limey faggot). Manning had gone off somewhere, perhaps to deliver a telephonic commination to *The Times* bureau in Washington. Sobbing Eve and her escort had also disappeared. Jim Swinney was there till the end. The guard had changed. It was still, however, all black. A young man with tortured eyes swung open the gate. He had his automatic pistol at the ready. The driver waited courtly by the open doors of the saloon. He had, he had told me, once been a driver for Government House, South Australia. The young black accompanied me to that door.

He said, "I'm coming with you, man. I'm getting outa here." He pointed his gun back at his former colleagues, who pointed in return. There was no question of anybody firing.

"In quick," I said, pushing him. He dithered and his pants were wet. The driver, glad of excitement after the long dullness of his wait, rushed to his seat and switched on the ignition. We started off on the desolate road to Los Angeles.

"Jesus," the young black said through his terrified sweat, "you don't know what it's like back there, man."

"I have an idea," I said and offered him a cigarette.

seventy-five

"What," I asked Melvin Withers of the *Los Angeles Times*, "did you get out of him?"

"The usual. What you'd expect. Beatings-up called the Lord's punishment. A rotational harem. He says his brother died under queer circumstances, but he can't prove anything. Nobody can. There's no point in him going to the police. Manning is very generous to the Los Angeles police. Your little black friend is in some danger."

I had known Withers for some time, off and on. I had once given him an exclusive story about the impending marriage between the sixty-year-old actor-singer Benny Grimaldi and a sixteen-year-old girl still at Hollywood High. He was a good journalist but he was going to die soon. At fifty he was on a bottle and a half of California brandy a day and four packs of Lucky Strikes. His clothes smelt as though they were steeped in tobacco juice. His white forelock was stained with it. He breathed a heavy reek of what the Irish call blind hash (spuds stewed with onions and a spoonful of Oxo), evidence of a strange metabolism. We sat in a dark bar. "Read this," he said. He meant the file he had put on the table before me. It was too dark to read with ease. "I can't lend it." He drained a neat brandy in one. "I'll be back in about an hour. Some copy to file."

So I squinted at Godfrey Manning's dossier over three more vodkas on the rocks. Soothing music played from the ceiling, a whole spectrum of my time, from "Darktown Strutters" to "I Could Have Danced All Night." A heavy man at the bar counter kept saying, "Yeah I guess so. They could at that, I guess."

Godfrey Manning's career began in the town of Pring, Indiana. His parents had died in a road accident near Decatur, Illinois, and he had gone to live with an uncle and aunt. The town of Pring was a Ku Klux Klan center where custom defied law and said that no nigger had better have the sun setting on his head if he didn't want buckshot in his ass. The uncle belonged to this organization and only went out of doors when it was time for putting a white sheet on and brandishing a fiery cross. He was not well enough to work. He received a monthly disability check from the government, something to do with his lungs and something that had gotten into them in the First World War. The aunt was reputed to have Cherokee blood. She worked in a tomato ketchup factory. Pring had seven churches, and young Godfrey, who was given to religion, attended them all. He liked to play at being a preacher and would make boys lie on top of girls so that he could accuse them of sin. He won every biblical quiz that was going at all seven Sunday schools. He was dogmatic and fierce-tempered, but only about religion. His preferred church, after a long time of sampling, was the Pentecostal Church run by the Holy Rollers. Sick of the racism of Pring, he dropped out of its high school whose principal was a loud voice of intolerance and enrolled in a school in the bigger town of Richmond. He talked of becoming a minister of religion. He left with average grades but several Bible prizes and entered Indiana University in Bloomington. There he did badly in subjects with an exact discipline but grew famous for his gabgift. He ran a Bible study group with a hot enthusiasm that sometimes appalled, always fascinated. He married a Bloomington girl, daughter of the keeper of a cigar store, who was five years his senior, Claudine Rogers, given to religion like himself but reputedly passionate in bed. He took her to Indianapolis where, though unordained, he became a pastor at the Eastbank Church. This city, home of the national office of the Ku Klux Klan, was even less tolerant of the doctrine of racial equality than Pring, and Manning was courageously preaching this doctrine. He was jeered at during church services; dead cats were stuffed into the church toilets; NIGGERLOVER was chalked on the church wall. He became a part-time student at Butler University, took ten years to get a bachelor's degree and was finally ordained as a minister of the Disciples of the Lord Jesus. During those ten years he spent some time in the wilds, preaching to village layabouts bored with pool halls, also to college students in bars and under campus oaks, and he wrote and published at his own expense a book which I had heard of, God knew, but not seen. I could imagine its content and style.

Sick of the dead cats on his returns to Eastbank Church, he decided to start his own sect, the Children of God, in a district of Indianapolis which was changing from poor white to poorer black. On a trip to Philadelphia, he went to listen to Father Divine, dispenser of love and chicken dinners. He admired his style. He admired his total control over his flock. He admired most of all that clue to Father Divine's success—faith healing.

He continued to suffer the enmity of racists. Talking to a black brother at a bus stop he was hit by a hurled beer bottle. His wife was spat upon in a supermarket. He saw his church as a garrison besieged by a mad and dangerous world. Like all garrisons, it had to be disciplined. He achieved loyalty not through eloquence and love alone but through punishments, some of them crassly physical. He formed a kind of ecclesiastic police force. None of his congregation loved him the less for his occasional, and unpredictable, shows of violence. The Mayor of Indianapolis gave him a seven-thousand-dollar-a-year job as director of a human rights commission. He spoke eloquently on behalf of love and tolerance but had rocks thrown at him. He received telephone calls which told him to get out of town. He stuck to his convictions. His congregation grew. Money began to come in. He served one thousand free meals a week to the destitute. He bought two old buses to carry singers, auxiliary preachers or warmers-up, and cheerleaders to spread the word in the Midwest on revival tent campaigns. He began to heal the sick, or those who thought they were sick. At his temple in Indianapolis hundreds crammed in to watch him cure arthritis, toothache, dyspepsia, calcified joints, cardiac disease, epilepsy, thrombosis. A cataleptic girl was brought in and he restored her to animation, crying, like his master, *Talitha cumi*. One evening he called out a name and a woman stood up to say she was suffering from cancer. Manning ordered her to go to the church toilet and pass the growth from her bowels. A cloth was brought in with a black odoriferous horror wobbling on it. Cries of hallelujah and praise the Lord. Manning's enemies alleged that this was a decayed chicken liver.

Manning preached a fiery sermon in the course of which he stated that he had received an angelic visitation in sleep. The angel had prophesied the destruction of the world by a nuclear holocaust. Fire and fallout. The seven places on the earth's surface which the disaster would not touch included the fringe of the Mojave Desert in California. There the Children of God might find their ultimate haven. And so it was to be. On May 17, 1956, Manning signed state papers making the Children of God a nonprofit California corporation. He kept in with the Californians. He founded an orphanage. He served on charitable committees. He started a fund for the families of cops slain in the line of duty. God, in both interpretations of the name, knew where the money came from, but the money was there. Manning, preaching at the Temple of the Children on Sunset Boulevard, brought local politics into his harangues as an aspect of the amelioration of a Christian society; he could sway, he could command votes. He was an admirable television performer. Bank managers and businessmen, disc jockeys and sheriffs believed in him. His choir sang and later gained a reputation nearly as great as that of the Mormon one in Salt Lake City. The coastal newspapers publicized his work. Manning went on the road with selected members of his congregation. They drove in their buses labeled GOD IS EVERYWHERE, EVEN HERE to the Fillmore and Bayview districts of San Francisco. Leaflets were like an autumn in the streets:

GOD MANNING . . . the Wonderful . . . the Incredible . . . the Beloved Disciple . . . See the work of God in miraculous cures which in no way contradict the teachings of modern medical science. The power of the healing hand is the rarest power in the world but it is acknowledged by medical practitioners everywhere. No man's healing hand is like unto God Manning's . . .

God Manning brings you not only Christ's message . . . he brings you Christ's own miraculous presence. Come and see. Come and believe. Come and join, all ye that are weary and heavily laden and he will give you rest. He will give you peace, love, assurance, satisfaction . . .

Bands, dancing, gospel singing, the Heavenly Choir, sermons of divine inspiration!

And, of course, donations.

Stories leaked out not altogether to Mannning's credit. He alone was permitted to eat meat. Liquor was banned but Manning had a well-stocked liquor cabinet. He was on pills of various kinds. Like the prophet Abraham he took unto himself handmaidens. Some of the disciples ran away, and some were brought back. Those who were not brought back got away from Redfern Valley as far as they could, but still feared the knock at the door in the night. The perimeter of the Home of the Children of God was guarded by armed men and fierce dogs. Manning had an escort of knuckledustered bullyboys. But those who heard him preach in public, or talk reasonably but eloquently on radio and television, were mostly convinced that here was a Savior Rarer than Radium. Some, listening to his repeated warnings of the imminence of the End of the World, said he was a nut, like folks that lunched off yoghurt, but none could deny that Christ too had warned of the impending consummation of all things. Okay, that had been two thousand years ago, right?, and it hadn't happened yet. Right, all the more reason why it might happen now. They had no nuclear fallout in those days, right? To tell people to be pure and honest and diligent and love the Lord was hardly to be construed as fanaticism. Jesus, the Pope of Rome was saying the same thing and he was real hardheaded.

I was not happy about the gist of a sermon that was reproduced among all these clippings and handouts. Manning's text was "Fear not them that kill the body." It was man's duty to live as long in the flesh as he could, since the Divine Being had constructed that flesh and the instincts and appetites that went with it, but the true life, as the Son of the Divine Being taught, was the life of the spirit, and the spirit was what was left when the body was taken away. When it came to the crunch, like with persecution and Armageddon, the true Christian martyr rejoiced in the coming loss of the body, since now the life of the spirit could truly begin. So all Children of God must be ready any time to put off this corruptible body and endue an immortal body which was made of the stuff of the spirit.

There was a lot of stuff in the thick folder, but my eyes hurt with the attempt at reading it in the dark. When Melvin Withers, preceded by his metabolism, came back in again and signaled for brandy at one of the cat-eyed waitresses, I said, "It's pretty well what I expected. A very American phenomenon. And I don't like it, Melv."

"Your little black friend stripped off his shirt and showed marks which looked like they might have come from a whip. He goes on swearing that his brother disappeared one night, just like that. But he can't get any place."

"Can't anybody investigate? A state governor's commission? The appropriate state senator or congressman?"

"You need real proof of irregularity or crime. With witnesses all lined up. Look, Ken, this is a religious organization and it's very very privileged. There's plenty of crime in the streets before the very eyes of the cops without them going to look for what might not be there. Leave God Manning alone and he shows his gratitude in a very tangible way. He causes no trouble to the community at large."

"I told you what he did to me. My great- or grandniece was evidently scared out of her pants—well, no, those are the only things she wasn't scared out of. Look at it from my angle—elderly author of international reputation lashed out of there with very opprobrious language. I don't like it especially when I was only doing my duty. That man is *bad*. I fear for my grand- or great-niece."

"She asked for it. Nobody asked her to join."

"She's just a kid. She knows no better. I saw a lot like her. Is there nothing that can be done?"

"I've done pieces before. I don't like the bastard and never did and I'm always glad to stick the rapier in. Only one of those pieces ever saw print, and then Manning fires broadside on with a libel suit. Settled out of court. What they call substantial damages. The big nicotine-stained finger was wagged at me." Strangely, Melvin's fingers were not nicotine-stained. Something to do with the way he held the weed. "You have to let it go, Ken."

"I used to know your state governor pretty well in the old days. That's when he was in Hollywood and I with him. He should have been in one of my things but wasn't. If I saw him?"

"He wouldn't do a damned thing. The cousin of his wife's sister is in there, praising the Lord. And there are certain times in our governor's life when Mr. Manning comes in very very useful. Election time, for instance. And if our governor, which he's always threatening to do, decides to aspire to the office of president—no, it won't do."

"Where the hell does all that money come from?"

"Astonishing how little bits mount up. Especially when there are no taxes to be paid. As they say, the Lord looks after his own. Ken, I've no spare cash. Your little black friend is literally and I mean literally spraying his pants. He has what he calls a uncle and a aunt in Arkansas. I think we ought to get him on a bus pretty soon. Can you help?"

I stayed the night at the Beverly Wilshire. It brought Ralph back to me and reminded me of my present loneliness. I telephoned Geoffrey Enright in San Jaime. Could he meet me in the Algonquin tomorrow, ready to accompany me back to Tangier?

"My dear, you'll never regret it. My only immediate problem is finding the money for an air ticket. No, wait. No sweat, no problem. Lubricious Labrick drew five hundred dollars from the bank this morning. I'll just take enough from his roll to get palpitant me to Fun City or the Big Apple or whatever they call it. No hurry to get to Tangier, is there? There are all sorts of things I can show you in the *dirtier* portions of Manhattan. My dear, we shall have a riotous time. *Tutti-frutti*."

It was, after the Children of God, a breath of moral sanity.

seventy-six

"Your old pal Pope Buggery," Geoffrey said, "looks to me to be getting premonitions of his Latter End."

We were at breakfast under the oleanders in the garden. Geoffrey, who regarded himself as a growing boy, insisted daily on eggs and rashers. I watched him indulgently *tuck in*, as I toyed with toast and Cooper's marmalade. He had yesterday's *Daily Telegraph* propped against the outsize coffeepot. Ali was no longer cooking for us. He had never much cared for cooking, and his repertoire had always been small. Now we had Hamid, who had been kicked out of the kitchens of the Miramar, while Ali had been promoted to majordomo.

"In Moscow?" I asked.

"In bloody Moscow. Poisoning his *borshch*, I shouldn't wonder. Insinuating rare Siberian toxics into his red caviar. Addressing the Presidium in immaculate Russian," Geoffrey improvised from the paper, "His Ballsiness was overtaken by a series of sharp stabs in the *kishkas*. He begged to be excused and everybody said *Da da da ochin khorosho*. Kremlin medicos were summoned and begged him to go easy on the brotherhood of man stuff for a bit. Taking too much out of the old bastard. Very hard work, the brotherhood of man. Heart, my dear," he said, looking up. "He has nobody to watch his heart, as I am so assiduous or is it insidious in watching yours."

"He has Dr. Leopardi. He had Leopardi back in Moneta. He's always sworn by the skills of Leopardi."

"Ah, but skills are not the same as love. He has nobody, poor old bar steward, to lerve him."

"If by watching my heart you mean the kind of excursion you took me on into the ah heart of the Casbah last night—"

"But, angelic Kenneth, you are fitter than you have ever been. You have been reawakened. You are engaging *life*."

That was true. Little brown boys, kif, cantharides. A good day's work at the long novel I swore I would be my last, a stiff gin and tonic before dinner, after dinner some little sexual adventure not untinged with danger. In bed the company of Geoffrey, who had taught my aging body new paths of rejuvenation.

"And now," Geoffrey said, having drained the coffeepot, "let us lash ourselves to labor."

We went in together. Ali was wailing some lovesong of the Atlas slopes as he polished the furniture. Geoffrey's workroom was neat and the sunlight was allayed by nylon curtains newly washed. His electric typewriter squatted ready, a pack of Effacil erasers stuck to its side. "This," Geoffrey said, "is what I wrote to that tiresome woman. Listen. 'Madam, I note your somewhat fanciful allegation that in my novel *The Affairs of Men* I have based a minor female character on your defunct sister. I never knew your sister, living, moribund, or defunct. Are you quite sure your defunct sister did not base her personality on that of my character? I have far too much serious work to do to engage myself in frivolities of the kind that seem to beguile what appears to me to be an excessive leisure. Get stuffed. Yours et cetera.' "

"I should cut out the *Get stuffed*."

"I didn't put it in, my dear."

"Fine then, fine."

We were really doing very well together. Too well, caution and a life of betrayals should have taught me. I was right to be scared of overmuch felicity. Still, my raddled old muse forbade complacency. She threw the most worn tropes and situations at me. The reviewers would say: "Toomey offers this bulky but overpriced novel as an elected swan song. One hears the cackling of the goose more often than the unlocking of the cygnic throat." To hell with them, as always. I worked. He worked. We worked. We lunched lightly off a herb omelette and a bottle of Vichy and a couple of peaches. We took the siesta together, and then tea, and worked until sunset. At sunset we walked the esplanade. Juanito, a boy who sold foreign newspapers, offered *Times, Mail, Express, Mirror*. Geoffrey, as he always did, said, *"No gracias. No se leer."*

"Wait," I said. "You seem to be right about the Latter End." I handed dirhams over and read the front page of *The Times*. The Pope had been rushed back to Rome by Aeroflot. He was far from well. Prayers prayers and prayers. Massive heart attack. "For God's sake, look at this." We sat at an outdoor table of the Papagayo and read that His Holiness, who was well known as an orphan of unknown parentage adopted by the Campanati family of Milan (to be more specific and say Gorgonzola might have seemed irreverent), had no adoptive relatives living. Domenico Campanati, the noted light composer, had died earlier this year of thrombosis. Campanati's widow, sister of the noted British author Kenneth M. Toomey, had been summoned from her home in Bronxville, New York, to attend the papal bedside.

"Why?" I asked, and Geoffrey: "Will she go? You always told me she hated the old bastard."

"But why? Why Hortense? What can they possibly have to say to each other?"

William Sawyer Abernethy, who idolized Father Rolfe and had written a book on him, shuffled toward us in his whites and panama, sat down uninvited, made a two-finger gesture to the waiter which meant raw Ricard with ice, and said, "It looks as if he's on his way. He was a great Pope." Abernethy had no religion. "He's done more than anyone to restore universal confidence in the Catholic Church. His *Ignis Cibi Inopiae* is a great humanitarian document. He has given back to humanity a long lost confidence in itself. The Kampala innovation was a stroke of genius. What's all this about your sister going to see him?"

"She may not."

"On the radio it said she would. Reporters on to her. She's taking a plane at Vatican expense. Traveling with the Archbishop of New York."

"That," Geoffrey said prissily, "is surely jumping the gun. The old bastard isn't dead yet."

"He's sinking fast," Abernethy said, and sank fast his Ricard. "Nice to see you chaps again. He was a great Pope."

Hortense, called mystery woman from New York by the *Daily Mirror* and, less gallantly, the piratical enigma by the commentator at the end of the BBC's European News Service the morning after her arrival at Fiumicino, was with Carlo from the moment of her admission to his bedchamber until his death less than two hours later. For over an hour of that time she was alone with him. Then the Cardinal Dean, the Cardinal Vicar of Rome and the *sostituto* came in. Hortense tried to withdraw, but the dying man frantically waved that she stay. The Cardinal Secretary of State anointed him. Carlo clutched that prelate's hand all through the oiling and prayed, to the slight disgust of the surrounding dignitaries, in the tongue of his adoptive mother. His last words were "Lord hear my prayer and let thy cry come unto me"—a transposition of pronouns that made sense. Hortense, leaving the chamber after his death, would tell no reporter what they had talked about.

He had insisted, on his return from Soviet Russia, on being helicoptered to Castel Gandolfo. It was summer, June 3, and it was right for the Pope to be there. For two days his corpse lay in state at this country palace, watched over by two Swiss Guards and lighted by a solitary candle. The faithful pushed and shoved each other on the staircases to get a good look at a corpse which began to decompose very early. Women wept and fainted. He had given instructions that no one should photograph him either dying or dead, having in mind what Galeazzi Lisi, the private doctor of his predecessor, had done—sold pictures of Pius in extremis and given a gruesome press conference on the causes of his death. Despite the veto, flashlights popped and thousand-lira notes changed hands.

The decaying body was then transported to St. Peter's in Rome in a motor hearse that kept a steady pace, slow driving being impossible to Italians, and outriders on motorcycles buzzed and rasped before, behind, to left, to right. Helicopters whirred above. The procession stopped briefly at St. John Lateran, the cathedral church of the Roman diocese, so that Cardinal Paolo Menotti, who tended it on behalf of its official bishop, could recite a psalm. Then the Mayor of Rome, a Communist, became responsible for the safe passage of the papal body to St. Peter's. Messages had come through from political terrorists to the effect that it would be immune from kidnapping and there was no need to guard it with tanks and machine guns. This was to some extent accepted as a sincere declaration of truce, but security was as vigilant as it can ever be in Italy, and there was a vaguely Chicago look about Carlo's cortège. In the Piazza di San Pietro, where Vatican territory begins, the Mayor was seen to wipe off the sweat of relief as he handed his burden over. The body was laid in the great basilica and the crowds came to wail over it. The click of rosary beads was answered by the snap of Odorokos, Oyayubis and Kugwatsus. The Vatican gendarmes brutally hustled the crowds forward, right turn, out. *Avanti avanti.*

Despite hidden electric fans, the air was foul about Carlo's body. He had left instructions not to embalm. Here was the corruptible that had to be put off. The face had turned the color of strong tea, the ears were black, the mouth gaped idiotically showing teeth still strong. My father, long corrupted in a Toronto graveyard, would have admired them and talked about waste.

Carlo had requested a funeral pious and simple, no catafalque, no monument. His monument was all about him, a world restored to a view of its own worth, dignity and essential goodness. His plain coffin lay on the ground in front of the altar, an open copy of the Rituale Romanum on it. The cardinals were in red, not black, and they wore miters to stress their episcopal functions. Bishops, like Saint Ambrose, were burly fighters with balls. The sculptress of the basso-relievo of the Ambrosian struggle and triumph was present, much noticed in her smart mourning from a Roman couturier with truly piratical eye-shade. The paschal Alleluia was sung: *Vita mutatur non tollitur.* The remains of Gregory XVII were laid to rest in the crypt of St. Peter's, not far from the bones of the bewildered fisherman who had seen the light of the world go out upside down. Carlo's will was published a few days after his obsequies. He had nothing material to leave. The wealth of the Campanati family had already been bequeathed to the children of Israel. He left to his brothers and sisters, growing in number at an annual rate of about fifty million souls, the beauty of the earth and the fruitfulness thereof, an assurance of God's benevolence, a sure hope of heaven.

seventy-seven

The death and burial of a beloved pontiff drove out from the front pages of the newspapers of the world, even in the countries of the Soviet bloc, such trivialities as riot, murder, and earthquake. But the nearer the newspapers were to the

Mojave Desert of California the less space they expended on the mourning and rejoicing going on in distant Rome, a city a hell of a way west of Tokyo. The ghastly dissolution of the Children of God shocked editors into the expenditure of their grossest headline type and made their staffs drain their Rogets.

Godfrey Manning was picked up by the police with little difficulty at Los Angeles Airport. He could disguise his head by removing his toupee and his upper lip with a false mustache, but he could not disguise his eyes. Passengers on international flights provoked suspicion by wearing dark glasses under the soft nighttime lights of the departure lounge, and dark glasses were swiftly whipped off by police at the boarding gates. Manning was attempting to travel on a genuine United States passport in the name of Carlton Goodlett: a bald mustached photograph looked out at the dirty world with eyes which, unsuccessfully, tried to dissimulate their prophetic fervor. He had booked a first-class ticket, one way, to Valparaiso. The case he carried contained one million dollars in notes of a hundred. The baggage already checked in was crammed with another million, as well as jewels donated by rich women who wished to go to heaven without too much altering their ways of life. Manning seemed somewhat relieved to be arrested. He had not been in the habit of running away from things, except the threat of nuclear holocaust.

His story is well known. It has even gone into books. In downtown Los Angeles he told it, in distress, ramblingly, repetitiously, over cardboard beakers of the coffee which had been an abomination before the Lord. He even smoked cigarettes, unhandily, like a girl smoking her first. Sometimes he wept. In his eyes everyone could see a strange mixture of horror and self-righteousness.

The daughter of U.S. Congressman Robert Lithgow, a girl of fifteen named Lydia, had attended a revivalist meeting run by Manning in Eugene, Oregon, in the company of a girl friend, and had been overwhelmed with the power and goodness that flowed from the man. She had announced herself a convert to the sect and had been driven back in Manning's own limousine to the Home of the Children in Redfern Valley. The girl friend, harder to seduce, had reported back to the Lithgow family, and Lithgow, then in Washington on his legislative duties, had invoked the Mann Act. On the allegation that his daughter had been transported over the state line for an immoral purpose, he had been able to secure the services of the Federal Bureau of Investigation in demanding entrance to the Home and the restitution of the person of his daughter, her soul being another matter. Lithgow and his wife had driven up to the gates of the camp at sunset on the very day that Carlo died. Behind them, in an official car, were four armed officers of the Bureau. Lithgow had demanded entrance and been refused it by the guards. The senior FBI officer had then demanded entrance in the name of the United States Government. This also had been refused. The officer drew his gun as an earnest of his intention to enter. A guard fired out of nerves, wounding him in the right arm. Another officer fired at the guard and killed him. The remaining guards retreated to the guardroom and used it as a blockhouse. Firing, once started, continued and intensified. Lithgow and his wife lay dead. Two junior officers of the Bureau lay dying. The senior officer fired at the window of the guardroom and was himself shot through the heart. The remaining officer, who was losing blood fast, got back into the official car and tried to speed off for reinforcements. One of the tires had been struck by shot and was flat. He got out to commandeer the Lithgows' car. On the way to it he joined the dying.

On hearing the news by telephone from the guardroom, Manning ordered that the jubilant bells be rung all over the camp, signifying immediate assembly in the great hangarlike Place of Prayer. All had to be there, children, sick, henchmen, secretaries, deputy ministers. This was an urgent matter: no time for devout shambling; running, running, under the whip if need be. It was, as always, a slow business getting the Children into the hall, all seventeen hundred of them. As the faithful entered, each was given the Body of the Lord wrapped in plastic, but this time a somewhat reduced Body, more like a pill. All, even Manning's aides, were instructed to hold in the palms of their hand the tiny seed of eternal life. At length they were all in. No organ played this time, no artful spots and floods conduced to a mood of devotion. Bare raw light from the roof emphasized that there was serious work at hand, not the fripperies of healing and prayer.

His homily was brief. He had always warned his Children that the time would come when the enemy closed in. The advance guard of the enemy had been foiled, but the destroyers would soon be approaching in mass, the forces of evil, the mechanists of destruction.

"Be not afraid of them that kill the body," he cried from the rostrum. "The hour has come for the putting off of this corruptible. We shall all meet again in a split second in heaven. Take ye and eat. This is my body." The guards at the gate had to find a less expeditious way to the next world.

Manning presided over the almost instantaneous deaths of seventeen hundred adults. The children did not die: they spat out the bitter host. He saw from his podium what he had often tried to imagine, his imagination being much assisted by pictorial evidence of Nazi camp slaughter: uncountable slumping bodies, as though awkwardly trying to get down to pray in the imposssible space between rows of bucket seats, eyes shut or glassy, the rictus after the bitter desiccation of the mouth, arms in automatic supplication heavily or gently dropping, and all this on a scale inacceptable to the horrified eye. There were noises, too—the rattle in the throat, the loosening of bowels and fecal odors threaded the air. He panicked about the wailing children and, worse, those children who did not wail but fixed him with the hard eyes of wonder. In this single huge family there was no nuclear family feeling. No couples lay dead embraced. No children tugged at dead parents to bring them back to life again. There was no mother, only a father. This father got down from the podium and approached a girl of thirteen who had refused her host, medicine, quietus. "See, my dear," he said, "we must all go together. I go last, because I have to tuck you all in for the night, for the day rather, the day that is already dawning for all these now free of the horrible world. Take the Body of the Lord, there's a good girl. Take the Body of the Lord, damn you." She shook her head and wailed and he wondered how best to kill her. Though to stun would be enough. He tried strangulation but she got free and ran up the central aisle between the rows and files of lolling dead. She ran knockkneed screaming out, the one living witness.

Desperate, and with little strength and much sweat, he tried to kill the smaller ones by smothering with his coat, then by strangulation or, in four instances, by picking them up by the feet and dashing their heads against the tops of the bucket seats. He was astonished at how long it took to smash an infant skull. Some he left to wail. He had to get out now. No, he was supposed to die with his flock. No, suicide was a deadly sin. And yet his absence must not be noticed from among the grotesque assembly of the faithful unto death. It must appear that he had gone to heaven with them, perhaps arriving and smiling ready to greet an instant before. He went backstage where cans of gasoline had long been kept for such an emergency as this. He had faced the prospect of death, though vicariously, nearly every day. He, though no smoker, had even kept the means of ignition in his pocket—a jeweled lighter from Tiffany's donated by a Mrs. Henderson, not of the flock but a believer in his work who kept her distance, whose vow to abstain from the foul weed and other Godless stimulants had been signaled in this gift. There had been times, trying to raise money from the corrupt and important, when he had offered lights as he had smiled indulgently at others' bottles. Make unto yourselves friends of the Mammon of Righteousness. Manning poured a whole canful of the eager combustible into the central aisle of the Place of Prayer. He remembered his aunt once saying of an Abbott and Costello film that the audience had died laughing. This guy kills me. He thought he heard gunfire at the front. He took out the lighter from Tiffany's and wondered whether to throw it ignited into the rich reeking fluid. No, it was a gift. He flicked on the spark, let it lick the outer edge of the gasoline, then saw fire whoosh. Flame leapt quickly into the dry air.

The locked trunk of his Plymouth, always parked at the back of the Place of Prayer, had always contained the rich luggage of possible exile: it was as safe a place as any to store loot. He got into it and effected a more benign ignition. The flames in the Place of Prayer had already reached the roof. There was a metal gate, flush with the metal fence, diametrically opposed to the main entrance of the compound and about a mile and a half distant from it. He drove toward this steadily along a sandy track. He wept on reaching the gate: he could not find the key to it. At length he did and unlocked, swinging it open wide. He saw again to his left garnet and amber flames rejoicing, crowned with an unworthy pall of rising black pollution. God's air should be kept clean. He left the Home of the Children of God and proceeded along a dirt track toward a secondary road. He would reach the airport without touching the city. Before arriving at that secondary road he knew he had better stop. He thought he would have to spend long minutes on the syndrome of horrorstricken grief. He found himself remarkably calm, as it were fulfilled. In the glove compartment he had some of the machinery of disguise. He turned himself into Carlton Goodlett, checking with the passport photograph. That passport had cost a lot of money.

"They were all better out of it," he told the police. "A vile and filthy world, and its vileness and filth could not be kept out of the abode of grace. I do not regret what I have done. I have sent them to a safe haven. Only fear of the Lord's punishment prevented me from dispatching myself in the same manner. Suicide is a terrible sin." And then he said, over and over again, and this confirmed the police suspicion that he was a nut: "Any salt of hydrocyanic acid. The cyanides contain the ion CN. They had been a long time waiting. I wondered if they would still work. Two thousand rats, they said, that's impossible. All too possible, I told them. You must use men's weaknesses to the glory of the Lord. Some would call it blackmail, a very dirty word. I got what we needed from him, a young man in the pharmaceutical industry who had sinned terribly. God will decide whether or not to punish, I told him, the punishment of men is nothing and may justly be evaded. But some sins merit punishment from the Lord's human ministers if they are committed within the Lord's precincts. They merit terrible punishment, even unto death. The Lord's ministers know themselves to be so through the favors of the Lord. In them the flesh is transfigured, and all the joys of the flesh. My name is God Manning. In me the human and divine conjoin. But it is not for me to judge the entire world, only those who are committed in the Lord's name to my care. I have always done my duty. I have always been faithful to the divine ideal. I wish to go home to my long deserved rest."

A psychiatric examination would decide whether Manning was fit to stand trial. At his first psychiatric session he seemed to will himself into a deep sleep. Voices spoke as it were from several layers of the psyche, all contending. Some howled or wailed in languages the waking Manning did not know. There was perhaps only one man qualified to deal with him, and he lay dead in Rome.

seventy-eight

And so, as I said many chapters back, my eighty-second year lay all before me. Ali drove from Luqa to Lija and parked the car by Percius's Garage. I got out and found the Poet Laureate, Dawson Wignall, chatting amiably to the two youngest children of Cicco Grima. They knew no English, he no Maltese. They compromised on Italian. They knew what a *gelato* was: they called it a *gelat*. Wignall gave them small Maltese coins and they ran to the little shop on the corner. Wignall came toward me smiling. He was in a cream tropical suit and carried a cane. "All right then?" he said. "They told me here what was going on. Jolly good. Got rid of him, eh? Better off without him. Too stimulating, I'd say. Come home to jolly sedative England."

I let us both in and took him into the bar. He liked it. "Very elegant," he said. "Very nice for a game of bridge. Very nice piece of wood, that bar counter. Gin and tonic, yes. Thank you. Jolly good."

We sat at a table. I said, "Yes, he's gone for the last time. During the near decade he was with me, off and on, he would run away and come back again, not too repentant. In my weakness I always took him back. He had some amiable qualities. These, in the last few years, have steadily decreased."

"And who'll look after you now?"

"Oh, I can manage. With Ali. Whether I stay here is another matter."

"Oh, come home. And bring dear Hortense home too. A very estimable woman. She's out of her element out there. There was an exhibition of her work, you know, at the Southall Gallery. Including that admirable bas-relief she did for Milan and which Milan stupidly rejected. She's being regarded now as one of the genuine twentieth-century British sculptors. I saw the strength of her work when I first met her in New York. I saw the strength of the woman herself. And the charm. And the elegance."

"Well," I said, "I came here because of Geoffrey. He didn't like Gibraltar when we holed up there for a fortnight, arranging transportation of furniture. He wouldn't go back to the States. In his innocence he thought that England might welcome him. He always had a remarkable innocence when it came to acts of transgression against morality, against the law. He just didn't somehow *get* the law. That was the Welsh blood in him perhaps. He honestly thought we could go on living in Tangier after what he'd done. Get the better of the bastards, he'd say."

"What had he done?"

"Incredible. There was a royal garden party in Rabat, to which we'd been invited. He publicly insulted His Majesty. Called him a wog and offered to fight him. Drunk, of course. The King was prepared to laugh it off, not knowing the term *wog* and thinking the aggression a kind of affection. But there were officials there who knew what was going on all right. The police in Tangier would be ordered to pick him up for something. Some of his sexual habits became, you know, aggressive. He'd been reading Sade and thought it would be a jolly good idea to try out some of the simpler adjuncts to perverted pleasure. He went too far, but the police hadn't found out yet. I got him on a flight to Gibraltar, told him to wait for me at the Rock Hotel while I sorted things out. They threw him out of the Rock Hotel, of course. They threw him out of several hotels. He could be very trying."

"Oh, it's not easy," Wignall said. "Oh, it's not at all easy. We can all be bloody fools, you know. When I woke this morning I felt very unhappy about last night. I didn't come too well out of it, did I? Of course, there was a general irritability around. That little Maltese poetaster was absurd. And those two children with their sex and Coca-Cola. I'm sorry I said what I said."

"That's all right. I mean, a poem is a thing of great specific gravity. To throw at you like that, I mean, casually, you know, something that obviously had bitter tears behind it."

He did not seem to know what I was talking about. "I don't remember. It was the other thing that worried me. It was in very bad taste, but of course I'd forgotten, you know, personal applications and so on."

I did not know what he was talking about. "I don't remember," I said. He should have let whatever it was drop. Instead, he uttered a word I remember seeming to have uttered, though in what context was at that moment not clear.

He said, "That nonsense about anthropophagy. It was very tasteless of me."

"Oh, yes. Very amusing, I thought. Tins of Munch or something."

"For my part, I don't believe there's ever been much of it in the world, you know. Cannibal—a word you throw at an enemy, like Zola, you know. I mean Zola threw it at the Paris mob. Quite figurative. It always is. Nearly always."

"Yes, I suppose so."

"So that's how it is," he said. He had drained his gin and tonic with hale thirst. Ali was now at the bar to serve him another. "Thanks awfully. Jolly good boy you have there, I can see that. Big bowl full of ice already set out and so forth. No," he said in the English manner, contradicting nothing, "I met this fellow at Columbia, said he knew you, spoke very warmly about you. Black chap called, as I remember, Ralph something, Welsh, that's right, Pembroke, straight out of *Pudd'nhead Wilson*. Fine book that."

"Good God." And again "Good God. He ought to be running an African dictatorship by now. In Columbia? Good God. Back home. No nonsense about that damned African name he took on. A very mature student, exceptionally mature. He got that from his poor sister, she was a mature student too."

"Oh no, not a student, Toomey. Member of the faculty. All these American universities have departments of what they call Black Studies now, you know. Ralph what yes Pembroke is very prized in that sort of thing. Actually been in Africa, worked there, speaks Swahili and the rest of the nonsense. He showed me the African mass."

"I beg your pardon?"

"Oh come come, Toomey, the African mass. He showed us a film of it. Very professionally made film, sound and everything, full color, but all done from a hide, you know, like wild animal life, this particular tribal group not greatly relishing being photographed at what I suppose they regarded as their devotions. You've seen it on your travels?"

"No. Only heard of it. The Kampala innovation and so on. What was it like?"

"Well now," shifting his limbs as though with anal irritation, "you can't translate some of these things, you know. Pembroke himself made that very clear afterwards. Not during the damned thing because we had these Columbia fuzziwuzzies shouting right on and get in there man and so on. Afterwards. Some of the local languages can't carry the weight of Western theology."

"You mean like not being able to count beyond two? Very awkward, I always thought, for the Holy Trinity and so on. Continue, this is very interesting."

"Interesting. I see. You obviously know nothing. Shouldn't perhaps have broached the business. The African mass, you see, is performed in full regalia of lionskins and cock's feathers and drums and stamping and shouting. The consecration is to the Western eye very barbarous. This is my body, this is my blood, they see that all right, but they don't see about changing it to bread and wine. In this film we saw the priest—a real ordained priest, mind you, despite the rippling black muscles and the ornate headdress—what he did was to consecrate real flesh and real blood."

"Oh Christ."

"Precisely. The body and the blood of the Savior, the real thing. Bits of cooked meat, jungle pig probably, and a calabash of warm pig's blood. They saw that all right, no communion under one kind chicanery. And highly rhythmical language. A cross up there with a painted Savior on it and the pigmeat attached in little strips with pins or something and the calabash underneath as though his blood were draining into it. Very successful, genuine religious fervor, like the American South, you know. Blessed by the Vatican, the fine flower of the Kampala innovation. Do you see what I'm getting at, Toomey? Pembroke said something about difficulties with the liturgy, problem of getting the Holy Ghost across. He said this too often worked out as an unclean spirit or taboo spirit or something."

"Look," I said, "where was this?"

"A little enclave in Rukwa where Pembroke worked. The Omo or Oma people or something. Some of them took this flesh and blood business a bit too literally. I don't think I have to say any more. You can understand perhaps now why I think you ought to get your delightful and talented sister out of an America full of very aggressive blacks. Right on, man, slay the white bastard. She's saying too many of the wrong things. Ralph Pembroke should have shut up. He should have known. There are things you don't say to certain people."

"Are you," I said, "in effect telling me something about my poor dead nephew? And his wife?"

"I'm not in effect telling you anything except that your sweet sister has got something very firmly into her head. I heard about the archiepiscopal visit you had yesterday—many belated happy returns, by the way—what you've been requested to do. There was a little item in the *Times of Malta*. Our American pals call that jumping the gun, Toomey. You'd better not start turning His late Holiness into a saint without consulting your sister first. That in effect is what I'm telling you."

"In effect you're telling me as I've already said that my nephew John and his wife Laura were not killed by terrorists. You're telling me in effect that they were killed by remote control with a death gun from the Vatican. Is that what you're telling me?"

"Your old friend Pembroke had to tell her about it, you know, everything. The state of the bodies. Oh, they may have been killed by terrorists with knives instead of guns. But terrorists don't cut off little strips of the flesh, you know. They just kill. They rape too, of course, if they have time. They rob, always time for that, Toomey."

"There's no proof of it."

"Oh no, no proof at all. No proof that your nephew and his wife were used as what are known as the accidents of the Sacrament of the Holy Eucharist. But your sister, who lost an eye prematurely in grief of bereavement—I know it all, we talked, we've talked on many occasions, Toomey—your sister is a woman and women take very short cuts in thinking. You know, you Catholics make fun of the Church of England—"

"I'm not a Catholic."

"Oh, yes you are. You're not a Protestant and you're not a Jew, neither do you subscribe to this children's nonsense of Zen. You have to be a Catholic. Do you ever consider that the real reason for the Henrican break with Catholicism is that the meat of Catholicism is a little too strong for reasonable appetites? British appetites especially. Along comes a Pope, dear dead soon to be canonized with your help God forbid Gregory the Seventeenth, and he wants to cut out the mumbo jumbo—unfortunate word in the circumstances perhaps, but never mind—bring the faith closer to the people. Examine the implications of that faith, Toomey, and it's damned hair-raising. It ends up in the jungle. Or in the vulgarities of Scouse."

"Of what?"

"Oh, I was at one of these damnable poetry festivals. A Liverpool beardie with glasses got up and began to recite something like 'When I feel proper umpty E makes me feel gear. Jus so I do credit to im he moodeys along wit me into de real best specs in dis world.' That, Toomey, is meant to be the Twenty-third Psalm. You have to leave well alone, get on with the job, don't examine too deeply the meanings of those terms which, I remember clearly, that Maltese poetaster threw at us last night—home, duty, love and so on. You and your sister ought to come home, Toomey. I'll have one more for the road—a lion-frightener or tigerfrightener, it all depends where you are."

Ali had gone out. I served Wignall.

I said, "By his lights he did the right thing. By Christ's lights. I can't blame him."

"Perhaps not, but your sister blames him very bitterly. Very dangerous stuff, Toomey. *Hoc est corpus meum*—hocus-pocus, as it became in the mouths of the ignorant. It was better as hocus-pocus, keep it distant."

"Your church," I said, "anticipated Carlo's reforms."

"My church knew what it was doing. It knew it would turn into a club for upper-class Englishmen. You may laugh at it, but it's a safe church, not like yours. It's tepid, because it knows that fire burns. It thinks fire should be imprisoned in an Adam fireplace, not held in the hand. Never despise tepidity, Toomey." The doorbell rang. "Right," and he drained his drink with a wag of wattles. "You have another visitor."

Ali came in and said, "*Policia.*"

I accompanied Wignall to the open front door, where the inspector from the station across the road stood with papers in his hands. He raised a hand to salute us both. Wignall saluted back with a wave of his cane and said "Jolly good." I asked the inspector to come in. He said no, hardly worth it. Wignall went off to lunch at the residence of the British Council representative, waving his stick jovially at everybody on Triq Il-Kbira.

The inspector said, "Asked by the Office of the Prime Minister to check certain things, sir. The gentleman who was with you has already left? I mean, the gentleman who was living here?"

"He left for the United States this morning. He will not be coming back."

"That is in order then. He had overstayed the time on his visa by three days. The servant you have from Morocco, he too will be leaving?"

"He's in my employ. He stays."

"Sir, you have been issued with a letter from the Prime Minister's Office confirming that you have permanent residence here on condition that you do not take paid employment."

"I've no intention of doing that."

"That is in order then. Your servant has overstayed his visa and must now be under notice to leave. He is employed by you. That is not allowed. Only Maltese citizens may be under employment. I have the notice here. Perhaps you could read it to him and explain."

"He has to go? I hadn't thought of that."

"Oh yes. He may leave the territory and enter again for a stay of three months. But not under employment, only as a visitor."

"Look, inspector, I have to go to Rome tomorrow. It's ah Vatican business connected with the visit I had yesterday from His Grace. I will be away three days at the most. May the matter rest as it is until I return?"

"No difficulty there, sir, we can always stretch a point. But he must understand that he is here illegally. We naturally overlook the illegality for so short a time."

"Thank you, inspector."

"It is my pleasure, sir." And he saluted. A bus crammed with screaming schoolchildren, holy inscriptions on its flanks and an electric-lighted shrine to the Blessed Virgin in its driver's cab, was coming round the corner, filling the width of the street and blocking the inspector's path of return. We heard a struck garbage can going over. "Once in Attard," he said, "I saw an old woman crushed to death by a bus." Wittily he added, "It is like the law."

For luncheon today there was an innovation Joey Grima had brought back from the Great Wall restaurant in Sliema: strips of pork in a plum sauce. I sent it away, contenting myself with a bit of bread and a half bottle of Pommery.

seventy-nine

The young dentist, grandson of the old dentist who had tended my mouth in Mussolini's day, drained the abscess efficiently, saw no need for extraction. "A fine set of teeth," he said, "for a man of your age. I only knew of one other man who could touch you. That was His Holiness Pope Gregory. He died with every tooth in his head."

"Good mastication," I said, "good digestion. That explains his optimism perhaps."

"Well, then, you must be optimistic too."

I paid him in cash. I had drawn a big bundle of ten-thousand-lira notes from the Banca Commerciale. Italian royalties. I left the surgery and walked for a little around the Piazza Navona and its environs: it was a glorious day, the baroque musculatures daring the gods to hurl thunderbolts, rainbows in the fountains. I had *spaghetti alla carbonara* for luncheon with a half bottle of chilled Frascati. Then I walked to the Raphael on the Largo Febo and went to my room for the siesta. I lay on my bed reading the newspapers. Riots, political assassinations, robberies. An American writer whom I knew, Martin Bergman, complained in the *Daily American* of the inefficiency of the police when it came to dealing with *scippatori*. He had just finished a book which had taken him a year to write and was carrying it under his arm in a Gucci case to have it copied at a Xerox shop. *Scippatori* had whizzed by and the pillionrider had snatched the case from under his arm. They would keep the case and throw the typescript into the Tiber. A year's work wasted. Why did not the police insist that all motorcycles carry a numbered *targa*? Were the police in league with the *scippatori*? There was a photograph of the police dealing with a divorce demonstration—riot shields and tear gas. Professor Amalfi, lecturing at Rome University, had been shot in the middle of his lecture. Bless you my children. Reading through the entertainment section of the *Messaggero* I was interested to see that my old film *Terzetto* was being shown at the Farnese, a *cinéma d'essai* in the Campo dei Fiori. I would, I thought, go to see if time had been good to it. Then I slept.

I had no bad dreams. I had never yet had a bad dream when sleeping in Rome, perhaps because all the badness of life there was reserved to the waking time. Here was the sewer of history, and it was an open sewer. There was nothing cynical about the glory of its art and architecture. Beauty was set on a line parallel to morality. Faith too had nothing to do with being good. What I dreamt of was trivial enough—eating a curry in an open-air restaurant in Vienna, a bottle of ketchup on the table, Christmas songs being played in waltztime by the orchestra—but I was buoyed up on a kind of air cushion of acceptance. I awoke sweating but rested.

After dinner I stood in the Campo dei Fiori, looking up at the statue of Giordano Bruno, the Nolan as Jim Joyce had called him. Whether he had been burnt on this spot in person or in effigy had never been clearly established. He had been chased all over Europe for teaching the heresy that soul or spirit cannot exist apart from matter, that dissension and contradiction between the elements of the multifarious universe are to be welcomed and blessed since they justify the existence of God as the only reconciler and unifier. Though a Neapolitan, he was a true patron saint of Rome, a president of discord. I went into the cinema. Going in I was stared at as an oddity because of both age and elegance. The audience was made up almost entirely of international youth, bearded and jeaned and unwashed. The auditorium stank of old urine. The lights went down to catcalls and there on the screen was a grainy copy of *Terzetto*. After the main titles I myself appeared on that screen, in a great garden with shaven lawn and swimming pool, seated on a cane chair in tennis clothes, behind me a table laden with all the expensive liquors that ever were. I was much younger then than now but still, in the view of the audience, a very old man. There were cries of *vafnculo* and *stronzo*, also raspberries and squeaks made by blowing at bits of the plastic that wraps cigarette packets. I had been made to speak good Tuscan. I told my audience that here were three of my stories brought to the screen, all based on events that I had either witnessed or been told of during my long life. Then came the first story, the one I had written when sailing to Singapore, about the planter's wife who grew faithless because her husband snored. The snores of the husband were, of course, augmented by carks and lipfarts from the audience. I, an aged intruder here, seated right at the back, grew angry. I cried *"Silenzio,"* but the response was petulance and greater noise. These young people were quieter for the second story, which was about a young American boy deep into drugs whose mother, out of a pelican love, stole money to buy him cocaine from the pushers. Then the screen signaled PRIMO TEMPO and the lights went up. Many now stared at me in puzzlement. I was like somebody they had seen somewhere, though of course much older. I coughed briefly and a Roman girl who looked like an American said *"Silenzio."* A fat sullen bald Roman brought a tray down the central aisle calling in a profound broken voice *"Bibite fredde."* The lights went down again and SECONDO TEMPO was flashed.

This third, last and longest story was the one, fairly well known I think, of the aged dilettante who dwells in a fine country house in Sussex surrounded by fine pictures, bronzes, priceless first editions. He has a lovely rosewood harpsichord on which he plays corantos and galliards by Byrd and Weelkes. A faithful old servant serves him exquisite food in dainty portions on silver plate; he drinks costly wine from a chased Florentine goblet. He is living in an ivory tower or Axel's Castle. Then the modern world breaks in in the shape of four louts with coshes and razors who proceed to smash up this hermetic retreat, having first beaten up the servants and left them for dead. The horror is that the leader of the louts knows precisely what he is doing. Throwing a first quarto *Hamlet* into the fireplace he discourses learnedly on the bad 1603 pirated edition of the play. He talks of incunabula. Before slashing Toulouse-Lautrec's oil (actually in the Kunsthaus in Zurich, but none of the audience seemed to know that) of the Fat Proprietor and the Anemic Cashier, he points out the weakness of the foreground detail compared with the masterly economy of the proprietor's head. All this time the suffering dilettante sits bound and gagged in a chair, listening incredulously to the sneering erudition of this lout with the cockney whine. The lout plays a coranto by John Bull before giving orders for the smashing of the harpsichord. The camera tracks slowly on to the old gray head and aristocratic features while the noise of gleeful destruction crescendos. The eyes stare, the breath grows more labored, the image blurs as he seems to

592

suffer a cardiac arrest, the image fades out. Fade in of him waking from sleep in a Queen Anne canopy bed. His butler, unharmed and suave, is bringing him tea. It was all a dream, thank God thank God. The audience, aware of being cheated, began to growl.

The aged dilettante, taking a walk with spaniel and silverheaded cane in autumnal Sussex, suddenly sees something and starts. It is a group of four young men, identical with those of his nightmare. They have lighted a little fire in a spinney and are cooking turnips on it. They are polite, dispirited. They have been in Kent for the hop picking but no farmer wished to hire them. They are jobless and after their half-raw turnip meal will trudge to the nearest casualty ward. The old man empties the contents of his wallet—fifteen pounds in notes and all his silver. The men are grateful but suspicious. They see him as he walks with old man's bones, spaniel and stick back to a big house on the horizon. The leader of the young men says, in a cockney whine, that if he can afford to give this amount of cash as a handout there must be plenty more where that came from. "Some are born to money," says the young man, "others to poverty. I've studied in the public library and where has it got me? I know all about painters like Toulouse-Lautrec but I can't afford even a picture postcard of the Fat Proprietor and the Anemic Cashier. Tonight we're going to break in there and grab what we can." But they go with their fifteen pounds odd to the nearest village and get drunk and disorderly. They are arrested and put in the lockup. They lie down to fuddled sleep and the educated young man has a vision of vandalism and carnage. He says: "No, that's not my line." He drops off. A final shot of the old dilettante in his gorgeous bed, smiling in his sleep. FINE.

Whether this would have happened anyway, or whether it was the influence of that last third of the film, pulsing through the air on those even who had not seen it, I do not know. I mean, what happened to me as I walked the dark sidestreet leading to the lights and taxis of the Via Arenula. I was eighty-one years of age and had lived in a violent epoch, but I had only once been subjected to violence. I had imagined it, written about it, but the chief pains I had known, apart from the agonies of the spirit which are tolerable and can be quelled with sleep and wine, apart from dyspepsia, twinges in the joints and the sort of mild toothache that had been quelled that morning, had been referred—my sister, the victims of the camps, poor dear Dorothy writhing in the pincers of cancer. Now, at an age when my body was not well equipped to take it, I was subjected to physical outrage which makes me doubt the capacity of literature to cope with human reality. Four Roman boys jumped me from a side alley. They were generic modern youth, with much hair, good teeth, mindless eyes, slim loins, strong fists.

They wanted money, and they took it. They took also my watch. The cigarette lighter I carried, Ali's birthday gift with the Maltese cross, they disdained so they threw it down the drain whose metal my head struck when I was borne over. Robbery was a mere preliminary to gratuitous violence. They could find a pretext for this violence if they sought not too hard: my age, their youth; my wealth, their poverty; my despicable foreignness despite the correct Italian vowels I uttered in words like *perche?* and *basta.* But violence needs no pretext: it is good in itself like the taste of an apple; it is built into the human complex. I was kicked. I was picked up from my blood and moans and, light as a bicycle frame but less solid, held by two while I was punched by the two remaining. I felt things break within me, dully but accompanied by a blaze of lights. I was hit in the mouth by something metallic and felt teeth go loose, one of them, I knew, the tooth for whose surgical extraction my dentist had seen no necessity. "*Sono vecchio,*" I groaned. Yes, they agreed, *vecchio*: that merited another crack in the dried-up testicles. "*Basta,*" one of them said. That was the last thing I heard.

I was, I gathered, in the Ospedale Fatebenefratelli on the Isola Tiberina. In, of course, a private ward with the smell of the river coming up to the quarter-open window. The nurses were male, members of a religious order of some kind, sweetsmelling and softfooted. Dr. Pantucci, young, bearded, balding, in a white coat, had studied for a year at Johns Hopkins: he insisted on speaking English. Multiple fractures, three teeth fell out, danger of pneumonia averted, averted with difficulty but averted. "You're a lucky old man," he said. I was encased in gesso and bandages. I asked, and with the impaired dentition my voice, I noticed, had an altered resonance:

"How long?"

"How long do you stay here? Oh, a long time. And when you go home you must be long immobile."

"I live alone. I've nobody to look after me."

"You must have nurses. In Malta there are good nurses."

"I have problems in Malta. I must find a way of getting through to my servant. I must contact the local police station."

"You must not be agitated. Agitation is inimical to recovery. Calm is needed, resignation."

"My servant will be thrown out of the state. I have not been able to regularize his position." I noticed a white telephone by the bed mounted on an expansible and contractable metal trellis. "If I could get the number of the police in Lija, Malta. Perhaps I could obtain it from the Maltese Embassy here."

"Do not think of that now. You are agitated. I must give you something to induce sleep."

It was two more days before I was able to have that telephone call made for me. Speaking to the inspector at Lija, I could hear my voice piping and whistling as in caricature of age. "Oh," he said, "I am very sorry to hear this. Law and order are necessary in any city. Your servant was told of his situation. He has already left. He complained that he had no money. We turned our eyes away while he took certain items of yours and sold them at the Indian Bazaar in Valletta. This had to be done, there was no alternative, you had not returned, we had heard nothing from you, now I see why, I am very sorry."

"What items?"

"A set of chessmen, I think. A small picture. You will see when you return. He has flown to Tunis. The keys to the house are with the Grima family opposite."

"Could you kindly inform the postman I wish to have my mail directed here? I shall be here for some time: 126, Ospedale Fatebenefratelli—"

"That is all one word?"

"That is all one word."

"Do not be away from Malta too long. There are these new housing regulations, as you know."

"What regulations?"

"Absence for a certain period of time is regarded by the Prime Minister's Office as permanent abandonment of residence. There is the new law about the confiscation of property."

"But, damn it, I can't help being broken and near dead. I'll be back when the medical authorities give me permission to travel."

"Gort verneyflood ablesforth nardfire."

That was the line breaking. I lay exhausted as if from a two-mile walk.

After two weeks mail began to come in. Two of the nursing brothers brought me a sack of it. I was not able to open any of it myself, one arm being totally disabled and fixed in the air like a fascist salute. The near imbecilic brother who did odd jobs and had, after a day's journey, brought my luggage from the Raphael, willingly sliced the envelopes open and crooned over the beauty of the exotic stamps. Another brother, quick and terrierlike, collected stamps and snarled for their possession. There were a lot of books—bound proofs which American publishers sent in the hope of a kindly publishable word. I donated them to the hospital library. After six weeks a book came from Geoffrey. This I did not donate. With the book was a letter. The letter I was now able to hold, though feebly, in both hands. It was brief. It said:

"Dear old dearly and genuinely though intermittently beloved bastard. I'm here in ah should have written the address at the top righthand corner and all that Sunday writing home to dear mater and pater ballocks, shouldn't I, here in the city of Seattle in the state of Washington and very nice too really, the street being Rainier and the number 1075, and I'm with Nahum Brady who is back in his native habitat to research some great scandalous blockbusting shithouse of a book about the Boeing aircraft people. I'm all right really and don't propose seeing you in London if that's okay with thee, so if thou wouldst be kind enough to remit sum in dollars to above address I shall be more than beholden. Which means that I have done what I was asked, old dear, to wit requesting your archives to be copied and sent to Malta, an easy job that one, and then, much more difficult, scrounging around Chicago after this evidence you were after, you know, Pope Buggery's miracle all that way back. Of course, what with it being His Ballsiness, everybody I met in the hospital line was all too ready to declare on oath they'd seen him turn horsepiss into Johnnie Walker, but I was very very firm as you know I can be, and I said there was one particular doctor and he was the man to make the opissial dispission, I was tight of course, not really been sober since I landed at O'Hare. Anyway, to make a short story long, I got the name, and there was the name in old ledgers and reports, and even on a plaque on the wall in letters of the Purest Gold as one who had served his country, saving life not taking it and the rest of the inflated ordure. This was a certain Dr. B. C. Gimson, M.D., well remembered by the old and admired too because he'd written and moreover my dear actually published a kind of memoir, the one you should have now in your hands or on your lap rather, unless ha ha it or both or all three are hotherwise hoccupied you come along a me sir don't want no trouble do we now—ah, how often those words have been addressed to yours truly. But of course there was just no copy to be found. Published 1948 and remaindered, and then Dr. B. C. Gimson suffers a slight fatality in the sport of gliding whereof he was most inordinately fond. So they send me to the widow, who lives in the posh suburb of Oak Park, where old Hem came from, and still as it was in his day, uncountable churches and no bars—thirsty me, you've just no idea. Nor did she offer me one, not having a thing in the house. Nearly almost completely and totally blind, my dear, but getting along on her own except for the neighbors helping with the shopping. She said look on those shelves there and you may find it—*Medic* it is called, *Medic*—I don't read no more, me eyes, see, charming old lady though really, take it to that table there, copy out what you want and then put it back where you found it, it is one of my most precious possessions, and then bugger off drinkless. Alas I took advantage of the old trout, pretended to scribble a few lines, made as to put the precious volume back but in actual fact, oh cunning shameless me, stowed it under my handsome handknit cashmere pushover. The crimes I have committed on your sodding behalf, you sod. So here it is. Page 153 is where you have to look. Don't forget the cash, be careful of those elegant though brittle limbs. A fall could be very very nasty at your age. I have something good coming up soon, I think, I hope, fingers crossed. Your loving faithless Geoffrey. XXXXXXXXX."

The book was still in its dustjacket. *Medic*, yes, with the rod of Aesculapius to whom Socrates owed a cock on the cover, and on the back a cheerful photograph of the author in military uniform. The face was not familiar. I was reluctant to get to page 153 too soon, so I leafed, with some pain, through the earlier pages. Here was a medical practitioner who, after fifteen or so years of varied hospital and private experience in Illinois, served as a medical officer in the U.S. Army from Pearl Harbor to the end. His aim was to show, rather in the spirit of Carlo, how good came out of evil, how he learned to believe in the essential benevolence and certainly courage of ordinary human beings, and how, after an adolescence of glum agnosticism, he came to accept the notion of a God sometimes enigmatic but always loving. As for his own craft of curing diseases, the area of the inexplicable grew as he practiced: patients died when they should have lived and vice versa. On page 153 he mentioned an inexplicable remission of disease in a Chicago hospital and followed it with a glib paragraph on the possible meaning of the term *miracle*. On page 155, which Geoffrey evidently had not read, he stated the name of the child cured by prayer and speculated on the possible future of one so signally picked out by the Lord for special favor. Here I felt my eyes must be deceiving me.

I asked that a call be put through to Monsignor O'Shaughnessy at his private apartment on the Via Giulia. When I got through to him I talked of the good old times. Those bridgeplaying days in Paris? How could he ever forget? The voice sounded slurred by whisky. Whisky, whiskey rather, had perhaps hindered his advancement. He was not even a bishop. He had a variety of odd jobs in obscure departments of the Vatican. One of the jobs was the making of saints. There were not, of course, many occasions for saintmaking. He said he would come round and see me, though he found getting about difficult these days. Anno domini, you know. He was seventy-nine, he said. I'm eighty-one, I said. Are you now, who would have thought it?

He shuffled in two days later. Old, yes, whiskeypickled, the long Irish neck I remembered, the eyes like watered milk blinking in Irish neurosis, the face a map of an unpopulous Irish county with dusty tracks leading nowhere. He sat down by my bed.

I said, "About the canonization of our late friend Carlo. I'm ready to sign the appropriate form. I definitely witnessed a miracle. And here, in this book just sent to me from the States, is corroborative evidence. The doctor himself.

Page one fifty-three. Could you read it out to me? I had a bad accident. My sight isn't so good."

He put on horn-rimmed glasses and smacked his lips. He was not particularly interested in my bad accident. "Fell, did ye? Ach, that's all too easy at our age. Giddy fits, then the bones break. Here we are, then." He held the book near his eyes and read: " 'I remember the name of the priest. He was the brother of a certain Mr. Campanati, a well-known Chicago businessman. Father Campanati was in the hospital, along with an English friend or relative, I forget which, because his brother was a victim of the bootleg racketeers who flourished in those unhappy days. He could do nothing for his dying brother but he went into the public ward near by where a child was dying of meningitis. This child was my patient and was in the hopeless terminal stage of the disease. With nothing more than a prayer Father Campanati reversed that stage and the child began to recover. The recovery was incredibly rapid. In two more days the child was sitting up and taking light nourishment. He had come to us from the Saint Nicholas Orphanage, a non-religious establishment despite its name, Saint Nicholas of course being the patron saint of children. As a bonus to his recovery the child was adopted while still in the hospital and left it with a new father and mother.' " Monsignor O'Shaughnessy looked up. "That seems definite enough. That can certainly go on file." He looked down at the book again. "Then he goes on about his skepticism about miracles and how it was cured by this event. Miracles he saw as a medical officer in the army. How one man said he'd drink himself clear of pneumonia and did. That's interesting, but it's not a miracle."

"Look at page one fifty-five," I said.

"Let's see. 'I never saw the child again after his adoption and discharge from hospital, but I often wonder what happened to him. I remember his first name, which was Godfrey. The surname he came in with I cannot remember, but I remember the name he went out with—Manning. The childless couple who adopted him were not rich but they were clearly loving. They took him away to live in a humble but loving home in Decatur, Illinois. Godfrey Manning it seemed to me was a good name, bringing God and Man together.' "

"Well," I said, with a mixture of emotions which I felt might break my body entirely if it had not been strongly encased in gesso and bandages. "Does the name mean anything to you?"

"It's a good name, I agree. Not that names mean anything. No, wait, the name rings some kind of little bell at the back of me mind. Wasn't the name in the newspapers?"

"It was in the newspapers about the time of the death of Carlo, His late Holiness I should say. A very terrible business. The body of Christ administered as a cyanide tablet. Nearly two thousand slaughtered in the name of the Lord. My great- or grandniece among them. And her baby."

"Oh Jesus. Oh holy mother of God. That was the man. Oh may the Lord save us. Oh sacred heart of our blessed Savior." He crossed himself many times but wildly, as a man might cross himself when suffering from Korsakoff's syndrome. And then, "Ach, it's not possible. It's a coincidence. It couldn't happen that way at all."

"And if it's not, which it's not, a coincidence?"

"The Lord gives all human creatures free will. If a man comes to a bad end it can't be blamed on the Lord. This is just a terrible thing that a human creature cut off from the Lord has done. You can't blame God for that terrible Hitler, can you now? Or for that Mussolini and the rest of the terrible people this terrible century's thrown up. Man's a free creature, and sometimes he uses his freedom in terrible ways."

"Yes," I said, not believing that affirmation. Had I been free? Not for one solitary moment of my life had I been free. "But if God deliberately chooses to interfere in his free-running creation, which is what a miracle means, if he saves one life rather than another, what then? Doesn't it mean that he has a special intention for that life? That he puts on the foreknowledge he usually denies himself to ensure human freedom?" That last sentence exhausted me. Enough for one day; let me rest, let me not think on the matter. "Like," I said, "that legend of Saint Nicholas, since Saint Nicholas has come into it. Ah, never mind."

"What you're trying to say about God it seems to me cannot be said ever ever, do you understand, about God. I read a novel about the life of Lazarus once—a wicked French novel I picked up on the *quai* in Paris. It made out that Lazarus had been brought back from the dead in order to live a life of riot and fornication. That was a wicked book. The human imagination is capable of a terrible amount of evil. God bless us, God save us from harm. Yes, yes, I know that story about the blessed Saint Nicholas. That Anatole France was a clever man but like so many clever men capable of great mischief."

"He kept it," I said, "in the realm of the imagination. God prefers the realm of action. If God hadn't saved that child— Oh, let it pass. Let me sign whatever has to be signed in order to speed Carlo on the road to canonization. And then let me be done with him."

"We have," Monsignor O'Shaughnessy said, "a lot of other miracles on record. Well, you know, things that will have to be looked into. An old woman in black recovered her sight when praying near his tomb. This communist leader in Bracciano found he could walk again. His Holiness had come to him in a dream. It didn't make him any less of a Communist. His Holiness himself was a Communist he said, forgive his stupidity. I think we can let this business go, very controversial. I think you'd best control your memory on that point, I know, I know, difficult at our age when our youth is the only thing we remember. I think this book had best be forgotten about. It's twenty-odd years old from the date on it I see, there can't be many copies around. There'll be enough support for his beatification which is the first step without bringing controversy into it."

"It could be entered on the side of the *advocatus diaboli.*"

"There you're joking. That would make him out to be really diabolic. No, we forget all about it. For the good of the lot of us. Isn't that the best way?"

"Fathers," I said, and it did not seem at first to be *a proposito*, "are terrible people. We can do without fathers." Coming at me with redhot forceps, had that been it? "Mothers are altogether different. Our Mother the Church. Our Father in Heaven. I wonder whether it's time for me to come back into the Church."

"Sure, you've never been out of it, isn't that so?"

"The nature of my sexual endowment," I said prissily, "obviated from about my fourteenth year on any possibility of my—" Breath, I needed breath. "It was in Dublin it happened, but let that pass."

"You're finished with the life of the flesh now," he said jauntily. "You'd better be back in again at your age and in your condition, what I can see of it. I'll get them to send in a priest to hear your confession."

"No," I said. "No, thanks. Thanks all the same, but no."

"I had a brother, Terence was his name," Monsignor O'Shaughnessy said, "who had some of these wild ideas, reading too many of the wrong books. He joined the IRA and was shot by his own people, can you imagine that? He said with Mother Church you could save yourself from the everpresent wrath of the Almighty but only if you concentrated on it as a foundation of Jesus Christ as the suffering Son who protected you from the Father. That the Father only showed himself in thunder and lightning and things of terror in the world. But the Son, he said, couldn't be the same as the Father. That was a shocking heresy, I used to cry at him. Arianism, if you know the term. Anyway, for yourself now, I should start preparing your confession, it must be a long time since you've approached the altar. And when you're ready I can have a priest sent in. To be frank with ye, I'm in deadly need of a drink. Would you have such a thing as a drop tucked away in that cupboard of yours there?"

"I could send out for something. We have a kind of errandboy brother but he tends to get lost on the way. It would take some time, I'm afraid."

"Ach, never mind. One final question. What was it your sister and the Holy Father talked about when he was at the point of death? I'm anxious to know if ye know yourself that is."

"He said," I said clearly, "that he loved her. But only as Dante loved Beatrice. She to him personified the Divine Vision made flesh. As for the flesh, he added that if they'd been able to meet early enough he would never have taken orders but would have asked her to marry him. He was not altogether *compos mentis* at the time."

"Ach." And, unexpectedly, " 'Eternal Woman draws us upward.' Goethe said that. Perhaps with all your learning you'd know it in German."

"*Ja*," I said. " '*Das Ewig-Weibliche zieht uns hinan.*' "

"That's the truth, and there's no denying it."

What accelerated my recovery more than anything was a letter from the Department of Housing of the Government of Malta informing me that, since my property in Lija had clearly been uninhabited for some time, this was taken as an indication of my intention to give up residence on the island. Abandoned houses of expatriates were to be taken over by the government as a means of easing the accommodation shortage for native Maltese. I was to be good enough to arrange for the keys to my property to be deposited in the office of the Department of Housing in Floriana at my earliest possible convenience. Your obedient servant, P. Mifsud. I wanted to get out of that hospital and onto that plane.

eighty-one

Mifsud did not come himself. He sent Azzopardi. Mr., not Fr. Probably no relation. I was in my self-propel chromium and leather wheelchair when he arrived. Maria Fenek, my eighteen-year-old nurse, opened the door to him. I interviewed Azzopardi, a dark young man with bland black eyes and deep sideburns, in my study with, behind me on the shelves, evidence of my long industry. Azzopardi made it clear to me that he was doing me an exceptional favor in coming at all: according to the regulations it was my duty to go to him, meekly rattling the metallic symbols of my submission to expropriation. I pointed out mildly my condition. That my absence from Malta was enforced by an act of gratuitous violence to my person, the necessary and I might add very expensive treatment, including value added tax, a total immobility which, as he could see for himself, continued, and that it was hardly seemly for a man in my condition and of my reputation to propel himself along busy roads the several miles between Lija and Floriana. He quite understood, that was why he had left his busy office to come to me. Now would I please hand over my keys?

Where was I myself to dwell on the completion of the act of expropriation?

That was not his concern. There were several hotels on the island. There were also hospitals and nursing homes.

And if I told him now that I had already sold the property to an Englishman desirous, ill-advisedly, of establishing residence in Malta?

That was against regulations with which clearly I was not conversant. Foreigners were not now permitted to sell property to other foreigners.

I said, "I am a very old man. I have worked hard all my life and had, I thought, sailed to my haven. If I am rich, and hence to be considered a legitimate prey to confiscatory upstart governments, the riches have been gained legitimately. I have paid my way, Mr. Azzopardi, and stolen from no man's pocket. On the other hand, I have myself been much stolen from, and I have had enough of it. I see very little difference between the violence done to my person in holy Rome and the violence your government is now proposing to do to my natural right to enjoy the possession and use of my own property."

Such a natural right did not exist. Rights were conferred by governments not by Nature.

"My books, my papers, my furniture—are these too under confiscation? Is there nothing here your government will allow me to call my own?"

If movables remained on the premises at the time of the government's taking possession in the name of the Maltese people, then these too must be deemed confiscate. However, the government was no monster. Three days as from this day would be granted for the removal of what could be removed.

"I have no telephone. Would you be good enough to contact on my behalf Messers. Cassar and Cooper in Valletta and ask them to arrange for the removal of my movables and their transportation to the United Kingdom and their storage in a metropolitan depot of their choice?"

I was asking a lot, but he perceived my difficulty and would of his goodness arrange for the implementation of what I had requested.

"There is one more thing you will do for me," I said, "and if you do not do it I will revile the name of your government in the world's press as the monster you say it is not. Do not underestimate the power of a pen universally known and, may I say, revered, Mr. Azzopardi. I will have press photographers here to record your brutal eviction from his own property of a man distinguished, old, injured, ill, wretched. Tell your Mr. Mifsud that. Tell that also to your Prime Minister. And to your archbishop. By the living Christ, there was a time when British destroyers would have blasted a capital from river or harbor at even the mere whiff of a hint of a suggestion that a British national was to be treated in the manner you are treating me."

Times had changed. This was no longer a colony. Britain no longer had any power in the world. Malta was not herself powerful either but she had powerful friends. My words were opprobrious. Let me beware of uttering calumnies against the Maltese state and the elected leader of that state. What was the other thing I requested to be done?

"You will have prepared," I said, "a large round plaque to be affixed to the façade of this property. On this plaque the following words are to be engraved or embossed in some durable form. Take down these words in your little notebook. Go on, sir, *take them down.* KENNETH MARCHAL TOOMEY, BRITISH NOVELIST AND PLAYWRIGHT, LIVED HERE UNTIL EVICTED BY THE GOVERNMENT OF MALTA IN SEPTEMBER 1971. Have you got that?"

That could not be done. That was not the responsibility of his department nor of any other department of government. That could be effected only by myself or by some interested private organization if, that was, the government permitted such a memorial of so little interest to the Maltese people on its own property.

"That bloody well will be done," I cried in great rage. "And now remove your nasty little bureaucratic presence from what is so long as I am on it still my property before I deliberately induce a terminal heart attack and curse you at the moment of dying. I, sir, have lived my life and am quite prepared to do it. Get out. Get out, you bloody nasty little grub in the cheese of the modern world."

It was not quite in this manner that I had foreseen my going home.

eighty-two

"I shall call it, I think," I said, "*Confabulations.*"

"That's a wet sort of title."

"Well, consider. In psychiatry, according to this dictionary here, it means the replacement of the gaps left by a disordered memory with imaginary remembered experiences believed to be true. Not that I see the difference. All memories are disordered. The truth, if not mathematical, is what we think we remember."

"There's another of these things," Hortense said. She was going through the mid-morning mail. The sight in her remaining eye was not good and she had to peer. "It seems to have been mailed in Toronto."

"The usual?" I asked, bundling my final manuscript together at the escritoire and squaring it off.

"They're sticking the pin in the heart part of the image. Do you feel a stabbing pain in your heart they want to know."

"Not at all. My heart is in very good fettle. Geoffrey is not going to kill me that way."

"Why does he want so desperately to publish?"

"Money money money. Thirlson at Doubleday told me that he'd get the second half of the advance when the biography is completed. It can't be completed till I'm dead. Meanwhile, there's this. *Confabulations*. It will, I hope, make his own work somewhat redundant." And I chuckled in the manner of a wicked old man.

"You wicked old man," Hortense said indulgently. In her mid-seventies as she was, she retained much of her youthful lissomeness, grace, fluidity of movement. I cannot remember what she was wearing that morning, just one week ago. The time is too close. But I remember the eyeshade, a matt beige to match something. Her shoes, probably, the beige shoes. She peered at her wristwatch, a big one, bigger than a man's. "They're open," she said.

I got up from the desk chair, stiffly, rightly, in my mid-eighties. The long ground-floor sitting room looked well in the Sussex summer morning sun that bathed it mildly from the seaward side. The french windows were open to it and the sloping garden, the recently shaven lawn and the apple trees. My furniture and bibelots had found, I was pretty sure, their final place of repose. It was a pity about that missing Picasso sketch, but Ali's need had been greater than his master's. The bronze bust of myself, which Hortense had threatened long ago to model and had at last achieved in her shed, a converted garage to the right of the cottage, dared me to take myself seriously, the Great Author. I had never, I thought, taken myself seriously. "Come then, my dear," I said. We went out by the front door, arm in arm. In the kitchen Mrs. Hill was mixing something loudly in a bowl. In the front garden her husband was pruning the old walnut tree. "Morning, Tom," I said. He intoned a groundrow of country vowels.

"Talking of Tom," Hortense said, as we walked, her steps short only to match mine, up the shallow hill toward the Royal Oak, "I think that flat parcel I haven't opened must be the long-playing record. We'll hear it over lunch."

"It's always the orchestra that sounds tinny in these rerecordings," I said. "And the voice seems to belong to another age. Nowadays voices try to chew your ear. That young lout on television the other night had the damned thing in his mouth, did you see that?"

"Morning Mr. Toomey, morning Mrs. Toomey," Jack Laidlow behind the bar said. It was easier that way. *Mrs. Campanati* would never have done in these parts: it would have been like having *spaghetti alla carbonara* on the Royal Oak luncheon menu. But that doubtless would come. I underestimated, having been out of touch so long, the capacity of even the rural British for adaptation to the exotic. After all, there was a pizza parlor in Battle now. Still, with the extinction of the Campanati family, there had not been much point in waving its pennant in the void, and Hortense had naturally reverted to the name she had been known by as a schoolgirl in these parts. Under the pressure of the new suffragettes or whatever they were *Miss* and *Mrs.* were being subsumed under the unpronounceable *Ms.* The Sussex mouth had never differentiated strongly between the two titles. Both derived from *Mistress.* The Hills assumed we were man and wife. We slept in narrow beds by opposing walls in the same master or mistress bedroom. If one of us cried out in the night the other was only ten stumbling paces away. The village rector, however, knew differently from the others.

"Half-pint of best, Jack please, and a scotch and water."

The village rector now came in, the Reverend Bertram Murdoch, a man of good Kentish family who did not have to rely for living on his living. "A large Gordon's, Mr. Laidlow, and a mere whiff of lime juice." Unlike the priests of reformed Catholicism, he kept, except for squash and cricket, to clerical black with dog collar. "A gorgeous day," he said, "but I fear a change in the weather. The farmers will, theoretically anyway, be pleased." A handsome irongray man in his sixties with very little humor in him.

I said, "An admirable sermon yesterday, if I may say so, rector. It was kind of you to quote from me. You needn't have done it, you know."

"It was altogether apposite. I have ah news for both of you." Hortense and I were perched on barstools close together. The rector got his head between our heads and said, in a lowered tone: "The mass in Latin. The Tridentine rite. It will be celebrated at dawn from next Sunday on in the house of Lady Fressing-field. I thought you might be interested to know. A young French priest named Père Chabrier will be the regular ah celebrant."

"Quite like Reformation times," Hortense said. "The mass in secret. Is there a priest's hole there or whatever it's called?"

"I thought you might be interested to know. I'll be turning up myself I think now and again. Though it makes Sunday a very long day for me."

"We're quite happy," I said, "with the monarch's brand of Christianity. When in England and so forth. Still, exciting to think there's a touch of crimi-nality in it. We must go, Hortense. We can even confess in French, I suppose, in the foredawn candles. One's sins always sound more dignified in French."

"Yes," the rector said, "like Baudelaire. Pleasant to think you don't have to cut yourself off from one communion in order to belong to another. That's a Gregorian reform we all have to approve of. Good morning, Mr. Amos, Mr. Catt, Mr. Willard."

"Aaaargh, rector."

"Do you know," the rector asked Hortense, "anything about medicinal plants?"

"I know the names of some of them. Argimony, bistort, butcher's broom, loosestrife, herb Paris, meadowsweet, hemlock—" She trembled a little on that.

"Figwort," I suggested, "wood sorrel, tansy, pasqueflower, avens, self-heal—Why do you ask?" It was as though we were being tested for the right to enter English rural life.

"I just wondered. The rural dean's coming to dinner. He has an obsession about these things. I'm quite ignorant. I wonder if you could both come. Thursday."

"Thank you, yes, we've nothing else on."

For luncheon that day Mrs. Hill gave us roast leg of lamb with mint sauce. "Funny," I said, "how France regards this as a barbarism. Mother, I remember, dutifully mixed chopped mint and sugar and vinegar for the rest of us but exclaimed on it as an Anglican heresy. These new French structuralists deny synchronic sweet and savory to the cuisine, no part of Western culture they say. How about the British, somebody asked. Roast pork and apple sauce and so on. I think it's Lévi-Strauss himself who says that the British don't belong to Western culture."

"Here's the song about Paris," Hortense said.

Tommy Toomey excavated from the past and singing and talking on LP to a new generation. That clear voice gave out my ancient words over the apple tart and cream:

> *When you have dined*
> *You'll find*
> *Some* boîte
> *Whereat*
> *They're inclined*
> *To* l'érotique
> *Keep her close entwined*
> *Till your mind*
> *Grows weak*

"All made," I said humbly, "out of my young imagination."
"Hush."

> *When you have danced*
> *Chance takes you where*
> *The air*
> *Is entranced*
> *With Paris spring . . .*

We took coffee in our armchairs and heard the other side of the record, Tom monologuizing. It was a matter of unhooking the loudspeaker from the wall of the dining room and bringing it, on its long lead, here into the living room. "I've never heard any of these," I said.

"Nor I. We were away. We weren't home."

Tom, though dead before the Nazi invasion of Europe, had imagined an occupied England with the youth of a rural school, like the one here just down the road, being indoctrinated by an *Erziehungsfeldwebel*. Here was the sergeant's voice: "*Ja*, mine kids, dere is vun ting ve learn before ve beginnen, and dat is very how do you say it gross. You see de Himmel, de sky up aluft? Dat is *high*. And you are little, yes? You are littler dan de sky, yes? So you point up at de sky and you say vile you pointing are *high littler high littler*. Is dat not gut? And ve have a leetle aitch in it so it become *highl hittler*. Is dat not beautiful?"

"Oh my God," I said, "that's just how it would have been."

"I've never heard this one either."

It was Tom as a kind but irascible mother with two children. They had moved to a new house and the children, during the removal, had been staying with an aunt somewhere. Now they were introduced to the new house and new furnishings. "Children, we will start as we mean to go on. You will not *touch anything*, do you hear? Underneath that cushion there is a five-legged animal that likes to live undisturbed. Disturb that cushion and it *bites*. There, what did I tell you? All right, suck it better, but *now you know*. Behind that picture called *Faithful Unto Death* there is a large square hole, and in it dwells a whole colony of creepy crawlies that *sting*. And in the lavatory cistern, children, there is a huge multicolored spider just longing for the opportunity to *lash out*. Leave well alone, do you hear, Hortense, Kenneth—"

"Oh my God," I said again.

"Leave well alone," Tom's maternal voice went, and then it coughed. It went into a spasm of coughing. "There, children, I should have left the cigarettes well alone, shouldn't I? Wugh wugh wugh, oh dear." The record had come to a stop.

"Poor Tom," I said.

"What do you mean, *poor Tom*?" Hortense said. "Tom was never to be pitied. Tom was the only truly good man I ever knew. If I believed in saints I'd pray to Tom."

That evening, as we nearly always did, we watched television. Our long lives were often refracted from the screen—a reference in an interview with the Archbishop of York to Neo-Gregorianism; a man with a microphone in an art gallery in Birmingham, with a small metal sculpture by Hortense glowing dully and disregarded in the background while he talked of the excellence of Ahmar or Kokinos or Vermelho; a contemptuous snort for Maugham or Toomey in a program called *Paperback Stand*; as tonight, an old movie with score by Domenico Campanati. "He wasn't bad," Hortense would say grudgingly as his muted trumpets signaled dawn at sea or his massed strings were a bed for physical passion. "I don't suppose any of us was really bad. We meant well, anyway."

The days and nights of calm and warmth dissolved that evening in violent rain and thunder and cryptic brief messages in lightning over the Channel. "He plants his footsteps in the sea," I quoted from Sunday's service while I looked out from the lashed french windows, "and rides upon the storm. The old bastard. Will he let us sleep?"

"He'll be persuaded to let us. That's my one article of faith."

The sky was still emptying as we went to bed. The thunder trundled over our roof and, in the very instant of a blue flash, I heard the crack and soaked leafy multitudinous tumble of, surely, that oak in Penney's field opposite. I waited, as I always did, for my sister to settle to calm breathing after her single barbiturate. Then I turned, old bag of bones as I was, onto my left side and addressed myself to the brief slumber which would, I knew, terminate with an hour's wait for the dawn chorus. I contrived, you will perhaps remember, an adequate beginning. I have always, all through my literary career, found endings excruciatingly hard. Thank God, or something, the last words were not for my pen and, thank that same something, their scratching or sounding could not, in the nature of things, be very much longer delayed. I hoped there would be no dreams.

MONACO, 1980